Penguin Books
The Michael Innes Omnibus

Michael Innes is the pseudonym of J. I. M. Stewart who was a Student of Christ Church, Oxford, from 1949 until his retirement in 1973. He was born in 1906 and was educated at Edinburgh Academy and Oriel College, Oxford. He was lecturer in English at the University of Leeds from 1930 to 1935, Jury Professor of English at the University of Adelaide, South Australia, from 1935 to 1945, and lecturer in Queen's University, Belfast, between 1946 and 1948.

He has published many novels – including the quintet *A Staircase in Surrey* (*The Gaudy*, *Young Pattullo*, *A Memorial Service*, *The Madonna of the Astrolabe* and *Full Term*) – several volumes of short stories, as well as books of criticism and essays, under his own name. His *Eight Modern Writers* appeared in 1963 as the final volume of *The Oxford History of English Literature*, and he is also the author of *Rudyard Kipling* (1966) and *Joseph Conrad* (1968). His most recent books are *Andrew and Tobias* (1981) and *The Bridge at Arta and other stories* (1981)

Under the pseudonym of Michael Innes, he has written broadcast scripts and many crime novels including *The Bloody Wood* (1966), *An Awkward Lie* (1971), *Appleby's Answer* (1973), *Appleby's Other Story* (1974), *The Appleby File* (1975), *The Gay Phoenix* (1976), *Honeybath's Haven* (1977), *The Ampersand Papers* (1978), *Going It Alone* (1980) and *Lord Mullion's Secret* (1981).

The Michael Innes Omnibus

Death at the President's Lodging
Hamlet, Revenge!
The Daffodil Affair

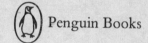 Penguin Books

Penguin Books Ltd, Harmondsworth, Middlesex, England
Penguin Books, 625 Madison Avenue, New York, New York 10022, U.S.A.
Penguin Books Australia Ltd, Ringwood, Victoria, Australia
Penguin Books Canada Ltd, 2801 John Street, Markham, Ontario, Canada L3R 1B4
Penguin Books (N.Z.) Ltd, 182–190 Wairau Road, Auckland 10, New Zealand

Filmset in Monophoto Bembo by
Northumberland Press Ltd, Gateshead
Printed in Great Britain by
Richard Clay (The Chaucer Press) Ltd, Bungay, Suffolk

Contents

Death at the
President's Lodging

Note

The Senior Members of Oxford and Cambridge colleges are undoubtedly among the most moral and level-headed of men. They do nothing aberrant; they do nothing rashly or in haste. Their conventional associations are with learning, unworldliness, absence of mind, and endearing and always innocent foible. They are, as Ben Jonson would have said, persons such as comedy would choose; it is much easier to give them a shove into the humorous than a twist into the melodramatic; they prove peculiarly resistive to the slightly rummy psychology that most detective stories require. And this is a pity if only because their habitat – the material structure in which they talk, eat, and sleep – offers such a capital frame for the quiddities and wilie-beguilies of the craft.

Fortunately, there is one spot of English ground on which these reasonable and virtuous men go sadly to pieces – on which they exhibit all those symptoms of irritability, impatience, passion, and uncharitableness which make smooth the path of the novelist. It is notorious that when your Oxford or Cambridge man goes not 'up' nor 'down' but 'across' – when he goes, in fact, from Oxford to Cambridge or from Cambridge to Oxford – he must traverse a region strangely antipathetic to the true academic calm. This region is situated, by a mysterious dispensation, almost half-way between the two ancient seats of learning – hard by the otherwise blameless environs of Bletchley. The more facile type of scientific mind, accustomed to canvass immediately obvious physical circumstances, has formerly pointed by way of explanation of this fact to certain deficiencies in the economy of *Bletchley Junction*. One had to wait there so long (in effect the argument ran) and with so little of solid material comfort – that who wouldn't be a bit upset?

But all that is of the past; when I last sped through the Junction it seemed a little paradise; and, anyway, my literary temper is for more metaphysical explanations. I prefer to think that midway between the strong polarities of Athens and Thebes the ether is troubled; the air, to a scholar, nothing sweet and nimble. And I have fancied that if these Oxford clerks who centuries ago attempted a secession had gone to Bletchley there might have arisen the university – or at least the college – I wanted for this story . . . Anyone who takes down a map when reading Chapter 10 will see that I have acted on my fancy. St Anthony's, a fictitious college, is part too of a fictitious university. And its Fellows are fantasy all – without substance and without (forbearing Literary reader!) any mantle of imaginative truth to cover their nakedness. Here are ghosts; here is a purely speculative scene of things.

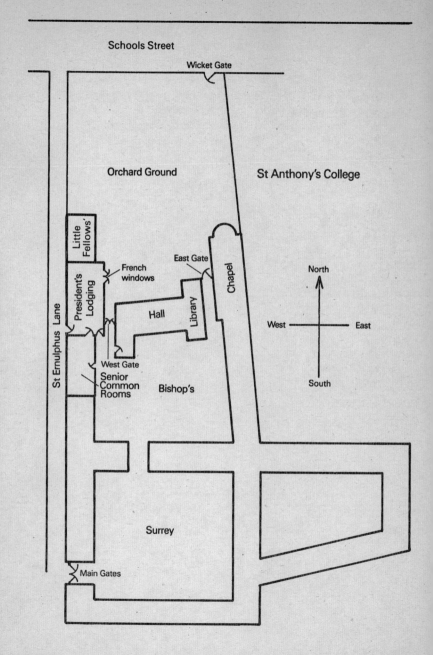

Chapter 1

I

An academic life, Dr Johnson observed, puts one little in the way of extraordinary casualties. This was not the experience of the Fellows and scholars of St Anthony's College when they awoke one raw November morning to find their President, Josiah Umpleby, murdered in the night. The crime was at once intriguing and bizarre, efficient and theatrical. It was efficient because nobody knew who had committed it. And it was theatrical because of a macabre and unnecessary act of fantasy with which the criminal, it was quickly rumoured, had accompanied his deed.

The college hummed. If Dr Umpleby had shot himself, decent manners would have demanded reticence and the suppression of overt curiosity all round. But murder, and mysterious murder at that, was felt almost at once to license open excitement and speculation. By ten o'clock on the morning following the event it would have been obvious to the most abstracted don, accustomed to amble through the courts with his eye turned in upon the problem of the historical Socrates, that the quiet of St Anthony's had been rudely upset. The great gates of the college were shut; all who came or went suffered the unfamiliar ordeal of scrutiny by the senior porter and a uniformed sergeant of police. From the north window of the library another uniformed figure could be glimpsed guarding the closely curtained windows of the President's study. The many staircases by which the medieval university contrived to postpone the institution of the corridor were lively with the athletic tread of undergraduates, bounding up and down to discuss the catastrophe with friends. Shortly before eleven o'clock a sheet of notepaper – unobtrusive, but displayed contrary to custom outside the college – informed undergraduates from elsewhere that no lectures would be held in St Anthony's that day. By noon the local papers had their posters on the streets – and in no other town would they have read as discreetly

as they did: *Sudden Death of the President of St Anthony's*. For in the
papers themselves the fact was stated: Dr Umpleby had been shot – it
was suspected deliberately and by an unknown hand. Throughout the
afternoon a little knot of lounging townsfolk, idly gathered on the
further side of St Ernulphus Lane, satisfied their curiosity by staring up at
the long row of grey-mullioned, flat-arched Tudor windows behind
which so intriguing a local tragedy lay. And local tragedy meanwhile
was becoming national news. By four-thirty hundreds of thousands of
people in Pimlico, in Bow, in Clerkenwell, in the mushroom suburbs of
outer London and the hidden warrens of Westminster, were adding a
new name to their knowledge of a very remote university town. The
later editions put this public on a level with the local loungers, for the
same long line of Tudor windows stretched in photographic perspective
across the front page. By seven o'clock quadruple supplies of these
metropolitanly-keyed news-sheets were being feverishly unloaded
within hail of St Anthony's itself. The cloisteral repose of the college
was shattered indeed.

But it is a troubled quiet that much of the university enjoys in
the twentieth century. Day and night the vast aggregation of London,
sixty miles away, clamours for supplies; day and night it sends out
products of its own. And day and night the venerable streets, up and
down which so many generations of scholars and poets have sauntered in
meditative calm, re-echo to the roar of modern transport. By day the
city is itself a chief offender; local buses and innumerable undergraduate-
driven cars jam and eddy in the narrow streets. But by night the
place becomes an artery only; regularly, remorsely, with just interval
enough to allow uneasy expectation, the heavy night-travelling lorries
and pantechnicons of modern commerce rumble and thunder through
the town. And day and night as the ceaseless stream goes by, the grey
and fretted stone, sweeping in its gentle curve from bridge to bridge,
shudders and breathes, as at the stroke of a great hammer upon the earth.

St Anthony's is fortunate amid all this. Alone among the colleges that
front the worst of the hubbub, it presents on this aspect a spacious garden,
the famous Orchard Ground. Behind the privacy of a twelve-foot wall,
topped by lofty ornamental railings, a spreading lawn thickly set with
apple trees runs back to meet the first and most massive group of college
buildings: the chapel, the library, and the hall. Beyond the great screen
of these, in Bishop's Court, the hum of traffic scarcely penetrates. And

beyond that again the oldest part of the college, the medieval Surrey Court, with its high Early English archway and main gates giving on St Ernulphus Lane, almost touches the inviolate calm of King Alfred's Meadows. The ancient town has its haunts for the dreamer still.

But the great garden of Orchard Ground had proved from time to time the haunt of anything but quiet activities. The St Anthony's undergraduates had rioted in it, hunted a real fox in it, smuggled into it under cover of darkness a very sizeable sow on the verge of parturition. Orchard Ground, therefore, had long been locked up at night; junior members of the college had no access to it after ten-fifteen. The senior members, the Fellows, could use a key: for four of them who lodged in Orchard Ground a key was essential ... And upon Orchard Ground, thus peculiarly insulated at night, opened the french windows of the study in which Dr Umpleby's body had been found.

2

It had been a quarter past two when the great yellow Bentley swung out of New Scotland Yard; it drew up outside St Anthony's just as four o'clock was chiming from a score of bells. Seldom, Inspector John Appleby reflected, had he been so expeditiously dispatched to investigate a case of presumed murder beyond the metropolitan area. And indeed, his arrival in the Yard's most resplendent vehicle was sign and symbol of august forces having been at work: that morning the Dean of St Anthony's had hastily seen the Vice-Chancellor; the Vice-Chancellor had no less hastily telephoned to the Lord Chancellor of England, High Steward of the university; the Lord Chancellor had communicated quite briskly with the Home Secretary ... It was not unlikely, Appleby thought as he jumped out of the car, that local authority might feel central authority to have been pitched somewhat abruptly at its head. He was therefore relieved when, on being shown by a frightened parlourmaid into the deceased President's dining-room, he discovered local authority incarnated in no more formidable shape than that of an old acquaintance, Inspector Dodd.

These two men offered an interesting contrast – the contrast not so much of two generations (although Appleby was by full twenty years the younger) as of two epochs of English life. Dodd, heavy, slow, simply bred, and speaking with such a dialectical purity that a philologist might have named the parish in which he was born, suggested an England fundamentally rural still – and an England in which crime, when it occurred, was clear and brutal, calling less for science and detective skill than for vigorous physical action. He had learned a routine, but he was essentially untrained and unspecialized, relying upon a pithy if uncertain native shrewdness, retaining something strong and individual in his mental, as in his linguistic, idiom. Beside him, Appleby's personality seemed at first thin, part-effaced by some long discipline of study, like a surgeon whose individuality has concentrated itself within the channels of a unique operative technique. For Appleby was the efficient product of a more 'developed' age than Dodd's; of an age in which our civilization, multiplying its elements by division, has produced, amid innumerable highly-specialized products, the high-specialized criminal and the highly-specialized detector of crime. Nevertheless, there was something more in Appleby than the intensely-taught product of a modern police college. A contemplative habit and a tentative mind, poise as well as force, reserve rather than wariness – these were the tokens perhaps of some underlying, more liberal education. It was a schooled but still free intelligence that was finally formidable in Appleby, just as it was something of tradition and of the soil that was finally formidable in Dodd.

The two men were likely enough to clash; with a little goodwill they were equally likely to combine. And now Dodd, for all his fifteen stone and an uncommon tiredness (he had been working on the case since early morning), sprang up with decent cordiality to welcome his colleague. 'The detective arrives,' he said with a deep chuckle when greetings had been exchanged, 'and the village policeman hands over the body with all the misunderstood clues to date.' As he spoke, Dodd turned towards the table, on which a pile of papers evinced his industry during the day. They were flanked on the one hand by a hastily-made but sufficiently clear ground-plan of the college and on the other by the remains of bread and cheese, and beer in stout academic pewter – refreshments which it had occurred to Dr Umpleby's servants, round about three o'clock, that the inspector might stand a little in need of. 'The St Anthony's beer,' Dodd said, 'is a good feature of the case. The village policeman is baffled, but he gets his pint.'

Appleby smiled. 'The village policeman has notably mastered his facts,' he replied, 'at least if he's the same policeman I knew a couple of years ago. The Yard still talks about your check-up on those motor-thieves ... you remember?'

Dodd's acknowledgement of the compliment in the reminiscence took the form of wasting no time now. Drawing up a chair for Appleby, he placed the pile of papers between them. 'I've been going a bit fast today,' he said abruptly, 'and what I've got here is limited by going fast. It's short all round but it gives us bearings. There has been ground enough to cover, and first on the spot must get quickly over all, you'll agree. I've taken dozens of statements in a hasty way. Any one of them might have put me direct on somebody making out of the country. But none of them has. It's a mystery right enough, Appleby. In other words, it looks like one of your cases, not mine.'

Dodd's handsome speech was sincere but not wholly disinterested. Fortified by the St Anthony's ale, he had been spending the last hour thinking, and the more he had thought the less he had liked the results. His mind, indeed, had begun to stray, shying from this case on which he could see no beginning to another case of which he hoped soon to see the end. For some time he had been working on an extensive series of burglaries in the suburbs, and this baffling matter of Dr Umpleby, obviously urgent, had come to interrupt his personal control of a round-up from which he saw himself as likely to gain a good deal of credit. He put his position to Appleby now and it was agreed that the latter should, for the time being, take over the St Anthony's mystery as completely as possible. As soon as they had come to an understanding on this, Dodd placed the plan of the college in front of Appleby and proceeded to outline the facts as he knew them.

'Dr Umpleby was shot dead at eleven o'clock last night. That's the first of several things that make his death something like the story-books. You know the murdered squire's house in the middle of the snow-storm? And all the fancy changes run on that − liners on the ocean, submarines, balloons in the air, locked rooms with never a chimney? St Anthony's or any other college, you see, is something like that from half past nine every night. Here's your submarine.' As he spoke, Dodd took up the ground-plan and ran a large finger aggressively round the perimeter of the St Anthony's buildings. 'But in this college,' he went on, 'there's more to it than that.' This time his finger ran round a lesser circuit. 'In this college there's submarine *within* submarine. At half past nine they shut off the college as a whole from the world. And then later, at ten-fifteen, they shut off one bit of the college from the rest. That is almost a pure story-book situation now, isn't it? Nobody gets in or out of the college after half past nine that the porter doesn't know of – *with certain exceptions*. Nobody got in or out from half past nine last night to this present moment that we don't know of – *with the same possible exceptions*. And after ten-fifteen, nobody can go to and fro between the main body of the college (submarine) and this additionally shut-off Orchard Ground (submarine within submarine) with, again, *the same possible exceptions*. Only' – and here Inspector Dodd suddenly spoke with a vigorous irritation – 'none of the exceptions appears to be a homicidal lunatic! And therefore the lunatic who did *that*' – and here Dodd jerked his thumb in the direction of the next room – 'ought still to be on the premises. *I* haven't found him, Appleby. Every man alive in this college is saner and more blameless than the rest.'

'Why necessarily look for a lunatic?' Appleby asked.

'I don't,' responded Dodd soberly. 'That hanky-panky through there rattled me for a moment,' and again he motioned towards the next room. 'You'll see what I mean presently,' he continued a little grimly, 'but the point I have to make now is about these exceptions. The exceptions, as you may guess, are certain of the Fellows of the college – not by any means all of them. They have keys – double-purpose keys. They can enter or leave the college with them through this little door on Schools Street. And you see where – if they're coming in – that lands them. It lands them straight in the submarine within a submarine, Orchard Ground. They can then use the same key to get them out of Orchard Ground into the rest of the college. And when I give you the facts of the case in a minute you'll see that the murderer of Dr Umpleby appears to have had one of those keys. Which is no doubt,' the inspector added drily, 'why *you* have been sent for in such a hurry.'

'I see the suggested situation, anyway,' Appleby replied, after a brief scrutiny of the ground-plan. 'Whereas in a normal college a nocturnal murder would probably be physically within the power of anyone within the college, *this* college is so arranged that *this* murder could apparently be carried out only by quite a few people – people who had, or who could get hold of, a key to this Orchard Ground. For the keys – you are maintaining, are you not? – gave the particular sort of access to Dr Umpleby that the circumstances seem to require.'

Dodd nodded. 'You've got it,' he said, 'and you can understand the perturbation of St Anthony's.'

'There is the obvious fact that keys are treacherous things. They're easier to steal usually than a cheque-book – and far easier to copy than a signature.'

Dodd shook his head. 'Yes, but you'll see presently that there's more to it than that. The topography of the business really is uncommonly odd.'

Both men looked at the plan in silence for a moment. 'Well,' said Appleby at length, 'here is our stage setting. Now let us have the characters and events.'

3

'I'll begin with characters,' Dodd said; 'indeed, I'll begin where I had to begin this morning; with a list of names.' As he spoke, the inspector rummaged among his papers as if looking for a memorandum. Then, apparently thinking better of it, he squared his shoulders, wrinkled his brow in concentration, and continued with his eyes fixed upon his own large boots.

'Here are the Fellows who were dining in college last night. In addition to the President there was the Dean; he's called the Reverend the Honourable Tracy Deighton-Clerk.' (There was an indefinable salt in the inspector's mode of conveying this information.) 'And there were Mr Lambrick, Professor Empson, Mr Haveland, Mr Titlow, Dr Pownall, Dr Gott, Mr Campbell, Professor Curtis, Mr Chalmers-Paton, and Dr Barocho.'

Appleby nodded. 'Deighton-Clerk,' he repeated, 'Lambrick, Empson, Haveland, Titlow, Pownall, Gott, Campbell, Curtis, Chalmers-Paton – and a foreigner who just beats me. Go on.'

'Barocho,' said Dodd. 'And only one Fellow, as it happens, was absent. He's called Ransome and at the moment he's said to be digging up some learned stuff in central Asia.' Dodd's tone again conveyed some hint of the feeling that Dr Umpleby's death had landed him among queer fish. 'Not that I've any proof,' he continued suspiciously, 'of where this Ransome is. That's just what they all say.'

Appleby smiled. 'The submarine seems well officered,' he said. 'If you're going on to extract a list of a couple of hundred or so undergraduates from those boots of yours I think I'd certainly prefer the baronet's country house. Or the balloon in the stratosphere – that generally holds about two.' But his eyes as he spoke were on the plan in front of him and in a moment he added: 'But the point seems to be that the undergraduates don't come in?'

'I don't think they do,' replied Dodd; 'at least it's *likely* they don't, just as it's likely the college servants and so on don't – and, as you've gathered, for simple topographical reasons. So the list I've given you may be important. And now, after the scene and the persons, I suppose, events and times. Here is the time-scheme of the thing as far as I've got it into my head.

'Dinner was over by about eight o'clock – as far as the proceedings in hall were concerned. But all the people at the high table – the President, Dean, and Fellows, that is – went across in a body as usual to their common-room. They sat in the smaller common-room for about half an hour, having a little extra, I gather, in the way of port and dessert. Then at about half past eight they made another move – still in a body – to the larger common-room next door. They had coffee and cigarettes there – all according to the day's routine still – and talked till about nine o'clock. Dr Umpleby was the first to leave: he went off through a door that gives directly into his own house. And if we're to believe what we're told, that was the last time any of his colleagues saw him alive.

'Well, the common-room began to break up after that, and by half past nine everybody was gone. Lambrick, Campbell, Chalmers-Paton are married men and by half past nine they were off to their homes. The others all went to their rooms about the college. All, that is, with the exception of Gott, who is Junior Proctor and went out patrolling the streets.

'At nine-thirty the locking up began. The porter locked the main gates. That is the moment, you may say, at which the submarine submerged: from that moment to this nobody can have got in or out of St Anthony's without observation – *unless he had a key.*'

Appleby shook his head in mild protest. 'I incline to distrust those keys from the start,' he said, 'and I distrust your submarine. A great rambling building like this may have half a dozen irregular entrances – or exits.'

But Dodd's reply was confident. 'The submarine may sound as if I've been reading novels, but I believe it's near the mark. It's something we have to know in a quiet way – and we could surprise some colleges by pointing out a good many smart dodges. But I've overhauled St Anthony's today, and it's *watertight*.'

Appleby nodded his provisional acceptance of the point. 'Well,' he said, 'the President is in his Lodging, the dons are in their rooms, the undergraduates are in theirs, and the great world is effectively locked out. What next?'

'More locking out – or in,' Dodd promptly replied. 'The President's butler locked three doors. He locked the front door of the Lodging giving on Bishop's Court, he locked the back door giving on St Ernulphus Lane, and he locked the door between the Lodging and the common-room – the one, that is, the President had used a little before. That was about ten o'clock. At ten-fifteen came the final locking-up. The porter locked the gates to Orchard Ground . . .'

Dodd had so far been delivering himself of this scheme of things without book. Now he paused and handed Appleby a sheaf of notes. 'I'd go over that again, if I were you,' he said; 'it takes a little getting clear.'

Appleby went slowly over the notes and observed, with something of the admiration that was intended, that Dodd had apparently let no discrepancy creep into his oral account. He looked up when he had digested the names and times, and Dodd went on to the crisis of his narrative.

'When Dr Umpleby left the common-room he went straight to his study. At half past ten his butler, Slotwiner, took in some sort of drink – it was the regular routine apparently – and then retired to his pantry off the hall. Slotwiner more or less had his eye on the hall during the next half-hour and nobody, he says, entered the study that way, and nobody came out. In other words, there was only one way into – or out of – the study during that period – by way of the french windows that give on Orchard Ground.'

'The so-securely locked Orchard Ground,' murmured Appleby.

Dodd took up the implications of the other's tone perceptively enough. 'Exactly. I suppose our first clue is just that – that we have to deal, from the outset, with so obviously artificial a situation. But here meantime is this butler, Slotwiner, in his pantry. The pantry is a mere nook of a place and normally he would have gone downstairs to where he has a room of his own beside the kitchens. But apparently on this night of the week, Mr Titlow – that's the senior Fellow – has been in the habit of calling on the President for a short talk on college business. He comes regularly just on eleven – pretty late, it seems to me, for a call, but the idea was that each could get in a couple of hours' work after the usual common-room convivialities were over. I believe, you know, that these folk do quite an amount of work in their own way. Well, Slotwiner waited upstairs to let Titlow in. He had to unlock the front door – this one opening on Bishop's Court – because, as you remember, he had locked it along with the other two doors at ten o'clock, following the rule in Umpleby's household. Titlow turned up as usual on the stroke of eleven and he and Slotwiner were just exchanging a word in the hall when they heard the shot.'

'The shot coming, no doubt,' said Appleby, 'from the study where Umpleby was supposed to be sitting *solus*.'

'Exactly so. And he was *solus* – or rather his corpse was – when Titlow and Slotwiner rushed into the room. Umpleby was shot; there was – if we are to believe these two – no weapon; but the french windows giving on Orchard Ground were ajar. Well, Titlow and Slotwiner (or one of them – I don't know which) tumbled to the situation surprisingly quickly. They saw it was murder and they saw the significance of Orchard Ground. If the murderer had escaped that way he was there still, unless – what didn't occur to them – he had the key to those gates.'

The inspector picked up a pencil this time and ran it over the plan. Very laboriously, once more, he made his cardinal point. 'You'll see how certain that is,' he said, 'when you get out there. On these three sides Orchard Ground is bounded either by an exceedingly high wall or by an arrangement of combined wall and railings that is higher still. The fourth side has the President's Lodging here at one end and the college chapel at the other, with the hall and library in between. These make a line of buildings that separate Orchard Ground from Bishop's Court, and there are just two passages through: one between chapel and library and the other between hall and President's Lodging. The only other exit from Orchard Ground is by a little wicket gate opening on Schools Street. And all three exits were, of course, locked. Escape from Orchard Ground without the key was impossible.

'So you see Titlow and Slotwiner decided they'd got the murderer safe. They didn't think he could get out because they didn't think he could have the key to those three gates. And they didn't think he could have a key because it didn't occur to them to think of a Fellow of the college.

'I suspect Slotwiner of taking the initiative. He's an old soldier and would be up to an emergency, whereas Titlow seems a dreamy soul enough. But Titlow's got guts. The look of that room was pretty surprising, but he stuck there guarding the window while Slotwiner ran to the telephone in the hall and got the porter across, called a doctor and got on to us. I was at the station late working at reports on my own case and I got enough from Slotwiner to be along with every man I could muster in ten minutes. Slotwiner and Titlow were in the study still with a porter to help them keep guard. We went through everything on the orchard side of those gates as if we were looking for a black cat. We worked on a cordon basis from one end to the other, ransacked the chapel and the little block of Fellows' buildings opposite and climbed every tree. Apart from three of the four Fellows (Titlow is the fourth) who live in Orchard Ground and were there undisturbed in their rooms, we found no one. We searched again by daylight, of course, and the gates are guarded still.'

Dodd paused for a moment and Appleby asked a question: 'There is no trace of any sort of robbery?'

'None at all. Money, watch, and so on still on the corpse. There is one point, though, that might conceivably be relevant.' Dodd picked up a small object wrapped in tissue-paper and tossed it down in front of his colleague. 'Umpleby's pocket-diary – and found in his pocket all right. Plenty of entries for you to study – until you come just up to date. The leaf for the last two days, and the leaf for today and tomorrow, have been torn out ... And now come along.'

4

The two men left the dead President's dining-room and crossed the hall to where, at the end of a narrow corridor, a stalwart constable stood guard over the study door. He stood aside with a salute and a frank provincial stare at Appleby, while Dodd, taking a key from his pocket, unlocked the door and pushed it open with something of a restrained dramatic gesture.

The study was a long, well-proportioned room, with a deep open fireplace opposite the single door and with windows at each end: to the left (and barred like all the ground-floor outer windows of the college), a row of small windows giving on St Ernulphus Lane; to the right, rather narrow french windows, now heavily curtained, but giving, as Appleby knew, upon Orchard Ground. The sombrely-furnished, book-lined apartment was lit partly by the dull light of the November evening and partly by a single electric standard lamp. Halfway between the french windows and the fireplace, sprawled upon its back, lay the body of a man – tall, spare, dinner-jacketed. So much, and so much only, was visible, for round the head there was swathed, as if in gross burlesque of the common offices of death, the dull black stuff of an academic gown.

But it was not at this sight that Appleby started a little as he entered the room. If Dodd had spoken of a lunatic he now saw why. From the dull dark-oak panels over the fireplace, roughly scrawled in chalk, a couple of grinning death's-heads stared out upon the room. Just beside the President's grotesquely muffled head lay a human skull. And over the surrounding area of the floor were scattered little piles of human bones.

For a long moment Appleby paused on the spectacle; then he moved over to the french windows and pulled back the curtain. Dusk was falling and the trim college orchard seemed to hold all the mystery of a forest. Only close to him on the right, breaking the illusion, was the grey line of hall and library, stone upon buttressed stone, fading, far above, into the darkness of stained-glass windows. Directly in front, in uncertain silhouette against a lustreless eastern sky, loomed the boldly arabesqued gables of the Caroline chapel. An exhalation neither wholly mist nor wholly fog was beginning to glide over the immemorial turf, to curl round the trees, to dissolve in insubstantial pageantry the fading lines of archway and wall. And echoing over the college and the city, muted as if in requiem for what lay within, was the age-old melody of vesper bells.

Chapter 2

For some minutes Appleby continued to stare out upon the fast-thickening shadows. Then, without turning round and almost as if in soliloquy, he began to feel for his own grip on the case.

'At ten-fifteen this court, Orchard Ground, was locked up. After that, anyone who was in it could get out, or who was out could get in, in one of two ways. The one way was by means of the key possessed by certain of the Fellows: with that one could pass either between the orchard and the rest of the college by one of the two gates giving on Bishop's Court; or between the orchard and the outer world by means of the little gate that gives on Schools Street. The other way was through these french windows, through this study and out by one of the doors in the President's hall – the front door giving on Bishop's Court, the common-room door giving indirectly on the same quarter, or the back door giving on St Ernulphus Lane, and, again, the outer world.

'At ten-thirty Umpleby, according to the butler, was alive. From then until eleven o'clock, according to the butler, no one passed from the study through the hall to Bishop's Court or St Ernulphus Lane – or conversely.

'At eleven o'clock, according to the butler and Titlow, there was a shot from the study. They went in at once and found Umpleby dead. They then claim to have had the route through the study under continuous observation until they handed over to you. And you had it under observation until you had searched study, Orchard Ground, and all the buildings in Orchard Ground thoroughly.

'Accepting these appearances we have a fairly clear situation. If Umpleby was shot when we think he was and where we think he was and other than by himself, then his assailant was *either* one of the three people discovered by you during your search *or* a fourth person having a key. That fourth person, again, might be *either* another of the persons legitimately possessed of keys *or* an unknown person in wrongful possession of one. It follows that there are two preliminary issues: first, the movements of the persons legitimately possessed of keys and, as an extension of that, the relations of such persons to Umpleby; secondly, the provenance of the existing keys – the history of each, with the likelihood of its having been abstracted and copied in the recent past.'

Appleby, as he worked out this concise and knotty résumé of the facts, spoke with a shade of reluctance. He was less ready than Dodd for anything savouring of a conventional mystery, and he was inclined to distrust inference from the oddly precise conditions under which Umpleby had apparently been murdered. As Dodd had shrewdly re-marked, the affair was obtrusively artificial, as if the criminal had gone out of his way to sign himself both ingenious and grotesque, calculating and whimsical. Within an hour of his arrival at St Anthony's, Appleby was finding a particular line of action imposed upon him – a line de-manding minute and probably laborious investigation into the conduct and dispositions of a small clearly marked group of people. He saw that he was confronted, actually, with two propositions. The first was simple: 'The circumstances are such that I must concentrate on so-and-so.' The second was less simple: 'The circumstances *have been so contrived as to suggest* that I must concentrate on so-and-so.' In pursuing the first propo-sition he must, at least, not lose sight of the second.

Appleby checked surmise and turned once more to Dodd for information. 'Which of the Fellows lodge in Orchard Ground?' he asked. 'Which of them have keys? How far have you traced their movements after the break-up in the common-room last night?'

'The four that lodge in Orchard Ground,' Dodd replied, 'are Empson, Pownall, Titlow, and Haveland. They're in a building next to, but not communicating with, this Lodging. It's just through here' – and Dodd tapped his finger stolidly on one of the scrawled death's-heads above the dead man's fireplace. 'The block is called "Little Fellows"'. There are two sets of rooms on each side of a staircase,' he continued with precision, 'and the men live like this.' And with a quick rummage Dodd produced another of his industriously prepared papers.

| *Upper floor* | Empson | Titlow |
| *Ground floor* | Pownall | Haveland |

'We found Empson, Pownall, Haveland each in his own room;

Pownall in bed, the others working. About Titlow's movements you know. Now about the keys; with them we come to the really extra-ordinary factor. These four people lodging in Orchard Ground all have keys. Being shut off from the rest of the college, they naturally have to. And you would expect that for convenience of getting at them, as well as to get in and out of the college by the wicket without rousing the porter, all their colleagues would have keys as well. But they haven't. You know, they're an unpractical lot.'

Appleby smiled a little grimly. 'There may be one among them,' he said, 'who is – efficient.'

'Well, for that matter most of them are efficient after a particular fashion. They're not vague, for instance. They're keen and precise, really. Only it's a preciseness, I reckon, that has all run to things a long way off or a long time back. For instance, there's Professor Curtis. He lodges in Surrey Court. I asked him if he had a key to the gates. "Gates, Mr Inspector," he said, "gates?" "The gates between this and Orchard Ground," I explained. "Yes, to be sure," he said, "there's a story they came from Cordova. The college had them from the third earl of Black-wood; he served in Sidmouth's second ministry." "But have you a key?" I asked again. "I relinquished my key," he replied at once, "at the end of April 1911." "End of April 1911," I repeated a bit blankly. "Yes," he said, "at the end of April 1911. Empson won both Cornwalls that year, you know, and we elected him to his Fellowship at once. He's done nothing since, either. He'll make an admirable President, no doubt. You did say poor Dr Umpleby was quite dead, did you not?" "Quite dead," I answered, " – and you're quite sure you haven't had a key since 1911?" "Quite sure," he said; "I gave up my key to Empson. I remember reflecting what an excellent thing a locked gate between colleagues might be. If you want a key, Inspector, the porter will no doubt lend you his."'

As Dodd concluded this remarkable feat of witness-box memory, he produced yet another paper. 'Here,' he added impressively, 'is a table.' And he laid it before Appleby.

× Deighton-Clerk	Bishop's
× Empson	Orchard Ground
× Haveland	Orchard Ground
× Pownall	Orchard Ground
× Titlow	Orchard Ground

Barocho	Bishop's
Campbell	*married*; Schools Street
Chalmers–Paton	*married*; suburb
Curtis	Surrey
× Gott	Surrey
× Lambrick	*married*; suburb

'I've put a cross,' said Dodd, 'against the people who have keys. There seems to be no system in it. For instance, Lambrick, who is married and lives out of college, keeps a key, but Campbell and Chalmers-Paton, who are in just the same position, get along without one. Gott and the Dean live in college and have keys; Curtis and Barocho also live in college and have not. So much for how the keys are distributed. And now for their history.' At this point Dodd broke into an unaccountable chuckle. 'You know, I was reading a story the other day which turned on keys – the provenance of keys, as you call it in your learned London way. It was the key of a safe that it was all about, and it couldn't have been stolen – had literally never been in unauthorized hands. And yet it had been copied. Do you know how?'

Appleby laughed. 'I could give a good guess, I think. But we don't know we have to search for any fancy tricks here. A key might very easily have been stolen and returned in the recent past.'

'Yes,' Dodd replied; 'recent past is the word.' And he looked almost slyly at Appleby as he spoke. For with a nice sense of the dramatic he had delayed the climax of his narration. '*The keys were all changed yesterday morning!*'

Appleby whistled. Dodd when he had heard the same news had sworn. It was the final and overwhelming touch of that topsy-turvy precision that seemed to mark the St Anthony's case.

Briefly Dodd explained. No one had taken much care of his key. A key is not at all the same thing to a scholar that it is to a banker, a doctor, or a business man. The possessions of the learned classes are locked up for the most part in their heads and to a don a key is more often than not something that he discovers himself to have lost when he wants to open a suitcase. And those Fellows of St Anthony's who possessed keys to the gates which had suddenly become so tragically important had for long been careless enough with them without anybody worrying. But recently there had been a scandal. An undergraduate had got into serious trouble during an illicit nocturnal expedition, and the mystery of how he had made his way in and out of St Anthony's had not been satisfactorily cleared up. The President had decided that a key had been copied. He had ordered fresh locks and keys for the three vital gates – and the locks had been fitted, and the keys distributed to the people concerned, only the morning before he met his death.

It was Dodd's view that this circumstance, though extraordinary in itself, introduced a welcome simplification into the case. It seemed likely to save an enormous amount of laborious and difficult inquiry – for nothing, as he had found in the interviews he had already conducted that morning, could well be more difficult, delicate, and tedious than pursuing a number of academic persons with minute questions as to their material possessions. Moreover, the circle of possible suspects seemed at once to be narrowed in the most definite way. If Dodd at that moment had been called upon to write a formal report on the progress of the investigations he would have risked a categorical assertion. Dr Umpleby could have been murdered only by one of a small group of persons definitely known.

And Appleby, as he reviewed the situation while pacing restlessly but observantly round the fantastic death-chamber, had also reached one definite conclusion. Mystery stories were popular in universities – and even among the police. Dodd, who still kept so much of an English countryside that read Bunyan and the Bible, and who was, besides, a monument of efficient but unimaginative police routine, was a case in point. His native shrewdness had at once led him to note the artificiality of the present circumstances. But (and such, Appleby reflected, is the extraordinary power of the Word) he was half-prepared to accept the artificial, the strikingly *fictive*, as normal. And he seemed in danger, as a consequence, of missing that most important *Why* in the case: *Why* had Umpleby met his death in a story-book manner? For that his death had been set in an elaborately contrived frame seemed now clear: the circumstance of the changing of the locks made this evident almost to the point of demonstration. Umpleby had died amid circumstances of elaborate ingenuity. He had died in a literary context; indeed, he had in a manner of speaking died amid a confusion of literary contexts. For in the network of physical circumscriptions implicitly pointing (as Appleby had put it to himself) to *so-and-so* there was contrivance in a literary tradition deriving from all the progeny of Sherlock Holmes, while in the fantasy of the bones there was something of the incongruous tradition of the 'shocker'. Somewhere in the case, it seemed, there was a mind thinking in terms both of inference and of the macabre ... A mind, one might say, thinking in terms of Edgar Allan Poe. Poe, come to think of it, was a present intellectual fashion, and St Anthony's was an intellectual place ...

An intellectual place. That was, of course, a vital fact to remember when proceeding a step further – when attempting to answer the question of which Dodd was perhaps insufficiently aware: *Why* had Umpleby met his death like a baronet in a snowstorm? There were two tentative answers: (1) because, for some reason, it was *useful* that way; (2) because it was intellectually amusing that way ... Intelligence, after all, had its morbid manifestations.

Appleby caught himself up. He was trying somewhat wildly, he saw, to find an approach to his problem on a human or psychological plane. He knew it to be at once his strength and his weakness as a detective that he was happier on that plane than on the plane of doors and windows and purloined keys. The materials of the criminologist, he used to declare in theoretical moments to colleagues at Scotland Yard, are not finger-prints and cigarette-ends, but the human mind as exposed for study in human behaviour. And of human behaviour he had as yet had nothing in the present case. He had been met, so far, not with human actors, but with a set of circumstances – once more the story-book approach, he told himself.

With an odd effect of thought-reading Dodd spoke. 'You'll be beginning to look for some of the livestock.' And as Appleby, startled by the odd ring of the phrase in the presence of what had been Josiah Umpleby, turned back from the window through which he had been staring, his colleague crossed the room to ring the bell. 'We'll have in a witness,' he said. And the two men adjourned again to the dining-room.

2

Mr Harold Tapp had been waiting for half an hour to be interviewed in connection with a murder, but he was not in the least nervous as a result. He was a sharp, confident person; he had all the appearance of being reliable and, according to Dodd, he enjoyed the reputation of being an excellent locksmith. Very little prompting was necessary to get him to give a tolerably connected account of his recent dealings with St Anthony's. His statement was impressively recorded by a sad and portly sergeant summoned for the purpose.

'The late Dr Humpleby,' said Mr Tapp, 'sent for me a week ago today. To be exack – which is what *you* want, you know – the late Dr Humpleby gave me a ring-hup.'

'To be more exact still,' said Appleby, 'did Dr Umpleby ring through to you direct, can you tell, or did somebody else make the call before Dr Umpleby spoke?'

The question found Tapp decided – the only point it was designed to test. Umpleby himself had summoned the locksmith, who had immediately presented himself at the President's Lodging. 'You see,' said Tapp, 'the late Dr Humpleby was in a nurry. He was in a nurry and a flurry about them locks. I don't think flurry's too strong to describe his 'urry: he was hanxious for the change. He explained the why and where-fore of it too – a nundergrad having been getting hout and all. Hanxious was the late Dr Humpleby.'

Appleby was regarding Mr Tapp with more interest than he had expected to feel.

'Well, you see,' continued the locksmith, 'it weren't what you'd call a big job nor it weren't rightly what you'd call a little 'un. So I fixed yesterday morning for fitting, and the late Doctor said it would serve so. Very interested he was in the way of the work too, and particular over the keys. Very proper notions over keys had the late Doctor. Ten keys there were to be and all going to him direck. And ten he got yester-day morning as soon as the locks were fitted and tested by myself.'

'Just how did he get them,' asked Dodd; 'and just how safe had you been keeping them?'

'Well, you see, I'd been on them all week myself and done all the assembling and finishing. And the drawing was in the safe, and the locks and keys in the safe, as often as they weren't in my 'ands. All that's a nabit, you see, with a nigh-class locksmith. Not that all my business is 'igh-class, you know. Still, this was – and treated accordingly. I fitted the locks yesterday morning and then I saw Dr Humpleby 'imself and gave him the ten keys as required. And from the moment I set file to them to the moment I 'anded them hover every one of them keys 'ad been treated like a bag of golden sovereigns. And they're not a thing you often see nowadays,' Mr Tapp concluded somewhat irrelevantly.

A little questioning substantiated the fact that the new locks and keys had been prepared under completely thief-proof conditions. Appleby's problem of 'provenance' was proving very simple indeed. He turned to the point in Tapp's statement which had particularly arrested his interest. 'You say that Dr Umpleby appeared anxious about the keys and gave you a reason – something about an undergraduate? Just how anxious was he? Would you describe him as agitated – really worried about the matter?'

Tapp answered at once. 'Hagitated, sir, I wouldn't nor couldn't rightly say. But he was in a nurry and a flurry – and that I *do* say.'

Appleby was patient. 'Not really agitated, but flurried. I wonder if you can make that a little clearer? Agitation and flurry seem to me very much the same thing. Perhaps you can give me a clearer idea of what you mean by flurry?'

Tapp reflected for a moment, 'Well, you see, sir,' he said at length, 'by flurry I wouldn't quite mean scurry, and by scurry I *would* mean hagitation. I 'ope that's clear. And certainly Dr Humpleby was in a *nurry*.'

This was as much information as was to be obtained from the locksmith and, after he had signed a correctly aspirated version of it prepared by the lugubrious sergeant, he was dismissed.

'Just how odd is it,' asked Appleby, 'that Umpleby should give the excellent Tapp *reasons* for changing the locks and keys? I don't see that, Dodd, do you? It strikes me as just a shade queer. It's a queerness that may be nothing more than a minute queerness of character. I may be noticing only a minute way in which Umpleby's behaviour has differed from the dead normal behaviour of a dead average Head of a House – or I may be noticing something much more significant. And the same thing applies to the other interesting point – that Umpleby was in what our friend called a flurry about the business; that he was within some recognizable distance, measured by flurries and scurries, of being agitated.'

'There's something strikes me as more significant than that.' Dodd was very stolid. '*There was an extra key.*'

Appleby gave his second whistle of the afternoon. 'Your point again! The Dean, Empson, Gott, Haveland, Lambrick, Pownall, Titlow, one for the head porter . . . Hullo! That's only eight. Surely there were two extra keys?'

Dodd shook his head. 'The head porter got one for his ring and another went as a spare in the safe in his lodge. But one key does remain to be accounted for. And an awkward complication it makes.'

'Umpleby himself perhaps kept a key?'

Dodd again made a negative gesture. 'I don't think so. At least he never, according to the Dean, used to. He had no need of one. He could walk out of his own Lodging into either Orchard Ground or the main courts. And similarly his own back-door let him out on the street. And, of course, we've found no key in his belongings.'

'A missing key,' murmured Appleby. 'Do you know, I'm rather pleased about the missing key. It represents a screw loose somewhere – and so far your submarine has been screwed down uncomfortably tight.' But he was speaking absently, and pacing about as he spoke. Then, with a sudden gesture of impatience, he led the way back to the study.

3

The black gown which had been found swathed round the President's head, and which had been replaced there, following police routine, after the police-surgeon had certified life to be extinct, Appleby now carefully removed. It was caked with blood, but only slightly, and Appleby laid it on a chair. He gazed with some curiosity at the dead President. Umpleby's was a massive and, for a spare-bodied man that he was, a surprisingly heavy head, bone-structure prominent about the brow and commanding nose – fleshy and heavy-jowled below. The mouth, sagging in death, had been rigid in life; firm to the point perhaps of some suggestion of cruelty; ruthless certainly rather than sensual. The eyes were open, and they were cold and grey; the features were composed – oddly at variance with the tiny but startling hall-mark of violence in the centre of the forehead. And death had brushed away a load of years from the pallid face: it was some moments before Appleby saw clearly that Umpleby had been an old man. At the moment he made no examination but picked up the gown again to do the office of a temporary shroud. As he did so something about it held his attention. 'I take it this is not Umpleby's gown?' he asked Dodd.

'No, it's not. And it has no name on it. I haven't, as a matter of fact, questioned people about it so far.'

'You needn't, I think, expend much effort on that. It's Dr Barocho's gown.'

A second thought and Dodd had taken the point neatly. 'You mean it's some sort of foreign gown, not an English one?'

'Exactly so, and Barocho follows as a good guess. But I doubt if it will be a case for bringing out the handcuffs. And now what about the movements of all these people? How far, to get back to where we were, have you traced their movements after the break-up of the common-room last night?'

Appleby was prowling round the study again. Dodd rustled among his papers as he answered. 'In the course of the day I've taken preliminary statements from everybody who seems concerned – or everybody who seemed concerned until this infernal tenth key started up. Some are apparently checkable as alibi-statements for the time of the shooting; others not. I'm checking up as fast as the three capable men I've got can work – incidentally they're *your* men now for the purposes of the case. Meantime here are the carbons of the different statements. You'd better hold on to them.' As he spoke, Dodd put the little pile of flimsies down in front of his colleague with an air that suggested plainly enough the symbolic shifting of responsibility latent in the act. Appleby turned to the first sheet.

Slotwiner, George Frederick (54). Entered the college service as buttery-boy at sixteen. Personal servant to Dr Umpleby on the latter's becoming Dean of the college in 1910. Has acted as butler since Dr Umpleby became President in 1921.

10.30 p.m. Took in drinks to study, finding President working at his desk and alone. Thereafter had a full view of the study door from his pantry.

11 p.m. Crossed hall and admitted Mt Titlow at front door. Titlow still speaking to him when shot heard. Entered study along with Titlow and discovered body. Returned to hall and telephoned doctor, porter, and police. Rejoined Titlow in study and kept guard until arrival of porters.

11.10 p.m. Took message from Titlow to Dean.

Corroboration: Titlow.

Titlow, Samuel Still (51) . . .

At this moment there came an interruption in the form of a heavy knocking at the door, and the melancholy sergeant thrust in his head and announced lugubriously: 'The valley has a message!'

The valley of the shadow . . . For a moment in the darkening room with its litter of dead men's bones, the effect of the words was almost startling; a second later they were explained by the appearance of a discreet black-coated figure in the background. A discreet voice remonstrated, '*Butler*, if you please, *constable*!' and added, to the accompaniment of a ghost of a bow to Dodd, 'The Dean's compliments, sir, and if the gentleman from London has arrived, he would be glad to see him in his rooms at his convenience.'

Appleby regarded George Frederick Slotwiner with all the interest due to the first intimate actor in the recent drama to present himself. Slotwiner bore little trace of any period he might have spent in the Army. Slight and sallow, he moved and held himself like a typical upper servant. Apparently somewhat short-sighted, he looked out upon the world through a pair of pince-nez glasses with an effect at once impressive and disconcerting – impressive because they contrived to elevate the mind from butlers to house-stewards, and from house-stewards to majordomos and grooms of the chamber; disconcerting because of a sudden doubt that their owner's stiff bearing was less the expression of professional dignity than the result of some chronic balancing feat on his nose. As this thought crossed Appleby's mind Slotwiner, who appeared to have been inwardly debating whether propriety permitted him any direct awareness of the gentleman from London's presence, made the ghost of a bow to him as well and, having effected this judicious compromise, waited impassively for a reply.

Appleby solved Slotwiner's difficulty. 'My compliments to the Dean,' he said, 'and I will be with him in half an hour. When Inspector Dodd rings the bell perhaps you will be good enough to take me across.' And as the butler turned to withdraw he suddenly added: 'One moment. When did the President last use candles in this room?'

The effect of this question was remarkable. Slotwiner swung round with a most unbutler-like rapidity and stared at Appleby. He was plainly startled and confused – more so even than the odd and abrupt question pitched at his back across the shrouded body of his employer, could warrant. But in a moment his look gave way to one of bewilderment; a moment more and he was wholly composed.

'The President never used candles, sir. As you will see, the room is very adequately lighted.' The man's hand went swiftly out as he spoke and flicked down a switch by the door: the single standard lamp which had been burning was reinforced by half a dozen further lamps set high up on the walls and throwing out a brilliant light over the ceiling. Appleby continued his questions. 'How did the President usually sit when he was here in the evenings? Did he use all the lights or merely the standard lamp?'

The butler answered now without hesitation. When at his desk or when sitting in his armchair near the fire, Dr Umpleby had been accustomed to use only the standard lamp. But if he had to move about among his books, or if he had visitors, he would turn on the other lights as well. They worked on a dual control and could be turned on from the fireplace as well as by the door.

'Last night at ten-thirty,' Appleby next asked, 'how were the lights then?'

'All the lights were on, sir. The President was selecting books from the far corner there while I was in the room.'

'And afterwards, when you broke in with Mr Titlow?'

'Only the standard lamp was burning.'

'Dr Umpleby would have turned off the others on returning to his desk?'

'I could not say, sir. It is possible.'

'Tell me what happened about the lights then.'

'Sir?'

'I mean did you, or did Mr Titlow, at once turn on the other lights when you found the body?'

Slotwiner hesitated. 'I can't say, sir,' he replied at length. 'Not, I mean, with any certainty. I believe I turned them on almost at once myself, but at such a moment the action would be mechanical. I do not positively recollect it. Later certainly all the lights were on.'

Slotwiner, feeling now that he was being interrogated in form, was speaking with caution and every appearance of conscientious precision. But Appleby broke off. 'I shall want your whole story later,' he said. 'Only one more question now.' He had half turned away, as if what was significant in the interview was over. Suddenly he turned round and looked at the butler searchingly. 'I wonder why you were so startled by my question about the candles?'

But this time Slotwiner was perfectly composed. 'I'm sure I hardly know, sir,' he answered. 'If I may say so, the question – *any* questions, sir – was a trifle unexpected. But I am unable to account for my reaction – you must have seen that I was quite perturbed. If I may attempt to express my feeling when you spoke, it was one of puzzlement. And I was puzzled as to why I was puzzled.' Slotwiner paused to consider. 'It was not over the overt content of your question, for I am quite clear that candles are never used in the Lodging. Dr Umpleby did not care for them, and with so much old panelling around I would certainly not sanction their use among the servants. To be as clear as I can, sir, I would speak a trifle technically and say that your question had a *latent* content. The feeling tone evoked was decidedly peculiar.' And with this triumph of academic statement Slotwiner gave one more ghost of a bow to Appleby and glided – levitated almost, to speak technically – out of the room.

Dodd gave a chuckle which would have been boisterous had his eye not fallen on the object stretched before the fire. 'You can see that you've landed among the dons,' he said. 'If you get that sort of cackle from the butler, what are you likely to get from the Dean, eh?'

But Appleby's smile in reply was thoughtful rather than merry. 'The feeling tone evoked was decidedly peculiar,' he quoted. 'You know, Dodd, that's an interesting man and he said an interesting thing. By the way' – Appleby glanced innocently at his colleague – 'what do you make of the candle business?'

Dodd looked bewildered. 'What candle business?' he said; 'I had no idea what you were getting at.'

Appleby took his colleague's arm for answer and led him to the far side of the room round which he had earlier made what had appeared to be a casual tour. Here the bookcases not only clothed the walls but projected into the room in the form of shallow bays. Islanded in one was a revolving bookcase containing the *Dictionary of National Biography*; in a second similarly was the *New English Dictionary* – the two sets of heavy volumes uniformly bound. But it was to the third of the four bays that Appleby led Dodd. Here was yet a third revolving bookcase – and Dodd found himself confronted by the fourteen bulky volumes of the Argentorati Athenaeus.

'The *Deipnosophists*,' Appleby was murmuring; 'Schweighäuser's edition . . . takes up a lot of room . . . Dindorf's compacter – and there he is.' He pointed to the corner of the lower shelf where the same enormous miscellany stood compressed into the three compact volumes of the Leipsic edition. Dodd, somewhat nonplussed before this classical abracadabra, growled suspiciously: 'These last three are upside down – is that what you mean?'

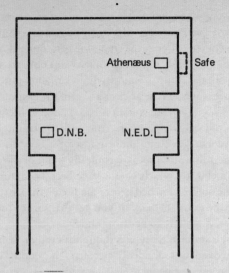

'Well, that's a point. How many books do you reckon in this room – eight or nine thousand, perhaps? Just see if you can spot any others upside down. It's not a way scholars often put away their books.'

Dodd declined the invitation. 'I thought you said something about candles. Is it all a little classical joke?'

Appleby straightened himself from examining the lower shelf and pointed gently to the polished surface, breast high, of the top of the book-case they were examining. A few inches from the edge farthest into the bay was a small spot, about half an inch in diameter, of what appeared to be candle-grease.

'Some cleaning stuff,' said Dodd. 'Beeswax preparation, perhaps. Careless servant.'

'A burglar – an amateur burglar with a candle?' Appleby suggested.

Dodd's response was immediate: he vanished from the room. When he returned, Appleby was on his knees beside the body. 'You were right, Appleby,' he announced eagerly. 'Only some sort of furniture cream is ever used on these bookcases. And they were done yesterday morning. The housemaid swears there wasn't a speck on them then – and she's a most respectable old person.' He paused, and seeing that Appleby's inspection of the body seemed over, he added: 'I've something of my own to show you in that alcove. It made me jump to your suggestion of

a burglar at once. We didn't ignore the nine thousand books altogether, you know.' He led the way back to the bay and paused, this
time not before the revolving bookcase but before the solid shelves of
closely packed books behind it. Putting his hand behind what appeared
to be a normal row he gave a sharp pull – and the whole swung easily
out upon a hinge. 'Dodge they sometimes decorate library doors with
– isn't it? And look what's behind the dummies.' What was behind, sunk
in the wall of the room, was a somewhat unusual, drawer-shaped steel
safe.

'The sort of burglar who potters about with a candle,' remarked
Appleby, 'wouldn't have much of a chance with that. Difficult to find
too, unless he knew about it. Not that I expect you knew about it?'

Dodd had not known. He had found the safe in the course of a
thorough search. The thousands of books had not been moved from
their shelves, but every one had been pressed back as far as it would go to
ensure that no discarded weapon lay anywhere concealed on the shelving
between books and wall. He was positive, however, that the searchers
were not responsible for turning the smaller Athenaeus. He had examined
its particular revolving bookcase himself – missing, he admitted, the
candle grease – and had found it unnecessary to take any of the books
out. He had also himself inspected the whole bay and had come upon
the concealed safe in the process.

Appleby's eyes travelled once more along the endless rows of books,
rapidly noting the character of the dead man's library. But it was the
physical appearance of hundreds of heavy folios on the lower shelves
which prompted his next remark. 'Lucky he was shot through the head,
Dodd. Do you see what a job that has saved us?' And seeing his
colleague's puzzled look he went on: 'Fancy it this way. Umpleby wants
to commit suicide. For this reason or that – just out of devilment, perhaps
– he decides to conceal the fact. Well, he takes any one of these books,
probably a big one, perhaps quite a small one' – here Appleby tapped a
stoutish crown octavo – 'and he hollows out a little nest in it – large
enough to hold an automatic. He holds it open with his left hand, close
by its place on the shelf. Then he places the pistol just where a careful
study of anatomy tells him, fires, slips the pistol in the book and the book
in its place, staggers across the room and falls – just where you see him!'

Following Appleby's pointing finger, Dodd strode across the room
to where the body lay. The small round hole, central in the forehead of

the dead man, reassured him – but he glanced with new curiosity nevertheless at the vellum and buckram and morocco rows, gleaming, gilt-tooled, dull, polished, stained – the representative backs of perhaps four centuries of bookbinding. But Appleby, with a gesture as if he had been wasting time, had turned back to consider the concealed safe. 'Finger-prints?' he asked.

Dodd shook his head.

'None at all?' pursued Appleby, interested.

But this time Dodd nodded. 'Yes,' he said, 'I'm afraid so. Umpleby's own. No one has been feeling the need of polishing up after himself. It looks as if the safe has been undisturbed. One thing's queer about it all the same – and it's this. Not a soul seems to know anything about it. I asked fishing questions of everyone the least likely – "Do you happen to know where the President kept his valuables?" and that sort of thing. And then I asked outright. Slotwiner, the other servants, the Dean, and the rest of the dons – none of them admitted to knowing of its existence. And there's no key. It's a combination lock and a combination lock only – not the kind where the combination opens to show a key-hole. Further than that I haven't had time to follow the thing up.'

At the mention of time, Appleby looked at his watch. 'I'm due for the Dean,' he said, 'and you for your supper and a rest. They'll want to take the body now, I expect.'

Dodd nodded. 'The body goes out to the mortuary,' he agreed; 'the room's locked up and sealed and you take the key. And it's for you to say when we bring a sack for these blasted bones.'

Appleby chuckled. 'I see it's the ossuary that really disturbs you. I think it may help a lot.' He picked up a fibula as he spoke and wagged it with professionally excusable callousness at Dodd. And with an association of thought which would have been clear to that efficient officer only if he had been a reader of Sir Thomas Browne he murmured: 'What song the Sirens sang, or what name Achilles assumed when he hid himself among women ...'

The fibula dropped with a little dry rattle on its pile as Appleby broke off to add: 'Nor is the other question, I hope, unanswerable.'

'*Other* question?'

Appleby had turned to the door. 'Who, my dear Dodd, were the pro-prietaries of these bones? We must consult the Provincial Guardians.'

Chapter 3

The Reverend the Honourable Tracy Deighton-Clerk, Dean of St Anthony's, contrived, though still in middle age, to suggest the great Victorians. His features were at once wholly strong and wholly benevolent, evoking, even to a hint of side-whisker, the formidable canvases of G. F. Watts. His manner was a degree on the heavy side of courtesy and not at times without that temerarious combination of aloofness and charm which used to be attempted, some two generations ago, by those who had once glimpsed Matthew Arnold. He had a fancy of himself in the rôle of *ultimus Romanorum*; the last representative of a clerical and leisured university, of an academic society that was not cultured merely but also Polite.

The psychologically-minded Slotwiner (who was said to model himself not a little on Mr Deighton-Clerk's manner) might have remarked that in the Dean's *persona* the episcopal idea had of late been rapidly developing. Indeed, the episcopal idea was hovering round him now, a comforting penumbra to the disturbing situation which confronted him as he stood, in elegant clerical evening-dress, before the fireplace of his study.

It was a room in marked contrast with the sombre and somewhat oppressive solidity of the dead President's apartment. Round a delicate Aubusson carpet, on which undergraduates instinctively trod as diffidently as if they had been schoolboys still, low white bookshelves enclosed the creamy vellum of the School-men and the Fathers. The panelling was cream, its delicate Caroline carving touched with gold. The ceiling was cross-raftered in oak and from the interstices there gleamed, oddly but harmoniously in blue and silver, the twelve signs of the zodiac. Over the fireplace brooded in austere beauty one of Piero della Francesca's mathematically-minded madonnas, the blue of her gown the same as that amid the rafters above. The whole made a pleasant frame – and the rest of the furnishing was ingeniously unnoticeable. Mr Deighton-Clerk and the Virgin between them dominated the room.

But at the moment the Dean was feeling in a scarcely dominant mood. He was doubting his own wisdom – a process he disliked and avoided. But he could not but doubt the wisdom of the action he had taken that morning. To insist on bringing down a detective-officer – no doubt a notorious detective-officer – from Scotland Yard because of this appalling affair! This was surely to court the widest publicity – to say the least?

Mr Deighton-Clerk's gaze went slowly up to the ceiling, as if seeking comfort in his own private astrological heaven. Comfort came to him in some measure as his eye moved from *Cancer* to the taut form of *Sagittarius*. He had taken energetic action. And was it not (but here the thought floated only in the remoter regions of the Dean's brain) – was it not the capacity for energetic action that was called in question when the possible preferment of a mere scholar was canvassed? At this moment the Dean's eye, voyaging still among his rafters, rested on *Aquarius*, 'the man who bears the watering-pot', as the rhyme has it. And by processes connected perhaps with the association *cold-douche*, the full mischief of the business was brought home to him more vividly than it had been yet. To be *mixed up* in a scandal under these outrageous circumstances of modern nation-wide publicity! Hardly helpful, he thought grimly; hardly helpful whatever solution of the business the police achieved. That there would be no sensational domestic revelation – it was for that that he must hope and pray. And it was of that that he had, in the course of the day, almost succeeded in convincing himself. (*Pisces*, as if they had ventured some contradiction, came in for a stern glance here.) In the long run it would not be left in any doubt that the crime (crime in St Anthony's!) was an outside affair – the purposeless stroke, perhaps, of a madman.

But here *Libra*, the scales, asserted themselves. There was matter to be balanced against that hope. Let this detective be anything but a model of discretion, let him have a taste for amusing the public, and there might be an uncomfortable enough period of startling, if improbable and unprovable, theories blowing about. The unlucky topographical circumstances of the deed, the Dean had realized from the first, set suspicion flowing where it should be fantastic that suspicion should flow . . .

He frowned as he thought of his colleagues under suspicion of murder. How would they stand badgering by policemen, coroners, lawyers? How, for that matter, would he stand it himself? Praise Providence, he and his colleagues were all demonstrably sane.

Those bones! They were mad. Last night, when he had viewed them, he had been annoyed by them. He had at first been more annoyed by the bones (he recollected with some discomfort) than distressed about the tragedy. He had been annoyed because he had been bewildered (Mr Deighton-Clerk disliked being bewildered – or even slightly puzzled). But later he had felt – somewhat incoherently – a possible blessedness in them: their very irrationality removed the crime somehow from the sinister and calculated to the fantastic. They were a sort of bulwark between the life of the college, in all its measure and reason, and the whole horrid business.

And then – and it was as if *Leo*, *Taurus*, and *Aries* had roared, bellowed, butted all in a moment – Mr Deighton-Clerk realized what a feeble piece of thinking this was. The first thing that this detective would suspect about the bones was that they were some sort of blind or bluff. How obvious; how very, very obvious! Indeed, were the man literate, his mind might run to some notion of the touch of fantasy, the vivid dash of irrationality, that it might please an intellectual and cultivated mind to mingle with a laboriously calculated crime ... A mixture, thought Mr Deighton-Clerk, somewhat in the manner of Poe.

Decidedly, he did not like the bones after all. And suddenly he realized that, subconsciously, they had profoundly disturbed him from the first. Sinister, grisly objects – surely they were striving to connect themselves with ... something forgotten, suppressed, unconsidered on the borders of his consciousness ... ? He was nervous. The dock (he heard his own inner voice absurdly exclaim) is yawning open for us all ...

Mr Deighton-Clerk pulled himself up. He was decidedly tired. More than tired, he was unsettled. Indeed it was a terrible, a shocking business. Murder – the human soul hurled all unprepared to Judgement – was equally awful in college or cottage. He had seldom seen eye to eye with Umpleby – but how meaningless their disagreements had been! How absurd this or that estrangement between them in face of abrupt and total severance – the quick and the dead! The Dean looked at his watch. Just half an hour to hall, and hall and common-room would be something of an ordeal.

At this moment there came a knock at the door and the announcement: Mr Appleby.

2

Mystery in the vicinity, the Dean was finding, was productive of irrational annoyances. He was annoyed again now, and it seemed for two most inadequate reasons. The stranger who had just been shown in upon him was remarkably young, and he had all the appearance of being – indeed quite plainly *was* – what Mr Deighton-Clerk still liked to think of under the designation 'genteel'. But if both facts were disconcerting both might well be advantageous. In a moment the Dean had advanced and shaken hands. 'I am glad to see you, Mr Appleby,' he said. 'I am very glad that it has been possible to – ah – detail you for this' – the Dean hesitated – 'this investigation. Sit down.'

Appleby displayed a suitable awareness of politeness intended and seated himself in the chair which had been indicated – one somewhat uncompromisingly central before the Dean's tidily-arranged desk. It was plain that, in the introductory exchanges at least, Mr Deighton-Clerk intended to lead the conversation. Tapping the arm of his chair deliberately rather than nervously, he began speaking in an even, rather cold but pleasantly modulated voice.

'You will have seen the extraordinary circumstances in which our President has met his death,' he began. 'The university, I need hardly say, is very much shocked, and it is the duty of the college to assist in every way what must, it is only too clear, be called the course of justice. As soon as I saw the gravity of what has happened, I determined that the college itself, for its own credit, must take ... energetic action' – Mr Deighton-Clerk paused meditatively over the phrase – 'and so overriding what I suspected might be tardy processes, I took steps to secure assistance from London at once. Nothing could be more satisfactory – more reassuring, indeed – than the promptitude of the response. We look to you, Mr Appleby, to clear up this terrible affair.'

The Dean paused at this, but even as Appleby was framing a reply he continued in the same somewhat formal strain. He had apparently delivered himself merely of a sort of exordium or proem and intended something like a speech. Perhaps, thought Appleby, it was simply the

academic habit of sustained utterance. Perhaps something more idiosyn-
cratic and revealing. Anyway, he sat tight, with an air of respectful
attention.

'I should not like,' Mr Deighton-Clerk continued, 'to say that this
tragedy has occurred at a particularly unfortunate time. It would be
a most improper thought. Nevertheless you will understand me when
I tell you that the five hundredth anniversary of the foundation of the
college falls to be celebrated in only two months' time. The occasion
is to be marked in – ah – various ways. It is known, for instance, that
Dr Umpleby was to have been knighted. That the college must enter
upon the sixth century of its history upon the morrow of its President's
violent death is, of course, terrible in itself. But it would be yet more
deplorable should we have to suffer from prolonged mystery and scandal.
And the longer Dr Umpleby's death is unexplained, the more scandal
– shocking though the admission be – will circulate. I know that, Mr
Appleby, only too well. And it is my duty as the acting Head of this
House to see that the living are not penalized, either in their peace of
mind or in their careers and material interests, by an ounce of avoidable
scandal – or suspicion.'

Here Mr Deighton-Clerk made a real stop, conscious perhaps that
in a somewhat wandering declaration he had spoken two words more
than was discreet. Appleby replied briefly. He was fully aware of the
likelihood of extravagant and irresponsible rumour. Searching inquiry
in various directions would, perhaps, be unavoidable, but in whatever
he did he would endeavour to act with all possible discretion. He hoped
he could do something to restrain the exuberance of the Press …
Appleby's tactful speech, terminated by an inviting pause, had the effect
which was intended. Mr Deighton-Clerk began again. And this time
he advanced from generalities to a specific position. Dr Umpleby –
he declared in fine – had met his death under certain complicated circumstances which the police would interpret. But a valid interpretation
must be congruous, not with physical or mechanical facts merely, but
with higher psychological probabilities as well. Obviously, a murder
in St Anthony's could not be a domestic matter.

This proposition – put forward with a good deal of complication
– Appleby in some measure met. 'I agree,' he said, 'that the physical
circumstances of the case are not in any way conclusive. They may
be very misleading – deliberately misleading. I recognize that they do

not point in any certain way either at any one person or at any group of persons. They are merely a total situation about which as yet I have very insufficient information.' Appleby let this sink in and then he added: 'There is the queer business of those bones. They may well be thought to point to a wholly irrational element in the affair. I remember something very similar, sir, in a case in Cumberland: homicidal mania accompanied by what is called, I think, obsessional neurosis. A man broke into a totally strange building – a public-house as it happened – and committed a murder. Then he turned everything he could move upside down, chalked up his own name on the wall and went home. They've never been able to discover at the asylum whether he remembers anything about it.'

That Mr Deighton-Clerk, fresh from his recent revelation on the likely official view of the bones, was altogether taken in by this reassuring anecdote is uncertain. But in combination with Appleby's manner it encouraged him to proceed with the train of thought he plainly wished to develop. Dr Umpleby's death, he agreed, might well be the work of a demented person – indeed he could imagine no other explanation. And that the bones pointed the same way he also thought extremely probable. Not that he considered that a matter of certainty: the bones might be some sort of blind – a point Mr Appleby had no doubt considered – though the very obviousness of this somewhat discounted the idea. But of one thing the Dean was certain: there existed within St Anthony's itself no circumstances, no relations, no individual that could, with the slightest psychological probability, be in any way connected up with an attempt on the President's life. The actions and motives of his colleagues and himself might quite properly fall to be scrutinized: he would not, for his part, object for a moment. But with what authority he might possess, and in the interests of a rapid elucidation of the crime, he would again state his simple conviction that, whatever physical circumstances might suggest to the contrary, the problem must be one which lay essentially outside the precincts of St Anthony's.

Was this gentleman, Appleby wondered, protesting too much? Or was he, in all this declamation, simply pumping up conviction within himself? And he wasn't finished yet. Standing up now with his back to the fire, the Dean looked directly at Appleby and began again. 'Mr Appleby,' he said, speaking in more abrupt tones than he had yet permitted himself, 'there's another thing. You may find your man, mad or sane, tomorrow. Or you may, as I have said, find it necessary to undertake a laborious investigation among us all. If you do, you may find – you certainly *will* find – disturbing circumstances. It is such circumstances which I suggest, very seriously, are only too likely to delude. In a college like this we have our own manners, and I hope they are the manners of scholars and gentlemen. But superficially – I deliberately use the word – there are jealousies, conflicts – quarrels even – enough. When you come upon them I ask you to do two things: first to weigh the gravity of such learned squabbles carefully against the well-nigh imponderable deed of murder; secondly to give some thought to the possible relevance of each before pursuing it to the point of publicity.'

This was Mr Deighton-Clerk's best speech, and he might have rested on it. But he had something to add and he added it forthrightly enough.

'I will quote an example. Only a few days ago Dr Umpleby and I had something approaching a personal quarrel – in public. Consider it, and you will find it pretty evidently not the quality of thing men commit murder over. Investigate it further and, while keeping that quality, it will reveal matter of minor scandal – matter which, in the interest of the college, I would not see made public without dismay. And so on. You must know only too well, Mr Appleby, that in any company of men minute perscrutation of act and motive may have the most miserable consequences … But I am at your disposal for such inquiries as you may think useful – and so, I am sure, are my colleagues. Mr Appleby, how would you wish to proceed?'

But Appleby, who was inwardly congratulating the Dean on this quite magnificent manner of admitting to a recent quarrel with a murdered man, was given no opportunity to reply. Indeed, the climax of the interview had all the appearance of being timed to the minute: even as Mr Deighton-Clerk ceased speaking the college bell began to ring.

'That is our dinner-bell, Mr Appleby,' the Dean explained. 'I am afraid we must defer further discussion until tomorrow – or later tonight should you choose.' And after a moment of apparent hesitation he added: 'May I ask what your arrangements are? You will need constant access to the college: would you care, I wonder – would it be regular, if I may so put it – to stay in St Anthony's? We would be glad to receive you if you should think it convenient, and I can promise you a quiet set of rooms from which to – ah – operate.'

Appleby reflected rapidly on this unexpected suggestion. No official objection, he felt sure, would be made to his lodging in the college if he considered it expedient. And it had several obvious advantages – not least that it made him free of the college buildings at any hour of the day or night. He accepted the proposal gratefully, explaining that he had driven straight to St Anthony's and that his suitcase was at the porter's lodge. He would be glad to sleep in college that night – and for longer should it prove necessary.

Mr Deighton-Clerk was pleased with himself. Here was more energetic action. It entailed, perhaps, some breach of the minor proprieties – but it was in a crisis in the college's history that justified the action fully. He took another glance at Appleby – the man was indubitably a gentleman – and plunged finally. 'Excellent,' he said, 'a most satisfactory arrangement. And you will of course dine with us now in hall. I only wish you were meeting the high-table on a more auspicious – ah, on a less melancholy occasion.'

This was slightly more than Appleby had bargained for and the official in him was moved to demur. But Mr Deighton-Clerk, having twirled a dial and murmured into an ivory telephone, was enfolding himself in his gown. 'Not at all, not at all,' he said, meeting what he took to be the reason for Appleby's objection. 'There is no need whatever for you to change. A number of the Fellows will not have taken the trouble. Mr Haveland, for instance, will certainly not be changed. He never does change. It annoys – dear me! – annoyed poor Dr Umpleby. Indeed, the manciple had to bring him a list every day, and if Haveland and his tweeds were to be in the hall the President as often as not stayed away. I fear they detested each other. Mr Appleby, let me lead the way downstairs.'

Appleby followed obediently, feeling that he had gained a point. The Reverend and Honourable the Dean, for the past half-hour so elevated and so correct, had condescended to a fragment of downright gossip.

Chapter 4

One of the nicest of academic fantasies is *Zuleika Dobson*, that pleasing narrative of Max Beerbohm's in which an entire undergraduate population, despairing of its heroine's affection, casts itself into the fatal waters of the Isis. The great touch, it will be remembered, comes at the end. Life goes on undisturbed; that night the dons file into the halls of their several colleges as usual; and at the high-table dinner proceeds, in complete unawareness of the deserted benches where armies of perished undergraduates had sat.

Inspector Appleby had this fable flitting in his head as he entered the hall of St Anthony's on the morrow of a less comprehensive academic fatality. The college had already assembled as he was guided up to the dais by Mr Deighton-Clerk. Round the high-table there stood, gowned and for the most part dinner-jacketed, the Fellows – looking grave certainly, but no graver than the ceremonial pre-prandial moment commonly demanded. Stretching down the length of the hall were the lines of those *in statu pupillari*: two tables of commoners in the oddly diminished, vestigial-looking gowns of their order; an equally long table of more generously-swathed scholars; a short and bunchy table of completely enfolded Bachelors. By a lectern near the high-table, ready to say grace, was the Bible-clerk, a blue-eyed cherubic undergraduate, doing his best to disguise an undisguisable constitutional breeziness. The few whispers in the hall died away as the Dean took off his cap and bowed gravely to the cherub – who bowed profoundly, if not exactly gravely, in return and proceeded to deliver himself with miraculous speed of a flood of medieval Latinity. The Bible-clerk bowed; the Dean bowed; the Dean sat down; the college – and Appleby with it – did the same; ritual was preserved. But there was no instant babble of voices such as customarily would have arisen. St Anthony's conversed, but conversed sparely and quietly. The high-table set the tone, and the cherub, in occasional brief remarks to his neighbour, the senior scholar, seconded. From around the lofty dark-panelled walls the vanished statesmen, divines, poets, and philosophers whom St Anthony's had in one century or another produced looked down on a decorum amply maintained.

Appleby considered his neighbours. A rapid count made one fact evident: all the Fellows of the college had made a point of turning up in hall. Decorum once more, thought Appleby. Decorum too in the fact that nobody seemed to regard him with any curiosity – and decorum finally, he reflected, required that he should not begin a too-curious circumspection himself. He was on the right of the Dean; on his own right there sat, as a murmured introduction had informed him, Mr Titlow – middle-aged, handsome, with a touch of encroaching flabbiness, nervous. And Titlow's present nervousness, he quickly decided, was something that went with a good deal of chronic irritability or internal excitement. Alone among the diners that night Titlow had the look of an imaginative man – a man, as used to be said, of quick invention. Those long, square fingers, alone preserved from some old portrait, would have suggested just that mobile mouth and lively eye. What they would not have suggested was so negative a nose. If features could be read, Appleby concluded, Titlow was a brilliant but unreliable man.

Directly opposite Appleby was Dr Barocho, a round, shining, and beaming person, eating heartily and happily. He was a clear specimen of the stage foreigner – the foreigner who remains obstinately foreign. Which by no means prevented him from being an equally clear specimen of the maturest thing in the world – Latin culture. Dr Barocho, Appleby's considering mind told itself, was master by right of birth of something in which his colleagues were laborious undergraduates still. And his mind would not work like theirs ... But of one thing Barocho was plainly not master – his colleagues' language. He was getting into difficulties now in the simple matter of explaining that he had mislaid his gown. (Would he be put off the capital grilled sole, Appleby wondered, if he knew what purpose it was now serving? Probably not.)

'You did not notice it please, Titlow, Empson, Pownall, I beg? You did not see me put the gown down, Pownall, at all – Titlow *no?*'

The appeal was not very politely received. A sardonic person who was to reveal himself as Professor Empson murmured that Barocho might well have mislaid his head, a response which the Spaniard at once contrived to muddle. 'Ah, yes, you said our dead Head!' – and he crossed himself and looked solemn over what he apparently took to be some obscure reference to the late Dr Umpleby. Then a thought seemed to strike him and he turned to Titlow. 'One thing I want to ask you. You speak of Heads of Houses, and that is university Houses – Colleges – *no*? And then you speak of Safe as Houses, and that is university Houses too, Titlow – *verdad*? You call this House safe?'

Barocho's mind seemed to work not so much differently as weirdly – or it had a whim for appearing to do so. Several people were looking at him with the sort of half-irritated tolerance which one bestows upon a familiar oddity. But one member of the high-table, an impassive featureless person who was to turn out to be Haveland, seemed, to Appleby's eye, to be attending with considerable concentration. The Spaniard was now embarked on random philological speculation and inquiry. For a minute his voice was lost, save to his immediate neighbours, amid such subdued talk as the high-table was allowing itself. And then, in a pause, it rang out in question:

'Do I say, then, that you will be *hanged*, or that you will be *hung*?'

Titlow's glass came down abruptly; equally abruptly Haveland's went to his mouth – it was impossible to tell to which the fantastic question had been addressed . . . Had the round innocent eyes of Barocho, Appleby wondered, meditatively sought his own in that disturbing moment? The Spaniard, he suspected, was neither witless nor concerned deliberately to give offence. He had simply conducted an experiment. Why?

In an instant Deighton-Clerk had taken charge, subtly but absolutely, of the whole table. He seemed to dictate alike the subdued conversations and the interspersed silences which marked the rest of the meal. He had determined, clearly, that there was to be no further incident – and there was none. Half an hour after dinner had begun, and without allowing a suspicion of haste towards the close, the Dean rose and murmured two words of grace. Chairs were drawn back, caps were handed, the occupants of the high-table filed out through the rows of standing undergraduates. Hall was over.

2

The little file of dons streamed over the narrow neck of Bishop's Court separating hall from common-rooms: Appleby, with his instinct for observation, brought up the rear. Away to the left, and clearly illuminated by a brilliant lamp, was the big, unimpeded archway between Bishop's and Surrey. To the right, close by, but illumined only accidentally by a light streaming from the open common-room door, were those problematical gates which had been locked at ten-fifteen the night before, and which were locked still now. Through the elaborate iron-work there flowed a velvet blackness, and the faint, sighing breeze that must be stirring the mist around the invisible trunks and branches of Orchard Ground. None of the little procession, Appleby saw, looked that way. But through that gate some lurking minion of Dodd's would presently have to admit Empson, Titlow, Pownall, and Haveland, if these were to pass the night in their own rooms . . . It was an awkward arrangement at best, this nightly splitting of the college in two with lock and key. It was a piece of practical awkwardness typical perhaps of the place. Had it been exploited with an equally typical intellectual finesse? This question took Appleby, in the wake of his hosts, into the smaller of St Anthony's common-rooms.

The room had the air of somewhat desiccated luxury characteristic of such places, but it was pleasant enough. A long mahogany table, lit by candles in heavy silver candlesticks, glowed with the ruby and gold of port and sherry, glittered with glass, broke into little rainbows of fruit. The only other light was from a generous fire in a generous fireplace. The walls, covered with innumerable portraits of Fellows dead and gone, swam in and out of shadow, surrounding the living with a company of fleeting ghosts – Victorian ghosts looking like Mr Deighton-Clerk; eighteenth-century ghosts sitting in libraries, walking in parks, striking postures amid fragments of the Antique; a few seventeenth-century ghosts holding prayer-books. The great of St Anthony's hung in hall; these were her illustrious obscure, appropriately perpetuated on a miniature scale. It was like a cloud of witnesses.

There was a moment of confusion. As Mr Deighton-Clerk crossed the threshold of the common-room, his authority – or rather the authority of the dead President now vested in him – was by some inviolable custom suspended. It fell to Mr Titlow to dispose the company around the table. But Titlow was still plainly in a state of agitation and he showed every sign of making a bad job of it. His gestures were vague and contradictory and there was a generally embarrassed shuffling and shifting before the company was settled down. Appleby found himself oddly placed at the head of the table, facing the single figure of Haveland at the other end – a double line of dons between them.

A modicum of confusion Mr Deighton-Clerk had suffered in the name of the prescriptive, but when the table was once settled he resumed control. He whispered to Titlow; Titlow and he severally whispered to the servants; and cut glass and decanters, fruit and finger bowls, vanished untouched. It was a portentous symbolism – and it induced a portentous silence. The ritual of dessert had been metamorphosed into the ceremony of a meeting. The servants had withdrawn and the Dean spoke. He spoke, Appleby noticed, without the slightly strained formality which unfamiliar colloquy with a policeman had induced earlier in the evening.

'We have here tonight Mr Appleby of the London police. Mr Appleby has been sent on our direct application to the Home Office, and we will help him in every way. He is staying in college, in the rooms just opposite my own, until matters clear up. We realize, I think, that that may take a little time. It is useless to disguise from ourselves the fact that the circumstances in which the President has died, as well as being quite evidently sinister, are possibly complicated. Mr Appleby will no doubt wish to see us all severally and discover what, if anything, we have to tell.

'Mr Appleby, I will name my colleagues. On your left is Mr Titlow, Dr Gott, Professor Empson, Professor Curtis, Mr Chalmers-Paton ...'

And so the Dean went right round the table. It was an uncomfortable proceeding, but sensible and efficient, and Deighton-Clerk went through it with a level severity. It was not, Appleby decided, exactly a matter of introductions, and the process was completed without bow or word spoken. Most of those named looked direct at Appleby; a few kept their eyes on the bare table in front of them. Only Barocho's eyes went circling round with Appleby's, and he smiled amiably on each of his colleagues in turn, giving much the impression that he regarded the roll-call as preliminary to the starting of some pleasant paper game.

For a moment there was silence, and then Haveland suddenly spoke from the lower end of the table. He was a pale, almost featureless person, but there was a rigidity about such features as he had that suggested a quality of intensity or concentration. He was dressed, as the Dean had foretold, in morning clothes – clothes which conveyed, in their soft but clear colouring and negligent flow, something of consciously-worn aesthetic sensibility. But the hands were lifeless and the voice cold, thin, impassive as the features. He addressed the Dean.

'I take it that you are not suggesting that Mr Appleby should begin by holding a conference. What information each of us may have, what impressions each of us no doubt has – all that Mr Appleby had better get by going round privately.'

Beneath the flat words, beneath the flat tone in which they were uttered, there was discernible some latent cutting edge waiting to come into operation. 'Information', 'impressions', 'going round' – there had been scepticism, irony, contempt delicately perceptible behind the successive words. Haveland continued:

'But there is something I take this chance of saying to everybody. It may deprive one or two of you of the pleasures of suddenly realizing that two and two are four, and give you an impression the less to convey to Mr Appleby. Please forgive me.

'You all know that Umpleby's study has been found littered with bones. I wonder where they came from ... Empson, can you think?'

There was some hidden art in this appeal: Empson seemed momentarily confused. But Haveland at once went on:

'I am sure you can. But I don't know if Mr Appleby understands as yet the significance of bones amongst us? I am certain it is a point his rural colleague – with whom I am afraid I shall reveal myself as having been improperly reticent this morning – would scarcely appreciate. I suggest you say a word to Mr Appleby on that, Deighton-Clerk.'

Deighton-Clerk, thus appealed to, looked first puzzled and then startled. 'Mr Haveland no doubt means,' he said, 'that anthropology is a strong subject with us at St Anthony's. Haveland is an anthropologist himself. Titlow's classical archaeology has got mixed up – please excuse the expression, Titlow! – with anthropology of late. And Pownall's ancient history and Campbell's ethnology have linked up with the subject too. The linking-up was fostered by the late President. Dr Umpleby himself came to anthropology through comparative philology, as did his pupil, Ransome, who is now abroad. In fact, St Anthony's has been famous for team work on ancient cultures for years now. As a student of comparative religion I have been interested myself. I suppose that is what Haveland means by the significance of bones amongst us — though such an odd notion would never have occurred to me ... And now, Haveland, if you have something to say, pray say it.'

Haveland had that look in his eye which a man might have who is putting a horse for a second time at a very stiff fence.

'Empson knew that I had a collection of bones in college. I wonder if anyone else knew?' His eye ran round the table, making a fleeting point before he continued. 'The bones are my bones.'

The common-room was hushed. None of Haveland's colleagues said a word, and Appleby said no word either.

'At least I presume they are my bones, for my bones have disappeared. And as mine happen to be of Australian aborigines they will be fairly easily identified ... I wonder if any of you has any thoughts as to how these exhibits of mine have come to be put to such a picturesque use?'

There was absolute silence.

'Or perhaps I might ask not *how* they came where they did, but *why?* What do you think ... Empson? Would you care to advance any theory?'

'I have nothing to advance ... Ask Titlow.'

Why, thought Appleby, ask Titlow? And Titlow seemed to think the same. He was looking with much the same indignation at Empson as Empson was looking at Haveland. A little more of this and all the subterraneous currents of this little community would be rising to reveal themselves on the surface.

'I can imagine their being put there to incriminate you, Haveland,' Titlow put in. 'Pownall, does that not seem possible to you?'

Pownall, thus dragged in (why drag in Pownall?), responded: 'I can imagine an explanation which is at once simpler and odder. Can you not, Haveland?'

It was as if Barocho had been right and some round game — a round game of which only a fragment of the rules was known to any one player — was in progress in the common-room. But now a venerable and bearded person sitting opposite the fireplace took up the conversation. 'I wonder if any of you know the curious Bohemian legend of the Bones of Klattau ... ?'

This was Professor Curtis, and to Appleby's ear and mind his perfectly irrelevant interjection had a curious effect. Its innocence – and, in the circumstances, absurdity – threw into sudden clear relief the animus with which the previous play of conversation had somehow been heavy. Pownall's 'Can you not, Haveland?' had said it, and now Haveland, ignoring Curtis and the Bohemian legend, squared himself to reply.

'Certainly I can imagine another explanation. There is a concatenation of circumstances that comes to my mind at once. Empson, I think you should give some account of a conversation I had with Umpleby in your presence a month or two ago. You know what I mean. And I don't think anyone else knows of it.'

'Pownall knows: I told him next day.' Empson had replied impulsively and seemed to regret it. 'I don't see,' he continued, 'that I need give any account of anything here. If you want all that out, out with it yourself."

The Dean stirred in his seat – half uneasily, half authoritatively. 'Haveland,' he said, 'is this expedient? If you insist on telling us something, tell us outright.'

'I am going to tell you something outright.' The retort was a neat and venomous imitation of the Dean's slightly magisterial accents. Haveland was certainly not playing for sympathy: the common-room could be felt to shudder at the impropriety of his tone. But he had controlled himself instantly and now continued unmoved. 'I am going to tell you – as Empson seems reluctant to do it – of a certain occasion on which I quarrelled with Umpleby – badly.'

From several quarters there rose protesting murmurs. The Dean, in evident perplexity, half turned to Appleby. But Appleby seemed lost in absorbed contemplation of the table-edge in front of him. And Haveland continued unchecked.

'It was a matter, of course, of one of Umpleby's usual thefts.'

If there was anything, Appleby decided, to be discerned in the expression of the late President's colleagues at this opening, it was comprehension rather than perplexity. The Dean, however, was moved to some attempt at remonstrance. Haveland – and with a trace of unrestraint – thrust it aside.

'Deighton-Clerk, don't be a fool. Consider what we are up against.

Umpleby, I say, had been stealing again. I needn't go into it all. Empson was there, and if he were not so uneasy about it could give you a cooler account than I. But I do remember one very definite expression I used.'

Haveland's fence, Appleby sensed, was full in front of him now. And the whole room seemed to feel the strain that was in the air.

'When I taxed him with it he simply would not meet my point. He talked about his own work among the tombs down the Gulf. And I said I would like to see him immured for good in one of his own grisly sepulchres ... That is correct, Empson, is it not?'

Empson made no reply. There was absolute silence. Haveland was impassive still, but even down the candle-lit table Appleby thought he could discern the drops of sweat that stood upon his brow. At length a voice broke the spell.

'Haveland, what madman's trick are you suggesting?'

It was Pownall who spoke. And if there had been silence before, there was utter stillness now. Appleby had the feeling of a sudden horrid sense of understanding, a catastrophic dark enlightenment, running round the table. But Haveland had suddenly got to his feet. He looked directly across at Appleby, and seemed now to address him rather than the room.

'And there you have material for two theories. Titlow said something about "incriminating": you can reflect on that. And Pownall said something about "simpler and odder": you can reflect on that too. Good night.'

And Haveland swung out of the room. For a moment the company sat staring rather blankly at an empty chair. But Deighton-Clerk had whispered to Titlow and Titlow had pressed a bell. Some soothing fragment of ritual was again being resorted to.

The door of the inner common-room was thrown open and the un-emotional tones of a servant announced: 'Coffee is served!'

3

The Dean motioned to Appleby and the two of them, together with Titlow, Barocho, and a silent person who had proved to be Dr Gott, passed into the next room – Deighton-Clerk because he was Dean,

Appleby because he was the Dean's guest, Titlow because he was Senior Fellow, Gott because he was at present a proctor, and Barocho probably because he had simply forgotten to remain behind. Appleby was helped to coffee by the Dean, and the others helped themselves. Deighton-Clerk made no secret of his distress to Appleby.

'Mr Appleby, it is a horrible business. Pray heaven you clear it up quickly! I am coming to feel some wretched tone or atmosphere spreading itself around us.'

Little more than an hour before Deighton-Clerk had been elaborately impressing upon Appleby, in direct contradiction to the strongest physical appearances, that Umpleby's death was the deed of some Unknown who had no part or lot in the life of St Anthony's. Plainly, he was not a little shaken from that confidence – if genuine confidence it had been – now. He had drawn Appleby into a corner and was continuing with increased distress.

'It was a most improper observation of Pownall's. Even if Haveland was inviting accusation, it ought not to have been put to him by way of insinuation like that. We were all exceedingly shocked.'

Appleby was in the dark as to the significance of this speech, but in a moment the Dean enlightened him. 'I am afraid it is my duty to explain to you, Mr Appleby, though it has much upset me. I had quite forgotten ... Did I remark earlier this evening when we were speaking of the bones that they were *mad* whereas we in this college were all demonstrably *sane*? At any rate, I think I implied it. And of course I had forgotten – though I was dimly aware of some sinister thing. I had forgotten the trouble poor Haveland had had. Some years ago, Mr Appleby, he had ... a severe nervous breakdown, and behaved for a time very oddly. Actually, he was found behaving very oddly among the sarcophagi in the Museum ... Where will this lead us?'

It might lead, Appleby thought, in more directions than one – but it did not look, at present, as if it would lead straight out of St Anthony's.

'There was never any relapse,' the Dean was continuing. 'The whole thing has been long overlaid and forgotten – until Haveland and Pownall so deliberately dragged it up. You will realize that it has been so when I tell you that Haveland has been regarded as a not unlikely successor to Umpleby – despite the fact that he is, as you know, uncompromising in certain social matters. Haveland's attack was regarded at the time as the aftermath of wartime strain, and he is a thoroughly equable person.'

There came back to Appleby upon this his first impression of Haveland, shortly before. Was it exactly of an equable person? He was *even*, yes. But was he even as a result of some constant control? Somewhere in the man there was high pressure – and where there is such pressure there may, conceivably, be chronic latent instability.

A few minutes only had passed since the break-up in the other common-room, and now, after the ritual interval, the other St Anthony's Fellows (who, while divorced from their seniors, had tonight been without the compensating advantage of an extra moment with the port) came in to coffee. The company split into small groups and Appleby presently found himself taken possession of by Professor Curtis. It seemed likely that he alone was to be privileged to hear in full the curious legend of the Bones of Klattau. But it was something else that the *savant* had in his head.

'May I ask, my dear sir,' he began mildly, 'if you have ever condescended to interest yourself in the imaginative literature of your profession?'

Curtis, Appleby reflected, should be approaching Dodd. But he answered that he was not altogether ignorant of the field.

'Then,' said Curtis, blinking amiably over the top of his steel-rimmed glasses, 'you may be acquainted with Gott's diversions? I am not giving away any secret here, I think, when I tell you that Gott is Pentreith, you know. I suppose his stories are now fairly well known in the world?'

Appleby agreed that they were, and looked round with interest for so distinguished a story-teller. But Gott, being a proctor, had departed on his nocturnal disciplinary perambulations of the city.

'It is a curious branch of literature,' Curtis was continuing; 'and I must confess, I am afraid, to being an indifferent scholar in it. Would you be inclined to maintain that Wilkie Collins has ever been bettered? Or Poe? Not that Poe is not, I always feel, inconsiderable – how curiously his reputation has been foisted on us from France! You younger men, I suppose, have passed beyond the Symbolists? But *The Purloined Letter* now; don't you think that is a little – *steep*, as they say?'

Appleby agreed that he thought it was. Curtis was delighted.

'I am glad to have my amateur's opinion – so to speak – profession-

ally endorsed. Yes, I think I should have spotted the letter myself –
almost at once. But I wonder if it was Poe's idea? I wouldn't be a
bit surprised if the basis of it was as old as the hills, would you? There
is an interesting story they relate in the Basque country ... But I will
tell you that another time, if you will let me. What Poe put it in my
mind to say was that these bones we hear of might *neither* be meant
to incriminate somebody *nor* be evidence of any sort of mental unbalance.
Not of mental unbalance in the strict sense, I mean. They might be
– how shall I put it? – some perfectly sane man's idea of the humorously
grotesque ... Do you know Goya's sketches? In the – dear me, what
are they called? Barocho, those war-things of Goya's ...'

And Professor Curtis wandered away.

Looking round the room, Appleby now saw standing conveniently
in one group three members of the common-room of whom he as
yet knew nothing: Lambrick, Campbell, and Chalmers-Paton. He was
particularly interested in Lambrick, the married member of the college
who retained a key to the fatal gates. And something about Campbell was familiar. Feeling that he might usefully pile up a little more
in the way of impressions before retiring to sort them out, he approached
this group and was presently sitting smoking and talking with them.
Nothing could well have been more irregular. But St Anthony's had
enough of its conventions to care very little, it seemed, for those of
the world. The college was taking it for granted that it should treat
a detective-officer come up to investigate a murder just as it would
treat an architect come up to design it a new library or an Academician
making water-colours of its courts. It was an attitude that made a superior
technique of investigation possible, and Appleby was not going to
quarrel with it.

The conversation was running on the proctorial activities of Gott.
The walk from hall to common-room had revealed a raw, unpleasant
night, cold and with a lurking vapour that caught at the throat. And
to Appleby's companions, comfortably smoking cigarettes in large
leather chairs, with a leaping fire, more generous even than that in the
outer common-room, pleasantly warming their legs, the thought of
their colleague pacing round the streets at the head of a little bevy of
university police appeared to be particularly gratifying.

'Think of it,' Lambrick, a large dreamy mathematician with a primitive sense of the humorous, was saying; 'in he goes to the Case is

Altered – two men drinking egg-hot – men duly proctorized and out goes Gott into the night, thinking of egg-hot. He goes across the way to the Mucky Duck (good pub that) – two men playing shove-halfpenny over a little rum shrub – proctorized – and out comes Gott thinking both of rum shrub and shove-halfpenny (capital hand he is, too). Over he goes to that flash place at the Berklay – half a dozen smart men having a little quick champagne. Old Gott half hoping for a rough-house. "Your name and college, sir?" – all answer like lambs. Then out again to prowl around that college next my tailor's (never can remember its name) until the Hammer and Sickle Club is out and safely tucked away in bed. What a life!'

'Did you ever hear,' asked Campbell, who was a dark and supple Scot, 'did you ever hear how Curtis when he was Senior Proctor proctorized the Archbishop of York?'

It was an excellent anecdote, but over-elaborate for Lambrick, who vanished suddenly as he sat into some impalpable mathematical world. But Chalmers-Paton kept the theme going by remembering an exploit of Campbell's. 'I say, Campbell, do you remember your climb up St Baldred's tower after that pot?' And despite something approaching positive displeasure on Campbell's part Chalmers-Paton told the story. It represented Campbell as a daring, even reckless man – and as a skilled climber. And then Appleby remembered.

'You went high, didn't you,' he quietly asked the Scot, 'in the Himalaya in 'twenty-six?'

Campbell flushed and seemed for a moment almost disconcerted. 'I was there,' he said at length. 'Didn't you and I once do the Pillar Rock together when I hit your party in Wasdale?'

Appleby in his turn admitted to this – much as he might have admitted to Mr Bradman that they had once played rounders together at a Sunday school picnic. But a subject had been started, and for a few minutes there was climbers' talk. Then Appleby dropped a casual question.

'Is there any roof-climbing in St Anthony's in these days?'

'I believe not,' replied Chalmers-Paton. 'A few years ago there was a club, but undergraduates come and go, and I believe it has lapsed.'

His companions, Appleby noticed, were quite evidently aware that something had at length been said relevant to the President's death. Addressing Campbell, therefore, he came more directly to his point. 'What is St Anthony's like for climbing in, out, or about?' he asked.

Campbell laughed rather shortly. 'I'm a mountaineer at times, as you know. But I assure you I'm not a housebreaker – or a steeple-jack, and I don't see that I'm qualified to give an opinion. Anyone could get on to the roofs through some trapdoor or other and scamper round; but I should say, for what it is worth, that that would be about all. I should imagine that climbing up or down, in or out, is almost impossible.'

'Even to a skilled climber?'

Campbell answered steadily.

'Even to a skilled climber.'

Chapter 5

Appleby sat in his bedroom and took stock — first, and by long habit, of his immediate surroundings; then of his mind. The room did not occupy him long. It was about eight feet square, eight feet high and for window it had a bewildering maze of traceried glass sweeping in a Gothic curve from the floor in one corner to the ceiling in another. St Anthony's, willing to cram into its venerable fabric an extra dozen of undergraduates, had carried out some curious internal alterations in the venerable fabric's structure. The room bore traces of its regular occupant in the shape of an empty jar labelled *Rowing Ointment*, a religious text decorated with an exuberant floral border, a half-tone representation of Miss Mae West, and ten uniform photographs in uniform frames of exceedingly uniform young men — the other ten, doubtless, of some school eleven of the recent past. Why the owner of these *keimelia* was not in residence among them had not been explained: perhaps he had had some difference of opinion with authority; perhaps (Appleby speculated) he was having measles or mumps.

Appleby turned to his thoughts. He was feeling, on the whole, more confident than when he had parted from Dodd. Going over Dodd's facts had given him certain physical contours of the situation — contours that must be regarded as significant by reason of the definition with which they appeared to point, limit, exclude. But around them Appleby had felt a complete darkness; they were no more than a sort of Braille recording of the facts. But later in the evening he had begun to see light, or the possibility of light — light flickering and uncertain, no doubt, as the dying fires in the common-room must be at this moment. From the stage and *décor* — that so elaborately constructed stage, that gruesome *décor* — Appleby had arrived at some view of the *dramatis personae*; at some glimpse, perhaps, of the protagonists ...

A certain amount of Appleby's work lay among persons of considerable cunning. Occasionally he had the stimulus of crossing swords with a good or excellent natural intelligence. But for the most part he dealt with sub-average intelligence, or with normal intelligence circumscribed and handicapped by deficient training and knowledge. And here was what might be intellectually the case of his life. Here was a society of men much above the average in intelligence, the product of a variety of severe mental trainings, formidably armed with knowledge. The secret was hidden amongst them and intelligence and athletic thinking would be needed to reveal it.

Of one thing that evening he had begun to feel convinced. His earlier cautious refusal to take as conclusive those physical facts that cried '*Submarine!*' to Dodd might almost certainly be abandoned. The extraordinary fact of the freshly fitted locks and freshly issued keys had been almost conclusive of that in itself. Directly or indirectly, the murder had been brought about by one or more of the persons with keys. The only alternative – that a malefactor had climbed out of the locked orchard – was sufficiently unlikely to be put last in any line of investigation. The keys held the key. They gave a formula:

Deighton-Clerk, Empson, Gott, Haveland, Lambrick, Pownall, Titlow, the college porter, a hypothetical X (possessor of the missing tenth key); one, or some, or all of these murdered Umpleby – or so disposed of a key as to be able to throw light on the murder.

Appleby looked mentally at this and saw that he had missed something. He brought out pencil and paper and wrote an elaborated formula down:

Slotwiner, Deighton-Clerk, Empson, Gott, Haveland, Lambrick, Pownall, Titlow, the college porter, a hypothetical X (possessor of the tenth key); one, or some, or all of these murdered Umpleby, or one of the nine last so disposed of a key as to be in a position to throw light on the murder. So far, none can be excluded, but if Slotwiner and Titlow are telling the truth they corroborate each other's alibis . . . Dodd is having certain further alibi-statements checked.

So much he had learned that afternoon in the President's Lodging – and so much his subsequent impressions had come to confirm. But what else had he learned later? What had he learned from his interview with the Dean? First, certain facts about the Dean himself. He had been anxious to have it found that the murder was an *outside* murder – that was natural enough. And he had advanced an argument which was simply in effect, 'Such things do not happen among us. And the quality of our knowledge that they do not so happen is really safer evidence than arbitrary physical indications to the contrary.' Appleby had given the argument fair weight, but he was abandoning it now – and the Dean, he suspected, was doing the same ... What else had transpired? The Dean was apprehensive that routine investigation would bring to light matters of petty scandal within the college. And he had recently had some sort of quarrel with Umpleby himself. That was about all. As to more general impressions, they were difficult to form as yet. The man was upset – even thrown off his balance. He would not have given way slightly to a latent pomposity, would not have made pointless reference to the celebrations in which St Anthony's was soon to indulge, had that not been so. But that he was insincere, that he was concealing any material information – of anything of this sort there was no evidence.

Appleby next passed to a review of the events in hall – or rather to the one significant event: the odd behaviour of Barocho. The Spaniard had possibly only the vaguest ideas on the circumstances of Umpleby's death, and was aiming something at random and for reasons of his own – at Titlow, had it been, or at Haveland? Or had there been no specific application; merely something tossed into the air for the purpose of watching the general reaction? Not much useful thinking, probably, could be done on the incident at present.

But on coming to the events in the common-room Appleby faced a complexity which made him feel suddenly cramped. He sprang up, and passed into the absent undergraduate's sitting-room – a big, rather dingy apartment, its walls entirely panelled in wood that had been overlaid with chocolate-coloured paint. Turning on the reading-lamp, Appleby began to pace softly up and down.

The outstanding fact was Haveland's admission – that oddly public admission – of the proprietorship of the bones. He ought to have admitted this earlier to Dodd. That the bones would be traced to him he must have known as fairly certain: why then had he delayed owning to them? Obviously, in order to do so under the particular circumstances possible in the common-room, with all his colleagues around him. He had wanted to show himself publicly as aware of the existence of a case against himself. He had appealed to Empson to reveal a most damaging story that he believed only Empson knew – the story of a quarrel with Umpleby which had led to his expressing a malevolent wish now almost literally fulfilled: 'I said I would like to see him immured in one of his own grisly sepulchres.'

It was a terrific admission to have to make, and Haveland must have been aware that Appleby would soon be in possession of information which would make it doubly – and more than doubly – terrific. Haveland had once experienced a fit of serious unbalance – and the circumstances had apparently suggested some morbid attraction to symbols of physical dissolution.

What had happened, then, was this. Confronted by these disquieting facts, Haveland had come forward and said, 'You are at liberty to believe that in a fit of aberration last night I killed the President and made good my wish as to his lying amid a litter of bones. Or you can suspect that somebody aware of all this has put a plant on me.'

Somebody aware of all this ... 'Empson knew I had a collection of bones in college: I wonder if anyone else knew ... ?' 'Empson, you know what I mean, and I don't think anyone else knows of it ...' 'That is correct, Empson, is it not?' Haveland had, in fact, as good as pointed to Empson. And what had Empson done? Perhaps the most striking fact, Appleby reflected, was that Empson, aware enough of the insinuations, *had not pointed back*. Empson, had, after a manner, pointed sideways. 'Ask Titlow ...' There was nothing in the words, but there had been no mistaking the existence of some significance behind them. There had indeed been an electrical atmosphere round that table, and now Appleby was feeling his way to recreating it – conjuring it up imaginatively in order to test and explore it anew.

The facts pointing at Haveland. Haveland pointing at Empson. Empson (like Barocho?) pointing at Titlow. And Titlow himself? 'I can imagine their being put there to incriminate you, Haveland. Pownall, does that not seem possible to you?' Had there been anything in that? Appleby thought there had – but amid all these charged utterances was he now reading a charge into something uncharged, casual merely? Anyway, Pownall in his turn had certainly pointed. It was he who had, at length, pointed back at Haveland: 'I can imagine an explanation which is at once simpler and odder ...' 'Haveland, what madman's trick are you suggesting?' Appleby knew how, on the level of intellectual dispute, these men would toss a ball around in just that way, each trying to embarrass the other. It was the habit in any mentally athletic society, no doubt; and no doubt the same progress would have its pleasures on the level of scandal and gossip. But when it was a case of murder that was in question ... ?

Appleby felt that he had run over the salient facts. Now he turned to contemplate those less obtrusive. And the less obtrusive facts, he well knew, were often finally the vital facts: the neglect of some minute observation, the leaving of a single fugitive query unattended to, was often the ruining of an elaborate and laborious detective procedure.

The candle grease. Slotwiner and the candles. The *Deipnosophists* upside down. The safe. Barocho's gown. The Dean, hitherto so reticent about college scandal, describing Haveland's old attack. Curtis so casually, so vaguely making sure that Appleby should know that Gott was Pentreith ... And finally there was Campbell, the man who had gone high; more significantly, the man who had scaled St Baldred's tower. He was married and lived out of college. He had no key. But he was an ethnologist and so connected with the Umpleby group. And although Appleby did not believe in the probability of Campbell scaling the heights of St Anthony's as it were alpenstock in hand, probability was not enough. Troublesome red herring as he might be, he must be kept in mind.

Appleby's thoughts swam up from these speculations to a consciousness of his surroundings. He had been staring unseeingly at a rather scanty shelf of books: *Stubbs's Select Charters, Poems of Today, The Forsyte Saga, Trent's Last Case* ...

He turned round and swung impatiently across the room. A kettle, a commoner's gown, a football 'cap' – its tinsel already tarnished by those vapours that were even now floating round the courts. Kneeling on a window-seat he threw open a window and looked out. It was black, damp, cold. But it was cold too inside, and Appleby was not at all sleepy. Obeying an impulse, he switched off the light, groped his way out to the landing and then softly made his way downstairs. There was a light under one door, and a murmur of voices. Excited undergraduates sitting up over the case, no doubt, and fortifying themselves lawfully within college with some of those pleasant potations denied to the unhappily prowling Gott. But by this time Gott would be comfortably in his bed in Surrey: as Appleby reached the open air there came to him, muffled and solemn, one deep note from a distant bell, followed by fainter chimes from other quarters. One o'clock.

The Dean's staircase, where Appleby had his rooms, was in the corner of Bishop's diagonal to the common-rooms. On the left, over the archway to Surrey, a lamp still burned. But it had been turned low and its light hardly reached across the gravel path to the edge of the lawn which Appleby knew stretched in front of him. The night was starless and obscure. Almost nothing could be seen except an uncertain line separating two contrasting textures of darkness – textures which would reveal themselves at dawn as stone and sky. And yet Appleby had never felt the place more keenly than under this spell of silence and night. He began to pace up and down the near side of the court, cleaving a path through the darkness, absorbed.

2

Two o'clock found Appleby still pacing. But the echo of the bells once more made him pause, and in the pause there came to him the second impulse of that night. Behind the screen of buildings in front of him lay Orchard Ground, and in his pocket reposed a key. It was now the only key, with the exception of the problematical tenth, not in the possession of his colleagues. The keys had been collected from their owners that morning (a bold exercise of authority by Dodd); a constable armed with one had stood guard all day; and a relief, similarly armed, was now sitting in the porter's lodge. Empson, Haveland, Pownall, and Titlow, once they had been let into Orchard Ground for the night, were thus virtually prisoners of the police until the morning. As things stood at the moment – and they could hardly so stand for long – no one could get in or out of Orchard Ground without applying to the constable on duty – or to Appleby. The latter's impulse to use his key now was quite irrational, for in the almost impenetrable darkness nothing certainly could be done. But impulses of this sort he did not think it necessary invariably to resist, and he moved cautiously off to the nearer of the two gates – that between chapel and library. Then suddenly changing his mind, he struck across the lawn, skirting the library and chapel, to reach the western gate instead – that between hall and the President's Lodging. This was, of course, the gate he had seen when moving to the common-room after dinner, and the gate through which the constable would have admitted the four Orchard Ground men to their rooms.

He rounded the last of the great south buttresses of the hall and found himself upon gravel – upon the path, that was, that led through the gates and skirted the President's Lodging before striking into the orchard proper. He walked warily on; the hall on his right, what must still be the common-rooms on his left. He felt for the key in his pocket, keeping his eye meantime on the faint gleam of the path at his feet. In the darkness distance was hard to judge; he put his hand out before him to avoid running full into the gate, and paced steadily on. And then suddenly he was aware of something inexplicable to his right: the hall, close to which he had been walking, had vanished, to be replaced by empty space. At the same time he dimly discerned the path at his feet forking right and left. He was in Orchard Ground. *The gate lay behind him.*

A moment earlier Appleby, though walking cautiously through the night, had been almost a disembodied intellectual machine, the emphasis of his attention turned inwards. Now he was a tense mechanism of physical potentiality and sensory awareness. For perhaps thirty seconds he stood rigid, listening. He sank noiselessly down to the ground, crouching with his ear to the earth. There was no suspicion of a sound nearer than the subdued intermittent rumble of the night traffic on Schools Street.

Softly he straightened up again and retraced his steps. The north angle of the hall loomed up a few feet away and he progressed slowly, his left hand feeling constantly along the wall until presently he came to the gate. One wing only was open: he had walked unaware straight through the narrow aperture. And now he halted and debated his course of action. To leave the gate unguarded would be inexcusable: here was the chance of a discovery which must be waited for till morning if necessary. He could, of course, shout and rouse somebody. He could even, by advancing only a few paces, command the archway into Surrey, and through that archway the torch he carried might just convey a signal to the constable at the lodge, were he vigilant. But both these courses might warn somebody who, if unalarmed, would walk straight into a trap. Appleby drew up to the wall and waited. He was prepared to wait with unabated vigilance until sunrise.

His back was against the hall; his left hand was on the cold iron of the open wing of the gate: playing up and down, it touched the lock. His body stiffened. In the lock was the key – the tenth, problematical key!

He set about exploring the gate thoroughly – or as thoroughly as darkness allowed. The open wing was so hung that it swung to of its own weight, and would then lock automatically. But in the wall of the hall was a catch by which the gate might be held back in the day-time, and this catch had been applied. Out of Appleby's pocket came a fine tool. He disengaged the key from the lock without touching it with his fingers and stowed it in his pocket-book. Then he stepped through to the Bishop's side and let the gate swing to behind him. He noticed a faint creak as it closed. All the keys were now in police keeping.

And now Appleby ran. Silently across the grass, rapidly through the archway and to the lodge. It was the work of a moment to beckon to the constable doing porter's duty to follow him, and both men were back at the gates within a minute of Appleby's leaving them. Appleby unlocked the gate and murmured: 'Somebody may come – from either side. Get him. And wait till I come back.' Then he slipped once more into the darkness of Orchard Ground.

He made first for the eastern gate, that between library and chapel. A glide across the grass brought him to it: it was closed and securely locked. And now he set off along the faintly discernible path that led in the direction of Schools Street and at the end of which he would find the wicket that connected St Anthony's with the outer world. Presently he lost the path and was groping among the apple trees. But still he judged it better not to use his torch, and after a few minutes' wandering he touched what he knew was the wall bounding the eastern side of the orchard. The grass ran up to the wall, so that he made his way silently forward. Presently he reached the wicket. It too was locked.

He turned round now and made off down the orchard, trying to recall to his memory the lie of the paths as he had seen them on Dodd's sketch-map. But he failed and had to proceed by judgement. Two paths in succession ran off to the right; he bore left till he came to a little cross-roads. He guessed where he was now: to the right was Little Fellows'; to the left the west gate where he had left the constable; straight on were the french windows of the President's study. Appleby went straight on. And presently he knew that something was wrong.

The french windows, he knew, had been bolted from the inside at top and bottom and locked in the middle. But now the window, like the west gate, swung open. Within was blackness. Appleby listened once more and then slipped inside. The curtains were only partly drawn back; as silently as possible, he drew them to behind him and switched on his torch.

The body had been removed that evening. But the bones had been left – and the bones were still there, as were the crudely chalked death's-heads on the wall. He stepped over to the door; it was locked, and he did not doubt that on the other side the seal applied by Dodd on leaving would be still intact. The french windows had simply been forced and the room rifled. Appleby turned on the light now and walked to the far end with a premonition of what he would find. In the bay by the *Deipnoso-phists* the dummy shelf swung loose. The concealed safe was open. Some documents lay scattered in it. Something, doubtless, was gone.

An observer would have found Appleby pale at this moment. He had lost a trick – perhaps a decisive trick. He ought to have insisted to Dodd on more surveillance than was represented by the constable at the porter's lodge. He ought to have had a team of locksmiths up from London, working at that safe all night ...

He set himself to an inspection. Nothing, as far as he could see, had been disturbed. The desk was untampered with. And the safe had not been forced. Whoever had been in the room had known what he wanted, where it lay concealed, and how to gain access to it. The safe, the very existence of which appeared to be unknown to the rest of the college, had held, even in the combination that opened it, no secret for this intruder. Who had the intruder been? Appleby turned to the probabilities. One of the four men sleeping in Little Fellows' next door could have broken in easily enough. He slipped once more through the curtains and examined the window. What had happened was clear. The burglar had made three circles with a diamond and to each of these he had applied a piece of sacking treated with some sticky substance; through this deadening medium he had then smashed the holes which enabled him to get at bolts and key. It was a trick out of fiction rather than out of current burglarious practice, and it was surprising that it had worked as well as it had done. A resounding splintering of the whole great pane ought to have been the result; as it was, the fractures had almost confined themselves to their diamond-scrawled boundaries and the noise would have been insufficient to penetrate either to the quarters of the dead President's domestic staff or round the corner to Little Fellows'.

It might have been one of the Little Fellows' men – but what then was the meaning of the open west gate? The key had been on the orchard side. If the burglary and the open gate were connected and if one of these four – Empson, Haveland, Pownall, Titlow – was responsible, he had gone on through the gate to one of the other courts – *and was there still*. Or somebody from outside St Anthony's had entered with this tenth key through the wicket, committed the burglary, and similarly gone on to the other part of the college.

But the indications might be deliberately misleading. Why had the key been left in the lock? As a deliberate false trail? Supposing the burglary had been committed not from the orchard side, but from the Bishop's side? The perpetrator might then have left the key on the orchard side to suggest the contrary. But what would that suggestion, logically followed up, imply? It would imply that somebody had passed from Orchard Ground (or perhaps from Schools Street) into the main courts of the college and had then (as a fictitious person could obviously not be discovered there) passed back, leaving the gate open and abandoning the key. The pretence was too thin to have been worth putting up. Almost certainly somebody had passed from Orchard Ground to Bishop's; and almost certainly that person was there still. For if (as the creak suggested) the gate had been left open to cut down noise pending a return and one final shutting of it, then the key might have been forgotten in the moment that such a procedure was decided upon. But if the person concerned had passed back to Orchard Ground his whole instinct would be to cover his traces: he would almost certainly take the very slight risk of shutting the gate, and would almost certainly repossess himself of the key.

If this was indeed the situation, if the burglar was now somewhere in the main buildings and had his escape to make through the gates, he was virtually in Appleby's hands. Leaving the gate open, with police possibly prowling round, had been a gross error of judgement; abandoning the key in the lock had been more careless still: both acts implied a sort of mind that Appleby had not hitherto associated with Umpleby's murderer. If this was the murderer who was operating now the St Anthony's mystery might be past history within half an hour. It was somehow a disconcerting thought.

And now Appleby glided into the darkness again and made his way back to the west gate – to find himself looking into the dimly gleaming barrel of a revolver. It was not a weapon with which the sturdy constable holding it was likely to be over-familiar, and Appleby was relieved when his identity was established. At least, this was a vigilant man; he might safely be left on guard alone a little longer. In a whisper Appleby gave directions. He himself was going back to explore Little Fellows'. The constable was to continue to keep watch and to make sure of anybody who came along. By lying low there was a chance of capturing the burglar neatly with his spoils upon him. A general alarm and search might discover somebody who would have difficulty in explaining his presence but that somebody would be unlikely to have anything incriminating still upon his person. Meantime, a search of Little Fellows' might discover one of its four occupants missing; and this would be evidence in itself supposing anything were to go amiss with the hoped-for capture by the west gate.

Appleby was on the point of turning back into the orchard when he became aware that during this prolonged night prowl he had grown exceedingly cold. And in front of him, after he had searched Little Fellows', lay what might be a long vigil beside his colleague. Just across the lawn, at the foot of the Dean's staircase, was hanging his overcoat, and as his course to it would be untouched by the dim light over the Surrey archway he decided he could cross once more without any appreciable risk of giving alarm.

With a word of his intentions to the constable, he set off and in a moment was round the corner of the hall and making for his staircase with fair certainty. He came upon the gravel path again just by his doorway and slipped inside. He groped his way forward to where he knew the coat hung. His hand had gone out to it when he sensed a movement in the darkness behind him. And before he could turn there came a smashing concussion. He crumpled up on the floor.

Chapter 6

In something under half an hour Appleby regained consciousness. His head was throbbing and he felt sick. Nevertheless, he had barely become aware of these circumstances before he was aware too that his brain was beginning to work clearly. Almost his first reflection was that he had by no means been made the victim of a murderous attack: he had merely been neatly and not unmercifully stunned. It required little thinking to tell why. His pockets, he discovered on passing a hand over himself, had been rifled and his key to Orchard Ground was gone. But not the key which he had found: that was safely in his pocket-book still – with whatever tell-tale finger-prints it might conceivably bear. The assailant had been content with securing *a key*: beyond that he had not stopped to think. And this was Appleby's second indication that night that something less than a perfectly efficient mind was at work.

The unknown had been content to secure a key; there was little doubt to what purpose. The west gate was guarded, but the east gate was not: as long as all the keys had been in police custody there had been no need for that, for whoever was lurking in these courts could get out only by the open west gate where the constable stood. But now Appleby's assailant was as good as a free man. All he had to do was to hurry down the east side of Bishop's, down the passage between library and chapel – all this being remote from the hearing or observation of the constable across the court – and let himself into Orchard Ground by the alternative route. Then if he were Empson, Pownall, Haveland, or Titlow he could go straight to bed; if he were an outsider he could let himself through the wicket and vanish.

Appleby got painfully to his feet. The movement started a trickle of blood from the wound on his scalp; as he bent forward it ran down his forehead and dropped suddenly and sickeningly into his eyes. Impatiently he made a rough bandage with his handkerchief, and wrapped his now shivery body in the coat which had been the cause of his downfall. For it was a downfall. Twice he had been outwitted that night: first in suffering the burglary of the President's study to happen, and now again in this closer and somehow more personal duel. For the second time he had the mortification of vain regrets. If only he had gone to Little Fellows' before consulting his comfort in the matter of the overcoat, what might he not now know! Something that he would not be given the chance, perhaps, to learn again.

At least he could go to Little Fellows' now. Bracing himself to hold at bay the giddiness and nausea that were upon him, he stepped out into the court. It had been cold in the little stone lobby, but it was colder in the open. The extra chill, numbing as it was, steadied him and he crossed the lawn confidently enough.

The constable had done the right thing: as long as Appleby was absent he had stuck to his post. But as time passed he had been in considerable perplexity and now he was anxious to know that he had committed no error of judgement. Appleby reassured him and dismissed him to an easier vigil in the President's study. To guard the gate any longer would serve no useful purpose: the bird had flown ... Appleby made his way once more into Orchard Ground. He looked at the luminous dial of his watch as he did so: it was a quarter to four – and impenetrably dark.

That anything would come of this final reconnoitre he had little hope. But it was preferable to going back to his room to think when his brain was too tired to think at its best. And if he went back he would, he knew, attempt to think: sleep immediately after defeat was impossible to him. So he rounded the corner of the President's Lodging and presently became aware of the bulk of Little Fellows' a few paces ahead. He would do a little burglarizing on his own. If one of the four occupants had been his assailant there was just a chance that some tiny indication of the fact might be discoverable. And if he were detected rummaging about the rooms of one of his St Anthony's hosts at four o'clock in the morning it might not be altogether unfortunate. A bare feeling that the police were uncompromisingly at work on a trail is a thing often surprisingly productive in criminal investigation.

No glimmer of light came from Little Fellows' as Appleby stepped into the stone-flagged lobby. Little Fellows' was a modern building, but it had been constructed on the old orthodox plan. Right and left of Appleby as he entered were the heavy outer doors of a set of rooms: Pownall's, as he knew, upon the left; Haveland's upon the right. Both doors were ajar and Appleby's torch ran cautiously round the little inner lobby revealed beyond each. Within the lobbies was one single door only; this would lead to the owner's sitting-room, from which an inner door, in turn, would serve as the only entrance to the bedroom beyond. In front of Appleby, and against the right-hand wall, the staircase ran up into the darkness to a similar lobby on the upper floor – the floor on which were the rooms of Titlow and Empson. Again in front of Appleby, and along the left-hand wall, a short passage led to a flight of stairs running downward – no doubt to some small service basement. There was little to explore here, but Appleby made a minute examination first of the paved floor of the outer lobby and then of the wooden floors beyond. Outside, it was slightly damp underfoot and there was the chance that a fresh footprint might give some clue to who had been stirring in the small hours.

But a careful search revealed nothing, and Appleby started on the staircase. Softly he mounted the bare wooden treads, scrutinizing them one by one. Half-way up was a small landing with a coal-locker, and then a full turn brought him to the upper lobby – and still nothing. He began to think that this in itself might be evidence, for in the lobby down below, and on the first few treads of the staircase, his own feet had left distinct traces. If anybody had passed indoors within the last two hours it seemed likely that traces would remain. But it was a doubtful point. Appleby himself had been walking a good deal on the grass; if his assailant had kept to the gravel paths his shoes might have remained comparatively dry. Or it was not unlikely that a careful man would have removed his shoes on the threshold.

And now Appleby decided to make sure that the occupants of Little Fellows' were indeed all in the building. He quietly opened the door of Empson's sitting-room and slipped inside. His flitting torch revealed a large book-lined room, handsome rugs on a polished floor, deep leather chairs, and, by the door where Appleby stood, a bronze bust on a pedestal. By an impulse of artistic curiosity that was natural to him he turned his torch for a moment full on this. The head, obviously, of a *savant* – and then he noticed a plaque on the pedestal: *Charcot*. Empson's master, perhaps – and Freud's.

Next – and again characteristically – the torch ran over the books. It was a severe library, almost without digressions, hobbies, or loose ends of any sort ... Ancient philosophy, massed together. Modern philosophy, similarly massed. *The International Library of Psychology, Philosophy, and Scientific Method* – uniform, complete, overwhelming. Academic psychology – what looked like a first-class collection. Medical psychology – a great deal of this, too. General medicine – something like the nucleus of a consultant's library. Criminal psychology. Straight criminology ... And that was all. Now for the bedroom.

Stepping deliberately from rug to rug, like a child on the pavement baffling the bears, he reached the inner door and heard, his own breath suspended, low, regular breathing from within. He turned the handle and opened the door a couple of feet until the bed was visible. Then he shone his torch upon the ceiling of the sitting-room behind him: the light was just sufficient to reveal Empson clearly. He was sleeping soundly, and in his sleep he looked worn and delicate. The lines of his mouth suggested pain; the skin stretched tight in a clear pallor over the cheek-bones and the jaw. Appleby recalled a slight hesitation – barely a stutter – in Empson's speech; recalled too that he was lame, walking with the assistance of a stick that even now stood beside his bed. The two disabilities were perhaps symptomatic of some congenital delicacy, and the dry, slightly acrid spirit of the man was the protective shell over a suffering and perhaps morbid sensibility. Appleby's mind went back to the books in the room behind him. The mainspring of such a personality as Empson's would be described there as the restless urge to power of one who feels in certain physical particulars subnormal. He softly closed the door on the worn almost bitter figure. He felt an unprofessional impulse of shame at his spying: a man appears so helpless in sleep – so helpless and so revealed ... Appleby passed out to the landing once more and entered Titlow's rooms.

He made no pause this time to scrutinize the sitting-room, for he wanted to be downstairs again without delay. Tip-toeing over to the bedroom door, he bent down to listen. There was no sound from within. And Appleby's ear was almost abnormally acute. Either Titlow was an exceedingly light sleeper or ... Appleby boldly opened the door. The room was empty. The bed-clothes were disarranged and Titlow's evening clothes lay on a chair – but Titlow himself was missing.

There was as yet no faint glimmer of light in the eastward-fronting windows of the rooms, and Appleby kept his torch burning as he made his way thoughtfully downstairs. He would wait for Titlow, and while waiting he would have a look at the two men below. He had recovered from his compunctions: if sleep was revealing he wanted more of it. Turning right as he got to the foot of the stair, he had his hand on Pownall's door, when he checked himself. Beneath the door was a thin luminous line. Within, someone had turned on the electric light.

Appleby's first thought was that it might be Titlow: while he himself was in Empson's rooms Titlow might have slipped down to Pownall's for purposes of his own. There was no murmur of voices from within: only the sound of slightly physical movements. Was Pownall still in bed and asleep, unconscious that he had a visitor – even as Empson had been a few minutes before? Appleby tried the keyhole – unenthusiastically. No aperture is more exasperating to the would-be spy than is a keyhole. It gives him a strip of floor, a strip of wall – even a strip of ceiling; but its lateral range is wretched. The thicker the door, moreover, the narrower the view and college doors are commonly good stout barriers. Through Pownall's keyhole Appleby could just discern movement, and no more. It seemed to be a case of either walking in or going away uninstructed. And then it occurred to him that the windows might be more hopeful. He slipped out into the orchard and was rewarded. The curtains of Pownall's room were drawn, but from one cranny there came a streak of light and by standing on tiptoe in a flowerbed he could just peer in.

Something large and black was moving about the floor, and it took a moment to sort out this appearance from its surroundings and impose an intelligible form upon it. Analysed it proved to be a pair of human buttocks, the curve of a human back, and the soles of two human feet. A dinner-jacketed form, in fact, was kneeling on the floor and crawling slowly over the carpet. It could not be Titlow – unless he had unaccountably changed out of one dinner-jacket into another. But at this moment the form circled round and rose to its feet. It was Pownall himself.

Inadequate as was his means of vision, Appleby was struck by the concentration on the man's face. Pownall was a clumsy man, and possessed at once of the bluest and the slowest eyes that the detective remembered. These eyes were cold now – were felt as cold even through the little chink of window-curtain – and the brow above them was heavy with effort. There seemed no fear that he would spot the dim face at the window. His gaze was intently fixed upon the floor; without shifting it he sidled out of range for a moment, and returned holding some small object with which he sank down upon the floor once more. Inch by inch he was going over his own carpet.

Appleby was as absorbed as Pownall – so absorbed as to start almost violently at the sudden murmur of a pleasant voice behind him. 'Ah, my dear Mr Inspector, you begin early – or continue late!'

Switching on his torch, Appleby swung round. It was Titlow – Titlow in pyjamas and a frayed but gorgeous silk dressing-gown, regarding him over that weak nose, through those luminous but fathomless eyes. There had been amused irony in the voice, in the 'Mr Inspector'. But suddenly there was concern as the Senior Fellow added, 'But bless me, man, are you not hurt – injured in some way?'

Appleby, pale, exhausted, with a bloody bandage round his head and clotted blood down his face, was discernible in the ray of light from the window as a sorry sight. He admitted drily that an unexpected mis-adventure had befallen him. Titlow continued concerned. 'If you have concluded your momentary observations, will you not come upstairs to my rooms? I have just been fetching myself a tin of coffee from the basement pantry here – I have wakeful fits sometimes. But you, if I may say so, need something stronger. And after that, I doubt if you could do better than go to bed ... Now, come away.'

Beside all this easy benevolence, Appleby discerned, was the same nervous excitement, the same irritability and impulsiveness that had struck him in Titlow already. And Titlow, if no more intense than say Empson or Haveland, was deeper than the others: there was layer upon layer to him – the several layers none too firmly bound together perhaps into any coherent personality. But he was smiling urbanely now, simply amused, it seemed, at having detected a detective in an absurd situation. And Appleby did feel a little uncomfortable. He experienced an idiotic satisfaction that Titlow had not come upon him while he was at the keyhole: there were several shades of ignominy, somehow, between keyholes and windows. He pulled himself together. 'I shall be delighted,' he said, 'if you will excuse me one moment.' And turning into the lobby of Little Fellows' once more, he went straight into Haveland's room, straight into his bedroom, discerned him indubitably asleep, and came straight out again. And this gesture accomplished, he followed the now frankly smiling Titlow upstairs.

2

Titlow's whisky was very good – or so it seemed to Appleby, who would have consumed the rankest poteen with relish at this melancholy hour of four-thirty on a November morning. Stretched in front of a large electric radiator, he sipped, munched biscuits from a large tin delusively labelled 'Msc. clay-tablets: Lagash and Uruk', and looked round him with interest. He had already – although Titlow did not know it – had a glimpse of this room; now he scrutinized it in detail. A living-room is always revealing, and particularly so when clothed with books. Titlow's books, like Deighton-Clerk's and unlike Umpleby's and Empson's, came up only waist-high round the room, but they were two deep everywhere on the broad shelves – an arrangement the inevitable inconvenience of which seemed enhanced by the completely haphazard arrangement of the volumes. Carelessly disposed along the tops of the low bookcases was a mass of ancient pottery – shapes subtle, free, and flowing; shapes angular, abstract, and austere; brilliant glazes, delicate crackles; textures that flattered the sense of touch through the sense of sight. Above the pottery on one wall was an enormous ground-plan of some large-scale excavation, a yearly progress marked on it in coloured chalks. Next to this, and set up for study it would seem rather than for ornament, was a series of large and technically magnificent aerial photographs of the same site, with sundry lines and crosses delicately traced on them in Chinese white. And next came a perfect miniature picture gallery, photographs and colour-prints covering a vast field of art – or covering rather all that field of prehistoric, barbaric, and pre-Hellenic culture which is still 'archaeology' to most although it has become 'art' to some. All the forms of natural life, the human figure chief among them, stylized and distorted to convey implications of permanence, rigidity, abstraction: the art of peoples who feared life. And hard upon these, in subtle juxtaposition, an art despising it: the art of the Middle Ages – an erudite collection, dominated by a big German *Danse Macabre*. And, single against this, in violent disharmony upon the opposite wall, all the physical glow and warmth of the Renaissance pulsating from a colour-print of Giorgione's Sleeping Venus.

Titlow in fact – it came to Appleby – was dramatizing an inner incoherence in this room. And in addition to the deliberate sounding of major disharmony there had been a scattering of little grace-notes of pure oddity. There was a stuffed dog, oddly reminiscent of Queen Victoria (who would scarcely have felt at home here); there was a small cannon; one of the chairs was simply hollowed out of some porous stone. But Appleby looked chiefly at the *Danse Macabre* and then at the Sleeping Venus. And he sipped his whisky and finally murmured to Titlow, with something of the whimsicality that Titlow had been adopting a little before, '*What truth is it that these mountains bound, and is a lie in the world beyond?*'

There was silence while Titlow's eye dwelt meditatively on a policeman conversant with Montaigne. Then he smiled, and his smile had great charm. 'I wear my heart on my wall?' he asked. 'To project one's own conflicts, to hang them up in simple pictorial terms – it is to be able to step back and contemplate oneself. You understand?'

'The artist's impulse,' said Appleby.

Titlow shook his head. 'I am not an artist – it seems. I am an archaeologist, and perhaps that is not a very healthy thing to be – for me. It is unhealthy to be something that one can be only with a part of oneself. And it is with a very small part of myself, I sometimes think, that I have become what I am. By nature I am an imaginative and perhaps creative man. But it is difficult to become an artist today. One stops off and turns to something else. And if it is something intellectual merely, so that other impulses lack expression, then perhaps one becomes – freakish. Irrational impulses lurk in one, waiting their chance ... do you not think, Mr Appleby?'

Odd the abruptly pitched question. And odd the whole man, talking thus under some queer compulsion to a stranger – and a policeman. Appleby's answer was almost at random: 'You think the thwarted artist ... unstable?' But it set Titlow off again.

'Artists or scholars, Mr Appleby – we are all unstable here today. It is the spirit of the age, the flux growing, the chaos growing, the end of our time growing nearer hourly! Perhaps one has not to live in imagination much amid the long stabilities of Egypt and Babylon to know that? But it is to the scholars, the men of thought, of contemplation, that the first breath of the whirlwind comes ...'

And pacing nervously, convulsively up and down Titlow talked ... of the rhythm of history ... the rise and fall of cultures ... *der Untergang des Abendlandes*, Decline of the West. He talked well, with a free, un-ashamed rhetoric, at once logical and full of bold ellipses. And Appleby listened quietly to the end. Titlow was talking as he was because Umpleby had died as he did.

'You know where we come from here – whence we derive, I mean. We are clerks, medieval clerks leading this mental life that is natural and healthy only to men serving a transcendental idea. But have we that now? And what then does all this thinking, poring, analysing, arguing become – what but so much agony of pent-up and thwarted action? The ceaseless driving of natural physiological energy into narrow channels of mentation and intellection – don't you think that's dangerous? Don't you think we could be a dangerous, unbalanced caste once the purposes have gone and the standards are vanishing? Don't you think it?'

Titlow had paused; he was perched outlandishly on his outlandish little cannon. What was the compulsion behind this queer talk – talk that was indeed but contemporary commonplace in substance, but, in some personal relationship in which the man now stood to it, so decidedly queer? Appleby remembered Deighton-Clerk talking – talking, it had seemed, to convince himself. And somehow – surely – Titlow was doing the same? Again he had concluded on a question, an appeal for corro-boration. Again Appleby had to evolve a reply.

'No doubt it is, as you say, the scholars and men of thought who feel the whirlwind coming. But do they really – give way? Is it not they who survive – survive because they are removed from the world? Do they not – well – guard, hand down?'

What, Appleby was wondering as he spoke, would Dodd think of all this as a technique of investigation? But his eyes were as searchingly on Titlow as if his question had related directly to the President's death. And there was strain, something even of anxiety or alarm lurking in Titlow's eyes as he replied.

'It should be as you say, Mr Appleby. Indeed, it *is* so – essentially.'

There was a silence of calculation. It was as if Titlow were feeling his way, testing the ground he would be on were he to abandon some position to which he had trusted – and all this with no reference to how he stood with Appleby. 'It is so – really,' he reiterated.

'But you think that a society such as this, in what you see as a disintegrating age, is unstable, erratic?'

Titlow made a gesture almost as of pain. And when he replied it was with an impersonality that plainly revealed the intellectual man's habit of striving for objectivity, for dispassionate truth. The personal pressure he had contrived for the moment to sink.

'Erratic, yes. But I have been overstating – or over-suggesting – greatly. Any fundamental unbalance there is not. What there is, is – nerves. And personal eccentricity, perhaps some degree of irresponsibility – our modern scholarship, I know, is essentially irresponsible. But basic instability – no. Except perhaps' – softly, firmly Titlow added – 'in such a one as myself . . .' Again he made his little gesture of pain.

'You would not say – regarding the matter untemperamentally – that the spirit of the age, and the rest of it, is likely to incline any of your colleagues to homicide?'

If there was a hint of irony in Appleby's question it was lost. Standing now before the fire, Titlow weighed it. And replied: 'No.'

'You would not think of any of your colleagues, while in his right mind, as remotely likely to murder?'

'Certainly I would not think anything of the sort – spontaneously.'

'Only on proof?' Sitting nibbling Titlow's biscuits and drinking Titlow's whisky, Appleby felt he could get no nearer direct inquisition than this.

And Titlow's response was enigmatic. 'What is proof?'

3

Appleby rose. Of all this there must be more on the morrow, or rather later this same day. Meantime it would be discreet to withdraw from a slightly uncomfortable position. But Titlow had something further to say. His restlessness, the characteristic nervous agitation which had expressed itself in his earlier talk, and which he had by some great effort controlled later, was back again now in full possession of the man. He had paced across the room; now he turned round with a new and tempestuous gesture, as if to say some conclusive, some final thing. But for a moment he seemed to seek delay on a minor theme.

'Who could have told, Mr Appleby, that *you* would come amongst us? Not one of us would have believed there was such a person – outside Gott's nonsense . . . Tell me, when were you here before?'

Appleby answered the unexpected question with some reluctance, but truthfully. 'Eight years ago.'

'Exactly – obviously! A good head that has had the right training – of course one knows it anywhere. But talk of erratic conduct ...! What of erratic walks of life? From our angle, you know, you yourself are the oddest thing in the case.'

'You mean,' said Appleby, remembering a facetious remark of Dodd's, 'that you expected Gott's other stock figure, the village policeman?'

'I say we should not have been inclined to count –' And suddenly Titlow was off on another tack. 'Did you ever read De Quincey's *Murder considered as one of the Fine Arts*?'

This was not the aimless belletristic habit which had prompted the venerable Professor Curtis to discourse on *The Purloined Letter*. Titlow meant something – was indeed poised again to take his plunge. But for a moment he wavered anew from the issue. 'Rather in your line. But poor stuff really – much slack erudition on a thread of feeble humour ...' And then he said what he had to say. 'It records an anecdote about Kant. You would find that interesting, if only because it deals with an academic attitude to murder. And if you turned it upside down it might even be illuminating.'

Appleby smiled. 'Thank you. I will look it up with all speed.' He moved to the door. And when Titlow spoke again it was easily, benignantly, as when he had first invited Appleby to his rooms.

'Well, you ought certainly to be in bed. You can get three or four good hours – and so perhaps can I. Put a notice on your door and the servants won't disturb you.'

Easy, benignant again – but with a difference. Titlow *was* easy now. It was as if, in giving some hint or pointer through De Quincey's essays, he had reached a position, or come to a decision on which he could rest. He moved to the door with his guest.

'Later – we shall see,' said Titlow. He gave his agitated little gesture – by way of farewell this time – and turned back into his room. Appleby went slowly downstairs. Through the orchard was seeping the first glimmer of dawn.

Chapter 7

Inspector Dodd walked down Schools Street in stolid satisfaction. The business of the burglaries was going well. In his pocket nestled a sheaf of notes for his London colleague that witnessed to the efficiency of his department. The morning was cold but pleasant, with gleams of sunshine filtering down the street, gilding St Baldred's tower, playing hide and seek in the odd little temples in front of Cudworth, exploring the dusty intricacies of the ornate and incongruous portals of the Museum, straying across the way to Ridley in an effort to brighten up the heavy-featured effigies of Jacobean divines. A group of undergraduates passing in riding-kit; a solitary and exquisite youth, in the most beautiful scarlet slippers, was crossing the street with the evident purpose of breakfasting with a friend in Joseph's; occasionally a female student, capped and gowned, bicycled hurriedly past in that zealous pursuit of early morning instruction proper to her kind. A small boy was sitting innocently on the door-step of the Warden of Dorset, selling an occasional newspaper to unenthusiastic purchasers. No one could have guessed that the same boy had been dashing wildly up and down Schools Street the evening before, waving the *Evening Standard* and bawling the death of Dr Umpleby ... The Master of St Timothy's, venerable, bearded, and magnificent, swept down every morning these forty years – plainly untroubled either by the decease of his colleague or by the reflection that St Timothy's rather than St Anthony's might have been the seat of the crime. It suddenly occurred to Dodd to rejoice that he was not a policeman in Chicago or Sydney or Cardiff. Praising heaven for his lot, he turned down St Ernulphus Lane.

Mr Appleby was to be found in Six-four. Meditating on this un-orthodox way of conducting police investigation, Dodd found Six – which was a staircase – passed Six-two with its unacceptable announcement, 'The Rev. the Hon. Tracy Deighton-Clerk: Dean', found Appleby's temporary quarters and knocked loudly. There was no reply, so Dodd walked in. A big fire was burning ruddily. Appleby's table was laid for breakfast; Appleby's coffee was keeping warm on the one side of the fire; a covered dish that was certainly Appleby's bacon and eggs was keeping warm on the other. But of Appleby himself there was no sign – until Dodd's eye lighted on a sheet of paper pinned to the inner door. Its message was short and to the point: 'Breakfast at nine – J.A.' Dodd looked at his watch. It was just nine-ten. 'Well I'm damned!' said Dodd, and was just about to penetrate into the bedroom when Appleby emerged.

'Morning, Dodd,' he said. 'Have some coffee? I expect there's plenty, and fairly warm still.' And then, noticing his colleague's doubtful glance at his still-bandaged head, he chuckled. 'Yes, I've been in a rough-house all right. Nocturnal rioting in St Anthony's. The police attacked with sandbags, lead pipes, and the butt-ends of heavy revolvers ... But I think this picturesque touch might come off now.' And Appleby disposed of the bandage before proceeding to fall upon his coffee and bacon and eggs.

Dodd looked at him wonderingly. 'You've really been knocked out?'

Appleby nodded. 'Knocked out, gently but firmly – and on the very verge of solving the St Anthony's mystery. I'm in disgrace.' He took a large gulp of coffee and nodded again in solemn assurance. 'One of your henchmen will be going home this morning with a sadly diminished respect for the conception of the metropolitan sleuth.'

'Who was it attacked you?'

'I don't know. But he – or perhaps she? – was the possessor of the tenth key. At least he was, and then I was, and then we did a bit of an exchange. I've got his tenth and he's got my ninth, so to speak. He took it from me after hitting me on the head.'

'Took it from you! And where did you take the tenth from?'

'The lock, Dodd; I found it in the lock. Natural place for a key, no doubt.'

Dodd groaned.

'And, by the way, Dodd, Umpleby's safe has been burgled – very successfully. Not a thing in it now – to interest us.'

Dodd fairly started to his feet. 'Burgled? Who in heaven's name can have done that? Someone in college?'

'I don't know.'

The local inspector looked at his colleague for a moment with what might have been positive distrust. 'Have you had *any* light on it – on the whole affair, I mean?'

'Indeed I have. Lots. Light comes flooding in from every angle – far too much light, from far too many angles. And I'm quite sure you've brought another surplus of it yourself ...'

'I've got something,' responded Dodd. 'But in a general way I'd like to be hearing what has happened. If you've got time, that is.' And he glanced with a sort of humorous severity at his watch and at the notice on the bedroom door. His admiration for Appleby was increasing rapidly. If he himself had lost that key he could never have contrived this air about it all. And Appleby, he felt, was doing something more than simply carrying the matter off: he was showing a quite natural and unforced faith in himself. He could be hit on the head and still remain in control of the situation – or so it seemed. If Dodd were hit on the head he would be hot and angry for days afterwards.

'Very well,' Appleby was saying. 'Here is an abstract of what has turned up.'

'First, your friend the Honourable and Reverend Tracy is in a stew. But whether he's simply worried about the reputation of the college, or whether he's worried somehow on his own account, I don't know. St Anthony's is due to come into the limelight in the near future, and he seems to have got his worries mixed up with that.

'Secondly, I know where the bones come from –'

Dodd sat up straight. 'Where?'

'Australia, my dear Dodd. Earth's last-found jewel. *Tierra Australis del Espiritu Santo.*'

Dodd looked bewildered. 'You're sure they don't come from Athens or Sparta?' he asked sarcastically, 'same as the *Deipno*-what-was-it in Umpleby's library?'

'The bones were abstracted from Australia – by no irrational ferrety, as Sir Thomas says. They were snatched from the pious care of an aboriginal posterity to gratify the scientific proclivities of one Johnnie Haveland.'

'Haveland! They're his?'

'They're his. And he was suitably apologetic about refraining from explanations when you were making inquiries yesterday. Apparently Johnnie kept the skulls and what-not in his own little toy-cupboard

– and now they're in Umpleby's study. He invites us to consider two possibilities about the murder. One, that he did it himself and left the bones as a sort of signature; two, that somebody has tried to frame him. And he as good as invited his learned friends to explain to me that there had been a time some years ago when he wasn't quite sound in the head. He seemed to think that would fit in with either possibility ... Oh! and he wasn't very nice about Empson.

'Thirdly, in the matter of keys, submarines, and scaling ladders. St Anthony's turns out to harbour a man who is likely to make the summit of Mount Everest one day – and who has already made the summit of St Baldred's tower in this city. That's Campbell – and I hope you have a little information about him in your pocket at this moment.

'Fourthly, President Umpleby was not beloved. Johnnie Haveland alleges that Umpleby stole from him in a learned way. And that, when you consider it, is more excessively unlikely than any number of murders – nevertheless, it undoubtedly struck some chord in the assembled confraternity.

'Fifthly, Umpleby's safe, as I've told you, has been opened by one X – who incidentally knew the combination. X had the tenth key. He came either from Little Fellows' or through the wicket from outside. X is erratic but brilliant. He left the west gate open behind him, apparently because it squeaked – an error of judgement. He left the key in the lock – a piece of colossal carelessness.'

'But,' Dodd interrupted, 'why should he come through the gate into the main body of the college at all?'

Appleby shook his head. 'After his successful burglary perhaps he wanted a little chat with somebody in the other courts. As I say, he is erratic – and brilliant. He found himself trapped when he came to get back – and he got out of the trap ruthlessly, effectively, and without losing his head and hitting too hard.' And Appleby stroked his own skull tenderly.

'Sixthly, under the prosaically named Giles Gott, at this time Junior Proctor in the university, is shadowed no less a person than Gilbert Pentreith.'

Dodd fairly leaped. 'And I never knew that!'

'Yes. He sits over there in Surrey giving his spare time to imagining just such pretty affairs as this. I told you there was a great deal of light flooding in.

'Seventh, Mr Raymond Pownall, an eminent ancient historian, spends his nights crawling about the floor of his room in a panic.

'Eighth – and, for the moment, lastly – Samuel Still Titlow lures honest policemen into his apartments, bemuses them with large and convincing talk of the end of the world, and just thinks better of concluding that the times are so out of joint that St Anthony's may well be a hot-bed of murder. And he counsels a little reading in the minor English classics. And he drops dark hints about being in at the death.'

'Would you say,' put in Dodd with his sudden shrewdness, 'that Titlow, like X, is erratic but brilliant?'

Appleby nodded thoughtfully. 'Yes,' he responded, 'he is. But it's just one of his points, I imagine, that that is a habit here. And I rather agree. I hope my next case is in Hull.'

Dodd smiled a slow smile. 'You just love this,' he said. And then a sudden thought struck him. 'What about traces of the burglar in that study? What about his slipping back to obliterate any later?'

Appleby shook his head. 'Your man's been sitting there all night since I recovered from my knock – I expect he'll have rung through for a relief by now. There was an interval, of course, after X got back from Orchard Ground, in which he could have gone to the study and cleared up. But I expect he'd pretty well obliterated himself already – even if he is erratic. I had a shot at the cigarette-ends and what-not earlier – and nothing doing. And I don't much look to find the damning thumb-print on the tenth key either.'

The two men were silent for a moment and then Dodd took his papers from his pocket. It was characteristic of Dodd that he always had something on paper ready to produce; he moved in an atmosphere of neat dockets and conscientious documentations. Appleby at the same time produced the notes and statements that had been made over to him the day before. As yet, his study of them had been superficial; direct contact with the personalities they dealt with had been taking up his time.

'Constable Sheepwash,' Dodd began in the peculiarly wooden manner he adopted when cautiously savouring the absurdities and ironies of his profession – 'Constable Sheepwash had a bite of supper last night with the Lambricks' cook. Earlier in the evening the lighting installation failed at the Chalmers-Patons'. Sergeant Potter represented the Electricity Department and after prolonged operations, mostly in the servants' quarters, the lights went on again. Constable Babbitt, as a Press reporter, failed to make an impression on the Campbell establishment yesterday, but he has done better as a milkman this morning. Station-Sergeant Kellett undertook to trace the movements of the Junior Proctor, Mr Gott, round the places of refreshment and amusement in the city for the material times. Kellett was unable to avoid the purchase of considerable quantities of liquor, but his report is nevertheless substantially coherent.' And Dodd, having had his little joke, became business-like. 'How would it be,' he asked, 'if you read out the statements as made yesterday and I followed each with my check-up here? That would begin to get us clear, I think, on these four people who were out of college on the night of the murder.'

Appleby nodded his agreement. 'We'll begin with Campbell,' he said. 'I see these are not *verbatim* statements in evidence?'

'No, they're simply abstracts of preliminary statements got out of these folk in a hurry. I don't think they could be evidence. I think you will have to take formal statements today. Anyway, we must have some before the coroner fixes the inquest.'

Appleby nodded and began to read:

'Campbell, Ian Auldearn (29). Became a Fellow of the college six years ago; has been married for four years; lives in a flat at 99 Schools Street; has never possessed a key to the St Anthony's gates. Declares that he has no knowledge whatever likely to elucidate mystery of Umpleby's death. Was associated with Umpleby in scientific investigation but was never in any sense a personal friend of the President's.

9.30. Left college and went home to flat. About half an hour later went out again to the Chillingworth Club in Stonegate.

11.50 (approx.). Left club for home, but remembered that he had certain business matters to discuss with Sir Theodore Peek, who lives at a house called Berwick Lodge up the Luton Road. Knowing that Sir Theodore keeps late hours he walked out there and arrived just at midnight. He had a brief conversation with Sir Theodore and then walked back to Schools Street, arriving home a few minutes before half past twelve.'

Appleby had no sooner finished reading than Dodd took up Constable Babbitt's report as a sort of antiphonal chant:

'Acting on instructions received entered into conversation with Mary Surname Unknown at 99 Schools Street 7.25 a.m. Subsequent to general remarks not necessary to record Informant declared (1) her employers kept fine hours, (2)

Mr Campbell came home night before last shortly after 9.30 but went out again about three-quarters of an hour later, (3) she believes she heard him returning long after midnight, (4) he remarked to Mrs Campbell at breakfast next morning that he had looked in on that old gargoyle Peek at midnight and found him in a sleepy, growly state (? a sick dog). No further information elicited.'

Appleby nodded and made a note. 'Questions at the club,' he said, 'and questions at St Theodore's – the sick dog! The material time was at the club, and it seems to hang together.' And without more ado he turned to his next note.

'Chalmers-Paton, Denis (40). Lecturer at St Anthony's – also at two other colleges. Married and lives at 12 Angas Avenue. Can make no suggestion on President's death.

9.30. Left college and went home. Read *The Decline and Fall of the Roman Empire* aloud to Mrs Chalmers-Paton. Mrs C.-P. then went to bed. C.-P. retired to his study and continued to read *D. & F. of R. E.* until shortly before midnight. He then went to bed too.'

Again Dodd followed with his subordinate's report. Chalmers-Paton had indeed come home, had read to his wife, and had then retired to his study 'a little before eleven'. But after that the servants knew nothing, and Sergeant Potter had not been authorized to approach Mrs Chalmers-Paton in any way. He had, however, timed the walk from Angas Avenue to St Anthony's and made it just twenty minutes. Chalmers-Paton had no car.

'Almost satisfactory,' said Appleby, 'and yet not quite. The man disappears into his study just too soon. If he was home at ten to ten and reading by ten, then "a little before eleven" *might* be twenty to eleven. And with the possibility of some emergency sort of conveyance that is just not good enough. And we don't *know* that he hadn't got the tenth key.'

'Just not a good enough alibi. And Campbell's at that club looks an uncommonly good one. Always sound to suspect the good alibi.'

Appleby smiled. This was the story-book Dodd speaking. But he did not altogether disagree. He turned to his next note.

'Lambrick, Arthur Basset (54). Fellow of the college for twenty-four years. Married and lives next door to Chalmers-Paton. Has had a key to the gates for a long time. Said to Inspector D.:"I cannot persuade myself that it was I who murdered our poor President."

9.30. Went home and stayed at home, "not knowing there was anything on".'

'Our humorous friend,' murmured Appleby. And he listened to Dodd's reading of Constable Sheepwash's researches. There seemed no doubt here. Lambrick had got home shortly before ten, played shove-halfpenny with his eldest son till eleven and danced to the wireless with his eldest daughter for half an hour after that. A housemaid who had still been up thought both proceedings immoral and consequently had them firmly fixed in her head.

'Not much good suspecting *that* good alibi,' admitted Dodd. 'But he might always have lent this key, you know.'

'And danced, so to speak, while Umpleby was cooling? It is possible. He might have lent his key, for instance, to Chalmers-Paton next door.' Appleby's tone was absent and it was a moment before he came back to his sheaf of papers.

'Gott, Giles (32). Came to St Anthony's six years ago. Has had key to gates since becoming Junior Proctor this year. Can give no information about Umpleby's death.

9.15. Left St Anthony's by the wicket gate and proceeded to the Proctor's office. Transacted university business there until 11.15. During this time he was quite alone.

11.15. The Senior Proctor returned from his rounds, accompanied by the four university officers on duty. Gott then took over, proctorizing various parts of the city in turn. He was later than usual, only dismissing the officers outside St Anthony's at about twenty past twelve.'

Appleby finished this recital with a shake of his head. 'No alibi there,' he said, 'nor the shadow of one. He was alone in his office until fifteen minutes after the shot and the discovery of Umpleby's body. And by way of the wicket that office is not more than seven or eight minutes from Orchard Ground.' Appleby's topography was remarkably sure. 'I don't see that your sleuth can have done anything useful about Gott?'

'Kellett has simply been round the town inquiring about the movements of the Proctors the night before last. It all squares so far. Between nine-thirty and eleven the Senior Proctor was patrolling about here and there. And after that Gott did apparently take on, going to various places until well past midnight. He wasn't seen before about eleven-thirty, but he might have slipped down from the office to St Anthony's and back easily enough without being recognized. It was a pretty dark night. Kellett, incidentally, hasn't made any inquiries direct at the Proctor's office, or seen the four officers. That would have to be done formally and openly, I think. As you say, there's no alibi – or rather any alibi there is is for the wrong time: it begins too late. Kellett has followed it all up, but it seems irrelevant.'

'Kellett has followed Gott up after eleven-fifteen? Better let us have it.' There were times when Appleby was a stickler for routine.

'Well, Gott must have gone straight to the railway station first. He and his men were there meeting the eleven thirty-two from Town. Then he went straight back to Town Cross and was seen by one of our men on duty there just after eleven-forty. He turned up at Stonegate and must have gone straight ahead, because just on midnight he was at the Green Horse.'

'What's that?'

'It's a dubious pub out on the Luton Road and a likely place to proctorize after hours. But Gott didn't spend long there, for he was back at Town Cross by twelve-fifteen, and went down Schools Street, presumably to St Anthony's, as he said.'

'About this Green Horse business. Did Kellett get his information from the people of the pub?'

'No, he got it from a farm-hand who had left a bicycle in the yard and was collecting it at midnight when Gott more or less ran into him. Kellett was uncommonly smart to tap him. The fellow knew what was up, of course; everybody in these parts knows the Proctor in his gown. And when he got out of the yard there were the four "cops" as he called them waiting.'

Appleby had got up and was striding restlessly about the room, seemingly in more perplexity than the St Anthony's mystery had yet driven him to. Suddenly he halted.

'Dodd, you haven't by any chance got a street-map on you?'

Without a word Dodd produced a map. Appleby opened it and pored over it for a minute. 'Odd,' he murmured, 'distinctly odd. And the first oddity that hasn't pretty well been thrust at us. And at the same time, as you say, irrelevant. I tell you, Dodd, there is too much light in this case – too many promising threads.' And he fell to striding up and down the room once more.

'Well,' asked Dodd, slightly aggressively after an interval of silence, 'what are you going to do now?'

'I think I'm going to go for a walk. But there is one other matter first. Can you spare a little more time this morning ... ? Well, I want you to send for Pownall to Umpleby's dining-room and take his formal statement. And I want the proceedings to last something over half an hour.'

2

Mr Raymond Pownall's was a colourless room. The books looked drab and were interspersed with unbound journals that looked drabber. The few pictures were of classical statuary – the kind of photographic reproduction in which the marble is thrown against an intensely sooty background. The carpet was a discouraged blue and a still more aggressive black.

It was the carpet that interested Appleby. Secure in the knowledge that its owner was closeted with Dodd, he crawled over it with every bit as much concentration as he had witnessed in the small hours of the morning. First, he studied the design – a largish floral one. Then, guided by the pattern, he made sure that his eye travelled over every inch of the surface. At the end of twenty minutes he had covered the whole area – and found nothing.

He straightened up, sat down, and thought. And then suddenly he shivered; his adventure of the night before had left him susceptible to cold ... *Cold.* He looked round the room. On this bleakly sunny and decidedly chilly morning every window of Pownall's room was open to its fullest extent. He began again, crouched over the carpet, not looking this time, but smelling ... After a few minutes he sprang to his feet and, stepping into the orchard, sent a lurking subordinate with a message to Dodd. He must have another hour. And he fell to the carpet again.

Pale blue had been turned to black. In eight symmetrical places the pattern had been minutely altered – and in eight places the faint smell of ink remained. A brisk rub with a handkerchief produced from eight places a faint but amply confirmatory smear: Indian ink.

'Of all the tricks ... !' murmured Appleby – and proceeded to rummage a packet of envelopes from Pownall's desk. Presently he was on his knees once more, industriously plying a pocket scissors.

3

In Two-six in Surrey the immemorial System was in operation. Mr David Pennyfeather Edwards, the Senior Scholar of St Anthony's and owner of the rooms, was squatting in front of the fire – appropriately, he had just pointed out – upon a large copy of the *Posterior Analytics*, superintending the preparation of a simple matutinal beverage mainly compounded of milk and madeira. Mr Michel de Guermantes-Crespigny, the cherubic Bible-clerk of the evening before, was lying on a window-seat with Sweet's *Anglo-Saxon Reader* upside down upon his stomach. Mr Horace Kitchener Bucket, an exhibitor of the college, was playing a rather absent-minded game of patience – involving four packs of cards and every inch of space – round the chairs and tables on the floor. And all three were improving themselves by conversation.

'The elimination of the Praeposital Pest,' said Mr Edwards, 'suggests a number of nice speculations. For instance, what would you do, Inspector, if you knew who had performed this useful and sanitary act?'

Mr Bucket, referred to as Inspector in allusion to the immortal masterpiece of Charles Dickens, wriggled a few inches across the floor to impound a ten of hearts, and shook his head.

'Dunno, David. Wait and see if there was a reward, I suppose.'

'I really believe,' murmured Mr Crespigny from the window-seat, 'that such is our Inspector's petty-bourgeois passion for the till that he would accept blood-money without a qualm. You shock me, Horace ... How's the drink?'

Horace, peering round the sofa in hope of a clinching ace, answered without heat. 'Aristotle – or perhaps it was Plato – was a shopkeeper – or perhaps the son of one: I forget. And your own namesake, dear Mike, the sage of Périgord, was a fishmonger. And you are a nasty, unwholesome, misshapen, degenerate, and altogether lousy scion of outworn privilege. And the increasing unpleasantness of your personal habits, your thick and incoherent utterance, your shambling gait, and above all your embarrassing and indeed painful inability to talk sense have long since convinced David and myself – though we have striven to conceal it – that you are already undermined beyond human aid by the effects of retributive disease. And your tailor – whose taste perpetually astonishes me, let me add – would be grateful for any blood-money *you* might raise on Umpleby: it would help feed the eight children your bad debts are deriving of sustenance.'

Long before Horace had finished these remarks he appeared to have lost interest in them. The words came automatically from his lips as his hands deftly manipulated the cards round the coal-scuttle. But presently he added, 'Who *did* kill Umpleby?'

'Umpleby,' Mike ventured, 'was stabbed by a dishonest serving-man, a rival of his in his lewd loves, and died swearing. Don't you think, David, that it must have been that crypto-Semite Slotwiner? Passion had run high between them over Mrs Tunk the laundress. And all to no purpose, for Mrs Tunk is firmly pledged to our own omnivorous and promiscuous Horace.'

'But what *would* one do,' asked David, suddenly jumping up to distribute the adulterate madeira; 'what *would* one do if one did really know?' Whereupon Mike swung himself erect on his window-seat, closing Sweet with a snap; Horace scrambled up from the floor, scattering his cards as he rose; and all three eyed each other attentively over their mugs. A moment before the rules of the game had required the slackest sort of interest, the laziest, sleepiest sort of wit. Now interest was allowed. It was rather like a flock of birds rising abruptly from the ground at the instance of a sudden and mysteriously communicated excitement.

'Would it depend,' asked Horace, 'on how bad we knew Umpleby to be?'

'Or on how good we knew the murderer to be?' asked Mike.

'What d'you mean – how good?' demanded David. 'If he was a good man and in murdering Umpleby did a bad act, his goodness couldn't be a relevant point in our decision, could it? He would have to be good in his character as a murderer, not simply in his character as a man, before we should have to begin reckoning with his goodness. I mean that if he murdered from some sort of ethically pure motive – then we should have to consider.'

Horace protested. 'Can one murder from a pure motive?'

'Well, suppose Umpleby were a very bad man in ways the law couldn't touch. Suppose he did things, and was bound to go on doing things, that would inevitably result in other people committing suicide and smothering their babies and being ruined by fraudulent speculation and all that. Would eliminating him be ethically pure?'

'Would the motive but not the deed be ethically pure?' asked Mike, who was untrained in these disputes but always put in a word.

'But suppose Umpleby a good man,' suggested Horace, '*chiefly* a good man, but with ... but with a kink or something. Suppose him a *split personality* – yes, now, suppose him just that – one of those people Morton Prince studied: one person one day and another person the next –'

'Jekyll and Hyde,' said Mike, very pertinently – and was ignored.

'Suppose he had two personalities, *a* and *b*. And *a* was, say, a blackmailer. And *a* knew about the existence of *b* but *b* didn't know about *a*. And now suppose his murderer happened to be a split personality too – with three personalities: *x* knowing about *y* but not *z*, *y* knowing –'

'Steady,' said Mike. 'Stick to the corpse – and to who struck Umpleby. When we find out that it will be time enough to debate whether we can morally seep in and collect the cash. And why *shouldn't* we find out – if Gott doesn't?'

'What d'you mean, if Gott doesn't?' asked both his companions.

'Gott could find out if he wanted to,' maintained Mike, who had boundless faith in his tutor; 'only quite likely he doesn't want to.'

'Quite likely it *was* Gott,' declared David. 'The man must have a morbid mind, turning out such tripe. A man who could write *Murder among the Stalactites*, with all that stuff about how long a well-nourished, middle-aged man would take to petrify, must be capable of anything. Did I tell you I tried pumping old Curtis yesterday evening, and he said the President had been murdered with "grotesque concomitant circumstances"? What do you think that meant? I wonder if Gott *disembowelled* him?'

Mike, ignoring this offensive suggestion, pressed his own point. 'I don't see why we shouldn't amuse ourselves by finding out. We haven't got the facts, but I expect a lot can be done just by intelligent thinking. And you and I are intelligent, David – and even Horace has his moments.'

Horace, secure in the classical man's consciousness of a superior training, was undisturbed. 'No doubt we're brighter than the police,' he said, 'although this Scotland Yard man is probably smart in a ferrety way. But we're no brighter than Deighton-Clerk or Titlow, and they know more of the facts.' Horace, in his turn, would maintain the almost ideal intelligence of his preceptors. 'They're more likely to guess than we are.'

There was a brief pause. Then David said, 'I have a fact.' There was another pause and he added, 'But what's more interesting: I have a notion too.'

In all tiny coteries there is always a leader, and David was the leader here. Attention was immediate. 'It's what no one will have thought of – and it opens a line. I'll tell you.'

And he did.

Chapter 8

Pownall, irritated and pale after his long interview with Inspector Dodd, halted, suddenly paler still, on the threshold of his room. For from beside the fire there rose to greet him Inspector Dodd's colleague, Mr Appleby of Scotland Yard.

Appleby was, as the occasion demanded, politely and conventionally apologetic. 'I hope you will forgive my waiting for you in your room. I thought I would wait a few minutes on the chance of your coming back. And I was tempted to sit down by your fire. It is a chilly morning.' And Appleby's eye, moving as lightly as his apology, swept the uncompromisingly open windows of the room.

Rather slowly, as if gaining time to collect himself by the act, Pownall shut the door. And having closed it he seemed to realize, with a fresh failure of composure, that he had thereby closeted himself with the detective. But he kept his eye steadily on his visitor as he crossed the room and sat down. He was a grey, dim creature, Appleby thought; his beardless, fresh complexion the sort that makes a close guess at age impossible; his greying hair cropped Germanically short. His head went a little to one side and his hands had a trick of falling lightly into each other in front of his chest – a gentle, almost feminine attitude that was strangely at variance with the hard chill of the slow blue eyes. The eyes, so cold in the small hours, were indeed cold again now – and they were unwavering as the man sat down opposite Appleby. He sat absolutely still. He was clumsy – and it was as if he feared that a single clumsy movement of body would bring some fatally clumsy revelation in its train.

'I have just signed a statement for your colleague, and been questioned at great length. And now, can I help you?'

Pownall spoke quietly and colourlessly – severity only hinted at in his choice of words. But as he spoke he let his glance glide over his room, a resolutely casual, yet cold and searching glance. And all the time his head kept its fixed, slightly sideways-inclined posture – oddly like the sooty photograph of Alexander the Great on the wall behind him.

'You have been unable to add anything to your informal statement yesterday?' Appleby too spoke colourlessly, but the question took an emphasis not of his giving from the pause of silence that followed it. At length Pownall replied.

'I have added nothing.' And again there was a pause.

'You are aware of no circumstances connected with the President's death that would be useful to us?'

'No.'

'In effect, you have just sworn to that position?'

Again there was a pause. And then Pownall suddenly sprang up and crossed the room. His objective turned out to be a little glass box containing cigarettes, which he apparently intended to offer to Appleby. But the oddly-timed gesture of hospitality never accomplished itself: the box suddenly slipped from Pownall's fingers and its contents were scattered on the floor. The touch of clumsiness about the man made the accident seem natural enough. But to Appleby there was no accident – only a fresh illustration of the general proposition that in St Anthony's minds worked well.

Pownall had stooped down instantly. His fingers, gathering the cigarettes, ran here and there over the carpet. And when he straightened himself again his face, which might have been flushed with the exertion, was even paler than before. For a moment the two men looked into each other's eyes. And then – obliquely – Pownall answered the question which had been directed to him a minute before.

'I can throw no light, by way of evidence, on the death of the President. But there have been certain matters, connected with his death, but not elucidating it, that I have considered it my duty to myself not to advance up to the present.'

'What you have signed before Inspector Dodd can be used in court, Mr Pownall. You must know that. And the fact of your having omitted material facts from your statement can be used too.'

'It is not perjury, Mr Appleby, to make one's own decisions as to what is relevant in a statement offered to a police officer.'

Appleby bowed his acceptance of this proposition. But an edge had come into his voice when he spoke. 'A course far short of perjury may, under certain circumstances, be very injudicious. It is injudicious, for instance, to spend the night following a murder in doctoring the floor of your room. As you have guessed, from every spot where you put ink I have taken a specimen; and what is under one or more of those spots analysis will reveal.'

Appleby had a good deal more faith in extracting a revelation from Pownall himself than from any chemical analysis. Pownall would realize that the doctored carpet was a most uncomfortable fact in itself, irrespective of what the doctoring might be proved to conceal. And he did realize. Coldly, abruptly, came the confession. 'The ink covers blood.'

There was a pause, and then Pownall made his first movement since he had sat down again – something like a gesture of resignation over what he had just said. And then he went on:

'You will wonder how an intelligent man could act in so foolish a way as I have been acting. Well, the answer is – *blood*. They say that to shed blood is an intoxicant – that one feels like an angel. I have been drunk too, and drunk from – blood. But not blood that I had shed. And I have not felt like an angel . . . No.'

There was another of the pauses which seemed characteristic of any conversation with this dim, still, clumsy creature. But this seemed – despite the incoherence of what had just been said – a pause of intense calculation, as if the man had made a first move at some intricate game of skill and was striving with complete concentration to assess the result.

'It was blood on the carpet. Just here' – and Pownall, rising, strode almost to the middle of the room and pointed with his foot. 'Not much, a little pool – two inches perhaps . . . and half clotted. I took blotting-paper. I remember wondering if it would work; if blotting-paper would absorb blood – clotting blood. It did, and there was left just half an inch of stain. On the black, it didn't show – only on the pale blue there. So I took the ink, a dead black Indian ink I have, and enlarged the pattern. It was a panic action – the fear of what had been planted on me drove me. And the panic kept coming back. Every time I looked at the carpet yesterday the irregularity – the minute half-inch irregularity – seemed to leap at me. But the ink on the blue seemed a perfect dye, giving exactly the normal black of the carpet. And it worked on me till I went over the whole carpet in the night, making it regular. It was only when I had made all those half-inch blots that I found it would smell. But with the windows open . . .'

Pownall stopped. He seemed simply lost in thought. And this time Appleby had to speak.

'Will you please give me a more coherent – a less dramatic – account?' Expressed in Appleby's tone was the conviction that the pressure under which Pownall appeared to speak was a fabricated pressure, that the man was playing a part. And yet he was not sure; the strange blend of agitation and impassivity with which he was confronted was almost baffling. And now Pownall took up the request simply.

'Yes,' he said, 'I will.' And after that pause which had established itself as an essential rhythm of the proceedings he added, 'It began, really, with a dream.'

Inspector Dodd, had he been treated to these confidences an hour before, would undoubtedly have betrayed some impatience at this point. Appleby did not. But he took a notebook and pencil from his pocket and began to make a shorthand entry. The action seemed to stimulate Pownall, who plunged into something like connected narrative.

'I keep early hours, usually breaking the back of my day's private work before breakfast. It is a habit I got in hot countries: I have done a good deal of archaeological research in Egypt as well as Greece. I am up normally before five and therefore I go to bed fairly early. The evening before last I got back from the common-room perhaps a few minutes before half past nine. I sat here reading for about twenty minutes. Then I got some hot water from the servant's pantry out on the landing there, washed, and went to bed. I must have been asleep before ten-fifteen: I like to be asleep a quarter of an hour earlier than that if I can.

'Well, it began, as I said, with a dream. I was a rowing man as an undergraduate and this dream was about the river. We were practising just as they are practising now – in tub fours. Our coach was shouting to us and I remember being worried by some quality of his voice – perhaps he was using a megaphone – I know I was unreasonably worried by something about the shouting . . . We were practising starts and the same shout ran through the dream again and again: *"Come forward – Are you ready? – Paddle!"* The last word was a tremendous shout, like the crack of a whip, and then we were straining up the river. There were other things that I forget, or perhaps the dream lapsed. But, anyway, the same situation came back again, a sort of recurrent nightmare. And presently some stiffness seemed to come over me and interfere with my stroke. The coach was calling to me over and over again, *"Drop them, Bow! Drop them, Bow!"* – meaning my wrists. But I couldn't get them away and finally I caught a crab.

'And that woke me up with a start. I was in a cold sweat of terror. But not terrified enough not to be puzzled by my terror. For though I sometimes have nightmarish dreams they don't leave me really scared. And then I knew somebody had been in the room. I don't know how I knew, but I suppose that my sleeping consciousness somehow told me. And a moment later I received confirmation. I heard a distinct, heavy sound from this sitting-room. If I had been in an accessible part of the college I might have suspected an undergraduate joke, although such things are rare. But only one of my colleagues, or the porter, could normally be in Orchard Ground at that hour. And although a colleague might quite naturally and properly enter my sitting-room, he would hardly be likely to come secretly into my bedroom while I was asleep. And I concluded therefore that a burglar had broken into Little Fellows'.

'I am not a particularly courageous man. It took me perhaps two minutes to compel myself out of bed and into the sitting-room. As I entered I was aware of a streak of light from the lobby beyond – and then the streak disappeared. Somebody had just closed the door. Oddly enough, I think (for I am, as I say, a coward), I went straight after him. And I got out just in time to see someone disappear into the darkness –'

'Which way?'

The sudden question came from Appleby like a pistol-shot. But he could not feel with any certainty that it had caught Pownall out. The man hesitated, but only for a moment. 'There is only one path,' he answered, 'and he was lost to sight long before it branches. I shouted, and I know he heard me, for he instantly broke into a run.'

Appleby's question was soft this time. 'Who was it, Mr Pownall?'

And this time Pownall did really hesitate – the old trick of marked pause again. Once more he seemed to be calculating effects and chances before he finally replied, 'I don't know.'

'You have no idea? It was just a back? What about the build, the clothes?'

Pownall shook his head – and returned abruptly to his narrative.

'I went back to my room, meaning to telephone to the porter at once. But as I glanced round to see if anything had been rifled or upset I saw –'

'You saw the blood, Mr Pownall – two inches of half-clotted blood. And you mopped it up with blotting-paper and got out your bottle of ink ... What else?' Appleby was really formidable now. The cold, measured disbelief in his voice might have unnerved a hardened criminal. But Pownall was entirely master of himself.

'That is so,' he said. 'I discovered the blood – and something else. Two charred pieces of paper in an ash-tray caught my eye – an ash-tray which I knew had been empty when I went to bed. And when I examined them I found that they were two pages torn from a diary – nearly all burnt, but not quite. There was a corner preserved with a fragment of the President's writing.'

Appleby, in whose pocket the dismembered diary of the dead man reposed at this moment, knew that here at least was something not sheer fiction. But he showed no sign of being impressed. 'This might have come out of the brain of Mr Gott,' he said – and half started at the unintentional two-edged nature of the remark. 'And you immediately concluded from these indications ... *what?*'

Pownall rose to his fence as Haveland had done the evening before. 'I concluded,' he said, 'that someone had murdered the President and was trying to blame me.'

'It is in Chicago surely, and not here, that that sort of conclusion is lying ready to come into people's heads? You seriously put it to me that you thought of that?'

Pownall looked coldly at his guest. 'I thought just that.'

'These rather odd facts – a spot of blood, a couple of scraps of paper, a night-prowler of some sort – actually suggested murder and conspiracy?' Appleby's tone was openly incredulous.

Pownall did not hesitate this time. 'It was the blood,' he said. 'It threw me off my balance – made me, in a way, drunk, as I told you. My actions became abnormal. The attempt at concealment was abnormal. But my inference was perfectly sound and reasonable. From these facts – the clandestine visit to my rooms, the blood, the half-destroyed fragments of Umpleby's writing – induction could take me to only one conclusion: Umpleby, incredible though it was, had been attacked or murdered – and the blame was in course of being put upon me. Probably the blood, the diary pages, were only first steps. Probably I had interrupted the plot. I ought to have been still asleep, allowing further stages of the plan – but now the plotter knew I was awake. Probably he had relied on the fact that I am a notoriously heavy sleeper to enable him to leave yet further traces in my bedroom. It is worth while remarking, by the way, that when we had an alarm of fire some years ago I slept so soundly through the hubbub as to become a college jest.

'I guessed, then, that the plotter intended to leave the body near at hand and then give the alarm and somehow direct the search to my rooms. And these things would be found, like fatal traces I had over-looked before going callously to bed. If I had not awakened when I did, the first thing I should have been aware of would have been being hauled out of bed to face a murder charge.'

Pownall spoke confidently and – beneath the resolute chill – even passionately. *Almost*, thought Appleby, like a man speaking the truth. And yet Pownall, in rising so resolutely to that fence, had made a mistake. And Appleby, with that effect of intuitive awareness that experience and training bring, knew that Pownall knew that he had made a mistake. (He thought, said Appleby to himself, that a knowledge of Umpleby's murder was necessary to explain his getting into a panic and monkeying with the carpet. So he has invented this story of guessing at it. And in doing so he has landed himself in simply psychological impossibility. He ought simply to have put up the story that he was scared by what had happened and acted out of mere indefinite, massive sense of danger. He has made a mistake which no talk about inference and induction can cover – and he knows it.)

Aloud, Appleby said: '*And you gave no alarm?*'

The mention of Chicago had been one absolute point. This was another. And Pownall took a moment to square himself to it.

'My hands were tied. Once I had – unnerved by the blood and with, I admit, the gravest folly – used that ink, I dared not risk another move. Hiding the blood-stain had been the result of some morbid streak of fear rising up in me: it rose again the next night when I continued to tamper with the carpet. And I felt at the time, I think, that I would rather be hanged than admit to it.'

The man could make a good come-back – knew what and when

to concede. They were all able ... what a case it was ...! And suddenly Appleby found himself shocked at the quality of pure intellectual pleasure that he himself could get from this wretched business – this wretched murder where murder had no reason to be. He remembered thoughts which had come to him pacing up and down Bishop's in the darkness that morning. The darkness, the silence, pregnant somehow with the spirit of the place, had brought him momentarily a strange bitterness – bitterness that he had come to these courts he knew as an instrument of retributive justice. And that mood had been succeeded by anger. He remembered touching the cold carved stone of an archway and feeling a permanence: something here before our time began; here while our time, as Titlow was to paint it, moved fearfully and gigantically to its close; to be here in other times than ours. He remembered a significance that the light over Surrey archway, shining steadily amid the darkness and vapour, had taken on. And he remembered how he had sworn to drive out the intrusive alien thing ... And now here he was with the problem coldly before him again – a frankly enjoyable intellectual game ...

And yet it was impossible altogether to suppress the element of emotion – of pity. Why was this scholar sitting here coldly telling fibs – in a matter of life and death? Had he taken a revolver and shot Umpleby in the head? After all, why should he do such an idiotic thing? A little wave of exasperation came over Appleby and he let himself go farther than he had yet done.

'Well, Mr Pownall, did your observation extend to the hour at which these interesting events took place?'

But Pownall was not to be rattled by a tone of contempt any more than he was to be shaken by disbelief. 'I looked at my watch as I got out of bed. It was ten forty-two.'

'Ten forty-*two*.' Irony emphasized the precision. 'But was not ten forty-two, sir, eighteen minutes before we know the President was shot? Just how was the living Dr Umpleby, do you think, persuaded to part with – well, even two inches of blood? There seems to be some difficulty.'

'I suppose it needn't have been Umpleby's blood. I suppose the plotter – whoever he was – was laying as many false clues beforehand as possible. Then he would simply have to kill Umpleby somewhere close at hand, run, and then cause the alarm to be given.'

'But we know that the President was shot in his study, where the shot would almost certainly be heard and mark the time. And then the President's body was found there, surrounded by Mr Haveland's bones. Does that square?'

'Yes, it does. Remember, the plotter knew that I had found out what was afoot. He had heard me call after him. And so he might abandon the plan of putting the crime on me and attempt to put it on Haveland instead.'

There was a long pause. Resolutely Appleby said nothing. And eventually Pownall added something more. 'Or the murderer might abandon his plan of fathering the murder on someone else. If he were an unbalanced person, for instance, and his elaborate plan miscarried, then –'

'He might turn round on himself and leave his own signature, as it were, openly on the deed? I see.'

Appleby got up. And then a thought seemed to strike him. 'By the way, if your first suggestion holds – if the murderer, knowing he had failed to frame you, decided to frame Mr Haveland, he must have counted on your unlikely folly in concealing what you ought immediately to have revealed.'

'I do not suppose my first suggestion to hold,' said Pownall.

2

It was a thoughtful and perplexed Appleby who walked slowly back through Orchard Ground to the President's Lodging. He felt a disposition to react against these odd little interviews by which the case seemed to be conducting itself. He had an uneasy feeling that his own favourite technique, which was that of sitting back and watching and listening, was somehow inadequate – dangerous, indeed – in this case: something more aggressive was required. In discussion, all these people would be endlessly plausible – and they would hardly ever make a mistake.

What had he really learnt? Or what, rather, had he really learnt that he was not *meant* to learn? His one success, so far, had been in this last encounter with Pownall: he had at least forced Pownall from one position to another – convicted him of very injudicious conduct. But that success had been the result of orthodox police methods: a little successful prying through a window, a little successful bullying. Had he made a mistake in trying to follow these people over their own discursive ground? And these palavers took time; the morning had slipped away without appreciable gain. He would not have another of these face-to-face interviews until he had done a little preliminary backstairs work. And the need for one piece of concrete investigation was pressing upon him vividly – had been pressing upon him when he told Dodd that he was presently going to take a walk. He had to solve a puzzle that seemed at once irrelevant to the case and at the same time too *near* the case to be really irrelevant ... And meantime he turned into the President's Lodging to persuade Dodd, if Dodd himself was impatient to be gone, to provide another officer sufficiently senior to go on with the business of taking formal statements. He was not yet prepared to give time to that himself.

He was still somewhat gloomy as he crossed the President's hall. Quick results were not to be looked for, to be sure, in a case so complicated as the present. Nevertheless, certain things should now have emerged or be beginning to emerge that had not in fact done so. Certain threads of motive there should be by now – and, actually, what was there? Umpleby had been disliked by Haveland and others, and there was a dubious story of his having made free with other people's intellectual property. Very insufficient, so far. What else might have emerged? The weapon ... ?

Appleby turned into the dining-room. At one end of the table the sad sergeant was gathering together a bundle of papers. At the other end sat Dodd, apparently in meditation. And on the polished mahogany between them lay a tiny gleaming revolver – a delicate thing with a slender barrel of chilly blue steel, a slender curved ivory butt. Barely a serious weapon – but at three or four yards just serious enough.

Appleby was analysing his surprise at this appearance when Dodd awoke from his meditations and beamed. 'The coppers,' he said, 'have managed a little more of the rough work for you' – he waved his hand at the pistol – 'and will now withdraw.' And he began gathering his own papers together.

'Without divulging the hiding-place of this interesting object?'

'To be sure – I was forgetting. We found it among the Wenuses and other fabulous animals.' Inspector Dodd had his own power of literary allusion.

'Quite so,' said Appleby; 'among the Wenuses. What could be more obvious?' And even the sad sergeant joined discreetly in the mirth. Then Dodd explained.

'Babbitt found it in the store-room of Little Fellows'. You know how a passage runs back on the ground floor to the little staircase that goes down to the servants' basement pantry and so on? Back there on the ground floor itself, just over the pantry, there is a little store-room or big cupboard full of all manner of junk. Babbitt' – Dodd continued with a momentary return to the meditative manner – 'was routing about there before you were facing that breakfast of yours ... Well, there is all manner of stuff, apparently, including a good many of Titlow's cast-off oddities. Quite a museum of a place: there's statues and mummy-cases and bits of an old bathroom floor – or so Babbitt says, but your learning will doubtless recognize a Roman pavement or such-like. And the door is more or less blocked by an old bath-chair that Empson used to use (it seems) when he was lamer than he is. And behind that are these heathen females, and the revolver had been chucked behind them again. Not a bad hiding-place, really.'

'It no doubt had its points,' Appleby agreed rather drily. He was staring thoughtfully at the little weapon. And for some moments he continued to stare.

'You seem to be waiting for it to jump up and out with the whole story,' said Dodd.

'I have a feeling that it has already told me something just as it lies. But I can't fix it. *Abondance de richesses* again. A few minutes ago I was feeling that perhaps I had learnt nothing at all. And now in a minute I learn far too much.'

'The approved cryptic manner,' said Dodd with a chuckle.

Appleby almost blushed – and suddenly became brisk. 'Got a railway time-table, Dodd? Good, Sergeant, have you had a jaunt to Town recently? Go over, will you, and get my suitcase from Six-two.'

'The Yard in action,' continued Dodd in the same humorous vein. 'And now, in my own humble way, I'm off after my burglars. Kellett will be here presently to continue taking statements and so forth as you want them. I think you said you were going to take a nice walk. Don't let them bludgeon you again in our rural solitudes. And if your learned friends aren't claiming you, will you meet Mrs D. over supper?'

Appleby accepted cordially: it would be a failure in propriety, he felt, to appear at the St Anthony's board again. The arrangement was just completed when the sergeant returned with the suitcase, and Appleby fell rapidly to work before a lingering and attentive Dodd.

'You don't think he'll have left finger-prints, do you?' the latter asked incredulously.

'You never can tell.' Appleby's fingers were busy twisting up a stout length of wire.

'I never heard of dusting for finger-prints with a sort of rabbit-trap before.' Dodd was amused and impressed and happy in the contemplation of these mysterious proceedings.

'Good Lord, Dodd; how out of date you shockers must be! You don't think I'm going to tackle what may be a hundred-to-one chance myself, do you? It's a job for the best chemist and photographers we have. And they will want the bullet, too, by the way, when it's available.' The little wire cage was finished as he spoke; the revolver, delicately lifted, fitted miraculously into it; the whole, together with the notorious tenth key, fitted into a small steel box. The box was locked and handed to the sergeant; its key pocketed. 'There you are, Sergeant, and there's the time-table. The first train to Town and then a taxi to the Yard. Mr Mansell in the east block. Time is an element in these diversions – so off with you. And you'd better stay the night: you might be useful to bring back reports. So have a good time.'

The sad sergeant went off transformed. And Dodd went off too. He carried away with him for meditation a new image of Appleby – an image, momentarily caught, of a startled and startling eye.

Chapter 9

Undergraduates were strolling through Bishop's – more of them than usual, perhaps, and more slowly than the bite in the air might seem to warrant. Some lingered to converse with friends at windows – and the windows of the court were remarkably peopled too. But Appleby, pacing in the filtered winter sunshine where he had before paced in darkness, was oblivious of his character as a spectacle. The excitement detected by Dodd was on him still.

To Dodd he had complained earlier of too much light – but it had been light, or a multiplicity of lights, playing brokenly and confusedly on a blank wall. Now the light had suddenly concentrated itself and revealed an opening, an uncertain avenue down which it might be possible to press. He was beginning that exploration now. And as he went cautiously forward the avenue narrowed and defined itself; the light grew ...

He knew now something that he ought to have known the moment he first entered the President's study. The shot heard by Titlow and Slotwiner could not have been the shot that killed Umpleby. Barocho's gown was next to absolute proof of this. Appleby had found it – carefully replaced as it had first been discovered – swathed round the dead man's head. And for this the murderer had surely had no time. Between the report from the study and the entry of Titlow and Slotwiner scarcely a quarter of a minute could have elapsed. To scatter the bones, to scrawl however hastily on the wall, and then to escape into the orchard would take every available second. The murderer would have had no time to wrap a gown round his victim's head – and he would have had no motive to do so either.

And all this, which should have come home to Appleby at once – which must, indeed, have been lurking deep in his mind from the first

– it had needed a chance piece of information from Dodd to bring to consciousness. And it had come to consciousness in the form of a vivid picture. For as he had stood in Umpleby's dining-room his inner vision had recreated for itself all the impenetrable darkness of a moonless November night – darkness such as he had himself experienced a dozen hours before. And through the darkness had lumbered a dubious shape, creaking and jolting – a shape indefinable until, stopping by the dim light from a pair of french windows, it revealed itself as a bath-chair in which was huddled a human body, its head swathed in black ...

And as the picture came now once more with renewed conviction to Appleby's mind he turned round and hurried into Orchard Ground. A minute later he had found the store-room of which Dodd had spoken. The bath-chair was there. Would it be possible to say that it had recently been used – that it had recently been outside? He fell to an absorbed examination. It was, even as it had presented itself to his imagination, an old and creaking wicker-work thing – a hair-raising vehicle for the purpose to which he suspected it of having been put. But it was in sound enough order. He studied the hubs. There was no trace of oil – slight evidence perhaps, that if the chair had been used it had been used in an emergency, without previous plan. And nowhere was there any blood. That, of course, would give the motive for the swathed head: nowhere must there be blood except in the President's study ... And next, Appleby turned his attention to the tyres. They were old and worn, the rubber hard and perished, with a surface to which little would adhere. But here and there were minute cracks and fissures which offered hope. In these, in one or two places, were traces of gravel – but all bone dry. Supposing this gravel to have been picked up a couple of nights before, could it be as dry as this? Appleby thought it could – and searched on for better evidence. And when he had almost finished minutely scanning the perimeter of the second wheel he found it. Between tyre and rim, caught up as the chair had scraped against the border of some lawn, was a single blade of grass. And that clear green, which clings even in mid-winter to an immemorial turf, was on it still. Recently – very recently – the bath-chair had been used.

Appleby turned to the back. The chair was propelled by a single horizontal handle of the kind that can be removed by unscrewing a knob at each end. Mechanically, following the routine search for finger-prints, Appleby unscrewed. And then he glanced round the little room.

It was, as Dodd had reported, full of lumber – and obviously of Titlow's lumber chiefly. There was a harquebus. There was a meek-looking shark in a glass case. And there were one or two plaster casts, including one of a recumbent Venus – the goddess, no doubt, behind whom the revolver had been found. Appleby, not venturing to sit down on the chair, sat down on this lady's stomach instead – and thought hard.

Umpleby alive in his study at half past ten. Umpleby shot, elsewhere, between that hour and eleven ... And suddenly there came back to Appleby another impression of the night before. The quiet of Bishop's, protected by the great barrier of chapel, library, and hall. The intermittent rumble and clatter of night traffic heard in Orchard Ground, increasing to uproar as one came nearer and nearer Schools Street. Every five minutes there must come, even in the night, a moment in which it would be safe to fire a revolver without fear of detection.

Umpleby killed here in Orchard Ground and his body trundled back to his study. Umpleby killed at one time and place and given the appearance of being killed at another time and place. At another time and place and *therefore by someone else*. Alibi ... no, that wasn't it: there had been the second shot. Stay to fire a second shot and you can't be establishing an alibi. *Destroying someone else's alibi* ... that was better ... And then to Appleby's picture of that grim conveyance emerging from the darkness there was added a new detail. At the feet of the dead man was a box – perhaps a sack – filled with bones.

He heaved himself up from the chilly and unyielding abdomen of Aphrodite and went slowly out of the store-room. In the lobby he paused. On his left, Haveland's rooms: the bones had lived there. On his right, Pownall's – and on the carpet, blood. He turned into Orchard Ground once more and fell to pacing among the trees – this time a spectacle to none. His mind was absorbed in testing a formula – a formula which ran:

He couldn't prove he didn't do it there and in twenty minutes' time – were some indication left that he was guilty. But he could prove he didn't do it here and now.

And he added a rider: *An efficient man; he reloaded and let the revolver be found showing one shot.* And then he added a query: *Second bullet?* and finally, and inconsequently, he appended a reflection: *Nevertheless I must take that walk still – best do it now.*

2

Appleby had not set foot outside St Anthony's since the big yellow Bentley had deposited him at its gates the afternoon before. And he was beginning to feel the need of a change of air. He had planned a little itinerary for himself which was to subserve both business and pleasure; the carrying of it out had been interrupted by the discovery of the revolver; he was resolved not to delay it longer now. A sandwich and a pint of beer at the Berklay bar and he would be off. He was just slipping through the archway to Surrey when he became aware of the approach of Mr Deighton-Clerk. And on Mr Deighton-Clerk's countenance there showed, in addition to its customary benevolent severity, the clear light of St Anthony's hospitality. Appleby's heart sank – justifiably, as it quickly appeared.

'Ah, Mr Appleby, I have just been seeking you out. Pray come and take luncheon with me if you can spare the time. I should much like to have another talk with you. Something simple will be waiting in my rooms now.'

Appleby scarcely *had* the time – and certainly not the inclination. But he lacked the courage to say so. Perhaps long-buried habit was at work: the habit of intelligent youth to jump to the invitations of its intelligent seniors. Or perhaps the detective instinct subterraneously counselled a change of plan. Be this as it may, Appleby murmured appropriate words and followed Mr Deighton-Clerk meekly enough. He took some pleasure in the mysterious handle of the bath-chair which he carried delicately with him. It would puzzle the Dean.

The luncheon was double fillet of sole, *bécasse Carême*, and *poires flambées* – and there was a remarkable St Anthony's hock. College cooks can produce such luncheons and undergraduates – and even dons – give them. But it was an odd gesture, Appleby thought, with which to entertain a bobby off his beat – or on it. About Deighton-Clerk there was some concealed uncertainty. His beautiful but rather precious room, his excellent but untimely woodcock, were the gestures of an uncertain man. And, once again, his conversation began uncertainly. With his colleagues, even in a difficult and untoward situation, the Dean was efficient, easy, and correct. But add to the untoward situation a stranger whom he had difficulty in 'placing' and he was frequently a shade out. During the meal his talk held frequent echoes of the formality and pomposity which had appeared in his first exchanges with Appleby. But now, as then, he managed finally to achieve forthrightness. He talked at length, but without more than an occasional suggestion of speech-making.

'You may remember my saying yesterday evening how particularly unfortunate the President's death was at this particular time – just before our celebrations. It was an odd and irrelevant thing to feel – or to imagine I felt – and I have been thinking it over. And it seems to me that I was really trying to invent worries that didn't exist in order to cloak from myself the worries that did – and do – exist. I was determined to repulse the idea that our President could have been murdered by any member of his own Society; I was anxious – at the expense of logic as you no doubt felt – to see the murder traced out and away from St Anthony's.

'I am impressed now by the extent to which – quite involuntarily – I ignored or even distorted evidence. I was inclined to see those bones, for instance, as evidence of some irrational outbreak *from without* upon the order and sanity of our college. I contrived to ignore the reflection that the interests of a number of my colleagues made it possible that they should have bones in their possession. And – what is more remarkable – I succeeded in repressing my memory of poor Haveland's aberration.'

There was a pause while the Dean's servant brought in coffee. Appleby remembered the periodical pauses in Pownall's room that morning. But while Pownall's pauses were involuntary, Deighton-Clerk seemed to contrive his for the purpose of underlining a point. If not an outside madman, then at least an inside *madman*. That, in effect, was what the Dean was saying – and his motive, as before, was thought for the minimum of scandal ... But now he was continuing.

'But what I want to say is: that last night I failed in my duty. The urgency of my feeling that this or that event or situation in St Anthony's *could* not bear any correspondence to murder made me, I am afraid, insufficiently communicative. I tried to impress upon you the fact that such disharmonies as have existed here are on another plane from murder. I would have been better leaving that – which I still of course believe – to your own common sense when you had heard a dispassionate account of what those disharmonies have been. That account I want to give you now.'

Most long-winded of the sons of St Anthony – Appleby was murmuring to himself – get on with it! Aloud he said, 'It is difficult to tell what may be helpful – directly or indirectly.'

'Quite so,' responded Deighton-Clerk – much as he would reward a discreet observation by an undergraduate – 'quite so. And I must tell you first – what indeed I hinted at before – that for some years now we have not been an altogether happy society. You heard the shocking remark that Haveland tells us he made to Umpleby, and you will have noticed other signs of friction. I mentioned to you a dispute I myself recently had with the President – of that I must tell you presently. But the first thing I must say is that for the disputes we have had amongst us I am unable to apportion blame. Irritations arising one cannot tell how have hardened into quarrels, enmities, accusations. There have been accusations – a thing shocking in itself – and accusations of mild criminality. But it is significant of the scale of the whole miserable business that a dispassionate mind would find it difficult, I believe, to say where the blame really lies.

'I should tell you something of Umpleby himself. He was a very able man – and in that, perhaps, lies the essence of the situation. We have no other intellect in St Anthony's which could touch his – unless, it may be, Titlow's. But Titlow's is an intellect of fits and starts compared with Umpleby's. Umpleby had all but Titlow's ability, and far more intellectual tenacity. The great strength of Umpleby lay in his being able to cover a number of fields – of related fields, I mean, and organize useful affiliations between workers in one and another. And here in St Anthony's he had gathered together a team. Only the team fell out.

'As I told you last night in the common-room, Haveland, Titlow, Pownall, Campbell, and Ransome were all pretty closely associated – and the association was really thought out and organized by Umpleby. I was interested in the work myself, in an inactive way – or at least in those aspects of the work that touched the Mediterranean syncretisms. So I had an eye on the relations between Umpleby and the others from early on and was aware of the trouble pretty well from the beginning.'

Appleby had brought out his notebook – not without a certain diffidence over the remains of the Dean's elegant and unpolicemanly luncheon. Deighton-Clerk, seeming to recognize the diffidence, made a permissive gesture – not unepiscopal in its rotundity – and proceeded.

'I would put the beginnings of a certain awkwardness about five years ago, after Campbell got his Fellowship. He was a very young man then – I suppose about twenty-three. And that would make him only two or three years younger than our other young man, Rowland Ransome, the research Fellow. Ransome had been working for some time, practically under Umpleby's direction, when Campbell came to St Anthony's and the two young men became close friends. Ransome is a clever creature but – well – intermittent: one thing he will do well and indeed brilliantly, and the next carelessly and ill. He is a careless, happy-go-lucky, and often obstinate person, with very little thought for his own reputation or success. And presently Campbell got it into his head, rightly or wrongly, that Umpleby was exploiting Ransome. Ransome, he thought, was content to work under Umpleby's direction to an extent not proper to his status, and Umpleby was profiting by Ransome's results as a man should not profit from the results of his pupil. And he convinced Ransome himself that this was so.

'As I said, it is a matter very difficult to judge. Umpleby was printing steadily – and printing without more than occasional reference to Ransome. But you have to remember that Umpleby was organizing and coordinating the work of a number of people with those people's consent – and a good deal to their advantage. I record here the opinion, Mr Appleby, that Umpleby never appropriated other people's intellectual property for any good it would do himself in the learned world.'

This was a dark saying and Appleby, remembering his own incredulity over Haveland's insinuation of plagiarism, challenged it at once.

' "For any good it would do himself" – will you explain that qualification, please?'

'You will find, Mr Appleby, that it explains itself presently. To put it briefly, Umpleby came to relish annoying people. And if he himself worked out, say, *Solution x*, he was capable of working still harder to persuade, say, Colleague A that *Solution x* was Colleague A's achievement – simply for the amusement of annoying Colleague A by appearing to steal *Solution x* from him later on.'

'I see,' said Appleby. (And what, he was wondering, would Dodd make of *this*?)

'I can now take up my thread again,' continued the Dean, 'without further emphasis on the fact that Umpleby was not an easy or amiable man. When he heard that Ransome, who had been his pupil since he came up, and whom he regarded as his pupil still, was complaining (behind his back, as he said) in the way I have mentioned he was furious. The situation was exceedingly awkward until Ransome went abroad four years ago. He was away for two years and when he came back the trouble flared up again. There were scenes – incidents, perhaps, is a better word – and finally Umpleby acted in what was generally thought a very high-handed manner. He had in his possession certain valuable documents which had always been understood to be preponderantly Ransome's. When I say valuable documents you will understand, of course, that I mean valuable in a learned sense: they constituted, in fact, an almost completely worked out key to certain inscriptions which promised to be of the greatest importance – I need not particularize. Umpleby simply hung on to them. When Ransome, he said, was out of the country again he might have them: Ransome's presence here was offensive to him and that was his only means of getting him away. Well, Ransome went, and has been away ever since. And over this arose my own quarrel with Umpleby – the quarrel to which I referred yesterday evening.'

Deighton-Clerk was absorbed in his narrative now: the self-consciousness, the orotundity were gone in the intellectual effort to attain the completest clarity. Appleby was listening intently.

'A few months ago I had a letter from Ransome saying that the documents had not come back to him. And he added some hint that set me making certain inquiries. And presently I found to my great uneasiness that Umpleby was proposing to print matter bearing on the decipherment of the inscriptions in question in a learned journal. I was told this in the greatest confidence by the editor, Sir Theodore Peek, and I at once approached Umpleby privately. I could get no satisfaction from him. And then I considered it my duty to bring the matter up formally at a college meeting. It was not strictly in order to do so, but I did it. And it caused high words. Superficially, it was not a very serious affair – merely an unfortunate dispute between colleagues over a learned matter. But underneath there lay this ugly hint of plagiarism – or theft. Remember, please, that it is not a simple business. I have not the least doubt that Umpleby was capable of work on those inscriptions of a superior order to Ransome's, and beyond the fact that Umpleby was acting high-handedly and unjustly in retaining another man's property – or part property – the whole matter is doubtful.'

'But other people besides Umpleby, Ransome, and Campbell were involved?'

'Yes, indeed; that is what I have come to. From the first the wretched business seemed to have an unhappy effect on the President. I think he was a wayward man. And when he came to feel that the weight of college opinion was against him in this matter he behaved wilfully. Or so it seems to me – though I would again say that such things are very difficult to disentangle. Umpleby quarrelled with Haveland. It was initially a sort of *teasing* of Haveland, I believe – a sort of mocking, "I'm going to steal *your* work next." Certainly it made Haveland both nervous and furious and Umpleby came to like that. And finally he evolved for himself what was really a sort of curious intellectual game. He liked, in some queer ironic way, to keep the college guessing about his intellectual honesty. And he started new quarrels. And he made alliances. In particular he allied himself with Pownall against Haveland, and then to make the fight less uneven he jockeyed Titlow into Haveland's support. And then recently he decided it would be better fun (it is really dreadful to have to put it so) to fight them single-handed – with the result that he precipitated a violent dispute with Pownall.

'It was a game with Umpleby and he never actually overstepped certain limits, never, you may say, broke the rules he had invented for himself. He was always formally courteous, and I think that fundamentally he was quite dispassionate – quite detached. He was simply running an intellectual man's somewhat morbid recreation. But it set a bad tone in the college. And the minor actors were less dispassionate, less detached. Pownall and Titlow in particular I suspect of being somewhat carried away against each other: there is very real dispathy between them, I am afraid. And others have been implicated in one degree or another: Empson, Chalmers-Paton, even Curtis – dear old man! What a setting, Mr Appleby, for this final horrible thing!'

Deighton-Clerk had come to the end of his narration. And as if in sign of this he threw himself back in his chair and fell for a moment into a gloomy and abstracted inspection of the dusky blue and silver of his ceiling. Appleby made a final note and fell to a no less abstracted study of the Aubusson carpet. And presently the Dean spoke again. 'And now if you have any questions to ask arising out of what I have said – or on anything else – ask them.'

But it was not Appleby's policy at the moment to worry his host with cross-questioning. He confined himself to a matter which had not been touched on. 'This affair of the changing of the keys to Orchard Ground – I wonder if you can throw any light upon that? It was Dr Umpleby's idea?'

'Yes. He told us at the last college meeting that he thought it was desirable, and that he would make what arrangements were necessary. Our Bursar died recently and the President took upon himself a good deal of the practical business of the college.'

'Do you think there was anything behind the resolution to have the keys changed – that Umpleby had the idea of protecting himself in any way, for instance?'

Deighton-Clerk looked startled. 'I hardly think so,' he replied. 'Umpleby had the idea that there were unauthorized copies of the old keys in existence. That was the motive for the change, and it certainly never occurred to me that he was in any personal trepidation in the matter.'

'But it was from the Orchard Ground angle, so to speak, that he was vulnerable? His study, for instance, is barred on the Lane side, and the doors to Bishop's and the common-room and the Lane were locked every evening. But from Orchard Ground entry would be easy enough.'

For a moment Deighton-Clerk's face brightened. 'That would imply,' he said, 'that Umpleby was apprehensive of attack by somebody other than an authorized possessor of a key – by some outside person who had got a copy of the old key?'

Appleby nodded. Deighton-Clerk considered for a moment. And then he shook his head. 'No,' he said regretfully, 'I don't think there can be anything in that. I am sure – I am *almost* sure – that Umpleby's concern was simply as he declared it to be. He *was* concerned, and I must admit to an odd degree. But it was genuinely over the reputation of the college. There had been rather an ugly business arising out of an undergraduate escapade, and he was determined to stop illicit egress from St Anthony's. Umpleby, by the way, had been a poor boy and he had certain rather morbid social anxieties. He liked a particular sort of undergraduate to come to St Anthony's – and nothing frightens good families away from a college like a vulgar scandal. I think the whole of his perturbation over the affair lay in that. I don't think he can have been alarmed for his own safety at the hands of an illicit holder of a key.'

But for a moment Appleby stuck to his point. And he inserted a pause of his own this time before dropping his next question.

'By the way, did Ransome have a key?'

Deighton-Clerk started in his chair. 'Yes,' he said, 'he did.'

'But he would not have one of the new keys?'

'No; I suppose not.'

'Just how did the President distribute the new keys, can you tell me?'

'As far as I know he simply walked round the college, handing them over personally.'

'In what order?'

Deighton-Clerk looked puzzled. 'You mean to whom he went first, second, and so on? I have very little idea. Except that he came to me last but one, saying he had only Gott's to hand over after that.'

'And this was about noon the day before yesterday?'

'Yes.'

Once more Appleby was silent. His luncheon had not been unenlightening. Only the light was breaking up again, playing brokenly here and there. That evening he would have to report to Dodd yet again, it might be, that there was too much light . . .

The Dean was looking at his watch. 'I have a meeting presently, Mr Appleby, and shall have to hurry away. But I wonder if there is any other matter you wish to raise?'

'There is one thing,' Appleby replied – and he picked up his enigmatical bath-chair handle as he spoke. 'I am afraid I must have the finger-prints of the Fellows of the college.' The policemanly demand at last: the bouquet of the Dean's hock and the savour of his excellent rendering of Carême's masterpiece haunted Appleby's palate as he spoke.

Certainly, Deighton-Clerk was slightly taken aback. 'Finger-prints!' he exclaimed. 'To be sure. But I thought that nowadays malefactors always wore gloves?'

'So they do often – and then, as far as that goes, we are baffled. Though in Germany they are claiming to have evolved a technique for getting prints through any ordinary glove . . . Anyway, taking prints – of course with the permission of the persons concerned – is routine work we are required to put through. If there is any objection –'

'There will certainly not be any objection,' the Dean interrupted firmly. 'I agree that it is a most necessary procedure. My – ah –

fingers and thumbs are at your disposal to begin with. And with the rest of us it will be the same.'

Nevertheless, there was a shade of reluctance or misgiving in the Dean's voice, and Appleby proceeded cautiously. 'In that case, Mr Deighton-Clerk, if I may send a sergeant round –'

The Dean's face brightened instantly. It had been a point of propriety that was worrying him. That Mr Appleby, who had dined at the St Anthony's high-table, should go round with a little pad of ink, jabbing scholarly fingers and thumbs upon police record-cards, was disagreeable. A subordinate was necessary.

'Certainly, Mr Appleby, certainly – a most proper suggestion. It will be – ah – quite a novelty. You have had no prints taken so far?'

'Only from the corpse,' said Appleby, a little disconcertingly. And, looking at his own watch, he got up and took his leave. The Dean concluded the interview on a note of polite inquiry as to Appleby's comfort in St Anthony's. But his eyes were meditatively on the wooden bar that Appleby bore delicately away with him. It was curiously like a symbolical truncheon.

Chapter 10

I

It is in our universities that the conservative spirit finds its most perfect expression. Long after the reform of our ecclesiastical institutions, medieval habits and conventions survive within these venerable establishments. 'The Monks' (as the learned denizens were indignantly described by the sciolistic historian of the Roman Empire) are seldom up-to-date. They loll deep in what economists call a 'time-lag'. They teach outmoded subjects by exploded methods. They remain obstinately unconvinced of the necessity of the modern amenities either for themselves, their wives, or their children. Only recently, indeed, did they *discover* wives and children. Only yesterday did they discover baths. Only today, despite much undergraduate example, are they beginning to discover the motor-car. It is notorious that the late Master of Dorchester, who died only a few months before Dr Umpleby, maintained to the last that the convenience of a private locomotive was far outweighed by the dangers arising from the proximity of the boiler: himself, he would always travel by rail, and in a carriage towards the rear of the train.

But the motor-car does gain ground. For one thing, unlike the train (another institution that won but tardy acceptance and distant sufferance), it can change its mind. And there is something in the mental constitution of the retiring scholar to which this is a grateful circumstance. How delightful to set off of a morning in pursuit of the high dry air of the British Museum – to end the day instead in Beaconsfield churchyard, meditatively scanning the epitaph of the poet Waller, *inter poetas sui temporis facile princeps!* And earlier on this same road – many miles indeed before one reaches Aylesbury – there is a spot especially associated with such changes of plan. A by-road branches off – perhaps in the direction of Bicester, perhaps in the direction of Tring – and brings the initiated truant after a few miles to a most excellent –

indeed a most Chestertonian – inn. Here one may lunch, here one may dine *well*: there is *bortsch* not inferior to that once known at Gurin's, and a simple *schnitzel* that would have won the commendations of the eminent Sacher himself. There is a good straight claret; there is a genuine Tokay; there is a curious Dalmatian liqueur. The garden is erudite, remarkable in summer and winter alike. If you are lucky, you will find no similarly knowing colleague there; only an alien and abstracted *savant* from the academic deserts of Birmingham or Hull, come to meditate in solitude the remoter implications of the quartic curve, or a London novelist of the quieter and more prosperous sort, giving a lazy week to the ruinous correction of page-proofs. Only one disturbing presence there may be: that of undergraduates – for undergraduates too, with a sad inevitability, have discovered this earthly paradise. But even undergraduates become more urbane, less restless, in the *milieu* of the Three Doves.

It was an undergraduate party that was in possession of the Three Doves now. Mr Edwards, Mr de Guermantes-Crespigny, and Mr Bucket were sitting over the remains of luncheon, engaging in quiet and ingenious obscenities at the expense of the only other occupant of the coffee-room, a fluffily-bearded old party who was consuming soup noisily in a corner while sitting huddled over an obviously learned volume. Not the novelist from London; quite possibly the Birmingham mathematician in retreat; almost certainly not the master of esoteric misbehaviours elaborated by the gentlemen from St Anthony's. But presently a look somewhat askance from the fluffy party, suggesting an awareness of comment which St Anthony's good manners did not intend, coupled with the necessity of lighting pipes (a thing forbidden by custom in the coffee-room of the Three Doves), took the trio to another room. And presently they had settled down to discuss the formal business of the day.

'I had a shot at Gott this morning,' Mike announced, 'but he was pretty close. I asked him who he thought had done it. Or rather I asked him who *had* done it. He said the murderer was almost certainly the Chief Constable – or just possibly the President's demented grandmother, who was kept in an attic and made scratching noises in the night. So then I tried the "But-seriously-now" note and he said he stuck to fiction. And he asked my advice about his new book.'

'Asked *your* advice!' exclaimed Horace incredulously. 'You mean tried bits out on you as a pretty average specimen of the *dumm* public?'

'No. Asked my advice. About an epigraph.'

'A what?'

'Epigraph. As in *The Waste Land*, you know. *Nam Sibyllam quidem Cumis ego –*'

'Silly ass! He didn't ask *you* for a Latin tag for his pre-adult fictions?'

'Not Latin. And not a tag exactly. You see he makes up excerpts from imaginery learned text-books and sticks them at the beginnings of his chapters. Scientific touch. This one was all about taking slices of criminals' brains and looking at them with gamma-rays or something.'

'What foul fatuity. And where did you come in?'

'I provided a title. "*Statistical Researches into Twelve Types of Homicidal Algolagnia* – by Professor Umplestein of the University of Göteborg" – that's in Sweden, you know. Gott accepted the title, but vetoed Umplestein. Quite right, no doubt. It was, as they say, not in Good Taste.'

'And *therefore* not suitable for one of Gott's lucubrations,' said Horace with heavy irony. 'What, I ask, is the University coming to? We shall be hearing of Deighton-Clerk doing advertisement copy-writing on the quiet next.'

'Did you say *lucubrations*?' asked David, bethinking himself of a belated pedantry. 'Wrong word. Means something done in the night.'

'Like Umpleby,' said Horace. 'He was done-in in the night all right. *And* I'm not convinced *he* wasn't really one of Gott's lucubrations.'

But David, ignoring this witticism, had produced a map. 'Gentlemen,' he said, 'let us confer.' They all stared rather vaguely at the map.

'It is a matter,' said Horace, 'of penetrating to the mind of the quarry. Did you ever read *The Thirty-Nine Steps*, Mike? An altogether healthier type of fiction than the morbid perpetrations of Uncle Gott. Well, there was a man there who wanted to pass as a Scottish road-mender. And he did it by thinking himself into the part. He gave his whole mind to *being* a road-mender. And as a result he survived the keenest scrutiny of the emissaries of the Black Stone – and all that. Now, all we have to do is to identify ourselves with the criminal; we can then put our finger down quite confidently on David's map and say: *There he is!*'

'It depends on the size of the map,' said Mike. 'I think he's in London.'

'Too far.'

'No, not really. And a capital place to hide – to lie concealed, as they say. At his club, quite likely. Terribly close London clubs are about their members if you go to inquire. Very nice point Gott makes of that in *Poison at the Zoo* –'

David and Horace gave a concerted groan.

'Anyway,' said David, 'do dons *have* clubs? I don't believe they do – except the very old ones who belong to a special place down by the Duke of York's Steps ... But Town's no good: we bank on a radius of about twenty miles. Let's see what that takes in.'

He busied himself with a pencil and presently announced: 'Just misses St Neots, takes in Biggleswade, goes through Hatfield, misses Amersham, goes through Princes Risborough, misses Kingswood by a few miles and Bicester by a good deal more, just misses Towcester, takes in Olney and a bit beyond –'

'Got it!' cried Mike suddenly, 'and we're all wrong!'

'Olney and a bit beyond,' David reiterated severely, 'misses Rushden – and so round to just short of St Neots again. And *now* what is it, Mike?'

'It is,' replied Mike in bubbling excitement, 'that we're miles out. Olney, you see, made me think of Kelmscott at once –'

'And why should Olney make you think of Kelmscott, you moron?'

'Because of the English poets, you ignoramus. And now listen. When I was, as the uninstructed say, a fresher, I made a pilgrimage one vacation to this Kelmscott – a *literary* pilgrimage. And making my way from Kelmscott to Burford I came to a hamlet of which the name escapes me. And outside the hamlet was a manor house or some such – much retired in its own grounds. And just as I was passing, out he came.'

'Out *who* came?'

'Our quarry – as Horace so picturesquely puts it. And even in those days, when I come to think of it, he nursed a criminal conscience. Because he started perceptibly on seeing me, as they say, and appeared, again as they say, to wish to avoid observation. In fact, he seeped out and was gone before I could really distinguish his features. But I recognized him absolutely and instantly by a trick he has – walking with his fists to his shoulders like physical jerks.'

'Is this thing *true*?' demanded Horace.

'Split true. Old David's prosing away brought it back to me. Of course it's *miles* away. But if my frail old car can get us there – let's go quick.'

David nodded his agreement. Horace, who had been lying in his favourite position on the Three Doves carpet, puffing smoke at a sleeping cat, scrambled up, and all three bundled out into the yard. Mike's frail old car – a thoroughly robust and recent De Dion which had cost a doting aunt a small fortune – was purring in a moment. And presently they were careering exhilaratingly through the tingling winter air in the direction of Farringdon. That there was any sense whatever in their operations none of them believed: they were simply diverting themselves after the complicatedly ironic fashion of their order – the order of more mental undergraduates. To lunch at the Three Doves, to spin through the country drinking the wind of their own speed like Shelley's spirits, to sing and chant and chatter, and in the intervals play this elaborate make-believe; these were excellent things. And so they ran through Wantage.

Suddenly Mike threw out his clutch and jammed on his brakes with a reckless abruptness that made Horace shut his eyes in the expectation of a catastrophe. But the De Dion merely glided smoothly and instantly to a standstill. Over the way was an unbeautiful brick building announcing itself as a Steam Laundry.

'Here,' Mike explained, 'we make a purchase.' And he climbed out. 'You may come too, if you like,' he added politely.

And so the three crossed the road and entered a damp and forbidding office, presided over by a severe – and already surprised and misdoubting – lady of uncertain years. Mike had already removed his hat. Now he bowed – the same bow he was accustomed to give nightly in his character as Bible-clerk to the St Anthony's high table.

'I wonder, madam, if your establishment uses – I believe they are called skips?'

'Skips? Yes, of course.'

'Of course you use them?'

'Of course they are called skips. *And* of course we use them.'

'Will you sell one?'

'Sell one, sir! This is a laundry, not a basket-makers. We haven't any spare skips.'

'My dear madam, are you sure? It is really quite urgent. May I explain? My grand-aunt – you may know her: Mrs Umpleby of St Anthony's Lodge – is sailing for India tomorrow, and she has always been accustomed to pack blankets and eiderdowns and things of that sort in a skip. And she has just discovered that her own skip has been damaged by mice, so she asked me –'

'Mice!' interjected the misdoubting lady incredulously.

'Asked me to see what I could do. I understand the usual price is about five pounds –'

Mike produced his pocket-book, and the misdoubting lady, now no longer misdoubting, produced the skip. It was an enormous wicker-work thing, secured by a formidable iron-bar, two staples and a padlock. Mike gravely superintended the hoisting of it into the back of the car, paid the surprised lady, assured her of his grand-aunt's gratitude, distributed substantial tips and waved his friends aboard. The De Dion purred on.

Mike, Horace thought, was probably Aristotle's Magnificent Man. His fun was on a lordly scale ... But the expenditure on the skip had rather shocked him. 'What's it for?' he asked.

'One cage for Bajazeth,' Mike replied – and continued cryptically: 'one city of Rome, one cloth of the sun and moon, one dragon for *Faustus* ...' The day before he had been deep in the study of Elizabethan stage properties. And presently he was declaiming:

> *And there, in mire and puddle, have I stood*
> *This ten days' space; and, lest that I should sleep,*
> *One plays continually upon a drum;*
> *They give me bread and water, being a king ...*
> *Tell Isabel the queen, I look'd not thus,*
> *When for her sake I ran at tilt in France ...*

And Horace, behind, was thumping the skip and answering:

> *I am Ulysses Laertiades,*
> *The fear of all the world for policies,*
> *For which my facts as high as heaven resound.*
> *I dwell in Ithaca, earth's most renown'd*
> *All over-shadow'd with the shake-leaf hill,*
> *Tree-famed Neritus ...*

And then David started on Pindar, and remembering a lot grew more and more excited in the effort to remember more. And the De Dion sang through the air like a thing of victory, and the other two listened much as when the world was young. And so they came to Lechlade and stopped in the square to consider. Presently they were nosing up narrow lanes and for a long time were completely and oddly silent.

'There has come upon us,' said David, 'a nasty sense of the possible reality of our quiet fun.'

And it was true. After all, it was *true* that Mike had once seen him near here ...

'This,' announced Mike presently, 'is my hamlet – and there is the house.'

The hamlet was small and unremarkable. The house was large, gloomy, and repellent – a raw red brick affair not unreminiscent of the steam-laundry, and an offence in this country of yellow stone. But it was decently hidden away behind a large well-timbered garden and high brick walls. There was a lodge with high iron gates and a postman's bicycle leaning against an open wing.

'I think,' said David, 'we will put a question or two in the village.'

Mike backed the car out of sight of the lodge and they all got out. It seemed an ill-populated hamlet. No one was visible except two very aged men, sitting against the side of a house and sunning themselves in the bleak and diminishing November sun. These worthies David approached.

'Good afternoon,' he said. 'We are rather lost: can you tell us the name of this village?'

One of the very aged men nodded vigorously.

'Oi, oi,' he muttered, 'powerful great pigs. True it is, there was never such come I was a lad. True it is.'

Conjecturing that this was part of an interrupted conversation rather than directed to his own question, David tried again – loudly.

'What place is this, please?'

Both aged men looked at him kindly and comprehendingly. The second appeared to be on the verge of revelation. But when he spoke it was himself to take up some anterior theme.

'And do 'ee tell oi so!' said the second aged man. 'And do 'ee tell oi so!'

Horace was giggling. Mike was making unintelligible signs. And then the first old man suddenly made contact with the new factor in his environment.

'This be Lunnontawn,' he said.

'London town!' repeated David and Mike blankly together.

'Noa! Not Lunnontawn; *Lunnontawn.*'

'And what,' asked Mike, taking up the running and slightly changing the subject, 'and what is that house there?' And he pointed to the aggressively red, steam-laundry-like building amid the trees.

'That be White House,' said the second old man, darkly and un-expectedly – and spat.

'White House: who lives there?'

The two aged men looked at each other apprehensively. And then, mysteriously moved by a common impulse, they both struggled to their feet. They were old, old men – gone at the knees and with hands like claws. And they tottered away. The first disappeared at once into the house against which they had been sitting. The second made for a decrepit cottage next door. But on the threshold he paused and shuffled himself painfully round.

'A terrible haunt of wickedness that do be,' he said. He spat, and disappeared.

Mike was shaking his head sadly at Horace. 'I heard the old, old men say, All that's beautiful drifts away like the waters ... Chaps, let us drift away.' And the three moved back, rather uncertainly, towards the big house.

'We will go straight in,' said Horace, 'and inquire.'

'Horace,' said Mike, 'scents *une maison mal famée*.'

'Come on,' said David, 'he was lurking here once and may be lurking here again.' The gate was still open and the postman's bicycle still leaning against it. No one noticed them as they went in, but they caught a glimpse, over a low hedge, of the postman gossiping with someone at the back door of the lodge. 'Straight on,' said David. The drive wound among shrubberies. Presently they rounded a bend and saw the White House – saw, that is to say, in addition to the large and garish red structure which was alone visible from the road a long, low, and rather dubiously white residence on to which it had been built. It was a depressing place; house and grounds alike seemed decently but lovelessly and unenthusiastically kept. From somewhere behind the shrubbery came a murmur of voices. The three stopped to listen.

And then an odd thing happened. Round the final curve of the drive in front of them there swung the figure of a man, coming from the house. But no sooner had he seen the three intruders bearing down on him than he plunged into the bushes – from the crashing noise that resulted, apparently the thick of the bushes – and disappeared.

'Was it him?' cried David. It had all been tremendously sudden.

'Of course it was him,' shouted Mike, and started blindly forward. He didn't really know, but he did want excitement. All three went galloping up the drive, Horace making blood-curdling noises by way of ironic reference to the sport of fox-hunting. The fugitive, by plunging through a few yards of laurel, had gained a narrow winding path and disappeared. But he could be heard still retreating rapidly, in a direction roughly parallel to the drive and towards the house. The pursuers followed in single file.

But presently the little path branched – and just ahead both branches could be seen branching again. And the hedges were high and thick. Horace, who was ahead, stopped, and pulled up the others. 'Bless me,' he exclaimed, 'if it isn't a regular maze!'

It was. And the fugitive could now be heard more faintly, as if he had put several thicknesses of hedge between himself and his pursuers.

'Split up!' cried Mike, jumping with excitement.

'No,' said David, 'keep together. We'll know then that any noise is *him*.'

David had the master mind: his would be the best First in Schools at the end of the year. Obediently bundled together, they explored ahead, stopping constantly in an endeavour to locate such noise as the fugitive made. Sometimes it was ahead and sometimes to the side; now it was fainter and now louder. But presently it became clear to the pursuers, as they swung round the abrupt angles of the maze, that they were astray. It could hardly be otherwise if the man ahead had his bearings. And at length the sounds died away just as the trio, turning a final corner, found themselves in a little clearing. It was the centre of the maze.

'What a mess!' gasped Horace. 'He's clean away – which will take *us* some time.'

But David pointed and ran forward. In the centre of the little clearing was a raised wooden platform reached by a ladder – a sort of gazebo from which wanderers in the maze might, if necessary, be directed. David was up in a flash.

'I can just see him,' he called down presently. 'He's nearly out too. Listen, Mike. Have you got any paper? We're for a paper chase now. Out you both go and I'll direct you. And leave a trail so that I can follow.'

It was the most efficient plan, but a tedious business nevertheless. The afternoon was already fading into twilight and David from his perch was only just able to trace out the path that led from the maze. It took him some twenty minutes to get his companions out and five minutes to follow by the aid of the paper trail himself. Finally, they found themselves reunited on the main drive, a little farther from the house than where they had broken off.

'Poor show,' said Horace.

'Distinctly where we step off,' said Mike.

'Down to the lodge,' said David: 'he's likely to have made a complete break-away. Come on.'

And down they went. And just as they came within sight of the gates they heard a loud and angry voice exercising itself in picturesque imprecation in front of them. It was the postman. And he was lamenting the disappearance of his bicycle. 'Come *on*!' cried David – and all three dashed into the road, with no more than a fleeting glimpse of the gesticulating official, a scared and surprised woman by the lodge, a gardener or groom hurrying up from a side path. On the open road no bicyclist was in sight – and indeed the fugitive might have pedalled off a good twenty minutes ago. The postman seemed just to have become aware of his loss: he had followed up his gossip, perhaps, by going within for a little refreshment.

'Which way – that's the question! Which way?' Mike, as he made for his car with his companions at his heels, threw the question desperately to the wind. But it was answered in an unexpected fashion – by nothing less, in fact, than the appearance of the two very aged men, gesticulating excitedly. They shuffled rapidly up the road, waving their sticks that were as crooked as themselves and screaming together in a weird, unpremeditated unison.

'There 'ee do be gone, there 'ee do be gone, zurs! There 'ee do be gone in his wickedness away!' And they pointed ahead down the narrow country lane.

In a moment the De Dion was purring. Another moment and it was roaring up the lane. 'I rather think,' Mike shouted, 'that this runs without a break to the Lechlade–Burford road. That's in about two miles. We ought to get him.'

He was right in his bearings. The lane ran winding between low hedges for something under a couple of miles, with no more break than here and there a gate giving upon bare fields. It seemed likely enough that the fugitive had ridden straight on. David was studying his map and by the time the car had slowed down to swing into the main road he had located their position.

'Left for Lechlade,' he said, 'with a cross-road about a mile along from Bampton to Eastleach. Right for Burford, and no cross-road until the Witney–Northleach road just short of the village. I vote for Burford.'

'Wait a moment,' exclaimed Horace. 'Here's a bobby who can probably tell us for certain.' A very fat policeman was cycling slowly towards them from the Burford direction. David called out to him.

'I say, constable, have you met anyone on a bicycle along this road?'

The fat policeman got off his machine with slow dignity. 'Yes,' he said, 'I 'as.' And his attention being directed to the matter, a new aspect of it seemed to strike him. 'Come to think on it,' he added, ' 'twas Will Parrott's bicycle.' He paused, broodingly.

'Will Parrott the postman?' David asked.

The policeman nodded. 'But 'twern't Will on un.' He brooded again over this reflection, and as he did so vague possibilities, undefined implications seemed to be hovering on the borders of his consciousness. 'Come to think on it,' he added slow, 'fellow on un were going fast and wild. Happen –'

He was interrupted by the sudden roar of an engine. The De Dion had dispatched itself like a bullet from a gun in the direction of Burford. The fat constable allowed himself a few moments to incorporate this fact in his reflections. And then light seemed to break on him. 'It be them dratted Lunnon gangsters come about these parts at last!' He turned his bicycle round and set off in heavy pursuit.

The short November twilight was closing into dusk. It was just on lighting-up time. Peering ahead, Mike and David could discover nothing. But Horace in the back with the skip suddenly called out. 'Chaps! There's another pack on the tail – a whacking great Rolls. Open out.'

It was evidently true. Mike was already driving fast, but only a moment after Horace had spoken a large grey Rolls-Royce loomed up in the dusk almost abreast. Its horn sounded urgently and at the same instant its head-lamps flashed into brilliant illumination. Mike swerved to allow free passage – and thrust at his accelerator at the same moment. The Rolls was in a hurry, but not suicidally so. It drew in behind and the cars tore down the road in single file.

Visibility was poor; it was the uncertain hour at which headlights just fail to help. And suddenly, just ahead, Burford cross-roads came into view. And somewhere the telephone must have been at work, for standing across the road were three policemen. And between cars and police was the fugitive, bending low over the handlebars of the purloined bicycle and pedalling furiously. The next minute was one of confusion. The cyclist was up with the policemen, two of the policemen had made a lunge, there were shouts, a stumble – and the fugitive, by swerving wildly, had got safely through the cordon and was shooting over the cross-roads to Burford Hill. Another second, and the police were jumping to the side of the road to let the pursuing cars sweep past. But Mike, who was perfectly level-headed when driving a car, had checked for the main road, and by the time the cars were across the bicycle was some way ahead again and just dipping down the steep slope.

'We'll get him!' cried Horace.

'If there's anything left to get,' said David grimly. 'He's going down a good deal faster than he meant to.'

It was true. Mike was plunging down the long steep street that is Burford as fast as was safe in a large, perfectly controlled car. But he was scarcely gaining on the cyclist, who had let himself plunge ahead as madly as if death itself were on his tracks. His continued equilibrium seemed a matter of miracle. But in a moment it was all over. The Lamb flashed by on the left, the church on the right; the road levelled and curved to the bridge; the fugitive, by some freak of control, was safely over; the De Dion was up with him and had edged him into the ditch. The quarry was run to earth . . .

'It's not him!' exclaimed Mike, gazing at the dazed, red-headed creature in the ditch. And he was conscious of the quite slender reason there had been to suppose that it was.

'It's a looney,' said David gently, looking at the red-headed creature's vacant eye.

'It was a looney-bin,' said Horace, looking with his inner vision at the dismal red structure known as White House . . .

The grey Rolls-Royce drew up with a swish of brakes. An excited but competent little person of medico-military appearance jumped out. 'Is he hurt?' he cried. 'Is his lordship hurt – damn him?' And he jumped straight into the ditch and began an examination.

'His lordship,' murmured Horace. 'This *is* where we step off.'

The little doctor was out of the ditch again. 'Nothing broken. Bit of a bruise – a bit of a daze – that's all. Yates! Davies! Help his lordship into the car. Leave that damn fool postman's bicycle where it is. Damn these policemen – couldn't stop a child on a tricycle. Nearly had a neck broken. Rogers! Turn her round. And now, gentlemen.'

The gentlemen eyed his lordship's warden warily. They were decidedly uncertain as to where they stood. But it did not occur to the little doctor, seeing three prosperous youths and a more than prosperous car, to see himself confronted by the villains of the piece. 'Much obliged to you, gentlemen, for your – ha – intervention and assistance. I think the circumstances will be clear to you. Lord Pucklefield is one of my patients – Dr Goffin of the White House. Nervous fellow – if anything occurs to startle him off he goes. Can't think what can have done it this time. Gates open too – gossiping postman – won't happen again – damme. Yates! Davies! Get in!'

And Dr Goffin took off his hat very punctiliously (Mike just got in his high-table bow) and jumped into the Rolls. A moment later Lord Pucklefield and his friends had purred smoothly away into the gathering darkness.

Horace thrummed meditatively on the skip. David took out his watch. 'Quarter to six and ever so far from home. We *could* just make hall – hurrying.' The suggestion was unenthusiastically made and unenthusiastically received. 'And I drop ten bob if we don't,' the errant Bible-clerk added.

'You've dropped five pounds already,' said Horace brutally, and giving the skip another slap. 'Another ten bob won't do *you* any harm. I think we'd better go and have a decent meal.'

David's pipe was alight. 'There's the Three Doves,' he said.

With one accord the party moved to the car; in a minute they were running down to the Fulbrook cross-roads to turn. And as they swept back to take the long hill down which they had recently come their lamps caught for a moment a ponderous figure who had dismounted from a bicycle and was contemplating the bicycle in the ditch. It was the fat constable. He must have missed his colleagues at the top of the hill. He was brooding over an impenetrable mystery.

2

The great De Dion, foiled but not ashamed, glided beneath the discreetly flood-lit sign of the Three Doves. In the lounge there was comfort in the great fires, rest in the mellow candle-light, refreshment in the preliminary sherry. The fantasy of the day was over – fantasy fortunately untouched by the fatality that had at one moment threatened. David had gone back to Pindar, Horace was lost in reverie, Mike was thinking of the dinner. They were early and the pleasures of anticipation might be enjoyed.

At the Three Doves things always fall out well. The sherry had been drained, the ode finished, the reverie dispersed, the wine planned; the moment at which anticipation turns to impatience was hovering on the clock – when the waiter hovered at the door and murmured the awaited words. They rose luxuriously, and in a formal sentence, Mike dismissed the cares of the day. 'You know, chaps, I should have hated really to catch him.'

They were the first in the long, dim, gleaming coffee-room and the smoked salmon was consumed before the next diner arrived. It was the fluffy old party of their luncheon speculations. He was without his book this time, and he ambled over to his table with his fists pressed oddly to his shoulders . . .

'*Tally-ho-ho!*'

Mike's cry was unearthly – and it sent the fluffy old party out of the room.

'*Gone a-way-ay!*'

The ensuing scene was unique in the history of a well-ordered hostelry.

Chapter 11

I

The ability to smell a rat is an important part of the detective's equipment. Appleby had smelt a rat – in the wrong place. But he was too wary to take it that a rat in the wrong place is necessarily a red herring: it may be a rat with a deceptive fish-like smell – and still a rat.

To be exact, this rat had been not so much in the wrong place as at the wrong time. Just an hour after the discovery of Umpleby's dead body two Fellows at St Anthony's, Gott and Campbell, had converged on one spot up the Luton Road. It might have been fortuitous: it might have been by design – but if by design the purpose behind the manoeuvre was obscure. At any rate, there was a field for investigation and Appleby had felt drawn to it when he first announced to Dodd that he wanted to take a walk. He was walking rapidly down Schools Street now and as he walked he concentrated on the first point he had to consider.

On the night of the crime Campbell had gone to the Chillingworth Club in Stonegate. He claimed to have arrived there before the hour at which Umpleby was last seen alive and to have remained until within ten minutes of midnight. That, as far as the murder was concerned, was Campbell's alibi and it would have to be checked, anyway. He would begin with it now.

The entrance to the Chillingworth Club from Stonegate is down a few yards of covered alleyway. This gives upon a meagre little court with a meagre little fountain and fish-pond – the whole about fifteen feet square and known to members as the 'garden' ... A subterraneous approach to the Chillingworth, Appleby decided as he traversed this retreat, was impracticable: there was nothing for it but a frontal attack upon the secretary. With this plan in view he rang the bell.

The secretary was an elderly person of great discretion. Appleby's credentials produced his assurance that the club would render all proper assistance with all possible expedition. Nevertheless, in a matter involving an inquisition into the movement of a member while on the premises, he was afraid he could not act without the sanction of the chairman. Could the chairman be consulted forthwith? Unfortunately not. Lord Pucklefield was in delicate health, and for some time his physicians had forbidden business matters being referred to him. An acting chairman? Well, yes; no doubt Dr Crummles's authority might suffice. Ring up Dr Crummles? The Inspector would realize that it was scarcely a matter to confide to a telephone conversation . . .

Appleby was accustomed to getting over difficulties of this kind and in something over an hour he had obtained from a succession of club servants almost all the information he required. And his requirements, as far as Campbell's movements were concerned, were minute. Campbell had arrived at ten-fifteen. Just before half past ten he had been served with a drink in the smoke-room. A few minutes later he had entered the card-room, with this drink still in his hand, and had cut in upon a four at bridge. The game lasted till half past eleven, and for ten minutes after that Campbell had remained talking to another of the players. But at exactly a quarter to twelve he had collected his hat and coat and gone out. Of the precise time of his leaving the servant concerned was convinced: just before getting up Campbell had looked at his watch, and this had had the effect of making the man glance at the clock. Moreover, something else had occurred to fix the matter in his mind. Campbell had gone out by way of the little court. But he had evidently forgotten something in the club, for a minute later he was seen in the building again. And then almost immediately he had finally left – this time by the side entrance that gave directly on Stonegate somewhat farther north.

This seemed detailed enough and Appleby did not feel disappointed when, on certain minute points on which he inquired, he did not succeed in getting a clearer picture. It was remarkable that of the casual movements of a member some nights before so much had been noted and remembered. Appleby was now almost certain that he was on the trail of something. Thoughtfully he emerged on Stonegate – as Campbell had done – and turned left for the Luton Road. His next call was to be on Sir Theodore Peek – and on Sir Theodore's neighbour, the Green Horse. For in this topographical fact lay the germ of Appleby's present proceedings. Dodd's street-map had shown him that the Green

Horse must be almost in the stables, so to speak, of the eminent scholar. And the exact topography, he hoped, would be finally illuminating.

It was. The entrance to the Green Horse Inn was from the inn yard. And the yard, which opened on one side to the high road, opened on the other to a secluded suburban avenue. And the nearest house was Berwick Lodge, Sir Theodore's home. Appleby spent a moment conjuring up the whole venue in the dark. Then he ran up the steps of Berwick Lodge and knocked at the door.

2

The city abounds in venerable men. Particularly are its suburbs thronged with scholars of enormous age. The fact is not immediately observable – because once having abandoned their colleges they never go out. But hidden there in that humdrum Ruskinian villa is a greybeard who remembers the publication of Lachmann's *Lucretius*; over the way, behind that imitation Tudor timbering, is the historian who quarrelled with Grote; down the road is an ancient whose infant head was patted by the great Niebuhr himself . . . Moreover, there is something special about the generation of these primigenous *savants*. They are themselves the sons and grandsons of scholars who, having given a long working life to the furtherance of human knowledge, and feeling, round about ninety or so, the first mists of senescence begin to gather about their minds, have retired from their intellectual pursuits to the solaces of matrimony and procreation. It thus comes about that the man who remembers Lachmann remembers too his father's anecdotes of Porson, and that he who received the blessing of Niebuhr preserves the liveliest family anecdotes of Bentley and Heinsius and Voss – the sense of personal contact scarcely growing dim until it disappears with Politian and Erasmus into the twilight of the fifteenth century. This is the tradition of the true University Worthies – and of all living University Worthies Sir Theodore Peek was the oldest and the dimmest, the most sunk in the long and foggy history of scholarship – and the most truly bathed, perhaps, in the remote and golden sunlight of Greece and Rome.

Appleby found him in a small and gloomy room, piled round with an indescribable confusion of books and manuscripts – and asleep. Or sometimes asleep and sometimes awake – for every now and then the eyes of this well-nigh ante-mundane man would open – and every now and then they would close. But when they opened, they opened to decipher a fragment of papyrus on his desk – and then, the deciphering done, a frail hand would make a note before the eyes closed once more. It was like being in the presence of some animated symbol of learning.

Sir Theodore was finally aware of Appleby, but scarcely aware of him in his character as a policeman. Rather he seemed to think of him as a young scholar who, having just taken a creditable First in Schools, had come to consult authority on matters of post-graduate study. It was only with difficulty that he was headed off from a discussion of the Aristarchic recension of Homer to a consideration of the reiterated name 'Campbell'.

'Campbell,' said Appleby firmly. 'Campbell of St Anthony's?'

Sir Theodore nodded, and then shook his head. 'Able,' he murmured, 'able, no doubt – but we are scarcely interested – are we? – in his field. Umpleby is the only man at St Anthony's. I advise you to see Umpleby. What a pity that he too had taken to these anthropological fantasies! You know him on Harpocration?'

'*Did* . . . *Campbell* . . . *visit* . . . *you* . . . *on* . . . *Tuesday* . . . *night?*' asked Appleby.

'Indeed, *you* might consider Harpocration,' Sir Theodore went on. 'He preserves, as you know, a number of passages from the Atthidographers, Hellanicus, Androtion, Phandemus, Philochorus, and Istrus – to say nothing of such historians as Hecataeus, Ephorus, and Theopompus, Anaximenes, Marsyas, Craterus –'

Appleby tried again.

'Yes,' he said emphatically, 'yes; Harpocration. *Was* . . . *it* . . . *about* . . . *Harpocration* . . . *that* . . . *Campbell* . . . *was* . . . *talking* . . . *here* . . . *on* . . . *Tuesday* . . . *night?*'

Dimly, remotely, Sir Theodore looked surprised. 'Dear me, no,' he said. 'Campbell knows nothing about it, I am afraid. He simply brought a manuscript for the Journal – we don't object to giving a little space to that sort of thing. He was here only a few moments. And now, if you should want introductions when you go abroad . . .'

Sir Theodore Peek was venerable, but exhausting. Respectfully, Appleby withdrew – and betook himself, for more purposes than one, to the Green Horse.

3

Appleby got back to his rooms in St Anthony's at half past eight. The visit to the Green Horse had not finished the day's ferreting. There had been interviews with surprised and uncertain clerks; telephone messages to the Senior Proctor, to the Vice-Chancellor; minute interrogation of pugilistic-looking persons clutching bowler hats ... But the evening had ended pleasantly in supper with Inspector Dodd, and in restfully irrelevant talk which would have been prolonged had not that excellent officer had to take himself hurriedly off. The very crisis of his operations against the burglars was approaching. Now Appleby, refreshed, was seeking the solitude of his room for a spell of hard thinking on the material available after the day's investigations. But he stopped as he opened the door. Sitting waiting by the fire, much as he himself had waited by Pownall's fire that morning, was Mr Giles Gott.

Mike's enthusiasm for his tutor was understandable. Gott began well by being in repose quite beautiful. When he moved, he was graceful; when he spoke, he was charming; when he spoke for long, he was interesting. Above all, he was disarming. 'Plainly' – he seemed to say – 'I am a creature whose life is more fortunate, more elevated, more effortlessly athletic and accomplished than yours, but – observe! – you are not in the least irritated as a result; in fact, you are quite delighted.'

Mr Gott rose gracefully now – and said nothing at all. But he looked at Appleby with a whimsical, tentative familiarity such as few men, being total strangers, could have achieved without some hint of impertinence. In this creature, it was most engaging.

Appleby saw no present need to decline the atmosphere suggested. Quite silently he sat down at the other side of the fire and filled his pipe. And when he spoke his opening remark seemed obligingly calculated to the slight oddity of the encounter.

'And so,' he said, 'you are a bibliographer?'

Gott was filling his own pipe, and he merely chuckled.

'You are,' Appleby pursued didactically, 'professionally a bibliographer – which is as good as being a detective. You make a science of the physical constituents of books and you are able, by means of the most complex correlations of the minutest fragments of evidence, to detect forgery, theft, plagiarism, the hand of this man or of that man in a text, an interpolation here, a corruption there – perhaps hundreds of years ago. By pure detective work, for instance, you have found out things about Shakespeare's plays that Shakespeare stopped to learn ...'

Appleby paused to puff at his pipe and stir the fire.

'And this technique – or at least the type of trained mind behind this technique – you have actually turned (I am told) upon crime. Pentreith's books are the best in their kind; pleasantly fantastic, but closely-reasoned. I fancy you must take quite a professional interest in the pleasantly fantastic, pleasantly closely-reasoned death of Dr Umpleby?'

Gott shook his head. 'Mr Appleby, you don't believe it. Amid all the sad puzzles in which this case is involving you, you have one or two certainties. And you know that although – to my embarrassment – I write thrillers, I did *not* plan this real murder.'

'I know that you planned – something.'

'To be sure. But remember *Don Juan*. "The fact is that I have nothing planned except perhaps to be a moment merry." ... What do you think?'

'I think that it is dangerous to make merry in the vicinity of murder. And I think it is wrong to make murder a matter of disinterested observation. It would be wrong to go into a thieves' kitchen and be simply *interested* in murder. And – sentimentally, perhaps – it is worse here.'

Gott had listened seriously. 'Yes,' he said soberly after a silence, 'that's true. But my affairs, you know, have nothing to do with the case.'

Abruptly, Appleby was emphatic. 'Mr Gott, I have spent all this afternoon over your affairs, and a good deal of preliminary thinking too. And it happens that, in a case like this, my time has a certain scarcity value.'

But this only brought Gott out of his sobriety. 'What's the Green Horse bitter like, Mr Appleby? And how did you find Sir Theodore? And I suppose you have worked it all out ... ?' His laugh was mocking and friendly, his speech at once confession and challenge.

'Yes,' answered Appleby, 'I have worked it out. It wasn't *very* difficult.'

'Ah!' said Gott ... 'Can I have your story?' It was cheeky but charmingly topsy-turvy – and there was no denying that Appleby liked the man.

'You can have my story from first suspicion to proof. And the first suspicion was pure chance. I was not very interested in anybody's doings round about midnight on Tuesday. I should not have been interested in yours. But a conscientious colleague, commissioned to check up on you earlier on, actually followed your movements – or what he thought were your movements – just as far as he could.

'The Junior Proctor was at Town Cross at eleven-forty. Just after that he was going up Stonegate. At midnight he was at the Green Horse. Oddly enough, another Fellow of St Anthony's, Mr Campbell, declared himself to have been going in just the same direction at just the same late hour. There was just enough coincidence (to use, I am afraid, a very unscientific term) to arrest my attention and make me call for a map. And the map was suggestive enough to make me take a walk. And the walk showed me why Campbell was visiting Sir Theodore Peek at approximately the same time as the Junior Proctor was visiting the Green Horse.'

Appleby paused. His visitor was contemplating him mildly through a haze of tobacco-smoke.

'Mr Gott, you and Campbell were faking an alibi for yourselves on the night of Umpleby's murder, but as far as that murder went you were faking it for the wrong hour. Your alibi was an hour too late.'

'Odd,' said Gott. 'But won't you tell me a little more of how you thought of all this? I like it.'

'When I remembered,' Appleby responded quietly, 'how a proctorizing procession moves, it became quite simple. The proctor doesn't go along with his marshals in a bunch; they follow him a good twenty yards behind. And when he enters a building they don't follow unless they are signed to: they remain outside.'

'You seem,' interjected Gott drily, 'familiar with the process. Please go on.'

'You and Campbell had eleven forty-five as a sort of zero hour. From eleven-fifteen to eleven forty-five both your alibis were genuine. I mean that you were each where you appeared to be: Campbell in his club, you proctorizing about the town. But at eleven forty-five you came up Stonegate and at the same moment Campbell emerged from the alleyway to the Chillingworth. The marshals saw him – actually recognized him, as it happened – but there was no harm in that. You greeted each other and Campbell made as if to draw you back into the alley and into the club. Nothing odd in that; during such a visit the marshals would simply wait outside. But once in the alley you slipped off your proctor's gown and handed it over to Campbell. You then simply lay low while Campbell, with the gown bundled up, passed through the club and, slipping the gown on himself, passed out into Stonegate again by the entrance further north. And so there was the Junior Proctor striding ahead of his marshals once more. If anybody recognized him in the street it would never occur to them that Campbell was not acting as a pro-proctor in a perfectly regular way.'

'It would read well,' Gott murmured.

'And so to the Green Horse – and Sir Theodore's. The marshals as usual wait outside. Campbell goes into the inn-yard and noses about for a minute in his gown. And anybody that's about knows that the proctor has been at the Green Horse. Not that that is important, because the marshals know – or think they know. Then Campbell offs with the gown again, passes out of the other end of the yard, and within a couple of minutes it is established that Campbell – the real Campbell – paid a fleeting visit to Sir Theodore at midnight. Two good alibis: one faked, and one, so to speak, faked-genuine.'

'And the get-away?' asked Gott softly.

'Campbell as proctor again just shows himself under the arch of the yard, signals to the marshals, turns round, and is off the back way – past Sir Theodore's, in fact. And so the marshals follow right to St Anthony's. And here's the last point. You usually return to college on these occasions, you know, by way of the wicket on Schools Street. But on this occasion you returned to St Anthony's by the main gate on St Ernulphus Lane, knocking for the porter in quite a regular way to let you in ... Oh yes, it *was* you. Campbell made the turn off Schools Street to the Lane, and there you were in the doorway. A quick change of the gown again and Campbell is sauntering home to his flat. And you, I say, walk down to the main gate, wait for the marshals, turn round, and cap them gravely. Off come their little bowlers. Good night, Mr Gott. And you knock for the porter. Again, Good night, Mr Gott ... *Actually, you had had from about eleven-fifty to twelve-twenty to do what you liked, and a nice alibi manufacturing for you all the time*. It was rather a shame to squander (fruitlessly, as you see) on crude actuality what would have done so nicely for a book!' And Appleby looked with a rather dangerous mockery at the celebrated novelist.

Gott puffed thoughtfully. 'It is very ingenious,' he said, 'but surely a little wanton? *You* might have made it all up surely, rather than Campbell and I? Until you collect a little evidence – someone who saw me where I oughtn't to have been or who saw that it was Campbell in the proctor's gown – it hangs a trifle in the air, does it not? And have you thought of a motive for all these surprising proceedings? Were we going to murder Umpleby at midnight, and were we forestalled?'

'Perhaps,' replied Appleby, 'it all had nothing to do with St Anthony's. My colleague Dodd here is grappling with the problem of a series of burglaries in the suburbs. Perhaps, Mr Gott, you are the master mind behind the gang?'

Gott laughed – a little shortly. 'You think it's a burglar I am?'

'Yes, I do.'

'In the suburbs?'

'No.' There was a moment's silence and then Appleby added, 'And now, am I to have *your* story?'

'If there were a story, you know, it mightn't be mine to spin.'

There was another silence while Appleby debated how to take this charming, cool, and unhelpful person. To Pownall he had been almost rude – a horrid technique. And he doubted if much could be extracted from Gott by bullying ... His thoughts had only arrived at this stage when there came an interruption. From outside the door of the sitting-room there suddenly arose a succession of bumping and creaking noises, followed by a loud thud and the sound of a number of rapidly retreating feet. Appleby sprang over to the door and threw it open. In a little lobby stood a large-sized wicker laundry-basket.

Gott too had risen and come over to the door and for a moment the two men regarded the problematical object in silence. And in the silence they became aware of equally problematical sounds. 'I think,' said Appleby, 'we may open up.' And he proceeded to remove the sizeable iron bar which kept the hamper fast shut.

There is something eminently absurd in the spectacle of a human being confounded with a laundry-basket – a fact known to Shakespeare when he fudged up *The Merry Wives of Windsor*. And it was a somewhat Falstaffian apparition that emerged now – a Falstaff in distinctly damaged theatrical disguise. For some species of paint was dripping down the apparition's face, and from one pink and angry ear hung the remains of a false, fluffy-white beard.

Appleby was quick on his bearings. His extended arm was helpful; his voice was bland.

'*Mr Ransome, I presume?*'

Chapter 12

Mr Ransome had gone off for a bath and a raid on the buttery. As he darkly remembered, he had *not* dined ... And Mr Gott was left to explain.

'Our whole story,' said Gott, 'may now, I suppose, emerge. You have no doubt heard of the business of Ransome's papers – those Umpleby was holding on to? Well, Ransome came back to England a month ago, furious that Umpleby hadn't sent the stuff on to him. And instead of coming openly up to college he stayed in town and sent for Campbell. He and Campbell were always pretty thick, and Campbell was all for taking drastic measures against Umpleby. Presently they decided to take the law into their own hands. And when they decided on that, they decided, too, to call me in as – an authority.'

Gott's pipe was going again. He was telling his story with disarming simple pleasure.

'I came in on it – very foolishly, you will say – and I half turned it, I suppose, into a species of game. We could simply have raided Umpleby and forced the stuff out of him – he wouldn't have cared for public scandal. But we decided instead to plan a sort of perfect burglary and I worked it out. There were the three of us – Campbell, Ransome, and I – and it was the alibi idea that interested me. I had to be in at the actual burglary, and so had Ransome –'

'Why the two of you?' Appleby interrupted crisply.

For a moment Gott seemed to see the question as almost awkward. Then he grinned amiably. 'I had to be there,' he responded, 'because the circumstances of the burglary required – well, rather a special sort of brain – you'll understand presently. And Ransome had to be there simply because I wasn't going to carry out this rather risky and indubitably foolish proceeding for him while he lay safe in bed ... It was the alibi notion that interested me. First, I reckoned that Ransome himself was all right; for all that anybody but our three selves knew he was thousands of miles away. But there must be an alibi for me and, if

Campbell were implicated, for Campbell. As I say, it was little more than a game. I didn't expect Umpleby to call in the police over the burglary and – forgive me – I didn't expect the police to dream of testing our alibis even if he did. Nevertheless, I tried to work it out thoroughly.'

'The experimental approach to popular fiction,' murmured Appleby.

'Perhaps so; perhaps I had it in my head in terms of a book. Anyway, you know how I worked the idea out. At eleven forty-five Campbell, as you guessed, was to slip into my shoes. I was then to go straight to St Anthony's and join Ransome, who would already have reconnoitred the ground. We reckoned to be through with the burglary by twelve-ten. I was then going to slip out and round to St Ernulphus Lane, where Campbell was due to arrive at exactly twelve-twenty, and at the same time Ransome was to make his own get-away. But we were going to make sufficient row on leaving the President's Lodging to rouse the household; in that way the burglary would be discovered at once and *timed* – timed at a moment when the supposed I, followed by the marshals, was yet some way off St Anthony's, and when equally, of course, Campbell could not have made the college on foot from Sir Theodore's. Campbell and I were to change places again while hidden from the marshals by the corner of the Lane; he would be back in his flat in two or three minutes. I would simply walk down to the main gate of the college (I could hardly seem to turn back out of the lane again, you see, for the wicket) and be let in by the porter, a comfortable ten minutes after the burglary was discovered.'

Appleby had been following closely. And now he asked a question. 'You say that Ransome was to have reconnoitred the ground before you joined him. Do you mean he was to have reconnoitred inside the college?'

Gott nodded. 'You are thinking of the business of the new keys? Of course they nearly caused some alteration of the scheme. They would have done so, but for luck. Ransome has always had a key to the gates and although we knew that fresh keys were making we didn't think they would be forthcoming so soon. It wouldn't have mattered very much, of course; one key was enough. But one for Ransome and one for me was better and it was a nuisance when, on Tuesday morning, Umpleby suddenly appeared in my rooms to say the locks were changed and to hand me my new key. Even if he had had one made for Ransome he would of course hold on to it.'

'Do you think,' Appleby interrupted, 'that the business of having new keys made had anything to do with keeping Ransome out of one – that Umpleby felt apprehensive in any way?'

Gott looked startled. 'I never thought of such a thing. I think the keys were changed for the reason given; I don't think Umpleby had Ransome on his mind in that way at all.'

Appleby nodded. 'You can imagine a prosecuting counsel, Mr Gott, making a good deal of the point.' The words were spoken drily.

'I see the prospects of awkwardness well enough,' Gott responded, 'otherwise I should not (as my fictitious crooks are fond of saying) be coming clean. There is obviously awkwardness in the fact that I got hold of the tenth new key – Ransome's key.'

'*You* got it, did you,' said Appleby tartly – and his hand passed reflectively over the still-tender crown of his head.

'Ah, I don't mean that time; I mean in the first place. I got it through luck and a simple trick. Umpleby came to me last, with two keys left in his hand. I took mine, and put down my old one on the table. Then I handed Umpleby a good fat folio I had been working on and asked his opinion on some point or other. He grabbed it nicely with both fists: he had a brain that could get the hang of anyone's trade in three minutes, had Umpleby – and he liked showing it. And, quite automatically, down went that last key on the table. I got him into a good hot dispute – to break any thread of connection in his mind – meanwhile palming the tenth key. Then presently I poked the old key with my finger: "Whose is this?" I asked casually, and he growled "Ransome's, if he comes back" – and off he went. Result. Ransome got his key.'

'Result,' Appleby amplified tersely, 'one step nearer a crime ... And now, what actually happened on this unfortunate night?'

'Nothing. Ransome slipped into college by the wicket at eleven-thirty to have a preliminary look round, and the first thing he was aware of was a mild hullabaloo and people tramping through the orchard. And then he heard Deighton-Clerk's voice shouting something about examining the wicket. So he took it matters were badly amiss, cut out of college, and came to meet me after Campbell and I had done our first swap. Of course I kept my date for swapping again in the Lane – and that was all.'

There was a momentary pause.

'Except that when you got back to college you heard that Umpleby had been murdered?'

'Yet.'

'You none of you came forward with your story?'

'We left all that to you.' The feeble repartee was absently made; Gott was plainly considering what yet lay ahead.

'Before you go on,' Appleby pursued, 'there is one particular question. Did any of you in this precious diversion actually succeed in entering Umpleby's study on Tuesday night?'

'Definitely not.'

'You were not there, for instance, earlier – when you purported to be in the proctor's office? You were not in the study, conducting any preliminary search?'

'Definitely not.'

'Nor Ransome, nor Campbell?'

'Campbell definitely not; Ransome – not if he's not lying.'

'You were not there, looking for a safe?'

Gott shook his head, 'I had done that much looking long before,' he replied.

'You were not there, messing about with a – *candle*?' The word was shot out.

Gott's denial was again absolute, and this time somewhat surprised.

'Mr Gott, you said just now that the burglary was a foolish proceeding. And the coincidence of the murder was really something rather appalling. What possessed you to persevere in the undertaking the next night?'

'Obstinacy,' replied Gott, 'and opportunity.'

'You mean the fact that you still had one key between you?'

'Exactly. The police had collected nine keys, and we had the tenth. I thought, incidentally, that your knowledge that there was a tenth key somewhere might make you keep up a regular staff of guards. But it didn't ... Well, there we were with access to Orchard Ground – and more or less to the study – still. And no one knew. We met yesterday afternoon and arranged the second attempt. It was a perfectly simple plan this time. Ransome had the key and at twelve-fifteen he was to enter Orchard Ground by the wicket. It was risky because, as I say, you might well have had men on guard. But somehow we had got dead keen ... He was then to open the west gate on Bishop's and let me into the orchard. And then we were to do what we could.

'It all went well – at any rate, at first. We broke into the study and got the papers from the safe –'

'You knew about the safe? You knew the combination?'

'I knew where there was something – that was all. I had had a sufficient prowl in Umpleby's study, long before, to spot that faked shelf. I guessed there might be a safe –'

'And were confident you could get it open? Even in stories that is surely difficult?'

Gott grinned. 'I trusted to my wits. That was why I had to be on the burglary myself. Writing thrillers – and perhaps as you suggest, my bibliographical training – has given me a certain facility ... Anyway, it *was* a safe, and I *did* get it open – didn't I?'

All Gott's simple pleasure in his narrative had returned. Appleby scrapped his official reserves. 'My dear man,' he said, 'in heaven's name *how*? Are you going to tell me you listened with a microphone to the fall of the tumblers – and all that? Perhaps you did. You broke into the study by a next to impossible story-book method – canvas and treacle, heaven preserve us! – and perhaps you got into the safe as absurdly?'

'No,' replied Gott modestly. 'I didn't listen to anything. I just looked.'

'Looked! What at?'

'At the faked shelf – and on evidence of Umpleby's whimsicality of mind. You won't remember the particular dummy books represented on the shelf?'

'Long narrow shelf with about fifty volumes of the British essayists,' Appleby responded promptly. His memory was often photographic.

'Exactly. The spines of fifty little volumes all neatly glued on a board. Perhaps you didn't happen to look at the last ten closely?'

'No, I didn't!'

Gott beamed. 'I did. And they were out of order. Not actual volumes out of order, remember – but dummies *fixed on* out of order. Something like *49, 43, 46, 41, 47, 42, 50, 45, 48, 44*. In other words, a handily placed record for Umpleby that the combination of his little safe was *9361720584*. Elementary, my dear –'

' – Watson,' concluded Appleby, and knocked out his pipe. 'And as you say, a trick displaying your late President as a man of whimsical mind.' He filled his pipe again and pushed across his tobacco-tin. He was becoming disposed to a good deal of further conversation with the celebrated Mr Pentreith ... 'And now,' he prompted presently, 'we come to a matter of some little delicacy.'

Gott pointed to the laundry-basket that still cumbered the lobby. 'It was Ransome done it,' he said, 'and you can't say he hasn't had tit for tat ... If it isn't an improper thing to say of a colleague, Ransome is a little pig-headed. He would not go straight out of college with his precious papers; he must come to my room for a drink to celebrate our victory – a victory over a dead man, come to think of it. So out we both came into Bishop's and at the gate he said something about his fixing the lock and my scouting ahead. I went ahead – and gathered afterwards that the silly ass not only left the gate open because it squeaked, but actually left the key in the blasted lock.'

Appleby chuckled. 'It was a number one size slip and puzzled me rather. I can see that you wouldn't have much confidence in Ransome as a single-handed cracksman. Not that he can't crack a skull with very pretty judgement. But perhaps you were standing by directing?'

'No, I wasn't. It would never occur to me to hit a man on the head – except in fiction. Much too chancy. In Ransome's circumstances I think I should simply have given myself up, or thought of a plausible lie. But he seems to have acted pretty smartly. He found his way of escape guarded, hovered around until he got on your tracks – and you lost the key again.'

'I lost a different key.'

'Ah, then he made yet another slip. Not much finesse about Ransome, but good in a tight place.'

'If it's not a laundry-basket,' said Appleby. And then he added, 'But why should Ransome be hanging about in the neighbourhood in that fancy disguise today?'

'I put him in the diguise originally myself,' Gott replied. 'I'm interested in disguises – how far they can really be made to work and so forth. Ransome had a naïve confidence in the whiskers and when he got a bit scared as a result of having hit a celebrated *agent policier* on top he decided to continue to lie low for a bit where he was. And very comfortable quarters he had taken up – until our young friends found him.'

Gott had risen and was prowling about the room. Coming to the bookcase, he found himself confronted, as had Appleby the night before, with *Trent's Last Case*. He picked up this bible of his craft and, opening it at random, seemed absorbed for a space of minutes. Then he snapped the book shut and spoke.

'And now do you believe all this, I wonder? I *could*, you know, make up several tales to fit the facts, quite as quickly as speaking. Do you happen to believe the tale I've told you?'

Appleby puffed at his pipe in silence, pondering. *Appleby's Greatest Case* ... and *Appleby's Most Irregular Case* as well. He was prompted to take a risk — but only because some final judgement in himself, a judgement in which he had faith, told him that it was no risk at all.

'I believe your tale,' he said, '*verbatim et literatim.*'

'And that I've kept nothing up my sleeve?'

'And that you've kept nothing up your sleeve.'

'Then,' said Gott blandly as if in reward for this profession of confidence, 'then it only remains for us to find the real murderer. And now, if I'm truly not under arrest, I will just slip across and fetch a little beer ... Mild or bitter, Appleby?'

'Bitter, Gott.'

Chapter 13

The reflections in which Appleby indulged as he sat waiting the return of the St Anthony's burglar and the St Anthony's beer were of mingled satisfaction and exasperation. The rat had really been a red herring. Its investigation had resulted in the acquisition possibly of a valuable ally – but was he any farther forward with the case itself? The answer seemed to be that he was, but not so much as he had hoped.

To begin with there were now certain eliminations. Campbell was out. His alibi at the Chillingworth for the relevant times was absolute. The vision of that eminent mountaineer scaling St Anthony's in order to murder its President was dispersed. Chalmers-Paton was out: the advanced hour of the murder made his alibi unquestionably hold. Gott was surely out. A man who planned a perfect burglary for midnight would not precede it by an imperfect murder – a murder, that was to say, which on the face of it he might quite easily have committed. Murder before eleven followed by an alibi for twelve made nonsense. And if Dodd or another should say that here was no sufficient ground for counting Gott out – well, Gott would be under pretty close observation.

What held of Gott held, in a way, of Ransome. And yet not altogether so. If Gott had proposed to murder Umpleby the whole burglary plot as he had contrived it would have been pointless – simply a following-up of murder with a risky joke. If Ransome had proposed to murder Umpleby the burglary plot would have had its place in the scheme – *for it had procured Ransome access to Orchard Ground.* But even so the *inception* of the burglary plot could have had no point for a Ransome projecting murder: it could have become a factor only after the changing of the locks ... Appleby permitted himself to record an impression that Ransome would prove to be out, but this time it was an impression to which he could not with confidence attach any weight. Ransome's movements on the fatal night, his movements in the period before he met Gott with the intelligence of his alleged interrupted reconnaissance at eleven-thirty, would have to be scrutinized. There was no physical reason why Ransome might not have entered the college and murdered Umpleby.

Entered the college ... In Ransome's known ability to do this lay the real progress that had been made through the elucidation of the red herring. Ransome had had the tenth key. And with the tenth key *placed* came the most significant elimination of all. The element of the wholly unknown was now excluded. Umpleby had been murdered by, or through the connivance of, one or more of a known group of people. Who?

'Who killed Umpleby?' It was Gott who spoke. Laden with considerable quantities of refreshment, he had just closed the outer door and was negotiating the laundry-basket. He appeared innocently to be seeking information.

'Umpleby,' Appleby reiterated aloud, 'was murdered by, or through the connivance of, one or more of a known group of people. On the face of it, the people who may have murdered him are Deighton-Clerk, Haveland, Empson, Pownall, Ransome, the head-porter, yourself. Any one of these might also have connived at his murder – made it possible, I mean, by providing some other person with a key. The people who, without themselves seemingly being in a position to commit the murder, might have conspired towards it in the same way are Titlow and Lambrick. And Slotwiner must be considered.'

'What of Mr X the locksmith?' Gott offered.

'Sufficiently eliminated.'

'Eliminate locksmith. Eliminate, for purposes of useful discussion between you and me, Gott. Eliminate the head-porter, who will have an alibi – and who didn't murder Umpleby anyway, nor connive and conspire. Eliminate Slotwiner; one should always eliminate the servants early, I think. The shadowy suspicious butler is inevitably a bore –'

'But have you any reason for eliminating Slotwiner apart from these dramatic proprieties?'

'Well, in his restrained way Slotwiner was quite devoted to Umpleby and most unlikely to plot his murder. But I don't see why you say he must be considered. He had no key himself and he doesn't seem to have had a chance to smuggle a confederate out through the Lodging.'

Appleby nodded. 'All right. Say I was wrong to include him among the possibles – on the face of it.'

Gott showed that he was not unaware of the significant reiterated phrase. But for the moment he pursued his own theme. 'Eliminate Slotwiner *pro tem*. And that leaves us with seven suspects – quite enough. And a good mystic number at the same time. Come to think of it, not a bad title. *Seven Suspects*. They need handling, though, when one runs as many as that. And they're bound some of them to remain a bit dim.'

Gott's hobby-horsical vein lasted only until he had apportioned the beer and settled himself down opposite Appleby with a pencil and a sheet of foolscap. Murder and mysterious crime were associated in his mind with recreation and amusement: now he seemed to turn to them a mind as serious and concentrated as that which he was accustomed to give to the problems of the sixteenth-century printing-house.

'This business of conspiracy,' he said, 'of *A* giving his key to *B*. On the probabilities, that is really a second line of investigation, is it not? Deighton-Clerk here or Lambrick at home handing a key to a hired assassin . . . ?'

Appleby took up the implied unlikelihood. 'Yes,' he said. 'I agree. It brings in a sort of First Murderer in a very unlikely way. Not that the whole affair is not unlikely enough.'

Gott smiled. 'So Deighton-Clerk has impressed on me – and on you too, no doubt. He sees me as the spiritual father of the crime. Like the painter who invents an improbable type of beauty – and sees it appear in the flesh in the next generation . . . But after all such things *do* happen. There was a most horrid murder in this very college in 1483.'

'A precedent,' said Appleby, 'is comforting, no doubt. But to stick to the probabilities of conspiracy: obviously the securing of an alibi for oneself would be as nothing against the risk of plotting with anyone who could be conceived as a ruffian hired for the purpose. But what of a conspiracy between colleagues here, based on the fact that colleague *A* has a key and colleague *B* not? The murder is committed the very day the keys are changed – in other words the keys are deliberately *thrust* into prominence. Say then that *A* gives his key to *B*, who murders Umpleby. *A* has an alibi and we have practically to prove the conspiracy before we can demonstrate that *B* had access to the crime.'

Gott shook his head. 'In *any* murder a two-man show is less likely than a one-man show. And here surely a conspiracy-theory strains psychological probability very far indeed. A two-man murder is a very different thing, after all, from a three-man burglary.'

Appleby nodded. 'Yes,' he said, 'again I really agree. It will be sound methodology not to cast about for a two-man effort until we are baffled on the one-man level.'

'Which leaves *five* suspects – Deighton-Clerk, Haveland, Empson, Pownall, Ransome. We're getting on.'

'On the face of it, five; actually, it may still mean seven.'

There was a minute's silence while Gott, again presented with this theme, thought it out. And then he went straight to it. 'Umpleby wasn't killed when we thought he was?'

'Exactly. Umpleby was killed some time between half past ten and eleven, in Orchard Ground or perhaps actually inside Little Fellows'.'

'You can prove that?'

'No – far from it. But there's a fresh blade of grass sticking to a bath-chair.'

Again Gott was on it instantly. 'Empson's old bath-chair – a good quiet hearse!' There was a moment's silence and then he added his complete comprehension. 'Titlow's hearse too, maybe.'

'Or Slotwiner's – if you weren't so sure about his devotion. Imagine it. Slotwiner takes those drinks into Umpleby's study at half past ten as usual. He gives a faked message: Haveland's or Pownall's compliments and would the President step over to Little Fellows' to see or do this or that? Out goes Umpleby with Slotwiner presently after him, and the shot is fired somewhere outside Little Fellows' at a moment when something really noisy is roaring down Schools Street. Slotwiner collects the bones, collects the bath-chair, collects Barocho's stray gown – you don't know about that – and pushes back to the study with the lot. He returns the bath-chair – but forgets about the gown: he will be in a hurry by this time, with eleven o'clock and Titlow's usual visit drawing near. He fixed the pistol with some gadget or wire or string in the study and gives a tug just as he is talking with Titlow at the door. And he has a chance to pocket his pistol and string in the confusion after the finding of the body. Or one can, of course, produce a very similar reconstruction for Titlow.'

'I should favour Titlow,' said Gott instantly.

'You think Titlow a likely murderer?'

Appleby had dropped the question casually but deliberately; the really unfair thing was to shirk being a policeman. And Gott's charity seemed to recognize this even while he stepped back from the trap. 'I shouldn't have talked at large about Slotwiner's sentiments – because I'm not going to talk about anybody else's. We can consider the facts, but we can hardly start tipping each other for the gallows. All I meant was that if Slotwiner had given such a message to Umpleby he could hardly have come up *in front* of him in the orchard and shot him, as he was apparently shot, through the forehead. But Titlow – or almost anyone else – could.'

For a few minutes the two men smoked in thoughtful silence. And then Appleby continued. 'Do you think, then, simply considering the facts, that we have a special line on Titlow?'

'Far from it. Titlow and Slotwiner merely come in again – that is all. We have nothing more than the suggestion that someone wanted to make Umpleby's death appear to have occurred at a different time and place from that at which it actually did occur. And any of the remaining suspects might have had reason for wishing that: there is no justification for confining the motive of such a thing to Slotwiner or Titlow. Why, for instance, suppose the manoeuvre was necessarily intended to establish the murderer's own alibi? Why should it not be intended to destroy somebody else's?'

'Yes,' said Appleby, 'I've got as far as that, though it took me longer than it has taken you. I got to somebody saying "*He could prove he didn't do it here and now; but he couldn't prove he didn't do it there and in twenty minutes' time – were some indication left that he was guilty.*"'

'Good,' responded Gott; 'that takes us to an exact review of times and movements.'

'And brings us right up against the psychological probabilities.'

'Which – as between this person and that – I don't think I should debate with you. But there are still plenty of facts – the bones, for instance. The bones are your focus at the moment. Within the field demarcated by the gates and keys they are the nearest thing at present to a pointer. What sort of a pointer are they on Haveland, their owner, for example?'

Appleby replied with another question. 'Last night in the common-room Haveland, you remember, virtually put forward alternative propositions about the murder: do you think they hold?'

Gott nodded his comprehension. 'Haveland in effect said, "Either I myself murdered Umpleby in circumstances only compatible with my being quite insane, or somebody else has committed the murder and has attempted to father it on me." Well, I don't see that the proposition really holds. Haveland might have committed the crime and yet be sane enough. That is to say, he might have been laborious enough to frame a frame-up against himself.'

'You mean that he might have left his collection of bones beside his victim not crazily and in order to give himself away, but to fake the notion that someone was framing him? It seems a bit roundabout, and unnecessarily laborious and risky.'

'Risky, yes. Unnecessarily roundabout and laborious, perhaps – but perhaps not. It may have seemed his best way to plant the murder on somebody else.'

'Plant the murder on somebody else by means of faking a plant against himself! My dear Gott, isn't that rather too subtle?' But Appleby was obviously weighing the suggestion rather than scoffing.

'Subtle, yes,' Gott replied, 'but, after all, you know, you've come – back, is it not? – to one of the more subtle parts of England. Of course the theory holds – implications.'

'Such as?'

'Well, such as that you've *missed* things. Or not been let run up against them so far.'

Appleby smiled. 'No doubt I've been missing things. But what exactly are you thinking of?'

'Of the subsequent clues on the false trail – the further indications that Haveland would leave about that he had been framed *by this particular person or that*.'

'For that matter he seemed rather venomously inclined towards Empson. Though I haven't discovered any clues against Empson so far – planted by Haveland or otherwise. As you suggest, I may have missed them. On the other hand it is just possible that I haven't missed them because they're not there – that your theory's wrong, in fact.'

Gott protested. 'It's not my theory. It's simply one suggestion. But "missed", I think, was a mistake. There would be no point in Haveland's leaving clues so tenuous that they *could* reasonably be missed. But they may be yet to come.'

Appleby chuckled. He enjoyed Gott. 'The second murder, perhaps, that throws some light on the first? And then the third and fourth murders, that eliminate two of the possible perpetrators of the second?

Let's try the exact review of times and movements. And we can begin with Haveland.' And – much like Inspector Dodd – Appleby produced a sheaf of papers. But at this moment there came the second interruption of the evening. Somebody could be heard negotiating the laundry-basket in the lobby and then there came a knock at the door. It was Haveland himself.

The visitor halted when he saw Gott and addressed himself to Appleby. 'I beg your pardon – I thought I might find you free. Perhaps I might come again . . . ?'

'Mr Gott and I have been discussing – my business here,' Appleby replied, and at the same moment Gott rose to go. But Haveland meantime had shut the door and his next remark embraced them both. 'Can I usefully place myself at the disposal of so formidable a conference?'

Haveland's should have been an easy and open nature. His physical contours were bland and the effect was enhanced by the pleasing, if somewhat consciously aesthetic negligence of his clothes – the clothes he refused to shed for the sober black and white required by the ritual of the St Anthony's high-table. But, actually, the personality he presented to the world was stiff, uncoloured, and – surely – utterly unspontaneous. He was, apart from the hint of irony which always lurked in the fall of his phrases, impassive, deliberately unmoved, deliberately remote. Appleby suddenly resolved to essay the rousing of him now.

'You come at a useful moment,' he said. 'We were just beginning an examination of your movements at the time of the murder. Do sit down.'

That Haveland might display some indignation, if not against the policeman at least against his colleague, it was reasonable to suppose. But there was no flicker. The visitor obeyed the injunction to be seated and said nothing at all. Any business of his own on which he had come he was indicating as put aside at Appleby's pleasure. It had the effect, somehow, of being a distinct score; Appleby had to plunge ahead at once. And he had to do so without being very certain of his ground. The statements collected by Dodd he had not yet had time to review in the light of the slightly altered hour of the murder. Nevertheless he turned coolly to his relevant scrap of memoranda.

'John Haveland,' he read quietly,

'fifty-nine. Fellow of the college since 1908. Unmarried. Occupies rooms in Orchard Ground. Can throw no light on the murder or on any of the circumstances attending it.

'*Nine-fifteen*: Left common-room and went to own rooms. Read. *Ten-forty*: Quitted Orchard Ground by east gate and called on Dean in Bishop's. *Ten-fifty*: Returned by east gate, going straight to own rooms. *Eleven twenty-five*: Discovered there by Inspector Dodd and informed of President's death. Appeared scarcely interested.'

Appleby pushed the paper aside. Dodd's final observation made good ground on which to pause. But Haveland challenged it at once. 'I heard of the President's death,' he said, 'most certainly with emotion and without regret.'

'And without surprise, Mr Haveland?'

'I must confess to surprise.'

'And curiosity?'

'Curiosity?'

'My colleague's note has something more to add on the further interview he had with you in the morning. You had no information to give – about the bones, for instance. But you yourself asked three questions. You asked if the President had been shot, if the weapon had been found, and if the time of death was determined.'

'My dear Haveland,' Gott murmured at this point, 'such friendly interest in the world is unlike your usual self. You must have been quite upset.'

Haveland showed what might have been the shadow of impatience. 'With my collection of bones on the man's carpet the time of death was obviously material to me. For that matter, it was obviously material to Deighton-Clerk. Umpleby was apparently shot at exactly eleven o'clock. Either of us therefore could just have done it. But if he had been shot at, say, a quarter to eleven both of us would have been nicely out of it – or up to the neck in a conspiracy together. Why shouldn't I ask questions? I don't want to be hanged, you know.'

Appleby gave his information guilelessly. 'Umpleby was shot a long time before eleven o'clock. Inspector Dodd hadn't got the facts straight when you interrogated him. And we *have* found the weapon.'

Without eagerness Haveland took up the first point. 'How long before eleven?'

'Anything up to half an hour.'

Haveland was impassive still – but not utterly without betrayal. Coming somewhere from the man was an impression that Appleby was now familiar with in the St Anthony's case – an impression of rapid calculation. Titlow, Pownall, Haveland – these men thought intensively before they spoke. In all of them it was perhaps merely the intellectual habit that gave the impression. And yet with Haveland, certainly, the impression was that of a man intensely calculating – calculating whether to suggest something, to reveal something, to venture some further question ... At length he said flatly, 'Then Deighton-Clerk or I might still have done it.'

'Deighton-Clerk might have shot Umpleby and left your bones in his study?'

'Yes, or I might.'

'When do you think the bones were purloined from your room?'

'Between ten-forty and ten-fifty, I suppose – while I was visiting Deighton-Clerk.'

'In that case they couldn't have been taken *by* Deighton-Clerk?'

'No. Not that I really know when they were taken. I only know they were in their cupboard – an unlocked cupboard – in the afternoon.'

'Was Deighton-Clerk an enemy of Umpleby's?'

'He hadn't picturesquely wished him rotting in a sepulchre, as I so unfortunately had. But they were not on good terms. Deighton-Clerk had taxed Umpleby publicly with improper conduct towards Ransome, the man now abroad.'

'Ransome isn't abroad,' interposed Gott easily.

'Indeed?'

'He's probably in bed by now – in this college. Not long ago he was in the laundry-basket you must have encountered coming in.'

'Indeed?'

Certainly it was a mask that Haveland presented to the world. Hearing of a colleague being kept in a laundry-basket he showed no flicker of surprise, no flicker of interest. And now he had got to his feet. 'I can only interfere with your activities. I look forward to anything your collaboration may produce. Good night.' And Haveland withdrew.

Appleby was chuckling. 'What do you think he meant by the product of our collaboration, Gott?'

'I suspect him of meaning that we are likely to do best spinning novels together. But why did he come?'

Appleby chuckled again, thoughtfully this time. 'He came for information. And he got it, I think – or all the whiff of it he wanted. And you see what we've got to do now?'

'Oh, yes,' responded the undefeatable Gott. 'We've got to carry out a little practical experimental work with a hearse. And the beer will keep.'

2

'The miscreant,' reported Horace on returning to David's room after a prolonged reconnaissance, 'has been released.'

'Released!' exclaimed his friends blankly.

'I'm glad to say,' replied Horace, who had apparently been thinking it out, 'released. Which means, I suppose, that he didn't do it. Which means, in turn, that we haven't caught a murderer. We never decided, you know, on the morality of dealing with him if we did. We were carried away – or Mike was – by the funny joke of delivering him neatly parcelled and addressed.'

'They've really let him go?'

'He's gone to his old rooms, had a bath, and an enormous meal, and Mrs Tunk has been summoned by telephone to make and grace his downy couch. Pork Adams has seen it all from his window.'

'They may only be giving him rope,' suggested Mike.

'They may only be giving *us* rope,' retorted Horace. 'Don't you think it very probable that we shall all be sent down?'

'Not a chance of it. Can you see Ransome going to Deighton-Clerk and complaining of what has befallen him while skulking round the old *mouseion* in a false nose?'

'Well,' said Horace doubtfully, 'if that's so we're well out of it.'

'Out of it?' It was David who spoke. 'Surely, Horace, you are not content to let our investigation *rest*? Didn't I tell you both that in addition to a *notion* I had some *information*? No, no, Horace: thy charge exactly is performed, but there's more work.'

Horace turned to Mike. 'He *is* a bore, you know. I've long suspected it – and there it is.'

Mike nodded gloomily. 'Yes, one sees it coming. Sir David Penny-feather Edwards, the celebrated Treasury bore. Pattering round suggesting a committee here and an inquiry there. Poor old David.' And Mike applied himself with ostentatious concentration to *Selected Sermons of the*

Seventeenth Century. Horace slid to the floor and was enfolded in the mysteries of Miss Milligan in a moment. In Two-six Dr Umpleby's death had ceased to compel.

But David knew his men. Gently, he talked to the air. And in a couple of minutes his companions were absorbed.

3

The beer had been abandoned. Gott was brewing strong coffee. Appleby had his watch out on the arm of his chair and was regarding it thoughtfully.

'An inconclusive experiment,' said Gott. 'He might just have managed it, but it would be a tight squeeze.'

'Yes; and at either time. The two periods Haveland had are just equal: ten-thirty to ten-forty and then ten-fifty to eleven. Even if you put forward his arrival on the Dean to ten-forty-three or even forty-five you must allow something at the other end for Umpleby's leaving his study and getting up the Orchard after Slotwiner had brought in the drinks at ten-thirty. A *very* tight squeeze.'

'Ah, well, my picture of Haveland trolleying his own bones plus corpse up the garden path was no doubt, as you suggested, a bit steep. But why did Haveland visit the Dean anyway, and what has the Dean to say about the times?'

'Just a minute,' replied Appleby. 'We'll go over the other people's movements now and begin with the Dean. Here we are.' And he produced the relevant note.

'Deighton-Clerk ... *Nine-thirty*: Left the common-room with Dr Barocho and went to the latter's rooms in Bishop's. *Ten-thirty-five*: Walked across to his own rooms, accompanied part of the way by Barocho. Visited a few minutes after he got back by Mr Haveland. *Ten-fifty*: Haveland left to return to his rooms. A few minutes later Deighton-Clerk rang up the porter's lodge on college affairs and then settled down to read. *Eleven-ten*: President's butler, Slotwiner, came across with news of fatality ...'

'It corroborates Haveland,' commented Gott. 'And if that telephone-call to the porter took any time at all it looks like clearing Deighton-Clerk himself.'

'Unless,' Appleby responded, 'he telephoned with one hand, so to speak, and shot Umpleby with the other.'

'Any shot would be heard in Bishop's.'

'He might have followed Haveland immediately into Orchard Ground, met Umpleby and shot him, telephoned from an empty room in Little Fellows', run out again, chaired corpse and bones, dumped them in the study, fired – for some reason – a second shot at eleven and then beat it for his own rooms.'

'Good Lord, Appleby, that's a tighter squeeze still! Can you really imagine Deighton-Clerk skipping about like that? And anyway, was there an empty room in Little Fellows' to telephone from? Haveland was back in his. What of the other three?'

'Just a moment. It *is* another tight squeeze, I admit – probably too tight. And if there was no telephone available of course it breaks down. But before we look at the other three let's take Barocho. His movements link up with the Dean's and perhaps we can get rid of him.'

'But Barocho hadn't a key.'

'Never mind. Let's look at him. I seem to remember he's out anyway. Yes, he is.

'Walked with Deighton-Clerk to the door of latter's rooms at ten-thirty-five and then went straight to the library, reading there until called out after eleven ...

There were a number of undergraduates in the library. Barocho's quite out.'

'If you're taking people without keys – what about old Curtis? Has he an alibi?'

Appleby shook his head. 'Curtis went to his rooms at nine-thirty. He says he didn't stir out again that night. The Dean had him out of bed a bit before midnight to tell him what had happened. And that's all we know.'

'What of Curtis as the dark horse?' Gott asked – and added soberly. 'Let's try to sum up to date. The people really in the running are Haveland, Titlow, Empson, Pownall, Ransome, Deighton-Clerk, and myself. All these had keys. For the purposes of this discussion, I'm out. Ransome's movements at the material time we have as yet no information on. Haveland would seem to have a tight squeeze. Deighton-Clerk's outness or in-ness depends on the movements of the remaining three. If he couldn't telephone from one of their rooms he just hadn't time to shoot Umpleby and the rest of it between ten-fifty and eleven. And he couldn't have used Haveland's telephone. So let's have Titlow, Empson, and Pownall – whose movements, incidentally, are vital in themselves.'

Appleby turned to another paper. 'Here's Pownall,' he said, 'according to the story he gave me this morning. He got back to his rooms in Little Fellows' a little before nine-thirty. He read for twenty minutes. Then he went to bed and was asleep by ten-fifteen. He was disturbed by somebody in his room at ten-forty-two.'

'The dickens he was! But that's too early to have been Deighton-Clerk at the telephone ... And he didn't leave his room after that?'

'No. He prowled about discovering blood and deciding Umpleby had been murdered. But he sat tight in his rooms all the same.' And Appleby gave Gott the gist of Pownall's narrative. Then he turned to Titlow.

'*Nine-twenty*: Returned from common-room and worked until ten-fifty-five, when he set off to visit Umpleby as usual. Passed through the west gate into Bishop's and rang front-door bell of President's Lodging just on eleven.'

Appleby paused. 'You can help there,' he said. 'Why should he go round to the front door? Why not knock at the french windows?'

'Point of ceremony, I think,' Gott replied. 'He always did on those occasions. It was a sort of weekly official visit – and the two men didn't love each other.'

Appleby nodded. 'Well, that's the story. No corroboration – nor anything against it. But for what it's worth it deprives Deighton-Clerk of the possibility of another telephone. And now, here's Empson. He got back to his room at nine-thirty and settled down to work. At ten-forty he went over to the porter's lodge by way of the west gate in order to inquire about a parcel of proofs. He was back within eight or ten minutes and remained undisturbed until the arrival of the police ... That's the lot.' And Appleby tossed aside his notes.

Gott sighed. 'What a scope there seems to be for lying about it all! Do you see how no one of these Little Fellows' people makes contact with any other? But if Empson's story is true it cuts out Deighton-Clerk. Empson was back at ten-fifty – before Deighton-Clerk could use his telephone and avoid being discovered. What do you think?'

'I think that unless Deighton-Clerk telephoned from his own rooms *immediately* Haveland left him, and not as the statement says "a few minutes later", that he *is* cut out. Indeed, I think he's out in any case. The squeeze is too tight quite apart from the telephone.'

'In which case,' said Gott, 'it's down to the Little Fellows' contingent and to Ransome and myself.'

'Exactly. But somehow I suspect the St Anthony's burglars less and less. The key to the mystery lies –'

'In Little Fellows'?'

'In Thomas De Quincey,' said Appleby.

Chapter 14

1

As Appleby crossed Bishop's a few minutes after Gott's departure he had a sense of making his way to the last important interview in the St Anthony's case. In Gott he had just left a theoretically-possible suspect; in Ransome there was an unknown quantity yet to be dealt with. But the belief was really growing on him that the mystery of Umpleby's death was somehow hidden in Little Fellows': at least it was on Little Fellows' that his mind was going to concentrate before it wandered further afield. And of the four men lodging there he already had more than a little knowledge of three. Haveland he had just been scrutinizing; Pownall he had interrogated; Titlow had deliberately provided him with a sort of set exhibition of himself. But of Empson he had had no more than a caustic word in hall and common-room – and a revealing glimpse asleep. Perhaps he was already asleep again now. But it was still a feasible hour for a call ... Once more Appleby slipped through the west gates into Orchard Ground.

Empson's dry voice answered the knock. Perhaps it was some sense of an unexpected contrast to this dryness that gave a peculiarly vivid quality to the moment at which Appleby entered the room. Empson was sitting by the light of the fire and a single shaded lamp. The severe library, concentrated so uncompromisingly on the man's own subject of psychology and mental science, had receded into shadow. Its owner, who had discarded his ordinary dinner-jacket for the faded silk of some wine-club of a past generation, was sitting reading in a high-backed, old-fashioned chair. His stick was between his knees, pale ivory matching the pale ivory of the fingers clasping it. And the ivory complexion, set off by the dead white shirt, was softened by the faded rose and gold of the old silk ... Empson had risen punctiliously to his feet and put aside his book – it was Henry James's *The Golden Bowl* – and to

Appleby it seemed pleasantly to complete a picture of mellow scientific relaxation.

'I wondered if I might trouble you – ?' As Appleby spoke, Empson set a chair; the action was markedly courteous – but it had not the air of being an extra politeness shown to an anomalous policeman. Interviews in St Anthony's, Appleby felt once more, could be very difficult. And casting round for a suitable opening he decided to take the only matter in which Empson had a demonstrable concern. 'I believe that some years ago you were in the habit of using an invalid-chair?'

'That is so. The trouble from which, as you see, I suffer' – and Empson lightly tapped the handle of his stick – 'was temporarily aggravated and I was obliged to change rooms for a while with Pownall below. For some months I had to be wheeled to lectures, into hall, and so forth.'

'You know that the chair is kept in a store-room in this building?'

Empson shook his head. 'I know only that it is somewhere in college. May I ask if it has assumed some significance for your investigations?'

'It was used on the night of the President's murder. I believe it was used for the conveyance of the body.'

For a moment Empson deliberated – the universal academic deliberation of St Anthony's. Then he spoke. 'The conveyance of the *dead* body? You have concluded, then, that the President was shot elsewhere than in his study?'

'Yes.'

Again Empson deliberated; but he might merely have been pausing to take in this new view of things. There was something guarded in his next question. 'You have proof of that?'

Appleby was prompted to admit the truth. 'Only the fact of the chair's having been used. But I think it almost conclusive.' And suddenly Appleby found himself being *searched*: it was as if Empson's every atom of professional expertness were turned upon the endeavour to assess the reliability of what he had heard. But when the psychologist spoke it was without emphasis. 'I see,' he said. And the eyes that had a moment before been essaying to pierce Appleby's mind turned away to stare thoughtfully into the fire.

It was the consciousness of Empson's vocation that prompted Appleby's next approach. 'There is a matter,' he said, 'on which I wish to ask your opinion – for your opinion, you will understand, as distinct from your knowledge of facts. And it is, of course, not at all necessary that you should answer me. But it is a matter you are peculiarly qualified to speak of – a matter of human behaviour –'

Abruptly, Empson interrupted – and it was a thing so much against both his deliberate habit and his courteous manner that Appleby was almost startled.

'The science of human behaviour is yet in its infancy. We are still far better trusting to the prompting of our experience. And yet experience too will betray us. Science will say of a man, "It is infinitely unlikely that he should do this": experience will add, "It is impossible that he should do it" – and then he *will* do it.'

In Empson there was always the undertone of bitterness. But in the colour rather than in the wording of this speech, Appleby sensed something different, a quality of response coming not from a set habit but from something like a fresh revelation. Empson was speaking not from an attitude long since adopted; he was speaking, surely, from a sense of recent shock – almost of recent outrage. Was it himself, or was it another, who had violated expectation?

'It is infinitely unlikely – it is impossible,' Appleby boldly prompted, 'that Umpleby should be murdered *here*?' And at Empson's nod he continued quietly, 'Mr Haveland has been at one time subject to some form of mental disturbance. Do you feel you can properly say anything about that? To be frank, would you connect it with homicidal tendencies? The matter of the bones –'

And once more Empson interrupted. 'Haveland did not kill Umpleby. The bones you speak of are an abominable imposture.' He spoke quietly, but with an extraordinary intensity in the face of which Appleby's next question seemed almost impertinent. But it was a question which had to be asked.

'Is that the fallible voice of science, or the almost equally fallible voice of experience?'

There was only one reply by which Empson could preserve a fully logical position. Would he make it? Would he say that he spoke neither with the voice of science nor with the voice of experience, but with the voice of knowledge? Somewhere in the room a clock ticked out the moments of silence.

'Science is fallible, but it is not nothing. And it will tell you with great authority that the bones are a damnable plant – a plant by someone ignorant of abnormal psychology. I earnestly entreat you, before rushing into a trap, to have Haveland quietly examined by eminent physicians I can name to you. They will substantiate what I say.'

'That Haveland did not murder Umpleby?'

Empson deliberated. And it seemed to Appleby that when he spoke again he spoke as one determined against personal impulse to follow the dry light of knowledge merely. 'Science would be very fallible if it claimed to tell you that. Science can only tell you that Haveland did not murder Umpleby and then broadcast the crime by scattering bones. That, I suppose, is conclusive. And to it I add my *conviction* that Haveland is innocent.'

'Your conviction – the voice of experience?'

'Just that. Again something fallible, but of some authority.'

'Haveland, then, is mentally ... normal?' It was a new question, and Appleby's subtle attempt to introduce it as a tail-piece to what had just been said was a failure. Empson drew back just as Gott had done.

'It is my duty, Mr Appleby, to declare my personal and professional conviction that the circumstances of the President's death are incompatible with what I believe to be Haveland's mental constitution. But I should do very wrong to go on to discuss his or any other colleague's mental constitution at large. You will have little difficulty in finding psychologists willing to discover something crazy in the whole lot of us.' Empson was considerate; the jest softened the rebuke.

'One must be one's own judge of duty,' said Appleby. And for the third time Empson interrupted – and this time in some queer flare of passion.

'The most difficult thing in the world!'

2

Appleby had turned to a fresh topic. 'You came back here from the common-room at half past nine, and went out again something over an hour later – at ten-forty to be exact – to collect a parcel from the porter's lodge. That took you eight or ten minutes and thereafter you did not leave your room until the police reached Little Fellows'. I believe that covers your movements?'

Empson inclined his head.

'Did you meet anyone on your way either to or from the porter's lodge?'

'I saw Titlow.'

'Will you tell me about that, please – just where you saw him and when? And whether he saw you?'

'I do not think he saw me. He was entering his rooms just as I came out of mine. He had apparently come upstairs and was just turning into his lobby when I opened the door there' – and Empson nodded towards his own sitting-room door – 'and noticed him.'

'That would be about ten-forty – just, that is to say, when you were setting off to the porter's lodge?'

'Exactly so.'

'I must tell you that Mr Titlow has declared himself not to have stirred from his room until ten-fifty-five. And then he went *downstairs* and straight to the President's front-door.' And Empson declining to take advantage of Appleby's pause on this the latter added: 'There is discrepancy, is there not?'

'Titlow has forgotten – or Titlow is not telling the truth.' Deliberately Empson seemed to speak without emphasis; there was suppression even of the customary dryness in his tone. There followed a little silence.

'There was nothing remarkable about your glimpse of him?'

'He seemed to have come upstairs rapidly: I had the momentary but convinced impression that he was panting for breath.'

'And that he was agitated?'

'I saw him for a second only, and in that second I had the impression – again the momentary but convinced impression – that he was very much agitated.'

With just such damning lack of emphasis, reflected Appleby, might a judge set some fatal point clearly before a jury. And the image prompted him to try the effect of sudden violence – the advocate's jump to the vital point. 'You think Titlow guilty?'

No change, he reflected ruefully a moment later, was to be got from Empson that way. A blank silence sufficiently indicated the latter's sense that his guest had asked an impossible question. But at length he spoke. 'I should be glad to see justice done, but I am far from able to accuse Titlow.' And then he continued, with something of the air of taking up a subsidiary point in order to rescue Appleby from an embarrassing situation: 'There was, for instance, what actually happened – the shot, whether fatal or not, heard while Titlow was in the presence of the butler Slot-winer.'

'That,' said Appleby, 'might have been contrived.'

'I suppose it might,' Empson stared once more thoughtfully into the fire. 'Have you discovered – have you considered how? Is there, I mean, any sign of such a thing?'

Appleby was evasive. 'The plan would defeat itself if any sign remained.' And abruptly he turned to another matter. 'Why, Mr Empson, did you go over to the porter's lodge at all? You have a telephone here; why did you not ring up to inquire if your parcel had come, and get them to send it across?'

'We do not unnecessarily trouble college servants. It did me no harm to walk.'

The reply was not exactly a snub, but it was conclusive. And Appleby felt he had only one more set of questions to ask. 'And throughout the rest of the evening – from nine-thirty to ten-forty and then from ten-fifty onwards – you were here and quite undisturbed?'

'Quite undisturbed.'

'No one called?'

'No one.'

'And no one rang up?'

'No one.'

Vain persistence, thought Appleby, and was rising to take his leave when something, the echo perhaps of a faintly perceptible tension in the last word spoken, prompted him to add one last query.

'And you yourself rang up no one?'

The pause ensuing was but a fraction of a second; the increased pressure of the fingers on the ivory stick might have been something fancied rather than actual. And yet Appleby had a sudden impulse of overwhelming excitement. In the mind with which he was grappling, he sensed, in this moment, calculation more intense than he had hitherto had any feeling of. *Empson was debating his reply: Yes or no.* And the moment, Appleby's temporarily ungoverned intuition asserted, was the cardinal moment in the St Anthony's case ...

Empson spoke as quietly as ever. 'I rang up Umpleby a little after ten. The matter was of no consequence.'

3

Tantripp, the head porter, had been in the service of St Anthony's since a boy. He was an intelligent man and appeared to realize that he must give all the help he could. But the feeling that with policemen ferreting about among the Fellows of the college the end of the world had come was plainly strong upon him. And so Appleby began with an impersonal point. 'I should like you,' he said, 'to explain the telephone system of the college.'

It turned out to be a subject on which Tantripp was inclined to enlarge. The telephone had arrived in St Anthony's long after he had, and the innovation was one of which he was disposed to be critical. Moreover, there had recently been innovation upon innovation – and of this he was very critical indeed. There was a telephone in the outer lodge for undergraduates, a telephone in the manciple's office and another in the kitchens, a telephone in the President's Lodging with an extension to his study, and a telephone in the rooms of each Fellow of the college. Originally all calls had gone through a switchboard in the porter's lodge. This system had worked well enough, but putting through calls had required the fairly constant attention of the porter on duty. Recently, therefore, a dialling system had been introduced with the object of rendering automatic all calls within the college. To send a call out of college the caller must dial the porter's lodge; but any instrument within the college could be rung from any other by dialling the appropriate symbol. Unfortunately, when first put into operation, the dialling system had not proved thoroughly efficient and as a result it had not immediately, as Tantripp put it, 'caught on'. Partly owing to this reason, partly to academic conservatism, and partly to academic absent-mindedness, Fellows of the college were still liable to put their intra-college calls through the manual switchboard in the lodge.

'Did Professor Empson,' Appleby boldly asked, 'put his call through that way on the night of the President's murder?'

'Yes, sir,' replied Tantripp – uncomfortably but not unreadily – 'he did. He rang through here about ten o'clock.'

'You remember what he said?'

'He said, "Put me through to the President, Tantripp, please." '

'And he could have got through automatically?'

'Certainly. He had only to dial 01. But he's one that never would use the automatic.'

'You are certain it was Professor Empson? You are certain the call came from his room?'

Tantripp appeared perplexed. 'Well, sir, I expect it came from his room. I know at once by the switchboard light, of course, if so happen I think of it. But usually I'm only conscious of the connection wanted. It was Professor Empson's voice, but, come to think of it, he might have been speaking from anywhere – anywhere else in college, I mean. And it was him all right, because I mentioned the call to him afterwards.'

'Mentioned it?'

'Yes, sir. His parcel had been here all evening and when he came across for it at a quarter to eleven it struck me I ought to have mentioned its arrival when he rang up earlier. So I said I was sorry I hadn't told him about it when he rang through to the President.'

'And what did he say?'

'He just waved his hand and said, "All right, Tantripp" – or something of the sort – and went out.'

'What other calls went through your switchboard that night, can you remember?'

'Only two, sir. The President put through an outside call. Of course, I don't know to whom: I just connected him with the city exchange.'

'What time was that – can you be certain?'

'Just before half past ten.'

'And the other call?'

'That was from the Dean, sir, about some gentleman who had been gated. And I remember that he finished speaking to me just as my clock there was on five minutes to eleven.'

For a few minutes Appleby interrogated Tantripp as to his own movements. Gott had been right about his having an alibi: Tantripp would have no difficulty in proving that he had been in his lodge during the period of the murder. And the Dean was now certainly out. But it was of Empson that Appleby was still thinking – and of whom he continued to think as he strolled through the dark courts a few minutes later. It was abundantly clear why Empson had not been able to deny having telephoned to Umpleby. Not only had he used the manual exchange, thus making himself known to the porter – he had tacitly admitted to the call when Tantripp had chanced to mention it later. And yet for a split second he had meditated denying it to Appleby, meditated a denial which would be inevitably exposed. And this though Empson's brain was not the sort to meditate even for a split second a course merely foolish ... But could there, after all, have been anything sinister about the whole incident? For a sinister telephone call why not the secrecy of the dialling apparatus? And yet Appleby could not rid himself of the prejudice that he had arrived somehow at the heart of the case ...

It was after eleven o'clock and he had turned automatically towards his rooms for the night, the second night of his sojourn in the college. But the thought of his rooms suggested Gott and with the thought of Gott came Gott's whimsical recommendation to lose no time in eliminating the servants. The head porter he had just disposed of ... Once more Appleby let himself through the west gate into Orchard Ground.

The violated windows of the President's study had been secured by a padlock to which he had a key; he let himself in, drew the curtains, and turned on the light. The gloomy room, the litter of bones, the dead ashes in the hearth and, above, the grotesquely chalked emblems of mortality; it was all ugly, dreary rather than eerie now, flat, stale, absurd – but mysterious still. Appleby wasted no time. He turned out the main lights, turned on the single standard lamp, settled himself in Umpleby's armchair, and rang the bell. Within half a minute Slotwiner had appeared, as normally, as imperturbably as if his master were still alive to summon him. But this time he made Appleby a bow as to one whose status within the college had been recognized. He was, Appleby reflected, a cool card – certainly not one to be rattled by hearing a bell ring in a dead man's room. And Appleby decided to try a disconcerting opening. 'Slotwiner,' he said, 'we have had to consider you as a suspect.'

'You must explore every avenue, sir.'

'It has become obvious that the shot heard by Mr Titlow and yourself was a fake.'

'Yes, sir. I have always had that possibility in mind.'

'Indeed! In that case you must understand the reason for which the fake might have been arranged?'

'I can imagine more than one, sir. But one would be to provide an alibi for Mr Titlow or myself – presuming one of us guilty. I trust the whole matter will be gone into with minute exactness.'

Slotwiner, his colloquial style apart, came well out of these exchanges. Appleby proceeded to a frank statement. 'If the President was not killed by the shot which you and Mr Titlow heard he must have been killed not in this study, but some way up Orchard Ground, where the noise of the traffic might drown the report. I have to calculate times on that basis. Now, can you tell me anything helpful about yourself?'

Slotwiner considered thoughtfully. 'I see what you mean, sir. And I think I have at least a partial alibi. I think I may take it that to follow the President through the study and up the orchard and later to return with – with the body and the bones would take seven or eight minutes?'

Appleby agreed. Actually, he knew a longer time would be involved – time to cover a journey back to Little Fellows' with the bath-chair.

'Well, sir, I was not, I think, alone for so long a period after ten-thirty. Mrs Hugg, the cook, was engaged as it happened upon the eluci-dation of a puzzle in the kitchen. And she several times ventured upstairs to the pantry to ask my advice. Beasts of seven letters beginning with "P" and that sort of thing, sir. I suggest that you question her closely. But for the period before ten-thirty – supposing, that is, that the President was no longer alive when I affected to take in his refreshment – I fear I am quite uncovered.'

'Don't worry,' said Appleby quietly. He was coming to have a good deal of confidence in Slotwiner. 'Don't worry. I know that the President was alive just before ten-thirty: he made a telephone call. You heard nothing of that?'

Slotwiner unstiffened a little. 'I am, if I may say so, sir, distinctly relieved. But I heard nothing of the telephone call: the President's exten-sion was operating and he could make a call without my being aware of it. He always spoke very quietly into the instrument and in my pantry at the end of the passage the sound would be quite inaudible. Indeed, when working there I am often unconscious of any conversation from this room. But I have to tell you of something which I did hear. It has come back to me since our previous interview. I believe I heard the bones.'

'Heard the bones?'

'Yes, sir. Some time before Mr Titlow's arrival I happened to emerge from my pantry into the hall. And I remember becoming aware of a curious noise from the study. It was not like the President moving books or chairs, and I could not quite place it. May I venture, sir – ?'

And at Appleby's nod the dignified Slotwiner bounded into activity. In a moment he had glided over the floor and collected the major portion of the scattered bones. Bundling them into a newspaper, he handed the bundle to Appleby, 'Now, sir, if you would be so good – ?' And Slotwiner vanished out of the room, shutting the door after him. Appleby was interested and amused. He waited until he heard a distant shout and then, tilting the newspaper, he let the bones tumble to the floor. They made a surprising clatter. And in a moment Slotwiner was back in the study – positively animated. 'That, sir,' he said, 'was precisely it!'

Appleby asked the vital question. 'Can you time it?'

'With fair confidence, sir – to within five minutes. It would be between a quarter and ten to eleven.'

Appleby allowed himself a moment to place the implications of this as exactly as was momentarily possible, and then he turned to a further interrogation of Slotwiner. But the man had heard nothing further, had no further light to throw on the events of the fatal night. And questioned in more general terms as to the relations of Umpleby with the various Fellows of the college, he became reserved. It was an uncomfortable line of inquiry, but in a matter of the sort Appleby never allowed the luxury of nice feelings to interfere. And presently his persistence was rewarded. Slotwiner, admitting to a pretty accurate awareness of the disquiets that had troubled St Anthony's of recent years, came at length to recount one particular scene of which he had been a witness not long before. Umpleby had been holding some sort of meeting in his study with Titlow and Pownall. Whether it had been a protractedly acrimonious meeting Slotwiner could not say. But he had been summoned in the course of it by the President – who was always apparently a punctilious host – to bring in afternoon tea. He had considered the atmosphere strained – although (or perhaps partly because) almost nothing had been said while he was in the room. But opening the door a little later with the intention of replenishing the supply of buttered toast he had heard Pownall speaking with an emphasis which had made him pause. And in the pause he had heard Pownall make a remarkable declaration: 'Mr President, you may rejoice that it takes two to make a murder – for you are a most capital murderee!' After which Slotwiner had retired to his pantry – with the buttered toast.

Appleby wondered if he had eaten it.

Chapter 15

On the second and last morning of his sojourn in St Anthony's Appleby was greeted, as on the previous day, by an early visit from Dodd. The burglars were safely under lock and key, having been caught in a masterly ambush in the small hours of the morning. As a consequence, Dodd was in strange and boisterous mood. He affected solicitude for Appleby's personal safety during the night, searched round the room to see if any of his belongings had been stolen, and then, switching to another topic, inquired after the progress of his studies – what the lectures were like, and when he would be taking his degree? And finally he asked, after a great deal of chuckling over all this – who had killed Dr Umpleby?

Appleby was cautious. 'Well,' he said, 'it might have been Ransome.'

'Ransome!'

'Oh, yes. Ransome has been hovering round us in false whiskers these many days. In fact, it was he who downed me t'other night.'

'There!' said Dodd emphatically. 'What did I say about their saying he was in Asia? They're a deep lot!'

'On the other hand, it might have been Titlow; it might very well have been Titlow, you know.'

Dodd had heard enough on the previous evening to have his understanding of this. 'The pistol–shot being engineered?'

'Exactly.'

Dodd stood in front of Appleby's fire. He seemed to expand. 'It's just possible,' he said, 'that we can give a little help.'

Appleby smiled. 'You've been doing some more of the rough work, as you put it?'

'Kellett has. A conscientious fellow, Kellett. He's been having another hunt round this morning.'

'Ah! Again while I was still heavily asleep. And what has Kellett found this time?'

'Kellett,' Dodd replied very seriously, 'thought he would have a look at the drains. It's wonderful how often, one way or another, the drains come in. Well, he was having a poke down some sort of ventilator or such-like in Orchard Ground when he found this.' And Dodd produced from his pocket a twisted length of stiff wire.

'Kellett found it twisted up like this?'

Dodd nodded affirmatively and Appleby after a moment took up the unspoken train of thought. 'It hardly seems long enough to be useful. I don't really see –'

'One can imagine some sort of gadget – weights and so forth – ?' Dodd tentatively prompted.

'One can imagine,' Appleby sceptically responded, 'a plumber clearing a pipe or drain.'

'*Leaving* it down the drain?'

'Plumbers are always leaving things,' Appleby replied with rather feeble humour – his thoughts seemed to be far away. But presently he added: 'I rather agree that a plumber wouldn't leave it down a drain – twisted up like this.'

'What about sending it to Scotland Yard to be photographed?'

Appleby started, and then chuckled. 'I wonder if your sad sergeant will bring us any news? Meantime, you and I will go and have a heavy talk with young False Whiskers.'

'Asia, indeed!' said Inspector Dodd.

Mr Ransome was found in his regular rooms in Surrey, in the middle of a perplexed telephone conversation with the proprietor of the Three Doves. That he was the guest who had left in such unseemly circumstances the night before; that he was really Mr Ransome of St Anthony's College; that it was quite all right; that nothing serious had occurred; that it was all a matter of a bet; that he wanted his luggage sent on – this was Ransome's side of the exchange. But the mention of the momentarily notorious St Anthony's in conjunction with such a thin story obviously caused alarm at the other end of the line. Ransome was pink and snorting by the time he turned to receive his official visitors. But he calmed himself at once and spoke up with what seemed an oddly guileless cordiality.

'Oh, I say, you know, do sit down! I'm most frightfully sorry about the other night – should really have apologized yesterday evening. But honestly that basket-thing was so dashed uncomfortable that I was quite *furious* – and just before dinner, too! Did I hurt you too terribly? Dreadful thing to have done, I'm afraid. I suppose you will have to prosecute me? Really dreadful – I'm so sorry. But then one has to go to all lengths for one's work, don't you think? Well, not all lengths – not murdering and things – but when it's just a matter of knocking a man out – well, don't you think, really? If you would put yourself in my place, I mean?'

This ingenuous, haphazard appeal seemed to come genuinely from Ransome. He was a sandy, egg-headed, untidily dressed young man, given to gestures as vague and rambling as his speech. That such an absent person had hit Appleby on the head with just the right amount of force must have been the merest luck, and he was certainly not one to engineer an efficient burglary on his own. A very pretty specimen of the remote and temperamental scholar in the making, consciously capitalizing, perhaps, the advantages of being a 'character' – such was Ransome. Or such, Appleby cautiously put it to himself, was the appearance which Ransome presented to the world. And now, feeling that Dodd was about to offer some minatory speech in this matter of an assault upon a colleague, he quickly interposed.

'We needn't discuss the minor incident now, Mr Ransome. Our concern is with the death of Dr Umpleby. I am sure you realize that your position is unfortunate. You were confessedly in the vicinity of the college secretly and in disguise, at the time of the murder. And you were on anything but friendly terms with the murdered man.'

Ransome looked his dismay. 'But hasn't Gott told you all about it – our burglary, and the alibis and the rest of it? And isn't it all square and above board – or above the board you say *you're* concerned with, so to speak – what?'

'The situation is quite simple, Mr Ransome. You have to account for your movements between half past ten and eleven o'clock on Tuesday night if you are to be absolved from the possibility of suspicion. And so has Mr Gott – and everybody else.'

'Bless me!' exclaimed Ransome with what seemed all but impossible ingenuousness, 'I thought it was clear it was going to be poor old Haveland, scattering bones and what-not –?'

'You must endeavour to satisfy us about your movements – or, at least, it will be prudent and reasonable for you to do so. Inspector Dodd here will take down any statement you may think proper to offer. And I have to tell you that any statement you make can legally be used as evidence against you.'

'Oh I say! I must have time to recollect, mustn't I?' Ransome looked round the room in a distracted but still easily vague manner. 'Don't you think you or your colleague might just ask questions? Way of sticking to the point, you know?'

'Very well. You came in from the Three Doves, I take it, on Tuesday night?'

'Oh, yes, rather. After dinner. Bus from the lane-end – got in just on half past ten.'

'And what did you do in the succeeding hour, before you attempted to reconnoitre the college at eleven-thirty?'

Ransome's reply was prompt but disconcerting: 'I tried to work out the Euboic talent!'

Heavy breathing from Dodd seemed to indicate a feeling that the majesty of the law was being trifled with. But Appleby was perfectly patient. 'The Euboic talent, Mr Ransome?'

'Yes. Quite off my line, of course – but I suddenly got an idea about it in the bus. Boeckh, you remember, puts the ratio to the later Attic talent as 100 to 72, and it struck me that –' But here Ransome broke off doubtfully. 'I say, though – I don't know if you'd really be interested –?'

'I should be interested to know just *where* you indulged in these speculations.'

'Where! Oh I say – is that important? But, yes, of course it is. I'm most frightfully sorry, but I really don't remember. I was rather absorbed, you see – so absorbed that I almost forgot all about the burglary business. And that of course was enormously important. I remember I had to run. That shows you it was pretty absorbing, because I was awfully keen to get my stuff back from that old beast ... Now I wonder where I could have been?'

'Do you remember, perhaps, any method you adopted in working on your problem; sitting down, for instance, to write?'

Ransome suddenly jumped up in childish glee. 'To be sure,' he cried, 'a sort of menu-card; I scribbled down figures on that. Yes, I went straight to a tea-shop – that place in Archer Street that is open till midnight. And I was there all the time, right up till about twenty past eleven. Isn't that splendid? What luck!'

'Do you think they would remember you there?'

'I'm sure they would, whiskers and all. There was a bit of a fuss. They brought me Indian tea . . . Often in that sort of place they do, you know' – Ransome concluded on a note of warning.

'Well, Mr Ransome, pending the verification of that, I don't think we need trouble you further. Just one other thing. What put Mr Haveland in your head as the murderer?'

Ransome was distressed. 'I say! Don't think I think Haveland's the murderer. It seems just to be the gossip going round – because he was a bit rocky, I suppose.'

'But that was a long time ago?'

'Oh, yes, rather. Though he had a bit of a relapse when I was home last – but it was soon all right. Good chap, Haveland – knows his Arabia.'

'Can you tell me about the relapse you mention?'

'Oh, it was a couple of long vacations or so ago. He felt a spot unsteady and went into a sort of rest-home for a bit – place a long way off – a Dr Goffin near Burford – so nobody knew. Nobody except me, as it happened: I visited him there on the quiet. All blew over.'

'I see.'

'But I say, Mr Appleby, there's something I'm most frightfully anxious about. Can I hang on to my stuff – the stuff, I mean, we lifted from the old beast's safe?'

'Mr Ransome,' said Appleby gravely – and to the scandal of the attendant Dodd – 'I advise you not to discuss the materials in question with the police until the police discuss them with you. Good morning.'

2

'And your remarks on the text,' Mr Gott declared, 'are merely a muddle.'

'Yes, Gott,' said Mike meekly.

'You see, Mike, you haven't any *brain* really.'

'No, of course not,' said Mike.

'You must just keep to the cackle and write nicely. You write very nicely.'

'Yes,' said Mike dubiously.

'Keep off thinking things out, and you'll do well. In fact, you'll go far.'

Mike's acknowledgements faded into silence and tobacco smoke. The solemn weekly hour that crowns the System was drawing to its close. The essay had been read and faithfully criticized. The remaining ten minutes would be given to pipes and to silence punctuated by desultory conversation . . .

'It's the Fifth of November today,' Mike presently offered. And his preceptor plainly failing to find this an interesting observation, he added: 'Silly asses, letting off rubbishing fireworks – and all that.'

'No doubt.'

'Like Chicago during a clean-up. Guns popping.'

'Quite.'

'D'you remember last year, Gott? Titlow acting as sub-Dean while the Dean was away, and Boosey Thompson chucking a Chinese cracker at him, and Titlow wading in and confiscating old Boosey's stinks and bangs?'

'Very unedifying,' responded Gott absently. And suddenly he looked hard at his pupil. 'Mike, who put you up to that?'

'Put me up –?'

'Mike dear, you're very nice. But as I've just had to point out, you have *no* brain. Who's been stuffing you?'

'Well, as a matter of fact, it was David Edwards that –'

'David Edwards's suggestion,' said Gott, 'will be conveyed to the proper quarter.'

There was silence for some minutes, and then Mike ventured: 'There's something more . . . David thinks it's a pity we haven't been told more of the precise circumstances attending the poor President's death.'

'What has the poor President's death got to do with David Edwards?'

'David thinks he might have some useful information – if he only knew, that is, what would *be* useful information.'

'I can hardly believe his logic is as rocky as that. But out with what you've been crammed with.'

'I think,' said Mike mildly and respectfully, 'that you're rather rude. But it's like this. On Tuesday night David was working in the library, quite late. Dr Barocho was there and several other people and David was sitting on top of one of the presses in the north window – you know how people do sit on the presses – and of course it was quite dark outside. But when David was just happening to look out into the darkness there was a sudden beam of light – and he saw somebody.'

Gott had laid down his pipe. '*Recognized* somebody, you mean?'

'Yes, recognized somebody. In the light from the President's study. The light just showed for a moment as the person came out –'

'Came out!'

'Yes; came out of the french windows of the study – and David just made out who it was. He wondered a little afterwards because he doesn't know if this person keeps a key to Orchard Ground and he wondered how he was going to get out if he didn't. But of course it was quite a normal person to be visiting the President, so David didn't know if it would be the least important. As he says, the circumstances of the poor President's death have been kept so dark –'

'What time was this?'

'Oh, just before eleven o'clock.'

For a minute Gott was lost in speculation. Then he asked: 'Who was it he saw?'

'David won't say. But we have the matter in hand.'

'*You* have the matter in hand!'

'Yes, Gott – David and Inspector Bucket and I. You see, David thought it *might* be important. So he investigated. And he discovered one thing about this person whom he had seen. He discovered he had a nice, secret, private way in and out of college –'

Gott sprang up. 'Do you mean in and out of Orchard Ground?'

'Oh no. Just in and out of one of the main buildings here.'

'You young lunatics – why haven't you been to the police? Where is David Edwards now?'

'Well, as a matter of fact, he's on the *trail*. And I think if you'll excuse me ...'

And before Gott could interpose Mr Michel de Guermantes-Crespigny had gone.

3

It was a positively excited bibliographer who accosted Appleby and Dodd in the court a few minutes later to report on the report of his pupil. Dodd was not inclined to scout the suggestion that St Anthony's was not a submarine after all; with an attitude of mind that was distinctly to his credit he soberly admitted the possibility of an oversight, and suggested an immediate and even more thorough inspection. But Gott had a preliminary problem to advance.

'Even if it does exist it's difficult to see how it fits in. For according to this precious Edwards it's not in Orchard Ground but somewhere here in the main part of the college. And he saw somebody come out of the french windows about whose possession of a key he was doubtful. But he must know that the four men lodging in Little Fellows' have keys. Somebody other than these four, and somebody who might normally be visiting the President, had therefore to get out of Orchard Ground. How did he do it? The fact of there possibly being a secret exit from somewhere in the main buildings seems irrelevant.'

'No doubt it's obscure,' said Dodd a little shortly. He did not approve of co-opting a layman – even a favourite author – as a colleague. 'I leave the obscurity to Appleby here and intend to test the truth of that young fellow's story.'

'Why not wait,' Appleby asked, 'till the enterprising Edwards comes back from the trail?'

But Dodd would have none of this. And he was just making off in the wake of Gott, who was called away by the demands of the System, when a diversion appeared in the shape of the sad sergeant – in whose dreamy eye some reminiscence of a night in London might still be detected. The sad sergeant had a letter for Appleby and having presented it somewhat hastily withdrew. Appleby poised the official-looking envelope for a moment unopened in his hand. 'Well, Dodd – what do you think? There were no finger-prints on my bath-chair handle: will they have had better luck with that pop-gun?'

'No,' replied Dodd stolidly. 'They will not.'

Appleby tore open the letter. There was a moment's pause and then he spoke quietly.

'Pownall's prints.'

4

The sandwich at the Berklay bar, postponed from the previous day, had been duly consumed and Appleby had set out on a solitary walk by the river to think things over. And he began with that formula which he had evolved as he stood mid-way between Pownall's and Haveland's rooms the day before:

He could prove he didn't do it here and now. He couldn't prove he didn't do it there and in twenty minutes' time – were some indication left that he was guilty.

There had been a rider to that, he remembered:

An efficient man: he reloaded and let the revolver be found showing one shot.

And there had been a query:

Second bullet?

Mentally, Appleby deleted the query now and altered the rider:

No reloading; no second shot; a suitable squib.

But a moment later an echo of the first rider came back:

An efficient man: he ... let the revolver be found ...

There was the rub. Or there, so to speak, was the absence of the rub – a good brisk rub that would have removed the last traces of finger-prints from the weapon. Pownall was a clumsy man – physically. And here, perhaps, after much ingenuity, had been some answering and fatal clumsiness of mind. It might be that he had done something to obliterate the prints, but had not been careful enough. The chemists could almost work magic nowadays: Appleby remembered the authentic report he had given to Deighton-Clerk of the German criminologists who were getting finger-prints through gloves ...

Would everything fit? First Haveland's times. Haveland was with Deighton-Clerk from ten-forty to ten-fifty. That would be the period that wouldn't do (*he could prove he didn't do it here and now*). Could Pownall have been certain of Haveland's leaving the Dean – being without an alibi (*he couldn't prove he didn't do it ...*) – by eleven o'clock? Surely there was a way by which he could have been quite certain. To begin with, he might easily know that Haveland had dropped in on the Dean for a *short time*. Suppose Pownall knew *that*, and had shot Umpleby in his own room in Little Fellows' at ten-forty ...

And then Appleby improved on that. Even with traffic near by, no one, surely, would risk a shot right in the building. At ten-forty Pownall had shot Umpleby in Orchard Ground – and had known: *Haveland is now with the Dean*. He had got the bath-chair from the store-room, put the body in it, stolen Haveland's bones and put them in the chair too – and wheeled the whole lot into his own room. All perhaps by ten-forty-five. And then he had waited. And while he waited, from Umpleby's body, head lolling over the side of the chair, he had suddenly become aware of a drip, drip on the carpet ... Appleby was striding along obliviously now. Was it going to fit? Next there was Barocho's gown – if only it could be proved that its owner had left it in Pownall's room! Pownall would have snatched it up to swathe the head and its little trickling wound. And then, a few minutes after ten-fifty, he had heard Haveland return to his own rooms opposite, had slipped to his door, maybe, to make certain he was unaccompanied – defenceless in the matter of an alibi. A minute later he would set off with his grim cargo on the hazardous journey to Umpleby's study. And then at once the un-loading of bones and body; the 'big bang' or whatever the particular pyrotechnic might be let off at the right moment; the swift return with the empty chair to the store-room; the revolver, too-hastily wiped, thrown down where Haveland in his recklessness or unbalance might easily have thrown it.

What else fitted? Pownall's own story, offered to explain away the fatal doctoring of the carpet, had possessed one significant element: it had contrived to point at Haveland even while it cleared Pownall himself. Haveland – such had been the suggestion – killed Umpleby, became aware that he had failed in a scheme to incriminate his neighbour, and then by some sudden freak of mind abandoned concealment and virtually signed his own name to the murder by leaving the bones. And two other facts fitted. It was Pownall who along with Empson had known of Have-land's wishing the President 'immured in a grisly sepulchre'. It was Pownall who, in an outburst of his own, had addressed Umpleby as 'a most capital murderee'.

And now, what did *not* fit? Here Appleby gave himself a caution. Everything needn't fit – there lay the difference between his activities and Gott's. In a sound story everything *worried over* in the course of the narrative must finally cohere. But in life there were always loose ends, minor puzzles that were never cleared up, details that never found their place. And particularly was this so, Appleby had found, of *impressions*: things at one time felt as significant in the course of a case simply faded out. And yet ... Appleby liked his smallest detail to fit, his impressions stage by stage to demonstrate themselves as having been in line with the facts.

First among the elements that didn't fit was Slotwiner's statement that he had heard the arrival of the bones between a quarter and ten to eleven. That was a little too early if Pownall were to set out only after he was sure of Haveland's having got back from Deighton-Clerk's. But on a matter of two or three minutes, too much emphasis must not be laid. Next was this still obscure story of Gott's pupil. Was it another red herring? If he had it accurately (but it had come to him in too roundabout a way for much confidence as to this) it seemed too closely linked to the case to be something incidental and insignificant. Someone, not a dweller in Little Fellows', had come out of the study *just before eleven*. And that somebody possessed a secret means of getting in and out of St Anthony's. It was an unsettling complication and the sooner young Mr Edwards was interrogated the better.

There was another element that didn't fit. It was Titlow and not Pownall whom this same undergraduate recollected as having, just a year ago, impounded Boosey Somebody's fireworks. But there was nothing very significant in this: the whole firework theory was unnecessary, re-presented indeed no more than an ingenious guess in the dark. There was no real reason to exclude two genuine revolver shots, even two revolvers. The more Appleby reviewed his facts the less substantial opposition did they seem to present to the reconstruction he had just built up. Apart from what might well prove a mere undergraduate joke, there was really *no* solid material objection. It was certain impressions merely, difficult to assign a just weight to, that continued to cause obstinate misgivings. Until these – or the more assertive of these – were fitted into place, the case, although it might *do*, would leave Appleby uneasy.

But often, he reiterated to himself, he had been obliged to discount mere impressions towards the end of an investigation: why was he so reluctant to do so now? And presently he believed himself to have penetrated to the source of his doubts. More vividly than usual, he had been impressed at St Anthony's by a number of personalities and he was reluctant to lose sight of any of them. The picture of Pownall plotting against Haveland did not, on this plane of impressions, take in nearly enough: it ignored sundry moments in his contacts with this man and that in which he had sensed himself as at the end of *some* thread leading to the heart of the case. Most vividly before him now was that fraction of a second in which Empson had hung mysteriously suspended between a 'yes' and 'no' – mysteriously, because in a matter in which he had proved to be without power to prevaricate. And there had been similar moments with Titlow – even with Slotwiner ... Slotwiner startled by the mention of candles. The spot of grease. The *Deipnosophists*. A length of wire. Something noticed about the revolver ... With these things Appleby's mind had come back to material factors: material factors which without positively being obstacles, yet did not *fit in*.

He had been pacing the river's bank in deep abstraction. But something suddenly made him aware of his surroundings – the rhythmical but laborious passage of an eight up the stream. It might, he idly speculated, be the St Anthony's boat, and in relief from his absorption he gave a critical eye to the oarsmanship. The crew seemed near the end of a longish spell; the boat was rolling slightly; the cox, a shrill and improperly plump little person, was doing his best to hold things together. 'Drive ... drive ... drive; *in* ... out, *in* ... out, *in* ... out ...' And the next moment a deeper voice shouted startlingly close to Appleby's ear; it was the coach darting past on a bicycle. 'Eyes in the boat, Two. *Late*, Six, *Late*, Six. One ... two ... three ... four ... five ... six ... seven ... eight ... nine ... ten ... *Drop* them, Six!'

Drop them, Six! That was another moment that stood out: Pownall's curious insistence on beginning his story with an almost detailed account of a dream. How could he feel such a thing significant, if he were innocent? What purpose could it be meant to serve, if he were guilty? If he were guilty ... And here Appleby found himself confronted by the real crux. Why should this rather dim ancient historian shoot Umpleby? Why should he commit the unspeakable crime of fastening the deed on an innocent man? Those psychological probabilities which Gott had very properly refused to discuss – they made the really baffling feature of the case. There was only one reasonably probable core to the thing – and the facts would not fit it. Unless ... unless a key lay, as he had mockingly hinted to Gott, in De Quincey's anecdote of Kant – that queer pointer given him by Titlow ...

Presently he had left the river and struck into winding country lanes. He liked nothing better than to do his thinking during a lonely ramble. And the thought of his solitude striking him now, he remembered Dodd's facetious injunction to avoid being hit on the head again in the course of a woodland walk. It hardly seemed a very likely contingency; Appleby's eye roved whimsically and appreciatively over the peaceful countryside around him. And in doing so it became aware of a succession of interesting circumstances.

The first was an old gentleman pedalling past on a bicycle – not a likely assailant, but an object of some curiosity as soon as Appleby had recognized a Fellow of St Anthony's. It was the venerable Professor Curtis, looking so absent that Appleby marvelled that he did not pedal placidly into the ditch. Perhaps he was meditating some interesting detail in the curious legend of the bones of Klattau. Conceivably he was pondering the equally curious fact of the bones of Haveland's aborigines. But if he looked absent he also, it occurred to Appleby, looked curiously expectant – a happy expectancy rather like that of a small child going to a party.

Curtis had pedalled about a hundred yards ahead, oblivious of Appleby, when the latter, happening to glance behind him, observed a car just coming into view round a bend in the lane. Appleby slipped into the hedge to observe, for to a policeman at least there is something singular in a powerful car doing a resolute eight miles an hour. It was a reticently magnificent De Dion; it contained three intent youths of vaguely familiar appearance; and it was keeping laboriously in the wake of the gently bicycling professor. The procession represented, it sufficiently appeared, Gott's pupil and Gott's pupil's friends 'on the trail'. It was a trail which Appleby could follow too. Letting the De Dion get a little way ahead, he fell in behind at a brisk walking pace. The November afternoon was chilly, with a light but keen wind blowing: what might be important business and what was certainly beneficial exercise had come conveniently together.

But the walk was scarcely stretching. In something over a mile Appleby came up with the car, abandoned by the side of the road. Proceeding some fifty yards further, he came upon a cottage standing some way back from the lane in the seclusion of a sizeable, trimly-hedged garden. Moving to the gate, Appleby could see Curtis's bicycle standing by the front door and Curtis's trackers crouching picturesquely by one of the windows. But even as this sight presented itself to him the young men scrambled up and began to beat a retreat – not precipitately as if they had been discovered, but rapidly nevertheless as if in some discomfiture. Reaching the gate they fairly bolted into Appleby's arms. Mr Bucket exclaimed distractedly: 'It's the detective!' The detective's eye ran critically over the trio and singled out his man. 'Mr Edwards?' he asked crisply.

'I'm Edwards.' The young man as he replied edged a little further away from the garden gate.

Appleby went straight to the point. 'Mr Edwards, do you assert that you saw Professor Curtis leave Dr Umpleby's study about eleven o'clock on Tuesday night?'

Mr Edwards answered readily, as on a resolution taken long ago. 'Yes, I did.'

'You are certain?' Again Mr Edwards was ready – and intelligent. 'Quite certain. It was long chances seeing anything and very long recognizing. But I did.'

'And now what is happening here?' Appleby's gesture indicated the cottage.

But this time Mr Edwards, like his companions, was uncommonly confused. 'Something that I'm awfully afraid is none of our business ... As a matter of fact, sir, I think it's what might be called the lady in the case.'

Appleby, without superfluous delicacy, strode up the garden-path to the window. It gave upon a scene of domestic felicity. Professor Curtis was consuming tea before a large fire; perched on the arm of his chair and plying him with muffins was a youthfully mature lady – the sole glimpse of femininity that the St Anthony's mystery affords.

5

'It was quite true,' Dodd greeted Appleby on the latter's return to college, 'it was quite true; I should have spotted it.'

'Spotted Curtis's bolt-hole?'

Dodd stared. 'You've found out?'

'I know who was the owner, but not quite what he owned: tell me.'

'Well,' said Dodd, 'it was pretty tricky, but I oughtn't to have guaranteed St Anthony's as watertight all the same. Curtis's rooms look out on a little blind-alley off St Ernulphus Lane. His windows are barred like all the rest – but if you go out there you'll find, just next door to them, a sort of coal-hole in the wall. It's quite firmly bolted on the inside. And then when you come into the court to investigate you find that the cellar is the breadth of the building, and that the door to the court is securely locked. The porter has the key. But when I thought that there was an end to the matter I didn't reckon with the queer way these places are often built. What has Curtis, whose rooms are next door, got, if you please, but a door of his own opening straight into the cellar – so that he can help himself, no doubt, to a lump of coal when he wants it? Not that there is any coal kept there now, incidentally; it's just a nice, clean, empty space. And all that old reprobate had to do was to slip in there, unbolt the outer door, and amble quietly away.'

Appleby laughed. 'I don't know yet that he's exactly an old reprobate – but I suspect he has some interesting information to give.'

'You've seen him?'

'I came across him in the course of my walk. He was a bit occupied, but I've arranged to see him in his rooms presently. Any further news here?'

Dodd nodded. 'Gott's out.' He spoke half-regretfully, as if the drama of having the celebrated Pentreith really implicated in a murder were something to be abandoned with reluctance. 'A perfectly flat and simple piece of routine work has ousted him. A certain Mrs Preston cleans the proctors' office, usually between seven and nine in the morning. But her daughter was to be married on Wednesday, so she did some of the cleaning late on Tuesday night instead – taking care not to be seen by the gentlemen. But *she* saw *them*. And she was aware of Gott off and on from the time he arrived till the time he went out again after the return of the Senior Proctor.'

'Unexciting but conclusive,' Appleby agreed. 'And Ransome?'

'Ransome was in the bun-shop all right. Made a great fuss, it seems, about his tea – and forgot to drink it when he got it. He sat scribbling until a bit after a quarter past eleven and then suddenly rushed out as if he had remembered something. It all squares. And now, what's to be done next?'

'Done next, Dodd? Nothing more – except a chat with Curtis and a lot of thinking. We shan't get any more evidence, you know.'

'No more evidence?'

'I think not. As I see it, I don't know what further evidence – Curtis apart – there can be.'

'Well,' said Dodd doubtfully, 'as long, of course, as you *see* it –'

At this moment there came a knock at the door and a junior porter brought in a telegram. Appleby tore it open – and for Dodd his expression became a gratifying study.

'The revolver,' he said. 'It has Empson's prints too.'

Chapter 16

1

'It has always appeared to me,' began Professor Curtis, 'that on retiring from my Fellowship here I could not do better than settle down. Actually, as you see, my marriage, although it is of recent date, has preceded that retirement.'

Professor Curtis placidly stroked his beard and looked with mild and luminous intelligence upon his guest. With just such a lucid little proem would he begin expounding the mysteries of the papal chancellery to his pupils.

'You may think it in some degree singular, Mr Appleby, that I have not communicated the intelligence of this domestic event to my colleagues. But to begin with I may − may I not? − plead precedent. Of course you remember dear old Lethaby, who was Dean of Plumchester Cathedral? He was an honorary Fellow here and a regular member of our common-room for ten or twelve years, coming up every week. But it was only when he died and Umpleby went down to attend his funeral that we became aware that he was a married man. He had not mentioned it.

'In my own case I saw distinct inconveniences, which I need not particularize, as likely to be attendant upon a public announcement. And for the remainder of my time − which is now merely a matter of a few terms − I determined, therefore, on reticence.'

'Mrs Curtis,' Appleby smoothly interposed, 'of course agreeing.'

'My wife, as you say, agreeing. She is a most meritorious female, Mr Appleby, and I am happy that she had the pleasure of meeting you today. But all this − save in one particular − is really irrelevant to the distressing and confounding circumstances to which I must presently come. Let me mention this particular at once: you will see later how it gained significance. Attendant upon keeping my marriage clandestine there were certain difficulties which you will no doubt apprehend. But these have been minimized by the fact that I happen to possess, adjacent to this room, a convenient and private means of egress from the college.'

'Yes,' said Appleby, 'I know: the coal-hole.'

'Exactly so. That is no doubt the purpose for which it is actually intended. For a long time, as I think I told your colleague, I have been without a key to the college, and this emergency exit' – and Curtis beamed at his little joke – 'has been most useful. By leaving the door – aperture perhaps I should say – that gives on the little blind alley unbolted at night I have on occasion been able to slip in that way. And now,' continued Professor Curtis with great complacency, 'I approach the agitating portion of my narrative.'

Appleby produced notebook and pencil. 'I shall ask you to sign your statement,' he said, 'and I have to warn you –'

Curtis nodded amiably. 'Yes, Mr Appleby, yes – and I believe I have got, as they say, on the wrong side of the law. But so bewildering – so very bewildering – has everything been, that I have paused during these last two days in order to watch the turn of the event. I think that expresses it: to watch the turn of the event.'

'The event might have turned more quickly if you had come forward at once with such information as you possess.'

'That is no doubt a just observation, Mr Appleby. And – well, *here goes.*' And Professor Curtis, after an appreciative pause over the dashing colloquialism, really went, if somewhat parenthetically, ahead.

'That I have the knowledge – if knowledge such a confused concatenation of impressions may be termed – of events on Tuesday night that I do have is purely fortuitous. It results from my having resolved, I suppose a little after ten o'clock, to pay a visit to Titlow. It was not a merely social call. A vexed point in a Carlovingian manuscript had been worrying me for some time and it suddenly occurred to me that Titlow might help. He is not, of course, in *any* sense a palaeographer, but then he *is* – is he not? – an epigrapher, and I thought he *might* help. The notion was most exciting and I put the document in my pocket and went straight across. Or rather I did *not* go straight across – and that no doubt was the trouble.

'I had entered Orchard Ground when it occurred to me to consult Umpleby. I did not' – Professor Curtis continued with some severity – '*approve* of our late President: for some years, it had seemed to me, he had turned controversy into dispute – always an unbecoming thing, Mr Appleby, in a scholar. But Umpleby was really remarkably intelligent. And being distinctly excited over my problem and seeing a light in his study, I tapped at the french windows – rather familiarly, I fear, considering our by no means intimate relations – and, in short, I stepped in and consulted him. He was very civil and immediately interested – it must be said of our late President that he was a man generously eager for the furtherance of learning – and I suppose we spent some ten minutes over the document.'

'That would take you,' Appleby interposed, 'to about ten-twenty-five?'

'Until about ten-twenty-five. Umpleby made one or two interesting points and then I left him in order to consult Titlow, as I had originally proposed. I left, as I had come, by the french windows, and that' – added Curtis as if with some memory from Pentreith's fictions of the proper formula for such matters – 'was the last occasion on which I saw Umpleby alive.

'Well, I went straight to Titlow's. Or rather – you must excuse my lack of lucidity – I did *not* go straight to Titlow's. For it occurred to me half-way to Little Fellows' that in addition to the document in debate I might advantageously have brought certain other documents showing analogous problems. So I struck over the orchard in the dark, intending to return to my rooms by way of the east gate and get what I wanted. I had quite forgotten, of course, the vexatious business of these gates being locked at ten-fifteen. I came up against the closed gate with such unexpectedness, indeed, that injury might well have resulted. Upon that, I turned back to Little Fellows': if the further documents proved necessary, Titlow, who had a key, could come over with me to my own rooms. And it was just as I was approaching Little Fellows' once more that I received the first great shock.'

'Can you fix the time,' Appleby gravely inquired, 'of the first great shock?'

'I believe I can. I was presently to be very much *aware*, and that awareness, by some retrospective operation of the mind, seems to include anterior events as well. I remember that the half-hour struck a moment before I came up so abruptly with the east gate. And in the dark it would take me three minutes – would it not? – to arrive at Little Fellows'.

'And then, Mr Appleby, I became aware of Haveland. He was standing just outside the doorway of Little Fellows' and the light from the lobby illuminated him, if not clearly, yet sufficiently. I believe I must have discerned, and been much struck with his expression: I cannot otherwise account for the fact that I pulled up immediately. For it was distinctly a second afterwards that I became aware of what he was holding. He was holding a pistol – rather delicately in both hands. And he was examining it, it seemed to me, with something like fascination. But he had paused for a moment only; the next second he vanished into the darkness, only to return almost immediately and disappear into Little Fellows'.

'Haveland, as you know, was at one time afflicted by a nervous ailment and my first thought was that he was about to make some attempt on his own life. In that persuasion I was about to rush into the building after him when I became aware of a disconcerting, indeed of a horrible impression. *I had the distinct impression that I had already heard a shot.* It had lodged itself in my unsuspicious mind as some noise incident to the abominable traffic by which the university has come to be afflicted. But now it came back to me as a *shot*. I could not tell *when* I heard it: it might have been any time after leaving the President's study.

'And then, Mr Appleby, I did what I believe was a weak thing. I ought, I know, to have accosted Haveland at once – or alternatively, to have sought other assistance. But some unreadiness of nature supervened and I took a turn in the darkness of the orchard to reflect. I was already perplexed: how much more of perplexity was to come!'

Professor Curtis paused at this and smiled comfortably at Appleby. Then he resumed.

'I paced about in great agitation for, I suppose, five minutes –'

'Ten-thirty-nine or forty,' said Appleby.

'And at the end of that time I determined to consult Titlow on the whole disturbing incident. Titlow is our Senior Fellow and a man of brilliant if volatile intelligence: he seemed at once a proper and convenient person in whom to confide. I therefore retraced my steps to Little Fellows' – and for the second time became aware of something *most* untoward. Titlow himself was just emerging, *dragging what was plainly a human body*. He hauled it just out of the circle of light from the doorway, pitched it down, to use a vulgar expression, like a sack of coals, and disappeared once more into Little Fellows'. I was very much shaken.

'I am humiliated to think,' continued Curtis with every appearance of the blandest ease, 'that my duty was once more clear and that I again failed in it. Indubitably I should have hurried at once to the victim and rendered what assistance I could. But I was horribly convinced that the body I had momentarily seen was a *dead* body – and I was, moreover, excessively perturbed. I retreated once more into the orchard and it was a few minutes before I was sufficiently calm to take action. Then I saw that my proper course, in circumstances so exceedingly grave, was to go at once to the President. I made the best of my way through the orchard to his study ... I would remind you, Mr Appleby, that the horror of these events was exacerbated by the inspissated gloom in which they were enveloped.

'Dr Umpleby's study was deserted – and it was only on discovering this that I remembered, in my agitation, his having remarked that he was going over to see Empson almost at once. Within a few moments of my leaving him he must have followed me through the windows. I had as yet no suspicion of his fate, but I saw that I had no resource save to return at once to Little Fellows'. I passed out of the window once more and had advanced a few steps on my way when I became aware of a mysterious object advancing upon me through the darkness. I was so unnerved by this time that I at once withdrew from the path and made no sign of my presence. And the object soon revealed itself as some species of conveyance; a moment later it had halted before the windows of Umpleby's study and I became aware of sounds of intense physical effort. Then the curtains were drawn for a moment aside, allowing a vision of yet another appalling spectacle. *Pownall was hauling out of a bath-chair what was plainly the dead body of Umpleby* – and a moment later he had disappeared into the study with his burden.

'I will not pause,' said Professor Curtis, who had just paused impressively over this lurid picture. 'I will not pause to particularize my feelings. I will merely say that I fled – and again passed some minutes in the darkness of the orchard in great agony of mind. At length I hurried back to Little Fellows' to throw myself for counsel – and I may almost say for protection – upon Empson. In the inferno in which I was trapped – I do not think my expression is too strong – it seemed plain to me that there remained only one sane man. I hurried upstairs to Empson's room. He was out. The resource had failed. I disliked the thought of Umpleby's study – but I disliked Little Fellows' yet more. I hastily sought the protection of the orchard once again and there formed what I believe was the most rational plan open to me. I would wait some minutes to allow Pownall to get clear of the study and would then enter it and call the assistance of the President's servants. Looking at my watch, therefore, I gave myself five minutes. Then, I boldly, I hope I may say, approached the study –'

'What time was this?' There was a tremor of excitement in Appleby's voice.

'It was between two and three minutes to eleven o'clock. I stepped straight through the windows and came upon Umpleby's body laid among a litter of bones. But I came too upon something far more appalling than that. At the far end of the room by one of the revolving book-cases, and so absorbed in some operation of his own that he was quite unaware of my presence, was – Empson!

'I had just volition to slip silently from the room once more – and then, to use a familiar expression, my wits deserted me. I was, as I said before, trapped: my only way out of Orchard Ground was by the President's Lodging, and that was blocked by the presence – the sinister presence I cannot but call it – of Empson. It is really disconcerting, Mr Appleby, for a retiring scholar to find himself incarcerated in a college court with a congeries of criminal lunatics.'

Professor Curtis lost himself for a moment in the placid contemplation of this alliterative effort. And then he continued. 'Of my movements during the succeeding half-hour I can really give no coherent account, I was conscious, shortly after leaving the study, of hearing another shot; I have a memory of wandering round the orchard in plain distraction. I came to myself only with the sound of voices and what I took to be a general alarm. I was standing in the farthest corner of the orchard, beside the wicket that gives upon the street – and suddenly I noticed that the wicket was opening. By the light of a street-lamp I discerned a bearded person whom I did not recognize step tentatively into the orchard and check himself at the sound of the shouting. But I had seen my chance and, making a dive for the gate, I caught it just before it shut to and made good my escape. To such an extent was I nervously indisposed that I felt momentarily incapable of any other action. A few minutes later I slipped exhausted into my own rooms here – by means of the coal-hole, as you accurately call it. And since then I have waited, as I expressed it, on the turn of the event – waited for what was most plainly a horrid conspiracy to unmask itself.'

'There was no conspiracy,' said Appleby.

2

After Curtis, Barocho. And from Barocho came confirmation.

Yes, he had at length recollected where he had mislaid the gown: he had left it in Pownall's rooms ... Yes, his embarrassing questions in hall had been aimed at Titlow. It was interesting to see how people reacted – and about Titlow since the murder there had been something provoking experiment.

'But you had heard that it was believed not physically possible for Titlow to have killed the President?'

'No. I had not the particulars. But it is not that. Titlow would not plan a murder.'

And then Appleby put the grand question. 'The Titlows: would they fake a text?'

And Barocho pondered and understood.

'The Titlows,' he replied at length, with a gesture that took in the whole academic world of Appleby's question, 'would not fake a text, for a text belongs to a realm of pure knowledge which they would not betray. There can be no question of expediency in that realm. But in the world of affairs, knowledge is not serene; it is often obscured – sometimes by human wickedness, often by human stupidity. In the world, truth may require for its vindication the weapons of the world – and the necessity will justify their use. The Titlows do not think of the world – *your* world perhaps, *Señor* – as very perceptive, as very pertinacious for the truth. They live themselves remote from the world – too remote today. And when the world suddenly thrusts its crisis, its decisions upon them, their response is uncertain, erratic – like that of children. But in intelligence, in pertinacious thought, they regard the world as a child. And so, although they will not fake a text to pass about among themselves, they might, to guide the world ... put out a simplified edition.'

Chapter 17

I

Once more the long mahogany table gleamed beneath the candles in their heavy silver candlesticks; once more the firelight flickered on dead and gone scholars round the common-room walls. Once more the ruby and gold of port and sherry, the glitter of glass, the little rainbows of fruits had been swept away untouched. Outside, the courts of St Anthony's were still hushed in decent quiet, but from the lane beyond and from adjacent colleges came the intermittent splutter and crackle of fireworks: it was the evening of the Fifth of November ... And once more Appleby was seated at the head of the table, the Fellows of the college assembled round him. And presently Appleby spoke.

'Mr Dean and gentlemen, I have to tell you that the circumstances in which your President met his death on Tuesday night are now known. Dr Umpleby was murdered by one of his colleagues.'

The formal announcement had its effect. The stillness was absolute. Only Dr Barocho, his eye circling speculatively round his companions' faces, and Professor Curtis, whose dim absorption might have been directed to Bohemian legends or Carlovingian documents, were without a uniform strained rigidity of attention.

'In a moment,' Appleby continued, 'I am going to call for a number of statements which will make the facts clear. But I believe you will find these facts less disturbing than they otherwise would be if you will allow me to make one preliminary point.

'We speak of murder as the most shocking of crimes. It is just that. Nothing stands out more clearly in my sort of experience than the surprising effects upon behaviour which the shock of murder can have. Faced by the sudden fact of wilful killing, called upon for action and decision, a man will do what he might never think to do were he merely coolly imagining himself in the same circumstances. For murder goes along with fear, and when we are controlled by fear we are controlled by a more primitive self. In such a condition our reason may for a time become a slave – something used merely to give colour to unreasonable things. And should murder suddenly erupt in such a quiet and securely ordered society as yours, this shock may be very severe indeed: it may master a temperamental man not for minutes merely but for hours or even days – and particularly is this so if the fear is substantial and real, the product of a danger which even the rational mind must realize. And on Tuesday night, as you will learn, danger took a strange course through St Anthony's ... But though shock and danger may drive us out of ourselves for a time, sooner or later the normal asserts itself. We test our actions by normal standards – and find perhaps that we have to confess a brief madness. I cannot usefully say more and I will ask for the first statement ... Mr Titlow.'

2

'I was convinced from the first,' began Titlow, 'that Pownall had murdered Umpleby. And very soon I was to believe that, in order to escape the consequences of his guilt, he had attempted to fasten the crime upon myself. But for the horror and, as Mr Appleby has truly put it, fear arising from that second belief I would no doubt more quickly have seen the truth about the first. The truth is that I had *almost* conclusive evidence of Pownall's guilt – but only almost. As soon as I realized this – as I did in conversation with Mr Appleby in the early hours of yesterday morning – I realized that I must narrate what I had done. When I dispatched such a narration to him this afternoon I had arrived, he would say, at judging my conduct once more by normal standards.

'Here is my story. I returned from the common-room on Tuesday night at about half past nine and settled down to read until it should be time to make my usual call on the President. I became interested in my book to the extent of letting two important things happen: I let my fire get low and I lost an exact sense of time. As a result of the one I felt chilly and got up to close a window on the orchard side; as a result of the other, I vaguely felt myself to have heard ten strike a minute or so before, whereas I must actually have heard half past.

I leaned out of the window for a moment to see if it was raining, wondering if I should need an umbrella to visit the President. And at that moment I became aware of the President himself just coming into the circle of light from the lobby. He was about to enter Little Fellows' when he was stopped by somebody calling to him from the darkness of the orchard. I was just able to hear; it was Pownall's voice, speaking urgently but at a low pitch. "President," he had called out, "is that you?" And Umpleby replied, "Yes, I'm going in to see Empson." I was startled at the response: "Empson is here, President. He has had a fall: will you help?" At that, Umpleby at once turned round and vanished into the darkness. I was on the point of calling out and hurrying down to assist when it occurred to me that the President and Pownall could do all that was required and that there was nothing that Empson would like less than a fuss. And so I returned to my book. But I retained an uncomfortable impression that the thing was a little odd: it was odd that Empson should have been walking in the darkness of the orchard. And after a time it struck me as disturbing that nobody had come upstairs; I was afraid that Empson was too badly hurt to be brought up to his room. And on that I decided to go and investigate.

'I stepped out to the landing – and received a distinct shock. *Empson was moving about in his room.* Nobody, I knew, had come upstairs – and yet I could not be mistaken. Empson has a polished floor with rugs and you will understand that the sound of his footsteps and stick together make a pattern with which I am perfectly familiar. For a moment I stood dumbfounded – and then I realized that Pownall must have made a mistake, calling out prematurely that the injured person he had discovered was Empson. I ran downstairs – and I think the natural thing would have been to knock at Pownall's door. I do not know what growing sense of strangeness and alarm sent me straight into the orchard, to light upon the body of Umpleby – a revolver lying beside him.

'The shock, as Mr Appleby has charitably argued, was very great; for a moment after I had distinguished that quite conclusive wound I could only stand and tremble. Then I looked at my watch. It was ten-forty. Actually, that would seem to have been only some eight minutes after the committing of the crime. But I did not realize that: I had believed it to be just after ten when I rose to close my window and in the succeeding interval my sense of time had remained confused. Well, I had only one opinion – certain knowledge rather – from the first. Pownall, under cover of calling Umpleby to Empson's assistance, had lured him into the orchard and done this unspeakable thing. There came back to me with tremendous force a scene at which I had been present only a few days before, a scene in which Pownall had told Umpleby that he was "born to be murdered" – or some such phrase. And already I was aware of the vital fact. I was the only witness to what had occurred – either in the orchard that night or on the occasion of Pownall's using the words I have just quoted ...

'Almost without knowing what I was about, I had begun half to drag and half to carry Umpleby's body towards Little Fellows'. And there, I suppose with some idea of confronting the criminal with his crime, I hauled it direct into Pownall's sitting-room. The place was in darkness and I switched on the light. I crossed over to the bed-room: if Pownall was there I was going to have him out. And he was there – asleep. It was the horror of that, I think, that finally determined my actions: less than an hour after doing this thing the miscreant was asleep!

'I stood and thought for what seemed a long time – perhaps it was only sixty seconds all told. Pownall had killed Umpleby, and Pownall had got away with it. On that revolver there would, I knew, be nothing; and for evidence there were only my stories – the story of a sinister phrase spoken, the story of uncertain observations made from an upper window in the dark ... And at that moment my eye turned to the body and I was aware that something immensely significant had happened. The wound was bleeding upon the carpet. *And the blood represented evidence*.'

The gathering round the long table was listening in a consternation which was turning to horror. Deighton-Clerk voiced the dawning understanding: 'You resolved to *incriminate* Pownall?'

Titlow continued unheeding. 'I referred Mr Appleby to a contention of Kant's. Kant maintained that in no conceivable circumstance could it be justifiable to lie – not even to mislead an intending murderer as to the whereabouts of his victim. Standing there over Umpleby's body I seemed to see quite a different imperative. If the cunning of a murderer could only be defeated by a lie, then a lie must be told – or acted. I saw a moral dilemma –'

For a moment the Dean's voice rang out in passionate refutation: in the pause that followed the sporadic explosions outside reverberated as from a battle-field. And coldly Titlow continued. 'Deighton-Clerk is right. And Mr Appleby too is right: a brief madness, no doubt, was upon me. I saw myself in an utterly strange situation and called on for an instant decision. And what dominated me was this: were I not to act, the thing was over – in the next room was a murderer who could never be touched. But were I to act – act on the plan the blood-stained carpet had suggested to me – then nothing final and irrevocable would have been done. If a shadow of doubt should later come to me, if reflection should dictate it, I should cancel the effect of action by a single word. I did not think I should be afraid to do so – nor have I. But that is unimportant. I acted. I tore a couple of pages from Umpleby's diary and left them, burnt but for a fragment of his writing, in an ash-tray. I dragged the body out into the orchard again – that was obviously necessary. And then I returned with the revolver.'

Titlow paused. And in the pause there was a touch of the histrionic, as if a flash of his ungoverned imaginative sense had come to ease for a moment the situation in which he found himself. 'I had remembered a vital fact. During the alarm of fire we had some years ago, Pownall had revealed himself as an exceptionally heavy sleeper. That gave my plan, I thought, a substantial chance. I returned with the revolver, held by the barrel in my handkerchief, and went into the bedroom. Pownall was fast asleep, his arms outside the coverlet. I took his right wrist with infinite caution and lightly pressed the pistol-butt to his thumb. He stirred in his sleep, but I had slipped from the room, as I thought without his being roused. I tossed the revolver into the store-room, where it would certainly be found, and then retreated upstairs to my own rooms. But that is only half my story. And if I needed confirmation of Pownall's guilt the other half brought it – and with a shock. For Pownall turned the tables on me.'

There was a stir round the common-room – a furtive shifting of limbs, here and there a cough. Dr Barocho was providently rolling himself a stock of cigarettes. Lambrick thought to lower the tension by turning with unconvincing heartiness to throw a log on the fire. Curtis was looking with vague interest at Appleby, as if trying to place an uncertain acquaintance. Titlow continued.

'I determined that I had better do what I had always done – go over, I mean, at eleven o'clock to visit Umpleby. When he was found to have disappeared from his study I could give something like an alarm

– and perhaps manage to direct the search to Pownall's rooms ... So I presented myself on the stroke of the hour at Umpleby's front door. I had hardly spoken to the butler when we heard the shot from the study. We both rushed in. I could do nothing else, but I knew at once that some devilry was afoot.'

'That some devilry was afoot!' It was the Dean speaking, a fascinated eye on his colleague.

'And there the body lay, in that litter of bones. I knew at once that I must have awakened Pownall and that he had contrived some plot. On the face of it it was a plot against Haveland – a plant. But I was wary enough to send Slotwiner to the telephone and hunt feverishly around. There was of course a smell of gunpowder in the room, but there was a smell too of something else – a badly snuffed candle. And then I saw: Pownall had contrived a plot against *me* ... It was fiendishly clever, and if I had not penetrated to the farther end of the room it would have caught me. He had arranged a simple demonstration that I had both killed Umpleby and attempted to incriminate someone else and secure an unshakable alibi for myself. He had reasoned like this. If a shot heard by Slotwiner and myself had killed Umpleby neither Slotwiner nor I could have killed him. From that it followed that if such a shot were heard and then proved to be a *fake* it must have been faked to provide an alibi for Slotwiner or myself. If in the faking of that shot there were used something that could be identified with me then the case against me would be clear – or clear enough to give me a very bad time. And that was what he contrived. On the top of a re-volving bookcase in a bay at the farther end of the study, concealed behind a few books, he had arranged just such an apparatus as I might have used to engineer that shot. It was an arrangement of a candle-stub and a burntout squib – just such a one as they are letting off around us now and just such a one as I was known to have impounded from an unruly undergraduate a year ago tonight. With a little practice such an arrangement could have been quite accurately timed by a person wanting to suggest an alibi in that way. And if I had not discovered it you see what would have been said: that I had not had the opportunity on which I had counted for removing the traces of my plot. As it was, I had time to thrust squib and candle into my pocket and the books back on their shelf before Slotwiner returned. My escape had been a very narrow one.'

Titlow's extraordinary narrative was concluded. And Appleby allowed no pause. 'Professor Empson,' he said crisply.

3

'I knew,' Empson began, 'that Titlow had murdered Umpleby.'

The common-room was passing beyond sensation. Deighton-Clerk looked as if he had shot his bolt of indignation; Ransome had plainly taken refuge behind further calculations on the Euboic talent; Curtis was asleep; Titlow himself was immobile in the face of the accusation.

'I knew,' said Empson, 'that Titlow had murdered Umpleby and that he had contrived a diabolical plot to incriminate an innocent man. And I knew that I was in some danger myself. The simple knowledge of Titlow's guilt would not have moved me to act as I did – nor, I believe, would the knowledge of my own peril. But when I saw dastardly advantage taken of another man's misfortune in order to send that man in his innocence to the gallows, I acted without a qualm. Titlow has always seemed to me unbalanced, and that impression enabled me to get hold of the situation more quickly than I otherwise should have done. For I could not see – and I still cannot see – any rational motive which Titlow could have had for murdering Umpleby and attempting to incriminate Haveland and possibly myself ... But that is what I saw him to have planned.

'It is remarkable what, in a familiar and secure environment, one can witness without question or alarm. On Tuesday night I actually saw Titlow dragging Umpleby's body through Orchard Ground – *and I suspected nothing*. It seems incredible. But it is true – and this is how it happened. About ten-forty I decided to go over to the porter's lodge in search of a parcel of proofs. They were of my new book and the expectation of them put me in mind of certain passages about which I felt misgiving: the thought of these no doubt served to preoccupy my mind as I went out of Little Fellows'. But I was not so oblivious as not to see Titlow, and not to see what he was doing. He was a little way off in the orchard – not far because the light behind me was sufficient to illuminate what he was about: he was dragging an inert human body towards Little Fellows'. And, as I say, I thought very little of it. To be exact, my mind distorted the image of what I had seen sufficiently to allow of a facile and quasi-normal explanation. Titlow, I thought, had found somebody almost dead drunk in the orchard and was charitably assisting him to his own rooms. A moment's reflection shows that that would be surprising in itself and the fact of my inventing and accepting such an interpretation rather than let myself be arrested by something positively disconcerting makes an interesting, but by no means extraordinary scientific observation. I half-resolved to look in and see if I could help on my return. And then I simply walked on to the porter's lodge, my mind wholly given to those sections of my book about which I was dubious.

'What occurred next has, I think, real scientific interest. The porter, who as you know is a most accurate man, happened to imply that I had recently put through a telephone-call to the President – which was not the case. Normally, I would simply have assumed that he had made a mistake: I might have taken the trouble to trace the source of the error; more probably, being sufficiently absorbed in a train of thought of my own, I should have let the matter slide. But on this occasion I was instantly *alarmed* – almost wildly alarmed. It was an extraordinary reaction. And a moment's – I suppose professional – introspection enabled me to connect my alarm *with what I had just seen in Orchard Ground*. Two slightly disturbing facts had made contact – and produced not disturbance but extreme agitation. And at once that distorted image of what I had seen corrected itself. I saw Titlow as doing what he really had been doing: furtively dragging a dead body through the orchard. And instantly an equal impression of the sinister communicated itself to the odd business of the telephone. A blind instinct of caution prompted me to offer no denial to the porter. I hurried out of the lodge with my head in a whirl. It had come to me overpoweringly that in this quiet college, in which I had spent the greater part of an uneventful life, danger was suddenly lurking. It was a fantastic notion. But its fantasticality was something of which I was merely intellectually aware; its *reality* was immediate and overpowering – something felt like ice in the veins.

'It would be hard to say what made me do as I then did. I suppose I had recognized *whom* Titlow was dragging, and that the recognition had sunk instantly into the subconscious. Be that as it may, in making my way back mechanically to Little Fellows' I tapped at the President's french windows – and looked in. And there my eyes met substantial horror enough. Umpleby was lying on the floor, his head queerly muffled in a gown. I went straight to him and felt his heart: he was dead. And as I straightened up I became aware of the grim scrawls of chalk and of the bones ...

'Such a situation would make a dull man's brain move fast. I thought it out, I suppose, in something under thirty seconds. Titlow with Umpleby's body; no alarm; this tableau with what I knew to be Haveland's bones – the series could mean only one thing. Titlow was attempting to incriminate Haveland. He was turning a weakness of Haveland's – long all but forgotten – to what was wellnigh the foulest use conceivable by man. But he had acted in psychological ignorance. I knew as a fact of science that Haveland could never murder Umpleby and deliberately give himself away after that fashion. Even had I not detected Titlow in the midst of his crime I could not have been deceived ... But facts of science are too often not facts at law.

'And then my mind came back to the false telephone call – as it now obviously was. That too could have only one meaning: I was implicated in some manner myself. And I realized just how urgent the danger was. If a man of Titlow's ability had contrived such a crazy thing he would have contrived it well. What further hidden strokes he had planned, what other crushing evidence he had contrived, I had no means of knowing. I knew only that discovery might be a matter of minutes. Within those minutes I had to act. And a moment's reflection showed me that there was only one certain way of escape. The crime must be brought convincingly home to the wretch who had committed it.'

Empson, who was now speaking in his driest manner, paused for a moment. And Deighton-Clerk managed to exclaim: 'Empson, you *too* are going to tell us – ?'

'That I did what you would have done yourself,' Empson replied, 'if you had managed to think of it. Consider my position. I had stumbled by the merest accident upon a very subtle plot in which Haveland and myself – in whatever relation or proportion – were plainly to be incriminated. I had no reason to suppose that by merely giving an alarm at that point I could foil Titlow. And that the police would get to the bottom of an elaborate piece of ingenuity planned by such a man I had very little hope. Nobody, I think, could have predicted the arrival of an officer of Mr Appleby's perspicacity.

'Well, I hit on a plan – just the plan which Titlow fathered upon Pownall in the very ingenious story he has just told us. *It must be made immediately obvious that Titlow had killed Umpleby:* that was the postulate with which I began. And if I could not actually show Titlow murdering Umpleby I could, I thought, show him as *avoiding* being so shown. I could show him faking an alibi. I relied on his continuing to act normally and making his usual call on Umpleby at eleven o'clock. If I could fake Umpleby's murder for the moment at which Titlow would be in the hall with the butler *and arrange matters so that the fake would then certainly reveal itself* I should have achieved my object.

'And then I remembered an incident that had happened just a year ago today. Titlow had been acting as sub-Dean and had had occasion to purloin certain fireworks from an undergraduate. And these fireworks I had reason to believe were still in a drawer in his room ... A couple of seconds after I had realized that my plan was formed.

'I slipped out of the study, let myself through the gate and into the deserted common-room here: I took a candle-end from one of the candlesticks on this table. And with that I hurried back to my own rooms and, leaving the door open so that I could hear Titlow's movements opposite, waited. Presently, as I had hoped, he came out: he was plainly going to make a show of visiting Umpleby as usual. As soon as he had passed the turn of the stairs I entered his room and in a moment had found what I wanted: a firework of a simple explosive kind. Then I hurried after Titlow and was back in the study before he could have got as far as the west gate. That gave me about a minute and a half. I went swiftly to the far end of the study, lit my candle, affixed it to the top of a revolving bookcase in one of the bays and hid it behind a few volumes taken hastily from the shelf. Then I simply waited until I heard the butler open the front door, ignited the touch-paper of the squib at the candle – which was later to suggest, of course, some primitive but practicable fuse – laid the squib too behind the books, and hurried as fast as my leg would let me from the room ... I do not know that I made any mistake.'

'Mr Pownall,' said Appleby.

4

'My action on Tuesday night,' said Pownall, 'was dictated solely by my knowledge that Haveland had murdered Umpleby and attempted to lay the crime upon me.'

Deighton-Clerk almost groaned; Barocho gave an approving nod; Curtis woke up and took snuff. And slowly and curiously gently, his head dropped characteristically sideways and his hands lightly clasped, Pownall told his story.

'Empson, in his appallingly mixed-up version of the affair, has mentioned how one can come across something odd without — if one is unsuspecting — thinking much of it. That was how my own adventures on Tuesday night began. As everybody here knows, I have the habit of going to bed exceptionally early — often at about half past nine. I was a little later than usual on Tuesday: it must have been just on ten o'clock that I stepped out of my room to fetch some hot water from the pantry. As I did so I heard somebody making a telephone call from Haveland's room opposite. All I heard was a voice saying "Is that you, President?" and then I passed on. But the voice had been Empson's and I was vaguely surprised that he should be telephoning from Haveland's room. I suppose I was thirty seconds in the pantry, and I had a view of the lobby all the time. I heard no more on my return, for the door of Haveland's room had been pushed to. But I saw something that I immediately thought puzzling — that I ought to have realized as very curious indeed. Glancing upstairs as I passed into my room I saw Empson himself. He was making his way to the little landing half-way down — apparently to get a lump of coal from the locker there. I wondered how he could have got back upstairs without my noticing — but I failed to wonder long or vigorously enough to see that his having done so was a physical impossibility.

'I went straight to bed and, as my habit is, fell asleep at once. But the curious incident was still on my mind and I believe it entered my dreams. I dreamt of somebody speaking in an odd, unnatural voice, and into the same dream was woven what I now believe to have been the sound of the shot that killed Umpleby. And I dreamt yet further of somebody or something clinging to my wrists. And with that I woke up, knowing, as I have explained to Mr Appleby, that somebody had been in my room.

'The story we have heard from Titlow I cannot attempt to explain, but the things he has mentioned — the blood-stains and the diary pages — I presently found in my room. And then, hurrying outside, I found the body of the President ... You know with what vividness one can sometimes recall a voice? In that moment there came back to me exactly what I had heard earlier that night and I recognized it with complete certainty as not being Empson's voice but Haveland's voice imitating Empson's. Under cover of that disguise, it was clear, Haveland had lured Umpleby over from his study to Orchard Ground. And having lured him there he had shot him and was plotting, by what variety of means I could not tell, to incriminate me.

'Haveland was a murderer. Upon that, there came to me an illuminating thing that had been told me by Empson. We all heard it the other night: it was the crazy sentiment Haveland had uttered to Umpleby about wishing to see him immured in one of his own grisly sepulchres. That gave me my idea: I saw how I might escape and at the same time see justice done.

'I ran to Haveland's rooms. He was out. I secured the bones, ran with them into the store-room and stowed them at the bottom of the bath-chair. Then I pushed the chair into the orchard, hoisted in the body, wrapped Barocho's gown round the head and retreated with the whole thing into my own sitting-room. I was just in time. A few seconds later I heard Haveland returning. As soon as he had closed his door I was out again and hurrying, chair and all, to the President's study. The rest you can guess. Within six minutes of finding Umpleby's body and the plot against myself I had arranged in his study a very tolerable version of what had been his real murderer's expressed wish when he had talked of grisly sepulchres. I thought it would be conclusive.'

Again there was silence in the common-room; it was broken by the Dean. 'Mr Appleby, what light have you to throw on this mass of contradiction? And where is Haveland? He is not at our meeting.' Automatically, everybody looked towards the foot of the table where Haveland had sat facing Appleby two evenings before. But his place was now occupied by Ransome – who gave an alarmed 'Oh I say!' at the sudden concerted scrutiny ... Quietly Appleby took up Deighton-Clerk's questions.

'There is no contradiction, Mr Dean. We have heard – as far as each man's actions are concerned – nothing but the truth. It so happened that on Tuesday night a certain member of the college who chanced to be present in Orchard Ground was witness to a series of transactions which tallies exactly with what has been said. It was the information given me by that gentleman which put me in a position to elicit the narratives you have just heard.

'These, Mr Dean, are the facts. I repeat that everybody has at length told the truth as they knew it. But everybody acted from contradictory beliefs as to what had really happened – contrary beliefs which proceeded first from the design of the murderer and secondly from the first fatal assumption of Mr Titlow ... You ask for Mr Haveland. Haveland, the murderer of your President, killed himself while resisting arrest this evening.'

5

'Haveland killed Umpleby,' Appleby continued, 'but he was far from intending to set his signature on the deed. That he would not do such a thing Professor Empson was prepared to state with all the authority of his science. But Professor Empson, although passionately concerned at what he conceived as a dastardly plot against Haveland, was unprepared to discuss the question of Haveland's normality in general terms: such a discussion, he plainly felt, would distract the lay mind from the one piece of scientific knowledge he felt as relevant – *Haveland was not the sort who would deliberately give himself away*. But that was not after all the basic fact. The basic fact was this: Haveland had that sort of abnormality which never loses at least its tenuous connections with reason. Take his motive. He was, as I learnt from you, Mr Dean, a likely candidate for the Presidency – and so, as I learnt from a remark of Professor Curtis's passed on to me by Inspector Dodd, is Professor Empson. When Haveland proposed to kill Umpleby and let the blame fall on Empson (for that was the original plot) he was acting with just that combination of moral imbecility and logical sense which characterizes his type.

'He had a remarkable power of mimicry: in this room a couple of evenings ago he shocked you by a momentary imitation of Mr Deighton-Clerk – and it was deftly enough done to strike a mind interested in such things ... He rang up Umpleby, then, at ten o'clock, in Empson's voice and using the porter's manual exchange so that the call would be remarked. Umpleby came over to Little Fellows' – to keep an appointment with Empson, as he thought – just after half past ten. Haveland's plan was perfectly simple. He lurked in the orchard until the appearance of the President and again used the ruse of an assumed voice – Pownall's this time – to lure him into the darkness. And under cover of the roar of traffic in Schools Street he shot him dead, leaving the revolver beside the body. On that revolver, as I can demonstrate, he had secured and contrived to preserve Empson's finger-prints. Having done so much he went straight to the Dean, paying him an ordinary visit of some ten minutes. And thereafter he went straight back to his rooms. That concluded his activities. The strength of his plan was, I say, in its complete simplicity.

'Mr Titlow found the body at ten-forty and unfortunately concluded that Mr Pownall was the murderer. Thereupon he took the extraordinary course he did to ensure that Pownall should not escape. But in doing so he roused Pownall from sleep. And the latter, discovering the murder, concluded first and rightly that Haveland was the perpetrator, and secondly and incorrectly that it was Haveland who had attempted to incriminate him, Pownall. He guessed correctly, that is to say, the implications of the telephone-call he had overheard, but he had no suspicion of Titlow's inter-position in the matter. Acting rapidly on the plan he thereupon formed, he had body and bones arranged in the study before ten-fifty – and just in time to be discovered by Professor Empson. And Empson, having seen Titlow hauling the body into Little Fellows' and alarmed by his discovery of the spurious telephone-call, concluded that Titlow had murdered Umpleby and was plotting to involve Haveland, and possibly himself, in ruin. He therefore evolved his plan to reincriminate Titlow – who 'however' on bursting into the President's study discovered the device of the faked shot in time to obliterate almost every trace of it.

'And the result of all these subleties, gentlemen,' Appleby drily concluded, 'has been an investigation of some complexity. The double inquest will reveal the insanity which brought about Dr Umpleby's death . . . Nothing more, I think, falls to be said.'

There was the longest silence that had yet been. Then Deighton-Clerk nodded to Titlow and Titlow pressed a bell. The door of the inner common-room opened.

'*Coffee is served!*'

Chapter 18

It was late. The yellow Bentley – dispatched as a gesture of official recognition in response to a brief announcement of success – waited at the gates. Appleby, already overcoated, Dodd, still faintly bewildered, and Gott, largely appreciative, were consuming liqueur brandy from enormous rummers in the latter's rooms. And Appleby was summing up.

'Umpleby was murdered pat upon the changing of the Orchard Ground keys – in other words under conditions which made access to him possible only to a small group of people. There were various possible explanations of that obtrusive point. One was that the conditions of access were not as they seemed: that the murderer had some hidden means of access and was utilizing the surface conditions to mislead. Another was that he had arranged things as he did for fun: that he was one of the group indicated by the conditions and was giving us a fair start that way. And yet another was that he was one member of the group wishing to *plant* the crime on another member and taking a first step by limiting the possible suspects to the group. And the theory of planted murder proved of course to be the key to the case. Everything that turned up fell in with it – only far too *much* turned up.

'First came the strong suggestions of a plant against Haveland. And soon I came to couple with that idea the name of Pownall. Pownall was concerned to *point* at Haveland: he had pointed at Haveland during a scene which subsequently turned out to have made manifest the pattern of the whole affair; and he pointed at Haveland later when putting up a story to explain his own strange conduct. It seemed reasonable to suspect that in that story Pownall was ingeniously turning the facts upside down. According to his version, Haveland had murdered Umpleby and attempted to plant the murder on him, only setting his own signature to it with the bones in a fit of craziness after his plan had been foiled. In reality (I conjectured), Pownall had murdered

Umpleby and planted the crime on Haveland. When it became apparent that both the time and place of the murder had been fudged I was able to see a likely motive for both deceptions. By fudging the time Pownall was making sure of Haveland's having no alibi; by fudging the place he contrived a particularly striking fulfilment of the rash wish that Haveland had once expressed.

'I allowed this more or less simple case against Pownall a long run. But it didn't seem good enough. For one thing the revolver had significantly given itself the trouble to turn up and I had been prepared to find it faked in some way to represent another link in the chain against Haveland. On the contrary it had Pownall's prints; if Pownall had shot Umpleby with it he seemed to have been almost unbelievably careless. Again, I had a very distinct impression about the interview I had had with Pownall – the impression that his story had been a complicated mixture of truth and falsehood. This complication, and much else that I felt as having a place in the case, my theory so far failed to cover.

'I was, for instance, convinced that in some way or another both Titlow and Empson came in. With both these I had had what I felt were significant interviews. Titlow, an erratic person it appeared at all times, was strung up *to believe some specific person guilty*. He had it all curiously involved with a philosophy of history – was obviously in a state of unwonted intellectual confusion – but it came down to this: if there was anything incredible about the idea of X having murdered Umpleby then he, Titlow, had some duty before him ... And then he gave me the strange reference to Kant: I was to turn upside down the contention that the duty of truthfulness overrides the duty to protect society from murder.

'There was something here which any theory of the crime must elucidate and incorporate. And that consideration held also of the results of my interview with Empson. Empson too had an X in his mind; was shocked that, contrary to the expectations of science and experience, X should have murdered Umpleby – that, at least, was what I read into his attitude. And his X was, of course, not Haveland; there was something like passion in his assertion of Haveland's innocence. And there were two other points. When the possibility came up that the shot heard from the study might have been faked he was anxious to know if any trace of a contrivance for effecting such a fake had been discovered: he was inquiring, in fact, for what would be evidence against

Titlow. The last point was his hesitation over the telephone call. That was enigmatical until the revolver was revealed as bearing Empson's prints as well as Pownall's. That revelation brought, of course, the suggestion of a plant against Empson and a faked telephone call fell into place as another attempted piece of evidence against him. Why had Empson *almost* denied making that call, when he knew the porter would seem to expose such a denial? And the answer came: because he knew such a call had been planted on him and he had been on the verge of taking the line of saying so ... At the same time I saw how Empson's finger-prints at least might have been got on the revolver. I remembered that the revolver had tried to tell me something, so to speak, the moment I saw it. It was a slight little weapon with a slim curved ivory handle – uncommonly like the handle of Empson's stick. I could imagine it tied to some actual stick and thrust into Empson's hand for a moment in one of those dark lobbies before being withdrawn with an apology for the mistake. The result, almost certainly, would be the slightest and most imperfect of prints – more imperfect even than the prints cautiously got by Titlow from the sleeping Pownall. But very poor prints – the impress of quite a dry finger on an indifferent surface – can be made susceptible of identification nowadays. Here we had an instance of a technical advance in criminology being exploited not once but *twice* in the same case. Which is as good as a word of warning, perhaps, in the field of "scientific" detection.

'Then came the twisted wire found by Kellett thrust down a drain. You might have guessed that, Dodd. It was the crumpled cousin to the wire contraption you had seen me make to protect possible finger-prints on the revolver! Enclosed in a little cage like that, the revolver could be handled and fired readily enough without obliterating or marring previous prints.

'By that time there was a most embarrassing wealth of clues of the possibly or probably planted sort. Against Haveland: the bones. Against Empson: fingerprints and a faked telephone call. Against Pownall (accepting some truth in his story): the bloodstains, the diary pages, and – again – fingerprints. Against Titlow alone of the Little Fellows' group there seemed to be nothing planted. So I tried him out for a bit as sole villain. I toyed with the idea of his trying to incriminate all three of his Little Fellows' colleagues. Then, taking it another way, I tried to see him concerned to establish his own alibi. I brought in

Edwards's suggestion of the firework and my own observation of the candle-grease on the bookcase there. But I didn't much like it and presently – I suppose for the sake of schematic completeness – I began to explore the possibility of the candle-grease being the sole remaining evidence of a plant against Titlow. I got as far, in fact, as seeing the possibilities of the planted faked shot as an instrument for incriminating him. But there I knew I was on very speculative ground.

'What I had got was the four Little Fellows' men involved in some queer chain of events. I began to search for a *direction* to it. A minute ago I said that, quite early on, Pownall had pointed at Haveland. That was in the common-room on my first night. But more had happened on that occasion. It would not be too much to say that the air had been heavy with insinuation. And an analysis of what had been said or hinted produced this: Pownall had pointed at Haveland, Haveland had pointed at Empson, Empson had pointed at Titlow, and Titlow had pointed at Pownall. Nothing could well be more schematic than that: it gave what was certainly a chain, and it gave a direction in which the chain went. Could I find any start to it all? Was there any correspondence between the way the pointing went and anything known or suspected as to the direction of the planted clues? I could get at only one correspondence: Haveland's insinuations were against Empson – and I had some reason to regard Haveland both as the likely imitator of Empson's voice (he had a talent for it) and as the person who had planted Empson's prints on the revolver (he had been concerned to know if the revolver had been found).

'So I made another tentative start there. *Haveland killed Umpleby and attempted to lay the blame on Empson*. That turned out to be correct. But I went on from it to another guess which turned out to be wrong. *Titlow had suspected Haveland's guilt and had arranged the bones as a means of bringing the crime home to him* – and he was now very properly worried over the morality of such a procedure and was anxious as to the certainty of his belief. But presently I had to discard that – for Titlow's insinuations had been directed against not *Haveland* but *Pownall* . . .

'But what I was not immediately prepared to abandon – having got so far – was Haveland's guilt. For, paradoxically enough, the notion of somebody's faking a case against Haveland now removed the chief obstacle to seeing Haveland as really guilty. A case faked against Haveland was really protecting him – because it was *unconvincingly* faked:

Haveland, as Empson knew, was not the man to sign his deed in the way suggested.

'And Haveland had always been the likely murderer. In searching for a murderer amid any group of people every detective knows the importance of a history of mental unbalance. In real life murderers are not, on the whole, found among the chief constables and Cabinet Ministers: they are found among the less normal portion of humanity. Anyone may behave more or less fantastically in the face of murder, but the commission of murder is – well – specialist's work. Deighton-Clerk, I believe, had recognized Haveland as the murderer and had instantly blanketed the fact in his own mind in a manner – as Empson would say – full of scientific interest. The first *spontaneous* remark Deighton-Clerk made to me showed the subconscious run of his thought. Between Umpleby and Haveland there had been detestation . . .

'At that point I had pretty well shot my bolt. By following up the chain: Haveland – Empson – Titlow – Pownall – Haveland, I might get things a little clearer in my own mind; might even arrive at a position from which I could begin to extract a little unvarnished truth from people. But of one thing I was almost convinced. I should never see either Haveland or anybody else in the dock. Whatever these four people had been up to they had between them produced a mass of complications which no defending counsel could muff.'

Appleby rose and set down his rummer. 'Titlow's story I was half counting on, but my anonymous observer in Orchard Ground was the simple bit of luck that enabled me to dictate explanations after all. And Haveland's choosing the way out he did has been a crowning blessing all round. It cuts down the scandal here; and if it deprives Treasury Counsel of considerable fees it spares a harassed policeman a good many sleepless nights.'

Appleby clapped Dodd on the shoulder and moved towards the door. Then he turned and smiled at Gott. 'We shall meet again, I hope. And meantime I have a parting present for you.'

'What's that?'

'A title for the book you may never be able to write: *Death at the President's Lodging*.'

Hamlet, Revenge!

A story in four parts

1 Prologue

The actors are come hither my Lord...
We'll hear a play tomorrow.

When you spend a summer holiday in the Horton country you must not fail to make the ascent of Horton Hill. It is an easy climb and there is a wonderful view. The hill is at once a citadel and an outpost, dominating to the north the subtle rhythms of English downland into which it merges, and to the south a lowland country bounded in the distance by a silver ribbon of sea. The little market-town of King's Horton, five miles away, is concealed in a fold of the downs; concealed too, save for a wisp of blue-grey smoke, is the near-by hamlet of Scamnum Ducis. And almost directly below, beyond a mellow pomp of lawn and garden and deer-park, stands all the arrogantly declared yet finally discreet magnificence of Scamnum Court. Perhaps it is not the very stateliest of the stately homes of England. But it is a big place: two counties away it has a sort of little brother in Blenheim Palace.

And yet from the vantage-point of Horton Hill Scamnum looks strangely like a toy. The austere regularity of its façades, the improbable green of its surrounding turf, the perfection of its formal gardens bounded by the famous cliff-like hedges imitated from Schönbrunn – these things give some touch at once of fantasy and of restraint to what might easily have been a heavy and extravagant gesture after all. Here, Scamnum seems to say, is indeed the pride of great riches, but here, too, is the chastening severity of a classically-minded age. Mr Addison, had he lived a few years longer, would have approved the rising pile; Mr Pope, though he went away to scoff in twenty annihilating couplets, came secretly to admire; and Dr Johnson, when he took tea with the third duke, put on his finest waistcoat. For what is this ordered immensity, this dry regularity of pilaster and parterre, but an assertion in material terms of a prime moral truth of the eighteenth century: that the grandeur of life consists in wealth subdued by decorum?

Here, shortly, is the story of Scamnum and its owners.

Thirty years before the birth of Shakespeare, Roger Crippen, living hard by the sign of the Falcon in Cheapside, had been one of Thomas Cromwell's crew. A sharp man, uncommonly gifted in detecting a dubious ledger – or in concocting one when need drove – he had risen as the religious houses fell. His sons inherited his abilities; his grandsons grew up hard and sober in the tradition of finance. When Elizabeth ascended the throne Crippens already controlled houses in

Paris and Amsterdam; when James travelled south Crippens stood as a power in the kingdom he had inherited.

The Civil Wars came and the family declared for the King. At Horton Manor thousands of pounds' worth of plate was melted down; and Humphrey Crippen, the third Baron Horton, was with Rupert when he broke the Roundhead horse at Naseby. But bankers must not be enthusiastic: Crippens too controlled tens of thousands of pounds that were flowing from Holland across the narrow seas to the city and the Parliament men – and during all the monetary embarrassments of the Protectorate they lost no penny. Meanwhile – themselves in ostentatious exile – they patiently financed the exiled court and at the Restoration the family of Crispin came home to a dukedom. Since the first grant of a gentleman's arms to Roger Crippen there had passed just a hundred and thirty years.

Crispin remained a banker's name. And on banking, in the fullness of time, Scamnum Court was raised. Far more fed the Horton magnificence than the broad acres of pasture land to the north, the estate added to estate of rich arable to the south. 'You can't', the present Duke would ambiguously remark, 'keep a yacht on land' – and the yacht, the great town house in Piccadilly, the Kincrae estate in Morayshire, the villa at Rapallo, Scamnum itself with its monstrous establishment ('Run Scamnum with a gaggle of housemaids? Come, come!' the Duke had exclaimed when he shut it down during the war) – these were but slight charges on the resources controlled by the descendants of Roger. For Crispin is behind the volcanic productivity of the Ruhr; Crispin drives railways through South America; in Australia one can ride across the Crispin sheep-station for days. If a picture is sold in Paris or a pelt in Siberia Crispin takes his toll; if you buy a bus or a theatre ticket in London, Crispin – somehow, somewhere – gets his share.

And here, from the windy brow of Horton Hill, the wayfarer can look down on the crown of it all, his reflections dictated by his own philosophical or political or imaginative bias. There lies Scamnum, a treasure-house unguarded save by the marble gods and goddesses that stand patiently along its broad terraces, or crouch, narcissus-like, beside its ornamental waters – Scamnum unguarded and unspoiled, a symbol of order, security, and the rule of law over this sleeping country-side.

The great wing to the east is the picture-gallery: there hang the famous Horton Titian; Vermeer's *Aquarium*, for which the last Duke paid a fortune in New York; the thundery little Rembrandt landscape which the present Duchess's father, during his Dublin days, had got for ten shillings in a shabby bookshop by the Liffey – and for which, ten years later, he sent a flabbergasted bookseller a thousand pounds. And that answering wing to the west is the Orangery. Sometimes, of a summer night, they will hold a dance or a ball there – the long line of lofty windows flung open upon the dark. And a curious labourer and his lass, seeing the procession of cars sweep into the park, will climb the hill and stretch themselves in the clover to gaze down upon a world as remote as that other world of Vermeer's picture – tiny figures, jewelled and magical, floating about the terraces in a medium of their own. Now and then, as the wind veers, wisps of music will float up the hill. It is strange music sometimes, and then the spell is unbroken, the magic unflowed. But sometimes it is a lilt familiar from gramophone or wireless – and man and girl are suddenly self-conscious and uneasy. And Scamnum in general has long understood the necessity of keeping its own hypnotic other-world inviolate. Many a Duke of Horton has unbent at a farmers' dinner, many a Duchess has gone laughing and chattering round Scamnum Ducis. But all have known that essentially they must contrive to be seen as from a long way off, that they have their tenure in remaining – remote, jewelled, and magical – a focus for the fantasy-life of thousands. We are all Duke or Duchess of Horton – this is the paradox – as long as the music remains sufficiently strange.

From Horton summit it is possible to see something of Scamnum's great main court and of its one architectural eccentricity. For here some nineteenth-century duke, a belated follower of the romantic revival, has grotesquely pitched a sizeable monument of academic Gothic in the form of a raftered hall. As it stands it is something of a disreputable secret: the hill-top apart, you are aware of it only from certain inner windows of the house, and aware of it probably but to regret the famous fountain which it has obliterated. In the family it is known sometimes as Peter's Folly, and more regularly – with that subdued irony which Crispins have assimilated with the aristocratic tradition – as the Banqueting Hall. It is a trifle damp, a trifle musty, and there is painful stained-glass. No use has ever been found for it. Or rather none had been found until the Duchess had her idea, the idea which was unexpectedly to draw the attention of all England upon Scamnum and to bring streams of chars-à-bancs with eager sightseers to the foot of Horton Hill.

Even now, strange events are preparing. But this flawless afternoon in June knows nothing of them yet: from the dovecot beyond the home orchard floats the drowsiest of all English sounds: the jackdaws wheel to the same lazy tempo above the elm walk; a bell in the distant stables chimes four; Scamnum slumbers. On the hill no tourist, field-glass in hand, disturbs the gently nibbling sheep or speculates on such activity as Scamnum reveals. There is no one to identify as the Duke the little knicker-bockered figure who has paused to speak to a gardener by the lily-pond; no one to recognize in the immaculately breeched and booted youth sauntering up from the stables Noel Yvon Meryon Gylby, a scion of the house; no one to guess that the tall figure strolling down the drive is his old tutor Giles Gott, the eminent Elizabethan scholar, or that the beautiful girl, looking thoughtfully after him from the terrace, is the Lady Elizabeth Crispin. Nobody knows that the restless man with the black box is not a photographer from the *Queen* but an American philologist. And nobody knows that the Rolls Royce approaching the south lodge contains the Lord High Chancellor of England, come down to play a prank with his old friend Anne Dillon, the present Duchess of Horton.

Scamnum, doubtless, is in the minds of many people at this moment. In Liverpool, serious young men are studying its ground-plan; in Berlin, a famous *Kunsthistoriker* is lecturing on its pictures; its 'life', brightly written up for an evening paper, is selling in the streets of Bradford and Morley and Leeds. Scamnum is always 'Interest': presently it is to be 'News'.

The Rolls Royce swings under the odd little bridge joining the twin lodges and purrs up the drive.

'And her Grace,' said Macdonald magnanimously, 'can hae as muckle o' roses for the Banqueting Ha' as she cares to demaun'.'

'Good,' said the Duke, concealing the consciousness of a victory un-expectedly won. 'And now, let me see' – he consulted a scribbled envelope – 'ah yes, sweet-peas. Enough sweet-peas to fill all the Ming bowls in the big drawing-room.'

'The *big* drawing-room!' Macdonald was aghast.

'The big drawing-room, Macdonald. Big party this, you know. Quite an event.'

'I'll see tae't,' said Macdonald dourly.

'And, um, just one other thing. Dinner is in the long gallery –'

'The *lang* gallery!'

'Come, come, Macdonald – a big dinner you know. Quite out of the ordinary. About a hundred and twenty people.'

Macdonald reflected. 'I'm thinking, wi' great respect, it'll be mair like the saloon o' a liner than a nobleman's daenner in ony guid contemporary taste I've heard tell o'.'

Macdonald was one of the curiosities of Scamnum. 'Have you met our pragmatical Scot?' the Duchess would ask gaily – and the favoured visitor would be taken out and cautiously insinuated into the head-gardener's presence and conversation. Nevertheless, the Duke felt, Macdonald could be *very* trying.

'Be that as it may,' said the Duke, unconsciously supporting himself on what had been the pivotal phrase of his celebrated speech in the House of Lords in 1908 – 'be that as it may, Macdonald, the fact is – carnations.'

'May it please your Grace,' said Macdonald ominously, 'I had a thocht it might be the carnations.'

'Carnations. The long gallery is to have a single long table, and they've raked up thirty silver vases from the strong-room –'

'*Thirty*,' said Macdonald, as if scoring heavily.

'To be filled with the red carnations –'

'Horton,' said Macdonald firmly, 'it canna be!'

When Macdonald resorted to this feudal and awful address – eminently proper, no doubt, in his own country – affairs were known to be critical. And the Duke had been expecting this crisis all afternoon.

'It canna be,' continued Macdonald with a heavy reasonableness. 'Ye maun consider that if ye hae a hunnert and twenty folk tae daenner in your lang gallery, I'm like tae hae a hunnert and twenty folk walking my green-hooses thereaufter. And ye maun consider that the demaun's already excessive: a' but a' the public apartments and forty bedrooms – let alone what the upper servants get frae my laddies when my back's turned! And it's my opeenion,' continued Macdonald, suddenly advancing from reasonableness to an extreme position, 'that flu'ers hae no place in the hoose at a'. Unner the sky and unner glause, wi' their ain guid roots below them, is the richt place for flu'ers.'

'Come, come, my dear Macdonald –'

'I'm no saying there's no way oot o' the difficulty. Maybe your Grace is no acquaintet wi' Mistress Hunter's *Wild Flu'ers o' Shakespeare?*'

'I don't know –'

'No more ye need. It's no a work o' ony scholarly pretension. But it's in the library and it might persuade her Grace –'

'Come, come, Macdonald!'

'– that Shakespeare's wild flu'ers doon that lang table would be mair appropriate than my guid carnations. Do you see to that, your Grace, and I'll set the lassies at the sooth lodge to get a' that's wanted fraw the woods... In thirty sil'er bowls too' – added Macdonald enthusiastically – 'it'll be a real pretty sight!'

The evasiveness of the Duke's response revealed him as judiciously giving ground. ''Pon my soul, Macdonald, I didn't know you were a student of Shakespeare.'

'Shakespeare, your Grace, was well instructed in the theory o' gardening, and it becomes a guid gardener to be well instructed in Shakespeare. In this play that's forrard the noo, there's eleven images from gardening alone.'

'Eleven – dear me!'

'Aye, eleven. Weeds twa, violet, rose, canker twa, thorns, inoculate old stock, shake fruit frae tree, palm-tree, and *cut off in bloom* – the thing ya shouldna dae. It's a' in Professor Spurgeon's new book.'

'Ah yes,' said the Duke incautiously, 'Spurgeon – clever fellow.'

'She's a very talented leddy,' said Macdonald.

Powerful, precise, world-wide, the Crispin machine ground on. And did Macdonald, bringing this interview to a triumphant close, ponder in his metaphysical Scottish brain some deeper irony – conscious, amid all this familiar ducal ineffectiveness, of the lurking dominance of that steel-hard Crispin eye?

Macdonald trudged down the drive to the south lodge.

The Rolls stopped in its tracks. Lord Auldearn stood up behind his impassive chauffeur and made a dramatic gesture as Giles Gott advanced.

'Barkloughly Castle call they this at hand?'

Gott shook hands – with the bow one gives to a slight acquaintance who keeps the King's conscience in his pocket. Then he laughed.

'There stands the castle, by yon tuft of trees.'

'Mann'd with three hundred men, as I have heard?'

'Presently to be manned with about three hundred guests, as far as I can gather. In the Duchess's hands the thing grows.'

'Get in,' said the Lord Chancellor with unconscious authority. And as the Rolls glided forward he sighed. 'I was afraid it would turn into that sort of thing. Anne must always pick the out-size canvas. A mistake her father never made.'

'Didn't she run old Dillon?'

'I think she did – as a clever woman can run a genius. She kept him to the portraits, picked the right moment for capitulating to the Academy, and so on.' Lord Auldearn paused. 'I know my part, I think. What's yours?'

'I'm producing. And I've built a sort of Elizabethan stage.'

'Good Lord! Where?'

'In the Banqueting Hall.'

'Mouldy, gouty hole. So it's all very serious – striking experiment in the staging of Shakespeare – crowds of your professional brethren watching, eh?'

'There is a bevy of them coming down on the night. And an American about the place already, I believe. The Duchess is never wholly serious – but she's working tremendously hard.'

'Anne always did. Worked underground for weeks to contrive a minute's perfect effect – a minute's perfect absurdity, it might be. That's how she got here. What's she doing – the dresses?'

'Not a bit of it. She's been reading up the texts. Got out the Horton Second Quarto and borrowed somebody's First Folio. I'm terrified she'll start scribbling enthusiastically in the margins. And she's been studying the acting tradition as well. She's impressed by the accounts of Garrick, particularly his business when he first sees the Ghost. She's almost ready to coach Melville Clay in it.'

'Coach Clay!' Lord Auldearn chuckled. 'Do him good. Make a noisy success of a part in London and New York – and then be coached in it by a woman for private theatricals. What's he doing it for?'

The question, abruptly pitched, seemed to make Gott reflect. 'Glamour of Scamnum,' he suggested at length.

'Humph!' said the Lord Chancellor – and a moment later added: 'And Elizabeth – how does she like it? Rather a thrill playing opposite Clay?'

'No doubt,' said Gott.

For a moment there was silence as the car sped up the drive. Macdonald, stumping past, touched his hat respectfully.

'And Teddy?' Lord Auldearn continued his inquisition. 'What does Teddy think of the size the thing's apparently grown to?'

Gott looked dubious. 'I can't quite make out what the Duke thinks – on that or anything. I'm a distant Dillon, you know, and the Duchess strikes me as essentially readable. But the Duke puzzles me. I shouldn't like to have to put him in a novel – or not in the foreground. He's a nice conventional effect while in the middle-distance, but disturbing on scrutiny.'

Lord Auldearn paid these remarks the tribute of some moments' silence. Then he pitched another question: '*Do* you write novels?'

Confound you, thought Gott, for the smartest lawyer in England – and replied with polite finality: 'Pseudonymously.'

But the Lord Chancellor, vaguely curious, was not to be put off. 'Under what name?' he said.

Gott told him.

'Bless my soul – mystery stories! Well, I suppose it goes along with your ferreting sort of work – just as it might with mine. And what are you writing now? Going to make a story out of the Scamnum theatricals?'

'Hardly a mystery story, I should think,' replied Gott. Lord Auldearn, he reflected, was not impertinent – merely old and easy. But Gott was shy of any mention of this hobby of his. And it was perhaps with some obscure motive of diversion that his hand at this moment went out to a crumpled ball of paper which he had discerned in a corner of the car.

'What's that?' asked Lord Auldearn.

Gott smoothed out the paper – to stare unbelievingly at the three lines of typescript on an otherwise blank quarto page. 'More Shakespeare,' he said, 'like our greetings a few minutes ago. But this isn't *Richard II*; it's *Macbeth*.'

Lord Auldearn was again vaguely curious. 'Read it out,' he said. And Gott read:

> 'The raven himself is hoarser
> That croaks the fatal entrance of Duncan
> Under my battlements.'

The Rolls had stopped – Scamnum towering above it. 'Curious,' said Lord Auldearn.

It was half-past seven. Noel Gylby sat on the west terrace, dividing his attention between a cocktail, *Handley Cross*, and his former tutor, who had sat down with a brief 'Hullo, Noel,' to stare absently and a shade disapprovingly at the beginnings of a garish sunset.

'There's going to be a decent party at Kincrae for the Twelfth,' said Mr Gylby presently. 'Last August Aunt Anne took the bit between her teeth and the moors were like an O.T.C. field-day. But Uncle Teddy's put his foot down this time.'

'Has he,' said Gott.

'He's asking you,' said Noel, turning *Handley Cross* sideways to look at an illustration. 'Going?'

Gott shook his head. 'I think I may be in Heidelberg,' he said austerely.

'Humph.' Noel had been an impressed observer of the Lord Chancellor's mannerisms during tea. And after a silence he added, 'I'm getting a new 12-bore.'

In the technical language of his generation Noel was an 'aesthete'. His normal conversation was much of his contemporaries the youngest poets. He ran a magazine for them and wrote editorials sagely discussing André Breton and Marianne Moore; it was rumoured that he had been to a tea-party with Mr Ezra Pound. But in the atmosphere of Scamnum some atavistic process asserted itself; he took on the colour of the place – or what a lively imagination prompted him to feel the colour should be. He read Surtees and Beckford; he made notes on Colonel Farquharson on the Horse. He discoursed on stable-management with the head groom; he spent hours confabulating with the one-eyed man in the gun-room.

'A half-choke, I think,' said Noel – and the subject failing to excite he added after a moment: 'Why didn't you take a cocktail?'

'Habit,' replied Gott. 'The old gentlemen at St Anthony's don't drink cocktails before dinner, and I've got the habit.' He smiled ironically at his former pupil. 'I'm at the age when habit gets its hold, Noel.'

Noel looked at him seriously. 'I suppose you *are* getting on,' he said. 'What are you?'

'Thirty-four.'

'I say!' exclaimed Noel. 'You'll soon be forty.'

'Quite soon,' responded Gott coldly.

'You know,' said Noel, 'I think you should –'

He was interrupted by the appearance of a dinner-jacketed figure at the end of the terrace. 'Here's your pal Bunney. I'll leave the *savants* together. Little chat about Shakespeare's semi-colons may do you good.'

'My pal *who*?'

'Bunney. Dr Bunney of Oswego, U.S.A. Dying to meet a real live Fellow of the British Academy. I suppose' – Noel added innocently – 'it's something to make that even at thirty-four? Well, cheery-bye, papa Gott.' And Mr Gylby strolled off.

Gott eyed the advancing figure of Dr Bunney with suspicion. The man was carrying a largish black box which he set down on a table as he advanced to shake hands.

'Dr Gott? Pleased to meet you. My name's Bunney – Bunney of Oswego. We are fellow-workers in a great field. *Floreat scientia.*'

'How do you do. Quite so,' said Gott – and assumed that charming, charmed, and tentatively understanding expression which is the Englishman's defence on such occasions. 'You have come down for the play?'

'For the phonology of the play,' corrected Dr Bunney. He turned and flicked a switch on the black box. 'Say "bunchy cushiony bush",' said Dr Bunney placidly.

'I beg your pardon?'

'No. "Bunchy cushiony bush".'

'Oh! Bunchy cushiony bush.'

'And now. "The unimaginable touch of time".'

'The unimaginable touch of time,' said Gott, with the suppressed indignation of a good Wordsworthian forced to blaspheme.

'Thank you.' Bunney turned and flicked another switch. Instantly the black box broke into speech. '*Say bunchy cushiony bush I beg your pardon no bunchy cushiony bush oh bunchy cushiony bush and now the unimaginable touch of time the unimaginable touch of time thank you,*' said the black box grotesquely.

Bunney beamed. 'The Bunney high-fidelity dictaphone. Later, of course' – he added explanatorily – 'it is all graphed.'

'Graphed – of course.'

'Graphed and analysed. Dr Gott, my thanks for one more instance of that friendly cooperation without which learning cannot increase. *Hee paideia kai tees sophias kai tees aretees meeteer.* There are drinks?'

'Sherry and cocktails are in the library.' And as Dr Bunney disappeared Gott chanted a little Greek of his own.

'*Brek-ek-ek-ex! Ko-ax! Ko-ax!*' said Gott. '*Brek-ek-ek-ex! Ko-ax!*'

'Giles, have you laid an egg – or what?' The Lady Elizabeth Crispin had emerged on the terrace, bearing a luridly-tinged cherry speared on a cocktail-stick.

'I was only telling a rabbit what the frogs thought of him,' said Gott obscurely – and began laboriously an unhappy academic explanation. 'Aristophanes –'

'Aristophanes! Isn't Shakespeare quite enough at present?'

'I think he is. Shakespeare and Bunney between them.'

'It was Bunney, was it? Has he black-boxed you?'

'Yes. Bunchy cushiony Bunney. How did he get here?'

'Mother picked him up at a party. He black-boxed her and she was thrilled. He's going to black-box the whole play and lecture on the vowels and consonants and phonemes and things when he gets home. Only mother hopes he's really something sinister.'

'Sinister?'

'The Spy in Black or something. Black-boxing secrets of state. Have my cherry, Giles.'

Gott munched the cherry. The Lady Elizabeth perched on the broad stone balustrade. 'Another hideous sunset,' she said.

'Isn't it!' exclaimed Gott, electrified at this agreement. But Elizabeth had returned to the subject of the American.

'I suppose Bunney's quoted Greek and Latin and the Advancement of Learning at you?'

'Yes.'

'And you've been eyeing him with the polite wonder of the St Anthony's man?'

'Yes – I mean, certainly not.'

'Dear Giles, this must be an awful bore for you – beaning Shakespeare to make a barbarian holiday. You're very nice about it all.'

'It's not beaning. Everybody's being remarkably serious. And I want to see Melville Clay on something like an Elizabethan stage. And I particularly want to see you.'

Elizabeth wriggled gracefully into a position in which she could inspect her golden slippers. 'I wish about three hundred other people weren't going to. How morbidly Edwardian-Clever Mother is! Don't you think?'

'Age cannot wither her,' said Gott.

'Yes, I know. She's marvellous. But who but an Edwardian-Clever would think of celebrating a daughter's twenty-first by dressing her in white satin to be talked bawdy to by a matinée-idol and drowned and buried to make a big county and brainy Do?'

This breathless speech had evidently been simmering. Gott looked surprised. 'You don't really object, do you, Elizabeth?'

Elizabeth swung off the balustrade. 'Not a bit. I think I love it. Clay's beautiful.'

'And extraordinarily nice.'

'Yes,' said Elizabeth. 'And – Giles – I do hope I'll speak it all so that you approve!'

'Ironical wench.' Gott was out of his chair. 'Round the lily-pond before dinner, Elizabeth!' And they ran down the broad steps together.

Returning, they met Noel waving a letter.

'I say – Giles, Elizabeth! The Black Hand!'

Elizabeth stared. 'Do you mean the black box, child?'

'Not a bit of it. The Black Hand. Something in Uncle Gott's own lurid line. Preparing to strike – and all that.'

Gott understood. 'You've had a scrap of typescript?'

Noel withdrew a quarto sheet of paper from the envelope and handed it to Elizabeth. All three stared at it.

> And in their ears tell them my dreadful name,
> Revenge, which makes the foul offender quake.

'From *Titus Andronicus*,' said Gott.

'Rubbishing sort of joke,' said Noel.

Far away, St James's Park was closing. The melancholy call, as of the archangel crying banishment from Eden, floated faintly through the open window. The Parliamentary Private Secretary, glancing obliquely out across the parade, could catch a glimpse of his old berth. He and Sir James were well past that stile together...but this was a nervous elevation. His fingers drummed on the window-sill.

'Here in a few minutes now,' said the Permanent Secretary unemotionally.

'In a Bag?'

'Hilfers is bringing it back...Croydon.'

'Oh.' The Parliamentary Secretary was frankly raw, frankly impressed. There was silence, broken at last by footsteps in the long corridor. An elderly resident clerk came in.

'Captain Hilfers here, sir.'

'We'll go over to the deciphering,' said the Permanent Secretary briskly to the Parliamentary Secretary. He picked up a telephone. 'And have the great men over from their dinner.'

At this the Parliamentary Secretary grew suddenly cheerful. 'Of course they must come over straight away,' he agreed importantly.

The Prime Minister summed up the deliberations of an hour.

'Get Auldearn,' said the Prime Minister.

'Auldearn's at Scamnum,' said the Parliamentary Secretary.

'Get What's-his-name,' said the Prime Minister.

'Get Captain Hilfers,' elucidated the Permanent Secretary into a telephone.

The near-midsummer dusk is deepening on Horton Hill. The sheep are shadowy on its slopes; to the north the softly-rolling downland is sharpening into silhouette; and below, Scamnum is grown mysterious. Its hundred points of light are a great city from the air. Or its vague pale bulk is the sprawl of all Europe as viewed from an unearthly height at the opening of *The Dynasts*. And here, as there, are spirits. The spirits sinister and ironic look down on Scamnum Court these nights.

2

There had been a time when Anne Dillon's large canvases were notorious. Lionel Dillon, moving dubiously amid the gay, indistinguished, and overflowing companies which his daughter gathered in their rambling Hampstead house, had been inclined to charge her with a merely quantitative mind. Dillon himself was austerely qualitative in those days. He would stand grim and baffled before a single canvas for a year on end, and count every moment not so spent lost – fit only for drink and violence, to be followed by confession, Mass, and renewed concentration afterwards. He was of the time before the nineties. 'One should do nothing to make oneself conspicuous,' was the motto of his quiet spells; and he painted in a dress indistinguishable from that of his father, the Dublin solicitor.

Anne, taking charge of the widower in her later teens, had had to change all that. It was in itself, she knew, not a good picture to present to the declining century; and it was otherwise dangerous. Brandy once a month was the fatal Cleopatra of that generation; she ruled it out and established instead more intimate and respectable relations with claret. 'Dillon,' she would say – for she exploited all the minutiae of the cult of genius – 'Dillon was born a glass too low'; and the daily glass, working out in practice at three-quarters of a bottle, was provided. There was nothing merely quantitative about the claret; it was the best one could readily buy in London, and it came into the cellars regularly twice a year even if the rent or Anne's dressmaker had to wait. And it worked. The awkward thought disappeared from the canvas to be replaced by the fluent handwriting that was acclaimed miraculous in London, in Glasgow, in Paris. And although Lionel Dillon knew the early studies as the things for which men would one day bid high he did not protest. It was not altogether Anne's doing: he had felt the twitch of his tether, knew both the level at which he had shot his bolt and the level at which he had a future. And the orthodoxy that had come upon him like a revelation in Toledo was still heterodox enough in England – heterodox enough for the picture Anne was composing.

The period of the big parties had been the critical time. Making scores of undistinguished Bohemian people interesting to each other, imbuing them with poise, confidence, and urbanity for a night, had been stiff labour; and even on unauthentic champagne-cup and mixed biscuits it had come expensive. But again it worked. A mere law of averages mingled in those promiscuous gatherings certain of the emerging Great. Selection came later.

Perhaps the turning-point had been the famous Academy Banquet. It might have gone like a damp squib, been written a tasteless fiasco: the paper probabilities were strongly that way. But Anne had brought it off. There had been hard work behind the perfection with which the dozen chosen young men had impersonated the venerable President of an august English institution – twelve snowy beards, twelve courtly stoops. And Anne kept her head. She vetoed out of hand the exuberant suggestion that the real President should be lured unawares to the party; she firmly locked up in a lavatory a young actress who came brilliantly disguised as the President's undistinguished wife. Dillon and his bosom friend Max Cope, each in his own bravura manner, dashed off for the occasion a couple of travesties of the most discussed 'pictures of the year'. And a powerful London dealer, catching with the prescience of his kind a something in the air, bought these broad jokes on the spot at prices far exceeding what was being asked for the originals at Burlington House. The whole affair was kept beautifully dark – something half London had in confidence – and it marked alike the height and end of the Hampstead period. The play-acting period, Dillon called it.

The nineties had been quiet. There was Wilde's too-beautiful white dining-room; later there was Whistler, and Lionel Dillon's emergence, under that dazzling stimulus, as a dinner-table wit. The big portrait-commissions came in; the assault on the fashionable world was accomplished classically, as an assault by the fashionable world. There followed frequentation of the great London houses: Dillon, grown not unlike Lord Tennyson and in a resplendent Order secured at the expense of two goodish pictures sent to Central Europe, moving blandly through parties at which there was always royalty at the other end of the room. Finally there came the *concordat* with the Academy and, about the same time, Anne's engagement to the Marquis of Kincrae, the Duke of Horton's heir.

All this is not to say that Anne Dillon was a careerist. Always she had been a creature fundamentally detached; a priestess, a famous wit had laid it down, of the Comic Spirit, dynamic with hidden mockeries. Her choice, she would say, had been most horridly limited; and squir-archy, any professional caste, any continental nobility would have bundled her out at once; only a great Whig house would have accepted her. And if she had grown into Scamnum with the years she yet kept something of her fallen days about her. Alone in the little Gibbons-style drawing-room, she would stand by the piano measuring herself against the girl who stood by the piano in Whistler's portrait on the wall. The identical poise was there; for what time had softened and subdued in the flesh that delicate and sombre artistry had softened and subdued on canvas long ago.

And still for the Duchess life must be delicately odd always, with phases of bolder comedy interspersed. It was the Dillon brandy-drinking coming out perhaps, this periodic indulgence in a larger scale. And the present frolic was an instance, a prank elaborated to a point at which even the Scamnum world would blink. Just such a big affair she would have organized in Hampstead times, her father now ridiculing and now joining in. But Lionel Dillon was dead these ten years, and of his set nobody remained but Lord Auldearn – Lord Auldearn and Max Cope, a crazy old man with a snowy beard and a courtly stoop, come down to bear this part by painting perhaps his last picture for the Academy: 'The Tragedy of Hamlet played at Scamnum Court'.

The play was only three days off. Members of the house-party had been arriving intermittently throughout the afternoon and the Duchess was still busy with introductions in the last minutes before dinner.

'Diana, this is Charles Piper, who is going to excite you tremendously. Charles, Proust put a cousin of Miss Sandys's in *Sodome et Gomorrhe* – or was it refused to put him in? Diana will tell you all about it. Diana, find out about Mr Piper's new book for me. Look at poor Dr Bunney!' Bunney, having apparently decided with a struggle that the black box would be an impropriety at this ceremonial hour, was standing before the fireplace without a motive in life. 'Dr Bunney, come and have introduced to you Timothy Tucker – the strikingly handsome man in the corner. He published Piper's book you know. Mr Tucker, let me introduce you to Dr Bunney: he too is passionately interested in phonetics.' The Duchess gave a commanding nod at the ugly publisher, who instantly entered on a subject about which he knew nothing at all; such gymnastics were demanded as a matter of course at Scamnum parties. 'And what,' asked Tucker gravely, 'do you think of this younger German school?' The question was ninety-nine per cent safe. Bunney was enchanted. Conversation went smoothly and efficiently on.

Melville Clay, the veritable handsome man in the room, was introduced formally and without comment to Lord Auldearn. Gott stood
by a window receiving squeaky but racy reminiscences of Beardsley
from Max Cope. Gervase Crispin, the Duke's elderly cousin, was coping
with a strange American lady and her disconcertingly identical twin
daughters. Elizabeth had been sent to insinuate to the little black man
– another of her mother's recent finds – the extent to which he might
properly discuss politics with the Lord Chancellor. Noel was conversing
with Gervase's Russian friend, Anna Merkalova, in the polished French
proper to a future member of the Diplomatic – and casting most un-
diplomatically venomous glances at Mr Piper, earnestly discoursing with
Miss Sandys, meanwhile. The Duke, cruising amiably round, estimated
the probable length of the dinner-table. He detested a meal at which
his wife was not within hail and general talk possible. It was a small
party, praise God, so far; but there would be another bevy by the
late train. And meanwhile the widow with the twin fillies, he supposed,
was his pigeon. He hurried round to the Duchess to refresh his memory
on this lady's name. Mrs Terborg. And just in time.

The minute hand of the Dutch bracket-clock dropped to the horizontal of eight-fifteen. Bagot, Scamnum's venerable butler, appeared
through a vista of opening doors. The Duke carried off Mrs Terborg
without more ado. Noel, releasing himself from Anna Merkalova an
improper moment before that lady was handed over to Bunney, made
across the room. He was too late. Mr Piper and Miss Sandys, in unbroken
talk, had been waved forward by their hostess. Timothy Tucker and
Melville Clay had a Terborg twin apiece. Elizabeth held on to the
black man, having to superintend – as Noel, gloomily returning,
explained to Gott – the special oriental nosebag. Gott and Noel, with
Gervase Crispin and Max Cope, went forward together as momentarily
superfluous bachelor familiars of the house. The Duchess followed with
Lord Auldearn. 'Mixed biscuits, Ian,' she said, 'and champagne with
an "h" in the Reims!'

The Lord Chancellor chuckled. 'And a barrel of apples in the studio
for those in the know.' To the Duchess of Horton, Lord Auldearn
admitted what a rocky manner still hid from the world: that he was
a man mellowed and appeased by success, slipping into that final mood
– reminiscent, yet remote, tolerant yet comprehensively critical – in
which one who has made his mark in the world prepares to take leave

of it. And because there existed between him and Anne Dillon a long-standing and delicately handled sentimental relationship he would speak his thoughts to her as to no one else. 'Not much more apple-picking for me now,' he said, giving the apples a characteristic twist into some remote literary allusion. 'And not much more Shakespeare either. Just a year, I think, with Horace and Chaucer – and then a hunt through Hades for a few affable and familiar ghosts.'

'We don't think of you as a ghost here, Ian. We've cast you, you see, as a very lively, wise old man.'

Lord Auldearn shook his head. 'A slippered pantaloon and a figure of fun. And Polonius is a ghost before the play's ended.'

The Duchess pressed his arm. 'So are we all,' she replied; 'except young Charles Piper, who must live to write a great many more conscientious novels.' Piper was to be Horatio.

'Did you know Gott writes novels?'

'Yes. But he's ashamed of them because they're *not* conscientious. He thinks they're time stolen from all this business of old texts. I've been looking at that sort of thing for the play and it seems to me rather immoral labour. I have a feeling that such good wits should be in the Cabinet.'

'My dear Anne, how seriously you've come to regard the burden of rule! What of seducing me from affairs of state for a week? But they do call in Gott's sort, you know – for an emergency. It's an odd thing, but there's nobody like your professional seeker-out of truth for inventing a four-square, coherent system of lies. When propaganda is needed the don is the master of it.'

'Touching lies,' said the Duchess, 'have you heard Gervase's explanations of his Russian friend there?' And she turned to arrange her table.

Gott, unconscious of his potential role as a well of deceit in times of national emergency, was looking round the gathering with a producer's eye. More and more he was realizing that the Tragedy of Hamlet played at Scamnum Court had assumed alarming proportions. It had begun as a family frolic. And now, although it would not be publicly reported, the dramatic critics were coming down as if to an important festival. Professors were coming to shake learned respectable bald heads over a fellow-scholar's conception of an Elizabethan stage. Aged royalty was coming to be politely bewildered. Most alarming of all, 'everybody' was coming – for the purpose, no doubt, of being where 'everybody' was. And even if it was a select and serious everybody – a known set before whom a Lord Chancellor might mime without misgiving – it was still a crowd, and its reactions were unpredictable.

The company that was to present *Hamlet* had one initial advantage. It was thorough. Its members possessed that tradition of thoroughness that goes along with Scamnum traditions of leisure and responsibility. The habit that would prevent the airy Noel from touching a cricket bat or a tennis racket without making a resolute onslaught on county form, the habit that would send Elizabeth forward from Somerville next year miraculously perfected in sundry dreary Old and Middle English texts, the habit that brought Gervase Crispin to his feet in the House of Commons to discuss battalions of figures with his eye innocently fixed on the roof – this would make *Hamlet* as good as efficiency could make it. But Gott was dubious all the same. Acting is such a difficult business that only one thing will make it pass – economic necessity. Act-or-out-you-go is the only really effective producer.

'Don't you think acting is the most unnatural thing in the world?' It was the voice of one of the indistinguishable Misses Terborg – Miss Terborg One – on Gott's right.

'I was just thinking so' – Gott noted to himself the absence of that sense of miraculous coincidence that had accompanied Elizabeth's observation on sunsets earlier in the evening. 'But some people would say that we most of us act uninterruptedly.'

'Ah, but that's different, isn't it? We are always impersonating our own idealized image of ourselves – our *persona*, is it called? – in order to shine in our own eyes or in other people's. Or we're shamming something quite false in order to get something that our real self wants. But this business of becoming someone else and taking on his image and *persona* and desires – pure falsification, in fact – surely that is unnatural?'

Gott on the one side and Melville Clay on the other regarded Miss Terborg One with some curiosity. Gott with his tutor's instinct was placing this young lady's mind provisionally among the good Two-ones; Clay was attracted by discussion of the theory of acting. He broke in eagerly:

'It is the most unnatural thing in the world. Which is why it's still thought rather disreputable – and why it's so absorbingly interesting.

One never *becomes* someone else. There's no someone else to become; it's only a bad and confusing metaphor. They talk about how the great actor lives his part and so on; but isn't that just woolly thinking too? Acting's *acting* – every exquisite moment when one's on form. And that's why it's difficult for amateurs; because it's all technique.'

'Well,' said Gott, '*Hamlet* is fortunately an almost indestructible play. And with the thing chiefly on your shoulders we'll scrape home with it.'

'Oh, more than that! This show's already been a revelation to me of how rapidly clever people can acquire a specific skill. Lady Elizabeth's good. And the Duke's marvellous. They've both found the vital truth. If acting is a hundred per cent technique, technique is about seventy-five per cent timing.' And Clay turned to enlarge on timing to the Duchess on his right.

Yes, in the rehearsals so far held, Elizabeth had been good – and the Duke marvellous. It was difficult to get the master of Scamnum on the stage; at the appointed hour he would be engaged in instructing his bailiff, being instructed by his agent, or playing austere croquet with the vicar's wife on the farther cedar lawn. His attitude to the whole affair was one of vague dubiety. But, once planted on Gott's great platform stage in the Banqueting Hall, his part fell upon him like a mantle. Whether or not it were a matter of technique, Shakespeare's cunning usurper Claudius stood completely realized amid his court.

'Anne,' the Duke was saying down the table, 'about those flowers for the Long Gallery on Monday. What about having Shakespeare's wild-flowers? I was looking at a book about them in the library, and at this time of year we could get almost the whole lot.'

'Daisies pied,' interposed Bunney firmly, 'and violets blue, and lady-smocks all silver-white.' He smiled round the table as one who has contributed neatly to the general elegance of the proceedings. Everyone looked kindly on Bunney except the Terborgs, who looked cold. Nowhere more than in the United States, Gott reflected, are there chasms.

'Let's go out and gather them,' said Diana Sandys.

'They would have to be gathered on Monday,' objected the Duchess, 'when we should be much too busy. But it's a nice idea.'

The Duke considered. 'We might persuade Macdonald to send some of his lads into the woods for them – or perhaps the children from the lodges. I'll speak to him.' And, nodding over the possibility, he proceeded to give Mrs Terborg particulars on Shakespeare's interest in gardening. Mrs Terborg, taking up the subject of flowers, made efficient conversation out of gloxinias, antirrhinums, chionodoxas, kolk-witzias – matters more familiar probably to Macdonald than to his employer. Charles Piper, some way down the table, attended with the undisguised concentration of a man who always makes notes before going to bed. Some lady in some future fiction would talk efficiently of gloxinias, antirrhinums, chionodoxas, kolkwitzias.

'Who,' asked Miss Terborg One, 'is the young man listening so attentively to my mother?'

'Charles Piper, the novelist,' replied Gott. 'He has just published a very successful book called *The Bestial Floor*.'

Miss Terborg One could almost be discerned flipping over some voluminous card-index in her mind. 'Of course: "The uncontrollable mystery on the bestial floor." I suppose it's about Christ?'

'No. It's about the childhood of Dostoyevsky.'

'Dostoyevsky', said Miss Terborg One firmly, 'was very interested in Christ.' Across the chasm, thought Gott, threads of connection can always be traced. 'Do *you* write novels?' asked Miss Terborg One.

Unconsciously, the Duchess came to the rescue. 'And I decided we must have firemen. Giles, were there firemen in the Elizabethan theatre?'

'There were fires,' replied Gott cautiously.

'Well, I've arranged for three men from King's Horton – and I've said they must bring helmets. There will be one at each door beside the footmen.'

'Anne,' came Max Cope's piping voice from up the table, 'have you arranged for a detective too? Don't you think a detective –'

'A detective, Max!'

'I mean, there will be a lot of jewellery and so on, won't there? And a mixed crowd. And you've already got some pretty queer –'

'Fish, sir?' murmured Bagot, deserting his wines and breaking silence with inspired indecorum. Everybody at Scamnum knew that an eye had to be kept on old Mr Cope. His wits were gone: there was nothing left in him but a mere, sheer painting. He was promptly taken charge of by Mrs Terborg on the one hand and Gervase Crispin on the other for the rest of the meal.

Lord Auldearn was conversing with the black man – with that

remorseful deference which the English raj accords the Oriental visitor to the heart of Empire. Timothy Tucker was entertaining Elizabeth with fantastic anecdotes of a fellow-publisher.

'. . . But Spandrel's best stroke was with the Muchmoss. You've heard of her? She was a nice old party living in Devon and she sent him, years ago, a manuscript called *Westcountry Families I Have Known*. Spandrel has a nose and he smelt not family chat but novels in her. And sure enough he turned her into a solid market success. She was a nice old party with a good brain tucked away, and soon the Muchmoss Westcountry was esteemed. So after a few years Spandrel decided to build up a school. He found several other parties, not quite so old, and most luckily the Muchmoss – kind old soul – thought no end of them all. So you see, the Muchmoss sold them and they in turn were healthy for the Muchmoss. Well, that was all right – until the Muchmoss died. She died, unhappily, a bit too soon – before the Muchmoss atelier could do all its own heave and shove. Spandrel was stumped for a bit, but one day he had a revelation. He was walking in the Park, he says, when it came to him quite suddenly: the knowledge that the Muchmoss was *still* enjoying the Muchmoss school no end – in heaven. So he arranged a séance –'

Noel, it occurred to Gott, was making surprisingly heavy going with Miss Terborg Two. He had plainly reached that desperate stage at which one drops this disconnected observation after that into a horrid well of silence. But at this moment one of these observations had a startling effect. Miss Terborg Two gave a loud scream.

The literary activities of the Muchmoss ghost, Lord Auldearn's polite questions on *yogis* and *gooroos* died, with other miscellaneous topics, round the table. Everybody looked askance at Noel – particularly Gervase, who jumped to the conclusion that he had retailed to an innocent virgin an anecdote which Gervase himself had published to the billiard room earlier in the day.

Noel was apologizing profusely and confusedly both to the lady and to the table at large. 'I'm most frightfully sorry; never thought of it as actually startling; just the story –'

'Story!' said Gervase grimly.

'Just the story of the Black Hand, you know.'

Miss Terborg Two made an agitated gesture upon her boyish bosom.

'Stupid of me. Duchess, I'm so sorry – but secret societies and things have made me scared ever since a kid ... The Black Hand!'

The Duke looked with mild severity on his youthful kinsman. 'What's this foolery, Noel?'

'Nothing at all, sir. Rubbishing joke ... Elizabeth's seen it ... sort of threatening message. Thought it might amuse. Most terribly sorry to have distressed Miss Bertog – I mean Miss Terborg –'

This was most sadly remote from the suave success with which Noel must one day dine about the embassies of Europe. Elizabeth took on the burden of further explanations. 'A type-written slip that came to Noel by post. It's just a scrap from Shakespeare; something about revenge.'

In the buzz of speculation that followed Gott glanced at Lord Auldearn. But the Lord Chancellor said nothing. That a similar joke had been played on himself he did not propose, apparently, to announce. Here, even in dealing with a pointless prank, was the statesman's impulse to keep mum. But another statesman reacted differently. Gervase Crispin took Elizabeth up sharply: 'Revenge! That's odd. I had the same sort of thing myself the other day.'

Mild curiosity ran round the table.

'Yes. I had a telegram at the House before coming down here. Just two words.'

This time Lord Auldearn spoke: 'Two words?'

'*Hamlet, revenge!*'

'Curious about those messages,' said the Duke when the men were alone. 'Who would play a trick like that?' He looked lazily and amiably round his guests; the very anti-type, thought Gott, of King Claudius of Denmark. 'Funny thing.'

'A *bad* thing!' said the black man suddenly and emphatically. It was his first utterance to the company at large, and everybody started. 'It is *very* wicked to send a curse!'

'I don't know about it's being a curse,' said Timothy Tucker easily. 'I think it's just what we call a practical joke; and rather a feeble one at that. It's curious that a person educated enough to know his Shakespeare should do such a futile thing.'

'Odd the people who do know their Shakespeare,' the Duke remarked.

'I discovered this afternoon, for instance, that Macdonald, my head-gardener, knows his inside-out.'

'Macdonald!' said Lord Auldearn sharply. 'Mr Gott, was it not Macdonald that we passed coming up the drive?'

Gott nodded absently. 'There's a little more than mere knowledge of Shakespeare involved,' he said.

At this Max Cope, who had all the appearance of dozing comfortably in his chair, suddenly burst into high-pitched speech. 'In fact, it's "Puzzle find the oyster-wife" – eh?' And looking cunningly round the table, he ended in the embarrassing giggle of great age. As far as Gott could judge, everyone except Lord Auldearn was bewildered by this. But no one seemed inclined to interrogate the venerable painter. Max slumbered again.

'Cope means,' Gott explained, 'that Crispin's message, "Hamlet, revenge", is not – as you may remember – actually from Shakespeare's play. It was probably a line in an earlier play, now lost, and is first quoted as a joke in Lodge's *Wits Miserie* in 1596: there is a reference there to a ghost that cried miserably in the theatre, like an oyster-wife, "Hamlet, revenge." It doesn't follow that our joker has any special erudition, but he does seem to have browsed about in an antiquarian way.'

As Gott concluded this explanation he looked speculatively at Melville Clay. Clay, it occurred to him, should not have been bewildered by the oyster-wife; during the past few years he had been displaying a pretty thorough knowledge of the roundabouts of the Elizabethan drama. But Clay dissipated this speculation now. 'Of course!' he said eagerly. 'I'd quite forgotten. And there are other references too. It was quite a familiar quip.'

Gott nodded. 'Yes. But it doesn't really help us to the identity of the joker. What about where the messages came from?'

'Mine,' said Noel, 'was posted in the West End this morning.' There was a pause in which all eyes were turned on Gervase Crispin. But Gervase kept silent until directly challenged by the Duke. Even then he spoke with a shade of reluctance.

'My telegram,' he said quietly, 'was sent off from Scamnum Ducis.'

At this it was suddenly clear to everybody that speculation about the messages, pushed forward idly enough, had reached some point of obscure uncomfortableness. Everybody except Piper, who saw nothing in the conversation that would write up, was interested; even

Max Cope could be discovered on scrutiny to have one eye open still. But equally, everybody knew that the subject must be dropped. The Duke rose, and taking Cope's arm, led the way to the drawing-room.

Fresh arrivals were expected and the party was keeping together to welcome them. The Duchess contrived to establish one large circle and start a general discussion of the play. For a time it ran on practical lines: dresses, make-up, the next day's rehearsals. Then it took a historical turn and the talk narrowed to those with special knowledge: Gott, the slightly uncomfortable specialist; Lord Auldearn, with rather more than a smattering of everything; Melville Clay, genuinely learned in the histories of all Hamlets that had ever been; and the Duchess, fresh from intensive reading. Garrick's trick chair that overturned automatically on his starting up in the closet scene, the performance on board the *Dragon* at Sierra Leone in 1607, Mrs Siddons and other female Hamlets, the tradition that Shakespeare's own best performance was as the ghost: the talk ran easily on. Mrs Terborg gave a formidably perceptive account of Walter Hampden's celebrated Hamlet in New York in 1918. Elizabeth remembered how Pepys had once spent an afternoon getting 'To be, or not to be' by heart. And this gave the Duchess her chance. She immediately turned Clay to presenting Mr Pepys delivering the soliloquy to Mrs Pepys. Anything that Anne Dillon had once been used to impose on obscure young men at Hampstead she would never hesitate to impose on the great and famous at Scamnum.

There can be nothing more trying to an actor than being required to extemporize before a drawing-room – even a drawing-room of quick and sympathetic spirits. But Clay showed no trace of annoyance; the difficulty of the odd task had wholly possessed and absorbed him in a moment. He stood with knitted brows for perhaps twenty seconds, and then – suddenly – Pepys was in the room. And Gott, with no great opinion of the wits of actors, had the feeling that this two minutes' *tour de force* – for it lasted no longer – was one of the most remarkable things he had ever seen. Anyone might know his Pepys and his Hamlet, but instantly to produce the sheer and subtle imaginative truth that was Clay's picture of Pepys *as* Hamlet was a miniature but authentic intellectual triumph. Looking round the room amid the ripple of delighted exclamations, Gott saw Lord Auldearn's eyes narrowed upon Clay as upon something suddenly revealed as formidable; saw that Charles Piper's mind was racing as a writer's mind will race when something extraordinary has occurred. And the thing had even got across to old Max Cope; the painter was cackling with delight. Only the intelligent Hindu was looking intelligently bewildered. No doubt he had – following the weird system of education imposed upon his country – been examined both in Shakespeare's *Hamlet* and Pepys's *Diaries*. But this sudden telescoping was beyond him.

For the Duchess all this led up to something else. She now turned to a subject she had already frequently debated with Clay: Garrick's Hamlet, and particularly his first encounter with the Ghost.

> 'On the stage he was natural, simple, affecting;
> 'Twas only that, when he was off, he was acting,'

quoted the Duchess.

'Yes, but this wasn't natural. It's clear he took it too slowly; theatrically, you would put it. The *St James's Chronicle* said so; even Lichtenberg said so – and Lichtenberg was an enthusiast.'

Here, thought Gott, was a man who could talk his own shop in a mixed company, without a trace of self-consciousness. And everybody was interested.

'And Garrick overstressed mere physical terror. That was Johnson's opinion, Fielding's opinion.'

'One sees you see it,' the Duchess let fall.

And Clay was obviously seeing it. He was on his feet still, his brow again knitted, his eye upon David Garrick on the stage of Drury Lane nearly two hundred years ago. 'The cloak and the big hat,' he said softly, 'it was all built up from them.'

In an instant Noel was out of the room, to return with an enveloping opera cloak and a soft black hat – a hat with a monstrously exaggerated brim such as undergraduate devotees of the Muses delight to wear. 'The hat's not what it was,' he explained cheerfully; 'it and I have been pitched into the St Anthony's fountain together before now. But it may serve.'

Clay took the cloak at once and threw it round himself; then he jammed the hat apparently at random on his head. Gott felt sub-acute discomfort in himself; divined it in others. They were confronted by something grotesquely incongruous: a man in exquisite evening dress, set off by the black and scarlet of a twentieth-century dandy's cloak, with a parody of a Montparnasse hat perched on his head – and now

proposing to convert this elegant drawing-room, with its Whistlers, Dillons, and Copes, its Ming and 'Tang, into the battlements of Elsinore. But Clay, with a glance round at the lighting, had stepped to a door and flicked at the switches to get the effect he wanted: one area of subdued light in a farther corner of the darkened room. 'Horatio,' he called gaily, 'remember your lines!' And he took up his position in the little circle of dim illumination.

And then quietly, without any attempt at dramatic illusion, and as a teacher might enunciate Shakespeare from behind a lectern, Clay spoke Hamlet's lines as they follow on the noise of revelry borne up to the battlements:

> 'The king doth wake tonight and takes his rouse,
> Keeps wassail and the swagg'ring upspring reels:
> And as he drains his draughts of Rhenish down,
> The kettle-drum and trumpet thus bray out
> The triumph of his pledge . . .'

And, obediently, from the midst of the little audience came the voice of Piper as Horatio:

> 'Is it a custom?'

Clay looked across and smiled – still Melville Clay reciting quietly in the Scamnum little drawing-room:

> 'Ay marry is't,
> But to my mind, though I am native here
> And to the manner born, it is a custom
> More honoured in the breach than the observance.'

And as the speech proceeded Clay imperceptibly, like a cinematograph trick, faded out and Hamlet – David Garrick's Hamlet – grew into being. Shakespeare in the eighteenth century – here was another scholar-actor's subtlety indefinably but lucidly conveyed. Gott, watching fascinated, heard beside him Bunney's gasp of astonishment as the very vowels and consonants came over with the shading of 1750. The knotty, difficult speech, that throws the hearer's mind into a half-darkness of its own, proceeded – accompanied by an increase of mere physical blackness. A turn of the shoulder began to hide the lower part of the face; an inclination of the head brought the hat over the eyes. For

a moment there was a mouth, a nose only; then blackness save for two eloquently moving hands. The voice searched on:

> '... these men,
> Carrying I say the stamp of one defect,
> Being nature's livery, or fortune's star ...'

One hand disappeared; then the other: the speech ended in darkness answering darkness, the voice dying away in the impenetrable obscurity of the final lines:

> '... the dram of evil
> Doth all the noble substance of a doubt,
> To his own scandal.'

The cloak had fallen annihilatingly round the immobile figure. There was a long moment's silence in which Gott had time for the fleeting reflection that Miss Terborg Two might well make this juncture occasion for another scream. Then Piper's voice:

> 'Look, my lord, it comes!'

No one missed the actual presence of the Ghost in the minute that followed. With the rapidity of an athlete Clay had whirled round upon himself and stiffened as instantly into a convention of retarded motion at once wholly theatrical and wholly terrifying. The hat slipped to the ground, the cloak fallen back. Legs straddled, left arm flung wide and high, right arm bent with the hand hanging down and the fingers wide apart, the whole trembling figure of the man answered to the fixed, glaring terror on the face. Second after second of absolute silence crawled by. Then, on the hiss of an outgoing breath, came speech:

> 'Angels and ministers of grace defend us!'

With what seemed shattering rapidity there followed Melville Clay's own musical laugh. The lights snapped on. The actor was patting Noel's hat into shape with ironical precision. He had not turned a hair. 'Garrick,' he said, 'was more effective, of course; but that was the idea.'

Gott looked round the room. Lord Auldearn had disappeared. Nearly everybody seemed to be under the influence of a species of stage shock: the evocation, and more the abrupt dissipation of a piece of supreme theatre, had left the audience somewhat in the air. It was the Duke

who lowered the tension. 'You know, if I were the Ghost I think I'd be the more scared of the two!' The Scamnum drawing-room recovered its momentarily shattered identity; congratulation, comment, animated discussion flowed on.

Nevertheless, Gott felt a hint of constraint in the air. Elizabeth was looking, in some remote way, troubled; the Duchess was working particularly hard; the Duke had retreated a little further into the light-comedy part he seemed to cultivate. And there was a perceptible feeling of relief when the purr of cars on the drive announced the distraction of arrivals by the evening train.

Ten-thirty at night is not a wholly polite hour at which to arrive for a long week-end: explanations, previously offered no doubt by letter, were reiterated now. Lord and Lady Traherne had been giving one of their colonial parties: never such oceans of colonials as this year! Sir Richard Nave had been lecturing to the Society for Improving Sex on 'The Psychological Basis of Matrilinear Communities'. Professor Malloch had been conducting viva-voce examinations in his native Aberdeen. The Marryats had felt that a week away from London so early would be an *experience*, but things turned up so that only five days were *possible*. Tommy Potts explained that in Whitehall now one was worked like a nigger; one might as well be in the second grade. Pamela Hogg had been stepping into the midday train when she had had the most frightful news about Armageddon – intelligence obscure and even alarming until one realized that the matter concerned a horse. Mrs Platt-Hunter-Platt had been demonstrating at the Albert Hall against something ill-defined but outrageous. An undevotional-looking banker was loud in laments at having missed the midday service: Paris–Croydon, it turned out to be – and the sequel of a novel and apparently remarkably hazardous route by land and water. A sparkling lady in full evening-dress declared herself as having come straight from her old governess's funeral. A podgy M.P., unconscious of a faint residual smear of lipstick on his bald head, murmured obscurely of committees.

Sandwiches, whisky, hot soupy stuffs as if after a dance; some three dozen people, almost crowding the little drawing-room, laughing, chattering, exclaiming, eddying: was it, Gott wondered, what Elizabeth had called it – a barbarian holiday? Or was it really a polite society, with sufficient of a common code – tastes, attitudes, assumptions, intentions – to go through with this elaborate affair in front of it pleasedly and confidently? Did the Lord Chancellor of England and Pamela Hogg belong to a structure still sufficiently solid, sufficiently homogeneous for the one to play Polonius before the other? Or had the Duchess fabricated the idea of such a society out of the novels of her girlhood – and was the whole thing going to be an uneasy sham? What did Lord Auldearn think of this growing gathering? But Lord Auldearn was still invisible.

Gott disengaged himself from Mrs Platt-Hunter-Platt, who wanted him to sign some sort of manifesto or petition to the government of Brazil; dodged Professor Malloch, advancing with technical Shakespeare-scholarship in his eye; dodged Sir Richard Nave, discoursing blandly of the twilight of the Christ mythus, and slipped out upon the terrace. An uncertain moonlight was haunting the gardens, glittering on a sheet of water far below, adding folds and shadows to the silhouette of Horton Hill beyond. The babble of voices floated out through the windows; Gott strolled down broad steps to find silence on the farther terrace below. He stopped where the long flow of balustrade was broken by a massive, dimly-outlined marble – a Farnese Hercules perhaps – and let his eye travel along the line of the downs. He was worried about this play.

Yes, decidedly there was some uncomfortableness in the air; an un-comfortableness which must not grow if disaster was to be avoided. And it had its origin, he now felt, in the trivial foolishness of the mysterious messages. To begin with, the whole *Hamlet* plan was a little out – a whim imposed on this Scamnum world rather than something growing naturally from it. He himself had been to Scamnum often enough, but always before he had shed here his professional role of scholar and antiquary. Talking and contriving Elizabethan theatre in the Duchess's drawing-room was disturbing; it induced a self-consciousness such as a Fellow of the Royal Society would feel if asked down to demonstrate the peculiarities of atom and electron. Centuries ago that sort of thing would have marched: when Fulke Greville and Giordano Bruno disputed on the Copernican theory in the drawing-rooms of Elizabethan London; when the noble family of Bridgewater moved through the stately dance and rhetoric of Milton's *Comus* at Ludlow Castle. But now shop was shop; and theatricals were theatricals – and the basic attitude of a scurrying contemporary society to them was that expressed by Sir Thomas Bertram when he put a stop to such nonsense in *Mansfield Park*.

Leisure had gone. Of these people gathered here the abler were absorbed in the increasingly desperate business of governing England, of balancing Europe. And the others were not so much leisured as laboriously idle: fussing over Armageddon or demonstrating against brothers in Brazil. All in all, the Tragedy of Hamlet played at Scamnum Court, however seriously taken up by the persons chiefly committed, had to come to birth in a precariously viable air. True, the Duchess had carried out a sort of air-conditioning process with some subtlety. Tucker, Piper, the American ladies so ingeniously materialized from Henry James: these blended with Scamnum – or with the aspect of Scamnum the Duchess was concerned to emphasize – well enough. And here Gott arrived at the view that it was not after all so much a matter of the people as of the place. In its comparatively brief two hundred years of existence this enormous mansion had contrived to become heavy with tradition; and it was not a tradition – despite its Whig pretension of accepting whatever interested or amused – that squared readily with eccentricity. Just as the whole physical pile frowned down upon Peter Crispin's Gothic hall, so the spirit of the place frowned rather upon the play that was to be performed there. Hence the effect upon the house-party of the scraps of typescript: they gave just that hint of a lurking, unfriendly presence which was needed to start this other feeling of a lurking incongruity in the whole affair – the incongruity which had been felt again when Melville Clay performed his dazzling tricks in the drawing-room.

Gott's hand, groping for a cigarette-case in the pocket of his dinner-jacket, closed upon a proof of the printed programme that would be distributed on Monday night. 'The play produced by Giles Gott, M.A., F.B.A., Hanmer Reader in Elizabethan Bibliography, Fellow of St Anthony's College.' Everyone else had been shorn of distinction; Claudius was 'Edward Crispin' and as Polonius the Lord Chancellor of England was plain 'Ian Stewart' as he had been in Hampstead long ago. But with her producer the Duchess – with a sound eye for effect, no doubt – had piled it all on. And Gott recalled the slightly satirical eye of Professor Malloch in the drawing-room. He was up to the neck in it and it must go through.

His mind turning to ponder over detail, he climbed back to the upper terrace at the eastern end of the main building. Here there is a colonnade, lit at night by a vista of subdued lights in the entablature.

Under the lights was the Lord Chancellor. And Gott suddenly saw that his own speculations and doubts of a moment before were something of infinitesimal significance in the world.

Lord Auldearn was pacing absorbedly up and down, with a strange, forward-lurching gait that suggested more than the beginnings of physical decay. Indeed, he seemed very old; older by ten years than when he sat gaily talking to his hostess at dinner. In his hand was what appeared to be an official document. On his face sat an utter gravity, the utter gravity of a great savant or a great statesman in some crisis of thought or action. Gott watched him for a long moment; then turned round and retreated as he had come.

3

Looking back on the days immediately preceding the play Gott was to see them – and that despite the practical bustle with which they were filled – as an orgy of talk. Serious, pseudo-serious, and idle, relevant to *Hamlet* and irrelevant, general and *tête à tête*, sustained and fragmentary; there was talk in every category. Most of it was talk that would naturally fade from the mind in a day. But soon circumstances were to compel Gott to dredge up every accessible scrap of it from oblivion, to sift and search it as he had never perhaps sifted and searched before.

Saturday morning saw an encounter with Charles Piper in their common bathroom. 'I can usually,' said Piper over the turning of taps, 'get five to eight hundred words out of a hot bath.'

'Often,' replied Gott, unwarily stepping into the position of a fellow-author, 'I get a new start from brandy and muffins.'

'Really... and *muffins*? I never heard of that.' Piper eyed Gott as one might eye a suddenly perceived object of minor but authentic interest in the Victoria and Albert Museum. 'And what,' he asked with sober interest, 'brought you to detective-stories?'

'Moral compulsion. The effort to give a few hours' amusement as a sort of discount on many hours' boredom.'

Piper dropped this response after a moment's consideration into some mental pigeon-hole – was it *Evasion* or *Unsuccessful Humour* or *Academic Psychology*? – and proceeded to further interrogation. 'Would you say',

he asked solemnly, 'that fiction proper and narrative melodrama are absolutely distinct kinds?'

'I doubt if there is necessarily an absolute line. Dickens wrote a mix-up of novel and melodrama – and very successfully.' Gott paused to turn on the shower. 'Of course fiction commonly uses a finer brush all through. It avoids labels except where they are functionally necessary: Hot, Cold. Melodrama runs on big splashy labels: Bath Mat. None of your aristocratic restraint.' And Gott pointed to the unembellished cork surface at his feet.

Piper, again with a pause for the docketing procedure, turned from question to statement. 'I think myself that they come from different parts of the mind. Fiction belongs to what's called the Imagination. Melodrama belongs to the Fancy; it's a bubbling up of the suppressed primitive, a subconscious on holiday, *fantasy*.'

'I think that's a novel notion,' said Gott, looking at Piper with an innocent and admiring eye. But Piper, delaying only to record *Irony* in his invisible notebook, pursued his thought.

'I see the difference in my own waking and dream life. My waking life is given to imaginative writing – writing in which the chief concern is values. But my dreams, like melodrama, are very little concerned with values. The whole interest is on a tooth and claw level Attack and escape, hunting, trapping, outwitting. A consciousness all the time of physical action, of material masses, and dispositions as elements in a duel. And, of course, the constant sense of obscurity or mystery that haunts dreams. If I wrote melodrama it would be out of my dreams.'

'And what of Shakespeare's drama of primitive intrigue, *Hamlet*? Is that an example of the melodramatic and the imaginative working together?'

Piper meditated. 'Perhaps,' he said, 'it's a failure on that account. The melodramatic material taken over by Shakespeare may not have been susceptible –'

But this was a theme on which Gott conducted some dozen laborious discussions with some dozen more or less laborious undergraduates every year. During some part of Piper's following remarks, in consequence, he was guilty – like the Great Lexicographer in similar circumstances – of abstracting his mind and thinking of Tom Thumb.

'. . . And I should find it irresistible,' said Piper.

Gott nodded comprehendingly. 'Irresistible.' But Piper was not deceived. He made his invisible note, *Donnish exclusiveness; inattentive to outside opinion*, and patiently began again.

'I probably suppress the melodramatic in myself: I don't read it, for one thing. But it's there waiting to bubble up. And as it doesn't get into my writing it would like, I think, to get into my life. If a sort of Ruritania came my way – cloak and sword adventure – I should jump at it. And, as I say, in real life I should find your sort of business – neatly disposing of a corpse and so on – irresistible.' Piper adjusted the large horn-rimmed glasses through which he normally contemplated the world. 'As irresistible', he added conscientiously, 'as a lovely and willing woman.' He threw open the bathroom window. 'Do you do deep breathing? I always do.'

It was possible, said the Duke as he hovered indecisively between the kidneys and the bones, that his mother might come over from Horton Ladies' for the play. Diana Sandys, sitting beside Anna Merkalova, observed that the dowager Duchess was a *very* strict old lady. Piper made his note, *All girls cats by twenty*; Noel looked reproachfully at Diana; Elizabeth looked speculatively at Gott. Bunney, surrounded by an irreproachable American breakfast, was interested. 'How old?' he asked the Duke.

'Eh? Oh – ninety-four.'

Bunney's eyes widened. 'Vigorous?'

'Uncommon.'

'Not – deaf, by any chance?'

Mrs Terborg was looking sternly at her countryman over her coffee. The Duke replied that his mother was certainly not deaf, but added that she now lived in almost unbroken retirement. Bunney nodded inexplicably. 'Most important!' he said. 'Do you think she would co-operate? Ninety-four and living out of the world; you see how important that is?' He looked almost pleadingly at the Duke. 'Your mother is probably substantially uncontaminated.'

'Uncontaminated!'

'Uncontaminated.' Bunney made brief calculations. 'I think,' he said – his eye fixed meditatively on Timothy Tucker – 'she will almost certainly say *hijjus*. And *indjin*,' he added – looking at Mr Bose. Suddenly a gleam came into Bunney's eye. 'She may even say *gould*! It would be a big thing to find a *gould*.' He turned to Gott as to a fellow sage.

'You remember Odger maintains *gould* to have died with the Lady Lucy Lumpkin in 1883?'

The Scamnum running breakfast was now at its busiest. Some twenty people were scattered round the big tables; three or four more were foraging among the hot plates. But Bunney had now attracted the attention of the whole company. And he expanded under notice. 'Your butler is an interesting man,' he told the Duke, 'a most interesting man. He was born, you know, in Berkshire, and so were his parents. But almost certainly the family came from Kent. There are certain slack vowels . . .' And just as interest in Bunney was dissipating itself he succeeded in recalling it abruptly. 'Bagot was good enough to co-operate last night. I asked him to repeat the Lord's Prayer.'

The Duke looked blankly at his guest. 'Asked Bagot to repeat the Lord's Prayer! Really, Dr Bunney, you must meet my head-gardener, Macdonald. You would interest each other.'

'The Lord's Prayer,' affirmed Bunney, beaming round. 'It affords a number of interesting collocations of speech-elements. Bagot was good enough to cooperate, and here it is.' And stooping down to his feet, Bunney produced the black box and flicked a switch. The table fell silent in somewhat shocked expectation. Then the black box spoke, in a high falsetto.

'I will *not* cry Hamlet, revenge,' said the black box.

There was a startled pause and then a dry voice spoke from down the table. 'An unfamiliar version, my dear sir.' This was Sir Richard Nave.

'Kentish or Berkshire, Dr Bunney?' This was Professor Malloch: both these had arrived since the mysterious messages had been in prominence.

Bunney was staring at his machine much as Balaam may have stared at his ass. Noel took it upon himself to enlighten the new arrivals. 'If Miss Terborg will steel herself, I'll explain. It's the Black Hand. He was operating yesterday and here he is again. Only he seems to have changed his mind; quite turned over a new leaf, in fact. He will *not* cry "Hamlet, revenge."'

'Why should he change his mind, I wonder?' It was the competent Mrs Terborg who took up the theme. The previous evening, no doubt, she had realized as Gott had done that the Black Hand was generally disturbing; now she saw the advantages of giving the subject an airing on a whimsical plane. 'I think Black Hands ought to pursue a more consistent policy if they want to impress. Not that Dr Bunney doesn't seem impressed.'

'It's a comfort to think,' Miss Terborg One carried on briskly, 'that even if we don't discover the identity of the Black Hand Dr Bunney will be able to identify his grandfather's and grandmother's home-town.'

'I think it's creepy,' said Miss Terborg Two.

Gott, Noel, Nave, and Malloch made their way to the Banqueting Hall together. It was rather awkward, Noel felt, about Malloch. *Crucible*, Noel's publication, did not usually much concern itself with the merely learned of the world; it contented itself with occasional shadowing of all such under the generic figures of a certain Professor Wubb and his assistants Dr Jim-jim and Mr Jo-jo. But it had taken notice of Professor Malloch; in fact it had reviewed his Hamlet study, *The Show of Violence*. And Malloch had written a dry little reply. Confronted now by Malloch as a guest at Scamnum, Noel was disposed to see this reply as having been, in a way, a compliment. At the time, it had seemed an incitement: Professor Malloch and Professor Wubb had in consequence been ludicrously interwoven in certain editorial paragraphs of *Crucible*. Noel had just read these over in bed and although they still seemed funny – Noel's editorials were usually considerably gayer than the productions of his contributors – they had struck him as distressingly childish as well. And here was Malloch in the flesh; dry, courteous, incredibly learned, and apparently a constant and critical reader of *Crucible* from cover to cover. It was really very awkward.

'And the story,' Malloch was saying, 'of the hydrocephalic children at the funeral of the girl who used to torture the cats – I wonder if the writer took medical advice?'

'I suppose he is a little unbalanced,' said Noel uncomfortably.

'Ah, yes. But I mean advice on the likelihood of the story. Nave, do you read Mr Gylby's journal? There was a story about hydrocephalic children . . .' And Malloch proceeded to enlist the physician in the task of demolishing the pathological basis of *Crucible*'s last masterpiece. Yes, he was incredibly learned; he seemed to know more about it all than Nave himself. That was always their way, Noel thought. Accumulate enormous stores of information – always the right factual brick ready to throw at you. Meanwhile, anxious Crispin courtesy was the rule. Respectfully, he drew attention to a magnificent Fantin-Latour on the wall. Whereupon, Malloch made certain knowledgeable observations on Fantin-Latour.

Gott had taken up another semi-medical theme with Nave. 'Have you noticed the American twins? It's impossible to tell them apart – until they begin talking. Vanessa is distinctly intelligent and Stella is almost witless. That's unusual, is it not?'

Nave nodded. 'Distinctly so. They're clearly identical twins' – he searched for the technical word – 'uniovular. That means that they have an identical hereditary equipment. If their intelligence is markedly unequal it's an extraordinarily interesting thing psychologically, because the difference must be an accident of nurture or environment. I must have a talk with them.'

The psychologist was plainly interested. But Gott had a problem of his own. 'They are physically identical to the naked eye – but would they be that microscopically, so to speak? What about finger-prints, for instance?'

Nave, who was probably unaware of Gott's hobby, looked vaguely surprised. 'I'm really not sure. But I should think . . .'

Malloch, walking behind with Noel, interposed: 'Galton investigated the finger-prints of uniovular twins. He found that, although remarkably similar, they were never indistinguishable.'

Gott abandoned an interesting possibility. Noel, pacing beside the invincible Malloch, could almost be heard to groan. At the door of the hall he positively embraced the hovering figure of Mrs Platt-Hunter-Platt.

And now one of Gott's nervous moments had arrived: his stage was to undergo its first expert scrutiny.

'Ah,' said Malloch, 'the Fortune.'

'Yes. The hall being rectangular, I thought it best to take something like the Fortune as a model.'

Malloch looked dubious. 'I should have been inclined to take the Swan. However unreliable De Witt's drawing may be . . .'

And the two authorities drifted away in a courteous battle of technicalities.

Meanwhile Mrs Platt-Hunter-Platt's voice rose in a squeal of protest. 'But there's no curtain!'

Noel grinned. 'Oh yes there is – a little one there at the back.' And the amusements of delivering himself in his old tutor's best lecture-room manner suddenly striking him, he continued gravely: 'It is necessary to remember that the Elizabethan theatrical companies originally presented their plays in the yards of London inns –'

'In public-houses?' exclaimed Mrs Platt-Hunter-Platt. 'A most disorderly arrangement!'

'So the puritan faction thought. They produced manifestos and protests about it which you would probably find technically interesting. Well, as I say, the players simply put up a platform in the yard of an inn and acted on that. The expensive part of the audience sat looking down from the galleries or rooms of the inn –'

'Or sat on the platform itself,' interposed Nave, who had abandoned the scholars.

'Or sat on the platform on three-legged stools beside the actors,' agreed Noel, 'the nasty ones spitting tobacco and crying "filthy, filthy!" '

'Disgusting,' said Mrs Platt-Hunter-Platt.

'And the common people simply stood on the ground round the platform; they were called the groundlings.'

'Why?' asked Mrs Platt-Hunter-Platt blankly.

'I think because they stood on the ground. They were also occasionally called the understanders –'

'Understanders?'

'Perhaps a joke. Well, the platform was surrounded on three sides by the audience, and the fourth no doubt abutted on certain rooms that the actors used for dressing-rooms, entrances, and exits, and so forth. When they began to build theatres of their own what they built was still uncommonly like a platform in an inn-yard. Here it is.' And Noel led the way forward and assisted Mrs Platt-Hunter-Platt to mount the low platform which projected from the middle of the hall. 'This platform is the front stage, where most of the action of a play takes place. It ought to be under the open sky, just as an inn-yard was. And, as you see, we shall try to get a similar effect on Monday by lighting it from directly above with arc-lamps. The audience, sitting around the hall, will be more or less in shadow. Gott felt a bit dubious about a modern audience feeling comfortable in a full light.'

'The effect', remarked Nave, 'should be rather like a boxing-ring in a stadium.'

'Boxing!' said Mrs Platt-Hunter-Platt, in tones that conveyed whole manifestos against Degrading Spectacles.

Noel nodded. 'Yes. Only here the platform or arena isn't actually islanded in the audience. On one side it runs back to what is the really interesting part of the theatre. You remember I said that in the inn-yard one side of the platform abutted on certain rooms and so forth? Well, the players used a bit of the galleries in that quarter as well. They liked to be able to act on two levels. So they used the first gallery at the back of the stage for "aloft" and that sort of thing. The upper stage, it's called. *Enter Lord Scales upon the Tower, walking: then enter two or three citizens below*.'

'Lord Scales?' said Mrs Platt-Hunter-Platt, looking dubiously round the hall for one of Scamnum's plentiful peers.

'In *The Second Part of King Henry VI*. And they used another gallery above that, maybe, just for blowing trumpets and so forth. But what is chiefly interesting is what happened *below* the upper stage, on the level of the front stage or platform proper. That's where a curtain comes in. They simply hung a curtain from the gallery and the result was something very like a modern stage on a smallish scale right at the back of the platform. It was just a deep recess, with its own entrances, and across which they could draw and undraw a curtain. It's called the rear stage. And just as the upper stage was used for "aloft" – Juliet's balcony, city walls and that sort of thing – so the rear stage was "within": Prospero's cave in *The Tempest*, Desdemona's bedroom in *Othello* –'

'Or the Queen's bedroom in *Hamlet*!' said Mrs Platt-Hunter-Platt with sudden enormous intelligence.

'Wrong, as a matter of fact.' It was Gervase Crispin who had strolled up and who spoke. 'The Queen's bedroom will be played on the front stage because the rear stage is needed for Polonius hiding behind the arras. Hamlet stabs through the curtain, pulls it back – and finds the corpse.'

'I think,' said Mrs Platt-Hunter-Platt, 'that Shakespeare is sometimes rather dreadful.'

Gervase laughed gruffly. 'Not so dreadful as some of the others. Tell Mrs Platt-Hunter-Platt about the Jew's trap-door, Noel.'

'There's a trap-door between the upper stage and the rear stage. We know it should be there from Marlowe's *Jew of Malta*. The Jew sets a sort of man-trap in his "gallery" – the upper stage, that is. He arranges a concealed hole in the floor, with a nice boiling cauldron underneath. Then he falls through it himself, the curtain of the rear stage is withdrawn – and there he is nicely cooking in his own pot.'

Piper had joined the group. 'But there's no trap-door here, is there?' he asked. 'It's not necessary in *Hamlet*?'

'*Hamlet* only needs a trap in the front stage. But Gott had the upper stage one built in, all the same. It's there,' Noel added as Malloch and Gott approached once more, 'to satisfy nice antiquarian sensibilities.'

Timothy Tucker strolled up. 'You know, this is very suggestive.' He waved his hand around and addressed Gott. 'It gives me an idea. You remember Spandrel's idea when he published *Death Laughs at Locksmiths*? It was a story that all turned on skeleton keys. So Spandrel bought up about three thousand yards of copper wire and enclosed a foot with every copy. And soon everyone was trying to make their own skeleton keys to pick their own locks –'

'Encouraging criminality,' said Mrs Platt-Hunter-Platt severely.

'Not at all,' said Richard Nave with equal severity; 'on the contrary, a healthy resolving of suppressed criminal tendencies in fantasy.'

'Skeleton keys are apparently all nonsense anyway,' said Tucker easily. 'But what strikes me is this. Here's a perfect material setting for a mystery: upper stage, rear stage, trap-doors, and what not. Why not write it up, Gott, and we could issue it with a cut-out model of the whole thing – Banqueting Hall, Elizabethan stage, corpse, and all? Toy shops have the kind of thing: "Fold along the dotted line," you know. I dare say we could run to coloured cardboard and a bright scrap of curtain. Everybody would set up his own model and study the mystery from that.'

The publisher wandered away. 'Dear me,' said Malloch, 'Mr Tucker seems to think you greatly interested in sensational fiction.'

Noel, having suffered so much on account of *Crucible*, was ruthless. 'Mr Gott,' he explained courteously, 'is the pseudonymous author of the well-known romances, *Murder among the Stalactites*, *Death at the Zoo*, *Poison Paddock*, and *The Case of the Temperamental Dentist*.'

Malloch turned to Gott with no appearance of surprise. 'This is most interesting. But in *Death at the Zoo*, now: I readily believe that the creature could be trained to fire the fatal shot. But the training of it by means of the series of sugar revolvers to swallow the real revolver? I asked Morthenthaler – you know his *Intelligence in the Higher Mammalia*? – and he seemed to think . . .'

It was Gott's turn to groan. To have an expert scrutiny of his stage remorselessly followed up by an equally expert scrutiny of his fantastic hobbyhorse was a stiff beginning to the day's exertions. But just as Malloch was showing dangerous signs of proceeding from the natural history of *Death at the Zoo* to the toxicology of *Poison Paddock*, a diversion appeared in the form of the Duchess carrying a telegram.

'Giles,' she said briskly, 'Tony Fletcher, the First Grave-digger, has mumps. I've sent for Macdonald and if you approve I'll ask him. Everybody would be delighted, I think; and with luck I can persuade him.'

Gott considered. 'I don't know that Macdonald is just the cut of a Shakespearean clown. I rather suspect him of being something much more like Prospero. But the Doric would be pleasant – and a real feast for Bunney's box. Try him by all means. Here he is.'

'Macdonald,' said the Duchess, 'I wonder if you would play the Sexton?'

Macdonald reflected, 'Your Grace will be meaning the First Clown?'

'Yes. The Grave-digger.'

'I could dae't,' said Macdonald, with conviction but without enthusiasm.

'And will?'

'Weel, ma'am, I dinna ken that I can rightly spare the time. Wi' twa ignorant new laddies aye speiring aboot matter o' elementary skill, and wi' the green-hooses like to be half-pillaged o' blooms...'

'But we're really relying on you, Macdonald. There's nobody else who can possibly get it up.'

There was a remote gleam of interest in Macdonald's eye. 'I'm no Kempt or Tarlton, your Grace, and I rather misdoot the songs. But there's no question but it's an interesting pairt. And wi' a verra richt-thochted reference to the gardening craft – though ill-confoonded wi' ditching and grave-making. And I'd hae to consult wi' Mr Goot here on the queer reference to Yaughan...'

'Why, Macdonald,' exclaimed Gott, 'you know the part already.'

'I hae a common reader's knowledge o' the text,' replied Macdonald with dignity. 'And though the time's short, your Grace, I'll no say ye no. I'll awa' to study it noo, and hae a guid pairt o' the lines by the afternoon.' And Macdonald composedly withdrew.

'Macdonald,' said Noel, 'knows the Elizabethan clowns and the *cruces Shakespearianae*; a village Gott, in fact; a mute, inglorious Malloch; a pendant guiltless of his pupils' blood.'

'Mr Gylby', explained Bunney to Lord Auldearn, 'is paraphrasing Gray's celebrated *Elegy*.'

4

By tea-time on Sunday Gott found his anxieties about the play lightened. His mind was now concentrated on this definite point and that; his more comprehensive doubts had dwindled. He felt that the tragedy of Hamlet was winning. That first lurking sense of uneasiness; the embarrassed feeling that the house-party was making itself a motley to the view; the apprehension lest some emanation of personification of Scamnum, like a ghostly Sir Thomas Bertram, might abruptly appear and bring all to a huddled and ignominious close – these things were gone. Instead, some thirty people had agreed to put an antic disposition on – and were enjoying it. The Duchess had worked hard; Mrs Terborg had talked amateur theatricals through the centuries: Elizabeth Kenilworth, Voltaire's Ferney, Mme de Staël's Coppet, Doddington under Foote, the Russian Imperial Court – she had talked, in fact, all she knew, which was a lot. The Black Hand, moreover, had gone out of business; or those favoured by its communications chose to be silent. And Macdonald's last-moment accession to the company – calculated stroke of a clever hostess that it was – was an immense success. Behind stage during rehearsals, the head-gardener held a sort of court. And he repeated the Shorter Catechism and 'The Cotter's Saturday Night' for the benefit of Bunney and – as he later discovered with some indignation – the black box.

The practical business of those final days, with all the actors assembled, was, of course, that of fitting everything together. The principal characters were already well-drilled and the main tones of the production, Gott felt, were satisfactorily established. Melville Clay, with infinite tact, had perfected what was in effect a first-rate amateur Hamlet: quiet, with a minimum of business and movement, relying chiefly on the formal beauty of the verse and prose. In that virtuoso display of his in the little drawing-room he had glided imperceptibly in sixteen lines of blank verse from an enunciation merely academic to the full compass of a great actor in the grand tradition. On the stage in the Banqueting Hall it was as if he had found, somewhere in that progress, just the right point at which to halt for the purpose on hand. With this nursing of the company by an acute theatrical intelligence, with the ready acquiescence of the others in Clay's simplified dramatic formula, with the absence of disturbing professional association which the novel staging would ensure, the play was likely to go well. All the principal players had amateur experience: the Duke had done that sort of thing – in Greek as far as he could remember – at school; the Duchess had played Portia to the satisfaction of Mr Gladstone; Piper had been in the O.U.D.S. – and so on. Nevertheless, to get a large amateur cast to run smoothly through a long play, far more rehearsal than that available would be necessary. There were bound to be hitches; Gott and Clay between them were busy foreseeing and eliminating what they could.

Much was to depend on the rapidity and continuity of action which the reconstructed Elizabethan stage made possible. The play was to begin at nine o'clock; there was to be one interval only, taken at the end of the second act; it was to be over just before midnight. There was no scenery to change, and few properties to manipulate. Now on one and now on another of the three stage spaces – front stage, rear stage, upper stage – the action would run smoothly forward. As the first scene, 'The Battlements of Elsinore', ended on the upper stage, Claudius and his court would enter in procession for Scene Two, 'The Council Chamber in the Castle', on the front stage. And as soon as the last characters in this scene had made their exit the curtain of the rear stage would be drawn back, revealing Laertes and Ophelia in Scene Three, 'A Room in the House of Polonius'. The curtain would no sooner be drawn again on this than Hamlet and his companions would appear 'aloft' for the meeting with the Ghost in Scene Four. In this way the play was assured something of the impetus it enjoyed three hundred years ago. An audience accustomed to the constant dropping of a curtain over a proscenium-arch and to a succession of elaborate stage sets might be disconcerted for a time, but they would be seeing *Hamlet* played in the manner in which Shakespeare himself had played in it.

No expense – as Bunney commented – had been spared. The hall had been divided in golden section by a tapestried partition in the centre of which, and fronting the larger area, had been inset rear stage and upper stage, with a sort of dwarf turret crowning all, and with the front stage projecting far up the hall to the tiers of seats arranged for the audience. In the part of the hall behind the partition, there had been adequate room for all behind-stage necessities, including a green-room and a number of dressing cubicles. The hall was thus a self-contained unit, a complete playhouse in itself. Once the play began, no scurrying about between hall and the main buildings of Scamnum would be necessary.

Just before the Saturday afternoon rehearsal, Gott was busy with a final review of properties. It was surprising, he was finding, how little paraphernalia – costumes apart – were either necessary or desirable when producing in the old way. A property too much and the non-representational character of the stage would be marred, with an uncomfortable result as of a fragmentarily set-up scene. Moreover, it was necessary to keep the front stage as·bare as possible. The Elizabethan producer had cared almost nothing for continuous visual illusion; he would thrust a mossy bank – or even a lady in bed – out upon the front stage in the middle of a scene without a tremor. But a modern audience must not be unnecessarily disconcerted, and there must be as little shifting of properties on the open front stage as possible. Gott had finally reduced the front-stage properties to two thrones, with two benches added for the play-scene, and a table added to that again in the last scene of all – furniture which servants could whisk on and off unobtrusively enough. To all intents and purposes the front stage was to be simply a bare platform throughout.

The rear stage was different; behind its curtain one could move on and off anything one liked. Here, therefore, there would be more properties: different tapestries in different scenes, and various pieces of Scamnum's most exquisite Jacobean furniture. Gott was contemplating the rear stage as set for the King's prayer scene when the Duchess entered.

'Giles, we can take that ungainly monster' – and she pointed to a bulky *prie-dieu* which took up a good deal of the scene – 'back to its home. I've got the most perfect faldstool – and a much better crucifix too.' As she spoke two footmen came in bearing a crate. 'I remembered the faldstool at Hutton Beechings, and I rang up Lucy Hutton and she's sent it and the crucifix as well.'

'It's not a crucifix,' said Gott when they had unpacked. 'It's a plain iron cross, which is perhaps better. And the faldstool is exquisite. They'll both do for the King in the prayer scene and for Hamlet to point to at "Get thee to a nunnery". By the way, has Yorick's skull come? I've decided I don't want any bones; only the skull.'

'Old Dr Biddle is coming over to dinner and bringing it with him.' Dr Biddle was a local practitioner, and he had promised to provide whatever remains of Yorick were required. 'And, incidentally, he's very keen to walk on. Do you think he could?'

Gott nodded. 'Certainly he can ... There are plenty of spare costumes and he'll make a most convincing attendant lord or venerable counsellor. I thought of putting Mr Bose on' – Mr Bose was the black man – 'but I'm afraid he would look a little *outré*; something strayed in from a *cinquecento* Adoration of the Magi. As it is, he's a capital prompter; knows the text backwards and has terrific concentration. I don't think his mind will stray for a split second throughout. See where he comes.'

'He would make a capital Ghost,' said the Duchess, and seeing that the approaching Hindu had heard something of this remark, added: 'Mr Bose, you should be the Ghost. Your movement is not earthly.'

Mr Bose smiled – and his smile was something on which Charles Piper might have sat up all night elaborating paragraphs. It had at once the subtlety of Mona Lisa and the spontaneous gaiety of a Murillo beggar-boy; it was remote and utterly intimate, limpid and fathomless – the paragraph would have to be stuffed with such contradictions. And above all it was a sort of disembodied smile, just as the motion to which the Duchess had referred was a sort of disembodied motion. In his fictions Gott sometimes permitted himself a mysterious Oriental who was credited – on what he had described to Piper as the Bath Mat principle – with moving like a cat. Mr Bose moved not in the least like a cat, but strictly like a spirit, an *esprit* who had been caught by a spell and constrained to talk a giggling, difficult English, to charm and puzzle and alarm. Mr Bose giggled delightedly now.

'I do not go tramp, tramp about your place, Duchess? It is because I do not eat too much, I think!' Mr Bose radiated his quintessence of gaiety. He could give to mere facetiousness, Gott reflected, a something that made the finest Western irony *gauche*. And when he took a plunge into seriousness, talking with alarming suddenness and simplicity of the soul, he made one feel – as Noel put it – a great pink lout. Yet Mr Bose was a Bath Mat Oriental as well; he was ingratiating and he was wily, undoubtedly wily. And if one were surrounded by millions of Mr Boses most certainly one would feel that only the wiliness counted.

'But in winter,' Mr Bose was proceeding more seriously, 'perhaps

I shall eat an egg. I have my father's permission for an egg – if constitutionally necessary.' Mr Bose looked dubiously into the future; the possibility plainly troubled him. He stood on one leg, his habit when feeling unhappy.

'I was saying,' Gott remarked, 'that you are better than the best professional prompter. You know every line of the play.'

Mr Bose forgot the threatening diet and giggled again with delight. 'In my country our education is *very* largely memory – *very* largely. A Brahmin of the old school would not teach from books; much is thought too sacred to be written in any book. It is part of our training to learn by heart many thousands of lines of sacred texts. And so memory is developed. *Very* quickly I know an English text by heart; but to know what it means – *that* is more difficult. So I found, studying for the B.A. degree at University of Calcutta. Now I understand nearly everything – even Chaucer and much of Mr James Juice.' Mr Bose sparkled to the Duchess in modest pride.

But Gott was apprehensive lest Mr Bose, despite his efficiency as a prompter, might be feeling out of it. 'I'm sorry,' he said when the Duchess had moved away, 'that you're not in the play. But you wouldn't fit the colour-scheme, would you? I wonder if the Grand Mogul or somebody had an ambassador at the court of Elsinore?' Mr Bose, Gott knew, delighted in banter of this sort. And now Mr Bose laughed.

'One day at the Duchess's place I will play Othello the dusky Moor! And meantime I learn much – *very* much. If the Queen, though, had a little black boy ... but that was later, was it not? And on this old sort of stage you cannot disguise people – eh? Black cannot be made white, nor old young, nor plain lovely?'

'No; that is one of the points that have emerged. Very little make-up is possible on a platform stage. And that makes it important that people should be like their parts to begin with.'

'Mr Clay,' said Mr Bose, 'is *very* like the Melancholy Dane.'

'Yes; but I doubt if Gervase Crispin is at all like Osric. And Bunney, whom we've had to call in, is an unconvincing Gentleman of the Guard. And the Vicar, unfortunately, is peculiarly unlike a Doctor of Divinity – though he is one. And think of Lord Auldearn: was Polonius that sort of disconcerting mingling of Shakespeare and Caliban?'

This was neat enough: the Lord Chancellor, with his dome-like forehead, heavy jaw, and characteristic lurch, suggested just this combination. But Mr Bose was rather shocked. 'Lord Auldearn,' he said emphatically, 'is a *very* good man, a learned and enlightened prince! He is a little infirm because of his great years. In my country we consider great years *very* holy.'

Convicted, thought Gott, of a barbarian lapse and gently reproved. But Mr Bose, with politeness, continued the theme just as if he had not been shocked. 'Lady Elizabeth, I think, does not look her part. She is too beautiful, is she not?'

This was percipience. Could one, after fifty years in India, say anything as understanding as that of an Indian drama? It went straight to a point round which Gott had been fumbling for days. Ophelia, so hopelessly under the weather throughout the play, should be forlornly pretty; never more than that. And Elizabeth's looks would not knit themselves to the part; they spoke too clearly of a spirit with which poor Ophelia could not be credited. What was Elizabeth's beauty? It was not something that could be dissociated from uncommon qualities of mind; but it was not, again, the highest and always tragic sort of beauty – heavy, fateful, perversely crossed by melancholy or intellect. It was not Rosamund, Cordelia, Desdemona, the Duchess of Malfi. In fact, there was no real place for Elizabeth in the Elizabethan age; she represented something of later birth – an invention of Fielding's, or Meredith's. And this astounding revelation of deficiency in the Elizabethan drama, so casually indicated by Mr Bose, was perhaps the chief intellectual shock which Giles Gott experienced during these by no means uneventful Scamnum days. Now he looked at his watch. 'Time to begin,' he said briskly.

Hamlet has thirty speaking parts, two or three of which are nearly always omitted. With bold doubling, one can give the play with nineteen speaking players. In addition, one needs a few supers: a Dumb-show King and Queen, two servants, and if possible an extra Player, Lord, and Lady. There is no crowd, but in Act Four, Scene Five, everybody not actually on the stage must be prepared to stand off and shout to represent 'Danes'.

These were the Scamnum arrangements. It would have been easy to avoid doubling; there was no lack of minor amateur talent available for the smaller parts. But partly because the original plan had been for an entertainment *by* Scamnum, and more particularly because Gott was concerned to avoid that common course of amateur disaster, an over-crowded green-room, the cast had been kept down. It would finally stand in the programme like this:

CLAUDIUS, *King of Denmark*	Edward Crispin
HAMLET, *Prince of Denmark, son to the late, and nephew to the present King*	Melville Clay
POLONIUS, *Principal Secretary of State*	Ian Stewart
HORATIO, *friend to Hamlet*	Charles Piper
LAERTES, *son to Polonius*	Noel Gylby
ROSENCRANTZ ⎱ *formerly fellow-students* GUILDENSTERN ⎰ *with Hamlet*	⎰ Thomas Potts ⎱ Timothy Tucker
OSRIC, *a fantastic fop*	Gervase Crispin
A Gentleman	Rupert Traherne
A Doctor of Divinity	Samuel Crump
MARCELLUS ⎤ BARNARDO ⎬ *Gentlemen of the Guard* FRANCISCO ⎦	⎡ Richard Nave ⎨ Edward Bunney ⎣ Peter Marryat
First Grave-digger	Murdo Macdonald
Second Grave-digger	Gervase Crispin
FORTINBRAS, *Prince of Norway*	Andrew Malloch
A Norwegian Captain	Peter Marryat
English Ambassador	Richard Nave
Messenger	Vanessa Terborg
Sailor	Timothy Tucker
GERTRUDE, *Queen of Denmark, mother to Hamlet*	Anne Crispin
OPHELIA, *daughter to Polonius*	Elizabeth Crispin
Players Andrew Malloch, Gervase Crispin, Anna Merkalova, Diana Sandys	
Dumb-show King	Giles Gott
Dumb-show Queen	Stella Terborg
A Lord	Henry Biddle
A Lady	Lucy Terborg
Attendants	
The GHOST of *Hamlet's father*	Noel Gylby

This represented, Gott believed, a body manageable within the space available. Just thirty people all told would have business behind the scenes: the nineteen speaking players, the seven supers (including Gott himself as the Dumb-show King and two footmen dressed in Tudor liveries as 'attendants'), Mr Bose as prompter, the Duke's man and two professional dressers, male and female, brought down from London. A vexed question at the moment was whether there should be a thirty-first in the person of Max Cope. Cope was working on two sketches: one from the minstrel gallery at the back of the audience's part of the hall; the other from a corner of the upper stage, where he would be tolerably unnoticeable and get an interesting angle on the front stage. He was undecided still as to which he would work at on the night. Gott wished him safely away in the minstrel gallery, but as it would doubtless be by Cope's picture that the Tragedy of Hamlet played at Scamnum Court would go down to posterity he could hardly insist.

The cast, as the cast in any amateur theatricals must always be, was odd in one or two prominent places and shaky in several minor ones. Lord Traherne, as a Gentleman, unfortunately lost the character the moment he stepped on the boards, and became instead an awkward, though gentlemanlike, schoolboy. Peter Marryat, one of the untried late arrivals with two small parts, appeared dangerously half-witted. He was absent-minded enough, Clay declared, to begin his Norwegian Captain's speech while making his brief appearance as Francisco in the first scene – and obstinate enough, Gott added, to carry firmly on with it to the end. Stella Terborg was fairly safe in a silent part; but as her business was that of being poisoned in the dumb-show by someone uncommonly like a Black Hand she might very conceivably break through the convention with a scream. The more formidable Vanessa as a boy messenger, and Diana Sandys as a boy player who should speak the prologue in the play scene, both had parts less considerable than their competence deserved. Gervase Crispin had rather too much; it was doubtful if his foppery as Osric and his clownery as the Second Grave-digger would be as distinct as was desirable. And Noel was rather an unfledged Ghost. The part had been marked originally for Dr Crump, the Vicar of Scamnum Ducis; but when Dr Crump found it involving acrobatic disappearance down a trap followed by a longish crawl beneath a three-foot stage, he had retreated to the more familiar business of officiating at Ophelia's burial. Noel, however, was shaping well. Being the orthodox Crispin six feet, and a master of the precocious bass, favoured on public-school parade-grounds, he had the essential qualifications. All in all, Gott reiterated to himself, things should go well.

And this first dress-rehearsal on Saturday afternoon began excellently. Peter Marryat gave it a good start, by some terrific effort speaking

Francisco's eight dispersed lines correctly and in the right place. Bunney, although he insisted on delivering himself according to his own theory of Elizabethan pronunciation, was a surprisingly military Barnardo. Sir Richard Nave, in life a most drily unpoetical person – as who must not be, the Duchess said, that wants to improve sex? – brought out the lyrical strain in Marcellus well enough. Noel's Ghost, coached by Clay, stalked and turned on the upper stage as if on fifty yards of frosty battlement.

The first scene, however, tells one little of how the play will run. It is a tremendous start and the interest it instantly commands has to be caught up and sustained in the succeeding council scene. Once that is got compellingly under way the play is launched. And now it was going as Gott wanted it to go. The right atmosphere was being generated.

Gott's *Hamlet* was not the *Hamlet* in which Clay was accustomed to play on the professional stage. It belonged to what Malloch dubiously called 'the new historical school'. It was a *Hamlet* in which, through all the intellectual and poetical elaboration of the piece, a steady emphasis was given to the basic situations of wary conflict between usurper and rightful heir. The sense of desperate issues, of wits matched against wits in a life-and-death struggle, was to be perpetually present. The battle of mighty opposites – one side the crafty king and his equally crafty minister Polonius; on the other the single figure of the more formidably because more intellectually cunning prince – this was to be the heart of the Scamnum *Hamlet*. Whereas Clay's usual *Hamlet* sprang in considerable part from the ruminative minds of Goethe and Coleridge, Gott's sprang not a little from the minds of Shakespeare's full-blooded predecessors.

Into this newer reading of the play, Clay – though it had meant much work – had thrown himself with enthusiasm. And now in the second scene the result was beginning to unfold itself. Here in Claudius and Hamlet were two men who must fight to the death; here was the opening of a duel that would be instantly clear to any Renaissance audience. And as the action proceeded it came to Gott that he was watching not merely a careful and competent amateur *Hamlet* but a *Hamlet* which was – as far as its embodiment of this main conflict went – positively remarkable. Clay was a great actor, a fact Gott had barely realized before this Scamnum venture, though he knew him to be brilliant and successful enough. And – what was something more remarkable – the Duke of Horton was a great actor as well. He had been startling on his few and scrappy appearances at rehearsal earlier; he was astounding now. And the play as a result was catching the drift that Gott designed. The meditative Hamlet was revealed as only a facet of the total man; the Queen and Ophelia were pushed back; the play showed itself as turning predominantly from first to last on Statecraft. And it was the statesmen who were important; on the one side the dispossessed Hamlet; on the other Claudius and Polonius.

Gott watched the play unfold with the discriminating delight with which one studies an infinitely complicated thing that one has studied long. Mysterious power of dramatic illusion! Here was Melville Clay fronting the Duke of Horton and Lord Auldearn on a bogus Elizabethan stage in this bogus Gothic hall – and impossible not to believe that the fate of a kingdom lay at issue between them.

> 'The play's the thing
> Wherein I'll catch the conscience of the King!'

Hamlet's voice rang out in triumphant anticipation of his plot. The first part of the dress-rehearsal was over.

Nave came up in the interval, watch in hand. 'How quickly it moves!'

'As quick as the talkies,' said Clay.

Gott nodded. 'The talkies help. They bring the ear up with the eye again. And you notice how the speeding-up is carried over from the play? Everybody's brisker. Look at the Duke – bustling about like a works manager.'

'I should be inclined to put it,' said Nave, 'that there is rather a species of rebound. They have all been acting, and now they fall back more than they commonly allow themselves on what they would call real selves. The carry-over from the excitement of the play brings out what used to be called the ruling passion – or what your Elizabethans called the predominant humour.'

Nave's science was young and pushing, and the man was always ready to preach, even in a bustling pause for rehearsal. Now, as Clay hurried away, he continued to talk to Gott. 'Look at young Gylby. He's after that girl Sandys. He's twenty-two, I suppose, and she's probably the first girl he's ever become extensively aware of – such, Mr Gott, are our extraordinary educational conventions! And the result? A high degree of infatuation, a high degree of bewilderment, and a painful lack of technical knowledge as to how to proceed. But masquerading as a projection of sixteenth-century superstition has loosened him up. He's come back to his dominating purpose with a bound, and is achieving a markedly enhanced degree of sexual efficacy.'

Gott was somewhat too old-fashioned a person to relish the psychologist's terminology. But he had to admit the justice of the observation. Noel was taking Diana Sandys very seriously. And at the moment, clad still in the Ghost's gleaming armour and with his helmet under his arm, he was going about his business with all the directness of a knight in some distinctly pre-Tennysonian Arthuriad.

'Do you know anything of the girl?' asked Nave.

'Miss Sandys? She's a school acquaintance of Elizabeth's, and rather older. And, come to think of it, she too is a psychologist.' He looked with just sufficient whimsicality at Nave to make the coming thrust pass inoffensively. 'Or rather an applied psychologist, working on the mass subconscious in the interest of soaps and stockings and patent foods. Copywriting, I believe it's called.'

Nave nodded coolly. 'Well, advertising is one of the more harmless perversions of science, after all. And whatever she is, she's as hard as nails.' The tone indicated that, for Sir Richard Nave, to be hard as nails was one of the major maidenly virtues. And now abruptly he changed the subject. 'By the way, what exactly are the relations between the Player King and Player Queen?'

Gott, perhaps because he was obscurely disturbed, failed for an instant to grasp the question. And Nave, misinterpreting the hesitation, added: 'I ask as an old friend of the family.'

'Gervase Crispin and Mme Merkalova? I am not in their confidence.'

But Nave would not admit Gott's system of reticences. 'In other words, you share the general impression that she's his mistress? But that's just what's curious. I don't see quite the mechanisms one would expect. A Russian woman in such a situation, and moving in this sort of society, would insist on certain conventions – a little extra distance and formality between them – which would make the matter conveniently plain to the instructed, and leave the uninstructed equally conveniently ignorant.'

'Dear me,' said Gott, honestly feeling that he knew less of polished ungodliness than a romancer ought, 'you instruct *me*, Sir Richard.'

'Instead of which they are – well, not exactly as close as innocent lovers, but as thick as thieves.'

Gott laughed. 'If Gervase Crispin wanted to make the biggest haul in England, he'd have to crack his own safe. I hardly suppose the lady can be his accomplice in crime.'

The later hours of Saturday afternoon saw the arrival of another bevy of guests. Tea on the cedar-lawn, with the players moving about in their costumes still, had the appearance and proportions of a charity pageant. Gott had the impression that Lord Auldearn, viewing the swelling throng, was none too delighted. And presently he had what seemed confirmation. Auldearn, who had been talking earnestly to the Duke, swung round and approached him.

'Mr Gott, I have to go away. In anything you do tomorrow somebody must read my part. I shall be back on Monday morning – God willing.' And with this abrupt speech Lord Auldearn disappeared into the house. Twenty minutes later he stepped into his car and was whirled down the drive. The Duchess, Gott thought, was not disturbed; there was something like an extra dash of resolution in the ready gaiety with which she was going round. And the unwonted briskness which he had noticed in the Duke after rehearsal was gone. The master of Scamnum was vaguer than ever.

Noel had lured his Diana away to croquet; she was pinning up the Ghost's closet-scene dress – a sort of dressing-gown – to prevent its getting in his way. Pamela Hogg, the Armageddon woman, was fascinating Tommy Potts with equine lore. Mrs Terborg sailed about, knowing most people; discovering with others common friends in Paris, Vienna, Rome; skilfully circulating Vanessa among judiciously selected intellectuals, skilfully circulating Stella among less warily chosen Propertied Oafs. And by all these things Gott was obscurely troubled.

Dinner that night was an expansive affair. Bagot, unable to cope with introducing the first course, was of the technical opinion that it was a banquet. His master, contemplating a wife diminished into the middle distance, was just discernibly of the opinion that it was a bore. Max Cope, observing Gott's eye on the Duke, transferred his own gaze significantly to the panelling over the fireplace. Gott saw the point. There hung Kneller's portrait of the first Duke: an oldish man, competently painted, competently turned out as a Restoration type – and with over the keen features the same veil of indifference that now distinguished the eighth Duke at the head of his table Gott looked round for this queer habit of the will in the other members of the family. Gervase had nothing of it. Noel, a Crispin in some collateral line, was going to have it one day. And Elizabeth? Elizabeth was a Crispin rather than a Dillon, but it was not there nevertheless. A hereditary characteristic, perhaps, latent in the female. And for the remainder of the meal Gott contemplated a very simple fact. He was not, and never had been, disturbed about the Tragedy of Hamlet played at Scamnum Court. It was not in his nature to be disturbed by such an affair, and any anxieties he felt were transferred anxieties. Fuss over x while preparing to plunge at y.

Curious how the keyed mind would cling to inessentials, to the merely practical consequences, all the corollaries on less bewildering planes. A Fellow of St Anthony's, for instance, could not marry a Duke's daughter and get away with it – be as he had been. Either, Gott knew, he would have to quit, or inevitably on old Empson's retirement he would be President. Elizabeth, now at college because she had an eccentric mother, would be planted in the President's Lodging, entertaining dons' wives, undergraduates, itinerant Bunneys.

Irrelevant anxieties – and wandering later through the moonlit gardens with Elizabeth he continued to start them in his mind. Twenty-one and thirty-four. Thirty-one and forty-four, forty-one and fifty-four, seventy-one and eighty-four ... And – more formidable still – it had once been six and nineteen. Elizabeth had been a familiar creature then; now, walking beside him where he could remember balancing her on her first fat pony, she was remote as the stars and secret as the farther hemisphere of the moon.

They were pacing silently down one of Scamnum's famous avenues, the high, impenetrable hedges stretching interminably as in a dream; the pedestalled statues, a whole Olympus of marble deities dimly marshalled in extended file on either side, ghostly against the dark, cañon-like cypress-walls. At the end of the vista, etched in moonlight, stood one of Peter Crispin's minor eccentricities, a picturesque cow-house. A cow-house is not a common amenity in a formal garden, but Peter Crispin had liked to have his curiosities within an easy walk. When there were visitors at Scamnum he had been accustomed to give orders that cows be installed; and his friends, taking their first stroll, would exclaim in dutiful delight when the animals were discovered commodiously lodged in what had outwardly all the appearance of a ruined priory. And now the cow-house was picturesque still, but a cow-house no longer: they kept chemical manures there. Just beyond it, concealed by a high wall, ran the main road to King's Horton.

Elizabeth had paused for a moment by an untenanted pedestal. 'The Pandemian Venus,' she said. 'My grandmother had it removed because she thought it was particularly indelicate. Like Dr Folliott, Giles, in *Crotchet Castle.*' The light irony was Crispin; Giles, after all, *might* have been Elizabeth's tutor.

Six more statues to the cow-house. And there were those horrid words of Nave's: 'Twenty-two ... a high degree of infatuation, a high degree of bewilderment, and a painful lack of knowledge as to how to proceed ...' Noel, twenty-two; Gott, thirty-four. Thirty-four and twenty-one, eighty-four and seventy-one ...

Three statues to the cow-house. 'Auldearn went off suddenly,' said Gott, baulking badly.

'He heard of something important.' It was an absent but possibly ominous reply.

Two statues ... one statue ... round the cow-house.

'Elizabeth –' began Gott.

Elizabeth laid a hand on his arm. 'Look!'

The figure of a man had appeared from behind the bogus priory. There was a low whistle, some small object flew over the boundary wall in the moonlight, there was an answering whistle and the figure had vanished. A moment later there came the smooth crescendo and diminuendo of a high-powered car.

'Some servants' intrigue,' said Gott.

'With a Daimler waiting?' There had come into Elizabeth's voice – astoundingly – a far-away echo of the Duke's lazy indifference. 'No; it's something we've had occasionally at Scamnum ever since my enterprising mother hit on making daddy an Elder Statesman.' She gave a little puckered smile. 'A species of excitement your austere art sniffs at, Giles. *Spies.*'

And in the early hours of Monday morning the Black Hand put up its most effective show. Suddenly and hideously in the darkness the whole great fabric of Scamnum re-echoed to the uproar of a tremendous bell. It reverberated through the corridors and flooded a hundred lofty rooms, first in peal after solemn peal and then in a wild gallop, grotesquely loud. And as the startled household hurried out of bedrooms and along corridors, and while the Duke, a surprisingly commanding figure at the head of the main staircase, was shouting that there was no danger of fire, the bell abruptly ceased – to be replaced a moment later by a thunderous but oddly familiar human voice:

> 'Ere the bat hath flown
> His cloister'd flight, ere, to Black Hecate's summons
> The shard-borne beetle with his drowsy hums
> Hath rung night's yawning peal, there shall be done
> A deed of dreadful note . . .'

Echoing bewilderingly from every direction, the speech could yet be distinguished as coming from somewhere below. It was Gott who, with a sudden gesture of enlightenment, ran downstairs. The voice grew in menace:

> 'Come, seeling night,
> Scarf up the tender eye of pitiful day,
> And with thy bloody and invisible hand
> Cancel and tear to pieces that great bond
> Which keeps me pale! Light thickens . . .'

Silence. Gott remounted the stairs. 'The radio-gramophone,' he said. 'Turn a knob and get as much volume as you like. And it changes its own records. First record, a carillon chime – the horror of the ringing bell. Second record, Mr Clay recording from *Macbeth*. Another petty jest.'

Clay, beautiful in a brocaded dressing-gown, nodded easily. 'I thought the voice had a homely ring,' he said. 'I made that record a long time ago, and I think it was a mistake. What was that most apposite quotation?'

Vanessa Terborg turned from calming Stella, her master-passion for showing herself always on the spot roused at once. ' "The clangour of the angels' trumpets and the horror of the ringing bell." Well, I don't think anybody's scared.' Her eye went back firmly to her sister.

Gott doubted the assurance – of others besides the timid Stella. He was scared himself. The mind that could contrive so violent an effect was a mind that thought in terms of violence.

5

(3, 4) *The Queen's closet hung with arras, represented by the rear-stage curtain.*

The QUEEN *and* POLONIUS

POLONIUS: A' will come straight. Look you lay home to him,
Tell him his pranks have been too broad to bear with.
And that your grace hath screened and stood between
Much heat and him. I'll silence me even here.
Pray you be round with him.

HAMLET (*without*): Mother, mother, mother!

QUEEN: I'll war'nt you,
Fear me not. Withdraw, I hear him coming.
    [POLONIUS *hides behind the curtain of the rear-stage.*
    HAMLET *enters.*]

HAMLET: Now, mother, what's the matter?

QUEEN: Hamlet, thou hast thy father much offended.

HAMLET: Mother, you have my father much offended.

QUEEN: Come, come, you answer with an idle tongue.

HAMLET: Go, go, you question with a wicked tongue.

QUEEN: Why, how now, Hamlet?

HAMLET: What's the matter now?

QUEEN: Have you forgot me?

HAMLET: No, by the rood not so,
You are the queen, your husband's brother's wife,
And would it were not so, you are my mother.

QUEEN: Nay then, I'll set those to you that can speak.
    [*Going.*]

HAMLET (*seizes her arm*): Come, come, and sit you down, you shall not
    budge,
You go not till I set you up a glass
Where you may see the inmost part of you.

QUEEN: What wilt thou do? thou wilt not murder me? Help, help, ho!

POLONIUS (*behind the curtain*): What, ho! help, help, help!

HAMLET (*draws*): How now! a rat? dead, for a ducat, dead.
    [*He makes a pass through the curtain.*]

POLONIUS (*falls*): O, I am slain!

QUEEN: O me, what has thou done?
HAMLET: Nay, I know not,
   Is it the king?
   [*He lifts up the curtain and discovers* POLONIUS, *dead.*]
QUEEN: O, what a rash and bloody deed is this! ...

Aged royalty, perhaps with royalty's instinct for keeping clear of anything a trifle odd, had decided not to come after all. So decorations had been put away; young ladies, hearing the news when half-way to the drawing-room, had scurried back to their rooms to change into more intriguing frocks; Bagot had had a busy half-hour putting away the plate which Scamnum produces only for members of a Reigning House. And now in the hall the Dowager Duchess was sitting in the front row in solitary state, on her right hand the two empty chairs that had been destined for the 'real' Duchess and the 'real' Duchess's lady. The Dowager was formidable enough in herself and Gott received with relief Noel's report that the old lady seemed disposed to take out most of the play in sleep. It was a quite unexpurgated *Hamlet*.

Peter Marryat had caused some anxiety. After dinner he had declared that he felt all muddled, and piteously inquired of Noel as to which *was* the one that came first: Francisco or the Norwegian Captain? And Noel having recklessly decided that the answer might be found in a good stiff brandy, the first scene had at moments conveyed the impression that the sentries of Elsinore were a trifle too familiar with the regimental canteen. But as Claudius's court was well known to be in a condition of festivity and swagg'ring upstart reels, this might have passed as the stroke of a venturesome producer; indeed, Gott could see in Malloch's eye the prospect of its being humorously so represented in many common-rooms hereafter. But there had been no major mishaps. The first part of the play had run rapidly and well and ended in a thunder of applause.

And now the audience, who in the interval had been wandering all over the stage and hall, to the accompaniment of that quite deafening chatter which is the hall-mark of large and polite parties, had been shepherded back to their seats; Bunney had set his black box going on the floor beside the Dowager; the players had returned to the green-room and Tommy Potts, who had turned out to be skilful in such things, heralded Act Three, Scene One with a flourish on a trumpet. A second flourish and the rear-stage curtain was drawn back on 'The lobby of the audience chamber'. The King and Queen, with Polonius, Rosencrantz and Guildenstern, came on in a little confabulating, plotting knot; and behind them came Ophelia. The second half of the play was launched.

3.1 bristles with technical difficulties; Gott, standing off-stage in his costume as Dumb-show King, was following it intently. Rosencrantz and Guildenstern had come off – heads together, plotting still. And the King's voice continued, tense and secret yet carrying clearly through the hall:

> 'Sweet Gertrude, leave us too,
> For we have closely sent for Hamlet hither,
> That he, as 'twere by accident, may here
> Affront Ophelia:
> Her father and myself, lawful espials,
> Will so bestow ourselves, that seeing unseen,
> We may of their encounter frankly judge ...'

The Queen came off; Ophelia was set with her book at the faldstool; the King spoke the ticklish guilty aside that prepares for his remorse in the prayer-scene; he and Polonius concealed themselves. Hamlet came on; walked far up the front stage.

'To be, or not to be ...'

To the actor, this is the most formidable speech in drama, formidable because it has established itself at the heart of English poetry, and every word is a legend. Now it came, grave and level, from Melville Clay:

> 'For who would bear the whips and scorns of time,
> Th' oppressor's wrong, the proud man's contumely,
> The pangs of disprized love, the law's delay,
> The insolence of office ...'

Slowly Hamlet was rounding the great stage, the rhythm of his movement answering the rhythm of the speech. Now he was approaching Ophelia:

> 'Thus conscience does make cowards of us all,
> And thus the native hue of resolution
> Is sicklied o'er with the pale cast of thought,
> And enterprise of great pitch and moment

> With this regard their currents turn awry,
> And lose the name of action ...'

He had seen Ophelia; there followed, Gott thought, the most beautiful lines in the play:

> 'Soft you now,
> The fair Ophelia – Nymph, in thy orisons
> Be all my sins remembered.'

And now the moment had come which was to tax the utmost limit of Clay's technique. Without direct word spoken, it had to come to the audience that Hamlet had recognized of a sudden that Ophelia's presence was part of a plot. From that moment he would be speaking to her – savagely – with the skin of his mind; all his faculties concentrated on his lurking enemies. This sudden understanding – because it is prepared for only by a fragment of business buried six hundred lines before – is extraordinarily difficult to convey. The point can be made broadly by the King or Polonius accidentally giving their presence away; but there is no warrant for that. It can be – and often is – ignored; but then Hamlet's brutality becomes revolting. If the thing is to be perfectly effective Hamlet must *recollect*.

Clay recollected. He froze.

> 'Are you honest ... are you fair?'

The words came as if from one in trance. And each succeeding speech, while tremendous in itself, was yet queerly automatic. The surface of the mind ran on, to finish in threadbare railing: women and their painting! For all the forces of the man were now concentrated elsewhere. Here was a Hamlet for whom only one fact was any longer real: the presence of his enemies hidden somewhere here about him; plotting, preparing their final trap. Here, in fact, was the Hamlet of the historical school come rather terrifyingly to life.

He was gone. If Gott had been given to conventional gestures he would have mopped his brow. And now Ophelia's voice – Elizabeth's voice – was moving clearly and tragically through her final soliloquy:

> 'O, what a noble mind is here o'erthrown!
> The courtier's, soldier's, scholar's, eye, tongue, sword,
> Th' expectancy and rose of the fair state,
> The glass of fashion, and the mould of form ...'

The King and Polonius were out of hiding again, heads together, Polonius eager to be hiding once more:

> 'My lord, do as you please,
> But if you hold it fit, after the play,
> Let his queen-mother all alone entreat him
> To show his grief; let her be round with him;
> And I'll be placed (so please you) in the ear
> Of all their conference. If she find him not,
> To England send him; or confine him where
> Your wisdom best shall think.'

Polonius, his plan to hide in the Queen's closet settled, withdrew. The King turned full to the audience and raised a dramatic hand in keeping with the rhetorical menace of his concluding couplet:

> 'It shall be so.
> Madness in great ones must not unwatched go!'

He stepped within the rear stage and the curtain closed.

3.2.

3.3.

3.4 . . . Again the rear-stage curtain had closed on the King, this time as he knelt at his vain prayers by the faldstool. At once the Queen and Polonius took the front stage for the closet-scene.

Mr Bose, crouched in his place to the side of the rear stage, was following the speech of the invisible players, syllable by syllable. Polonius's injunction to 'lay home'; Hamlet's call for admittance; the rustle of the rear-stage curtain as Polonius slipped through from the front stage to 'silence himself' . . .

The altercation between Hamlet and the Queen grew. The Queen's cry rang out:

'*Help, help, ho!*'

From the rear stage came the echoing voice of Polonius:

'*Help, help!*'

Mr Bose, his eye fixed on his text, stirred in his seat. A pistol-shot rang through the hall.

2 Development

Good now, sit down, and tell me, he that knows,
Why this same strict and most observant watch? ...
What might be toward, that this sweaty haste
Doth make the night joint-labourer with the day:
Who is't that can inform me?

I

Mr John Appleby of Scotland Yard was at the theatre. Being the new sort of policeman he was at the ballet, waiting for *Les Présages* to follow *La Boutique Fantasque*. Being paid the old sort of wage, and having the most modest of private fortunes, he was sitting in what his provincial childhood had known as the Family Circle. But being unmarried he was unaccompanied by a family, and being serious and shy, he was without the distraction of a female friend. As a consequence, he was able to devote the interval to reflections on ballet as Pure Muscular Style. Appleby contrived to read the latest books on such things. He was just meditating the awkward case of Japanese tumblers – they were certainly not ballet, but might they not be Pure Muscular Style too? – when the lights were lowered and Tchaikovsky's music, heavy with observations on the Mysterious Universe, filled the theatre.

The constant patrons, who treat the stalls so impressively after the manner of a drawing-room, were strolling and edging back to their places. The woman next to Appleby shut her chocolate-box and stowed it under the seat. Portentously, the curtain rose on Masson's sub-Dantesque stage: hit or miss, Appleby thought, whether you were excited or felt that here was a nice design cruelly run in the wash.

The puce ladies, vaguely Spanish from the neck down; the green and brown gentlemen, ever so slightly ashamed of themselves (one ashamedly and philistinely suspected) from the neck up; Action, in pleasing pleats and extracting miraculous grace from impossible angularities ... they were all at it again, thought Appleby – who was half-way to being a hardened amateur. And certainly it was exciting; Pure Muscular Style – in stately capital letters – scarcely put the matter excitingly enough. The trouble was that these galvanic figures were obscurely up to something, insinuating something, endeavouring – the fatal image would come – like the deaf and dumb to utter through a laborious periphrasis of gesture. And now, against the backcloth, the gentlemen were leaping from wings to wings in three unbelievable hops; now they were charging across the same path in couples, the ladies held out in front of them, head-high, like battering-rams. And all, evidently, with the largest cosmic intent ... articulative, like the music, of the Nature of Things. But the oftener you came, thought Appleby, the less satisfactorily did it build up, the more did you get your pleasure from the fragmentary movements – the exquisite precision, for instance, of the *pas de deux* which the programme called Passion. Yet what delighted him most in *Les Présages* was something essentially dramatic, the entrance of Fate. It was a pity that Fate was got up like a queasy Ethiopian in off-black; it was a pity that he had to make that merely pantomime exit backwards on his heels. But his entrance perfectly blended the dramatic and the choreographic.

Appleby remembered his uncle George, who used to recite at parties a poem beginning 'A chieftain to the Highlands bound' – and at 'bound' *bound* into the middle of the room ... Fate did not come on like that. On the great stage the common traffic of life was proceeding with an even, untroubled rhythm – and then Fate was *there*, his entrance unnoticed, his menace waiting to strike home.

It was nearly over. The gentlemen had appeared in a new and yet more cosmic kit; they were machines, they were infantry crossing broken ground under fire. The evil in Man, as the programme had it, had aroused the angry passion of war – and the puce ladies, also metamorphosed, were themselves subjected by the martial glamour. If only as mere miming, this was impressive; the symbolism pierced to the contemporary nerve. And now the finale: dubious victory; the Hero leaping to a tableau on somebody's shoulders, stretching out arms – perhaps to the Future, but unescapably as if to an invisible trapeze, so that one thought of tumblers again and half expected the *corps de ballet* to clap hands and make admiring Japanese noises.

The woman in the next seat groped for her chocolate-box.

Appleby emerged from the theatre and walked luxuriously through the London night, discoursing with himself on his own character as a modified philistine. He worked hard as a policeman, he often made his work his play, it was pleasant to have given three hours to something that could have no possible bearing on shop – the monotonous pursuit of burglars in Earl's Court and injudicious philanthropists in the City. Coming down the Duke of York's Steps, his eye rested on the Admiralty and travelled along the jumbled line of government buildings. One had Palmerston to thank that the Treasury – or was it the Foreign Office? – was not a monument of Ruskinian Gothic. High up, just beyond Downing Street, there shone a solitary light. Were his more orthodoxly gifted contemporaries who had made their way here similarly immersed in a dull routine? What were they doing up there now?

Appleby had one of the humblest flats in one of the largest blocks in Westminster; his three rooms, he suspected, had originally been intended as a bathroom, a kitchenette, and a shoe-cupboard for some more magnificent tenant. But the situation gave him St James's Park as a detour to and from work; his living-room window commanded Mr Epstein's admirable Night while ignoring his less admirable Day; and sitting up in bed he could distinguish the upper half of the flag-staff on Buckingham Palace. Approaching the entrance of this building now, Appleby quickened his pace. A car was standing outside, a car which meant business. A moment later he became aware of a second car, and whistled. And when he saw a third car – a car which every policeman must know – he ran.

The night-porter, usually inaccessible to any under six-room tenants, came scurrying out of his cubby-hole to say something Appleby didn't stop to hear. The lift-boy, hitherto familiar and conversible, looked at him on this occasion with awe. He ran along the corridor and burst rather breathlessly into his room.

It was an overwhelming spectacle. The Chief Commissioner was pacing up and down the available eight feet of floor. Appleby's immediate superior in the CID, Superintendent Billups, stood, plainly bewildered and slightly affronted, in a corner. In the only easy chair sat the Prime Minister, holding a large gun-metal watch some three inches from his nose.

'Good evening, gentlemen,' said Appleby. The words represented, he felt, one of the major efforts of his career.

The Prime Minister exploded. 'Is this the man? Haddon, if you have a plain Number One man don't let him clear out of sight again. Theatres have names, you know, and theatre-seats numbers. Ask your doctor.'

While prime ministers speak to commissioners thus, detective-inspectors look modestly down their nose; Appleby attempted this. But now the Prime Minister tucked away his watch and sat back as if he had simply dropped in for a chat. 'And *where* have you been, Mr – um – Appleby?' he asked amiably.

'*Les Présages*, sir.'

The Prime Minister shook his head. 'The ballet's gone modern since my day. When Degas was painting, now ... but the point is the Lord Chancellor's been shot. At Scamnum Court, playing at *Hamlet* apparently – a strange play, Mr Appleby, a strange atmosphere about it.

Shot thirty-five minutes ago by goodness knows whom. But whatever it's about the business has no political significance. You understand me?'

'No political significance,' said Appleby.

The Prime Minister rose. 'But, you know, I like *Les Sylphides*. And now, Mr Appleby, come along and don't stand there talking. I'll tell you about it in the car.'

Appleby opened the door, and felt the blood tingling in his finger-tips as he did so – perhaps it was with the increased physical consciousness that follows ballet. '*Les Sylphides*, sir?' he murmured demurely.

'Yes. Damn it – no! Auldearn.' The Prime Minister turned conciliatingly to the Commissioner. 'Excellent plan coming on here, Haddon; got our man at once. Advise keeping that lead on him another time, though.' His eye strayed to Superintendent Billups. 'You'll see that Mr Dollups works a machine or net or what not in town here if it's necessary? I suppose he'll get his instructions direct from Mr Appleby at Scamnum.' The Prime Minister was innocently oblivious of the hierarchies of the police. And having during the proceedings sacrificed some forty seconds to the conscientious whimsicalities that endeared him to the electorate, he now pushed Appleby into the lift and cried 'Down!' so fiercely that the already overwrought lift-boy lost his head and shot them straight to the top floor. It was, Appleby thought, an excellent prelude to adventure.

And so was the fire-engine. Billups would not have thought to requisition a fire-engine; the Prime Minister had. Its bell, he explained, gained more respect than did a police siren – and in addition the sound was somewhat less disagreeable. So the fire-engine tore through the rapidly thinning night-traffic towards Vauxhall Bridge, the Prime Minister's car followed, and the police-car – it was the great yellow Bentley that always gave Appleby a schoolboy's thrill – brought up the rear.

Appleby looked cautiously at the silent figure of the Prime Minister humped in his corner; he was not quite sure that he was not part of a dream. Only fifteen minutes before he had been skirting the Horse Guards', murmuring against routine and looking as from an immense distance at an enigmatical light in the Foreign Office that had symbolized the very vortex of Empire. Now, far out on either side of him, Earl's Court with its burglars and the City with its twisters, were hurtling into the thither darkness at forty miles an hour – a sweeping turn at the Oval and the pace was working up to fifty on the Clapham Road. It was a gorgeous and fantastic procession, and Appleby thought comfortably of the fourth car going off in another direction, with a grim Commissioner giving Billups a gloomy lift to bed. He stole another glance at the great man beside him. Yes, it was true. This was the Prime Minister and ahead of them lay one of the famous houses of England. *Death at Scamnum Court* – what a title for Giles Gott!

The Prime Minister had out his ostentatiously rural watch again; when the road narrowed in New Wimbledon and the pace dropped he swore. It was his only utterance until, a mile down the Kingston by-pass, the fire-engine swung right for Putney and disappeared. Then, as the cars opened out, he talked.

'Lord Auldearn motored down to Scamnum on Friday afternoon. He meant to stay five or six days and join in this *Hamlet* business ... you don't know the Duchess?'

Mr Appleby confessed to not knowing the Duchess.

'Remarkable woman – and fond of that sort of thing. Daughter of Lionel Dillon – fellow who could make prosperous counter-jumpers look like saints in El Greco. Well, Auldearn went down on Friday and that same evening' – the Prime Minister hesitated – 'something important came in. We sent it straight down to him.'

'To the Lord Chancellor.' The matter-of-fact amplification was as near to a fishing question as Appleby thought it discreet to go. The Prime Minister took up the implication easily; he pursed his lips, evidently feeling his way.

'Auldearn's death', he said carefully, 'is a terrific blow – not merely personally to many of us, but nationally. He had more political wisdom and experience than anyone. And a wonderful brain. And he had a curious career – for a lawyer. He was Foreign Secretary, you remember, at a very ticklish time.'

'Of course,' said Appleby. There was a long silence. Some unidentifiable South London common was slipping past, at once banal and mysterious under the garish London sky. Far to the east a train whistled – the profoundly disturbing whistle of a train in the night.

'On Saturday afternoon,' the Prime Minister continued quietly, 'Auldearn decided he must come back to town. On Sunday there were various ... discussions. But he made it a point of honour to return to Scamnum for the play today. You will readily guess that he made no sacrifice of public duty to do so. Only ... he took with him for study another document. Mr Appleby, I wish to God he had not done so.'

The Prime Minister, so shortly before practising his pertinacious eccentricity of speech and manner, had become direct and grim. 'At eleven-five tonight they brought a telephone into my dressing-room – an urgent call. It was the Duke of Horton. He told me that Auldearn had been shot dead on the stage, apparently in circumstances which afford no light on his assailant. That is very extraordinary, but I suppose it may be so. Horton either knew or guessed that public issues might be involved. He said he was holding everybody tight and he begged me to act at once. He particularly asked for somebody who would not be scared by a high and mighty mob; he was referring, no doubt, to the sort of house-party he has down there. When I got hold of Haddon he named you.' There was a pause. 'Much may depend on you.'

Appleby said nothing. He would not have liked to swear that at the moment, at least, he was wholly unscared. But when the Prime Minister suddenly thrust forward a cigar-case his hand was perfectly steady under the other's gaze. It was a sort of ritual of confidence. Efficiently, Appleby supplied matches.

The Prime Minister drew a rug round himself and spoke again. 'There is no reason to suppose that this horrid affair is other than an act of random madness or of private vengeance. All public men are a mark for such things. And for that reason I cannot afford to go straight to the Intelligence. Who is known and marked there one can never know, and the knowledge that they had been sent down might be undesirable. And so we send' – the Prime Minister smiled wanly – 'a straight policeman.'

Appleby asked his first question. 'Was he guarded?'

'He would never hear of it. I am sure they would never let me get away with such an attitude, but Auldearn carried it off.' The Prime Minister eyed his own detective sitting beside his chauffeur and sighed. 'He was a powerful man.'

The cars swerved through Esher. 'Please Providence, Mr Appleby, this document is now safe and undisturbed in Auldearn's dispatch-case. But should it be involved you will be able to carry on for a time without being at a disadvantage with the specialists. If they have a line on anything at Scamnum at present the information will be waiting for us at Guildford, where I shall leave you. Have you struck the fringes of that sort of thing – espionage?'

'Yes, sir,' said Appleby briefly.

'So much the better. It's a crazy and surprising business; a complicated game that every country plays at – with a big bill and, just occasionally, a successful piece of mischief to show. What is to be remembered, I think, is that it is crazy – continually offending against probability, like bad fiction. You never know who's in on it, particularly – I'm told – among the women. To put it absurdly, Mr Appleby, don't trust anybody, not even the Archbishop of Canterbury should he be there. Trust nothing but your own nose.'

Appleby pondered these skilfully imparted instructions for a few moments before venturing on a question. 'Can I have more information on the nature and importance of the document, sir?'

The Prime Minister answered readily. 'The document concerns the organization of large industrial interests on an international basis, in the event of a certain international situation. The general drift towards the matter such a document embodies cannot, you will realize, well be secret; nothing big can be secret. But the details may be. And this document might be useful in two ways: the detailed information might be useful to one powerful interest or another; and accurate possession of the details, as circumstantial evidence of something already known in general terms, might be useful to an unfriendly government. And that is why I am gravely concerned: the document at this moment would be a lever, a lever where a lever is being looked for. Or call it a switch, Mr Appleby; a switch that might release a spark.'

Again there was silence. The Prime Minister contemplated the glowing end of his cigar. And Appleby had before him in the darkness – and with a new impressiveness – Masson's angry stage and Massine's loam-coloured personifications of conflict, beating out their obscure warfare to that mounting chaotic music. 'War?' said Appleby, carried to generalities despite himself; 'the springs of war are surely not in spy-work and filched papers?'

His companion regarded him with a new interest. But his voice was harsh and rapid as he answered. 'War! No, no – that is something no bigger than a man's hand. It must remain so.' He tapped the window at his side. 'Do you know this part of the country? Out there somewhere, a couple of miles short of the river, there's a little place called Mud Town. War means Mud Town for Europe, Mr Appleby. And do you know what's ahead of us – just north of Bisley, suitably enough? Donkey

Town. War means that too. Certainly its springs are not in filched papers! Its springs are in the profound destructiveness deep in each of us, the same madness that has killed Auldearn — yes, however calculated that killing may turn out to have been. But these things, documents, plans' — he returned obstinately to his former figure — 'can be levers; damnable engines.'

He let the dead ash fall from his cigar. 'Well, Mr Appleby, so much you must certainly know, if you are to face the unexpected. And you must know how to identify the document. It is endorsed *Ministry of Agriculture and Fisheries: proposed Pike and Perch Joint Scheme*.' He smiled on the astonished Appleby as he revealed this Cabinet secret.

'Auldearn's last joke,' he said. 'And not without salt.'

Just beyond the environs of Guildford the car drew to a halt. And almost instantly a dim figure appeared at the window and opened the door. The Prime Minister, followed by Appleby, got out.

'Captain Hilfers?'

'Yes, sir; beaten you by five minutes. There's no report whatever. I've had the Scotland Yard people up since I left you, and our own people as well. There has been trouble at Scamnum twice in the last five years. Once when you yourself were there an undesirable guest was discovered and quietly turned out; and once a servant was found to be taking money from a well-known agent. But just now — we have knowledge of nothing.'

'You're an experienced man; just how much does that mean?'

'Little enough, sir. But if there's been shooting I think the thing incredible. And on the other hand I've found myself sparring with the incredible before now.'

The Prime Minister nodded impatiently in the darkness. 'Yes, yes. No government, no bureau would venture such a thing. But no doubt there are amateurs . . . irregulars.' He laughed shortly. 'Well, we have our own irregular. Hilfers, you know Inspector Appleby? Mr Appleby, come along.'

To the north the sky still held the ruddy smear of London; to the south were stars and a low-riding moon. They trudged in silence to the police-car. Huddled in the back were the Yard's best searchers, man and woman — evidence that the Prime Minister left little unthought of. Appleby, wasting no time, sprang into the front. The Prime Minister shut the door, tossed in his cigar-case. 'You may have time for another. And you'll find there the telephone-number I'll be at the end of for the next twelve hours ... Did you see Woizikowsky?'

'In *Les Présages*, sir? Yes, as Fate.'

'Fate? ... Well, good luck.' The Prime Minister turned on his heel and with Captain Hilfers – that mysterious Mercury – melted into the darkness.

'Let her go, Thomas,' said Appleby. The Bentley rocketed south.

Just at twelve-forty, with some eight miles to go, they met the first car – a large limousine dimly lit within, and with a footman beside the chauffeur. 'Nobs,' said Thomas as they flashed past with dipped head-lights.

'The Brazilian Minister,' Appleby responded absently; he had spotted the flag. A moment later Thomas had to swerve violently to avoid a sports car cutting a vicious corner in the darkness. It held a hatless youth in tails, one hand on the wheel, one resigned to a lady submerged in white fur. And close on its tracks followed an enormous scarlet sedan.

'Earl of Luppitt,' said Thomas, well-informed on the equipage of one of England's sporting peers. 'Party on somewhere hereabouts.'

'Thomas, what's down this way?'

Thomas considered. 'Nothing much except Scamnum, sir.'

Another car flashed past and then another. Away to the right, along some ridge of downland, a succession of gliding, swerving lights sped westwards towards Hampshire. 'Push along,' said Appleby quietly.

Thomas pushed along, only to draw up abruptly on the crown of a little bridge, the Bentley's bonnet almost touching the running-board of a dapper coupé, awkwardly stalled in the middle of the road. Its sole occupant was a man, an opera-cloak on his shoulders, the immortal in-vention of M. Gibus on his head, and a look of uncommon anxiety dis-cernible on his face. He was thrusting angrily at his self-starter.

'Hullo, Happy!' The gentleman in the opera-hat jumped at the voice from the darkness. 'Thomas, this is Mr Happy Hutton; as part of your education – mark him well.' Appleby leaned across the Bentley and swivelled the spot-light. Mr Happy Hutton's anxiety was clearly revealed as changed to abject terror; his engine spluttered into life, his clutch engaged, he lifted his opera-hat nervously, and bounced on into the night.

Appleby chuckled. 'Happy's always polite, even when scared stiff. Useful information, Thomas, but not our quarry. Push along.'

This time Thomas pushed along unimpeded. The remaining miles melted away. The Bentley pulsed up the south drive of Scamnum Court.

2

Take a revolver down to the far end of the garden for a little target-practice and your neighbours (unless they be timorous folk) will merely complain of your 'potting away'. Let fly at someone you dislike in the street and the resulting disturbance will be supposed by nine bystanders out of ten to come from a motor-bicycle. But fire a revolver in a raftered hall and you will produce the equivalent of a thunder-clap.

The unknown – presently to be revealed as death – had irrupted upon the Scamnum theatricals with an effect of astounding violence; and it was because of this, perhaps, that the audience felt everything that followed as pitched incongruously low. The shot brought several people to their feet; brought cries from others. But the audience was quickly still again – waiting and watching. They saw Melville Clay hesitate in front of the curtain towards which he had been advancing with his rapier – hesitate with the actor's instinct to gain time when something has gone wrong. Then he took a swift step forward and vanished through the curtain. An agitated voice called out 'My Lord!' and a moment later the Duchess rose and slipped quietly off stage.

A minute went by and then the Duke of Horton, King Claudius's wig limp in his hand, appeared from the rear stage and said: 'There has been a serious misadventure: please all stay where you are.' A murmur – acquiescence, support, concern – answered him as he disappeared. A few people began to whisper, as if in church; most were silent; but all heads turned sharply when Giles Gott, still in his costume as Dumb-show King, walked rapidly down the hall, spoke to the fireman at the farther door, and returned silently behind the scenes once more. Five minutes later the Duke appeared again. With an ominous slowness he traversed the whole depth of the front stage and it was seen that he intended to speak to his mother. He dropped down from the stage, and taking her hand, spoke earnestly a couple of sentences. Then he climbed back to the stage and faced the audience. The hall was very silent.

'I have bad news. The pistol-shot you all heard was aimed at Lord Auldearn. He is dead.' The Duke paused to let the ripple of horror produced by the spare announcement subside. Then he added: 'For the moment, nobody must leave the hall. And it will be best that none of you should come upon the stage or behind the scenes. I ask you to stay where you are until the police arrive.'

Again there was a docile murmur, this time not a little awed. A guest of consequence − a stray ambassador who had turned up at the last moment − called out: 'We will do just what you direct.' And at this the Duke nodded and retreated again.

By this time the crowd in the hall was conscious that it was behaving well in difficult circumstances; that it was helping to handle an appalling situation efficiently. The lighting had not been changed and for the rows of people sitting in shadow there was perhaps something hypnoidal in the empty stage with its sharply focused arc-lamps; everybody continued to sit still as the minutes went by. It was as if that peculiar merging of consciousness which comes upon an audience watching drama had been furthered rather than broken up by the advent of veritable catastrophe: the audience for a long half-hour behaved as a single impassive spectator. Only a judicious murmur of conversation was kept up here and there to minimize the strain.

There was little to observe. The Duke came back to speak for a few minutes to his mother; he was followed by Gervase and then by Dr Biddle, who had succeeded in walking on as an attendant lord and who now brought the Dowager a drink in his everyday capacity as medical attendant to the family. After he had retired old Max Cope made a slightly disconcerting appearance on the upper stage, surveying the hall placidly, palette in hand, as if nothing whatever had happened. Presently he was joined by Melville Clay − clad in a sombre dressing-gown, as if he kept a stock about him for all emergencies − and led off. A minute later Clay emerged below, crossed the front stage and dropped down beside the Dowager. He sat down and talked quietly, the soothing murmur of his musical voice audible in snatches to the people near by. Then he went away again, returned with Max in tow, set the old man safely down beside the old lady, and disappeared once more. Twice a telephone buzzer could just be heard behind the stage; the murmur of voices there occasionally rose into a half-distinguishable phrase. Then at eleven thirty-five the door at the rear of the hall opened and a police sergeant and three constables entered, ushered by Bagot.

One constable stopped by the door, the others walked rapidly down the hall, eyes front. They disappeared behind the scenes.

And that was all. *That* – several people remarked next day, with the changed attitude that the chasm of sleep will bring – was all that the audience got from the violent death of a Lord Chancellor. That and an extra cup of coffee, for at eleven forty-five footmen wheeled in quantities of this decorous refreshment. For fifteen minutes cups were handed and accepted; sandwiches were handed and either declined as frivolous or consumed as a species of funeral baked meat according to the temperament of the individual. At three minutes past midnight the Duke appeared for the last time. He was brief and quiet as before, but in his voice some subtle change – it might have been relief – was distinguishable.

'It is not necessary that you should stay longer. Will those of you who are stopping with us go back to the house? There will be no need for you to stay up longer than you want to. For the others the cars are coming round now. It will be best that we on this side remain in the hall a little longer.' Again the Duke descended to speak to his mother; he secured two ladies to look after her and then steered Max Cope behind the scenes. The guests filed out. It was the end of the Tragedy of Hamlet played at Scamnum Court.

When the last tail-coat had vanished and the doors were shut once more the players began to percolate by ones and twos into the main body of the hall – foraging. One of the big coffee urns was empty, but the other was full; they fell to. They ate the sandwiches without delicacy; theirs had been the chief shock and they were beyond fancied proprieties. The two footmen in their Tudor liveries, together with the Duke's man, handed salvers with something like imperturbability. The two dressers from London sat in a corner and sipped and nibbled, scared and a little indignant. The police sergeant had gone off with one constable – for the orthodox purpose, it was said, of interviewing the servants – and a second was invisible on the rear stage, guarding the body. Macdonald waited on the Duchess, still considerably more like Prospero than a First Grave-digger. Most of the players had felt it seemly to discard as much of their theatrical appearance as possible, but all had not been equally successful. The women had removed the slight make-up from their faces and thrown on cloaks. Gervase had abandoned Osric's grotesque cap but not his fantastical doublet. Noel had cast Laertes's cloak over the Ghost's nightgown. Dr Crump had hastily taken off his vestments but forgotten his tonsure. Dr Biddle's white hose were stained with blood. All in all, it was discernibly the ruins of King Claudius's Court at Elsinore, disrupted by a mine more deadly than any Hamlet had devised, that stood or wandered about Peter Crispin's folly. A queer sight . . . and the courtyard clock was tolling one when the door opened and a young man strode rapidly in, swept up the scene at a glance and said: 'The Duke of Horton, please. I am from Scotland Yard.'

The tone was unaggressive, but it represented all that firm control of a situation which the Duke himself had been sustaining these two hours. And now from the Duke something seemed to fall away.

'Then surely we can get this cleared up.' The Duke looked irresolutely round his guests. 'Well – come, come.'

The Duchess sighed. And everybody had the irrational feeling that after an evening's madness the normal had reasserted itself.

But presently the Duke, emerging from the rear stage with Appleby and conducting him to the deserted green-room, thought it desirable to concentrate once more.

'Lord Auldearn was shot during the progress of the play and where you have just seen his body, in the curtained recess, that is, what they call the rear stage. He was playing Polonius and there comes a point' – the Duke looked speculatively at Appleby: the higher constabulary might be expected to know a little Shakespeare – 'you will remember there comes a point at which Polonius hides behind a curtain in the Queen's closet. He calls for help when he supposes Hamlet to be attacking the Queen, and then Hamlet stabs through the curtain, draws it back, and discovers that he has killed Polonius. It was at this point that the thing happened. Auldearn had just called out when his voice was drowned by the report of the revolver.'

'And why,' said Appleby, 'should one shoot Lord Auldearn?'

Thirty minutes ago the Duke had been listening to the Prime Minister authenticating this young man with some enthusiasm from a public telephone-box in Guildford. Nevertheless he looked at him warily now. 'I thought,' he said, 'that somebody might be after something he might have. That was why I shut up the hall and held on to the whole gathering.'

'But later you let the audience go?'

The Duke's wariness modulated imperceptibly into weariness. 'In the particular aspect I imagined – it was a mare's nest.'

'Agents after a document?'

'Yes. We found it.'

'Found it?'

'Just at midnight. On him – in a manner of speaking.' And the Duke produced a slender roll of paper from the folds of King Claudius's raiment – produced it and put it away again.

But Appleby in his turn brought out a fountain-pen. 'I'll give you a receipt,' he said briefly.

'I beg your pardon?'

'May it please your Grace, a receipt.'

There was enough of Macdonald's technique in this to make the Duke blink. A receipt and the portentous document – *Pike and Perch Joint Scheme* – changed hands. 'Please go on, sir,' said Appleby politely.

'Not on; back,' said the Duke a trifle pettishly – and thought for a moment. 'Auldearn was just calling out when the shot was fired. I made for the sound and came on the rear stage from behind. My kinsman, Gervase Crispin, was kneeling on the floor, with Auldearn's head on his lap. Clay – Melville Clay, that is, who has been playing Hamlet – was standing beyond, his rapier in his hand; I think he had just come through from the front stage. And a Mr Bose was standing a little to one side. Gervase said "Dead, I think"; and at that I hurried behind scenes again and stopped some of the other players who were running up from coming in. Then I called for Dr Biddle – he's our family doctor, and was in the play – and for Sir Richard Nave; he too is a doctor, but taken to something eccentric, I believe. Then I crossed the rear stage again, passed through the curtain and spoke to the audience of a serious accident, asking them to keep quiet. When I turned back to the rear stage, both Nave and Biddle were beside the body, and both said "Dead." Auldearn, as you saw, had simply been shot through the heart at close range. He was one of our oldest friends.'

The Duke paused on this and Appleby said nothing. The Prime Minister and his fire-engine, the mysterious Captain Hilfers, the grim talk of documents that might be levers and engines towards war – these things had receded, it seemed, and in front lay plain police-work. And Appleby was relieved; in plain police-work you could usually go straight for the truth, whereas in work with political implications a halt was often mysteriously called when the truth was in sight. But now the Duke continued, edging away from the hinted personal aspect of the cata-strophe by way of momentary generalization.

'When somebody dies in this way – is shot, murdered – one's first feeling is not of mystery, but of alarm. One looks round for a maniac brandishing a revolver and threatening further lives. There's a young man upstairs who might bear that in mind when he next writes up that sort of thing.' The Duke did not stop to elucidate this. 'But there was no maniac. My second thought was of robbery, robbery of no common sort. I seized the most reliable fellow beside me and sent him to secure the door behind the audience. There is only one other door – behind the green-room here – and I went straight to that and locked it myself. We had had a telephone put in so that we could communicate easily with the house. I went to it and was through to the Prime Minister by eleven o'clock, within five minutes of the shooting. Then I rang up the local police at Horton. Then somebody suggested that Auldearn's bed-room should be guarded and I agreed; I was for every precaution. I let my cousin Gervase and the man I'd sent to the farther door – a kins-man of my wife's – out by this door here and locked it after them. The next important thing was to prevent the audience and the players from mingling. Behind the scenes I had a manageable crowd, and a crowd I could take drastic measures with if necessary. But the audience was a mob and it included one or two diplomatic people; one can't go through an ambassador's pockets, can one?'

Appleby agreed monosyllabically. He was equally fascinated by the efficiency of the proceedings narrated and by some indefinable remote-ness in the narrator. The Duke, he was almost inclined to put it to him-self, was not interested.

'If something were gone, you know, and there was a possibility of it having been successfully conveyed to a confederate in the audience, I should have had the responsibility of deciding for or against the scandal of a general search – a thing I can imagine Cabinet debating for a day, can't you?'

Appleby did not admit to any vision of His Majesty's ministers in council. Instead, he made a shorthand note.

'Be that as it may,' continued the Duke, 'there was every chance of preventing anything of the sort. We were isolated from the audience and could remain so. I went out upon the front stage again, crossed it and jumped down to break the news gently to my mother; she is a very old lady and was sitting alone in the front row. Then I climbed back and announced straight out that Auldearn had been killed. And nobody, I said, must either leave the hall or attempt to come behind the scenes.'

'What control had you on that?' asked Appleby.

'As it happened – complete control. There are only three avenues of communication: across the open stage in full view of everybody or by the curtained entrances at one or other side of the stage. And by each of these entrances we had a fireman. Players and audience were as cut off from one another as could be.

'At eleven-twelve my cousin Gervase came back from Auldearn's room and I let him into the hall. He had startling news. The room had been burgled. Professionally it would seem, for the safe had been cracked.'

'I see,' said Appleby.

'I beg your pardon?'

'Please go on. Is a safe, by the way, a regular feature of your bedroom furniture?'

'People come sometimes with foolish quantities of jewels. We have found small wall-safes in some of the rooms the least bothersome way to cope with them. Well, the news was, I say, startling – if after murder anything can be called startling. I knew very well that Auldearn had this ticklish paper.'

'He had shown it to you?'

'No. But he had mentioned it. And mentioned a joke about it: it is endorsed *Pike and Perch Conciliation Board*, or something of the sort. Well, here in Auldearn's room was evidence of at least attempted robbery. And this attempt could scarcely have been made by the murderer *after* the shooting, for nobody could have got out of the hall – nor would there have been time to crack a safe in the seven or eight minutes that elapsed between the shot and Gervase's reaching the bedroom. I concluded that – unless there was a gang at work – the shooting had taken place because the burglary and safe-breaking had been unsuccessful; that what had been sought for in vain in the bedroom had later been sought for on a person, a person who had been murdered to facilitate the seeking. One sees objections, of course – but that was my first thought.'

If the Duke was rather weary now he was also very lucid. And lucidity is something that one does not often get hard after violent death; now it was saving Appleby hours.

'There was an obvious thing to do. With Dr Biddle I searched the body. There was nothing there.'

'I understood you to say –'

'Wait. There was nothing there. Then it seemed to me that the situation was grave and I knew that I must hang on, continue to hang on to everybody not merely until the local police arrived but until somebody came down who had been in touch with London. I wondered what I could best do in the interval. I thought of the weapon.'

The Duke took a restless turn about the green-room and came to a stand before a long table littered with theatrical debris – wigs, swords, a crown, the Ghost's helmet. Aimlessly he picked something up and Appleby saw, not without a start, that it was a skull – Yorick's skull.

'It seemed unlikely that anyone should have ventured to retain a revolver about him and it could not have been got right away. So I cast round. But I found no trace ... dear me!'

The exclamation was a mild one. For with a little clatter there had fallen from skull to table a tiny revolver. 'Dear me,' said the Duke, 'Giles would like that. Well, so much for the weapon. Might it have finger-prints, do you think?'

Appleby stared – not at the weapon but at the man. In this moment he discovered what Scamnum had now known for some time: the Duke of Horton was a born actor. No man could be other than startled at so queer a coincidence of word and event. But the Duke – for no conceivable reason, surely, save the pleasure of the thing – had given a bizarre display of impassivity. And now in a moment he was proceeding with his narrative. It would be easy, Appleby decided, to become too interested in the Duke – for here was a man with some suppressed instinct to hold the centre of the stage.

'Nothing more happened – barring a little subdued and uneasy discussion and moving about on this side, and a little uneasy shifting on hard seats on the other – until just after half past eleven. Then your local colleagues arrived. I have some faith in specialists; so I immobilized them.'

To immobilize country policemen is no doubt one of the privileges of a master of Scamnum. But Appleby, who had as yet seen only a stolid constable guarding the body and a nervous constable who had met him under Scamnum's *porte cochère*, felt that he might himself come in for some species of recoil. 'Immobilized them,' he echoed courteously.

'To be precise, I told them of the burglary and they have gone after that. There is a sergeant and he said something about questioning the servants. You know, he'll find a devilish lot of them.'

Appleby doubted if his rural colleagues were as simple as they were pictured; the picture seemed to merge with a discernible ducal taste for conventional sub-humorous effects. But he said nothing.

'So again we marked time, though I got down on paper as complete a list as I could of people's whereabouts behind stage for the relevant period.' The Duke smiled tenuously as he thus jerked Appleby back to the fact of Crispin efficiency. 'And then I thought of our unfortunate audience. I consulted my wife and she said "Feed them" and telephoned to the house for coffee and sandwiches. Her organization is always remarkable; the stuff was thrust through the bars, so to speak, within ten minutes. And then Mr Bose discovered the document.'

'You mentioned Mr Bose as on the rear stage when you first entered it. He was a player?'

'Prompter. An intelligent Hindu. My wife, you know. And he found the document.' The implication was plainly that intelligent Hindus – even Hindus intelligent enough to find vital documents – were more in the Duchess's line than the Duke's. But in the tone of the final sentence Appleby thought that he detected something more. The words rang with a curious finality. The safety of this document once established, they seemed to say, Scamnum's special responsibilities ended; blood-hunting was for others.

'Mr Bose found the document by accident. Just on midnight I became aware of him standing beside me – one never notices him approach – and looking miserable. It occurred to me he wanted to be helpful; he's a friendly little person enough. So I asked him to find my daughter Elizabeth; I meant to send her forward to my mother, about whom I was a little anxious. He went through the species of curtained corridor you will find behind the rear stage, and in doing so he nearly slipped on something that had apparently rolled off the rear stage itself. It was a little parchment scroll which Polonius was designed to carry throughout the play; part of his stage business was that of referring to it from time to time in a slightly fussy manner. Well, Mr Bose picked it up – and noticed a different coloured paper inside. He is an alert and subtle creature and he brought it to me at once. That is what I meant by saying that it had, in a manner of speaking, been on Auldearn all the time. And at that I let the audience go. If there had been an attempt on the document Auldearn had outwitted it. Perhaps he knew there was to be an attempt. Perhaps the inexplicable messages had warned him.'

'Messages?'

'*Hamlet, revenge!*' said the Duke mildly – and explained.

It was now twenty to two and the hall was still a sort of discreet gaol. The prisoners had by this time some right, perhaps, to murmur – but Appleby would make no move with them until he had a stronger grip of the case. The spy-story seemed to be fading fast into the realm of fantasy; emissaries of foreign powers do not commonly advertise themselves by clamours for revenge, and of the burglary in Lord Auldearn's bedroom Appleby had his own opinion. But there seemed to be one further crucial test: the time-element which the Duke had already hinted at as a difficulty in the spy theory. No calculating criminal would shoot in order to steal unless there would be reasonable time for the stealing. Had there been this? Almost certainly not; the shooting itself had been an extraordinary hazardous action and only the peculiar construction of the rear stage had given the criminal even a fifty-fifty chance of escape.

The rear stage was simply a large rectangular curtained recess into which one could slip through a parting on any of its sides. But because the single curtain had been found insufficient to deaden green-room noises, further curtains had been hung on the three back-stage sides, giving the effect of a corridor with two right-angled turns. This multiplicity of thick and in places overlapping drapery would have given a bold man a chance to slip into hiding unobserved at some favourable moment, and a less substantial chance of so manoeuvring after the shot as to escape discovery. And it seemed that this must, indeed, have happened. Suspicions might yet be reported, but had anything damning been observed there would surely have been denunciations long ago. Diligent ferreting, such as the Duke claimed to have begun, lay ahead if the movements or whereabouts of some thirty people were to be pinned down for the fatal minutes round ten-fifty-five.

But Appleby's preliminary problem was simpler. Who first got to the rear stage after the shot, and how long after it? On how many seconds could the assailant reckon for an attempted theft, and for escape? Appleby picked up the weapon that had so dramatically revealed itself, dropped it – wrapped in a handkerchief – into his pocket, and together with the Duke made his way to the other part of the hall. He was now to confront more at leisure the main body of players whom he had glimpsed on coming in.

The scene was reminiscent of a species of abrupted revelry with which he was professionally familiar – of one of those dismal occasions on which, in the midst of frolic, certain stalwart and hitherto most frolicsome gentlemen disentangle themselves from false noses, paper caps, balloons, and streamers, bar the available exits and admit a bevy of uniformed colleagues to count the bottles, sniff at the glasses, and take down the names and addresses. Three more constables had been sent into the hall by that sergeant who was still obstinately engaged elsewhere: one was standing shyly in a corner, apparently scanning the rafters for concealed gunmen; one was grudgingly permitting Bagot to replace an exhausted coffee-urn by a full one; and the third, being the fortunate possessor of a tape-measure, was solemnly taking the dimensions of the front stage. The company sat huddled in groups, half-heartedly consuming further coffee and beginning, Appleby surmised, to regard one another with some dislike. Several he recognized at once. Gervase Crispin, that high-priest of the Golden Calf, was covertly playing noughts and crosses with a young man of vaguely Crispin appearance. Melville Clay, still in Hamlet's black beneath an enveloping dressing-gown, was unmistakable. The Duchess of Horton, very pale, was plainly engaged in looking after the young women; one of the young women, evidently her daughter, was equally plainly engaged in looking after her. Lord Traherne was wandering about with a plate of sandwiches, as if at one of his 'homely' colonial parties – but was failing to offer them to anyone. The black man had withdrawn into a corner and seemed engaged in meditation, or perhaps purification and penance. Everybody looked up as Appleby appeared.

'I want to know, please, who was the first on the scene of Lord Auldearn's death, and how soon after the shot.'

At this the black man called out very softly, but so as to be clearly heard from the corner from which he now advanced: 'It was I.'

'A moment before I got through the front rear stage curtain,' said Clay.

'Mr Bose? Will you come up, please?'

Appleby turned back towards the rear stage and after a few paces halted under the impression that Mr Bose had failed to follow. Whereupon Mr Bose, who had been just behind, bumped into him and there were apologies. It was Appleby's introduction to the movement which the Duchess had described as 'not earthly'.

'He is ... quite dead?' asked Mr Bose gently.

'He died instantly.'

Mr Bose made a gesture of resignation – a queer, expressive gesture which Appleby could not afterwards fix – and said: 'And now ... I must tell you?'

'Please.'

'My place was here.' Mr Bose led the way off the rear stage and into the curtained corridor behind. At the extreme end of one of its shorter sides was a stool. 'My place was here, because from here I could see both the front stage and the rear stage.'

'You could *see* the rear stage?'

Mr Bose looked obscurely troubled, but answered readily. 'Why, yes. It is most necessary sometimes. Here is a slit through which I see the front stage and here is one by which I see the rear stage too.'

Appleby considered for a moment in some perplexity. 'But you saw nothing strange?'

'Remember, please, I was prompter. The eye must be on the text – though I know the text *very* well. Occasionally I look through the curtain – but to where the suffering is.'

'The suffering?'

'The drama – action. And at this time I glance perhaps at the front stage where there are Hamlet and the Queen and much action; but on the rear stage is only Polonius alone, waiting.'

Mr Bose appeared somewhat obliquely inclined, but what he meant to say seemed clear. And here was remarkable information. Anyone slipping through the rear-stage curtain with intent to murder and steal did so under the known and substantial risk of being observed by the prompter through his spy-hole. The possibility seemed to Appleby to double again the already remarkable hazardousness of the deed.

'And after the shot, Mr Bose – did you not at once look then?'

'I started to my feet in alarm. For a moment I stood still. Then I caught at the curtain to pull it aside and enter. But I was confused and pulled the wrong way. When I broke through to the rear stage it was – save for the body and gunpowder smoke – empty. But a moment later Mr Clay came from the front stage.'

'And then?'

'I ran out, in great fear for the life of Lord Auldearn, and called for the Duke. Mr Gervase came first and then the Duke. Then the physicians came.'

Before Mr Bose Appleby felt curiously baffled. He had a sense of subterraneous processes beneath these answers – processes perhaps profoundly deceitful, perhaps merely profoundly strange. But then it might be that this was a stock response; that one confronted the Oriental mind with such a sense ready-made.

'Mr Bose, this now is the important question. Between the shot and your breaking in upon the rear stage – how many seconds?'

The black man considered. 'With *very* great accuracy?'

'Please.'

The black man produced a watch. Then he meditated. Then he looked at the watch and at the same time began to murmur some fragmentary text. Then he looked at his watch again. 'Five seconds.'

Appleby rather supposed the procedure employed to be intelligent and reliable; Mr Bose's sense of time was bound up, no doubt, with ritual recitation. 'And then Mr Clay –?'

This time Mr Bose simply studied the second hand of his watch with concentration. 'Two seconds.'

'Thank you. And can you give me any further information?'

Mr Bose looked at Appleby in discernible perturbation; made an equally perturbed gesture. 'It is a *very* evil thing!' he said.

Perhaps the Western world still seemed to Mr Bose – despite an advancing familiarity with the works of Mr James Juice – a morally unaccountable place; perhaps he felt that he was really giving Appleby information. Or perhaps the odd answer represented evasion. At the moment Appleby was held less by the words than by the glance that accompanied them. It is easy, looking at a dark face, to speak of a flashing eye; but Mr Bose's eye held at this moment more than a common fire. He was, indeed, an almost unearthly creature, the youthful raw material, surely, of a character wholly contemplative, wholly spiritual.

But Appleby, if he saw the saint, suspected too the tiger. He felt it would be useful to know something of Mr Bose's way and rule of life. 'You are a Brahmin, Mr Bose?'

'I am a Warrior!'

The reply, given with a sudden lift of the head, was more than a simple statement of caste. It acknowledged the implications of the question it answered, was perhaps a threat – or a promise or a challenge. And a second later it might have been none of these things – and here merely a scared expatriated Oriental.

Appleby resolved that his next question should be public, so he proceeded to the front stage, strode down it like a player about to deliver a soliloquy, and surveyed the company at large. 'Mr Clay, what interval elapsed between your hearing the shot and entering the rear stage?'

Clay answered promptly. 'Seven seconds.'

This tallied remarkably with Mr Bose's estimate. But Appleby expressed surprise. 'You are sure it was not less? It seems a long time.'

'A second's pause on the shot. Something under four seconds across the stage; I was making time until it was clear the scene must be broken. Something under two seconds in front of the curtain, making time still. Then a fraction of a second getting through.'

'Mr Clay,' said the Duchess, as if anxious to substantiate her guest's credit, 'has an uncanny sense of time on the stage. I believe the interval was just as he says.'

The Duchess's impression, for what it was worth, was the only substantiation that could be got from the players; all the others had been behind the scenes. But now a severe person, sitting hand to forehead beside the Duchess, made a suggestion. 'What of Dr Bunney's contrivance? Was it not making some sort of record?'

'Sir Richard Nave – Mr Appleby,' said the Duke, apparently feeling an introduction desirable.

Appleby pounced on this. 'The machine that gave one of the messages? It was here recording?' Whereupon Bunney, with an incongruous mingling of pride and alarm, produced the black box. 'Science', he began ponderously, 'never knows to what uses –'

Nave interrupted brusquely. 'What may be useful is the recorded interval between the shot and the next succeeding audible words: Mr Bose's calling out "My Lord!" No doubt he was summoning the Duke.'

Mr Bose nodded vigorously. He had been summoning the Duke. Appleby promptly took charge of the black box – though without much faith in its detective qualities. Then he considered.

Anyone entering the rear stage to shoot Auldearn had had five seconds to make good the first part of his getaway – behind the curtains. But all the time he might have been under the fatal observation of Mr Bose. Would any man wishing to steal a document adopt such a method? He thought not – or in the case of a document of the kind involved. It was possible to conceive of a document – an unopened letter, for example, giving information on a grave crime – which might be worth securing on such bloody and dangerous terms. But a state document is stolen neither in passion nor as a last desperate act of self-preservation; it is stolen, almost certainly, for mere gain – a little, perhaps, for the excitement. And – as the Prime Minister had observed – the sort of person involved in such things does not kill; certainly not when the chances are heavily in favour of instant detection. Auldearn's murder, with its dramatic *locale* and theatrical preliminary warnings, represented – Appleby was persuaded – an altogether different kind of affair. And the spy story was fantasy, fantasy evoked by the mere fact that the dead man was known to have possessed an important document and to have safeguarded it in a somewhat eccentric yet rational way.

And looking round the shocked and jaded people in the hall Appleby doubted if an attempt to grapple with such a large company in the remaining small hours would be useful. Common sense and the facts of the case as they stood counselled him to send them all off to bed without more ado. But there still remained a doubt, a doubt that the thread before him might not be single. And he knew well enough that his whole reputation was going to stand or fall on his handling of an affair with which, in a few hours, all England would be ringing. And he determined to be utterly cautious – which meant being uncommonly bold. He spoke briefly to the Duke and then turned to the company.

'I am going to require something which some of you may judge unnecessary. Please remember that Lord Auldearn's death is inevitably going to cause a tremendous sensation. Everything that has happened tonight – everything concerning the preliminary handling of the situation by the Duke of Horton and myself – may be debated and criticized by thousands of people with no very marked ability to see their way through a complicated set of facts. They will ask certain stock questions; there are newspapers that take up such things with clamour. Because of this – and for other reasons – I believe that it is in the general interest here that each one of you should submit to a search before leaving the hall – as I hope you may shortly do – for the night. There are several magistrates here to whom I could go, but I think perhaps you will not stand on any form.'

It was a successful speech. Some of the company felt that by going through an unpleasant formality they would in some way avoid scandal; the more perceptive were put in good humour by the consciousness of being more perceptive and of so appreciating this young policeman's wiliness. Only Bunney protested, but he was assured by Malloch – confidentially and as between scholars – that in good society in England one never objected to being searched by the police. Peter Marryat, who had been beguiling the time by trying – *sotto voce* and with the assistance of Tommy Potts – to get the abandoned Norwegian Captain right at last, interjected an intrigued rather than an indignant 'I say!' The Duke expressed curt and slightly absent agreement and the Duchess, knowing the next move to be with her and seeming to recognize herself as still too shaken for effective action, murmured to Mrs Terborg. And Mrs Terborg promptly took charge: if the police had a respectable woman there would be no difficulty.

This gained, Appleby made discreet haste to another point. 'After leaving the hall nobody, I hope, will be disturbed again for the night. But a constable will be in the green-room and you will please go in one by one as you leave and give names; I must have a record, I think, in that form. And one other thing. It may be that some of you have something to say that you feel should be said soon, but which is too indefinite for other than the most confidential communication to the police. You will all understand me. While Lord Auldearn's death remains a mystery there must be suspicion, weighing of doubtful circumstances, possibly significant recollections. And any matter of that sort with the least substance it is your duty to advance. A word to the constable will bring me at once.' And having with these words baited a traditional but often-successful trap, Appleby gave certain further directions to the constables and then turned to the Duke. 'And now, sir, I must find the sergeant and the missing guest – the one who stayed guarding Lord Auldearn's room.'

'Ah yes,' said the Duke. 'Yes: Giles Gott.'

Appleby's response had just that quality of vehemence which made Stella Terborg jump.

'Giles Gott!'

3

'Hullo,' said Gott – whom, when excited, nothing could surprise.

'Hullo,' said Appleby. The two men looked at each other in silence and with profound satisfaction – a proceeding which Sergeant Trumpet, who was versed in the literature of crime, interpreted as that intent matching of swords proper to the first meeting of fated antagonists.

'My eye's been on him,' said Sergeant Trumpet heavily.

Appleby nodded gravely. 'Quite right, sergeant. The man Gott has planned many a murder before tonight.'

'Has he now!' said Sergeant Trumpet, deeply gratified and edging a little nearer to his suspect.

Gott spread himself more comfortably in Lord Auldearn's easy chair. 'The sergeant thinks I must be the central figure because I alone have broken away from the pack. He has given it out that he's sleuthing the third boot-boy, but actually he's been hanging on to me grimly.' He looked at Appleby lazily. 'And what may this mean that thou, dear corse, again, in complete steel, revisit'st thus the glimpses of the moon? Whence comest thou, shade?'

Sergeant Trumpet frowned. Appleby sighed – he thought he knew this mood. '*Les Présages*,' he answered absently. 'Sergeant, a word.' He led his colleague from the room and presently returned alone. 'That better?' he asked.

'Inspector Buxton,' said Gott, 'has the chicken-pox and Inspector Lucas has gone on holiday as far as Bridlington, where his late wife's sister keeps a boarding-house not far from the front. I had it all from the sergeant while his eye was on me, but during the last half-hour it palled ... Well, here's a mess ... what's happening below?'

'Search. Which has at last lured away your sergeant. Now talk. Better than the Duke if you can – and he's not bad.'

'On the Duke's suggestion I came up here with Gervase Crispin. The room was, of course, unlocked. Nothing seemed disturbed. But Gervase knew of a safe – behind the Walcot dry-point there – and it was cracked. Gervase went back and I sat down on guard, and to think – if I could. Presently the sergeant came and sat down to guard the guard. In the intervals of strained conversation I continued to attempt to think.'

'Good,' said Appleby. 'Results, please.'

'The shooting has to do with the play. It's been thought out in the context of the play. They'll have told you of the messages? Someone with a real sense of effect. Motive: perhaps just effect.'

'At least, not documents of state?'

'I don't know.'

Appleby had been inspecting the safe. Now something in his friend's voice made him turn round. 'Giles! –' He was interrupted by a question – and by the knowledge that Gott, despite his lazy way, was as much in earnest as himself.

'Have they found this damned thing, John? You forget I don't know what's happened down there. I only know there was something, and that this safe's cracked.'

'Yes, they found it. Auldearn was keeping an eye on it, though in a precious queer way. He'd stowed it in a sort of scroll he was due to hang on to, apparently, throughout the show.'

'I see. And you've decided the spies are moonshine?'

'It seems very probable that they are.'

'Materials for sensational fiction, not dealt in by Messrs Appleby and Gott?'

'Clearer-headed reasons than that, I hope. Everything points to quite a different sort of affair.'

'Everything except what Elizabeth – the daughter, that is: by the way, John, I want to marry her – everything except what Elizabeth and I saw in the garden.'

'Good luck to you ... What?'

Gott told of the flitting figure in the moonlight and of the mysterious something tossed over the wall. Appleby shook his head. 'I think Lady Elizabeth jumped to conclusions, though I know there has been spy-activity here before. I suspect I know something about this safe-cracking business that might interpret what you saw. Briefly, there's circumstantial evidence that a certain cracksman and jewel-thief, one Happy Hutton by name, has been operating hereabouts. And what you saw was not improbably Happy making contact with his inside stand.

I shouldn't be surprised to find some of the other safes like this one cracked too, and that it has nothing to do with the nasty business downstairs. And why should spy-business be thought out, as you say, in the context of *Hamlet*?'

'Why indeed. But you believe, don't you, in the delicate processes we lump together as feeling something in the air?'

'Yes. And so, no doubt, does the sergeant. But talk about the people first, the whole bewildering crowd of them.'

For a moment Gott looked querulous. 'But I'm still trying to think. And why aren't you superintending your search?'

'Because I'm hoping that when left to the simple and unintimidating rural bobby somebody may be moved to drop dark – and misleading – hints. I've left half an invitation that way. And as for thinking, think as you go.'

'Very well, I'll talk. I'll talk like Marlow in *Lord Jim*, who made a habit of delivering a hundred thousand words – uncommonly well – to casual after-dinner audiences while contriving to smoke a succession of cigars.' During this empty prologue Gott kicked off the Dumb-show King's slippers and undid his ruff. Then he plunged, slightly eccentrically, into exposition.

'Talking of Conrad, I hope you read Wodehouse. If so, you will have realized that the Duke cultivates the part of Lord Emsworth – you remember? Mark him, and you expect to mark that immortal porker, the Empress of Blandings, round the corner. The man cultivates ineffectiveness and it is moderately amusing. Obviously enough, he is able; and his hobby-horse is the first thing, no doubt, that gives one the feeling of Scamnum's keeping a good deal below the surface.

'The Duchess, who is a sort of relation of mine, is clever, charming, and oddly determined to have me for a son in-law. In that ultimately, I suspect, lies the genesis of *Hamlet* played at Scamnum Court – and so of this old man's death.' Gott paused. 'Auldearn was her friend chiefly and – I believe – part of her past, in a respectable way. In fact Auldearn was to the Duchess what I, with bad luck, may be to the Duchess's daughter – but that is by the by.

'In the present generation Gervase, as you probably know, is the centre of all things Crispin. He controls a big whack of the planet; too big, I imagine, for him to deal in miching mallecho and mean mischief. Scamnum is, as it has always been, simply the Crispin show-case, dukedom and all. And the Duke has a show-case role. He's an Elder Statesman. When the public shows signs of getting worked up about something the Prime Minister and such-like come down and consult him. Scamnum is put on the picture-page with an inset of the Duke in knickerbockers – faintly evocative of the Empress – or at his desk writing a monograph on trout-fishing. The effect is soothing and England stands firm. One has some respect for the technique. But whether the Duke is actually deep in the counsels of our rulers I don't know. Gervase, of course, is a junior minister from time to time but doesn't much exert himself along those lines.

'Kincrae – the heir, that is – is eccentric and has gone to govern a Crown Colony. He writes fish-monographs rebutting his father. Then there is Elizabeth. Elizabeth is twenty-one, serious, romantic, practical, childlike, mature, passionate, detached, ironical, and baffling.'

'Quite so,' said Appleby. As Gott talked he was systematically examining the dead man's bedroom. 'Now go on to the mob,' he directed.

'It's rather a large order. Shall I begin alphabetically? A's for Auldearn, the man who was shot. B is for Bunney, the man who was not. Very little to say about Bunney. He's rather like yourself – same policemanly figure and something of a detective mind. C is for Clay –'

'It might be better,' said Appleby, 'if you didn't go right through but simply picked out the type of the amazingly foolhardy murderer.'

'You think he – or she – must have been that?'

Appleby nodded. 'He walked out on the rear stage, shot Auldearn almost point-blank in what might have been full view of the prompter, was lucky in having five seconds to get off and amazingly lucky in manoeuvring into some uncompromising position thereafter without exciting remark. I call him foolhardy.'

'But I think,' said Gott, suddenly serious again, 'none of the conditions you have been describing necessarily holds.'

Appleby stopped exploring and sat down. 'Explain,' he said.

'Well, begin this way. You must thoroughly explore from a likely premise before you go on to one less likely. Now a likely premise is: the murderer exposes himself to as little risk as possible; he is *not* foolhardy. Take that and base a question on it. Why did the murderer, being resolved to expose himself to as little risk as possible, choose for his act the precise place and time that he did?'

'Why indeed.'

'Because, John, he could foresee your mind moving on the level on which it has actually begun to move. Literally, *level*. Did you look up when you were on the rear stage?'

'Yes,' said Appleby, 'and I see what you mean. And it didn't occur to me. And I hope the reason that it didn't occur to me was that it won't do.'

'Immediately above the rear stage there's what is called the upper stage. It has a trap-door. And in a shadowy corner of the upper stage was an old gentleman painting a picture. And anyone lying flat on the upper stage would be invisible to the audience –'

'It won't do,' said Appleby. 'Auldearn, as it happens, was shot from floor level. I'm almost certain of that at this moment, and I think the medical report will prove it. And I doubt if the distance could be more than six feet – though that's for experts too.' He looked at Gott and added: 'Giles, you have another shot in the locker!'

'I think I have. It comes from having produced the play. I suggest that Auldearn might have been shot *where* he was because one would immediately begin to think in terms of someone coming through the rear-stage curtains; of an "amazingly foolhardy murderer", as you said, who would half-announce his intention in sinister messages and so forth. But I think there's another *Why*. *Why* was Auldearn shot *when* he was? Conceivably because he had just lain down, preparatory to being discovered "dead" after Hamlet had stabbed through the curtain. And a shot from above when he was *prone* would carry on the suggestion that he had been shot from a level *when standing*. And the distance would be about eight feet.'

There was a little silence – and then Appleby smiled. 'Round One to you,' he said. And getting up he resumed his inspection of the room.

'So you have one suspect,' continued Gott, ' "aloft". And you have a possible maximum of – let me see – twenty-seven suspects "within".'

'Twenty-seven,' said Appleby. 'Excellent.' He was examining a bowler hat. 'By the way, had Auldearn a man with him, do you know?'

'He had no man – and kept nothing of the sort, I understand, in town. He lived very simply in a service-flat. His only establishment was in Scotland somewhere. But I'm giving you the biographies – by express invitation – of twenty-seven suspects.'

Appleby had turned to examine the contents of the dead man's wardrobe. He seemed to consider the process as of some importance, for he delayed Gott's further narrative with absent-minded banter. 'I say, Giles – what if you were all in it together? Twenty-seven conspirators getting up all this *Hamlet* stuff. But why should twenty-seven people wish away a Lord Chancellor?'

'Because,' said Gott sadly, 'the Lord Chancellor is a wholesale black-mailer and keeps twenty-seven micro-photographs of compromising documents permanently secreted beneath a wig and false skull ... Are you ready?'

'Where were the originals?' asked Appleby seriously; he was peering inside an old and shabby deer-stalking hat. 'Well, never mind; I'm ready.'

'There were thirty-one behind-stage folk. Subtract Auldearn – thirty; the Duchess and Clay, visible on the front stage – twenty-eight; old Cope, the suspect "aloft" if you like – twenty-seven. Twenty-seven suspects "within". And beyond that it's a matter of which of them can swear to which. Elizabeth, Noel Gylby, a girl called Stella Terborg, and myself you will find swearing to each other; we were in a group. And I can swear to one of the two footmen; I had him in the corner of my eye when the pistol went off. You will probably find other more or less authenticated alibis; but you will find too that people will be remarkably confused. Quite apart from the notion of a Royal Academician sniping from the heavens, I'm really not convinced of any absolute foolhardiness. The man knew his bloody game. On an occasion of this sort – for acting, you know, is a curiously exacting business even to the least nervous amateur – it's remarkable to what an extent each individual off-stage is wrapped up in himself. One would almost hazard that the criminal had a developed sense of crowd psychology – like the fellow Nave or the advertising girl, Sandys.'

'Suspicions,' said Appleby, 'crowd thick and fast upon us. Nave I remarked; the advertising girl, not yet.'

'I don't know that it's much use my talking about the people in detail before you've more than glimpsed them. But I was going to say something of the party in general, and of feelings in the air. I find I have two conflicting impressions about the party. First, it was particularly pleasant and well-contrived – one of those socially skilful mixtures in which each element finds the other charming, and so on. Secondly – and quite contradictorily, I'm afraid – it was on edge from the first. And the messages ... well, worked something up. If I say another word I shall be dealing with things so tenuous as to appear fanciful. It's best, perhaps, to go back to the statement that everything was bound up with the play – the first thing it occurred to me to say to you. The murder has been woven somehow into the play – and the play had woven itself into the party. Not the mere fact that we were play-acting, though that did at times engender a curious self-consciousness. I mean the particular atmosphere aimed at – by men, heaven help me! – in this particular production of the play *Hamlet*. The conflicts which are in the play were present with us as we sat at dinner; that sort of thing.'

'I see,' said Appleby; and there was no fear that Gott should feel him to be taking this difficult exploration lightly even when he added briskly: 'Well – to seize on something more concrete – I think there's no doubt that friend Happy has been present with us too. In fact I suspect this of being his hat.' And Appleby poked the bowler that had interested him.

'Happy's? Why not Auldearn's? It's a gentleman's hat, as they say.'

'Oh, for that matter Happy is quite the gentleman. He comported himself in a most gentlemanlike way – and with a hat – the last time I saw him. But not Auldearn's hat because not size of Auldearn's hats. See wardrobe. And probably Happy's because I see what Happy's been doing – gate-crashing. When I met him making a get-away some hours ago he was wearing a high hat – but of the collapsible sort. You see, Giles?'

Giles didn't altogether see.

'He specializes in raiding houses when there's a big affair on. And to get at the bedrooms his best chance would be to pass as a valet; half a dozen people have probably brought men-servants – some quite strangers to the Scamnum staff. Dark coat, appropriate sort of scarf, bowler discreetly in hand, upper-servant walk – and Happy might successfully make this bedroom or that. Business in bedrooms over, he abandons bowler, produces opera-hat – a thing easily concealed – puts scarf in pocket, opens dark overcoat on immaculate tails – and stands an excellent chance of snooping round usefully among the sahibs before being politely asked to leave.'

Gott sighed. 'You certainly know the habits of your friends. Round Two to you. But are you not jumping about more than your habit was?'

'Perhaps because there looks to be an uncommon lot to jump about between. But the likelihoods about Happy are part of my main drive at the moment – eliminating the spy-notion finally. Point is that this safe was cracked by a professional person in the way of ordinary business, and with no thought of secret documents.'

'Yes, I think the spy-scare is out of court.' Gott paused in sudden perplexity. 'But there was some other reference to spies, if I could remember; besides Elizabeth's in the garden, I mean.' His brow cleared. 'Oh, it was just an earlier joke of hers, or perhaps of Noel's. That Bunney was the spy in black; his black box must have suggested the phrase. A lot of blacks we were bandying; spy in black, black box, black hand, black man –'

'Meaning the Indian who found the document?'

'Mr Bose. It was Bose who found the document? Curious; he was first with the body too.' Gott's eyes suddenly narrowed. 'John – *when*? *When* did he find it?'

'Midnight,' said Appleby quietly. 'Remember, they have all been searched.'

'An hour after the killing! Well, there's something I should have been at the lodge gates to tell you, and it's come to me only now. Searched! Did you get Nave or Biddle to do a little trepanning – to look inside their skulls?'

'Out with it, Giles.'

'The black man's memory. It's like a photographic plate. If he could contrive to read through a longish document once – even in covert snatches – I believe it would be in his head next to *verbatim*.'

'And so – just conceivably – re-enter the spies.' If Appleby's tone was sceptical his action was decided. He strode to the telephone by the bed-head. And just as his hand went out to it it rang. He picked up the receiver.

'*Les Présages*,' said Appleby presently, causing Gott to stare. And after a longer interval he said steadily and formally: 'I am aware of a probable channel and have a good chance of getting the situation under control.' A moment later he had rung off and swung round. 'Giles, is the house isolatable?'

'Yes. Designed by a rectangular mind. Foursquare with two wings and broad terraces on all four sides, even towards the offices. And you can floodlight them.'

Appleby snatched up the telephone again. 'The green-room, please ... Sergeant? ... Is the search over ... all gone? How many men have

you? ... Good ... turn them all out on the terraces this instant, light
up and patrol. And if anyone tries to make a getaway they can hit
hard ... Yes, of course.' Rapidly he added some further instructions.
'Hurry.' Again he rang off.

'*Les Présages*?' queried Gott, taking up the first point of bafflement.

'Sort of pass-word — as used in sensational fiction when there are
spies about. And they *are* about; right back in the centre of the picture.
That was one Hilfers, a spy-fancier. Somebody in your respectable
audience celebrated his release by sending a wire from a local call-box:
the thing had been worked and the goods would shortly be despatched.
A dark message but intercepted, Hilfers says, on its way to a recipient
that puts the thing beyond doubt. There has been miching mallecho
with that document, all right. But if your playbox was as tight shut
as is made out we have half a grip on the thing yet. And now we'll
find the little black chap.'

He strode to the door and opened it — and then Gott heard an oath
he had never heard from Appleby before. In a moment he discovered
the reason. The little black chap had not been far to seek. His corpse
lay across the threshold.

4

Looking back upon this stage of the Scamnum affair Appleby was to
ponder, in unprofessional perplexity, on the vagaries of human emotion.
Lord Auldearn had died full of years, dignity, and achievement; almost
the last of a line of scholar-statesmen whom he profoundly respected.
The books which represented the dead man's incursions into literature
and theology were on his shelves in the little Westminster flat; and in
the midst of a world dipping towards chaos Auldearn's name had stood
out, for him as for many others, as a point of resistance and of sanity.
If the Duke of Horton were a show-case Elder Statesman Auldearn had
been the real thing.

Auldearn had been murdered; and within an hour Appleby had heard
talk of confusion and craziness drawing nearer as a result. It seemed
as if the Scamnum *Hamlet* had yielded a full measure of irony; that
on the make-believe Elizabethan stage Auldearn had died amid tragedy
actual and profound — died guarding a wretched paper which, philo-

sopher as he was, he must have believed to represent no more than the organizing of madness against madness. And these things – brutal murder, murder followed by the distant murmur (baseless, perhaps, as many such murmurs are, and yet, perhaps *not* baseless) of unimaginable calamity – these things had left Appleby almost unmoved. As a police-man he had been excited and as a policeman he had worked like a machine; he had debated with the unexpectedly-discovered Gott with the elaborate detachment which had established itself long ago as a con-vention between them. But now an unknown black man, a waif from the Orient, a murderer it might be and a fomenter of mischief, had been tumbled lifeless before that other dead man's door. And Appleby, who had seen a score of violent deaths, was shaken profoundly. He stood up, pale to the lips, and said not quite steadily: 'Another dead man.'

It was steadily enough that Gott responded, but he responded with a single word: 'Nightmare.' And Appleby knew that Gott at least, col-lected as he was, had been facing nightmare for hours. Amid this general horror he had his own distress. These things had happened in the house in which – perhaps on the night on which – he had thought to speak to the Lady Elizabeth Crispin of marriage.

An instant more and Appleby was speaking with decision. 'The ser-geant is on the rear stage; he must stop there until the ambulance comes. And the others are inside. I want you to come with me. Go and get somebody reliable to stay here, Giles. And get one of the doctors.'

Gott stepped carefully over the body – stretched like some slumbering guard before an eastern monarch's chamber – and departed silently down the dimly-lit corridor. Once more Appleby knelt down. There was no question but that Mr Bose was dead: the thin lips were drawn back over the perfect teeth in a grimace of sudden overwhelming agony; the lustre of the dark complexion had turned to livid in irregular smears, as if here were a player who had hastily begun to swab off his make-up. Death had come from a dagger-thrust hard below the left shoulder-blade. And the weapon stood – horribly – in the wound still. Appleby scrutinized it coolly enough, rapidly searched the body. Then he stood up and half-murmured in perplexity: 'I could have been almost sure . . .' And then he shook his head. 'Far, far too remote!'

A minute later Gott came back, bringing Noel and Nave. Although fashionable Harley Street psychiatrists are not commonly called to examine two violent deaths in a night, Nave's perturbation seemed no more than a convention of distress conceded to lay bystanders. He knelt for a long time, perhaps a full minute. Then he got up. 'He is dead,' he said, 'and he was instantly killed. A blow from behind.'

'A skilled blow?'

Nave's eyes went again to the dagger. 'It might be an anatomist's blow,' he said gravely, 'or it might be an evil chance.' There was silence for a moment and he added: 'Shall I stay here ... or take any message?'

Appleby shook his head. 'There is nothing to be gained by your staying. Mr Gylby is going to stay for a time.'

Nave glanced dubiously – perhaps with a sort of masked kindliness – at Noel, who looked strained and more than usually young. Then he nodded and went away. Noel looked resolutely at the body. He felt sorry for Mr Bose and wanted to say something restrainedly distressed. But a trial of his voice told him it would be risky and he found safety in being practical. 'Mr Appleby, must it stay here? Could we move it into the bedroom? These other rooms are occupied ... any of the women might come along.'

Appleby nodded. 'We can move the body. He wasn't killed here.' With Gott he stooped to the burden – it was strangely light – and bore it into what had been Lord Auldearn's room. Then for a moment they hesitated.

'On the bed,' said Noel with the sudden authority of Scamnum. He threw off the upper coverings and they laid the body face downwards. Noel picked up the fine linen of the counterpane. 'It won't ... damage anything on the knife?' Appleby made a negative sign and they shrouded the body. For a moment they looked at the grim little pyramid which concealed the haft. Then Noel offered something practical again. 'That dagger – I don't know if you know – it hangs with some stuff on the wall outside the ... the black man's room. Medieval French, I think.'

'Is his room next door?' asked Appleby.

'Lord, no. Some way off, round a couple of corners.'

'And these rooms are nearly all occupied?'

'Yes. Most people have gone straight to bed – or at least to their rooms – after the search. A curiously shaming process it was. But a few have been fluttering about to jabber.'

Appleby shook his head in plain bewilderment – a habit, it occurred to Noel, never indulged in by Gott's fictional sleuths. And then, almost as if he had read Noel's glance, he smiled. 'Decidedly the time-honoured stage at which nothing fits!' But his voice instantly went hard. 'And we can't give our time to sitting back and thinking, Giles; some crazy logic of events is working itself out around us now. Come.' He strode back to the door and turned to Noel. 'Mr Gylby, do you mind – for an hour, perhaps?'

'I shan't doze off,' said Noel drily. 'Don't bang the door.'

In the corridor Appleby paused. 'He wasn't killed where he lay; there would have been a nasty sound we should have heard.' He walked half a dozen yards down the corridor and called softly. 'He was killed – where we'll presently discover. There is blood as far as this that we can probably track. But here it stops, and here I take it the body was simply picked up, rushed the last six yards, and set gently down on our doorstep – and Auldearn's. Now follow the trail, probably to his room.'

'Intimidating scale the place is on,' said Gott absently. The corridor along which they were walking was some eighteen feet wide; dark parquetry with six feet of patternless cream carpet down the centre.

'Somebody wasn't intimidated – nor concerned to avoid a mess.' Appleby's eyes were on the carpet; on the two clearly discernible furrows made in the deep pile by the dead man's heels and on the steady sequence of congealing gouts of blood. 'You see, Giles, how the evidence points different ways. The *show* of violence . . .'

Gott started, made a gesture at Scamnum flitting past in the subdued light: vistas of dark panelling and soft enamels; the basic design elegant everywhere and a little dry, but relieved by the glow of rich stuffs, the gleam of fine cabinet-work; the whole eloquent of tranquillity and a large security – the Peace of the Augustans.

> 'We do it wrong, being so majestical,
> To offer it the show of violence . . .

The play is impressing itself on you too, John. Here is Bose's room.'

Mr Bose's room was dominated, startlingly and appropriately, by a Gauguin: dusky figures crouched in a vibrant shade, a hot, dark composition that seemed to cast its tropical glow far into the cool greys and greens of the lofty room. And the apple-green carpet was flecked with blood; it was as if the mangoes that made fiery points in the picture had tumbled out and been crushed to an ooze about the floor. Gott sat down abruptly, almost as if he had been hit in the stomach. 'It's

Elizabeth's room,' he said, 'she moved out when this mob came – there's a limit even to Scamnum's resources.' And then he said – and with bitterness – something that Appleby had said to himself in the Prime Minister's car: 'Death at Scamnum Court!'

Appleby, who had already begun a swift exploration, paused. 'Yes?'

'It would be a learned joke. Perhaps somebody's having a learned joke ... *Scamnum*.'

'*Scamnum*?' Appleby frowned in perplexity. 'A bench?'

'Yes; it was arrogantly named after old Roger Crippen's usurious counter. But it's the same word as something else.'

Appleby shook his head.

'*Shambles*, John. For God's sake let's get something done!'

Appleby was on the point of saying: 'Steady!' Instead he said quietly: 'Come and look at the bureau.'

The bureau stood to one side of the outer wall beneath a curtained window – a slender Chippendale piece. Near at hand, and overturned on the floor, was a low-backed mahogany chair. Appleby looked back at the door by which they had entered and then at another door in the side wall close at hand. Gott followed his glance. 'A bathroom, I think, converted from a dressing-room and with a second door giving direct on the corridor.' He moved swiftly across, disappeared, and returned in a moment. 'Yes.'

'Then that is how he entered. Coming through the bathroom door he had only to take two strides – and stab. And he stabbed while the black man was –'

'Writing!' said Gott softly. They both stared at the narrow writing space of the bureau. A fountain-pen lay in the corner, amid a splash of ink suggesting that it had tumbled there from a surprised hand. The Scamnum notepaper was undisturbed in its place; Mr Bose had been writing on a common scribbling-block. And from this block some pages had been hastily ripped away. The exposed surface was blank; nevertheless Appleby picked up the block delicately and studied it with infinite care. 'If things are as they seem,' he said, 'we're both beaten. As a policeman I'm out-witted and as a fantasy-weaver you're blown clean out of the water. Just cast about the floor, Giles, for the stub of the unique cigarette or the accidentally dropped scarab.' But as he spoke Appleby himself was casting about the floor in a search that was wholly serious. And Gott, instead, cast about in the air.

'Little Bose – Emissary A – kills Auldearn, snatches the damned paper, contrives to commit it to memory and then "discovers" it. As soon as the search is over he comes up to his room and gets it down on paper. Then an unknown B – a rival Emissary – stabs Bose . . .' He buried his head in his hands. 'John, it's not *impossible*; it's not even *unlikely* merely because it's grotesque. The document is grotesque in itself – and yet there it is, with hard-headed people in London worrying their heads off over it. I suppose that there are scoundrels and scoundrels at the game; and that Bose, being one, should be stabbed and robbed by another seems likely enough.'

'And yet,' said Appleby, 'you get a feeling from the air that Auldearn's death is basically a piece of theatrical effect, and mysteriously bound up with *Hamlet*. And what did you think of Bose, anyway? He's in the middle of the picture now. Describe him.'

Gott – avoiding the area between bureau and doors – strode up and down the room. 'Like most of the Duchess's finds he was charming. But there's nothing easier, I suppose, than to find a charming and un-earthly black man, and perhaps the process is just one of being taken in. If it had fallen on me to pronounce an emergency Last Judgement on Bose I should have sent him straight among the Saints, though he would have found their beliefs and proceedings absurd. But one can only have confidence in sizing up one's own sort. The little man was far too remote . . .'

'Exactly,' said Appleby. He drew back the window-curtain, threw open the window on the summer night and leaned far out. Below was a brightly-lit terrace with two constables constituting a very adequate patrol. He turned back into the room, locked the bathroom door, picked up the writing block once more and moved towards the door by which they had come. And then he paused to repeat the burden of his thoughts. 'If the substance of the document has really passed from Bose to unknown hands I'm next to beaten – and not all the constables in the home counties can help me.' He opened the door and transferred the key to the outside. 'Come along, Giles. There's some hope. There was the way we dealt with Bose's body – and there is the Duchess. I promised not to disturb people again tonight but you must take me to her all the same – now.'

Nevertheless Appleby stood a moment longer, his eye steadily on the further wall. And Gott realized with a start that in this, the crisis of his career, his friend – unobtrusively enough – was pausing to give proper attention to a noble picture. And for some reason his spirits rose.

Carefully, Appleby locked the door of what had been the Lady Elizabeth Crispin's room. Now it was to hold a ghost, a dusky presence that would hover before the uncertain shelter of that equatorial leafage, the half-recognition of those glancing eyes, the dubious kinship of those brown and glistening limbs.

5

Moving about Scamnum at night, it seemed to Appleby, was like moving in a dream through some monstrously overgrown issue of *Country Life*. Great cubes of space, disconcertingly indeterminate in function – were they rooms or passages? – flowed past in the half-darkness with the intermittent coherence of distant music, now composed into order and proportion, now a vague and raw material for the architectonics of the imagination. Here and there a light glowed still over a picture – on this floor pastel copies of family portraits scattered elsewhere: gentlemen extravagantly robust for the fragile medium into which they had been translated, ladies arbitrarily endowed with the too-heavy features of Anne and with dresses cut low over low, vaguely-defined breasts. And the scale of things wavered as in some hypnogogic trance. A low chair in the distance started into a randomly disposed grand piano at one's elbow. A hand extended to a door-knob fell upon air; the door was a door of unnatural size ten paces away. Appleby tried to imagine himself feeling at home amid this vastness and signally failed; he felt an inexpungeable bourgeois impression of being in a picture-gallery or museum – a well-contrived museum in which each 'piece' had air and space in which to assert its own integrity and uniqueness. He recalled the great palaces – now for the most part tenantless – which the eighteenth century had seen rise, all weirdly of a piece, about Europe. Scamnum, he knew, was to be a different pattern; would reveal itself in the morning as being – however augustly – the home of an English gentleman and a familiar being. But now it was less a human dwelling than a dream-symbol of centuries of rule, a fantasy created from the tribute of ten thousand cottages long perished from the land.

Thus Appleby reflected as he was piloted about Scamnum by Gott in search of the Duchess of Horton. And the nocturnal prowl so tinged his consciousness that he would not have been surprised to find in the Duchess – though he had eyed her attentively enough in the hall – a lady who had sat in Marlborough's tent or drunk chocolate with Bolingbroke in the seclusion of Chanteloup in Touraine.

The Duchess had not gone to bed. She was writing letters in a minute apartment which she had made peculiarly her own, a sort of porch-closet in Vanbrugh's manner, enshrining a bewildering display of photographs such as the most refined of the middle classes – it occurred to Gott – no longer think Good Form. The Duchess indicated two not very comfortable knob-chairs, looked very attentively at Appleby and laid down her pen.

'I've written twelve out of twenty,' she said, counting rapidly. 'We shall do no more entertaining until Scotland, and people must be let know. I've used the same formula twelve times and perhaps at the twentieth it will make me weep; if one could charm oneself into being the weepy sort it would be easier. But it's some good having something to do.'

'And Elizabeth?' asked Gott.

'I hope she is asleep. When she came up to her room her maid decided to be rather hysterical. Elizabeth quieted her, got her to bed and then went to bed herself.' The Duchess turned to Appleby. 'Have you seen the Duke again?'

'No, madam.'

The Duchess smiled – a smile which it would have been accurate, if banal, to call sweet. 'He won't join in the hunt much, I am afraid; far less for Ian's murderer than if the victim had been a mere acquaintance. It was different when he thought there was this secret – the paper – at stake. I can't explain it; his particular vision of good and evil drives that way. I suppose it is that there are people who, when the spectacle of evil opens at their feet, will stand insulated and immobile before that black pit. It appears as a sort of fatalism in face of personal calamity.' The Duchess sighed. 'Teddy is Hamlet,' she said. 'Which is why he made such a capital Claudius on the stage: Mask and Image.'

This was a glimpse of what had once made Anne Dillon more than a mere beauty in Edwardian drawing-rooms. It was fascinating and penetrating – but why was it offered? Appleby did not pause to speculate, but it would have been the answer, perhaps, that the Duchess possessed a genius for establishing personal relations. She had discerned in Appleby a certain temper of mind; someone to whom it would be best to present her own mind in its natural movement and colour. 'I very much hope,' she said, 'that *I* can help. I am not Prince Hamlet.' And she shivered. She had not failed – Gott supposed – to notice her last allusive utterance as a trick bred of long acquaintance with Lord Auldearn.

Appleby recognized the quotation but not the cause of the shiver. He plunged straight at his matter. And the straightness of the plunge indicated, perhaps, that the Duchess had established herself where she would have wished. 'You can help at once by telling me about Mr Bose. He too – it is very bad news – has been murdered.'

For a long moment the Duchess sat quite still and silent. And then it became very clear that if she was without tears she was not without passion. Her eyes blazed. 'Vile,' she said, 'oh . . . *vile!*' Then she controlled herself and added quietly: 'But, Mr Appleby, this means . . . a maniac? There is still danger? . . . you have adequate men? And where did this happen – when?'

Appleby answered slowly. 'I do not think that Mr Bose was killed in mere madness and without reason. He was killed – stabbed – not more than half an hour ago in his bedroom.'

The Duchess's thought was what Gott's had been. 'In Elizabeth's room!'

'It is very necessary – urgently necessary, which is why I have disturbed you – that I should know about your acquaintance with Mr Bose, in detail and from the beginning. Would it be too much to ask you to attempt that now? And I will put off an explanation of the importance of the matter until afterwards, if I may.'

'You are asking almost for a story.' Perhaps, despite her real distress, there was a faint undertone of eagerness in the Duchess's voice, for a story was something she loved. 'But I will be as brief as I can; you must ask me if I don't mention the relevant things.

'I first came across him in the British Museum. You see, Nevil – my son, that is, who is abroad – is interested in fish.' The Duchess paused rather challengingly, as if to assert that fish were a perfectly rational object of interest. 'And quite often I look things up for him in the library here. But a couple of years ago he became involved in a controversy in something called *Zeitschrift für Ichthyologie und tropische Tiefseekunde* – you will know it, Giles.' The Duchess had boundless faith in the universality of the learned of her circle.

'So then, when we were in town, I used to go to the British Museum sometimes and look things up there. I noticed Mr Bose the very first time. There are so many queer-looking people in the Reading Room – sandals, you know, and bearded sages in semi-religious robes and muddled women doing Higher Thought – that anybody who is remarkable rather than queer strikes one at once. And, of course, Mr Bose was remarkable. He used to drift about, very shy and looking rather lost. I don't know what his work was exactly, but I think it was all half-mysterious to him – a ritual that would bring him at last to the secret of the astounding and alarming West. One thought of the Reading Room as a temple whenever one looked at him; and – as you will hear – he thought of it as a temple himself.' The Duchess paused a little dubiously, as if aware of an incongruity in these reminiscences at three o'clock in the morning. 'But you cannot want all this, really?'

'Please. Just as it comes to you, cutting nothing out.'

'He worked for the most part in the room behind the Reading Room, where they give you the older books. It is quite a small place, no bigger than an ordinary library like our own here.' Gott, who was himself a frequenter of the twin vastness of 'the room behind the Reading Room' and of Scamnum's library, smiled at this description, but the Duchess continued unnoticing. 'Sometimes I went in there myself to look at the big monographs that need a whole great table to lay them on. There was one enormous and lovely thing by a man called Bloch – lovely plates of the most unbelievable creatures – and one day like a fool I tried to carry it back from table to counter myself. And, of course, I dropped it – two great volumes. It was more than rather dreadful! There is a superintendent who sits in a sort of pulpit and he stopped writing and put on an extra pair of glasses and *looked* at me. And an old gentleman with one of those French ribbons in his buttonhole got up and walked very quietly up and down, waving his hands – quite restrainedly – above his head; I suppose I had broken an important train of thought. I hadn't felt so bad since I made a perfectly thunderous mistake once, visiting Elizabeth at Cheltenham.' The Duchess plainly controlled an impulse to diverge on this and continued. 'Professor Malloch was there and he began to come across at a sort of modified, courteous trot. But the little black man was before him and gathered up Bloch – though I'm sure Bloch was far too heavy for him – and carried it to the counter. After that I felt entitled to get to know him if I could. I thought he might be interesting.'

The Duchess smiled as she touched on this foible. 'Unfortunately other people had thought the same thing. One of the Higher Thought women – I discovered afterwards – had invited him to tea and prepared a room all draped in purple – and with joss-sticks, I think – and asked all her friends to share the mysteries. So he was naturally rather shy. Then one day I happened to take sandwiches, thinking it would be pleasing to eat them on the steps as I did long ago, when I used to take – go with my father for a day with the marbles. You know how people sit on the steps and under the portico and colonnade and feed the pigeons. Well, I noticed Mr Bose and he seemed to be *wanting* to feed the pigeons. He had sandwiches with him himself – a very small packet – and he seemed several times to be on the point of throwing something to the pigeons and then to think better of it. I went and joined him and I am afraid my interpretation of his actions was primitive, really gross! I really thought he hadn't brought enough and was hesitating between his own maw and the birds'. So I said – like a fool – "I have too much here; let's feed the pigeons." He was dreadfully worried at having to demur and made a great business of explaining. He regarded the Museum as a holy place and the pigeons were surely sacred birds. And he believed that the Higher Thought ladies who were sitting about, scattering crumbs, had it as a sort of ritual charge to care for them. And because these were not his rites he rather doubted the admissibility of joining in – though he wanted to feed the pigeons. He would have to consult his father, he said, who gave him various dispensations from time to time such as were necessary for moving in Western society.'

'Like the egg!' said Gott. 'Do you remember? When winter came he had his father's permission to eat an egg, if constitutionally necessary.'

The Duchess nodded. 'And then he talked to me very simply about caste and about his family – very old landowners, it seemed – and finally he told me that I was like his mother. At that I felt the horrid triumph of the successful collector; just like Mrs Leo Hunter, no doubt, when she had secured the exotic Count Smorltork. But I was mistaken. Mr Bose led me a long dance after that.'

'You mean,' said Appleby, 'that you had great difficulty in … in carrying the acquaintance further?'

The Duchess raised a whimsical eyebrow. 'It wasn't quite a matter of pestering him; indeed, Mr Appleby, I would try not to do that. He liked me, I believe, and was always pleased when we met and he would talk very much as if I had been truly his mother. But afterwards he would retreat slightly and I had to begin all over again. He had learnt that I was what he called a ranee and perhaps he felt that I ought to make all the advances. So it was slow and difficult. You see, I didn't just want to trap him in a room with purple curtains and flummery.

'But we finally cemented our friendship one afternoon in Rumpelmayer's. I felt it as rather tragic at the time that his Achilles' heel was, so to speak, his stomach after all. It was when I had introduced him to that paradise of sweet and sticky delights – and particularly to the chestnut things that Elizabeth became so fond of in Vienna, Giles – that he finally opened his heart to me.' The Duchess pulled herself up. 'But his heart is not part of the story. Well, even later it was extraordinarily difficult to get him to come down and stay here. And when he came it was to his death. Invading him as I did seems terribly wanton now. He enjoyed himself, I think, and it was because I knew he would that I brought him. But now –'

The Duchess, despite the animation of her narrative, was clearly exhausted and only by an effort remaining other than distraught. Appleby rose. 'You have told me all I wanted to know. And if you will excuse me? . . . Minutes may be valuable now.'

'Then go at once. Servants will be up all night; coffee, anything you may require, they will bring. And there will be a man continuously in the telephone-exchange; anybody in the house you will be able to rouse instantly from such sleep as they are likely to get. And now, I will finish my letters.' The Duchess, seeing that Appleby wanted to waste no more time with her, wasted no more time on him.

'Now . . . the terrace.' Appleby, as he made his way down the great staircase with Gott, appeared lost in thought. Presently he roused himself. 'It makes the position no better; what do you think, Giles?'

'Once more, that the spies are a fable. Bose was no spy. That was not the story of how a spy worms himself into a house.'

'Quite so. That was the first fact I wanted; that the Duchess went after Bose and not Bose after the Duchess. And – you know – we had an instinct that Bose was all right when we were getting his body decently on Auldearn's bed.'

Gott gave a sort of sigh of relief. 'Not a Bath Mat Oriental' – and without pausing to explain – 'I'm glad.'

'And we have learnt why he was killed.'

'Yes.' Gott had no flair for being a Dr Watson. 'He was sending the whole story of murder to his father – thousands of miles away – and imploring guidance. But it seems pretty mad.'

Appleby shook his head. 'Not mad. Only – as we said – very remote. I thought he evaded a question of mine; he would not, I think, tell a direct lie. We were a very queer people to him, I suspect – despite his labours in the British Museum. He was not sure if I realized that the prime fact of the matter was that something evil had been done. And imagine yourself in a rajah's palace, Giles – a rajah's palace in a rajah-ruled world. You peer through a curtain in the middle of certain crazy proceedings and you see *A* wipe out *B*. I think you would be in some doubt. And Bose may have had fundamental philosophical difficulties; rather like those the Duchess attributes to the Duke, but more so. With what ought one to meet a particular sort of evil, and in particular circumstances as a guest? – and so on. If his code required him to consult paternal authority before feeding a pigeon or eating an egg, one can imagine its requiring something of the sort in the face of bloodshed. And so the murderer, who knew Bose knew, got his chance.'

'And Bose memorized nothing; that was just my novelist's fancy. And the spies are a fable.'

They had emerged on the terrace – to be pounced on by a constable. He recognized and saluted Appleby. 'Your photographers are in the theatre, sir – in the little stage place, with the sergeant. And the ambulance has come and we've sent it into the court. All been quiet apart from that, sir.'

They walked the breadth of the upper terrace and turned to look back at the house. It rose before them, a great expanse of stone still fretted with half a score of lights, colossal and mysterious as a liner looming out of the night – the soft line of encircling illumination bathing the terraces like foam. But Gott, watching the steady pace of the patrolling police, had another image in mind. 'A platform before the castle,' he said. 'Quiet guard ... not a mouse stirring ... The play haunts us still.'

Appleby laughed harshly. '*Hamlet*? ... Spy-stuff off a bookstall. Sprung to life with God knows what ingenuity.' They made the long round of Scamnum, verifying the efficiency of the cordon, before he spoke again. 'I may have been too late with this guard,' he said, 'and it may be all over now. Or I may be losing the game this moment through having an insufficiently elastic mind. Giles, do you know anything about wireless?'

Gott exclaimed: 'It doesn't fit ... it's nonsense! We're faced with some private, passional thing.'

Appleby shook his head. 'You forget —' He broke off to stare into the darkness and then back at the house, his gaze travelling between the twin bulks of Scamnum and Horton Hill. 'Do you see any light – any flicker of light – on that hill?' He called up a sergeant – the place seemed now swarming with police – and spoke rapidly.

'We thought of it, sir,' said the man, stolidly but with pride. 'There's a man far out to each quarter watching the house and others on the roof looking the other way. If they see anything but steady lights they'll report.'

Appleby moved off a few paces with Gott and sighed with satisfaction. 'And the Duke thinks the county police should be immobilized! Perhaps they're not quite adequately energetic in the matter of poachers. But it may all be too late. Back to your play-box now.'

'Are you not putting rather a lot of faith in your telephone friend? His report stands alone now against all appearance; and I suspect that sort of person is oftener wrong than right.'

'No doubt. Read unvarnished accounts of spy-work and you see that muddle's its middle name. And I have no doubt that if Auldearn were being stalked with the object of theft and then this killing happened, a spy in the audience might jump to the conclusion that his friends had acted a little more vigorously than expected and send off a rash promise from the first call-box. In fact Auldearn's death may have been, as you say, a private affair and the document never got at all. But I can take no chances. And so, back to your theatre.' He looked at his watch. 'Three o'clock.'

6

The door of the hall, thrown open by a discreetly impassive constable, became – disconcertingly – a valve for the release of exceedingly angry voices. 'Hamlet and Laertes,' said Gott, 'quarrelling by Ophelia's grave.'

And certainly the scene revealed looked like a quarrel in a play. Dr Biddle and Sir Richard Nave, undeterred by the dubious glances of another constable in a distant corner, were standing plumb centre of the front stage, under the full glare of the still burning arc-lamps, and only too evidently very much displeased with one another indeed.

'Clearly the localized form,' Nave was vociferating. Recently so cool among the corpses, he was now quivering like an athlete on his mark. '*Leontiasis Ossium* –'

'*Leontiasis* fiddlestick!' Dr Biddle, an amiable little old gentleman to all normal seeming, was dancing – dancing in something grotesquely like a low-comedy convention of indignation. 'Simple, generalized Paget's – plain as a pikestaff! If Harley Street ideologues –'

'Sir,' thundered Nave, 'you are impertinent!'

Appleby nudged Gott briskly forward. 'What they call consultation, no doubt,' he murmured, 'but of whom this honourable interest in diagnostic minutiae?' When Appleby fell to sarcasm it was a sign of outrage; and indeed the scene was more indecent than funny. A few yards away, behind the rear-stage curtain from which there came a low murmur of voices, lay the body of Lord Auldearn, with a bullet in his heart and surrounded by police photographers. High words in such a presence were sharp exemplification of something Appleby knew well enough; that the shock of violent death will obliterate and transform social responses in a very remarkable way. But now both men made an effort to control themselves, and it was in his normal manner that Nave addressed Appleby.

'Dr Biddle, who is police-surgeon, has done me the honour to include my signature on the preliminary report that must be signed, it seems, before the body is moved. That is why we are here. But Dr Biddle proposes, I understand, to offer a contribution to knowledge as well.'

The tone insinuated that country doctors – even those who attend on dukes – do not commonly make contributions to knowledge and it almost sent Biddle off his balance again. He contented himself with a frown – but the anger was there, and apparently it was going to unleash itself on the police. 'I wish to say,' said Biddle belligerently, 'that it would have been proper of you to consult me at once on the cause of death.'

'The cause of death!' said Appleby in genuine astonishment.

'Tcha! The manner of death, if you prefer it. Suicide. I am convinced that Lord Auldearn committed suicide and that this intensive police investigation is unnecessary and . . . and highly indecorous.'

'Suicide . . . unnecessary . . . indecorous!' It was Nave who broke in, and for a moment he seemed angrier even than before. Was it, Appleby wondered, the common enough irritation of an able man before a donkey-colleague? And was Biddle a donkey?

Biddle continued resolutely. 'Suicide, I say. Lord Auldearn was a sick man; a dying man, in fact. He was suffering from a not common but nevertheless unmistakable' – he shot a venomous glance at Nave – 'unmistakable disease which has only one end. And he took a quick way out.'

Appleby glanced at Nave. 'You disagree about his having been mortally ill?'

'Most certainly I do not. But clearly –'

Appleby interrupted smoothly. 'I see, you were discussing the technical details when we came in. But, Dr Biddle, have you any reason to suggest for Lord Auldearn's choosing such – well – such a striking occasion for his deed?'

'He had a damned queer humour,' retorted Biddle. And beneath the competent and humane, if momentarily upset, old practitioner Appleby seemed to see for a moment a raw medical student to whom most sophisticated attitudes would be inexplicable.

Nave said drily: 'And so – if it was suicide – must other people have had – damned queer. Somebody, for instance, picked up the revolver and humorously hid it in Yorick's skull –'

Appleby whirled on him. '*How do you know that?*'

Nave looked mildly surprised. 'The Duke told me – my good sir!' He turned back to Biddle. '*Your* skull, by the way, Dr Biddle. And then that somebody, or another somebody, fell into the spirit of the evening and stabbed the unfortunate little Indian.' He looked blandly from the startled Biddle to Appleby. 'Dr Biddle and I were so absorbed in scientific talk that I forgot to tell him. Somebody has thrust a dagger into Mr Bose's heart. And I have come to the conclusion – mere student of the mind that I am – that the result has been death.'

Biddle, shocked apparently by the news and goaded afresh by Nave's irony, again exploded against the police. 'If there has been another death I should have been sent for at once. I shall speak to the Chief Constable. And I want to know if I am to be detained throughout the night. I have had a message that a bedroom has been got ready for me. I don't want a bedroom! I want to go home! In fact I demand to leave! I have my practice to attend to. I don't even know what urgent calls there may have been.'

The first rumpus, thought Gott – and said aloud: 'Hadn't you better stay? Then you can be led to the deaths as they occur.'

Biddle jumped. 'Deaths?'

'There is an unknown person, callous of human life and apparently utterly reckless, at large in this house. I don't know what may happen but I do know that in such a situation it is – well – highly indecorous to badger the police. Unfortunately by this time we are all thoroughly tired and on edge.'

'Mr Gott is right,' said Nave. 'And – Dr Biddle – we have been hasty. I apologize.'

Appleby seized upon this favourable moment. 'I am afraid, Dr Biddle, that it may be necessary to detain everybody for some time. I am very sorry. Any urgent messages would have come through by telephone and been referred to you at once. And any message you wish to send out may be sent out through the police.' It was not a generous concession but Appleby made the most of it. And presently, sure enough, Biddle was wooed to something like amiability. But he reiterated his conviction of suicide. Auldearn's choosing to shoot himself in the middle of the Scamnum theatricals was queer; but sick men do queer things. Whereas murder would be sensational and appalling; and the sensational and the appalling simply had no place at Scamnum. As for the violent death of Mr Bose, Biddle was obviously unprepared to believe in it without the evidence of his own senses. And to acquire this, and make appropriate official memoranda, he was presently successfully despatched under the guidance of a now courteous and remotely amused Nave.

Appleby moved towards the rear stage looking faintly perplexed. 'I suppose,' he said, 'that Harley Street ideologues and Sussex G.P.s are naturally a sort of pike and perch. But it seems to have been an unnecessary flare-up.'

'I suspect Nave of having forgotten a good deal that lies outside the psychiatry he makes his money by. And if he was simultaneously cocky and hazy that would infuriate Biddle.'

'What was Biddle in the play?'

'He petitioned to come in at the last minute. We made him an attendant lord.'

'Well, he seems just such a minor figure. Only not very strong, perhaps, in the courtier's patience and self-control. And now, Giles, for the constabulary's star turn: scientific detection. But I'm afraid you'll find it lacking in novelty.'

The rear stage was certainly a highly-conventional effect. In one corner a lounging young man stood amid a litter of those large glass bulbs, filled with a gleaming silver-foil, used by press photographers; he was loosing them off in a bored way for two muttering and exclaiming persons with large cameras. Looking up, Gott saw a third camera peering down from the trap-door of the upper stage, and the head of a third muttering and exclaiming person bobbing about behind it. A severe little man with glasses and a bald head, very like a distinguished scientist discoursing on shaving-soap in one of Diana Sandys's advertisements, was industriously and impassively applying a miniature vacuum-cleaner to the surroundings of the corpse. In the background a brother scientist was puffing some sort of powder through a machine at the faldstool. To one side stood Sergeant Trumpet and two local constables, impressed, respectful but latently antagonistic. It was nothing if not a highly-coloured scene. Gott ran an agitated hand through his hair, indicated the manipulator of the vacuum-cleaner with a polite little-finger. 'John – I say – is that Dr Thorndyke?'

'It must be,' said Appleby.

Dr Thorndyke switched off his machine and addressed Gott with a disturbing fusion of American *camaraderie* and London accent. 'There was an old girl once thought her husband a bit dusty-like. Laid him down on the mat just like this 'ere' – Dr Thorndyke jerked a thumb innocent of irreverence at the body – 'and vacuumed him proper. Twisted all his po'r bleeding inside and he had to go into 'orspital. Almost knocked him off. Yes, siree.'

This was presumably Dr Thorndyke's favourite semi-professional anecdote; all his colleagues had plainly heard it before. 'You see,' murmured Appleby, faintly apologetic, 'they go to study these things in New York.' But Gott had turned to the person puffing at the faldstool. 'And I take it,' he said, 'that this contrivance is ... is what I call an insufflator?'

Appleby looked with subdued irony at his friend. 'I suppose it is rather macabre; the Gott *genera* coming alive, so to speak.'

'It's like stepping through the looking-glass,' said Gott morosely. He had never seen Appleby in this full professional setting before.

Appleby raised his voice. 'Nearly through?' There were affirmative noises. The young man with the flashlights draped himself in flex and departed. The faldstool was carried out to be photographed elsewhere. The army of criminologists melted away.

'Is all that useful?' asked Gott.

'Your insufflator's useful; finger-prints still catch criminals by the pint. And an expert gunsmith is useful. And good photographs serve sometimes to hold the attention of a tired jury. The rest's hooey, more or less. But I have to think of the fuss there's going to be if we're held up for long. Questions in Parliament: was such-and-such attempted and does the Home Secretary know of the advanced methods of the Kamchatkan police? I've been caught before by scamping the window-dressing. But now I must have a word with them and then we can look round.'

When Appleby returned he was carrying the heavy iron cross that the Duchess had obtained along with the faldstool from Hutton Beechings. 'Found on the floor,' he said. 'It was part of the rear-stage set?'

Gott nodded. 'Yes. Standing on the little ledge of the faldstool.'

'Then it just conceivably suggests a slight scuffle – or it may have been knocked over during the getaway. They thought Auldearn might have snatched it up to defend himself. But it's clear of finger-prints.' Appleby paused to pace out the dimensions of the rear stage. 'They agree with me about the shot. Getting on for close-up but distinctly outside suicide range – nothing in Biddle's theory. And certainly not from as far as the shelter of the curtains. But just conceivably from as far as the trap immediately above.'

They both looked up to where the trap-door had been left open. 'Still the spot, then,' said Gott, 'from which a venerable Royal Academician may have committed the first of two imbecile and beastly murders. Shall we go up?'

They went behind scenes and climbed to the upper stage. Cope's easel and canvas were still in position in a corner and his palette and a wooden box, with about a dozen very large tubes of paint, lay on the floor. Appleby took up a position behind the easel and looked out over the body of the hall. 'Was the lighting like this? He could be seen, surely, by the audience?'

'Yes, just like this – a half-light representing the battlements at night. The true Elizabethan upper-stage must, I think, have been pretty shadowy. But even so, he could, as you say, be seen. He wanted to paint from here and I felt that his presence, just discernible in the shadow, wouldn't spoil the play.'

'The question then would be whether he could get to this trap-door in the middle without being detected. I'll give the fellow at the far end of the hall there a shout. It would be from the back that he could be seen, if from anywhere. Just get behind the easel, Giles, move about a bit and then make for the trap-door as well as you can.' Appleby advanced to the low balustrade of the upper stage and called out to a constable at the extreme end of the hall: 'Just look up here, will you, and tell me what you can see besides myself in the next two minutes.'

The constable looked – open-mouthed but keen-eyed. Gott stood behind the easel; moved right and left of it once or twice; withdrew behind it; got cautiously down on his knees, on his stomach; squirmed towards the trap. Gaining it, he paused a moment, wriggled round, returned as he had gone and in a moment was appearing right and left of the easel again as if studying the composition before him.

'Well?' called Appleby.

The constable lumbered up the hall and climbed on the front stage. 'I saw the gentleman dodging about behind the picture,' he said. 'Then he disappeared for a bit like, and then he showed up again, dodging about as before.'

'What do you mean – disappeared for a bit?'

'Well, sir, happen he were just standing still behind the picture. It's all in shadow and hard to tell.'

Appleby nodded. 'Well, that's all right; quite possible. So tell me about Cope.'

Gott hesitated. 'He's imbecile, or thereabout. Which need not suggest the perpetration of imbecile crime. It's simply that the age is in and the wits are out. And there is a sense in which one feels that he might do any crazy thing. One's not a considerable artist without plenty of inner stress, and when one's mind and control begin to break up conceivably the stress may let fly in a perfectly helter-skelter way.'

Appleby looked dismayed. 'This latest tendency to psychologize your fictions, Giles. It sounds well, but I don't know that there's much record of considerable artists embracing the straitjacket by way of multiple homicide.'

But Gott was pursuing his thought soberly. 'No, but there are plenty of suicides recorded among them. And the two mechanisms are not altogether remote. However, it's the Bose factor that seems vital.'

'Quite so. Cope could have shot the recumbent Auldearn from here and nothing neater. But could Bose have known? You must do that reconstruction all over again, Giles. When I say Go.'

Appleby descended from the upper stage and took up Bose's position on the prompter's stool between the two thicknesses of heavy curtain. Applying his eye to the peep-hole commanding the rear stage he cried: 'Go!' And within a few seconds something significant happened; he was conscious of a stealthy slithering noise from above – Gott crawling cautiously over the boards. So far so good; Bose, who as prompter would be giving his whole consciousness to sound, might well have had his attention attracted in this way to the upper stage – and so, by a natural transition, have directed his glance through the peep-hole and upwards. So he peered in and up. And in a moment he saw some movement in the shadows – it was the trap-door sliding back – then, clearly, a pointing hand. It was Gott's, a finger extended as if aiming to shoot. Bose, then, could have known. What was more important, as explaining his presumed reluctance to speak, he could have suspected without knowing positively. A revolver thrust through the trap from the upper stage must *almost* certainly have been in the hands of Cope. Bose could have almost known. But how could Cope have known that Bose almost knew?

'How,' said Gott, coming down, 'how could Cope have known Bose knew – supposing, I mean, it was so?'

'Exactly. But the answer is simple enough if you psychologize. A single glance between the two afterwards would have told him.'

'Yes, a look could no doubt tell all. But the Cope theory, remember, is another thrust towards oblivion for the spy theory. I don't know

Cope's subsequent movements, access to Auldearn's body and so on; but if one shot to grab, one would hardly shoot from another storey.'

'Perhaps the grabbing is another story, very little connected with the shooting? And though the Cope theory is beguiling it's the grabbing I must hold on to now. And for that the vital point is the hermetic sealing.' And on the hermetic sealing, Appleby went to work. The structure of the hall, the floor, the doors, the windows; the chance of throwing something through a window, of thrusting something through a ventilator, of catapulting something through the darkness of the rafters to the far end of the hall – everything was considered. It was plain, to begin with, that nobody could have got away. There were only two exits from the hall. That behind the green-room had, as it happened, been under the observation of Gott, Noel, Elizabeth, and Stella Terborg at the moment the shot was heard and Gott had stood by it until the Duke arrived, locked it, and sent him to see to the other door – that behind the audience. And at this second door there had been a fireman, who could speak absolutely to nobody's having come or gone. Until the Duke dismissed the audience, therefore, nobody had left the hall except Gott and Gervase Crispin when they went to Auldearn's room.

'It seems a hundred to one,' said Appleby – and to Gott he appeared almost restless – 'that it's as you say. Either this Hilfers person has made the merest muddle or there really were people after the document and one of them, being in the audience and seeing what happened, jumped to conclusions and sent an over-confident message to his pals. And yet –'

'But any *danger* is gone, surely. The thing is in your pocket; Bose turns out overwhelmingly unlike a spy and so it's irrelevant that he had a memory like a photographic plate –'

'And so,' said Appleby, 'we might turn to this: Sergeant Trumpet's instinct was sound.'

Gott frowned – and started. 'To hang on to anyone who had left the hall! John, have you got your eye on me?'

'I have not. But there was also –'

He paused at the startled look on Gott's face and then swung round to confront the advancing figure of the Duke. And the Duke, who had been so impassive in the contemplation of murder, was moving in something between daze and distraction. He walked straight up to Appleby and spoke as if out of a trance. 'Mr Appleby, I have just been to my cousin Gervase Crispin's room. I happened to go in quietly by the dressing-room and he failed to notice me. I came away at once. He failed to notice me because he was sitting at a desk manipulating . . . an instrument.' For a moment the Duke's knees seemed to sway beneath him.

'It was a little camera,' he said.

There was only one question on which to pause. And the answer to it was uncompromising: it had certainly been Gervase's suggestion that Auldearn's room should be inspected and guarded. At this Appleby hurried behind-stage with directions; half a minute later he and Gott were running upstairs. Neither said a word but Appleby noticed that Gott was almost as disturbed as the Duke. In a night that had included two murders and the rumour of more than private calamity there had been nothing as simply dark as this. That an enigmatical Indian should have a memory like a photographic plate and employ it in mischief-making had been one suggestion; that Gervase Crispin might have been about the same job with an actual camera was another. It belonged to a different world of blackness. And to the quick imagination of Appleby the dimly lit vistas of Scamnum, as they flowed past once more, took on a new unsteadiness, as if the foundations of the place were rocking above a subterraneously exploded mine. But Gott, as he ran up the great staircase, was hearing again the frantic bell that had pealed so wildly there just twenty-four hours before and the voice that had rung out in sequel:

> '. . there shall be done
> A deed of dreadful note.'

The words had been from *Macbeth*. And the deed had been treason.

'Better knock,' said Appleby, pausing coolly before Gervase's door. He knocked; there was no answer. He turned the handle and walked in. Darkness. He flicked on the light. There was no sign of Gervase Crispin in the bedroom; the dressing-room and bathroom were empty too. Without wasting a moment, and perfectly methodically, he began to search the room. 'Perhaps the Duke's gone queer in the head,' he said presently. But his search was ruthless and the remark – half whimsical, perhaps, and half apologetic in intention – rang harshly when it was uttered. And then he put the case plainly. 'Gervase Crispin shoots Auldearn, gets the document, suggests searching Auldearn's room, leaves you there, and hurries to his own. He takes the photograph – perhaps gets the plate off to a confederate – and then returns to the hall and manages to get the document into the scroll. It seems to hold.'

Gott was analysing this in a flash. 'It won't hold. If he had a confederate waiting somewhere up here, he would surely give him camera and all: it couldn't be got away too soon. And he would have no reason to be fiddling with the camera afterwards when Scamnum was teeming with policemen. And if he had no confederate to get the thing away he would be taking a frightful risk. If the search in the hall had been followed by a search in his room – and there was half a pointer that way, for he had been out – he would have been caught.'

'There was more than half a pointer, Giles. And – Lord help me! – I missed it. As for frightful risk, frightful risks enough have been taken in Scamnum tonight; think of trundling Bose's body past all these bedroom doors! But tell me about Gervase straight, while I finish this rummage. Then, if he doesn't return, we must be after him.'

'If there's anything in this, then when I spoke of nightmare I spoke too soon. He's a Crispin. Indeed, as I said, he's *the* Crispin. And they're at the heart of England. It's fantastic.'

Suddenly, and while still searching like an automaton, Appleby spoke with something like passion. 'York's the heart of England – and Stratford and Preston, perhaps, and Huddersfield. Scamnum! ... didn't you say yourself it was a show-case – and the Duke and his fish and his pigs show-case stuff, too? And what's the real Crispin, this Gervase's Crispin? We were talking about grab – isn't that him? The honourable history of grab. First hundred years – grab in England and Holland; second hundred years – grab about Europe, India, and the Levant; third hundred years – grab round the planet! Gervase is big at his game – really big, I grant – and that's where something of the incredible comes in. But the heart of England is sob-stuff. Gervase is money, the root and heart of money. And for all I know his home and his allegiance may be wherever money spawns quickest at the moment. I've no more reason to trust him than I have a labourer out in the Crispin fields – less, in fact.'

'I didn't know you were a Jacobin, John.'

'No more I am. I'm probably violently reactionary. Even when *Hamlet* was being written Crispin was still Crippen, pushing a trade honest men didn't favour. But all that's irrelevant. Here's my point, though.

I know almost nothing about this document that's in my pocket now, and I probably wouldn't learn much more if I sat straight down to study it. It's about international industrial organization, as far as I can gather, and it may be far more a matter just of Grab than of the Union Jack. It was put to me in terms of this country and that, and with rumours of conflict in the background. But I know that once one touches the fringes of an affair like this, one is fated to work half in the dark. For all I know it may be just a racket that's going to cripple Gervase in Germany or Gervase in North Africa – that sort of thing. And you can't deny that the Duke, having been smart enough to see the significance of a camera, was sufficiently impressed to come forward – rather heroically – with the story. He may know that the document is in some way connected with Gervase's interests, which would be a reason for his instant extreme concern. And I'm not sure that I wasn't given half a hint not to trust ... well, the family.' Appleby was thinking of the Prime Minister's remark about not trusting even the Archbishop of Canterbury.

'But mightn't Gervase be in on the document-business anyway?'

'Not necessarily. He's not in the Cabinet, for instance. But tell me about him – as a private person, I mean – while I prod this sybaritic spring-mattress.'

Gott considered gloomily. 'Gervase has the family feeling for a role,' he said. 'In the play he took Osric and the Second Grave-digger, and that more or less represents what the Terborg girl calls his *persona*: something midway between the fantastic and the buffoon. His jokes have deliberately no sense to them; you know the sort? But one is aware all the time that he is the able banker and all the rest of it; one would be aware of something of the kind at a first meeting and without knowing anything about him. As for the rest, the Russian woman is his mistress –'

'Ah, the heart of England again. Go on.'

Gott smiled. 'Certainly it adds a neat touch to the cosmopolitan-villain picture. It's a recent affair, but I believe honourable enough or she wouldn't be here. The Duchess is ironical about it but actually approves. They can't marry I understand, because she has a husband in a mad-house.'

'It looks rather as if she had a lover in one too. Tell me more about them, if you can.'

'There's something a little puzzling about their relationship. Nave, for instance, was questioning it the other day. He has a nose for the psychopathic that he would do better to keep for his consulting-room. And – though I knew the story – I didn't discuss it with him. The point is, I understand, that Gervase doesn't in any sense keep the Merkalova. She's an independent creature, contriving to make some sort of living out of fashionable journalism, and she's temperamentally a virginal creature as well, so that it is one of these affairs that are laced with long-term platonics. It was the feel of that, perhaps, that baffled Nave.'

For a moment Appleby had looked startled. 'It's just possible –' He checked himself as if before a hazy speculation. 'But it's interesting about Nave. After all, he's a professional observer. What exactly did he think about them?'

Gott hesitated. 'It may have been his idea that they had less the air of lovers than of colleagues. But –'

'But you think – being full of reactionary prejudice yourself – that Nave would be baffled before anything outside farmyard relations. Maybe so. And here, surely, is friend Gervase returning.' Appleby punched the mattress and looked calmly round the ransacked room. 'I'm afraid that – like Wilkie Collins's traveller – he's going to find a Terribly Strange Bed.'

Footsteps had made themselves heard in the corridor. They ceased and there came a half-hearted – almost an inattentive – *rat-tat*. Appleby wrinkled his nose in disgust. And then the door opened and admitted Max Cope. 'I'm seeking Gervase,' he said placidly and with something of the North Country idiom it had always pleased him to retain. 'It's Gervase I'm seeking. Have you seen him, Gott? Is he about?' He advanced into the room and stopped to contemplate the cascading pile of rifled bed-clothes in the middle of the floor. 'How very, very pretty!' he said – and sat down and nodded his own lovely and cascading white beard.

For a moment it seemed as if this irruption of another Scamnum exhibit was too much for Appleby. Then he spoke briskly. 'I'm glad you like it; it's the lighting, no doubt, that gives the effect. Did you know that Mr Bose is dead?'

Cope looked dreadfully upset. 'Bose – the little dusky fellow who moved so well? Dear me, how dreadfully sudden!'

'Bose was murdered – *too*.'

'Worse and worse,' said Max Cope; 'worse and worse. It makes it much more dreadful. One wonders could a girl ... could a girl, one asks oneself ...' He paused doubtfully, looked very seriously at Appleby. 'You see, before I say anything to the police I feel I should consult Gervase. I should ask Gervase, I think, before speaking to the police. Don't you think, Mr —?'

'Appleby,' said Appleby.

'Appleby,' said Cope. 'Appleby – quite so.' His eyes strayed to Gott – and lit up. He wagged a cunning finger. 'The oyster-wife, you see. I kept the oyster-wife in mind. And then there she was!' He gave what in another man would have been a leer – for beauty still hung oddly over all Max Cope's gestures – and then he chuckled crazily. Suddenly he stopped, his eyes widening on Appleby. 'But didn't you arrange that search? The search – wasn't it you –'

'Yes,' said Appleby.

'I *see*.' Cope turned to Gott. 'Gott, this is a policeman. And little Bose is dead ... where's Gervase?'

'Missing but not, we hope, very far away.' Gott felt as baffled before Cope as Nave had felt before his problematical lovers. He wondered if this quasi-lunatic discussion was evoking in Appleby the irrational irritation that it was evoking in himself. Nevertheless he continued civilly: 'You wanted him very much?'

'He seemed the best person. Gervase seemed best. One must be so careful these days. I mean, there's just a suspicion of a thing and then they write about it. The mere suspicion might ruin the girl. The girl might be ruined –'

'What girl?' asked Gott – positively sternly.

Cope stared. 'Diana Sandys, of course. Gervase seemed –'

Appleby made a big effort to control the proceedings. 'Diana Sandys – one of the players? Mr Cope, tell me please, what is this about Diana Sandys? *What about her*?'

For a moment Cope seemed scared by the concentration behind the question; scared or simply, perhaps, lost and confused. 'Diana Sandys? Oh, no bone – don't you feel? No interesting bony structure. Pretty and illustrative ... determination or something of the sort. Pressure about the mouth ...' And as Appleby was on the point of giving up Cope seemed suddenly to emerge. Quite simply he said: 'She burnt something, you see.'

In the little silence that followed Appleby was aware that this rambling old person, as he made his announcement, was eyeing him intently. And as if to avoid reciprocal scrutiny Cope now ambled across the room and into shadow, to sit down and fidget by Gervase's rummaged desk. 'Burnt something,' he repeated with a species of gently imbecile guile. 'The child burnt something. And what, we wonder, did the child burn?'

How many of the pleasant people who had gathered at Scamnum – it suddenly came to Gott – were going to be pleasant no longer? Twelve hours ago Max Cope had been crazy and wholly amusing; now he appeared crazy and not a little nasty. Perhaps the nastiness was not in Cope; perhaps it was a poison in the air, a distorting medium that would soon people these stately rooms with knaves, a destructive element that would overwhelm all normal human confidence and make honest people eye each other with suspicion and fear. An exclamation of impatience was on his lips when he was prevented by Appleby – and by Appleby's favourite phrase.

'Tell me about it, will you?'

And ramblingly, repetitively Cope told. While the players had been waiting about the hall and shortly before the arrival of Appleby, one of the Terborg twins – he couldn't remember which, not that they were in the least indistinguishable as people maintained – one of the twins had remarked that there was sure to be a thorough police search. Whereupon Diana Sandys had said, 'I simply must have a cigarette,' and – though nobody was smoking – had gone off to one of the dressing-rooms to get her cigarette-case. And Cope had followed – followed, as he said, simply because it would be kind to hint that nobody had thought it proper to smoke. But on sticking his head round the corner of a curtain he had observed her applying a match not to a cigarette but to several small sheets of paper. And on this it had come to Cope, apparently, that Miss Sandys was what he called the oyster-wife, the person who had been responsible for the 'Hamlet, Revenge!' messages. The notion of a police search having been suggested to her she was hastening, he supposed, to rid herself of a little stock of similar messages. What it had to do with Auldearn's death he didn't know. But there it was.

'You thought it was messages?' asked Appleby – and continued evenly: 'It didn't occur to you that she might be burning notes made from the document?'

Cope's eye, he felt, was again narrowing upon him. But Cope's voice came out of the shadows in helpless bewilderment. 'Document, Mr —'

Appleby sighed. 'And you thought you must speak to Mr Gervase Crispin about it? You hadn't by any chance an appointment with him?' The question was shot out.

'An appointment with Gervase? Dear me, no. I thought it would be wise to speak to him. If the poor girl had been perpetrating this joke ... and then if this had happened...' Cope, fidgeting still at the desk, allowed his voice to falter into bewilderment and silence.

'I see. But Mr Crispin doesn't seem to be coming back. I think, Mr Cope, you should stop worrying now and go to your room for a little sleep. You will be able to consult him in the morning.'

And he humoured the aged painter like a tired child from the room. But when he turned back it was to exclaim: 'I wonder!' He took a turn about the room. 'A fresh trail? A red herring? A deep game of some sort? Giles, is the old rascal as daft as he appears?'

'I think he's daft all right. But he might be up to a deep game all the same. But what? Is he telling lies about this girl?'

'And in with Gervase? You know while he was rambling away I thought he was sizing me up with a pretty queer concentration.'

Gott started. 'I rather imagine —' He crossed over to the desk and came back holding a piece of paper. 'A habit of Cope's,' he said, 'and accounts for the calculating eye. And it's worth about thirty guineas, so hold on to it.'

Appleby stared dumbfounded at the vigorous pencil impression of John Appleby. He read the inscription: 'With best wishes for good hunting – M.C.'

'Oh my God!' said Appleby, swearing for the second time in Gott's knowledge. 'Of all the nights.'

Gott crossed to the window and drew back the curtain.

'Getting on for dawn,' he said. 'The dawn, ah God, the dawn – it comes too soon.'

7

Appleby caught at a suggestion from the *aubade*. 'I suppose that's where Gervase is,' he said. 'With the lady.'

'Perhaps. But as I said –'

'Quite so. And they may be just colleagues. But in any case we must try to get hold of him. He's the centre of the picture still, despite this story of Cope's. Question is – who's to fetch him?'

Gott considered. 'You might use the telephone. "Mme Merkalova? – may I speak to Mr Gervase Crispin?" But it seems indelicate. The obvious person to send is the Duke, but I think the Duke might be spared contact with Gervase at the moment. After all, he has practically suggested he be put in gaol. And the next most obvious person is the other member of the family – Noel.'

The proprieties must be preserved, even in nightmare. 'Then,' said Appleby, 'will you find him – once more? He'll long since have been relieved of his lyke-wake.'

Gott fetched Noel, whose sleepy eyes grew round as he surveyed Gervase's devastated room. 'I say,' said Noel, 'is this affair entirely non-stop, Mr Appleby – a sort of detective marathon? Do we feed you through a pipe as you sleuth?' He was a charming youth, tall, slim, obstinately pink and white, and now enfolded in beautiful green silk. And a murder seemed to have approximately as much effect on him as an aspirin tablet; there was a slightly depressant action lasting about an hour.

'There is something rather difficult I want you to do,' said Appleby. 'It's to get Mr Gervase Crispin here at once.'

'To be sure. And I don't suppose it's just in order to see him to bed. Have you got an eye on old Gervase for the shooting and stabbing?'

'He's got himself suspected,' said Appleby abruptly, 'of tampering with a document of state.'

'My good sir!' Noel's expostulation was as immediate as a reflex action.

'And the person who first suspected him was the Duke.'

Noel's eyebrows went up. 'Giles, it isn't that Mr Appleby's . . . feeling the strain?'

'It is not.'

Noel sat down on the bed. 'Friends,' he said soberly, 'give me your instructions.'

Appleby thought for a moment. 'We think Mr Crispin may be talking things over with Mme Merkalova. Go to her room –'

'Oh Lord!'

'Go to her room, knock, and call for him. If he reveals himself as being there – or if he doesn't, for that matter – say this.' Appleby paused to consider Noel's conversational style. 'Say: "*Gervase, will you come and deal with this detective? He has turned your room upside down and now he wants to convict you of stealing the secret treaty with Ruritania.*" And –'

Mildly, Gott made as if to protest. 'Isn't that rather dangerously giving away –'

'And be sure,' said Appleby, 'that the lady hears every word. Then come back; a member of the family won't be amiss. And now hurry. The night's gone and we've no grip of this business yet.'

Noel departed. Appleby was still prodding about the room. Gott sat down beside Gervase's spacious fireplace and stared thoughtfully at the soot which had been the sole result of Appleby's explorations there. His inner eye kept turning back to the rear stage in the hall, tenanting it anew with that fairytale squad of detective-officers photographing and vacuum-cleaning round the body of a Lord Chancellor of England. They were a symbol of the clamant fact: a pistol-shot – still utterly mysterious – had tossed Scamnum into a world as fantastic as any in the whole domain of his own Elizabethan drama. His mind switched to the bloody carpet in Elizabeth's room; that, he felt, had been less a symbol than a menace, a portent of danger lurking no one knew where. And remotely but convincingly before him he discerned the possibility of a reaction to experience that he had never thought to know – the reaction of panic. 'John,' he said, 'I think I'm going to be panicky.'

'You mean you're anxious about Lady Elizabeth. I hope we'll be too busy presently to be envisaging unlikely dangers.'

It was not a very sympathetic speech, perhaps because it had been absently framed. Appleby's mind too was on the rear stage, a rear stage that kept presenting itself in disconcerting fusion with that other and vaster stage on which he had watched Massine's obscurely struggling destinies. A queer cinematographic cross-cutting of *Hamlet* and *Les Présages* . . . he dismissed it as the muddle of a brain beginning to grow tired.

Noel returned. 'Coming,' he said. 'He started like a guilty thing upon a fearful summons – I don't think.' He paused with relish on the vulgarism and then added: 'If you ask me, he's annoyed.' And Noel sat down on the bed with something of the air of an expectant *habitué* of the National Sporting Club.

Half a minute went by. There was a brisk but deliberate tread in the corridor. The door opened and Gervase entered. He took an un-hurried glance round the room and said: 'May I have an explanation of this extravagant proceeding?' It was true that he did not look guilty. But neither did he appear angry – until quite quietly he added: '. . . you imbecile baboon?'

Noel wriggled luxuriously on the bed. Gott made a deprecatory noise which immediately struck him as donnish and ineffectual to a degree. And Appleby said: 'Sit down.'

Gervase's eyebrows went up, much as Noel's had done some time before. But his person went down, ponderously, into the most com-fortable chair. 'Mr Inspector,' he said, 'I don't mind your gambolling among my things a bit. It's a comparatively harmless employment until we get you taken away. But I object extremely to being hunted about the house as I have just been hunted. And my resentment is less with you than with my cousin here, who behaves like a bell-boy while presumably claiming the character of a gentleman. And now, what do you want?'

'The camera,' said Appleby.

Gervase's eyes narrowed. 'My dear man,' he said, 'you're wasting your time.'

Imbecile baboon or dear man appeared all one to Appleby. He said: 'As you probably know, the house is now very efficiently isolated. Go back, please, and bring the camera.'

What, it occurred to Gott, if the Duke had made a mistake? One cannot tackle the Gervase Crispins of the world like this and escape unpleasant consequences if one's ground gives way beneath one. But Appleby seemed perfectly assured.

'I have told you that you are wasting your time.' Gervase paused and shifted his ground slightly. 'Will you explain just what is in your head?'

'That you brought a document out of the hall, secured a photographic reproduction of it after you had left Mr Gott in Lord Auldearn's room, and then deposited it where it was eventually found on the stage.'

It would have been difficult to affirm that Gervase was not dumb-founded. And certainly he was angry; Appleby scarcely remembered an angrier man. He turned on Noel. 'So that's what you meant by Ruritanian treaties!' He turned back to Appleby. 'Apart from this fantasy about myself, have you any reason to believe that the document has been tampered with at all?'

'Yes.'

'And you have no other line to work on except this that you are putting over on me?'

'At present, nothing so circumstantial.'

'And you've been here for – what – four hours?'

'About that.' Appleby's resentment in face of this inquisitorial method was all assumed. Let the other man take the lead and there is always the chance of his heading in a significant direction. 'About that,' said Appleby in grudging admission.

'And a document – of importance apparently – has been tapped. And your net progress consists in turning this bedroom upside down and asking me fool questions about – a camera, did you say?'

'Yes,' said Appleby. 'The camera. Will you go and get it, please?'

Noel chuckled audibly. Gervase raised his hands to his head in a sort of despair. 'And it hasn't occurred to you that you are building wildly on next to nothing? That against this story of a camera that you've got hold of stands the solid blank unlikeliness of my having shot a guest and old friend of the family in order to pick his pocket? Had you not better at least *begin* with something less improbable and come back to me, you know, if all else fails?'

'I have to begin with what first significantly presents itself. And you rather pile on the unlikeliness. The murder of Lord Auldearn and the tapping or attempted tapping of the document may be matters essentially unconnected.'

Gervase stiffened. 'No doubt. And you want me for the tapping?'

'I want that camera. And if you don't fetch it I must fetch it myself.'

Gervase sprang to his feet in so evident a passion that Appleby found himself involuntarily bunching his fists. But there was no attack; with a noise that Noel likened to that of a sealion diving Gervase steadied himself. He walked to the far end of the room, turned, and spoke on the first stride back. 'Mr Appleby, on my coming in I spoke to you offensively. You're not a fool.' There was something about Gervase that made this admission an almost adequate apology for apostrophe as an imbecile baboon. 'No doubt you know your job and what you must go for. And surely you see that the ... matter you wish to discuss is probably irrelevant? Will you take my word as a gentleman that it is so?'

'Mr Crispin, you're wasting my time. I am aware of the probabilities but I can't deal in them yet. If I were investigating the loss of my own cheque-book I'd take your word at once. As it is –'

The sentence was never finished. Without warning the door flew open and Anna Merkalova swept into the room. 'Gervase,' she demanded tragically, 'have they found out?' And she tossed a sharp metallic object upon the bed.

Gott wondered if too much concentration on the Scamnum *Hamlet* was inclining him unwarrantably to assess things in terms of stage effect. The Merkalova's entrance had been excellent theatre. Noel, who had apparently decided for the time being to contemplate the distressing and confusing events of the night with all the aesthetic detachment which an editor of *Crucible* could command – Noel was obviously gratified by the turn the proceedings had taken. He twisted his neck to contemplate the exhibit which the Merkalova had cast on the bed and then straightened it to observe the more compelling exhibit of the Merkalova herself. She was not very adequately clothed. Perhaps she was content with the garment of psychic virginity piously attributed to her by Gott. But she had none of the appearance of one riven between Artemis and Aphrodite; she was a maturely and unambiguously attractive female, her Russian eye (thought Noel, quoting the poet) underlined for emphasis, and lit up, at the moment, with the most lovely intimations of passion. The lady, he said to himself, is about to throw a temperament.

'It's a sort of camera,' said Noel placidly into the momentary silence that had fallen upon the room.

What followed was not without its perplexities. The Merkalova's language – addressed to Appleby – was fortunately obscure; or obscure to all but Appleby, who happened to know some Russian. And the camera-business was obscure; Appleby took one step towards the bed, looked at the instrument – and smiled rather wryly. He turned to Gervase. 'Mr Crispin, I half-suspected this – until I felt no man would be obstinate enough to conceal anything so trivial. If my time has been wasted it has been wasted by you. You have played the donkey, sir.'

Noel sighed happily. Gott listened in some surprise to the urbane Appleby's apparently joining a slanging match. But in a moment he saw that the attitude turned on some shrewd reading of character. Gervase, after one indignant shout, was no longer an angry man. He gave a low guffaw of laughter and tumbled into a vein of extravagant humour. 'In fact, the fable of the donkey, the baboon, and' – his glance went to the still voluble lady – 'the humming-bird ... Anna, for God's sake be quiet.'

Perhaps Gervase was brusque because he had been caught in what was essentially a chivalrous action, or perhaps that was the suggestion which – amid much *outré* humour – he was now contriving to establish. Gott, noting these alternatives for future consideration and wondering if Appleby were doing the same, eyed the tiny camera and listened to the chivalrous story. And certainly the two fitted together. The camera might be presumed capable of photographing documents, but that certainly was not the purpose for which it had been designed. The Duke had called it 'small'; actually – while being obviously an instrument of precision – it was a mere matchbox of a thing. In fact it was a spy's camera in a very special sense: the sort of camera with which audacious persons obtain for public gratification pictures of occasions too intimate, awful, or exalted for overt recording. Gott remembered a recent batch of such snapshots in a magazine: surprising glimpses of what had been called a 'cheery party for sub-debs'. And the smart journalizing Merkalova, desiring doubtless with laudable independence to earn her own guineas, had apparently adopted the not-laudable plan of introducing such a machine to profane the wholly decorous, but intriguing mysteries of the Scamnum *Hamlet*. There would be a handsome cheque in it and no particular mischief beyond a gross abuse of hospitality. So it was a likely enough tale. And so was Gervase's account of subsequent events. The Merkalova, thoroughly scared after the pistol-shot, had thrust the embarrassing apparatus upon him and begged him to get it away. He had realized what she had been about, foreseen the possibility of search, and taken the opportunity, incidental to his suggestion of visiting Auldearn's room, to throw the mildly incriminating object into his own. Later – and this was what the un-fortunate Duke must have happened upon – he had thought it discreet to remove the film pack from the camera, chop it up, and put the fragments down a drain.

Thus Gervase's story, which he concluded with the vigorous sym-bolism of pulling an imaginary plug. And plainly the story had to be accepted, as Appleby had ingeniously accepted it before it was told. It covered the facts. And, as Gervase went on to point out in his own peculiar idiom, it covered the facts in a probable and almost prosaic way. 'I'm afraid, Mr Appleby,' he said with a grotesque gesture over his face, 'that it strips away the false whiskers and the sinister leer of the unscrupulous magnate. I suppose unscrupulous magnate was the phrase in your head? Well, well – the melodrama turns limp comedy. A pity ... such a damned good story it would have made – eh, Giles? But elderly back-benchers with drab City backgrounds just don't cut out for that sort of part. The whiskers sit awry on the blunt and honest face and the leer turns out to have been all in your own mind. And though Anna is quite the sinister Roosian –'

'She is nevertheless,' Appleby took him up with a polite inclination to the lady, 'as English as you are; is that it?'

Evidently, it was not it. Gervase's expostulation was brief, the Merka-lova's was sustained – but the indignation of both was extreme. Appleby made apologetic murmurs. He had been quite wrong in this as in the major issue; the matter was irrelevant anyway, everything had been explained. He made tentative movements as if to gather up Gott and Noel and leave the room. But the Merkalova had been touched in the vitals – with a nice economy, Gott felt – and now, very decidedly, she had something to work off. What it was emerged in a variety of the languages of Europe. But it was not philological interest in a virtuoso display of cosmopolitanism that caused Appleby to give some attention as the harangue progressed. It was the matter. How infamous – so ran the gist – and that the police should waste their energies trumping up a tale about Gervase carrying off a document and photographing it when a little inquiry would satisfy them of the guilt of somebody else. Whom else? Whom, of course, but the Sandys – *cette saligaude!* ... *Búrlak!*

A diversity of responses followed this outburst. In Gervase there was uncomfortableness and impatience, as if the wrong coda were being clapped on a hitherto well-constructed piece. Noel manifested rage as extreme as Gervase had been displaying some time before. Gott felt mild distress and traced it down to resolutely romantic views on what Bunney, he unjustly suspected, would call Woman's Higher Moral Number. But Appleby's reaction was to frame particularly careful questions. 'Ah, yes,' he said: 'now we come to something important. Can you remember, please, exactly what Mr Cope said?'

It pulled the Merkalova up. 'Cope? ... *ce radoteur-là*! I know nothing of Cope, *Isprávink-Mudr'yónui*.'

'Then you saw the burning yourself?'

'*Akh! Bozhe moï*! Burning? *Aber geh ... n'en sais rien*. She was writing – she. Scribbling ... no? *Deprisa, ligera, heimlich, in piccolo ... no-no*? Secret writing – *bátiushki moi*! ... *Voilà la conduite qu'elle tient*, the smug pug, *salope*!' The Merkalova turned passionately to Gervase. '*Golubchik – próchol*! ... *Proshtchaï*!'

And having delivered herself of this reckless linguistic grand tour the Merkalova swept from the room with a final '*Ukh!*' followed by a dubious Gervase and a resolved Noel. Gott and Appleby were left as they had been – lords of Gervase's ravished apartment.

Gott looked at his watch. 'A grain of comfort,' he said, 'lies in the unfaltering approach of the Scamnum breakfast. But what do you make of all that? And why was the lady so angry when you doubted her true-blue hyperborean blood?'

Appleby got up. 'As you say, breakfast. Now I wonder –?'

He disappeared into the bathroom and emerged a minute later lathering his face with two fingers and brandishing one of Gervase's razors. 'Must keep smart for your friends, Giles. Well, as we were saying – did you look at the lady's legs?'

Gott raised an austere eyebrow. 'They were certainly there to be looked at,' he said.

'You didn't find them suggestive?'

'My dear John!'

'Think of Degas, Giles. And moonlight and muslin.'

'Ballet!'

'Yes. The Merkalova's past is in ballet. You remember the only jury-man to laugh at Serjeant Buzfuz's joke about greasing the defendant's wheels in *Bardell Against Pickwick*?' Appleby could be like this when excited – or baffled. 'He laughed because he'd greased his own chaise-cart that morning. I spotted the Merkalova – that turned-out stance of hers – because I've just come from ballet. And I happen to have enough Russian to notice that her Russian is just two streets ahead of mine. I expect she was in the Imperial Schools for a bit before the war. And – as a point of minor psychological curiosity – I expect her profession explains old Sir Richard What's-his-name's puzzlement over the happy couple's love-life. Ballet people are a species by themselves, getting all the common relations of life a bit odd.' Carefully – for strange razors are tricky things – Appleby finished shaving. 'But where are we, Giles? Where are we now?'

Gott looked at his watch again. 'For one thing, we're at five-fifteen. And our other whereabouts are up to you. I should put them at the moment as somewhere between pillar and post. Where are we, indeed, with Gervase and the Sandys and Cope and Happy Hutton and Timothy Tucker –'

'Who's Timothy Tucker?'

'One of the dozen or so exhibits not yet shown.'

Appleby waved Mr Timothy Tucker aside. 'Order,' he said; 'method; the little grey cells! Or in other words we are where we are and have to begin from there. Now Gervase –'

'Haven't we moved – or been moved – on to the Sandys? Are you not hurrying after her at once?'

'I think that's what your Noel's doing, and she'll keep for a little as far as I'm concerned. Hold on to Gervase for a moment and give me your estimate. Imagine youself editing a text in your own learned way. There's a disputed reading. One variant is: "Gervase's story of the Merkalova sneaking photographs of Scamnum celebrities for gossip-papers is true." And the other variant is: "Gervase was after the document either with this camera or another, and his story represents either a planned getaway or a brilliant improvisation." Now bring all your knowledge to bear and attempt a numerical estimate of the probabilities involved.' Appleby, though putting the matter in this odd way, was obviously wholly serious.

Gott considered. 'Allowing pretty generous weight to everything against Gervase – a certain pat quality about the Merkalova's appearance, for instance, that may well have been fortuitous – allowing that I should still put the odds at about forty to one in favour of Gervase's story being the true reading.'

'I was going to say fifteen. But it's impressive odds at either estimate, particularly if you remember the first effect on us of the Duke's disclosure about the camera. Anyway, as soon as I saw that snapshot-snooping toy I knew there was no further pushing that way; the story would be watertight. The long chance remains and all we can do is to note it and look elsewhere. But pushing the spies into limbo again, what about an estimate of Gervase simply as a murderer?'

'An impossible question. Almost anyone *might* murder. Ten to one against might be a rough assessment of my feelings. But if, as you say, we shelve the long chance of Gervase doing spy-work and still look for spy-work *somewhere* it seems to me we are up against the Sandys as a last chance? But the situation's safe. The evidence suggests that she contrived to scribble an abstract of the document – a desperately difficult thing to manage, I should imagine – and was then forced to destroy it under threat of search.'

'That's the story. But – without knowing the Sandys – I'm inclined to see her less as a possible principal than as a possible inspiration.'

'Possible what?'

'Inspiration,' repeated Appleby innocently. 'And that would, of course, lead us back to recasting the odds.'

Gott sighed. 'I think', he said, 'I'll go and have a bath.'

'You'll be the brighter for it,' said Appleby cheerily.

8

Resolved but apprehensive, Noel paused for respite at the first turning of the stair. He flung up a window and surveyed the world. It was undeniably the familiar world – the world on which, rising early to canter on Horton Down, he had flung up his own bedroom window just twenty-four hours before. In the farther park two textures of moving grey were sorting themselves out: mist drifting, eddying, dispersing; sheep beginning to move in the dewy feed. Already the day declared its season; already the scent of the syringas, heavy as orange-blossom, was blowing up from the gardens. The hubbub dawn-chorus had thinned to distinguishable notes: willow-warblers monotonously tumbling downstairs, chaffinches as unvaryingly revving-up, and suspense provided only by the wrens, who pleased themselves as to whether or not they should add answer to question. And dominating and insistent, as if he were aware that a fortnight, a week now might command him to silence, the cuckoo called from the oak woods. To Noel, who associated birds – a few moorland varieties apart – with clerkly nature-lovers and girl-guides, these effects came confusedly. But as mere massive sensation their familiarity disturbed him and he looked round almost anxiously for sign of change.

It was there. It was there in a curl of smoke rising – a full hour early – in the middle distance: Mrs Manley at the south lodge, aware that the skies had fallen and determined to face the unknown with the day's routine well forward. It was there – more obviously – in patrolling policemen. It was there in a little group of people toiling hastily up the brow of Horton Hill: a gesticulating person in front and behind a knot of persons with impedimenta – cameras, this time, of the cinematographic and telescopic sort. And it was there – had Noel known it – in the couple of cars that flashed over the visible rise of the Horton road: the press making hell-for-leather for Scamnum Court. And it was there – again if he had known it – in the farthest puff of white on the horizon. For that was the express hurtling the London dailies south and west, all with the Scamnum story in two inches of smeared red – or all save the *Despatch-Record*, whose news editor, having pushed his stop-press button with some extra minutes to spare before going to bed, had built in a flaming streamer that became Fleet Street talk for days.

Noel leant out further inches, automatically estimated the possibility of spitting on a policeman's helmet below, and then turned his eyes sharp right along the east façade. In the remote distance he could just discern a fugitive line of blue. 'The sea,' he chanted, 'lay laughing at a distance...' He waved to the astonished constable below. 'And in the meadows and the lower grounds was all the sweetness of a common dawn.' And having keyed himself up in this fashion Noel slammed down the window, bounded up the remaining stairs and knocked briskly at Diana Sandys's door.

' 'Llo,' said Diana. She was sitting up in bed with a gold pencil behind her ear, and eating chocolates. 'Come in.' She looked rather uncertainly at her visitor. 'You can climb on the bed,' she said firmly.

Noel climbed on the foot of the bed. There was a pause that would have been embarrassing if both Noel and Diana had not known that one was *not* embarrassed. 'I'll call it a night,' said Noel presently.

'One helluva night.' Diana's idiom was at times affected. The Terborgs would have disliked it.

'Hasn't etiolated you, though,' said Noel politely.

'Hasn't *what*? Have a chocolate.'

'Give sickly hue to person.' Noel took a large chocolate and bit into it. 'I say, Diana –' Then he changed his mind and returned to the chocolates. 'I've always been told that women devoured these things in secret – particularly the ethereal kind that shudders away from the honest thrice-daily public trough. But wenches naturally tending to plump out –'

'They're nauseous things!' said Diana fretfully. With her right hand she stretched out for another; with her left she beat out a tattoo on the soles of Noel's beautiful green slippers. 'It's only that I've got to sell them.'

'Sell them?'

'They're coming out in August and I've *got* to sell them. And I've got three boxes here and before the rumpus I meant to get one of those Terborg girls in a sunny corner and eat them all with her. To get the feel of it.'

Noel stared at her blankly. 'Feel of it – and wouldn't I do?'

'No, you wouldn't,' said Diana, becoming animated. 'Not the way I'm analysing it out. Do you know the chief difference between chocolates and tobacco?'

'If it's a riddle I give it up. But look here, Diana. Something frightfully –'

'It's like this. Tobacco – except snob-cigarettes – is nearly always sold homosexually – Chaps Together, you know. Or occasionally one builds on the over-compensated Oedipus – Dad Advises Sonny-boy. But chocolates are quite invariably sold heterosexually – Boy Brings Girl Box. But with these I'm going to try Women Together. Women stuffing them after *tête à tête* teas, women clutching half-pounds at chummy matinées. And I'm going to have them called the Sappho Assortment. A good name, I think; splashy and prodigal associations, exotic word, and yet difficult to mispronounce –'

'First rate,' said Noel with dubious heartiness. Noel thought Diana wonderful. Part of him thought the wonder to consist specifically in her adherence to the Newer Womanhood; but part of him – the part representing, perhaps, the tutelage of Mr Gott – sometimes saw this as being on the contrary the snag. And, finding this business-as-usual attitude disturbing, he canalized his dubieties into a minor channel and said: 'But I don't know about pronouncing. I rather think you'll have female dons – all tense and arm in arm, no doubt, as you want – going to their favourite sweet-shop and asking for *Sap-foh*.'

Diana made a note. 'I'll go into it. But there will have to be snob-appeal too. Boy Brings Girl Box runs much further down the income-levels than Women Stuff Box Together. I shall be going for the eight-room-upwards public, which means they must sell at a higher price than they intended. Have one of the twirly ones.'

'If they charge more will they improve the quality?' Noel was interested in this irrelevant business of the Sappho Assortment despite himself.

'Cut down on it, possibly.'

'Oh,' said Noel – and added: 'Not very honest?'

'Most contrariwise. And not good policy. Half our troubles come from pious Victorian-minded manufacturers who think they can take the quality out of the product if they're putting it into the advertising. But that sort eliminates itself. It's inefficient.'

'Good,' said Noel. It sounded like a sort of feeble moral fervour. There was an awkward pause, during which Diana ceased fiddling with the slippers. 'Sleep well after the shambles?' Noel asked.

'Didn't have a shot at it. I've been trying to remember something and get it down on paper ... what are you jumping at?'

'Jumping? Dunno. Pretty awful end to the play, wasn't it?'

'Bloody. I can't bear to think of it. And I can't even get my mind to planning out these dam' chocolates.'

Diana, it occurred to Noel, was in her present phase remarkably a person of one idea. And suddenly he seemed to see, very far away, possible light. Carefully, he located Diana's big-toe beneath the blanket and secured it firmly between finger and thumb. 'I say,' he said, 'how do you really like it?'

'Nix – it's marzipan. And I've told you they're *all* nauseous. But one has to discover what it feels like to be full of Sappho Assortment –'

'I don't mean that. I mean all the racket; the lone girl's career.'

'Oh!' Diana turned up a childlike but resolute chin. 'It's no sort of Sweet Seventeen affair. And it's not like being a duke or a don or a black-beetle; you don't stretch down comfortable roots into the job. And the line of talk you deal in wouldn't make the best illustrative matter for a treatise on the Beautiful and the True. In fact it would be a poor life if the pace weren't so snappy; that's what makes it fun. It's a dog-fight and you're on top only as long as you produce tip-top copy six days a week. No room for amiable inefficiency in national advertising — it costs too much per inch. If you go stale and your copy turns lousy — out you go.' Diana scrutinized Noel's face and was prompted to add: 'I'm not out yet. And remember I was kept in hygienic wrappers at expensive schools until I was twenty and now I'm twenty-two and pulling twelve pounds a week. While you're a twenty-three-year-old caterpillar on the commonwealth still. So there.'

Noel after some search found the companion big-toe. 'Get on top of you ever?' he asked cautiously. 'Ruling passion, fixed idea — that sort of thing?'

Diana regarded him apprehensively. 'Please stop playing at being a crab — two crabs,' she said; 'I suspect it of being a morbid form of Bedside Manner. And why this indecorous visit at all?'

Unhappily, Noel let go the toes. 'Well, you see, I thought I'd better tell you. You know there was something missing — or thought missing — or tapped or something? And that that's why there was a search? Well, there's a story got about — the police have it — that you —'

'Noel,' said Diana abruptly, 'draw the curtains and let in Sol.'

Noel did as he was told and returned chanting with unreal ease:

> 'Busy old fool, unruly Sun,
>   Why dost thou thus,
>   Through windows, and through curtains call on us?
>   Must to thy motions lovers' seasons...'

'Why, Diana!'

Diana was crying. And Noel was as alarmed as if he had been confronted with a woman in process of cutting her throat, or one fallen suddenly into childbirth. 'Oh, I say...' he mumbled.

Between sobs Diana said: 'Such a helluva show-down ... up ... down. I wish I was beastly dead!'

'Diana — Diana darling...'

But Diana's extravagant woe had to spend itself. Presently she stopped and without pausing for handkerchief or powder-puff asked: 'Noel, will these awful policemen know about my job . . . will they?'

'Well, I expect so. You see Appleby – that's the man from London – is getting case-histories and thumb-nail sketches from Grandpa Gott.'

'And they'll want to know . . . what it was?'

'Perhaps – in general terms. It was suspicious, you see. Writing and then consigning to flames when search impended. Quite *à la manière de la main noire*. And the police mind –' He floundered unhappily. 'Let me wipe your eyes . . . Perhaps if you told me – vaguely, I mean – and I passed it on quietly. This Appleby's a decent chap – gentleman – and it appears quite a familiar of Gott's. And, for that matter, he's likely enough to have guessed. Alpha brain.'

Diana took no comfort in the quality of Mr Appleby's breeding or brain. But she said: 'Yes, I'll tell you, Noel . . . emetic process . . . probably good for the system. Get a bit of scribbling paper from the table.'

Diana scribbled. And as the scribble grew Noel firmly improved on the toes. 'I see,' he said at last. 'Quite enormously ingenious – Diana, you're frightfully clever! But certainly not comfortable to be found with amid the sorrowing friends afterwards . . . Never mind.'

'You see,' said Diana miserably, 'one learns to squeeze an idea out of everything. It's a rule that just everything that happens must be squeezed . . . Of course that poor old man doesn't come into it. It was just the general idea of violent death that gave me the notion . . . and it *is* a new tie-up . . . with gangster magazines, action fiction . . . just the public for the product, too! And I felt I just *had* to get it down. But of all foul inspirations to be caught having –' She paused at the sound of footsteps in the corridor. 'Noel, is that the flatties?'

'I expect it is.'

'Lock the door.'

Noel obeyed. A moment later there was a knock and Diana called out: 'Is that the policeman?'

'Yes, madam.'

'You can't come in. It's indecorous. Besides' – Diana felt Noel's arm about her and her spirits rose outrageously – 'I have a gentleman here already.'

'Madam, I would not presume. One question only: last night – did you happen to engage in any abortive professional activity?'

Diana gritted her teeth. 'Yes,' she said, 'I certainly did.'

'Thank you.'

The footsteps retreated. 'He's gone!' said Diana.

Noel scrambled to the floor. He crumpled up the scribbling paper. 'Must be pushing too. No hacking about today, I'm afraid; looks like being prisoners within the moated grange. But there's always squash.'

In the corridor outside the hall Murdo Macdonald had sat, motionless and vigilant, for a space of hours. Now he stiffened. The door had opened from within; the constable on guard stood aside; a little procession emerged – stretcher-bearers, under the directions of a sergeant, bringing out the body of Lord Auldearn. Macdonald stood up, drew into what remained of early-morning shadow in an alcove and bent his head as bearers and burden went slowly past. His lowered eyes were watchful beneath their heavy brows. Some yards down the corridor the sergeant halted and called back to the constable by the door; the constable moved towards him as if to receive a message. Macdonald glided into noiseless and rapid motion. Though elderly he was spare and agile; in a moment he had darted from shadow to shadow and gained the hall. He looked rapidly round. No one was visible; only the constable outside, returning to the door, might look inside as he closed it. Macdonald ran to the front stage, clambered up, and had gone to earth down the Ghost's trap before he heard the door shut on the apparently untenanted hall. So far – good.

For a full minute Macdonald crouched unmoving in the darkness beneath the low stage. Then he began to make the laborious progress which Dr Crump had rejected – subterraneously behind-scenes. He emerged close by the back curtains of the rear stage – again undetected – and slipped within the double folds. 'Dinna fash,' he murmured to himself. 'A wee bittock luck an' ye'll get awa' wi' it in a' preevacy!' He tiptoed to a parting of the curtains and peered through to the rear stage. A constable was standing guard, wearily but efficiently. Macdonald's eye roved over the little stage. Then he retreated and looked out the other way. There appeared to be a clear field to the green-room – a rectangular, match-boarded structure a dozen paces away. He emerged, stepped out towards it boldly and was presently surveying it from the somewhat precarious shelter of a curtained doorway. The green-room too was guarded by a constable. Macdonald eyed him warily and then once more began to cast about, scanning the litter of properties and effects scattered around the room. Presently his gaze concentrated itself in a corner, and then turned to the guardian policeman again with something like desperation. 'Ten to yin it's either that or the Assize,' he muttered in perplexity – and felt a tap on the shoulder.

'Now then, what are you after and how did you get here?'

Macdonald turned round to confront a highly suspicious Sergeant Trumpet. But he seemed at no loss. 'Get here? I walkit in by the faur door.'

'The far door . . . nonsense! It's guarded.'

Macdonald shook his impressive head. 'Yin o' you laddies was clacking wi' your sairgint up the corridor a wee. But the door was open and I walkit in. I'm for my horrn.'

'Your what?'

'I'm for my snuff-horrn. Somebody coupt a cup of coffee when I had the horrn in my haun' and I put the horrn by tae tak up the coupit cup and disremembered it.'

Sergeant Trumpet was incensed. 'And you think you can come skulking about after a peck of snuff as though there hadn't been murder done? Don't you know that murder –'

'Laddie,' said Macdonald, 'Murdo Macdonald needs no sairmon frae you on the weight o' the Sixth Commaun'ment. But twa' oonces o' Kendal Broon bides twa' oonces o' Kendal Broon. And in my graun'-faither's horrn foreby! We'll look th'gither.'

They looked together. But no snuff-horn was found.

Charles Piper, towelling after an early shower, had retreated hastily from the bathroom on hearing the approaching footsteps of Giles Gott. Now he was doing his exercises in the security of his own room and feeling – as active young novelists must often feel – the want of several brains to pursue simultaneously the variety of thought which battled for the single organ he possessed. Pursue one idea with concentration and you so easily lose all the others for good – hundreds of potential words, proper for elegant embodiment in Timothy Tucker's character-istic fount, whirled fatally into limbo.

First, he had a thought – a chronic thought this – about thinking during the exercises. If you don't (he thought) concentrate on the exercises they don't work. Labourers, though they exercise their muscles all day, fail to develop beautiful bodies because they don't concentrate their minds on the idea of harmonious muscular development. Then stop thinking (thought Piper to himself) during the deep breathing; concentrate on the breathing *qua* breathing; picture, perhaps, the mysterious cavities of the lungs – spongy, soot-lined, slowly filling out, slowly sinking. Perhaps one could really see them if one tried very hard; hysterical people could see their insides ... and the surrealists. But let the mind rest. Simply contemplate through the open window the fluid line of Horton Hill – itself rhythmical as good exercise – and count: *one – two – three*.

There was a crowd of people up there, a crowd that was an abrupt reminder of the gruesome term that had been put to the Scamnum *Hamlet* ... Gott's *Hamlet*. And Gott offered another train of thought. What reason could be put forward to himself for retreating from Gott in the bathroom? Perhaps he felt uneasy now at having discussed the man's absurd hobby with him the other morning. It must, when one thought of it, be an uncomfortable position, this finding himself involved in an extravagant actualization of his own species of fantasy. Rather like a surprised Pygmalion receiving undesired advances from his Galatea ... the image was not bad. Or perhaps he had retreated from the bathroom because he felt a little awkward on his own account? Had he not made rather naïve remarks about his own willingness to plunge into a sort of blood and thunder existence if it should turn up in real life – to accept a stray embrace from the other man's Galatea, in fact? Something about being ready to play pass-the-buck if confronted with a corpse and something about a hankering after picturesque international intrigue – that was what he had said. And it had been very foolish; such conversation was quite embarrassingly foolish in retrospect – reminiscent of the vaguely sinister remarks which everyone had to make in turn, no doubt, near the beginning of *Murder at the Zoo*. Piper swung up and down – touching his toes, sometimes getting the palms of his hands almost flat on the floor – and Horton Hill swung up and down outside like a green sea across a rolling port-hole.

There was a knock at the door.

It had been Melville Clay's habit to stroll across the corridor while dressing and consume, amid desultory talk, Piper's neglected and tepid morning tea. But this morning tea was still an hour off and Clay, like Piper, was newly bathed. He was in beautiful black and white:

white slippers, black pyjamas, black dressing-gown with an exaggeratedly robust white cord – and his face almost hidden behind a mass of white lather. 'How now, Horatio!' he articulated with odd clarity through the soap, 'you tremble and look pale: is not this something more than fantasy?'

'Pale?' said Piper pettishly but apprehensively – his face was red from the toe-touching – 'nonsense! Though I've had a shocking night.'

'Never mind. Good copy. Do Gott's stuff straight from life now. As they say – more than fantasy.'

This sentiment – delivered somewhat in the manner of Clay's departed colleague, Mr Jingle – hit disconcertingly on one of the thoughts. The reactions of all these people to sensational and mysterious murder would make good watching in the immediate future. But Piper felt the suggestion of copy must be snubbed as unseemly. He continued doggedly at a gesticulating exercise by the window and allowed a minute to elapse before he said briefly: 'A horrid business.'

'Horrid.' Clay had moved over to the other window and begun to shave. He was, Piper thought, a beautiful creature – with the proud bodily beauty that comes from heaven and not from a system of exercises. Perhaps he had a feminine streak – the little silver mirror he had taken from his pocket was too elegant; his deft movement as he caught the light with it under chin and nostril was too much that of a conscious beauty. Piper reflected rather jealously that he had no feminine streak himself – an invaluably informative thing to have.

'You know, you are quite extraordinarily beautiful,' said Piper, by way of conscientious experiment.

As experiment it was ill-timed; Clay might have blushed like a girl or he might not – the lather still obscured him. 'Ah, yes,' he said indifferently, 'one grows that way when one's bread and butter's in it. And rather showy too. Public means which public manners breeds. I'd as soon be out of it.'

Piper eyed him curiously. 'You haven't been in it long. You've risen like a rocket.'

'Soon to decline, perhaps, like a falling star. There may be copy in me too.'

Piper ignored the reiterated jest. 'But what,' he said, 'do you think of all this?'

'I think' – Clay had finished shaving and turned to look out of the window – 'it's already a first-class sensation, if one may judge by that crowd on the hill.'

'Pretty morbid, isn't it – turning out just to stare? And they've been mighty quick.'

'Oh, that's not what they're about; that lot's still to come. I guess these are Press People, training all sorts of ingenious cameras on us at this moment. Good publicity – Mr Charles Piper doing remedial exercises at his window shortly after the fatality.'

Piper drew hastily back. 'Disgusting!' he said – with some reminiscence of Mrs Platt-Hunter-Platt. 'But I've hardly got the hang of what's happened yet. What was the search supposed to be about? Was someone supposed to be hiding a revolver?'

'I think something had been stolen – from the body.'

'Robbery!'

'I rather gathered from something the Duke let fall – robbery of a special sort. A secret document – that sort of thing.'

'Spies!'

'Exactly.' Clay looked lazily at Piper. 'Again not in your line, I suppose? The missing treaty. Sort of contemporary version of cloak and sword adventure, you know.'

Piper almost jumped. It was the identical silly phrase he had used to Gott. Slightly fussily he began to get out his own shaving things. 'I wonder,' he said vaguely, 'who did it?'

'I didn't,' said Clay.

David Malloch lowered stiff legs from footstool to floor as the little tray was set down beside him. The footman looked without curiosity at the unruffled bed – there was nothing remarkable in anyone's having done without sleep that night – crossed to the window, drew back curtains, raised the blind. He went out at the other door; in a moment there was the sound of running water; an eddy of steam drifted into the bedroom. Still Malloch did not move. His hands, fingers extended, lay Pharaoh-like along the arms of his chair; his mouth might have been hewn in basalt; his eyes were fixed and sightless as eyes that gaze out over Karnac or Memphis.

The man came out of the bathroom, moved towards the door. 'There is no change in the hour of breakfast, sir.'

Malloch inclined his head and the man went away. For a long time there was neither sound nor movement in the room; next door the water ran unchecked. Presently Malloch's eyes, staring through the window as if across some vista of desert, faltered and changed focus. He got painfully to his feet – it was breaking the posture of hours – and moved slowly across the room. From the centre of the white blind, in silhouette against the light, hung a slender cord and silken tassel. He took the cord in his hands, looped it, thrust the head of the tassel within the loop. The head tilted to a macabre angle: it was a manikin that he held suspended in a little silken noose. For a moment his mouth tightened another shade; then he tossed the tassel lightly in the air and it fell to its normal position, straight and free. He turned and hurried to his bath.

3   Dénouement

See you now;
Your bait of falsehood take this carp of truth:
And thus do we of wisdom and of reach,
With windlasses and with assays of bias,
By indirections find directions out.

Once more Appleby stood on the rear stage. Here, he knew, lurked the heart of the mystery; as often as he moved from this spot, so often he was in danger of losing himself in a maze of irrelevant or subsidiary detail. Here, during Act Three, Scene Four of an amateur performance of *Hamlet*, Lord Auldearn had died. This was the one fact; as yet all else was speculation. And the fact was of an extraordinary fascination. To begin with, it was bizarre – almost as bizarre as any criminal act he could remember. And the place and the victim – Scamnum, a Lord Chancellor of England – gave it a colouring alien to mere police news, threw over it a half-light of history that was not without its own beguilement for an imaginative mind.

But it was the technical problem that was absorbing. What could one get from the specific way in which the thing had happened? The odd locale, the dramatic moment – were these things a structural part, so to speak, of Auldearn's murder, or were they decorative merely? Gott had talked of feeling behind the catastrophe the working of a mind theatrically obsessed; a mind outlandishly absorbed, over and above any practical motive for murder, in the contriving of an astonishing effect. And certainly it would be hard to deny at least an element of mere display in the circumstances surrounding the deed. The threatening messages of the preceding days could only be interpreted as a preliminary flourish of melodrama, a prologue to the melodrama being prepared within the framework of the Scamnum *Hamlet*. And that framework had been itself more simply melodramatic, apparently, than modern *Hamlets* commonly are. The show of violence ... and then a show of violence within the show.

The show of violence ... in the small hours Gott had quoted the context of that – a speech by Marcellus when the guard had tried to stay the Ghost:

> We do it wrong, being so majestical,
> To offer it the show of violence;
> For it is, as the air, invulnerable,
> And our vain blows malicious mockery.

You can't beat Shakespeare, thought Appleby irrelevantly – and for a minute his mind strayed over what he could remember of that tremendous opening scene – the scene in which they bring the sceptical young student Horatio to confront the uncanny thing that walks the battlements of Elsinore at night:

> How now, Horatio! you tremble and look pale:
> Is not this something more than fantasy?

More than fantasy . . . that was the next point. Was there something more than a mere effort after fantastic effect behind the manner of Auldearn's murder? Had it been exactly so because, for some reason, it had to be exactly so? By every conceivable theory save one – the theory implicating Cope 'aloft' – the deed had been extraordinarily hazardous. Was that hazardousness gratuitous – something accepted, it might be said, for fun – or had it been accepted after calculation as necessary to some specific end? The murder of Bose was evidence here. For Bose's murderer had dragged the body of his victim with a crazy bravado down a long corridor, known to be tenanted, in order to pitch it wantonly on Auldearn's threshold – and Appleby's. Bose had been murdered, almost certainly, because he *knew* – or almost knew; his murder was a crime of calculation and prudence. But to swift and efficient action had been added this grace-note of pure sensationalism: the body had been moved, at great risk, for the single pleasure, apparently, of securing a momentary effect. Might there be a similar mingling of motive, then, in Auldearn's murder? Had the deed itself been rational, directed to some practical end, and the hazards accompanying the specific manner of its accomplishment been accepted for the sake of added melodramatic colour? Or had – conceivably – the melodrama been all, an end in itself; had the effect been the sole motive; had the whole thing been the resultant of some ghastly perversion of aesthetic instinct?

Or – third and final possibility – was Auldearn's murder rational through and through, had there been – once again – cold reason for every hazard? These were the questions, it seemed to Appleby, which lay at the centre of the case. What, then, of the business of the document?

It was very difficult to connect the facts he had been considering with any designs upon the Pike and Perch paper. Spies, he had agreed with Gott, do not go about their work to an accompaniment of threatening messages. They rarely shoot; they very rarely shoot eminent statesmen; positively, they do not shoot in circumstances which make their chances of subsequent successful theft exceedingly tenuous. Even if spies had broken into the safe in Auldearn's room and, having drawn a blank, concluded that the paper they wanted was on his person – even so, and even supposing them prepared for desperate measures, they would hardly have chosen to shoot when and where Auldearn had been shot – at excessive risk and in a hall that could instantly be sealed like a strong-room. And there was no reason to suppose that it had been spies who cracked Auldearn's safe. Three safes in all, it had turned out, had been cracked and Happy Hutton was in all probability responsible. Indeed – once more Appleby came back to this – there was no reason to suppose the presence of spies at all – except for the intercepted message which Hilfers had reported. Save for that the spy-theory had its sole origin in the Duke's first alarm. That alarm had been reasonable, but it had been based on no positive evidence beyond the cracked safe and the unsuccessful search of Auldearn's body. And when the document had turned up – in a sufficiently ingenious hiding-place – that alarm had been allayed. Gott had revived it with his startling leap upon the possible significance of Bose's photographic brain. Then the Duchess had dissipated that possibility; Bose was *not* a spy, nor the kind that makes a spy. After that there had been two further alarms: the Duke's alarm over Gervase, Cope's and the Merkalova's alarm over Diana Sandys. But if Miss Sandys – and it seemed next to impossible – had contrived to copy the document before Bose discovered it, she had subsequently had to destroy her notes and no harm was done. Besides which, there was a perfectly reasonable explanation of her conduct to which Appleby, who knew something of advertising people, had jumped at once. And Gervase and the Merkalova, similarly, had a perfectly reasonable if equally embarrassing story. Only one thing gave Appleby pause here; he had mentioned it – with a mischievous obliqueness – to Gott.

There was a slightly disturbing coincidence between the two stories – the Merkalova's and Diana's. Both ladies had been pursuing an essentially innocent, but nevertheless uncomfortable professional acti-vity: the Merkalova taking press-photographs on the quiet; Diana getting down a commercially-useful suggestion which had been prompted, pre-sumably, by some aspect of the murder in the hall. It was not a startling coincidence; nevertheless it was something on which to pause. Suppose that Gervase or the Merkalova had detected Diana making professional hay, so to speak, by the lurid glow of Auldearn's murder: might this not have suggested to them their own story when they came to feel that a story might have to be put up? But at most this was to say that to Gervase and the Merkalova there still clung some fragment of suspicion: with the Merkalova's or another camera the document might have been photographed after all. And it seemed to Appleby that while this one conceivable channel did remain, he must maintain his blockade of Scamnum; or maintain it, at least, until he had positive orders from the Prime Minister himself to desist. Again there was no evidence; nothing but suspicion – and his suspicions of Gervase Crispin as a spy continued to be tenuous. If the Merkalova had appeared at moments to be putting up a set show – and this was the only point of significance he could find – that might well be because she was, just as much as Melville Clay, a creature of the stage.

All of which was not to say that the spies had no probable existence. Appleby was less disposed than Gott had been to dismiss Hilfers's report as unreliable. That there had been spies about he believed – and one of them had doubtless sent away an over-sanguine message. But the spies represented a different thread from the murder – just as there was a third thread in Happy Hutton. These three threads might not be tied up with each other at all; were probably quite without significant interconnections. Happy Hutton, indeed, appeared the merest side-show. He had wormed himself into Scamnum, cracked three safes, left a bowler-hat – and left no other mark on the case. But the spies, though their presence might have been ineffective in the end, had complicated the whole affair – had already given a peculiar twist to the conduct of it.

Appleby had abundantly gathered that for the Prime Minister the safety of the document was an issue to which even the apprehending of Auldearn's murderer came second. And he had placed it first himself; was still proposing to maintain elaborate precautions over it. But, in point of the murder, it was a distorting factor in the investigation, a red herring. And now Scamnum spies were fading fast into ineffectiveness – and six hours were gone since Appleby had arrived on the scene. On the business of the document he had gone – as Gott had hinted – from pillar to post and it was impossible to tell what he had missed that he would not have missed had his attention been concentrated on the single issue of murder. Now, given the maintenance of the blockade and a careful watch on Gervase and the Merkalova, he could concentrate on that issue in security. And the first step to the finding of Auldearn's and Bose's murderer would be a careful sifting of movements among that unwieldy crowd of back-stage suspects – Gott's twenty-seven suspects together with old Max Cope 'aloft'.

So Appleby paced the little stage, reviewing a tolerable confusion of materials and planning the morning's attack upon them. He was interrupted by Sergeant Trumpet, who brought news of difficulty with Scamnum's awakening domestic staff. You may isolate some two hundred people without much inconvenience during the hours of the night, but in the morning what of the butter, the milk, and the eggs; what of those outdoor servants who came into the servants' hall for meals; what of the bevy of chauffeurs at the Scamnum Arms who would expect breakfast in the steward's room; what of the guests, not involved in the play, who would presently be proposing to pack? The last question, obviously, was one for the Duke when he should be available: the others Appleby resolved to turn to the solution of himself. He would hold the blockade rigidly if possible till noon, by which time he should be able to report comprehensively to, and get further instructions from, London. Meantime it was simply a matter of organization; butter and eggs and chauffeurs must come in and nothing must go out. Appleby went in search of Bagot, whom he supposed the fountain-head of authority of Scamnum's menial affairs.

Bagot was already performing his first duty of the day – superintending the arrangement of a little ocean of silver on the breakfast-table. He was a silvery and ineffective old person – rather more like a domestic chaplain, Appleby thought, than a butler – and extremely bewildered. And in his bewilderment he was inclined to retreat on an anxious maintenance of Scamnum customs and forms. Of course he could go round with Appleby and arrange effective police supervision of all comings and goings in the offices. But he ventured to think it might really be Mr Rauth's province. Would the inspector see Mr Rauth? Mr Rauth had risen; indeed, Bagot had just seen him in his room – Mr Rauth never, of course, left his room – and he was very upset, exceedingly so. The inspector had better, perhaps, remember that Mr Rauth was exceedingly upset.

Very naturally, agreed Appleby – and asked to be directed to Mr Rauth, whom he conjectured to be someone in the exalted position of a house-steward or major-domo. A footman conducted him; nothing easier than to find old Mr Rauth, he said, because Mr Rauth *never* left his room – had never been known to. But everyone had his own idea of what you might call a life, he supposed – and tapped respectfully on a door.

Mr Rauth, certainly, had all the appearance of a picturesque recluse: he was lank and dim and dusty, with a sorty of peering stoop and the gentle voice of one who for long has communed only with abstractions. But he was distinguished, suggesting a librarian, perhaps, or an eminent antiquarian bookseller. And somehow one guessed that here was the very hub of Scamnum and that in the extreme neatness of the clerical paraphernalia by which he was surrounded was symbolized that virtuoso efficiency which made Scamnum among other things a great smooth-running machine. Behind Mr Rauth – around Mr Rauth – one sensed the accumulated experience of generations on the job.

'Yes?' said Mr Rauth. 'Yes...?' He shambled forward, peering up at the visitor. Then he shook his head. 'No, sir, no. I really couldn't do it. Science may be science, sir, and cooperation cooperation; but this morning No. I am too upset.'

Having an active mind, Appleby presently realized that he was being taken for the philologically zealous Dr Bunney – doubtless notorious below stairs since his treatment of Bagot. Laboriously he explained himself and Mr Rauth at length understood. But the only immediate result was that Mr Rauth removed his glasses, polished them, and re-iterated: 'I am very Upset.' The voice was gentle but its weight was great. Mysteriously, every sentence of Mr Rauth's had an august and solemn close.

'A great shock,' said Appleby, paying a timely tribute to the properties before getting on.

Mr Rauth at last looked at his visitor approvingly. 'As you say, a great Shock. Such a thing has not happened here – if my memory is sound – for Years.' He returned his glasses to his nose – or rather his nose to his glasses, with a disconcerting ducking motion. 'Of course,' he said, 'I know that it is often Done. I know that sort of thing Occurs. As a general thing, we cannot Deny It.'

Appleby looked at Mr Rauth a little blankly. He hardly seemed a helpful ally; one might almost suspect that he had indulged the whim of never leaving his room to a point which had endangered his sanity.

'Of course,' said Mr Rauth, 'it is the younger people who Do These Things. One hears Stories. There was the venison party at Hutton Beechings. There was the grassy corner pudding at poor Sir Hubert Tiplady's. One acknowledges the Fact.'

'The fact?' said Appleby. Scamnum, it seemed, always had a trick up its sleeve with which to overwhelm one. This was more unnerving by a long way than Max Cope.

'But,' said Mr Rauth, his voice mysteriously diminishing in volume as it gained in emphasis, 'here there is always ample provision made. Two bath olivers, two rich tea, and two digestive in every room. Replenished daily and changed three times a week. The bath olivers go to Mr Bagot – he has a Partiality for Them – and the others to the servants' hall. I am Dumbfounded. And at the very moment when there has been a death almost in the Family! I am more than dumbfounded; I am Aghast.'

'And all despite the fact,' said the now enlightened Appleby gravely, 'that an ample variety of sandwiches was served shortly after the late Lord Auldearn's death – decease.'

Mr Rauth looked at Appleby as if he had at last found an embodiment of Perfect Comprehension. That an unknown reprobate – certainly a guest – should asperse the hospitality of Scamnum by breaking into a pantry in the night and purloining half a tin of biscuits – this was very terrible to Mr Rauth. But there was something comforting – soothing indeed – in the ready understanding of this sympathetic stranger. 'But let that Pass,' said Mr Rauth, with a friendly peer at Appleby and returning to his interrogative manner. 'Yes...?' And in a couple of minutes he was being a most effective ally after all. He flicked out a plan of Scamnum, telephoned to the lodges, the bailiff, the home-farm, the kitchens, the King's Arms; directed the locking and unlocking of doors. In ten minutes the complicated traffic of the Scamnum offices was reorganized on a basis of easy and adequate police supervision. Perhaps Mr Rauth had a hope that it would all lead to the unmasking of the violator of the pantry; certainly, he worked with a will. And Appleby got away from him under twenty minutes all told – the morning's last fragment of time to be sacrificed to the ghostly suspicion of spying that still clung to Gervase and the Merkalova.

Very soon the unwieldy household would be beginning to assemble for breakfast. Appleby wished he could observe their reactions to each other but failed to see how this could comfortably be managed; no doubt Giles would report. So he went to the green-room and set about organizing it as a sort of headquarters. He made various routine arrangements with the local men. He sent off several telegrams; one of these it rather pleased him to hand to Sergeant Trumpet – for it read with a fine mysteriousness: *advise h huttons size in hats*. If Happy, that very minor fish, could be proved an illicit swimmer in the waters of Scamnum he might as well be caught. And then Appleby returned obstinately to the rear stage. Here – he reiterated perseveringly – lurked the heart of the mystery. On this place – on all the implications of this place as the site of the murder – he must concentrate his mind. And suddenly Appleby felt enormously hungry.

He had enjoyed a not particularly substantial dinner just thirteen hours before. Since then there had been various excitements: ballet, a ride behind a fire-engine with the Prime Minister, murder, spy-hunting, and a number of interviews, all of a more or less exacting and lively kind. During this time he had had no sandwiches, neither had he broken into any pantry for biscuits – and he was just allowing his thoughts to stray a little anxiously to the problem of how Scamnum was likely to treat detective-inspectors within the gates when he heard a gentle but unmistakable rattle in the green-room. He hurried. An expansive breakfast was being wheeled in on a series of trollies – and under the superintendence not of Bagot but of an ugly and cheerful person in tweeds. Sergeant Trumpet was looking doubtfully at the ugly and cheerful person; much less doubtfully at the breakfast. And the ugly and cheerful person gave the advancing Appleby a friendly wave. 'I'm Timothy Tucker – late Guildenstern, of Rosencrantz and Guildenstern, twisters,' he said amiably. 'It occurred to me you might like to be in advance of the pack and I dropped a hint to Bagot and here we are. And I'm uncommonly hungry myself; I wonder if I might join in? Gott may come, but family ties are around him – if only by adumbration, you know ... Obviously, there are kidneys.'

Gott, it was presumably indicated, was going to breakfast with his Lady Elizabeth. And Appleby was in no mood to reject the appositely named Mr Tucker. 'I shall be very glad,' he said. 'My name is Appleby. I'm frightfully hungry.'

The long tables – already cleared of the properties which the police had removed, searched, and inventoried – were spread with a magnificent meal. There was a table for a little shifting army of constables, a table for Appleby's men now returning from labours in Auldearn's room, a table that was a species of sergeants' mess and a table for Appleby himself, Tucker, and Gott if he came. And Appleby surveyed the scene wryly; it suggested that a riot rather than a murder-investigation was the business in hand. When he got rid of this crowd he would begin to feel the possibility of getting on.

Timothy Tucker swallowed much tomato juice, buried much butter in the warm heart of a roll, and halted a descending fish-slice to point at the group of burly constabulary. 'And are those,' he innocently inquired, 'what you call the Flying Squad?'

'County police, Mr Tucker. I have a great many men at the moment patrolling the outside of the house. When there has been murder, you see, it is always possible that someone is thinking of slipping quietly away.'

'Come, come!' Tucker, imitating the Duke, smiled inoffensively.

Appleby smiled too. 'Have you come to pump the police?'

Tucker shook his head. 'Oh, no,' he said. 'Not that at all. Egg?' He waved a hand in the direction of the sergeants. 'They stopped me telephoning a telegram – or rather they censored it. *Ultra vires* I'm sure, Mr Appleby. Not that I complain – nor am curious about that side of it, rumours of missing papers and so on. But I expect you've been sending telegrams or telephone messages yourself?'

'Yes,' said Appleby, wondering where this led.

'People's careers, interconnections, all particulars; that sort of thing?'

'Just that,' said Appleby. Tucker, he noticed, was no longer exuding easy cheerfulness; he had thrust away his fish and was stabbing half-heartedly at Scamnum's celebrated pork cheese as if some considerable weight were on his mind.

'Last night,' said Tucker, 'you said something about speaking up. I rather took it to be a walk-into-my-parlour move. Inviting the criminal to pass the buck.'

'Possibly so,' said Appleby.

'But, of course, one must speak up all the same. I don't mean that I saw anything in particular last night – not at all. Do you know Spandrel?'

'The publisher?' Appleby shook his head.

'Yes, the publisher. I'm one too. Spandrel and I both do a fair amount in the way of memoirs; mismemoirs, a good many of them – but all the thing just now. You know: *Recollections of a Political Scene-Shifter* and *My Long Life of Love*.' Mr Tucker shook his head mournfully – presumably over the depravity of the reading public. 'Well now, about a year ago an old gentleman called Anderson sent me a manuscript called *A Waft from Auld Reekie* – an excellent title, for it was a distinctly highly flavoured book. I don't know that there was anything positively actionable in it when it came to me, but it was plainly full of lies. So I sent it back.' Tucker paused over his modestly insinuated glimpse of virtue and then added with some complacence: 'After that, of course, Anderson had a shot at Spandrel.' He paused again, this time to reach for a bone and investigate the Devil sauce; once launched on the process of speaking up he seemed to have recovered his spirits. 'Spandrel, as you may know, is a rash young man. He agreed to publish the book. Whereupon old Mr Anderson died – and exchanged Edinburgh, I don't doubt, for all the sad variety of hell. And that didn't leave Spandrel in too good a position. He was contracted with Anderson's spawn, administrators, assigns, and so forth, and he was left, of course, to stand any racket himself. So he cut a bit and delayed a bit – and the result is that the book is coming out next week. In other words there are scores of advance copies floating about England at this moment.' Tucker took more coffee. 'So you will understand my position. If I had refused the book and it had then gone into limbo I should be the possessor of confidential information of a sort and in a difficult position. As it is, I am merely telling you of what you can read for yourself in a day or two. Because whatever Spandrel has cut out I think it very unlikely that he will have cut out all the business of Auldearn and our good Professor Malloch.'

'Ah!' said Appleby with a becoming inscrutability. He reached for the marmalade – a beautiful dark kind with whole quarters of peel.

'One needn't suppose,' Tucker went on, 'that Malloch knows about the book yet. And if he doesn't it will be a bit of a jolt – and would have been for Auldearn too. This Anderson had a flair for the ridiculous and he succeeded in making something quite tolerably diverting out of the relations of these people getting on for fifty years ago.'

Appleby looked curiously at Tucker. 'Fifty-year-old stuff? And ridiculous and diverting merely?'

'In the main, ridiculous and diverting merely. But shading off finally into hints of darker matter – matter that might smoulder till the end of a lifetime. That's what I didn't like about friend Anderson; his dropping hints. The courts don't like it, you know.'

'Quite so. But failing a copy of *A Waft from Auld Reekie* will you give me some details?'

'Sure. Auldearn – Ian Stewart, as he was then – and Malloch were contemporaries at Edinburgh University. Auldearn was by some years the older; had been three or four years, I think, in a country solicitor's office first. Anyway, they both started square and on the same line – the grand old fortifying classical curriculum. One doesn't know much' – said Tucker with the placid assumptions of the Cambridge man – 'of how these Caledonian academies conduct themselves. But I gather there is a great deal of top-boy feeling all through. No waiting three of four years to see who is the better man but much importance given to the results of Professor Macgonigal's fortnightly test.'

'Dear me!' said Appleby.

'Yes. Well, Ian Stewart and David Malloch were twin top-boys from the start and remained so all the way through. And – what didn't necessarily follow – they were rivals – and enemies. Not real enemies from early on, I suppose, or they would probably have ignored each other. They were friendly rivals at first, but with a real and deepening spirit of antagonism between them which they cloaked for a time in various boisterous ways. Both, as it happened, were distinguished in the primitive sports of the day, and were rivals there too. And that helped to make their rivalry a matter of public concern to the whole student body. There were two factions: the Jacobites, supporting Stewart; and the Mallets.'

'Mallets?'

'Yes. It was a joke, apparently, thought of by Stewart. Some time in the eighteenth century there had been a person called David Malloch occupying an obscure position in the Edinburgh High School; he went to London and set up as a literary man and changed his name to Mallet. And Dr Johnson, it seems, objecting to disguised Scots, made fun of him and his name in the *Lives of the Poets* and elsewhere. It was just the sort of little literary joke to annoy David Malloch the younger. Anyway, the Jacobites and the Mallets were famous in their day. There were wild doings – both between the factions and between the principals themselves. Malloch captured Stewart and hung him in chains – not by the neck, fortunately – over something called the Dean bridge. Later Stewart captured Malloch and succeeded in conducting him, tied head to tail on a donkey, a good way down Princes Street. Later still, there were rumours of a duel. And then their time was over and Stewart came straight to read for the English Bar and that was an end to it.'

Tucker was filling his pipe. Appleby regarded him curiously. 'And you are putting forward these events, which happened nearly half a century ago, as a possible motive for murder?'

'I am putting them forward,' said Tucker placidly, 'as a subject for laudable curiosity in policemen. But when I said that was an end of it I meant that was an end – or all but an end – in friend Anderson's narrative. Anderson writes all this up and then leaves off with a hint: so much for the amusing doings of these wild young men; how sad that a darker turn to it all was to follow – that sort of thing. Well, I went after a little information on my own and it was partly what I came on that made me finally turn down Anderson's book. All this talk of wild students now grown to eminence one could get away with. But if there had been anything serious, anything that this gossip and hinting might tend to rake up, then the thing would be highly offensive and it would be mug's work to touch it. So I found a Modern Athenian of enormous age who had been in on the doings of that time and he told me a lot – without vouching for the truth of what he was telling me. Anderson's stuff was more or less true, if a bit coloured up. But beyond that there was a rumour of matters that had been kept very dark. A girl had come into the affair and complicated it. Or rather she had simplified it, making the rather involved, half make-believe enmity wholly deadly. The two men fought a solemn duel by moon-light on Cramond sands – it was the period of R. L. Stevenson come to think of it – and Malloch got the bullet and Stewart got the girl. And after that Stewart came south in a hurry – which is why he ended his days as Lord Chancellor and not as Lord Justice General. So there you are. And if Spandrel knew there was this lurid legend on the fringes of this book he's putting out he wouldn't be at all happy.' Tucker smiled comfortably.

Appleby was silent for a minute, contemplating the extraordinary motive for murder which Tucker – wasting little time – had presented to the policemanly curiosity. Revenge delayed through almost a lifetime: it was a thing fantastic enough to contemplate – and yet not unknown to criminal science. But revenge, when it was long delayed, was commonly delayed because of some physical barrier, some long-standing practical

obstacle. Men had paid off old scores after ten years in prison; emigrants, after far longer periods overseas, had come home and rekindled within themselves the lust for some half-remembered rival's blood. But in such a case as was here to be supposed delay would be inexplicable, un-motivated ...

'Mr Tucker' — Tucker almost started at something subtle that had happened to the young policeman — 'Mr Tucker, what of the relations of these two people as you have observed them? They have been together, I suppose, rehearsing? And — if you will give me your opinion — what sort of person is Malloch?'

Tucker set himself to answer the last question first, and with precision. 'Malloch is what they call a systematic scholar — and of tremendous eminence, I believe, in his own line. Clear, retentive brain — very retentive — and has had his jacket off working hard for sixty years. Crawls over texts comma by comma, you know, and coaxes surprisingly interesting results out of the process.'

'Rather Gott's line.'

'Yes. But Malloch is positively an *Ober-Gott*. Better brain.'

'I see.' Appleby was rather dubious. He knew how Giles's mind could leap.

'But that's not all that's to Malloch. These people usually pay for their concentration in narrowness, it's said. Illiterate after 1870; never buy a new book.' Tucker shook a gloomy head. 'But Malloch's informed all round and lives quite in the world. Not that his learning's so relevant as his character, which I don't know much about. He's a correct, tartly courteous person, but showing an occasional streak of savage brilliance that suggests those old Edinburgh days. And that comes out in his writing, which can be very good — particularly in a destructive way. I'd like to have him on my list.' This was obviously Mr Tucker's furthest word in intellectual commendation.

'And his relations with Lord Auldearn?'

'I don't know much about that. Malloch only came down on Friday night and I didn't see them much in each other's company — not that I have any impression that they avoided each other. And I've never stopped in a house with the two of them before, though I seem to remember their passing the time of day at stray parties. The Duchess would know most about all that.'

'Yes,' said Appleby. 'Yes ...' He rose with the polite finality of the

Prime Minister himself pronouncing brief valediction on a deputation. 'Thank you very much. Now I must get hold of the document in the case.'

'Anderson's book?'

Appleby opened innocent eyes. 'Dear me, no. Shakespeare's play.'

2

'It came into my head,' said Piper to Gott, speaking across Elizabeth and not very amiably – for like most of the people scattered round the breakfast table he was feeling uncomfortable and frayed – 'it came into my head that in this business you must feel rather like Pygmalion when his statue came alive. You think out these things – and here you are.'

'A most felicitous idea. And what about the story of Frankenstein? – there is some possible application to be worked out there too. You might elaborate something good.'

Elizabeth, setting an example in the eating of an unagitated and adequate meal, frowned at her plate over this passage of arms. And Mrs Platt-Hunter-Platt, who had been explaining to the Duke how essential it was that she should be allowed to leave Scamnum when she pleased, did not improve matters by attempting a discussion on the dangerous influence of the cinema on the lower classes – so many films full of stuff that was a standing incitement to crime!

Nave injudiciously rallied her. 'And what, my dear lady, of the play you came to see? Does that not, according to the argument you suggest, invite us to adultery, incest, parricide, fratricide, murder, and revolution – to say nothing of going off our heads? No, no, these things, films of criminal life, stories of ingenious homicide – they are all safety-valves, madam, safety-valves.'

Gott cracked an egg in gloomy silence.

'But Shakespeare,' said Mrs Platt-Hunter-Platt – with some obscure sense, apparently, of sustaining an argument – 'Shakespeare was a poet.' And this failing to provoke comment she added: 'And in my opinion the Duke should send for a detective.'

'A detective?' said Noel politely from across the table. 'You mean a real detective – not like the police?'

'Exactly – a real detective. There is a very good man whose name I forget; a foreigner and very conceited – but, they say, thoroughly reliable.'

Gott made the little hair-rumpling gesture which he resorted to when the world seemed peculiarly mad. And unexpectedly Elizabeth murmured: 'Giles, couldn't you clear it up – solve it?'

Gott looked at her with something like alarm.

'I mean that they're right, in a way. What they're getting at. It is rather your sort of thing.'

'You mean inspired by sensational fiction?'

Elizabeth considered. 'No. Murder is obviously inspired by something more solid than that. But the way the thing was done, the setting, the technique – it seems the product of the same sort of mind that writes a complicated story. You might have an insight into it.'

'Not the insight Appleby will have. I don't think I'd make a very good real-life detective. I'm not foreign and ... but come and meet Appleby.'

They had reached the door when they were arrested by Clay, who had snapped his fingers impulsively and addressed the Duke and the company at large. 'I say, it occurs to me there is something that ought to have been put to the police. About your apparatus, Dr Bunney. Did anyone explain to them its extreme accuracy? I mean the chance of identifying the voice that used it to deliver one of the messages – "I will not cry Hamlet, revenge", wasn't it? Do you believe you could really do that? I remember Miss Terborg suggested something of the sort at the time.'

Bunney, who had been the dimmest of figures during breakfast, brightened at once. 'I am sure I could,' he said eagerly. 'You see, it's impossible to disguise the human voice against modern phonometric tests – *my* phonometric tests. Not even you, Mr Clay, could defeat them. All I should need would be control recordings.'

It had become a convention at Scamnum to consider Dr Bunney and his black box as a mild joke – which was doubtless why nobody had pursued this possibility before. But Bunney's confidence had something impressive in it now. Even the Duke was interested. 'And you've kept the cylinder – record, whatever it is – of that message?'

'It's in my room now.'

'And the machine?' asked Malloch.

'The officers have that.'

Gott struck in. All this seemed to him more for Appleby than for the company at large. 'Then will you come along now? I think this should be put to Mr Appleby at once.'

Bunney had not thus been in the centre of the picture since the notable occasion on which he had proposed to switch on the Lord's Prayer. He joined Gott and Elizabeth with alacrity. At the door they met the Duchess, always a late arrival at breakfast. 'Has anything been discovered, Giles? And what are their plans?' Gott was already the recognized intermediary between Scamnum and the new power so disconcertingly planted in its midst.

'Nothing startling, I believe. All of us back-stage people will be questioned this morning – and meanwhile we and everybody else are fast prisoners. I don't know what would happen if anybody rebelled, but so far there is only a little grumbling from Mrs Platt-Hunter-Platt.'

'And from me.' Nave had come up behind. 'But if Mr Appleby will despatch a telegram for me to an exalted patient who must be tactfully put off I shall be placid enough. I will come and see him now if I may.' Nave plainly liked it to be known that he had exalted patients.

They found Appleby, who had abandoned the still-populous green-room, sitting dangling his legs over the front stage and absorbed in the prompt-copy of *Hamlet*. Elizabeth wondered if Mrs Platt-Hunter-Platt would have been impressed; it was somehow distinctly reminiscent of the reliable foreigner. But Gott broke in upon these studies abruptly, anxious to get ahead of Nave and the pother about a telegram. 'Dr Bunney believes he could identify the voice that used his dictaphone for one of the Revenge messages.'

Appleby looked at Bunney in surprise. 'I had hoped we might narrow down the possible access to your instrument, and to the other means by which messages were given. But I understood the Duke to say that the voice was disguised? And surely a carefully disguised voice, coming through the medium of a dictaphone –'

Bunney broke in impatiently. 'You don't understand. This is not a commercial dictaphone. It is an instrument of precision for the scientific study of the minutiae of speech. I should like to explain it to you if you will have it brought here. I have shown several people how it works: it is very easy to understand. It *measures*, you see – measures relative intervals, stress, which nobody could disguise. Of course one would make no show with such a thing in a court of law: it would be ridiculed. But for us – for you – it can point. All I need is control speeches from

everybody concerned. Come to reckon on it, I have got them all already. It is just a matter of comparing each minutely with the cylinder which has the message and the job is done – you see? It's not a quick business, though, rather a long one. But the cylinders are all up in my room. I may get them? And you have the machine?'

Bunney's eye was gleaming. He was a detective in his own line and now the instinct was up in him. His slightly comical pomposity was gone; the words tumbled out impressively. And Appleby was prepared to suspend disbelief. 'Get them by all means,' he said. 'It's something wholly new in criminology – at least in England.' And at this gracious speech, Bunney bounded away like a schoolboy.

'It seems worth Dr Bunney's working on,' said Appleby candidly to the others, 'while the very laborious business of sifting movements – both in relation to the messages and the murders – goes forward. For we are up against a long job, I am afraid, and people must be patient.'

Gott looked curiously at his friend during this speech and the subsequent negotiations over the telegram. He had told the Duchess that nothing startling had been discovered; now he was not so sure. He suspected that something had turned up sufficiently odd to catch at Appleby's imagination. And Appleby's next words scarcely seemed to lead directly to the laborious investigation he had promised. 'Giles, what would you say was the chief problem in *Hamlet*; the thing one puzzles over when one begins to analyse the play?'

'I suppose one is chiefly troubled to account for Hamlet's delay in revenging himself upon King Claudius. There seems no reason for it. That was almost the first difficulty raised by early critics of the play. And it has been discussed ever since.'

'Delayed revenge.' Appleby swung upon Nave. 'Now what if Lord Auldearn was murdered as he was murdered – right in the heart of *Hamlet* – in order to make the statement: "Thus dies Lord Auldearn, by a long-delayed revenge"?'

Nave's eyelids drooped over alert eyes. 'Are these professional consultations that you are holding? Are Mr Gott and I going to unite our crafts and work the thing out together?'

'Perhaps something of the sort. I feel that Lord Auldearn's death and the play *Hamlet* may be in some way implicated with each other, and that the manner of death constitutes a statement, a statement intelligible and satisfactory to the murderer though necessarily enigmatic to us. And conceivably the statement is just this: "At last, long-delayed revenge!" '

'This is much better than turning our pockets out and so on last night; it should get you much further!' Nave was obviously stirred to interest. He leant against the stage, hands deep in pockets, and knit his brows at the floor. 'A statement, yes: nearly every homicide has its aspect as a statement, a manifesto. And here that seems to be pronounced. At once pronounced and enigmatic; a clamant riddle. There really is matter for a psychological approach.' He glanced keenly up at Appleby as if assessing the policeman's ability to conduct anything of the sort. 'A riddle to which the solution lies deep within an unknown mind – it is an interesting idea. Not an affair as in your stories, Gott; no footprints, no flakes of that unique East Loamshire clay.'

Appleby smiled. 'You are behind the times in that sort of thing, sir. Stories of the kind always have a psychological drift now.' He looked mischievously at Gott and added mendaciously: 'For instance the elaborate analysis of the gorilla-mind in *Murder at the Zoo –*'

Nave turned to Gott. 'Dear me – I had no idea! Another use, it seems, for psychology; just as with the advertising.' This was a neat retort upon a joke now some days old and it seemed to put Nave in good humour. 'But what exactly is the problem for the psychologist here? The likelihood, I presume, Mr Appleby, of the sort of "statement" you suggest. "At last, long-delayed revenge!" I don't know if you have some particular suspicion in mind – but I see the general idea as possible enough. Suppose someone with a lust for murder; suppose him directing it on a particular victim and crediting himself with a motive which he calls "revenge". His head is full of revenge and he nurses the idea. He thinks of himself as delaying his vengeance and finds pleasure in that. He is playing cat and mouse –'

'Which,' interjected Elizabeth, 'is one interpretation of Hamlet's conduct.'

'Very true, my dear Lady Elizabeth; perhaps an important point. In any case, the delay has been part of his pleasure; his sense of power is implicated with it; he could strike but he has delayed. And then remember, as I said, that nearly every murder is a manifesto – and nearly always a manifesto – so to speak – of self, a piece of exhibitionism. The criminal looks forward to his appearance in the dock as the martyr to his martyrdom – and for exactly the same reason: it is limelight, it is a supreme manifesto of self – nothing more.' For a moment there was a fanatical gleam in Nave's eye – but he came back to his reasoning swiftly enough. 'He is proud of the power, the control that has gone into his delay. And so the delay must go into the statement. It may be gloried in in the dock or – better – it may be declared doubly in the way of the killing itself. *Hamlet, revenge!* And Hamlet procrastinates – and then at length kills.'

'But,' Gott objected, 'here it was Polonius who was killed, whereas in the play Hamlet is out for the blood of the king – it is there the revenge lies – and the killing of Polonius is merely an accident.'

'Yes,' said Nave vigorously. 'Yes! But in acts like this, remember, it is not wholly the rational waking mind that is in control. The primitive is at work. And the primitive uses – just as dreams use – rough and ready symbols – and uses them *illogically*. Here, it would be quite enough for the purpose of statement, of manifesto, that the murder should take place in a context of delay; in the middle of a play the main problem of which is procrastination.' Nave made an excited and nervous gesture; obviously he had a pleasurable feeling of power himself in this analysis. 'Yes; I believe you may be on it, Mr Appleby!'

Appleby was drumming a finger on his copy of the play. 'But can we come down to types, Sir Richard? What sort of person nurses thoughts of revenge – and for how long – or about what? Lord Auldearn has been shot by someone of whom we know only one thing: that he or she is what ordinary people call "normal". There was nobody in the hall who is not commonly regarded as a responsible agent. Very well –'

'What,' Nave put in drily, 'of the eminent Mr Cope?'

'An old man grown eccentric, no doubt. But what I am trying to put is this. Here are so many people we may suspect and all of them are – within certain elastic limits doubtless – normal people with normal lives behind them. How does our idea of darkly declaring a nursed revenge and so on accord with this very rough limitation of types that we can establish? Would you expect to find such a thing only in subjects patently un-balanced?'

'Certainly not. A very normal-seeming type might, I believe, do just such a thing. Strange things bubble up even in the godly, you know – uncommonly strange things.'

'No doubt. But can you imagine this: a normal-seeming person – indeed, an intellectually-distinguished person – nursing the idea of revenge for some passional injury over a very long period of time;

husbanding up murder and finally producing it from hiding-places more than forty years deep?'

Nave looked startled, and so did Gott and Elizabeth. Plainly, Appleby was not intending to use a mere figure of speech. And to look for a motive for Auldearn's death more than forty years back, was drastically to narrow the field. Nave straightened himself. 'You have some specific thing in mind,' he said, 'and it would not do to give any sort of scientific opinion rashly. I don't know. But I should venture that murder voluntarily delayed over forty years, and by such a type as you describe, would be disconcerting even to a morbid psychologist – and, believe me, we are not disconcerted readily. But do not misunderstand. I am speaking of a murder in which the motive centres wholly in a remote past. One can imagine a long-standing, but still present motive – some stolen thing still flaunted, some deadly and irreconcilable ideological conflict even, which might span a great stretch of years. But such speculation is worthless; we have nothing sufficiently precise before us. Here is Bunney.'

The approaching footsteps, however, were those of Sergeant Trumpet. The Prime Minister was on the telephone.

Appleby had already sent a message that the document was in safe keeping. And now, excusing himself, he hurried to the green-room without enthusiasm. During the last hour he had been feeling that the hunt was up – and it was a hunt that had nothing to do with Pike, Perch, or Prime Ministers. Despite the continuing blockade the whole spy-business had been becoming progressively unreal.

'Well,' came the Prime Minister's voice, 'you've got it and so far so good. Hilfers is going down for it straight away. Can we be easy in our minds? From this second intercepted message I rather suppose we can.'

'I haven't had any second intercepted message,' said Appleby.

'Haven't? Then I suppose Hilfers is bringing it down to you. It says something like this: "Regret premature advice have to report failure and no further opportunity probable." Some fool, you see, thought that because a shot was fired his friend had certainly got what they were after. Surprisingly stupid some of them are. Not like the police, Mr Appleby.'

'Thank you, sir,' said Appleby gravely.

'But it shows there was mischief afoot – that sort of mischief. Some precious scoundrel down there with you still. Don't let him hit you on the head before you hand over to Hilfers.'

arrangement of pigeon-holes. And in each pigeon-hole was a hollow metal cylinder coated with some waxen substance; that and a little descriptive card. Only one was missing, but the corresponding card was still there. It bore simply a date and the significant words: '*The curious message*'.

They had taken Bunney into another bedroom. Appleby, pacing up and down with a set jaw, was alone with Gott. He stopped in his stride. 'The swift, ruthless devil! Tell me, Giles, how did this come up? – before you came with Bunney to the hall, I mean. Was there a sort of public canvass of the possibility of identifying the voice?'

Gott nodded. 'Yes. Clay brought it up at breakfast. It suddenly came into his head and he came out with it. And at that Bunney said yes, he believed he could collate the cylinder bearing the message with known recordings of our voices and so identify the perpetrator. And at that I brought him along to you.'

Appleby made a slight, uncontrollable gesture of bafflement. 'And it gave the alarm and the murderer decided to act on the spot! I should have thought of it. I should have known that from that moment Bunney was running a risk – poor devil. Who was there, Giles? Who was at breakfast?'

'At that moment, I should think about half the house-party. I could give you a good many names, but not a complete list. It would be another case of laborious inquiry.'

'Yes. But it gives a control on all the other alibi-occasions we shall come to. Opportunity to send the messages, to shoot Auldearn, to stab Bose, to overhear Bunney's plan and attack him: when I tabulate everybody on all that I shall begin to get somewhere – perhaps. And it looks the quickest road now the Bunney hope has gone.'

Briskly, Appleby made for the door. And Gott felt that he was becoming an angry man.

3

The unwanted guests – those who had been staying at Scamnum merely to be spectators at the play – were gone. In silence, or discreetly murmuring premeditated words, or mumbling whatever came into their heads, they had shaken hands with the Duke and Duchess and been bowled away to freedom and importance: once back in town they would be in the greatest demand for weeks. Pamela Hogg had departed in tears, the morning post having brought news of Armageddon that was very bad indeed. Mrs Platt-Hunter-Platt had offered to interview either the Home Secretary or the reliable foreign detective – whichever the Duke pleased. And the Dowager Duchess had returned to Horton Ladies' without ever knowing that an American philologist, now just edging away from death's threshold upstairs, had wanted to compare her linguistic habits with Lady Lucy Lumpkin's as reported by the learned Odger. They were all gone and Scamnum, with less than a score of remaining guests, seemed for a time like a great school when only the holiday boarders are left.

In the green-room Appleby, Bunney's possible short-cut having been snatched out of reach, was taking the long and laborious way. He was as yet without any eye-witness evidence; as far as the murders went no one had reported seeing a sinister thing. And, a common type of revolver apart, he was without material clues; nothing of the footprints and unique Loamshire clay variety had turned up. What he had was an isolated motive – pitched abruptly at him by Timothy Tucker – and a number of significant places and times. On the basis of these last, he had suggested to Gott, it should be possible to elaborate a table of eliminations – to prove that this person and that could not have done all that the criminal had done. Of course it was theoretically possible – quite apart from what was almost certainly a parallel activity in the spy or spies – that many hands were involved. The two murders might be unconnected. The person responsible for the messages might not be responsible for the deaths. Each of the five known messages, even, might have a source independent of the others. But all these were fantastic hypotheses, to be neglected until the likely hypothesis had been explored. And the likely hypothesis was that in these messages and murders one hand was at work. One hand had shot Auldearn, stabbed Bose, stunned Bunney, and contrived five messages.

In these circumstances as they lay before him, Appleby thought that he detected a familiar thing: almost reckless daring. The murderer had wantonly multiplied the dangers he must run; and always for dramatic effect.

(i) He had shot Auldearn under the possible eye of Bose. Even if he proved to be old Max Cope he had done that. For Bose, as a simple experiment had made it clear, had only to look up at the vital moment to see enough of what was happening through the trap-door to know that the shot came from the upper stage – the upper stage of which Cope was in possession.

(ii) He had risked carrying his weapon, a revolver, with him from the rear stage. And this was a big risk in itself. Without it, he might have been detected emerging from the curtains after the shot and yet – for lack of positive evidence – been tolerably safe. But with the revolver on him, he had only to be resolutely challenged by an observer, held, and searched and his fate would be sealed. And this risk, again, he had taken for a small, but startling effect: that of secreting the little weapon in the grisliest possible place, Yorick's skull.

(iii) He had dragged Bose's body past a dozen tenanted rooms. And for an effect again – a sort of gesture of defiance.

(iv) He had contrived, by one means and another, five threatening or sinister messages. And in these, it seemed to Appleby, a new factor appeared. Here again was risk: five cumulative risks. Each message might conceivably be traced; and even a doubtful or inconclusive association with a given person would become formidable if made in the case of three, or even two messages. There had been cumulative risk; had there been cumulative effect? For the murderer's eye for effect was, in its own peculiar way, excellent; it was a master of the startling and the macabre that was at work. Had not there been something superfluous in the management of the messages? Wholly effective in the light of subsequent events had been the one found by Gott in Auldearn's car: the lines on the fatal entrance of Duncan under Macbeth's battlements found at the very moment of Auldearn's arrival at Scamnum. And wholly effective had been that other passage from *Macbeth*, ringing through the sleeping house its warning of an imminent deed of dreadful note. And effective too, if only because of the oddity and ingenuity of the method of communication, was the message delivered through what Scamnum had light-heartedly called Bunney's black box. After that, however, there was a drop into comparative pointlessness. Noel had been sent a message through the post and Gervase had been sent a telegram. And about neither of these did there seem to be any special appropriateness or force. From the point of view of the artist – and as an artist the murderer had, strangely, to be regarded – these two messages marred a certain pleasing economy in the contriving of sensation.

But (said Appleby to himself) look at it this way: look at the *method* employed for each communication. And he made a list: (*a*) *by hand*, (*b*) *by radio-gramophone*, (*c*) *by dictaphone*, (*d*) *by post*, (*e*) *by telegram*. Was this not what Nave would call a manifesto; was it not the action of the boxer who, sure of his invulnerability, amuses himself by tapping systematically now here, now there? One might say that only radio proper was missing – the Black Hand could scarcely capture the air – radio proper and the telephone. And Appleby wondered if a sixth message by telephone had actually been sent to someone who chose to remain silent. Or – conceivably – if a telephone message were yet to come.

The messages, then, served two purposes. They created sensation and they were a challenge. Look – the Black Hand said in effect – at the variety of channels I can use – use and get away with. A piece of typescript through the post may be hard to get a line on; but what of a telegram, a note delivered in an eminent statesman's car, dealings with other people's gramophones and black boxes? Appleby felt that even if an investigation into the origins of the messages yielded nothing, the mere fact of their being so clearly a challenge was not without its light.

He decided to make this investigation his first concern. His assistant, Sergeant Mason, who had arrived from London with Captain Hilfers some time after the attack on Bunney, could meanwhile begin sifting people's movements at the time of the two murders – a vital business to which Appleby himself would turn as soon as preliminary data had been collected. In this way he hoped to save himself time on blind-alley interviews with people who could produce clear alibis.

The first point about the messages, he reflected, was that out of all five there survived the physical vehicle of only two. The note tossed into Auldearn's car, the note posted to Noel Gylby, the telegraph form received by Gervase – all these had been destroyed. At the time of their reception they had been no more than imbecile anonymous communications and they had passed by way of the wastepaper basket to limbo. The dictaphone cylinder which had so signally failed to offer up the Lord's Prayer had been successfully stolen – it was a hard thought – from under the very nose of the police. What survived was two gramophone records and – possibly – the original of the telegram sent to Gervase. Even if the telegraph message had been telephoned to the post office at Scamnum Ducis, so that no written original existed, a date and hour of transmission would still be on the post-office files.

As well begin with Auldearn's message. Appleby got hold of Gott, one of the available witnesses, and went with him to find the other, Auldearn's chauffeur. The man was grimly polishing his dead employer's car; he was bewildered, angry, and anxious to help.

The message, Gott said, had been in typescript on a quarto page of common paper. He had noticed it, a crumpled ball, in a corner of the car a few minutes after getting in and just before drawing up at Scamnum. The chauffeur, Williams, who had looked at the clock on his dashboard on arrival in order to time the run, could name the minute: four-twenty-two. By about four-twenty on the Friday afternoon, then, the message had been in the car. What of an anterior limit? When had it certainly *not* been in the car? It had not been in the car, Williams could swear, when Lord Auldearn got in outside his London house; had it been there he, Williams, would have spotted it when arranging the rugs. And that had been at two-five. But it might have been tossed in within the next five minutes, when he had gone to his place at the wheel and they were waiting for a stray suitcase to be brought out. Would Lord Auldearn not have noticed it himself if it had been in the car throughout the journey? And would he not have been likely to notice its being tossed in? No, said Williams; his Lordship was distinctly short-sighted and often failed to notice more conspicuous things than a ball of paper. If they had not picked up Mr Gott he would certainly have found it himself sooner or later: probably on handing out to the footmen on arrival. And, of course, he would have given it to his Lordship; he would not take the responsibility of destroying what might be of consequence. When one was with a Lord Chancellor –

Quite so, said Appleby – and turned to the next point. After starting from town what opportunities would there have been? Williams looked doubtful. Anywhere until clear of London, perhaps, when going slow or in a block; but how could the fellow know just where to reckon on that? From another car it might be possible – with skill. But once they had got clear of London he doubted if it could have been managed.

'And when you got to Scamnum?'

'Well, I went very slowly up the drive, as Mr Gott knows. Gentlemen who have deer are sometimes very touchy about pace through their parks.'

'I see. But was there anyone on the drive?'

'There was Macdonald, the head gardener,' Gott struck in. 'I remember him touching his cap to us as we went past.'

'Macdonald?' Appleby was about to mention that curious behaviour of Macdonald as reported by Trumpet but checked himself before the chauffeur. 'You would have noticed if anyone had thrown the message in while you were in the car, Giles?'

'Probably. But not certainly,' said Gott cautiously. Then a thought struck him. 'You came by the south lodge?' he asked Williams.

'Yes, sir.'

'That's a possibility.' Gott turned to Appleby. 'There are twin lodges there, joined by a sort of mock-battlemented bridge you drive under. And there's an outside staircase and anyone is allowed up. There's a view.'

'I was going very slow there,' said Williams.

And that was all that was to be discovered. Two-five to two-ten in town was a likely time; two-ten to four-ten on the route was possible but not probable; four-ten at the south lodge was likely again. A suspected person would have to be cleared in relation to these times. Going back to the house, Appleby tried another line. Gott didn't remember anything special about the text of the message – any sign, say, of its having been taken from a particular edition? Gott smiled at the ingenuity of this, but remembered nothing of the sort. The message had been in modern spelling, as most Shakespeares so deplorably were, and might have come, say, from the old Cambridge text – of which there was a copy in every fifth house in England.

And that was that. Valuable times had been fixed, and yet Appleby felt that on the whole here was one up to the Black Hand. There was opportunity in London and opportunity near Scamnum – a point all in favour of the unknown.

Next came Noel's letter. No time need be wasted on it – nor could; there was nothing whatever to be done. It had been posted in the West End on Friday morning; Noel remembered that. But it requires only the most moderate ingenuity to arrange for the posting of a letter where one pleases. There was no road that way.

Appleby turned to the gramophone records and the opportunities of access to the radio-gramophone at about two-thirty on the previous morning. If the records were new there would be some chance of wringing information from them. Neither the carillon nor Clay's reading from *Macbeth* would be big-selling recordings and the manufacturing company's files would show what retailers could usefully be questioned. Appleby sent for the records; they were much scratched disks and both recordings were old. If the Black Hand had bought them when new, the transaction probably lay too far in the past to get any line on. And if he had picked them up recently and second-hand there would be needed a very elaborate net indeed, if there was to be even a slender chance of successful inquiry. Nevertheless, Appleby communicated with London at once. He then considered the matter of access to the machine and found no progress was to be made. It stood in a small ante-drawing-room, close to a service door. Anyone could have gone down in the middle of the night, set the machine going, slipped through the door, and returned to an upper corridor by more than one pair of service stairs. Scamnum was a building made for such tricks. And in the alarm, occasioned by the pealing bell, nobody had been on the look-out for suspicious movements. From all this there was derivable only one inference: the Black Hand had a fair familiarity with the house. Which told one really nothing. So far, Appleby said to himself, the enemy was winning all along the line.

An understanding of Bunney's box and private access to it some time before breakfast on the Saturday morning, were the next points. The most important witness here was not available; it would be some time before Bunney could again be on speaking terms with the world, but significant facts were to be gleaned. Bunney had arrived after luncheon on Friday and had lost no time in bringing his machine into play – as Gott had discovered on the terrace before dinner. Mysterious phonetic nicety apart, there was nothing particularly novel about the machine, except that it combined recording and reproducing units in an unusually compact way. But Bunney, being proud of it, hawked it round. Late on Friday night he had been demonstrating to all comers in the library; in the library just short of midnight, the somewhat reluctant Bagot had repeated the Lord's Prayer; and in the library, finally, the machine had been left for the night. The Black Hand had merely to walk in. Which was not helpful, thought Appleby – and turned to his last chance.

Gervase's telegram seemed more hopeful. It was the earliest of the messages, having been received at the House of Commons on the Monday afternoon – a week before the play. And the office of origin was Scamnum Ducis. In other words the telegram had been sent from a hamlet within a mile of Scamnum Court – and sent some days before the majority of the house-party was assembled. And Appleby doubted if it could very readily have been telephoned. You can dictate telegrams from the right sort of public telephone-box. And there was such a one, he discovered, some miles along the Horton Road. But from there, it appeared, you would get not Scamnum Ducis but King's Horton as the office of origin. Another possibility was that a telegram could be telephoned in fair secrecy from Scamnum itself. That depended on just what the domestic arrangements in such matters were and for a moment Appleby debated another interview with the alarming but efficient Mr Rauth. But it occurred to him that the local post office would have to be tackled in any case; and moreover that thirty minutes given to walking there and back might serve instead of the night's sleep he had missed. So he got his directions and set out briskly through the park, challenged occasionally by one of his own local auxiliaries. He had withdrawn the men from the terraces but was going to make sure, all the same, that nobody now at Scamnum should quit without formal farewells.

Appleby drew deep breaths of June air as he went briskly down the drive. The summer was advanced in this southland country; from somewhere came the scent of the first hay and already the oak-leaves were darkening. Over his left shoulder he looked up at Horton Hill. Across the crown there must be some right-of-way, for no attempt had been made to eject the people gathering there. It was quite a crowd now: idlers in the neighbouring towns, reading the stimulating news in their morning paper, had hurried to get out the car and motor over to see what they could. And soon there would be similar arrivals from London; people 'running down for the day'. And portents these, thought Appleby, of a society running down in another sense: clogged by its own mass-production of individuals who, let loose from a day's or a lifetime's specialized routine, will neither think nor read nor practise any craft, but only gape. Hence an unstable world, in which Pike and Perch Documents can have a real and horrid power.

But his immediate concern with that was over. Appleby's eye, travelling along the hill, rested on a red and white object moving towards the crowd on the summit. It puzzled him for a moment; then he saw that it was an ice-cream barrow. Commerce follows sensation.

Scamnum Ducis is a tiny village; the cubic space of all its buildings put together would go several times into one of the wings of Scamnum Court. A queer proportion of things, thought Appleby, still in sociological vein and yet not so blighting as the constant proportion of biggish villa and smallish villa that now makes up most of presentable England. He looked about him. There was – inevitably – a Crispin Arms: he noticed in a quartering the three balls that told how an early Crispin had married a decayed Medici. There was no church, for the church was within the park; it was more convenient for the family so. There was an institute erected by the belatedly romantic duke, with a bas-relief of Shakespeare, Milton, Wordsworth, and Lord Macaulay holding a committee-meeting. And there was a post office, the sort of post office that is also a general shop. There were picture postcards of Scamnum and cardboard boxes of slowly melting sweets in the window and the whole was of such modest proportions that Appleby, who remembered the classics of his nursery, would scarcely have been disturbed to find it presided over by Ginger and Pickles or Mrs Tabitha Twitchit. But it wasn't. It was presided over by a young girl most startlingly like the Duke of Horton.

Genetic law makes no scruple to confront you with embarrassing memorials of your ancestors, thought Appleby – and introduced himself. But the girl, on learning that she was in the presence of Scotland Yard, gave out a scared, gulping sound unworthy of the Crispin spirit and dis-appeared into the recesses of the shop. Her place was presently taken by a venerable but sharp-eyed woman who studied Appleby with the greatest concentration. And Appleby regarded her in turn with considerable hope. A knife-like and restlessly-curious old body, she might just possibly represent the sudden downfall of the Black Hand. 'I'm tracing the sending of a telegram,' he told her; 'a telegram sent from this office not very long ago. I'm going to ask questions. But I don't want anyone to begin thinking they remember what they don't remember. I've come in just on the off chance – you see?' Appleby had found this a useful technique in the past; people's memories are better when they don't feel something urgently expected of them. But the sharp-eyed old person looked at him with some indignation. 'There's not many tele-grams come into this office that *I* don't remember,' she said firmly.

This was excellent – though scarcely an attitude that would have been endorsed by the Postmaster General. 'It's rather a curious telegram, too,' said Appleby. 'It was just two words: "*Hamlet revenge*." '

'Ah,' said the old person; 'there's been plenty like that.'

Appleby was taken aback. He had been hoping a good deal from the wording of Gervase's message; it should have held attention in transmission. But he had forgotten something which the Black Hand had not: for some weeks past Scamnum had been sending out telegrams about the play with all the prodigality of a great house. And in these, as often as not, the word 'Hamlet' had occurred. As the old woman said, there had been 'plenty like that' and the message *'Hamlet revenge'* would not in itself attract particular attention.

'Plenty like that,' said the old woman. 'A fortnight come tomorrow, now, Mr Rauth himself came in with two. One was to Jolce and Burnet, St Martin's Lane: "*Reference Hamlet duelling properties not delivered please check despatch – Gott.*" And the other was to Miles, Oxford Street: "*Despatch ten copies New Cambridge Hamlet by return – Horton.*" And the same afternoon a stranger came in – a tall gentleman in a grey suit and a green tie, just the height of our Tim, who's six foot exactly, with grey eyes and one or two freckles across his nose like a girl – and he stood over there making up his telegram and putting his hand through his hair. And then he brought it across. It was to Malloch, Rankine Lodge, Aberdeen: "*Hamlet revived and Hamlet revised stop our motto back to Kyd exclamation looking forward discussion – Gott.*" Then the next morning ...'

Appleby regarded the sharp-eyed old person, thus steadily forging through a fortnight's telegrams, with something like professional envy. Her description of Gott was only a shade less miraculous than her verbatim memory of a piece of academic banter that must have been incomprehensible to her. His hopes soared once more. Even if there had been 'plenty like that' the old person seemed to have a virtuoso gossip's grip of the whole corpus. 'Then,' he said, 'you may remember this telegram, "*Hamlet revenge*", and its sender.' But a puzzled, almost cheated look had come over the old person's face; she shook her head sombrely. 'It's not long ago,' he said encouragingly; 'just eight days – a week ago yesterday.'

'Monday!' The old person was extremely indignant. 'You expect me to remember anything about a telegram handed in here on the Monday? Have you never heard of Horton Races?'

So that was it. That was why Gervase had received his message when he did. There was one day in the year on which anybody could send off a telegram from the little post office of Scamnum Ducis without the slightest chance of being remembered. And that was on the day of the local race-meeting, when the village became an artery for streams of cars, and when scores of these stopped hourly at the post office to enable their owners to wire or telephone bets. Not only could anyone have driven down from London or anywhere else and sent the telegram in perfect safety; anyone from Scamnum could safely have sent it too. For there had been two strange assistants working hard, and the Duke himself could have handed a telegram to one of these without anyone being the wiser. And, finally, the message had been handed over the counter, not telephoned. The old person found it without difficulty, duly endorsed as having been despatched at two-fifteen p.m. It was a common telegraph-form with the message pencilled in neat block capitals – a thing with which nothing could be done outside a fairy-story.

Appleby walked back to Scamnum with the feeling that in the matter of the messages he had come off second-best. All he had gained was certain exiguous facts of time and place. Setting aside the thoughts of agents and accomplices, he had it that the Black Hand had been in Scamnum Ducis post office at two-fifteen on the Monday before the murders and that a few days later – on the Friday – he had been *either* outside Auldearn's London home just after two *or* in the neighbourhood of the Scamnum south lodge just after four or – less probably – somewhere on the route between these places at the time of the passing of Auldearn's car. But this information, if slight, was not valueless; it might serve to eliminate – at least in a tentative way – this person and that from what was an alarmingly large body of suspects. And in conjunction with the other similar tests a good deal of progress might be made. Take, for example, Malloch as a suspect. One would ask could he, on his verifiable movements, have (*a*) thrown the message into the car, (*b*) sent the telegram, (*c*) shot Auldearn, (*d*) stabbed Bose, and (*e*) attacked Bunney. By this means, laborious as it would be to apply to over a score of people, one should get a long way. And this was a fact that the murderer must have reckoned on; it was his rashness again. And suddenly Appleby halted in his stride; he thought it likely that he had got somewhere already – and not where he wanted to be.

He had taken Malloch as an example – involuntarily. Tucker's story had been extraordinary; quite extraordinary enough to make him, in the almost complete obscurity in which the case was still enveloped, eye the subject of it as a benighted traveller eyes a glimmer of light in the east. At the moment he would be sorry to see Malloch go. And Malloch, it suddenly came to him, lived in Aberdeen. He was said to have arrived from Aberdeen late in the evening of the Friday on which the message had been pitched into the car. Unless he had faked his movements – and to do so beyond the likelihood of detection would be difficult – he must have been hurtling through the midlands in an express train at the moment when Gott was smoothing out the crumpled message in Auldearn's car. And what about the previous Monday afternoon – the relevant time for Gervase's telegram? Would Malloch prove to have been south of the Tweed? Appleby – rather regretfully, rather rationally – doubted it. Here was the technique of elimination beginning to work – and to dispel what hope of light there had seemed to be.

There was one further immediate inquiry to make in connection with the messages. Appleby made a detour and visited the south lodge. It was, as Gott said, a curious twin affair, bridged across on the upper storey – one dwelling, apparently constructed on this fantastically inconvenient plan to gratify a melancholy taste for symmetry. And there were two pairs of twin staircases: a pair going up from within the park walls and a pair going up from the public road. Anyone who wished could go up and prance on the lodge-keeper's roof. Appleby, whom ill-success was making more and more radical-minded, felt that he could work out this gesture as a pretty symbol of what Crispins offer the world. But instead he ran up the steps and pranced on the roof himself – or at least walked round it and lay down on it. The bridge-affair had a three-foot parapet; by simply sitting down and appearing to sun oneself against the wall one could lie in wait, concealed from the road. It was the ideal place from which to launch Auldearn's message.

Appleby went down to the lodge and made inquiries about the Friday afternoon. But nothing had been observed. The gates stood open all day and when a car drove through it was not, it seemed, part of the lodge-keeper's duties to appear. You could hear people on the roof sometimes – walking-folk mostly – if you were in the upper rooms. But nobody would carry such a recollection in his head; there might have been somebody up there on the Friday or there might not. So Appleby came away not much wiser. That, for a moment at least, was the end of the messages.

And now to take up what Mason had been beginning to attack: the accounts people could give of their own or others' whereabouts at the time of the murders. And there was a considerable difference between the two. For the shooting of Auldearn there was an exact moment fixed; for the stabbing of Bose there was no such precision. Auldearn had been shot when everybody concerned was confined within the restricted area of the back-stage part of the hall; Bose had been stabbed when these same people had scattered to their rooms. The crucial moment, then, was the moment of the shooting. Who had been there – with whom – seen what? And here, Appleby felt, one might reasonably suppose oneself to be on extraordinarily promising ground. But he had a doubt. And he was canvassing this doubt in his mind when, approaching the house, he noticed Nave pacing moodily about the upper terrace. With a sudden thought he ran up the shallow steps and joined him. 'I wonder if you would allow me another professional consultation?'

For a second Nave looked at Appleby vacantly, as if the question had broken in upon some more than commonly absorbing train of thought. And for that second it seemed to Appleby that he saw more in those eyes than vacancy – he saw what might have been the hint of some intolerable strain. But Nave was alert in a moment. 'I will help if I can,' he said quietly.

'I have just been reflecting on the moment of the murder – Lord Auldearn's murder. There were nearly thirty people in the comparatively restricted area round about. And the murderer, even if he had been lurking within the curtains for some time before the shot, must have slipped away from them immediately after. He must have slipped out of them immediately after the murder had announced itself resoundingly. And yet nobody appears to have seen any suspicious movement – or at least nobody has come forward with anything of the sort. That seems to me strange. Surely the murderer was taking a tremendous risk? Or rather two risks: the risk of being immediately detected and the risk of the other people being able to vouch for each other's whereabouts so readily that one could come down to him by a process of elimination? What I am wondering about, you see, is the quality of people's attention and memory. Here was this shattering event. Would not the moment, the visible scene, be vividly printed upon every consciousness present?'

Nave took time to consider. 'It is an interesting point. And the answer depends entirely on the magnitude of the shock. If something interesting, surprising, or even thoroughly disconcerting happens one tends to

remember the setting, the concomitant circumstances, more or less
detailed and vividly. That is true of everyone almost without exception.
But it is a different matter when one comes to a substantially traumatic
event – an event, I mean, involving a very considerable degree of shock.
When that happens we are found to be split into types. Take being
run over by a bus in the street. Some will have afterwards a complete
picture of the occurrence down to the position, looks, gestures of the
bystanders, and so on. Others will come from the same experience
either in a state of amnesia about the whole affair – completely without
memory of it, that is – or, what is more common, with a memory
of it which is distinctly confused and unreliable. It is venturesome to
attempt a numerical estimate, for there has really been no reliable statistical work done. But the people who remember vividly are certainly a
minority.'

'This unexpected and shattering pistol-shot in the hall: would you
class that, Sir Richard, as a substantially traumatic event – an event
following upon which most people's minds would be confused?'

Nave appeared to consider almost anxiously. 'That again is interesting
– very interesting indeed. I will tell you why. If the shot had been
fired on some other occasion – say when we were all seated at dinner
– the effect would have been startling, of course – but not, I believe,
shocking in a technical sense. In the middle of the play it was different.
I don't know if you have experience of the atmosphere of amateur
theatricals; it is distinctive and peculiar. Everyone is oddly wrapped
up in himself and his part. One seems to attend to other people without
in fact attending to them. In making your inquiries about what was
happening before the shot you will, I imagine, be surprised to find
how vague everybody is about everybody else.'

Appleby nodded. This agreed significantly with something Gott had
said.

Nave continued. 'And it was upon this absorbed company that the
pistol-shot irrupted. The effect upon most of us present behind the
scenes may not have been incomparable with the effect of being run
over. Certainly I should expect a good deal of blurring and confusion
of memory.'

'The murderer could have counted on that?'

'If the murderer has a flair for psychology – yes.'

'He has a flair for display,' said Appleby.

'That,' said Nave, 'is abundantly clear.'

Noel Gylby and Diana Sandys walked round and round the lily pond. And conversation would not take the straight line it ought; it went round and round like the path. Partly it was because the gardens were without their usual privacy. Policemen – some meditative amid the beauties of Scamnum, others awkward before its splendours – still haunted the middle distance with unobtrusive efficiency. And partly it was because Noel and Diana had their minds on different things. Noel wanted Diana's view on the universe – but was shy on the job. Diana wanted Noel's explanation of the Scamnum murders – and was persistent. Irritation was just round the next curve.

'It's absurd,' said Diana. 'Here's almost a whole day gone and nothing seems to have happened at all. I don't believe they know anything. Who do *you* think did it?'

'Some silly ass,' said Noel with exasperating vagueness. 'Silly-ass thing to do.'

'It all seems to me remarkably smart. Everybody's baffled.'

'Yes, just as you'd be baffled by some kid's trick that you can't get the hang of because it's simply too silly. Murders are done by people with kids' minds. Arrested development. Peter Pans – have you ever thought what a sinister affair that is? And if I had to pick among the people here for the murders I'd pick the prime silly ass, Peter Marryat. But I don't know that it's interesting. The poor devils are dead – and let the police do what they can about the loonie responsible.'

'That's just the air the Duke has,' said Diana. 'I suppose it's Crispin hauteur.'

'Oh, come, Diana –'

'Exactly. "Come, come." And as for Silly-ass Marryat I don't know that he's more arrested than anyone else – though his mental age *is* about eight. If you were going sleuthing on those principles you'd have to tip almost the whole distinguished company.'

'All half-wits, you mean?'

'No. Just kids. All – or nearly all – with the motives of kids just underneath. Peter Marryat simply lacks a protective covering of conventional adulthood – that's all.'

'Isn't that rather a desperate view – average mental age human race eight?'

'I don't know. But you can't sell soap and toothpaste without knowing that people in general are sub-adult. Perhaps it's just in our time – a sort of progressive dotage. That's what I thought when I was doing Woman's-page before I got to copy-writing. The average mental age seemed to drop every week. In fact, we had a rule. If a thing was just too steep to put over – too unfathomably childish and imbecile – we simply put it in a drawer for a month or six weeks. Then folk were ripe for it. I suppose that's what's called history.'

'Yes,' said Noel hesitantly. He had got his discussion of the universe after all – and it rather alarmed him. 'Then what's to be done? Let the eight-year-olds and homicidal adolescents rip and look out for oneself?'

'Well, isn't that what you were putting over? The deaths of Auldearn and the little nigger man not interesting: let's talk about Life and Woman and Art and –'

'I meant –' began Noel, aggrieved.

'Never mind. But when one's sold soap and written up Woman's-page and seen people such trapped helpless mutts one feels that if one knew an honest, no-gup uplift one would go for it all out.'

'Yes,' said Noel – more happily. He was a fundamentally serious youth and much concerned to establish Diana's seriousness.

'Or perhaps just do a good mop-up where one happens to stand. Hunt out this public nuisance of a murderer, for instance.'

'Yes,' said Noel – with only a hint of doubt. This basing of a pertinacious interest in Lord Auldearn's murder on impressive if sketchy ground of high moral principle was not perhaps altogether consistent with Diana's first reactions to the same event in the hall. But it would have been a maturer Noel who could have reflected on this. 'Oh yes,' he said. 'Certainly he should be hunted out. Appleby's job, though.'

'That,' said Diana, 'is what the Duke thinks.'

'You don't suppose we could take a hand ourselves? We haven't any of the information that the police have – and I can't see that we should have a single advantage over them.'

'I'm not sure. For instance, Noel, take people in the most general categories you can think of. And begin placing the type of the criminal that way.'

Noel considered dubiously. 'Oh well – to begin with I suppose it's a man's crime –'

'Exactly!' said Diana, at once triumphant and indignant.

'I say, have I been tactless? Women's rights and all?'

'No. Just over-confident – as this policeman will be. Too much guts in the affair to think of a woman.'

'I doubt if Appleby will take for granted –'

'He thinks he won't but he will,' said Diana firmly. 'And, anyway, you and I are going to canvass the ladies.' She glanced at Noel, saw that she had gained her point, and promptly added: '*Please*, Noel.' To study the masculine temperament was – after all – part of her job.

4

It was late afternoon. Appleby and Sergeant Mason, sitting in the green-room with pencil and paper before them as if playing a parlour game, had been joined by Gott.

'I never thought we'd get as far,' said Mason soberly.

'It's not far enough,' said Appleby, looking at the lengthening shadows on the floor.

Gott looked restlessly from one to the other. 'Are you on a sound track?' he asked. 'I should imagine that if you work purely on eliminations the evidence will almost certainly stop before it becomes useful. How many do you reckon left now?'

'Four,' said Mason. He had little enthusiasm for amateurs.

'That's impressive. But even so –'

'We may get something more yet,' said Appleby. 'And anyway, Giles, do you see any other method open to us at present – *any* other way of getting at the truth?'

'I think we've got it.'

Mason sighed. 'You mean you *know*, sir?' he asked gently.

Gott looked doubtfully from one professional to the other. 'Yes,' he said, 'in a sense that one knows where the kettle is – at the bottom of the sea.' He frowned at the tips of his fingers. 'It sounds very absurd, no doubt. But I feel that at the bottom of my mind, I *know*. And it's just a matter of getting it up to the surface.'

'I see, sir,' said Mason.

But Appleby was really interested. 'In other words, we have sufficient evidence before us – if we could see it. May be so. But surely, Giles, it's not a merely intuitive feeling you've got – a vague sensation in the back of the head? You must feel that your feeling comes – so to speak – from *this* and *that*?'

Gott nodded. 'Yes, indeed. And first and foremost is the strong impression one has of the dramatic aspect of the affair. In the light of that alone we should see our way farther than by all this alibi business.'

Mason, an intelligent man, reacted unexpectedly to this. 'I think you have a line, sir; I don't think it's impossible that you may get there first just by fishing in the depths of your own mind. I wouldn't like to be short with a thing merely because it's not my own way. But what about summing up our facts first – alibis and everything else? It might give you the start you want.'

Gott nodded. 'By all means. And perhaps my innings later.'

Appleby looked at his friend attentively. From Gott's mind, he believed, something really was going to emerge. He recognized in him just the same excitement that he had himself felt earlier in the day on making the significant link between Tucker's Malloch–Auldearn story and the delay-theme in *Hamlet*. Such starts of mind may be will-o'-the-wisps – or they may be arrows to a mark. But now he turned to Mason. 'Go ahead,' he said briefly.

'Yes, sir. I'll begin with the first murder, although there are earlier events to be considered. Lord Auldearn was shot through the heart just on eleven o'clock last night. Owing to the construction of what they call the rear stage no one could see what happened, with the probable exception of the prompter – the Indian gentleman – who seems to have paid for his knowledge with his life. But we have a certain amount of evidence as to what occurred, nevertheless. There is the remarkable fact that the shot was not fired from the shelter of the double curtains: the experts swear to that on the strength of the powder-marks. Just conceivably the shot might have come from above when Lord Auldearn was in the act of lying down; in other words, just conceivably the shot might have come from the painter, Mr Cope. But it seems more likely that the shot was fired by a person who walked straight across the rear stage to effect it – risking the observation of the prompter in doing so. There may have been a moment's struggle or flurried movement, because an iron cross was knocked off what they call, I think, the faldstool; or this may have happened when the murderer was making his hurried escape back to the curtains. We must notice that the revolver – a small foreign weapon which it will not be easy to trace – was carried off the scene of the shooting and hidden in a very odd spot in this green-room here. And there's a point where I differ from you a little, sir. You see that as evidence of deliberate hardihood – one of a number of such pieces of evidence. But whatever we may think of placing the gun in the skull, I feel that carrying it away would be automatic. Calculation would no doubt tell the murderer to drop it before attempting his getaway through the curtains – I admit that. But calculation may not have come in. It isn't a man's instinct to drop a gun after firing; he makes off, gun and all.'

'A good point,' said Appleby quietly. 'Perhaps I was astray.'

'Well, sir, the next point is: no finger-prints, no material clues. And nobody saw anything; at least nobody had anything to report. At this stage – except for what's coming in the matter of Mr Bose – we seem to be faced with a perfectly successfully accomplished crime. We know that it must be the work of one of a defined but large group of people – the behind-stage people – and we know nothing else.'

Mason paused for a minute to take his bearings. 'The next point – or rather *not* the next point – is the presence of spies who are concerned to steal a document from Lord Auldearn. I say they are *not* the point in our case. They are distinct from it, run parallel to it, and by tackling them we won't get nearer Lord Auldearn's murderer. For a time it seemed that they might have succeeded in taking advantage of the murder. But that supposition is now dissipated. One of the spies – we presume there was a little gang of them – at first sent his principals a hopeful message: he thought either that the shooting had been a successful stroke of a confederate's or that a confederate had successfully taken advantage of it. But later he corrected himself, reporting that Auldearn's death was another affair altogether, and that their chance was gone. We take the spies, therefore, as having been present, but ineffective. They merely lead away from our business now.'

'No doubt true,' said Gott, who had been following Mason's methodical recapitulation with considerable respect. 'But nevertheless it seems likely that there is a spy among us still. It would be satisfactory to know who he or she is.'

'Yes, sir. But we must have concentration on the vital object before indulging miscellaneous curiosity.'

It was a crushing reply and Gott acknowledged it as such with a gesture. Mason plodded on.

'Next and as a matter of routine we look for bad characters. And we find reason to believe that a cracksman called Happy Hutton has been on the premises and has broken into three safes. Conceivably, he may later have insinuated himself among the audience during the interval. But after the interval he would be as cut off from behind-scenes as anyone else. Therefore, like the spies, he is irrelevant. We have his hat, it seems. But we can't jug him on that. Happy fades out.'

Appleby interrupted. 'Sorry; there's been a telegram you haven't seen.' He rummaged for a form on the table. 'It wasn't Happy's hat after all – not his size. So we've got nothing on him whatever except that I saw him scuttling for town like a scared rabbit some eight miles from Scamnum – and that the safe-work was his technique. That hat is another guest's as like as not.'

Gott chuckled. 'And how you crowed over it, John! Happy Hutton's habit with high hats and the vivid account you gave of them – well, well!'

Mason, possibly not without amusement, looked stolidly at his own large fingers. 'Happy fades out,' he repeated. 'And next we come to the second murder, that of Mr Bose. It seems next to certain that Mr Bose, as prompter, saw enough of what happened to be a mortal danger to the murderer. But instead of coming out with the story he went off in an outlandish heathen way to write home about it – as the custom was with him, it seems. And so he was killed too. His death has just two points of significance for us: it gives us – though much less precisely – another place and time at which the criminal was active; and it gives another of the evidences – undoubted this time – of something like foolhardiness in the criminal's conduct of the affair: he dragged the body about the house just for display. And the theme of display, as we all seem to be agreed, is a crux.'

Gott was stirring slightly impatiently again. His mind was too rapid for this stolid march; it wanted to leap about. But Mason, who felt there had been enough leaping about, went steadily on. 'This murder was planned, deliberately and at obvious risk, to take place bang in the middle of Shakespeare's *Hamlet*. And it was preceded by various more or less lurid messages, the burden of which was the idea of revenge. The point there, then, is clear. Vengeance – and vengeance in highly theatrical and sensational circumstances – is either the *real* motive or a *fake* motive for Auldearn's murder. For there is always the possibility that this *Hamlet revenge* business is a screen and that some quite different motive is at work. When we come to the people concerned – the definite number of people who *could* have killed Auldearn – we have to look about both for one sort of motive and the other. And we do come to the people now, after just one minute more with the messages.

'The messages, although they were launched with great cunning, give us certain further places and times. And one of them turned out to be dangerous to the sender – dangerous because Bunney's machine is an instrument, as it happens, of such phonetic precision that a voice recording for it would not be secure against identification however disguised. Hence the attack on Bunney and the stealing of that particular record from his collection.

'And now we come to the thirty-one people who were concerned one way or another with the play. We have to scrutinize their movements and – if we can – their minds and their pasts. In other words, we have to look for the cardinal things in a murder investigation: opportunity and motive. But we needn't trouble over motive where there was no opportunity whatever.'

Mason, Gott was thinking, was unafraid of the obvious. And yet Mason, maybe, was the type of the successful policeman; beside him John Appleby seemed to have something of a lingering and speculative mind – a mind of which the true territory lay, possibly, elsewhere. But now Appleby interrupted with a hard saying: 'That depends entirely on the class of motive involved.'

Mason looked at him dubiously. 'I don't quite see –'

'What I say applies both to the shooting and to the sending of the messages. Take the point you're on now, the actual shooting. You say we needn't trouble over motive where there was no opportunity whatever. That holds, I say, only if a particular sort of motive is involved, the sort of motive that practically rules out conspiracy. If we were certain that the motive here were what it seems – a matter of private passion and long-cherished revenge – we would be justified in hunting only among the persons who had an opportunity to commit the crime. But suppose the sort of motive that is compatible with conspiracy to murder – murder for the sake of great gain, political murder, murder resulting from some anarchist or terrorist ideology, and so on – then what you say wouldn't hold. We might find the motive most readily in the mind or past of some-body who had not the opportunity, and go on from that to establish the fact of conspiracy with someone who had the opportunity. And again, there is the possibility of an actual murderer who is not so much a confederate as an agent or creature – who might himself be unaware of the ultimate motive behind his deed. And, obviously, the same considerations apply to the messages. Grant the possibility of the sort of murder to effect which men combine and the whole business of eliminations takes on a different aspect. To clear anyone of Auldearn's murder it will then not be enough to show that he could not have murdered Bose or attacked Bunney or been concerned with this or that message; his confederate may have dealt with these.'

Gott was about to come rather indignantly to the assistance of Mason when Appleby forestalled him with a nod. 'Yes, I know. It's not Mason's summary I'm attacking but my own earlier position. And even at that it may be I'm no more than making an academic point – or if academic is an ill-used word, say pedantic.' He smiled at Gott. 'I can't see any room for conspiracy. But let us say two things: we look for opportunity and motive alike just where we can find them; and we remember, as a theory to fall back on if necessary, that more than one hand may have been at work. And now, Mason – go on.'

'We come,' said Mason patiently, 'to thirty-one people and begin to eliminate. And I suggest we begin by eliminating Lord Auldearn.'

Gott thought he might be pedantic as well as Appleby. 'It's quite certain he didn't shoot himself?'

'If he did,' replied Mason tartly, 'it's quite impossible to find sense or coherence in any of the previous or subsequent events; that's all.'

'It's not all – fortunately,' said Appleby. 'Mr Gott here could spin a yarn in which Auldearn shot himself and yet all these other things – Bose, the messages, Bunney – would have some sort of coherence and plausibility imposed upon them. Couldn't you, Giles?'

'I'm afraid,' said Gott morosely, 'I could.'

'No, we've better ground than that. There was only one wound; the bullet came from the gun we possess, and we have expert evidence that it was fired at not less than two nor more than five paces. Quite apart from the weapon's having been removed, the evidence against suicide is conclusive. Eliminate Auldearn.'

'Having eliminated Auldearn, then,' Mason continued, 'I take it we can go on to the next victim and eliminate Bose.'

'Suppose,' said Appleby, 'that Bose sent the messages and shot Auldearn – a sort of political or ideological crime. And suppose that the Duke, say, found out and killed Bose. The Duke, after all, is a curious creature. In the business of the document – when he conceived something like national danger to be involved – he reacted normally and efficiently. But his attitude to murder is enigmatic – except in one point. He has clearly no enthusiasm for policemen and formal justice.' Appleby looked apologetically at Gott. 'You may think that fantastic and gratuitous. We are both convinced that Bose was not that sort of person, and no doubt you have – quite justly – the same conviction about the Duke. It's simply that we mustn't think we're locking doors when actually we're not. The theoretical possibility remains.'

'That the Duke stabbed Bose in the back in his own daughter's bedroom, and then hauled the body about Scamnum Court for the sake of a sort of wild justice,' said Gott, 'is not my idea of a theoretical possibility. It's a laborious absurdity. And it still leaves you with Bunney on your hands. If Bose sent the messages, then only Bose would have an interest in attacking Bunney and getting the dangerous cylinder. And Bose was dead long before Bunney was hit on the head.'

'Very well,' said Appleby briefly – and gave Mason a nod.

'If we count Bose out,' said Mason, 'we're down to twenty-nine. The next people we eliminate are the Duchess and Mr Clay. They were on the front stage, in full view of the audience, and yards and yards from the rear stage. In a story, of course, it would *have* to be one of these two, just because they were where they were. Mr Gott' – Mason added with friendly irony – 'will know just how it could be done.'

'It would need,' said Appleby, 'a revolver previously trained and released from a distance. A sort of infernal machine, in fact – and that never writes up convincingly.'

Gott meditated for a moment. 'Oh, no it wouldn't. You've forgotten something – or rather you've failed to guess at something which hasn't perhaps been mentioned. When that shot was fired in the hall it echoed and re-echoed about the place like a little salvo. All Clay, say, would have needed was an exceptionally loud one-bang firework on a time-fuse. That would go off when he was approaching the rear-stage curtains; he would pause for a second and then dash through and shoot Auldearn with a small pistol. The actual shot the audience would take to be one of the final echoes. What they would take for the actual shot would be just a squib, the remains of which Clay would promptly pocket.'

The impassive Mason was shaken at last. He stared at Gott round-eyed. 'But isn't that just what may have happened?'

Appleby interposed. 'No, it's very ingenious – but it won't fit this case. Clay was too long in getting through the curtain for the reverberations to be anything but very faint. Indeed, they must have been quite over. He was marking time because he didn't want to break the scene.'

Mason got out a large handkerchief and blew into it vigorously. 'I haven't come across anything so ingenious since I read a crazy thing called *Murder at the Zoo* –'

'Clay and the Duchess out,' said Gott hastily. 'Twenty-seven.'

'And I suppose twenty-seven more battles,' said Mason. 'At which rate we'll be talking here till midnight.'

'The battles are healthy,' said Appleby. 'We can't have too much of them. Twenty-seven. Go ahead.'

'Well, sir, at this point – keeping in mind what you have said about possible confederates – we have to make a distinction. We have to put people in three classes: those who are vouched for by other people at the moment of the shooting (though there again conspiracy might come in); those who could not have stabbed Bose or attacked Bunney or been concerned with one or more of the messages; and those who have no alibi for any of the relevant matter at all.

'I'll take first the people who are vouched for by other people. And there is, as it happens, a simplifying factor there – one that seems to rule out conspiracy in that regard. People were in groups. Wherever a person is vouched for he is vouched for by two or more companions. That is the greatest luck we've had; and I'm inclined to say the only luck we've had. It means that these people – a wild improbability of multiple conspiracy apart – really do go out. And here they are.

'The two dressers and the Duke's valet were together by the dressing cubicles and they had just called up one of the two footmen. That's a group of four. And the other footman was under the eye of Mr Gott and one of the American ladies, Miss Stella Terborg – vouched for by two. Mr Gott himself, this Miss Stella Terborg, Mr Noel Gylby, and Lady Elizabeth Crispin were all together – a group of four. Mr Piper, Mr Potts, and Lord Traherne were together – group of three – and Lord Traherne says he saw the parson, Dr Crump, and Miss Sandys a little way off. And as these two vouch for each other, each of them is thus vouched for by two. Finally, there were Mr Tucker, Dr Bunney, and the other Miss Terborg – Miss Vanessa. In a way that group is a special case, Bunney's testimony not being available. But I think we can accept it all the same. And that is as far as we have been able to get. As I say, we've been lucky to get so far. We might have had impressions and doubts to weigh up and we haven't; the evidence as far as it goes is decided and clear cut. When you allow for the confusion and shock we counted on it's good going. Twenty-one people are eliminated outright. Ten are left for the other categories.'

'I can't see,' said Gott, 'that it's really good going. I was prepared for confusion – and yet it seems to me quite extraordinary that at the moment the shot was fired there should have been ten people in that back-stage area, each invisible to the other or to anyone else. *And* each, it seems, able to give a plausible account of his or her whereabouts.'

Mason shook his head doggedly. 'It followed partly from the lighting, sir, and partly from the rather elaborate way the area had been partitioned off – the number of little cubicles and so on – and partly just from flurry and confusion. And they do all give a reasonable account of themselves; I haven't been able really to rattle a single one of the ten.' He turned to Appleby, 'Shall I go over that ground?'

Appleby nodded.

'The Duke, when he came off after the prayer scene, went straight to the little telephone hutch behind the green-room. He had remembered some instructions he wanted to give about the calling round of people's cars after the show. He was just about to pick up the instrument, he says, when he heard the shot and hurried to the rear stage. Nothing shaky there. Mrs Terborg was alone in her cubicle; Macdonald and Dr Biddle the same; Mr Marryat was alone in the sort of general men's room that the men's cubicles give upon. So far, there are two points to make. All these people account for themselves perfectly naturally; and all profess to have been at a considerable distance from the stage. But that last point is not conclusive: a sharp person could, I believe, have slipped about fairly freely. Still, these people were in considerably less interesting positions than the remaining five to whom I am coming.'

Mason, it seemed to Gott, was a man resolved to get somewhere – confident that he was getting somewhere minute by minute. Beside him Appleby, very still and absorbed, seemed a personification of wary doubt. They made, unquestionably, a formidable combination. Gott began to feel his own imaginative tinkering with the case a very ineffective method of attack indeed.

'Five people,' said Mason. 'Mr Cope, Sir Richard Nave, Professor Malloch, Mr Gervase Crispin, and Mme Merkalova. Cope, we know, was on what is called the upper stage – immediately above the scene of the crime; he was alone and if he shot Auldearn he shot through the little trap. So much for him – he was close enough anyway. And so was Malloch. Malloch affirms that at the moment of the shot, he was climbing up the little staircase to the upper stage; it had come into his head, he says, to take a glance at Cope. Again, it's a likely enough story, I suppose; and he could easily be there without being seen, for the staircase is quite elaborately match-boarded in. But there he is too, as close to the scene of action as could be. And next Nave. Nave had been close to the back curtains of the rear stage, listening to the prayer scene. At the close of it he lingered a minute or so and then turned round and walked towards the green-room. He was a little more than half-way when he heard the shot. So he also was warm. And finally Mr Gervase Crispin and the Russian lady. They were together in the green-room when it occurred to them to have a look at the audience – again a likely enough story, particularly in the light of the affair of the snap-shot camera: no doubt the lady wanted to see who was where. Well, they came out of the green-room and moved towards the stage. But at the back of the rear stage, they separated, Mr Crispin going to the left and the lady to the right, so that they were hidden from each other by the rear stage itself. Each, that is to say, was going to peer through one of the entrances to the front stage – the entrances that flank the rear stage on either side. Once more, it is perfectly reasonable – and yet one could see it as the first movement in a concerted attack. There they were, both free from observation, and in a dead line between them – and separated from each merely by the double curtains that form the rear stage – was Lord Auldearn.'

Appleby stirred. 'Bose,' he said. 'Within these double curtains, close by where Gervase Crispin went to stand, was Bose, the one man who might have had an eye on the rear stage.'

Mason nodded. 'That carries on the idea of a concerted attack. Mme Merkalova, say, was to shoot Lord Auldearn while Gervase Crispin somehow distracted Bose's attention. Only Gervase Crispin failed.'

'That's a theory,' said Appleby; 'or a bit of one. And now let's have the last batch of facts.'

'Yes, sir. The final facts concern the movements, at the other significant times, of those ten people who are unvouched for at the time of Auldearn's murder. They relate to the messages, to the stabbing of Bose and to the attack on Bunney. And they are facts, we are agreed, which may be considered as positively carrying the eliminative process further only if we neglect the possibility of conspiracy. Here they are as far as they go – for we haven't yet finished checking up. I needn't go into details, I think. I'll just sum up:

'The Duke could not have got the message into Auldearn's car either in town or subsequently. He could not have attacked Bose; he could not have attacked Bunney; he could not have been at the post office in Scamnum Ducis within two hours of the time endorsed on Mr Gervase Crispin's telegram. And the same holds of Mr Marryat: he could have done none of these things. Mme Merkalova has not a set of alibis like that but she has one. She cannot account for herself throughout the periods within which occurred the attacks on Bose and Bunney: on both these occasions she claims to have been alone in her room. Nor can it be shown that it was impossible for her to have sent the telegram; she was already staying here on Monday and she had gone out for a longish walk in the park, alone. But she could not have got the message into Auldearn's car. Dr Biddle has a similar partial alibi – one similarly conclusive on one point. He could not have stabbed Bose: we have that on the authority of our own local men – he was down here, fussing round them, all the time. But he seems unable to bring evidence that he wasn't lurking on the roof of the south lodge, or that he didn't send the telegram or that he didn't go upstairs after breakfast and hit Bunney on the head. Nave is in the same position as Biddle. He can clear himself on one point only – the attack on Bunney. He was in the hall with yourselves and Lady Elizabeth during the whole period at which that could have happened. And Gervase Crispin, finally, has an alibi on all counts but one. He couldn't have run down and sent himself a telegram; he couldn't have attacked either Bose or Bunney: but he could have been up on the south lodge pitching a message into Auldearn's car. And that is as far as we have got, the remaining four people not yet having been fully questioned. At the moment it comes down to this: if we allow the possibility of conspiracy we have ten suspects for Auldearn's murder and no very clear means of getting further: if we rule out conspiracy we are down to these four people who remain to be questioned – and it may be possible to eliminate some of them. Notice that there is nobody who has failed to produce an alibi – sound alibi, I guarantee – for at least one event yet. And the four people left are Macdonald, Mrs Terborg, Cope, and Malloch.'

There was a little silence. Mason sat back in the consciousness of honest work accomplished. It was Gott who spoke first. 'It would be uncommonly injudicious to abandon the notion of conspiracy while it stares one in the face.'

'Two things stare us in the face,' said Appleby. 'And one involves conspiracy and the other virtually excludes it. You are back on the old ground of Gervase and the Merkalova, Giles – and certainly here they are again in startling enough concert. They bear down on the flanks of the rear stage at the critical moment with more than a suggestion of deliberate manoeuvre. And then when we come to study people's movements in relation to the other events, we find their alibis over the series coming together like the pieces of a puzzle. The one thing the Merkalova couldn't do – get the message into Auldearn's car – is the one thing Gervase could do. As you say, it stares us in the face. But what of a motive – a motive of a conspiratorial sort? They weren't after a document of Gervase's own composition. Then what were they after? At the moment one sees no glimmer of motive. The only motive that one sees anywhere is the motive one can attribute to Malloch. That, of course, is the other thing that stares us in the face. And it takes us right away from conspiracy: we agree, I suppose, that if the motive is a stored-up revenge from the remote past the notion of confederates and so on is an unlikely one.'

'It comes to this,' said Mason. 'If there was no conspiracy we have four suspects: Macdonald, Mrs Terborg, Cope, and Malloch – with a strong line on Malloch. If there was conspiracy we must add to these as possible murderers of Auldearn: the Duke, Marryat, Biddle, Nave, Gervase Crispin, and Mme Merkalova. With a line, in that case, on the last two. But not, I put it, a strong line. The interlocked alibis and the movements at the time of the shooting are startling at first, I admit. But they're a good deal less impressive after you've had a steady look at them. You were impressed, Mr Gott, because you had these two people linked in your head earlier on, when the document was on the carpet.'

This sound observation Mason apparently designed as his last word for the moment. He applied himself to stuffing a pipe and looked expectantly at Gott, as if awaiting the promised innings. Logic had got as far as it could: if imagination could get further – let it. But Gott, too, was filling his pipe; and having lit it he puffed silently until prompted by Appleby. 'What do you think, Giles: have we got anywhere?'

'I'm bound to think you have. I don't see Auldearn's death as a conspiratorial affair. And that being so, and taking your eliminations as valid step by step, I admit that you are confronted by four suspects: Macdonald, Mrs Terborg, Cope, and Malloch. But they don't impress me as I feel they should.' He looked apologetically at the impassive Mason. 'In fact, as suspects they don't appeal to me.'

But Mason was not to be drawn. And Appleby's formula came as usual: 'Go on.'

'Just consider them. Macdonald has worked in the gardens here – man and laddie as he would say – for something like forty years. You've gathered his type: severe, steady, dignified, and a bit of a tartar – a compendium, in fact, of all the most uncompromising Scottish virtues. It's simply unbelievable that he should break out into murders and murderous assaults. And there is nothing whatever against him except the local sergeant's story that early this morning he was found lurking about the hall. Somehow I can't attach much importance to that.'

'Quite so,' said Appleby.

'It needs explaining, all the same,' said Mason.

'Then Mrs Terborg. Isn't she another type one just *knows* about? Polite New England with a lot of Europe on top. And we're to suppose her guilty of two murders, a murderous assault and miscellaneous activities including dragging a dead body about the house in the small hours. I don't see it.'

'Quite so,' said Appleby. 'She and Macdonald, in fact, belong to the two most inflexibly virtuous traditions that the Western World has produced. The kind who might, perhaps, commit a crime under some severe provocation, but who would *not* embark on a series of consequential crimes to save themselves. It's an impressive psychological argument. Go ahead.'

'Max Cope. One can just conceive a crazy old man determining to kill Auldearn because of some mortal grievance buried in the past. And one can conceive Cope sending the messages. He knew the sources of

Gervase's message: *Hamlet, revenge!* And I remember his asking the Duchess if there was to be a detective in the house: you might consider that suspicious. And he's a cunning old man – and perhaps malevolent. But I can't see him as having the drive to put through the whole series of events. I've seen quite a lot of him and unless he has been simulating a failing brain for years he just doesn't possess the intellectual grasp and tenacity to proceed, move by move, as the criminal has done. For you'll agree, I think, that there has been more than just cunning at work. There has been something like incisive intellect.'

'Quite so,' said Appleby. 'And now Malloch – the last man in.'

'Don't forget,' said Mason, 'that even these four are in only negatively, so to speak. They're just the four that are left over at the moment and to be questioned by Inspector Appleby presently. It may be possible to eliminate more of them.'

'It may be possible,' said Gott, 'to eliminate them all.'

'Malloch,' interposed Appleby invitingly: 'the great scholar. And you can't say, Giles, that scholars don't at times behave in a distinctly curious way.'

'No. I've no psychological arguments to advance about Malloch. And if Tucker's story is true it's impressive.'

'It's true all right,' said Appleby, 'as far as the stuff being in Anderson's book goes. It's all here – the whole story of the Jacobites and the Mallets.' And he tapped a book on the table.

'You've wasted no time. But my point about Malloch is simply that he will probably eliminate himself out of hand on our no-conspiracy basis. He came straight from Aberdeen on the Friday.'

Appleby nodded. 'Yes, I know. And we'll be certain soon. But I'm leaving him to the very last – to cook.' He looked at his watch. 'Which reminds me: we're not going to be left entirely in peace much longer. The local Chief Constable's on his way here now. He's come pelting over from Ireland.'

'What sort?' asked Mason.

'A very gallant officer. And quite new to the job.'

'Ah,' said Mason darkly – and added after a moment: 'But Mr Gott hasn't given us those ideas of his yet.'

Gott shook his head. 'I haven't exactly got ideas. I just think there are other possible lines to take up – that material is before us which might lead straight to a solution. I think we want to know just why

Auldearn was killed when and where he was. That it was simply to set his death in a context of *Hamlet* and so make an enigmatic statement or manifesto about delayed revenge – the Malloch theory in short – seems to me ingenious but not quite adequate. The circumstances of the murder were not merely decorative but structural – you understand me? That is my first feeling.'

'Yes,' said Appleby; 'I did some thinking along that path too. It was so because it had to be so. I find that satisfactory as a general proposition; I mean I feel the criminal to be the sort of person who would like it that way. But at the moment I can't drive the idea further.'

'That is my one point,' said Gott. 'And the other is this. Something went wrong.'

Mason stirred in his seat. 'Wrong, sir?'

'With the showmanship – the producing. Even if the dramatic manner of the thing served some practical purpose which we can't at present place – even so, the dramatic manner of the thing was something that the murderer delighted in for itself. And there was a hitch. Something went wrong.'

Appleby was tidying accumulated papers on the table. Mason looked at Gott with a sort of perplexed respect. 'How do you make that out, sir? I mean, how do you know?'

'I'm quite prepared to believe I'm making an ass of myself. Or perhaps something canine – believing I can usefully work by smell. But I seem to know out of a dramatic sense – akin to the murderer's, I suppose – that has been sharpened at the moment by the business of producing the play. But you mustn't attend to me too seriously. I know how much it is something in the air.'

Appleby finished straightening his papers. 'The Chief Constable,' he said, 'will find our dockets on the table even if our ideas *are* in the air. And I've had sufficiently airy beckonings in this case too, goodness knows. For one thing, I should like to spot why I'm so constantly beckoned by Fate in *Les Présages* –' He stopped to stare at Gott. 'Giles, what on earth –?'

Gott's eye had fallen on the topmost paper of one of the little piles. And now he had sprung up, seized the pile, and was beating the air with it like a maniac.

'Giles – for heaven's sake! It's only the telegrams sent out for people this morning. What's come over you?'

But Gott was pacing about in a blaze of excitement that made even Mason's eyes grow round. 'Yes,' he cried presently. 'Yes ... yes ... and yes!' He whirled about on Appleby. 'I will *not* cry Hamlet, revenge!' He paced about the room again; stopped. 'There's a snag – of course there's a snag.' He flung out an arm, snapped a finger in extravagant bafflement. Decidedly, thought Appleby, Giles had never behaved like this before. 'There's a snag – a horrid snag. But there it is – *there it is!*' And he swung round the green-room, chanting:

> 'Come, seeling night,
> Scarf up the tender eye of pitiful day,
> And with thy bloody and invisible hand –'

From the door of the green-room came a respectful but desperate cough.

'The Chief Constable,' announced Sergeant Trumpet.

5

'Sandford's come,' the Duke announced. Sandford was the Chief Constable – but from the tone he might have been the Last Straw. 'Took it upon himself to hurry back from a holiday in Ireland. When we were getting on very nicely with that unobtrusive young man.'

The Duchess looked at her watch. 'How rather awkward! Will he stop to dinner?'

'And take a short view of the suspects over the soup?' suggested Noel.

'You can't have murders without these awkwardnesses turning up,' said Mrs Terborg placidly. 'Perhaps, Anne, he will like to dine with the detective – and confer, don't you think? The detective seems quite –'

'Yes,' said the Duchess. 'But I don't know that I could just suggest it.'

'The last time Sandford came here to dinner,' said the Duke, 'he began by talking nonsense on dry-fly, went on to a boring description of the Harrow match, and ended by being impertinent about the port. Nevertheless, Anne, you must ask him – and let him have a view of us as Noel says. Go along.'

The Duchess rose with a sigh. 'Teddy,' she said, 'they don't suspect you by any chance – or you, Noel? And they can't suspect Elizabeth?'

The Duke shook his head. 'I don't think they can reasonably suspect any of us.' He glanced in surprise at his wife's troubled face. 'And I don't know that we need exactly commiserate ourselves over it. I've no desire to be gossiped about as Ian's possible murderer.'

'No, of course not.' The Duchess crushed out a cigarette. 'But I wish I hadn't been sitting in sober innocence on the front stage. And I wish the family *weren't* clean out of it. We ask a lot of people down and Ian and Mr Bose are murdered. And we keep well clear and have Colonel Sandford in to suspect the poor wretches round the dinner-table. It's rather mean.'

'There's still Gervase,' said Noel cheerfully. 'I'm not sure they're not hot after him still. So there's a chance for the family yet. Bear up, Aunt Anne.'

Mrs Terborg interposed briskly. 'This is great nonsense. To begin with the poor wretches take the police and so on as quite in the day's round. This horrid thing has happened and we must expect to be badgered. And for another thing, Anne, you don't care twopence for the poor wretches. You care only for what's been and done with – and anxiety for the feelings of your guests is merely defensive social disguisement. And for a final thing I'm sure they can't suspect Mr Crispin. They're much more likely to suspect his –'

'Friend,' said the Duchess firmly. 'Perhaps you're right, Lucy – and you're a great comfort. And now for Colonel Sandford.'

The Duke got up. 'I'm coming too. Bagot must go down and find a bad Bordeaux. I promised myself never to give that man Scamnum port again.'

Noel was left on the terrace with Mrs Terborg. He eyed her warily, misliking his job. But the exigent Diana stood behind him in the spirit, as ineluctable as some invisible Homeric goddess commanding the hero to engage. For a few minutes they conversed indifferently. Then Mrs Terborg prepared to rise. 'Almost time to go up,' she said.

Noel did not like to contemplate what would happen if he missed his chance. 'I say,' he said, 'did you ever go round to Peter's Gothic pavilion, Mrs Terborg?'

'Gothic pavilion?'

'Yes.' Noel was guardedly eager. 'Everybody doesn't know of it; it's tucked away beyond the rock-gardens. I'd like to show it to you.'

Mrs Terborg may have been shrewdly surprised at the attention, but all she displayed was mild gratification. 'How interesting – such an interesting man Peter must have been! If we have time –'

'Oh, yes,' said Noel. 'Do come.' And artfully he held out to Mrs Terborg the bait of polite learning: 'A Gothic pavilion convertible into a greenhouse. I believe it was taken from Repton's *Theory and Practice of Landscape Gardening*. Long afterwards, of course, because Repton died – didn't he? – quite early in the century. We go round this way.' And he led Mrs Terborg through the gardens.

Diana had prepared a questionnaire; getting it skilfully across, she had said, would be good diplomatic training. Noel rather wished he had it before him in black and white. It had run so smoothly when rehearsed by Diana – was such an innocent excess of friendly curiosity. But now it went so badly that Noel felt that, like Peter Marryat with the Norwegian Captain, he must be muddling it all up. Or perhaps it was just that Mrs Terborg's responses didn't end where they ought, so that there was difficult steering to the next point. Still, Mrs Terborg seemed unaware of guile, and by the time he had got to Question Six Noel was beginning to have some confidence in his ability to extemporize approaches.

'What magnificent Dorothy Perkins!' said Mrs Terborg.

Noel leapt at an opportunity for Question Seven; he didn't understand it but Diana thought it particularly important. 'Frightfully prickly, though,' he replied. 'You need gardening gloves before you think of touching them. By the way, did you happen to leave a pair of kid gloves in the hall last night?'

'I'm sure I didn't,' said Mrs Terborg firmly – and gave Noel what might have been described as a long look.

Noel felt a little trickle of sweat down his spine. The thing was like a horrible drawing-room game in which you have to insinuate outlandish words into your conversation undetected. And that last attempt had been almost fatally clumsy and precipitate; he must go slow and strive for the authentic Crispin finesse. So he abandoned the questionnaire during the inspection of the Gothic pavilion and talked glibly about Repton and Capability Brown.

> 'At Scamnum, Croome, and Caversham we trace
> Salvator's wildness, Claude's enlivening grace,
> Cascades and Lakes as fine as Risdale drew.
> While Nature's vary'd in each charming view.

The Rise and Progress of the Present Taste in Planting Parks – you know it? Very amusing.'

This was what Mrs Terborg liked; the expedition to the convertible greenhouse became for a time a great success. 'Mason,' Noel continued easily, 'in his *English Gardens* – a romantic tragedy of landscape gardening, you know – Mason is thought to describe one of the Scamnum conservatories; not this one but the classical one beyond the orangery:

> High on Ionic shafts he bade it tower
> A proud rotunda; to its sides conjoin'd
> Two broad piazzas in theatric curve,
> Ending in equal porticos sublime.
> Glass roofed the whole . . .

Odd to bring a design for a greenhouse back from the Grand Tour. Have you been in Greece much?'

Mrs Terborg had been in Greece, knew Turkey – and yes, she had been in Russia several times. This, on the other hand, was perhaps an over-ingenious approach to the groups of questions dealing with Movements and Interests, but eminently it had finesse. Noel was once more rather pleased with himself and all went well until, when they were again in the rock-gardens, he got to Question Fifteen, which was almost the last. But at Question Fifteen, although Noel considered it particularly adroitly introduced, Mrs Terborg halted.

'Mind your own business,' said Mrs Terborg.

Noel was overwhelmed. 'Oh, I say, I'm most frightfully –'

But Mrs Terborg had stooped down to the border. 'This one with the tiny flat leaves,' she said. 'Such a quaint name: mind your own business! And everything is here: elecampane, birthwort, lovage, rosemary, clary . . .' And she held to her own favourite species of polite learning until they reached the house. Noel made no attempt to deflect her; he concluded – as he presently explained to Diana – that there had been a Hint.

But still Diana would not be put off. 'We're getting on,' she said.

'Getting on! I've been getting on Mother Terborg's nerves, if that's any good. And I don't see that the women offer any field at all. There's only the Merkalova that's fishy –'

'She's a wrong 'un, all right,' said Diana viciously.

'And we're only down on her, really, because she spat out nasty about you. In fact – I think this is where we stop.'

'The next thing,' said Diana, 'is to get into the hall. Do you think we can? I want to nose round.'

'Nose round?'

'Just that. *Nose*, Noel. Noel, *do* get me in – *please!*'

'Well,' said Noel, melting but judicial, 'as long as there's no more Terborg-stalking stuff, and provided the heavies aren't still lurking there after dinner, I expect we could reconnoitre.'

'Oh, good. But, Noel, there *is* more on the Terborgs. Think of the twins.'

'I have in the past. But at the moment I'm not promiscuously minded.'

'Thanks. But *think* of them.'

Noel made a resigned gesture. 'I suppose this to be the way my un-mellowed Aunt Anne treated the young Teddy. All right; I'm thinking of them. Then what?'

'Don't you see –' Diana paused as Gott came out on the terrace and stood looking at them dreamily. 'But here's an authority. Please, Giles Gott, if you were writing a mystery story – one all about x being here while y was over there – wouldn't you find two people who might pass for one another uncommonly useful?'

For a full ten seconds Gott stared at her.

'Invaluable,' he said, 'Miss Sandys – invaluable.'

Colonel Sandford put down the telephone with a clatter. 'That was the Home Secretary,' he said. 'Inspector! – the Home Secretary. We must act.'

'Did he say we must act, sir?' asked Appleby mildly.

'No, no. Not that. But he is concerned – gravely concerned.'

'We're all concerned, sir,' said the sober Mason.

'Quite so. But we must prepare to move in this affair – to move, you know. Now, Inspector, where are we? I have great confidence in you – confidence. Now what grasp have you? Grasp on it – grasp.'

Appleby did not think the pompously agitated Chief Constable too bad a fellow. He replied carefully. 'At the moment it's like this, sir. We're trying to get people into three groups. The first group comprises those who could not have shot Lord Auldearn. The second group comprises those who could have shot Lord Auldearn but who could not have committed one or more of the other acts: sending messages, stabbing Bose, attacking Bunney. The third group – one we're trying to establish – comprises people who could *both* have shot Auldearn *and* done everything else. And shortly before you arrived we had four people left to deal with. These were the only four people left who *might* have done everything. So you see where we were. We had, so to speak, four chances left of proving the possibility of its having been a one-man affair. If all those four people could prove that they belonged to the second group – the group of those who could have shot Auldearn but not done something else – then we should be faced with the certainty of a conspiracy; the certainty that a criminal and one or more accomplices must be involved.'

'I see, I see. In fact if these four establish themselves as in the second group you're back nowhere.'

'Not at all, sir,' said Appleby patiently. 'We should merely be back with a larger group of people – ten, to be precise – who might have shot Auldearn but who could not have done one or more of the other things; for whom, in fact, we should have to find an accomplice or accomplices.'

'Yes, I see. You mustn't expect me to be as quick as you are. I see. But, if these four make their getaway to the second group, at least it's a set-back?'

'Quite so, sir. And we're now at our last chance. The four remaining people were the head-gardener, Macdonald; old Mr Cope; the American lady, Mrs Terborg; and Professor Malloch.'

'Cope – that old fellow? He painted my grandfather – deuced well.'

'Yes, sir,' said Appleby politely. 'Well, we were interested in Macdonald because he behaved in a suspicious way early this morning – he was found prowling about the hall and invented some story of looking for a snuff-box. But I hadn't much hope of him because of the message that was thrown into Lord Auldearn's car. He could only have had an opportunity for that when he passed the car some way up the south drive and it would have been exceedingly difficult. And, in fact, Macdonald routed us. He couldn't have murdered Bose; he couldn't even have sent the telegram from Scamnum Ducis. So he goes very clearly into Group Two.'

'But still suspect of something? What about this business of skulking about the hall?'

'I got an explanation out of him about that – though with a good deal of difficulty. It's odd – quaint indeed – but I feel inclined to accept it. A few days ago Macdonald was induced, it appears, to repeat the shorter Catechism and one of Burns's poems for the American philologist, Dr Bunney. And he discovered afterwards, to his great annoyance, that these recitations had been recorded by Bunney's apparatus – the machine, as you know, sir, through which one of the messages was delivered. And when Macdonald heard about that – about Bunney's machine being mixed up with the messages – he got really worked up. For he believed that we would try to trace the perpetrator by means of Bunney's record – which is just what we were going to attempt when Bunney was attacked – and that everything about the machine would inevitably be exhibited in court. Well, he wasn't going to stand for the outrage of his versions of Burns and the Catechism being reproduced at the Assizes and he determined to get possession of the relevant cylinder – which he conceived to be still in the machine. The machine was in the green-room and that was what he was stalking. As I say, it's odd. But it's true to character, it seems to me, and I don't disbelieve it.'

'Well I'm dashed,' said Sandford. 'I suppose he ought to be prosecuted. But if that's all there was to it, I think we'll let it alone. I don't altogether blame him.'

'No, sir. And the immediate point was that as a single-handed criminal Macdonald was out. And – to be brief – Cope and Mrs Terborg have established themselves clearly enough in Group Two as well. So it's a case of one beer-bottle sitting on a wall.'

The Chief Constable meditated the proprieties for a moment and decided to laugh. He laughed loudly. 'And if *that* beer-bottle has an accidental fall – well, there was more than one person in the game. Malloch, you say? Is he any more hopeful than the rest?'

'Yes, sir – in a way. I've left him till the end on the chance that it may rattle him. He's in a special position – the only person against whom there's any suggestion of motive so far.'

'Ah, motive!' said Sandford eagerly. 'Motive; yes, of course – enormously important. Glad you've been on to motive. I'd forgotten it. Shocking thing – my mind hadn't turned that way. Motive.'

'Yes, sir. There is a story – with considerable foundation apparently – of something like deadly enmity between Malloch and Auldearn. Something dating from their student days.'

'I say!' said Sandford. 'Better have Malloch in. Embarrassing, chivvy-ing gentlemen – but it must be done. I'll keep quite quiet, you know – just sit by. Better have him in.'

'Yes, sir.'

Nave entered his bedroom and closed the door. A sunbeam, dropping towards the horizontal, broke upon the dress-clothes laid out on chairs; the man had been and gone.

He moved to the window and looked out for a moment abstractedly; then his gaze travelled to the summit of Horton Hill. The crowd, the ice-cream barrows – they were there still. He smiled grimly at the distant audience, smiled as the student may smile at a predicted result. Then he turned and paced the room – up and down in some mounting agitation: it might have been anxiety, bewilderment, some ungovernable impulse from within. He halted as if to steady himself, undressed delib-erately, went into his bathroom, and turned on the bath. He came back.

Standing in the middle of the bedroom he let his eye travel – but reluctantly, mesmerically – to a far corner. Resolutely, he brought it back to the business of cuff-links; uncontrollably it strayed again.

He strode to the bookshelf. And warily, as if it were a forbidden act, he took down a book.

With serious politeness Mason set a chair.

'Professor Mallet?' said Appleby.

'Malloch.' Malloch was not more severe than an eminent savant should normally be. And he did not seem disturbed.

'Malloch – I beg your pardon. And I am sorry to have left you till the last – and so near dinner-time. We have asked people to come in and discuss matters in quite a random order, I am afraid.'

'No doubt,' said Malloch. And he looked square at Appleby across the table. It was to be a real duel – this Appleby instantly knew, and knew that Malloch had deliberately given away that fact to him. It was a declared duel, with buried deep in it the strange enjoyment that such things can have.

'Mr Malloch, you have particularly interested yourself in *Hamlet*, and came to Scamnum to take part in the late production for that reason?'

Malloch considered this line of attack carefully. Appleby wondered if he would protest at once, as he well might. It was an opening more proper to a barrister in a court of law than to a policeman soliciting statements from possible witnesses. But Malloch replied deliberately and fully. 'Yes, I have published a study of the play called *The Show of Violence* – chiefly in the province of literary criticism.' Literary criticism, the tone implied, was a scholar's relaxation from severer things. 'And when I was invited to come up I was very glad to accept. Mr Gott, though chiefly a textual worker, has stimulating ideas about the drama generally. I welcomed talk with him.'

There was a pause. It was rather – Sandford reflected – like the opening of a test-match: slow and infinitely cautious. And, forgetting his conviction that the Home Secretary expected immediate action, he settled down to listen.

'And, like most of the other people, you had agreed actually to take part in the play before you came?'

Malloch answered both question and implication. 'Yes, I did not think I should feel awkward in it. There was to be sober company enough.' Which was true. There could be no ground for saying that he had shown a suspiciously unprofessorial levity in getting himself where Auldearn's murderer had been – in the play.

'By the way, you knew the family?'

'I knew the Duchess slightly. But I came, as I have said, chiefly through the instrumentality of Mr Gott.'

'You knew Lord Auldearn?'

'We were students together at Edinburgh. And we have met fairly frequently since.'

'And you know Mr Cope well?'

'Cope? Only by reputation. I am not aware of having met him before.'

'I see. I thought you might be friends, since you were going up to visit him on the upper stage, it seems, almost at the moment of Lord Auldearn's death. Might your visit to him not have disturbed the play?'

'I was merely going to stand in the shadow for a moment and glance at his canvas. He had invited me to do that earlier, when we were having some talk on the progress he could make during the performance.'

Appleby knew this to be true and that it was one of Malloch's strongest cards. But it was wholly without emphasis that Malloch laid it on the table.

'But you did not actually go up?'

'No. I was half-way up the little staircase – I suppose there are no more than a dozen steps – when I heard the shot. I stood still for a few seconds wondering what could have happened. Then I smelt gun-powder and guessed it was something serious. I turned back and got down just as a number of people were hurrying up. I understand that none of them noticed me come down the staircase. There was a good deal of confusion.'

'Quite so,' said Appleby. 'But here you were, sir, remarkably close to the actual crime; closer perhaps than anyone except Mr Bose. You cannot help us in any way; you have no information, nothing to suggest?'

Malloch took time. 'I have no special information or you would have had it despite our delayed interview' – he smiled gravely at Appleby – 'long ago. And my thinking on the subject is unlikely to have done more than parallel your own – if that. Primarily, I should conceive that the number of spaced-out acts committed by the criminal would be a great factor in his detection.'

This sounded like confidence – but it might be bluff. 'Yes, we must come to that presently. But my mind is on *Hamlet*; on the fact that Lord Auldearn died in the middle of *Hamlet*. I wondered if, with your knowledge of the play, you could help us there?'

'I don't think I can,' said Malloch.

'I was thinking particularly of motive. Here is an imaginative criminal –'

'A gratuitous assumption, inspector. Say a fanciful criminal.'

Appleby accepted this academic correction smoothly. 'Here then is a criminal of fanciful or fantastic mind. He kills Lord Auldearn in fanciful or fantastic circumstances; accepts a good deal of risk in order to do so. Why?'

'Conceivably because the criminal, like Hamlet, thinks of himself as in pursuit of vengeance. To kill his man in the middle of the play would be – in a rough and ready and a fantastic way – to say so.'

There was a silence. Then Appleby renewed: 'Thinking along those lines – which I confess have occurred to me – can one get any further? Can one qualify, for instance, the sort of vengeance with which Hamlet – and thus conceivably our criminal – is concerned?'

Malloch responded slowly but without hesitation. 'It is a tenuous line, perhaps, but certainly one can carry further – and in more than one direction. There is, for instance, the motive of Hamlet's vengeance: the theme of fratricide, incest, and usurpation punished. In the criminal here you might look for something equivalent to that. Or you might neglect the motive of Hamlet's vengeance and consider its character. Predominantly, it is a procrastinated revenge. That is what has always been debated about *Hamlet*: why the delay?'

This time there was a longer silence. Malloch was as steady as a rock. It was clear that he had the whole case against himself in his mind and had deliberately made the discussion of it inevitable. Had he some power in reserve? Appleby greatly feared he had: an unshakable alibi in Aberdeen. He took up another line.

'Mr Malloch, the safest way to commit murder is colourlessly: a shot in a lonely place, a knife in a crowd. When a murder takes place in curious circumstances – as Lord Auldearn's has done – there are two likely explanations. One we have touched on. The criminal, a person perhaps of unbalanced mind, wishes to actualize some fantasy, to kill startlingly or grotesquely. The other explanation of a murder accompanied by odd and striking circumstances is that there has been an attempt to involve an innocent person – a plant or frame up. The marked peculiarities of circumstance are there because they point at somebody. You follow me?'

'I suspect,' said Malloch, 'that I precede you.'

Colonel Sandford blinked at the grimly facetious repartee; Mason stolidly took notes; Appleby said, 'I believe you do.' And there was another silence.

'If you are inviting my opinion,' Malloch continued presently, 'on the likelihoods of an attempted plot to incriminate an innocent man, I will give it. I think it unlikely.'

This was too cool. Appleby came abruptly into the open. 'I suggest that some unknown person – having read Anderson's book or being possessed of other information – shot Auldearn after having concocted all this *Hamlet, revenge!* business in order to incriminate yourself, Professor Malloch. You think that unlikely?'

Malloch inclined his head gravely. 'You no doubt wish to suggest that it is a theory that should have its attractions for me. Maybe so. But as one a good deal accustomed to weigh evidence I cannot accept it.'

'Will you tell us why?'

'Certainly. My first reason is that it is nonsense. There is nobody – knowing Anderson's forthcoming folly or not – who would wish to incriminate me in a murder charge. That is a thing which a man may be presumed to know. Secondly – and this will impress you more – the suggestion will not stand logical examination. In contriving the messages and shooting Auldearn as he did the criminal incurred grave risks. Before he did so he would, we may be sure, want to be reasonably certain of his object – that of incriminating me. Could he be reasonably certain of a situation in which he would be safe and I would be compromised? I think not. And – more conclusively by a long way – his method of incriminating me as you suggest it would be the very way – almost certainly – to let me out. The messages – which are, after all, only a feeble pointer in my direction – would actually be, in all human probability, fatal to the plan. It is inconceivable that he should be so minutely familiar with my movements, minute by minute and hour by hour, as to be certain that for one or more of these messages I had not a solid alibi. And on a single solid alibi the whole risky and laborious plot would break at once. Your kindly suggestion won't hold.'

'I am inclined to agree,' said Appleby. Inwardly, he was contemplating a wall without beer-bottles – and the remote and stony streets of Aberdeen. Neatly enough Malloch had come round to what would be Appleby's breaking-point as well – alibis on the early messages.

'And the fact,' said Malloch quietly, 'that I am possibly uncovered for any of the relevant times is a remarkable circumstance on which your supposed criminal could not conceivably reckon.'

For an instant the words rang meaninglessly in Appleby's ears; then he realized their bearing. 'Ah yes,' he said equally quietly, 'we must come to that now. You will understand that questions intended to establish alibis are of a routine nature and put to everyone.'

'No doubt,' said Malloch.

'That the information with which you are volunteering to help us you may if you wish withhold, or defer until you have taken legal advice.'

'Quite so,' said Malloch.

'And that anything you say will be taken down and may be presented in evidence against you or otherwise.'

'No doubt,' said Malloch.

'And now, if you will be so good, we will work backwards. The attack upon Dr Bunney between nine-thirty and ten o'clock this morning. Nobody has mentioned you as in their company, so I presume –'

'Immediately after breakfast I went to the library and stayed there, alone.'

'Thank you. Did you meet anyone going or coming?'

'No.'

'The murder of Mr Bose between one-forty and two this morning.'

'Shortly after the search in the hall I went to my room and stayed there.'

'Thank you. Most people, of course, did just that. And the time of Lord Auldearn's murder we have discussed. So now we come to the messages. I understand that you came from Aberdeen –'

Malloch calmly took out his watch and looked at it. 'I would not wish,' he said, 'not to change. Perhaps it will shorten matters if I explain that I was in London for over a week before I came down to Scamnum.'

Appleby looked at him very gravely. 'There is a general impression –'

'Quite so. It is a matter of social prevarication. I was pressed to come earlier but, although I looked forward to the play itself, I rather fought shy of long preliminaries. So I pleaded pressure of work in Aberdeen and arranged to come south on the Friday, arriving here after dinner. That was the course of things I actually expected. But I found myself able to get away a week earlier and took the opportunity to go to London and put in the time at the Museum. I then came here on the Friday evening as arranged. And I judged it not necessary to explain my previous movements.'

'In fact you gave it out that you had come straight from Aberdeen?'

'By implication – possibly so.' Malloch was unperturbed.

'There were five messages that we know of. Working backwards again, there was the message on the radio-gramophone early on Sunday morning. I do not suppose that you, more than anybody else sleeping in the house that night, have an alibi for the effecting of that?'

'I am sure I have not.'

'Nor for the message that came through Dr Bunney's apparatus at breakfast on Saturday? I think you had the apparatus explained to you shortly after your arrival on Friday night?'

'Yes. No alibi.'

'Nor – again like everybody else – for the letter posted in the West End to Mr Gylby on Friday?'

'No alibi. And anybody could arrange for such a thing.'

'Quite so. And now, can you detail your movements on Friday – everything before your arrival here?'

'I was at the Museum at ten and worked, under the frequent observation of people who know me, till half past twelve. Then I took a cab to the Athenaeum and kept a luncheon appointment with the Provost of Cudworth – an erratic scholar but a credible witness. He had only an hour; we parted at a quarter to two and then the fine afternoon tempted me to walk in St James's and the Green Park. I took a cab back to the Museum a little after three.'

'You met nobody you knew during this walk?'

'Nobody.'

'You could have been outside Lord Auldearn's flat off Piccadilly a little before two o'clock and tossed a message into his car?'

'If I had known Auldearn's car was standing off Piccadilly I could no doubt have kept an appointment with it.'

'Thank you. There is only one other relevant time, that concerning the telegram sent to Mr Gervase Crispin from Scamnum Ducis. Can you take your mind back to the Monday of that week – eight days ago?'

'Yes,' said Malloch. 'That was the day I went down to Horton Races.'

The lead of Mason's pencil snapped on the page: it might have been a revolver shot. Then Appleby said: 'And you still reject the idea of a plant?'

'Yes. No danger of drowning would make me clutch at it. I am convinced that nothing but coincidence is involved.'

'Will you give us an account of your racegoing experiences?'

But Malloch was not to be shaken by sarcasm. 'Certainly. I like – perhaps because I am a man of the people – to mingle with common life. It is not a matter of curiosity and observation; it is just that I like a vulgar crowd. I keep it a private foible – a matter of occasionally slipping away. And on the Monday I simply went down with the crush on the excursion train, mingled with the crowd on the course, and returned as I went.'

'And you met, of course, no one whom you knew?'

'Fortunately not. Or perhaps unfortunately not. For I take it I really am one of those who fulfil all the conditions you want – who could, in fact, have done everything?' Malloch was stony still but pale.

'Professor Malloch, supposing all these acts to be by one hand, you are the only person who could be responsible.' Appleby paused. Then, in a deadly stillness, he enumerated: 'The two murders, the assault on Bunney, the five messages –'

Sharply, the house-telephone interrupted: an urgent buzzing at his side. Appleby picked up the instrument. 'Hullo –' His chair fell backwards with a crash; he sprang to his feet. He depressed the receiver-arm, released it, was calling urgently: 'House-exchange ... where was that call from ... where ... ?'

He put the instrument down, looked at his companions. 'The sixth message,' he said; 'another line from *Hamlet* and again about revenge: "*The croaking raven doth bellow for revenge.*" It looks as if there may be miching mallecho still.'

Mason put his notebook in his pocket; Sandford swore. 'Where from?' he cried. 'In heaven's name – did they know?'

Appleby hesitated. 'Well, sir,' he said, 'plainly not from Professor Malloch.'

And he ran from the room.

Ten minutes later Appleby came downstairs and ran into a gracefully dinner-jacketed Gott.

'Now that Sandford's here I daren't approach,' said Gott. 'How are things?'

'Backwards. No beer-bottles sitting on the wall. Malloch was the last and he's just had his accidental fall. So it's as you prophesied. As far as a one-man show goes everybody is eliminated. Conspiracy is now the word.'

Gott shook his head. 'If I prophesied that I was wrong. And I don't think I did. My point was that in all this eliminating business there were too many quirks. One might trip. And one has. I can find you a single-handed murderer yet.'

Appleby stared at his friend. 'The dickens you can! And, I suppose, tell me all about the sixth message?'

'There's been a sixth message? Perhaps I can tell you what it was. "*The croaking raven doth bellow for revenge.*" '

Appleby fairly jumped. 'Giles! how did you know?'

'By applying your own favourite method, John. Elimination.'

Appleby took him by the arm. 'This,' he said, 'is where the shy scholar has a quiet talk with the police.'

6

'I am sure,' said Colonel Sandford, square before the fireplace and speaking in a politely diffident yet discreetly fatherly way, 'that it has been a very trying time for you all – very trying indeed.'

The arrest had been made; the news had gone round; the first stupe-faction was abated, and in its place was dawning an enormous relief: the nightmare of uncertainty and suspense was over. And now at half past nine the Chief Constable had collected a small group of people in the little drawing-room. Plainly he was pleased – exultant in the knowledge that he had taken action and that there was calm in Whitehall. But he was decently subdued, semi-official to just that degree which becomes a soldier playing policeman at Scamnum Court – in fact altogether correct. The Duke might have repented about his dispositions in the matter of port.

'A time of bewilderment and anxiety,' amplified Colonel Sandford, 'and I think you are entitled to some explanation of how the matter has been cleared up.' He considered for a moment. 'That is perhaps a prejudicial expression – let me say rather – entitled to an explanation of how we have reached our present position. And as all of you here will, in the nature of the thing, be required as witnesses I don't think I ought to risk the appearance of laying down the police case to you now. It might not be quite correct – not *quite* correct. But I am going to ask Mr Gott – who pieced things together, you know, pieced them together – to give you his own brief outline of the affair. If you would be so good, Mr Gott.'

Mr Gott looked as if he had very little impulse to be so good. But around the room was a little circle of expectant faces from which there was no decent escape; to decline would be the part of a conjuror who walks off the stage with a much-advertised trick still in his pocket. Gott edged himself a little further into the shadow of a generous chair and began cautiously and informally.

'The affair has been full of contradictions; even now it's difficult to thread one's way through them. For instance, there was all the appearance of premeditated murder – and of murder heralded, almost literally, by a blast of trumpets. But I don't know that murder was intended. And I am quite certain that there was no intention of shooting Lord Auldearn.

It was when one had a first suspicion of that, indeed, that one might have seen a first gleam of positive light.'

A murmur, discreet and fragile as the Ming and 'Tang about the walls, ran round the little drawing-room – a muted version of the expectant buzz that greets the entrance of the Disappearing Lady.

'Again, the mystery appeared baffling. But in a sense it wasn't meant to be that. And it was when one got the idea that it wasn't meant to be baffling that there was a chance of its ceasing to baffle. If that is rather enigmatic I will put it this way. The thing was theatrical. It had, as we all felt from the first, an element of showmanship or display. Just what was being displayed? On that question I was present at an interesting conversation between Mr Appleby and Sir Richard Nave. We explored the notion that a motive was being displayed, that the peculiar circumstances in which Lord Auldearn died constituted a cryptic but very real manifesto of motive. Well, there was the motive – already declared in the messages – of revenge. And taking the central problem of *Hamlet* into account we hit on the conception of delayed revenge. We were not altogether astray there, for that notion did, I think, come in. Nevertheless the pursuit of a displayed motive was, in a way, an obscuring factor. It obscured the question: Was anything else displayed?

'And failing an answer to that question, a solution was, I believe, a very long way off. Mr Appleby, after analysing the entire series of events with which he had been confronted, came to the conclusion that an element of conspiracy was essential in the case. And he was finally faced with a considerable number of people – I think ten – any one of whom might have been Auldearn's murderer, but each one of whom would have required a confederate to carry out one or more of the other actions which appeared to be bound up with the case. Now, inquiry strictly along those lines would eventually have exhausted itself – for the simple reason that there *was* no conspiracy. And after that it would have been natural to inquire by what device the criminal succeeded in doing everything himself while making it appear impossible that he could have done everything without a confederate. But that inquiry would have been unsuccessful too, because it would have been wrongly grounded. The facts are these: it appeared to Mr Appleby that no one of the persons involved could have done everything; actually one of the persons involved could have done everything; but the appearance to the contrary was something not devised by the criminal but fortuitous.

'I say, then, that a solution was far off – failing an answer to that obscured question: Was anything else besides motive deliberately displayed? And that question was not adequately pursued; it just happened that at a certain stage an answer to it thrust itself under my own nose. You will see the point that I am making here – though to make it is really to anticipate. There has been in this affair an element of deliberate duel. The criminal displayed certain things which one might or might not spot – introduced, in fact, a perverted sporting element. And in the whole conduct of the affair the criminal made no mistake: only where a clue was offered has a clue been found.

'But now let me take up certain questions in the order in which they presented themselves.

'Why was Lord Auldearn killed in the middle of *Hamlet*? That was the first question and one couldn't look at it long before feeling it to be insufficiently precise. It was better altered to: Why was Lord Auldearn killed at Act III, Scene iv, line 23 of the Scamnum *Hamlet*? For then there was an obvious answer: Because Lord Auldearn was alone in a small enclosed space, and because at that moment he was expected by everyone within ear-shot to act in a particular way. *He was expected to call for help.*

'Now, from technical evidence – a matter, I believe, of slight powder marks – we know that Lord Auldearn was shot at fairly close range. Barring a suggestion that he was shot from above, it is certain that the murderer walked out to the middle of the rear stage. That gave a second question. Why did the murderer do this? Why forsake the safety of the curtains, from the shelter of which it would be possible to shoot, and walk out under the possible observation of the prompter? Three things suggested an answer: the messages; the answer to the first question; and a certain haunting memory, confessed to by Mr Appleby, of the ballet called *Les Présages*. Mr Appleby's memory was of Fate or Destiny, a figure of whom one suddenly becomes aware as standing, threatening, on the edge of the stage. Fate, retribution, revenge – you see how Mr Appleby's mind had moved. And you see, too, what was designed to happen on the rear stage. The avenger, who had already so explicitly threatened Auldearn in the message thrown into the car, was to step boldly out – at whatever substantial risk of observation by Mr Bose – and confront the victim. And you see the peculiar pleasure proposed. In those agonized seconds in which Auldearn recognized his attacker and his attacker's intention he would be helpless. He might cry out for assistance in the instinctive words that would come on such an occasion – and not a soul in all the hall would take it to be other than as Polonius that he was calling. "What, ho! Help, help, help!" That, structurally, was why the murder occurred where it did in *Hamlet*, and to that any decorative notion of a manifesto of motive inhering in the play was secondary. It was a diabolically-conceived thing.'

Gott paused – and paused amid a dead silence. For a moment the nightmare had darkened even as it was being dissipated. But presently the quiet, almost reluctant voice continued.

'I believe that Mr Appleby – though he will say nothing about it – had arrived at all this long before I had. But the next point was peculiarly my opportunity. Just as he had an obstinate sense of that fleeting parallelism with *Les Présages*, so I had an obstinate sense that – somehow and in terms of our own show – the thing hadn't gone right. The effect had not been as it should be. I puzzled over this and could make no headway with it for a considerable time. As directed against Lord Auldearn the thing had been perfectly effective. And then I saw that there was something lacking to it in another aspect – its aspect as something presented to the audience. For something was assuredly being presented to the audience; we are all certain of the sense of showmanship involved. An artist was at work and I felt – being keyed up, I suppose, in matters of theatrical effect – that something had fallen out as this very formidable mind could not have designed. And I hunted it down at last. It was the way the murder announced itself in a pistol-shot. The pistol-shot was startling enough – but how much more effective if Hamlet had simply drawn back the curtain in the normal course of the play and found Polonius – Auldearn – really dead! Why was Auldearn killed so noisily – why not, for instance, quietly stabbed and left for Hamlet to reveal to the audience? I looked at that question for a time and thought I found it, as you may find it, fanciful – a mere imaginative refinement. So I put it by. I didn't realize that in contemplating it I was contemplating the heart of the case.' Gott paused again. 'I didn't realize,' he added – absorbed and wholly unconscious of contriving a grotesque effect – 'the essential connection between Auldearn's having been shot and Mr Appleby's friend Happy Hutton's not having left a hat at Scamnum after all.'

There was another silence. Somewhere at the back of the room Peter Marryat, who had slipped in uninvited, sighed in perplexity. All this was running away from him.

'I don't know that one could have hit on the truth at that point. But in the early hours of this morning I overheard a conversation which really should have given a key. If either Mr Appleby or I had contrived to leap upon that we should have solved the mystery in something like a dramatic manner – and not, as it has been solved, on evidence which the murderer, in that pervertedly sporting manner, has deliberately provided.

'Now let me turn for a moment to motive. The pursuit of motive, I have said, in a sense obscured one question – the question of other things that the murderer might have built into the manifesto, the display. Nevertheless the pursuit of motive did take us somewhere. The crime – the original murder of Auldearn to which the subsequent murder of Bose was merely consequential – seemed to be a passional crime; one, likely enough, of revenge or retribution such as the face-value of the messages suggested. Revenge or retribution over what? And, if one of the implications of the *Hamlet* situation was to be accepted, delayed or suspended revenge over what?

'I think Mr Appleby, though conscious of the structural reason for Auldearn's death taking place where it did – the getting the victim, I mean, in a situation in which he could call for help in vain – retained some faith in what may be called the manifesto-significance of the situation. He took as dominant in the play the notion of delay and then tried to interpret the crime as an act of vengeance for a certain personal injury that occurred a very long time ago indeed. But for my part, I was impressed by something said by Sir Richard Nave in a conversation I have already mentioned. He implied, I took it, that a very long-delayed revenge would be – at least at a certain intellectual level – surprising, unless the cause of the supposed injury were still in some way present: he instanced a stolen thing still flaunted. Now, in the case Mr Appleby was tentatively constructing, and which I need not particularize, there had been – according to a legend that came his way from Mr Tucker – a stolen thing. But there was every reason to suppose that this stolen thing had disappeared from the picture long ago. So I was inclined to ponder another suggestion Nave put forward. Delayed revenge, he suggested, might be the consequence of some deadly and irreconcilable ideological conflict which had extended over many years. I say that interested me. For whereas Mr Appleby's theory involved a young and passionate Ian Stewart from very long ago – too long ago, it seemed to me – this other suggestion might involve the contemporary Lord Auldearn – I mean the statesman, the philosopher – and the man who sometimes invoked his power as a statesman to enforce his philosophy in its practical implications. In fact I felt that, seeking some such motive as this, I was approaching – if only approaching – psychological probability in respect of the intellectually and speculatively inclined people gathered in this house. You will say that men do not commit murder to defend an ideological position – much less as a sort of demonstration in its favour; they commit murder out of fear or cupidity or some variety of sexual passion. But perhaps that is not fully to take account of our time.'

Gott hesitated, as if seeking some brief expression of what lay in his mind. 'All over the world today are we not facing a rising tide of ideological intolerance, and are not violence and terrorism more and more in men's thoughts? And this dressing-up of the lawless and the primitive as a ruthless-because-right philosophy or world-picture or ideology that must and will prevail – is this not something to haunt and hold naturally unstable men, whatever their particular belief may be? The modern world is full of unwholesome armies of martyrs and inquisitors. We bind ourselves together by the million and sixty million to hate and kill – kill, as we persuade ourselves, for an idea. Are we to be surprised if here and there an individual kills simply because he hates – and simply because he hates an idea?

'At this point it would I believe have been possible, granted a good enough brain, to solve the mystery. But I was far from having such a brain and Mr Appleby, all this time, was preoccupied with an alien, but very grave matter on which I shall presently have to touch. And so the solution came not dramatically but by chance. I say chance without exaggerating one iota. It so happens that the criminal has a certain relative. That relative does not impinge upon the case in the least. But if that relative did not exist, we might never have discovered – and it is a humiliating thought – that the criminal had boldly signed to the murder, not once, but again and again.'

★

Slowly, the little drawing-room was dissolving into shadow; the last glow from the west had climbed to touch the shoulders of Whistler's Anne Dillon by the piano and disappeared; the blue and silver nocturnes, the early *pointillist* Copes, the hot and flashing Dillons were swimming together on the walls. A cooler breeze stirred at the open window, whispered through a great bowl of flowers, caused somebody to slip timidly from the window-seat to a warmer place. And Gott's voice talked on, remote, growing colder ...

'If Sir Richard Nave, I say, did not have a brother – a brother who like himself practises medicine – he would be unsuspected still.

'He invited suspicion. I believe that he knew his own craziness; that the sporting chance he gave represented his own sane self, looking with his own scientific ruthlessness at his own growing madness and endeavouring to ensure that the madman should not escape. Perhaps that is too subtle, too much one of the quiddities of his own craft. We shall never know. And I do not forget that in a legal sense Nave is not mad, is very far from mad; I don't deny that in the last issue he is not a criminal lunatic, but a criminal.

'He invited suspicion in a series of displays, not insinuating his motive cryptically but declaring his identity almost outright. These displays – I mean, of course, the messages – were investigated diligently enough. But that very diligence tended to hide the key they contained. The questions Mr Appleby asked about the messages were: *When?* and *How?* When were they sent? In what manner? Which one of the possibly suspect persons could have contrived this message and that? There was, of course, another question: *Why* the messages? But the answer seemed so obvious that one didn't pause over this aspect long. The messages were simply the showman-criminal's way of announcing his purpose. *Hamlet, revenge!* That was the first message – the one sent to Mr Crispin at the House of Commons – and there seems nothing to pause over. It is simple and appropriate, conjoining menace and the projected play. Next Lord Auldearn's message is seen, in the light of later events, to add to this a grim dramatic appropriateness; in the car that brought him beneath the walls of Scamnum were found Lady Macbeth's words on another fated victim:

> The raven himself is hoarser,
> That croaks the fatal entrance of Duncan
> Under my battlements.

'The next message, that to Mr Gylby, was a couple of lines from *Titus Andronicus* – lines which did no more than reiterate the idea of revenge:

> And in their ears tell them my dreadful name,
> Revenge, which makes the foul offender quake.

' "Foul offender" gave perhaps something more. Nevertheless it was at this message, I think, that Mr Appleby paused to ask a very acute question: Why *all* these messages? They were not all equally effective; why should this criminal, so careful of his effects, send as many as five messages of varying effectiveness? Mr Appleby's answer was certainly accurate: the diversity of messages was a challenge. The criminal was saying in effect: "See how many messages I can send – each in a different way – and get away with it." But there was another question besides the question: Why so many messages? There was the question: Why just *these* messages?

'And this question should have become clamant with the next message – the message that came through Dr Bunney's philological box: *I will not cry Hamlet Revenge*. The method of delivering the message was effective but the message itself seems pointless. What point, again in the light of subsequent events, could be thought to attach to that re-cantation? And at this stage I must say that I am ashamed of myself. My mind failed to go at once to the source of this message. And with a sort of obstinacy with which Professor Malloch, perhaps, will sympathize, I avoided looking it up. I didn't see the matter as significant and I wasn't going to be beaten over something I certainly knew. Actually, the phrase *I will not cry Hamlet Revenge* comes from Rowland's *The Night Raven*. The fact came back to me in the instant that I happened to glance at Nave's telegram – a telegram he had despatched through the police this morning, putting off a patient. Commonly one signs a telegram with one's surname only; but because Nave has a brother, also a practising physician, he has a different habit. And I looked at the signature "*R. Nave*" and saw the anagram at once.'

There was a little pause. Peter Marryat, too enthralled to be diffident, called out: 'I say – please – what's an anagram?'

'When you take the letters constituting "*R. Nave*",' said Gott soberly, 'and form from them the word "*Raven*", you make an anagram. In other words, Nave had – if in the rather tortuous way that is characteristic of the modern medical psychologist's mind – set his signature to two of the original five messages – indeed to three. The raven was hoarser; *The Night Raven* was quoted; and the second passage from Macbeth – the one that came through the radio-gramophone in the night – was cut off by me just before it spoke – if not actually of the raven again – of the *crow* and the *rooky* wood. When Mr Appleby told me this evening that a sixth message had been received I was able to guess the very words. For there was one message, the most pat of all, that had not come – a passage in which the raven and revenge and *Hamlet* are all bound up together. Most of you will remember what I mean – Hamlet's exclamation in the play scene: *The croaking raven doth bellow for revenge.* Mr Appleby had half-expected a further message. And these words of Hamlet's were actually spoken to him over the telephone a few hours ago – and spoken, as the man in the house-exchange was able to tell him, from Nave's own room. When Mr Appleby hurried up there he found Nave's own Shakespeare beside the telephone and open at the page. And a fraction of an inch below the line in question treatment revealed the fresh imprint of the index-finger of Nave's right hand. Which was the end – or all but the end – of the affair. There was something in Nave, I repeat, that would not let the murderer get away. He gave the police their clue and then, when they appeared to be making no headway, he gave it them again. *The croaking raven doth bellow for revenge.*'

Gott stirred in his chair. 'I said all but the end of the case. Even at this stage there was a snag. But before I come to that let me put briefly what I think occurred, and bring in some important matters which I haven't yet mentioned: for instance the iron cross.

'But for the iron cross there might, I believe, have been no murders. And but for the iron cross there would not have been that hitch to the affair in its aspect as something presented to the audience. But I must begin at the beginning.

'Here, then, is Lord Auldearn, a veritable symbol of a certain old order of things. He is, I say, a statesman, a philosopher, and a theologian. His writings are famous; to be found on most thoughtful people's shelves – including I know, Mr Appleby's. And here again is Sir Richard Nave, another typical figure – a scientist, a hard-boiled nominalist, an aggressive atheist – as many of you know who have conversed with him – and a life-long contemner of superstition, priests, priestcraft, and all the rest of it. What then happens? Does Nave decide to make away with this symbol of all that stands against him? I think not. But he does something else. Partly from some necessity of his own inner nature and partly – I have suggested – worked upon by the ideological terrorisms of our time, he begins to weave a fantasy of destruction round the figure of Auldearn. Two phrases of his stick in my head – I think they were spoken with reference to crime stories and crime films: "a healthy resolving of suppressed criminal tendencies in fantasy" and "safety-valves". Now it may be possible that inventing imaginary crimes is a "healthy resolving" and the rest of it – I don't know. But what Nave did was something different: he began envisaging a crime against a real person whom he really hated. To imagine that that was a safety-valve was just bad psychology. And the moment came when the impulse stepped outside the borders of fantasy and began to actualize itself – actualized itself by degrees.

'This is what I meant by saying that the murder was, in a sense, not premeditated. Even when the messages were sent the position was no more than this: that the fantasy had got ominously out of hand. I don't know when Nave provided himself with a revolver, but it would be to that action that I should point if I had to indicate the moment at which unreason got the upper hand. He was arming himself against eventualities.

'But – as I have said – he didn't mean to shoot Auldearn; the revolver was a precaution. What held him, and now impelled him forward, was the unique dramatic opportunity, the opportunity to confront Auldearn in the very character of Nemesis and kill him in the moment that he was calling in vain for help. I think he meant to stab Auldearn, just as Bose was stabbed; to stab him, and leave the body for Hamlet to find. It was a compelling fantasy; you may say that the circumstances were conspiring to unbalance him finally. But even yet it might have remained fantasy merely and the messages a harmless folly that would never have been explained. It was the arrival of the cross that was fatal.

'Here, ready to hand on the faldstool, was to stand a heavy iron cross. To what a terrific power would the representative, the ritual power of the act be raised if he should snatch up this symbol and with it dash out his victim's brains! So he abandoned whatever dagger he had meant to use – but the revolver he retained against emergency.

'Why, then, did the plan miscarry? Why the shot? Ideally, it would have been possible to arrive at the answer – and in consequence to get very near to the identity of the criminal – on the strength of two things I have mentioned: an overheard conversation; and the hat that was not Happy Hutton's hat. Briefly, Mr Appleby found a hat in Lord Auldearn's room and concluded it was not Auldearn's because it was bigger than Auldearn's other hats. But there is a certain condition in which one's new hat will be bigger than one's old: it is if one happens to suffer from Paget's disease.'

If Gott relished the odd turn his narrative was taking he gave no sign. His voice flowed on without emphasis. 'Lord Auldearn was gravely ill. But why was there such passion behind a technical diagnostic discussion between Nave and Dr Biddle – a conversation overheard by Mr Appleby and myself in the hall? I can remember what they said. "Clearly the localized form," Nave said, "*Leontiasis Ossium.*" And Dr Biddle replied "*Leontiasis* fiddlestick . . . simple generalized Paget's." And over that Nave was passionately angry. Why? Well, I need not and cannot be technical. Put it this way. What, in effect, Nave was saying was, "At the moment I was going to strike my rather rusty general medicine came back to me; I saw that I was proposing to crack a morbidly sick, morbidly hard, and ivory-like skull: as I couldn't risk failing to kill I dropped the cross and shot instead." And what Dr Biddle replied was, in effect, "You were wrong; the skull was certainly abnormally thick; but it was far from being abnormally hard – rather the reverse." In other words, Nave used the revolver as he did, and in doing so marred his intended effect, because, suddenly becoming conscious of Auldearn's morbid condition, more precise knowledge failed him in the sort of lightning diagnosis he then made. He supposed himself to be in the act of hitting at something like a billiard-ball. Actually it was not so; he might have hit out effectually enough. And his vanity was injured by the mistake. Dr Biddle tells me that if Nave's general medicine had not been distinctly in disrepair he would have recognized the significance of Auldearn's bowed walk and other symptoms long ago.

'This matter of the changed plan is the most remarkable feature of the case. It is the one point at which the criminal came up against the unexpected and the one point at which he might have been caught on ground – so to speak – other than that which he voluntarily gave away. The right man – an acute medical jurist, I suppose – hearing this technical conversation in the hall, might just conceivably have got somewhere on the strength of it. At any rate, it is the point at which the sheerly bizarre is most evident in the case; in telling a story for effect one would stop at it. Nevertheless, there is another matter of some importance that I must explain.

'Even with all this there was a snag – a hitch in the case against Nave. Mr Appleby, you remember, had got to a stage in his investigations at which he had ruled out the possibility of single-handed crime. Reviewing the events linked up with Auldearn's death in relation to what was known and provable about people's movements, he found that nobody could have done everything. The murderer must have had an accomplice. Had Nave, then, an accomplice? The sort of crime which we are imputing to him – a crime actualizing a private fantasy – is not the sort of crime in which one would expect conspiracy. What, then, was the exact position? It could not be shown that Nave was unable to send any of the messages. It could not be shown that he was unable to murder Auldearn. It could not be shown that he was unable to murder Bose. But it could be conclusively shown that he was unable to attack Dr Bunney. At the moment that attack was made Nave was talking with Lady Elizabeth, Mr Appleby, and myself in the hall. It would seem at first logical to look for the accomplice that Nave must have had. But he had no accomplice.

'Consider the relationship of all these events on which Mr Appleby was relying in his eliminative process. The messages, plainly, hold together among themselves and cohere with Auldearn's murder. Unmistakably, the person who sent them was directly concerned in that murder. Next take the death of Mr Bose. Of that only one explanation was found to be reasonably tenable: he was killed because he knew something about Auldearn's killing. But now we come to the attack on Dr Bunney.

'Was this attack, equally with the other events, bound up with the original murder? The accepted version took it that this was so. At breakfast this morning Mr Clay happened to suggest that Bunney's apparatus, being a phonetic instrument of unusual precision, might hold a clue. It might be possible to identify the voice which, carefully disguised, had delivered through it the message *I will not cry Hamlet Revenge*. And at this – it was suggested – the murderer took alarm and shortly afterwards attacked Dr Bunney in order to obtain the potentially incriminating cylinder. To support this interpretation is the fact that after the attack the cylinder in question, indexed as "The curious message", was found to have disappeared. But it has to be asked whether this is the only conceivable explanation of the attack on Bunney, whether it is the best explanation one can suggest, whether it is a good, or even possible explanation. Why, for instance, half-murder a man in order to filch from his room something that might have been stolen without violence? There was plenty of time for such a theft between Mr Clay's remark at breakfast and Bunney's going to his room. Well, I think it can be shown that the attack upon Bunney was no part of the murderer's work, nor of an accomplice's; that it belongs to another affair altogether.

'It is common knowledge now that the events we have experienced have been complicated by an alarm of espionage. Lord Auldearn had in his possession an important paper, the safety of which was feared for. Actually, the paper was not in danger; nevertheless, the alarm was not baseless. Spies – and spies indeed seeking that paper – there have been amongst us; their possible activities formed that grave preoccupation of Mr Appleby's of which I spoke. They were ineffective, however, at their job; they had nothing to do with the murders; and they have been thought of as having dropped out of the story. But they do make this one and not altogether ineffective appearance at the end. For the attack on Dr Bunney represents their last attempt to get the paper.

'Let me ask two questions. Exactly how was Bunney attacked? He was hit on the head from behind in a darkish corridor outside his room. Where was this paper when he was attacked? In Mr Appleby's pocket. Please look at Mr Appleby.'

Electric lights snapped on. Everybody stared at Appleby. It was an eminently successful if slightly flamboyant effect that Gott had allowed himself at the end of his recital.

'You see what I mean at once. The first thing I casually mentioned to Mr Appleby when speaking of Bunney was the fact of a certain resemblance to himself. And the same thing, Mr Appleby tells me, misled Rauth, the steward, this morning. The spies, then, guessing that the document had been transferred to Mr Appleby's possession, made one last throw. But the person they thought was Mr Appleby going to Bunney's room to investigate the business of the cylinder was actually Bunney himself. And when they found that their plan had miscarried they very adroitly stole the "curious message" cylinder, thus removing suspicion of the attack from themselves and transferring it to the murderer. With the realization of this simple sequence of events Nave's last defence breaks down.'

A long silence in the little drawing-room was presently broken by an advancing tinkling sound from without.

'Ah,' said the Duke. 'Whisky? Well – come, come.'

4 Epilogue

What, has this thing appear'd again tonight?

'Yes, they've gone all right,' said Noel, peering through. 'And very naturally too. It's all settled now except for the chaplain's final snuffle over the fallen infidel.'

'*Get on!*' said Diana fiercely. And she thrust Noel before her into the hall.

Gott stared at Appleby. 'You mean you would have held your hand? You didn't find it convincing?'

Appleby wandered restlessly – oddly expectantly – about the room. 'There was no holding my hand when you'd spilt Sandford all that. And, of course, it was convincing – overwhelmingly so. Only, my dear Giles, you were having it all your own way. One thing was lacking.'

'That being?'

'A competent criminal lawyer to laugh you out of court.' Appleby's tone was dry but without rancour.

'It's as bad as that?'

'Well, consider the business of Auldearn's skull. Is that going to be convincing – convincing in court, with a subtle mind working against it?'

'It all fits.'

'Quite so. I think it is a triumph. But do you think they'll miss the point that it's a triumph of your own craft – a bit of ingenious fiction? It *may* have been so. It sounds beautiful. But there is just no shred of evidence that Nave ever picked up that cross or thought about the consistency of Auldearn's skull or spoilt a dramatic effect by outing with a revolver. Counsel wouldn't be at it for ten minutes before it was just a lovely picture in the air.'

'You don't believe –'

'But never mind about me! It's my job to think of a judge and jury. And when I do that in this business I'm scared. Say I want evidence.'

'The messages.'

'Planted.'

'Nave's fresh finger-print on the line "*the croaking raven doth bellow for revenge*". You find that three minutes after the message had come

from his room. It's that that's conclusive. As you said yourself: finger-
prints still catch criminals by the pint. Nave knew to leave nothing
on the revolver or cross; but running his finger down a page of Shakespeare – he never thought.'

'Yes, that finger-print' – Appleby was kicking absently at an imaginary
object on the carpet – 'it was on the strength of that finger-print that
I gave a sort of agreement to Sandford's acting. To put it ignobly:
if Nave is tried and acquitted that finger-print will save me from
ignominy.' He stood stockstill. 'He says he was in his bath.'

'At the moment of the sixth message? But what does he say about
the print?'

Appleby shook an almost indulgent head. 'Bless us, he doesn't know
of that yet. That's to keep a bit. And I promise you it needs adding
to. Evidence needed – that's the word. By the way, Giles, about the
motive – you don't think you were a bit carried away?'

'Perhaps I ran it up a bit.'

'Quite so. What an unstable world we live in nowadays. And therefore
did one Richard Nave, Knight, having one set of convictions, feloniously
kill one Ian Stewart, Baron Auldearn, having –'

'Really, John.'

'All right. But I'm only putting what will be put in court. They
will boil it down to look just like that. And what evidence have we?
With Malloch we had at least an actual deadly feud about which we
could have brought witnesses. But with Nave we have no single specific
record of his having cherished one fleeting impulse of hatred for
Auldearn from the moment of his birth to this. What you say about
the power of impersonal, ideological hatreds may be abundantly true.
But the jury aren't going to be what you called "intellectually and
speculatively inclined men". They're going to be butchers and bakers
– perhaps fortunately so. And they're going to be thoroughly disconcerted when they're told that there is no personal or private element
in the affair and that Nave is a murderer because he is a hard-boiled
nominalist who rejects the validity of the subjectively apprehended
epistemological problem of –'

'I don't –'

'But that's what they'll say! And I put it to you myself that the motive's
weak. It came partly from your own habit of mind, Giles. For talking
of hatred, nobody hates a forthright, aggressive atheist like Nave so

much as a muzzy and apologetic agnostic, consciously steeped in the benefits of Christian tradition, like yourself.'

Gott ran quick fingers through his hair. 'That's fair enough,' he said. 'I believe you could presently persuade me that I've made an unholy ass of myself.'

'It's a matter of us, not you. But the point is – evidence. Just put it at that at present: we're short of evidence.'

'Yes, but I want your own conviction now, John. Taking the case against Nave as I outlined it, is there anything you blankly disbelieve?'

'Yes, there is – and it's what makes me feel that we're not through yet – certainly that without more evidence we shall be lost in court. I don't think you really got round to the snag – the business of Bunney, I mean, and Nave's undoubted alibi for that. I admit the full force of your main position there: Why a murderous attack when a simple theft was possible? But beyond that I can't go. I don't see these spies tracking me about Scamnum. And whatever you and your precious, short-sighted Rauth may say, I don't see myself as that Bunney's double. If it were a case of real doubles – like the Terborg girls, for instance – I could swallow the story. But the fact that there is a resemblance is not good enough. Before hitting a man on the head like that, one makes sure. It's what counsel would detect as another tinge of fiction about your version. I want a better explanation of Bunney. As it stands, I know it's going to be a weakness in the story.'

Gott looked at Appleby thoughtfully. 'I believe you distrust the story altogether.'

'No.' Appleby spoke very carefully. 'If I had distrusted the story altogether, I would have opposed the arrest – as a matter of principle if not of policy. There is a case against Nave too strong to distrust altogether. His arrest was justified. But I have certain doubts. And at the back of them – to some extent at least – is the fact that the case is yours, Giles – is so brilliantly yours. Don't misunderstand. I'm simply scared by a sense of your extraordinary facility in these matters. You created a magnificent case – or at least a magnificent effect. But some people would say that you could have done the same with half a dozen other suspects.'

'In fact, the irresponsible romancer. It wasn't just like that, you know.'

'I don't say it was. I'm sure you weighed up the probabilities responsibly enough before you let me lead you off to Sandford. But you know what I *do* mean.'

'You mean that my wretched fancy will work on anything. Give it a start and off it goes. Which is true enough. But I've rejected a good many starts because they were plainly nothing more than an invitation to fancy. I've dredged through everything that happened in the past week and all sorts of notions have started up as I did so. Things that this or that person said which the romancer – I suppose – could build on.'

Appleby was still restless – roaming about while pulling heavily at a pipe. 'Yes . . . yes. Such as?'

'Well – Piper; I told you about that. Piper displaying a dark and yearning zest for miching mallecho. One might build on that.'

'Anything else?'

Gott made an irritated gesture. 'Futile fancies,' he said. 'The Duchess, for instance. Coming up the drive in his car, Auldearn said something about the Duchess that might have been a beautiful dramatic irony. The Duchess was one who would work underground for weeks to contrive a minute's perfect effect. And a little later Elizabeth said something equally dark about Bunney: that he was the Spy in Black, black-boxing secrets of state.'

Something snapped. Appleby caught at his pipe as it fell, took the bitten-off mouth-piece from his lips and looked at it. Then he looked at Gott. And then he moved towards the door.

'John, what on earth is it? And where are you off to?'

'It's the truth – the first glimmer of the truth. And I'm off to chum up with Nave. It will be only discreet.'

The door opened as he approached it. Mr Gylby's head appeared. 'I say, may we come in? Diana thinks she's busted the *auto-da-fé*.'

'She's *what*?'

'Spiked the chivvying of infidel Nave. You see –'

'Get on!' said Diana from behind. A moment later she was in the room and had thrust a limp white object at Appleby. 'There!' she said.

Appleby looked at it. 'Yes. But everything, you know, has been examined –'

'Examined!' said Diana. 'Well the examiners haven't got noses. Smell it.'

Appleby smelt it. 'Yes,' he said – and handed it to Gott. Gott sniffed and shook his head. Appleby turned to Noel. 'And you?' Noel, too, shook his head. Appleby tossed the object on a table. 'As one would expect,' he said, 'very faint indeed. And, though Miss Sandys and I detect it, it isn't evidence. But it's a clue.' He turned to Diana. 'It is Mme Merkalova's?'

'It is,' said Diana with deep satisfaction.

'And the confederate' — Appleby made some effort of memory — 'is one of five persons: the Duke, Gervase Crispin, Dr Biddle, Clay, Cope.'

Gott stared at him. 'Why, in heaven's name, these?'

'Because they were the five back-stage people who had some conversation with the Dowager Duchess of Horton.'

Clay and Elizabeth were walking down the long corridor together towards their bedrooms. 'I've been feeling glad it's over,' said Clay; 'but really, of course, it's not over yet. The police-court and the trial and so forth will all be rather horrible.'

'It seems a pity they can't quietly shut him up. It seems the rational thing to do.'

Clay shook his head. 'Possibly so — but only after a trial. Mad or sane, he must have his chance. But mad or sane he's dangerous and — I suppose — tormented. Better dead. I for one will be glad when he's hanged.'

Elizabeth shivered slightly. They had paused at Clay's door. 'I'm afraid,' said Clay, 'you must feel a bit shaken after it all? While there's mystery the tension keeps one going. But afterwards one finds one is badly shocked.'

'No,' said Elizabeth — firmly and with something of Diana's reaction — for Clay's 'one' seemed directed at her sex. 'It hasn't left me shocked. Only distinctly hungry.'

'Bless us! Well, have a biscuit.' And Clay dodged through his door and reappeared with a little silver bedside box.

Elizabeth took a biscuit; then stared in surprise. There were at least a dozen biscuits left. 'Why,' she cried, amused, 'it was you who rifled the pantry and upset Rauth!'

'I know nothing about that,' said Clay.

'But there are never more than six —' Elizabeth glanced at Clay; their eyes met; she stopped. He had made a mistake — the first, perhaps, in the whole affair – and he knew it. And she knew it. And he knew that too.

Elizabeth took a heroic bite at her biscuit. 'Stupid of me,' she said – hardly knowing what the words were. 'And thank you. Good night.' And unhurryingly but with a whirling head she went on to her room.

She closed the door and leant against it, waiting for her brain to stop rotating and come clear. She knew that she had no new knowledge. All along – or ever since Clay had performed those dazzling tricks in the little drawing-room – she had known – something. Now it was simply that her knowledge had been revealed to her . . .

'Silly!' said Elizabeth aloud, and conscious of herself as watchful against hysteria. Then, regardless of her astonished maid, she opened the door and went out again into the corridor. It might be a mere brainstorm. Anyway, she was going to see it through.

Down the corridor and round a corner; once more she was outside Clay's room. She had a momentary impulse to knock at Charles Piper's door opposite. But she suppressed it and raised her hand to knock on Clay's door instead. A voice was speaking within and something – something perhaps in its quality as conveyed in mere murmur through the solid wood – made her pause again. She was suddenly aware that she was on the verge of veritable danger, that common decencies were suspended, that there was a job of work she could do. Her hand, raised against the panel, fell to the door-knob, turned it, gently opened the door a fraction of an inch. And Clay's voice, guarded but vibrant at the house-telephone, came clearly.

'Anna . . . are you alone? Listen. In fifteen minutes – ten perhaps – they'll have it all worked out. Can you make the cow-house straight away . . . you know? Take nothing . . . no . . . there first . . . it's hidden there. Over the wall they'll be cruising round . . . quick now . . .'

Softly, Elizabeth closed the door. *The cow-house straight away . . . hidden there . . . they'll be cruising round . . .* She turned and ran back to her own room, burst in. 'Jean, find the police, Mr Gott, Mr Gylby. Tell them to come to the cow-house at once. *At once* – you understand? Go . . . now!'

Anything might happen at Scamnum in these days. And Jean was from Kincrae; she had been unnerved once by these strange events and was determined not to be so again. 'Yes, my lady,' she said and ran from the room.

Elizabeth kicked off evening slippers and thrust on shoes. Then she ran out and along the corridor, going left to avoid the route by Clay's room. In a minute she was downstairs and out by a side door.

'Run, girls, run!' murmured Elizabeth. Her views on female athletics were Dillon and satiric. But her spirits as she plunged down the terraces were Dillon and Crispin both. She took the final steps with a leap. Her heart was pounding as she ran: *it's hidden there . . . it's hidden there.*

Charles Piper sat in his room and made notes on the events of the day. Having his own ideas of what was interesting and what was not, he was far from giving his attention exclusively to the queer and deplorable affair of Sir Richard Nave. He had enjoyed some conversation with Vanessa Terborg – an interesting type – and he made notes on that. He thought out a short story set in Venice for someone rather like the Duchess, and then changed Venice to Pienza as less hackneyed. And then he thought of Melville Clay.

Of all the people at Scamnum, Clay interested him most. It was not Clay's meteoric career, appearing from nowhere and rising to eminence in a few years; rather it was something integral to the man himself. There was, for instance, that feminine streak . . . the way he had stood that very morning, posed with his back to the window, tilting the little shaving-mirror now here, now there on his face.

Piper frowned; the frown gave place to something startled. In the hall after the murder, when he had glimpsed Clay through the curtain talking to the Dowager Duchess . . . surely there had been some similar impression connected with that? A contrived ease – that was it! an ease of poise and movement that was actually, to a more than commonly sensitive eye, the result of terrific concentration. Why? . . . *why?* And then something further about that fleeting picture in the hall; something that had registered itself just off the focus of consciousness in Piper's then agitated mind . . . something surprising . . . a surprising appearance. *Surely the old lady had been asleep.*

And that mirror . . . Piper leapt to his feet with something like a shout, looked round as if in search of a weapon, then ran out and across the corridor to Clay's door. He paused before it for a moment. Then he opened it and walked straight in – straight into a world of melodrama. Clay was gone. But a lady's maid – Elizabeth's maid – lay bound and gagged upon the carpet.

And Piper whirled into action. He got the girl free, he got the story, he telephoned, he sent her to the police. And then he leapt to the window and vaulted to the sill. He dropped to an architrave, to the *porte cochère*, to the colonnade, to the ground. And ran. His pumps were split and his feet were bruised – but undoubtedly one saved thirty seconds that way.

He ran steadily and well, as people who practise deep breathing are able to do.

2

Elizabeth paused cautiously on the threshold of Duke Peter's picturesque cow-house. It was utterly silent. She was here before them. And with luck the police would be here before them too – catch them in ambush; unless – it was an ugly thought – they were already here in a kind of ambush themselves. And Elizabeth realized that she was standing in idiotic silhouette under the arched doorway. Hastily, she slipped into shadow.

The cow-house, commonly so pleasing an absurdity, was eerie now. A low-riding sliver of moon was fleeting amid gathering clouds; the uncertain light came and went about the bogus ruin, gliding up the steps so ingeniously hollowed as if by generations of pious feet, playing on the crisply chiselled draperies of saints who stood as they had been fashioned without heads or arms. The mouldering tower, no more mouldering than on the day it was built, rose with an impressive appearance of insecurity overhead; the pale ivy stirring about it in the night breeze like myriad-tongued green flame, the bats flitting round, a single owl hooting from some crenellated fastness. All, Elizabeth thought, as Peter would have liked, but unnerving on the present occasion. For a moment the moon went; she slipped inside. It was wholly dark. In a sudden impulse of panic she whirled round on herself, as if a dagger threatened her where a dagger threatened Bose. Nothing. But she pressed her back against the wall and stood quite still, palms pricking. The little wind rustled in the ivy. The moon came again; she searched the dissolving darkness, the outlines of the forming shadows; suppressed a cry. Close to her feet the pale stone floor was flecked with drops of red.

But queerly luminous red. And her breath went out in a wary sigh of relief; she looked up to the fictively shattered traceries of a rose-window – and to the ruby-coloured lights of fictively shattered stained glass. 'Oh, Peter,' she breathed to herself, 'you did give me a truly Gothic thrill!' And she moved boldly forward again. In this Radcliffean world you took your courage in both hands and all was well; no mystery too horrid to plumb. But let go and you would outyelp Stella Terborg.

It was hidden here. If she knew just what the hidden thing was she would have some idea where best to look for it. And she wanted to get it. Somebody, something – a car perhaps – was cruising round – waiting for Clay and the woman over the wall. And if Clay were here, say, within two minutes he might conceivably be ahead still of the police. And get away – get away with *it*.

The cow-house was used as a store for garden things; shelves had been built round the old cattle stalls to take flower-pots, bags of lime and manure, miscellaneous implements. She crossed rapidly to the end stall and her eye, as if abnormally acute, went in an instant to the upper shelf. There stood a row of little sacks – uniform, but from one a little trickle of whitish stuff had fallen to the floor. She reached for it. The mouth was folded under, but unstitched. She plunged in her hand. 'Got it!' Elizabeth was exultant in her swift success. And in the same instant she heard a sound outside, a sound that was neither wind-stirred ivy nor bat nor owl.

In a flash she scrambled over into the next stall and crouched down. The moon vanished. When it came again she saw a raised arm – no, the shadow of a raised arm – groping for the rifled sack; a second later came Clay's subdued curse. Elizabeth crouched very still, not three feet away. Her heart, she thought, must make Duke Peter's well-cemented ruin quiver like a mill-house. And she recalled – it was less a recollection than something probing to a nerve – the sheer sensory acuteness of the man near her, his every-day effortless vigilance, his perfectly coordinating ear, eye, and hand. And now he was very still too, listening. His picture rose up before her as he had been in the nunnery-scene – Hamlet, tense, straining his senses towards his concealed enemies. He had only to search and she was done for. Where were Giles, Noel, the police? They must have had Jean's message long since.

He was searching the stalls. And always, searching the stalls, he would be between her and the door. So she was done for. With some idea of finding a weapon her fingers groped, touched something, explored.

It was only an empty paint tin, but it gave her a plan. Above the door was a trefoil aperture unglazed. If she could get the tin through she might have a long chance yet; if she failed she would be no worse off than staying still.

It was dark again. She waited for the ivy to rustle and cover the sound of slight movement; then she lobbed at the scarcely distinguishable target. And the tin went through. From outside the cow-house came a splendid rattle – suggesting, she rather deliciously thought, the true Radcliffean ghost in chains. In a flash Clay was outside and in a flash Elizabeth was after him and pressed behind a buttress.

The wind was rising; the moon was playing hide-and-seek with little, heavy scudding clouds; the moonlight was coming and going – a mild lunar lightning – about the gardens. She saw Clay standing, a revolver in his hand, some ten yards away; his eye swept round and past her; he turned and ran back into the cow-house. But she was not safe yet. Straight before her lay the long path to the house – a furlong and a half between towering hedges and oblivious deities. Down that path she must go. Up that path help must presently come – but there was no sign of it yet. And in seconds Clay would be out again. And not till she was a hundred yards or more down the path would she have some chance of escaping unnoticed.

To her left was a little track leading only through and round a shrubbery. Could she – conceivably – trick him a second time precisely as she had tricked him the first? Elizabeth made no pause to weigh up the unlikelihood. She picked up two heavy stones from Duke Peter's carefully dumped rubble; she gave a little panicky cry; she hurled the stones in rapid succession as far as she could into the shrubbery. It *might* have been somebody blundering a way through – but to Elizabeth it sounded just like two stones falling. She could hardly trust her eyes when Clay ran out and flashed past her in pursuit of the sound. He moved beautifully – like a panther. Nevertheless, Elizabeth reflected, to be taken in like that he must be rattled – more rattled than she was. And she picked up the skirts of her trailing frock once more and ran. The great dark cliff-like hedges, the pale deities dimly outlined against them, flowed past.

She was half-way, more than half-way. And then Clay's voice came from far behind her, carrying clearly through the night in a long-drawn call of warning:

'*A – nna! Com – ing!*'

Almost in the same instant a flicker of moonlight passed over the end of the path for which she was running and for a second she saw a figure standing there, waiting. It must be the woman – the Merkalova. And she would be armed. And behind, Elizabeth could now hear Clay approaching – searching as he came. On either side of her were the impenetrable, soaring hedges. Of help there was as yet no sign.

She was trapped.

Appleby dashed back from his garaged Bentley; slipped as he ran the safety-catch of the heavy revolver he had snatched from it. The others were fifty yards ahead ... forty ... thirty-five ...

Clay turned on the Merkalova. 'You've let her through!'

'No! But does it matter? You have it?' She seized his arm. 'Quickly, back and over the wall.'

Clay swore, scanned the shadows. '*She* has it ... and you let her through ... you must have!' He stopped abruptly. From somewhere in the darkness came the sound of running feet. 'All right ... back.' He swung round – and as he did so the moon came out full. '*God!*' He raised his arm and aimed – upwards. And in the same instant a figure rose from the dark base of the hedge, like a Red Indian from the earth, and swung a blow at his jaw.

Clay staggered; Charles Piper leaped at him; the Merkalova ran at Piper to shoot point-blank – and took Clay's bullet as she ran.

For a shocked moment the two men looked at each other across the body. Then again Clay took aim. 'Turn round,' he said, 'and go back.' And again Piper leapt at him. There was a flash, a report, and Piper staggered, only half-dazed from a graze on the temple.

'Damn you,' said Piper very seriously – and again advanced. This time Clay took his time. His revolver dropped to the line of Piper's heart; his face – calm, intent – was held by a shaft of moonlight that might have been limelight on a stage. And then from forty yards away came a deeper report. The heavy bullet took him square in the forehead, lifted him perhaps half an inch from the ground, tumbled him backwards like a felled tree.

★

Appleby stood up. 'Both dead.'

There was a silence. The moon had almost disappeared. Noel flashed an electric torch, measured with his eye. 'Lord, Mr Appleby, what a shot!' The beam of the torch, playing at random on the ground, flitted across what had been the face of Melville Clay. Rather abruptly, Noel leant against the pedestal of a dimly outlined goddess – looked again at the bodies. 'Even at the base of Pompey's statue,' he said a little crazily.

Again there was silence. And then the statue spoke from the darkness. 'I should like to get dressed now,' it said firmly.

Everyone jumped. Noel exclaimed. 'Who on earth –'

'The Pandemian Venus,' said Elizabeth mildly from her pedestal.

3

Bunney sat up in bed, his head swathed in bandages, his eyes sparkling with excitement. 'Science never knows,' he said, 'to what uses –' He paused as if realizing that he must conserve his strength, and picked up the cylinder. 'And Lady Elizabeth brought it perfectly unimpaired through all her adventures!' He slipped it into the black box and flicked a switch.

... what wilt thou do thou wilt not murder me help help ho help help my lord there has been a serious misadventure please all stay where you are there is very bad news mother about Ian I am just going to tell them he has been shot I have bad news the pistol-shot you all heard was aimed at Lord Auldearn he is dead for the moment nobody must leave the hall ...

... sit still Aunt Elizabeth Biddle is coming across in a moment thank you Gervase I have no desire to run about Biddle may come if he wants to this is very sad very sad we must not be too agitated drink this then my dear lady presently we shall be able to get away I hope you will be all right if I go back now a very great shock memorandum of cabinet emergency organization basic chemical industries date two six thirty –

'Thank you,' said Appleby.

Happily, Bunney switched off.

'And so,' said the Duchess to Appleby, 'it was a spy-story after all – every atom of it!'

'Every atom; but designed to bear a very different appearance.'

The Duchess placed delicate hands on the stone of the balustrade, already warm in the morning sun. She looked from Appleby to the Duke and from the Duke to Appleby. Then she looked away to the crown of Horton Hill. 'Ian is dead, and poor Bose. And Elizabeth is alive only because of Piper's courage, and Piper only because of your marksmanship, Mr Appleby. Perhaps I should wish never to hear another word about it all. But I am curious and I want you to tell it as a story; if only in return for the story – Bose's story – I told in the small hours.'

'Yes,' said the Duke, 'interesting to hear it all cleared up – a second time too. But I'm afraid I can't stop. Must see Macdonald – wreaths and things, you know. Extraordinary shot that of yours, Mr Appleby. Extraordinary. You must come to Kincrae some time. Good-bye, goodbye.'

The Duchess watched her husband disappear. 'He will never speak of it again,' she said. 'But I am different, I fear. *Now*, Mr Appleby.' She tapped the balustrade.

Obediently, Appleby sat down.

'The story begins with the Merkalova. She was the original spy; she became familiar with Mr Crispin, I am afraid, simply because in doing so she came very close to the sources of power and information. It is interesting that Nave detected something out of the way in their relationship and that several of the ladies – less tolerant than yourself – thought, well, unfavourably of her.'

'Gervase regarded himself as having married her,' said the Duchess briefly.

'Which makes it extraordinary that she elected to continue prosecuting her profession, if one may call it that. But there she was; and she – I suspect – brought Clay in. And Clay was bloody, bold, resolute, and an artist. An artist chiefly: one must believe that he took to the game simply because it offered new and incomparably exciting scope for his craft. Certainly there was no money in it comparable to what he made on the stage. And that is all the good – if it be good – that can be said of him.

'These two converged on Scamnum, probably with no very definite mischief in mind; the Merkalova because Mr Crispin brought her and Clay because it was at least a promising field for this most exciting of all games – espionage.'

The Duchess raised forlorn hands. 'And I thought I had exercised such skill in getting him!'

'But presently a less indefinite prospect showed. Auldearn was coming;

to Auldearn the gravest matters were constantly being referred; and – it may be – Auldearn's slightly eccentric habits of taking important papers about with him and so forth were known. It was at this point that Clay thought it worth while to make preliminary plans. He was an imaginative and a ruthless, reckless man – qualities which spies, contrary to popular opinion, do not commonly possess. And these qualities went into his plan, to our very great confusion – I am ashamed to say – in the early stages of the investigation. I must confess that we were caught saying: "Spies don't work this way" – which was just what Clay designed that we should say.

'Everything was to be violent, catastrophic, and – in the word Giles found so early – theatrical. And this was to serve two purposes: it was to give the affair an atmosphere remote from espionage except in the wildest fiction; and at the same time it was to satisfy Clay's real craving for theatre – for dramatic effect. Long before there was a definite prospect of anything important being with Auldearn he amused himself with envisaging murder. And he and the Merkalova began to send the messages.'

'And so to incriminate Nave.'

'Yes. But the attempt to involve Nave in any crime that might be committed was not at that stage designed very seriously. All that Clay was planning was a run of circumstances which would set the police hunting, for a time at least, after some private passionate crime. It amused him to think of us tumbling at length to the anagram and worrying Nave. And I think the Revenge messages may have been prompted as well by a sight of Anderson's book; that is to say he thought we might be persuaded to waste time over Malloch too. But, as Malloch himself pointed out to me, there was very little prospect of such a planted case being ultimately convincing. Clay could not reckon on Malloch being so uncovered in the matter of times and places as he was. Much less could he reckon on the amazing case built up against Nave by Giles Gott – *Leontiasis Ossium* and all the rest of it.' Appleby chuckled.

'It was a very good case,' said the Duchess with spirit. 'And according to Dr Biddle the *Leontiasis* whatever it was was perfectly sound. And if you didn't believe it yourself, Mr Appleby, you acted in a very irresponsible way.' She glanced at Appleby. 'Or Colonel Sandford did,' she said.

'The responsibility for arresting Nave,' Appleby said seriously, 'was morally mine, even if technically it was the Chief Constable's. I *was* inclined to believe the story – all but a fragment of it, as I'll explain. And anyway –' He checked himself.

'And anyway,' prompted the Duchess with sudden perception, 'you thought it might loosen things up.'

Appleby looked at her with real admiration. 'It sometimes happens that way,' he said. 'A criminal is at a strain; suddenly he seems to see the last danger removed; and for a moment he goes off his guard. Which was exactly what happened. Clay's guard failed for a second and Lady Elizabeth got his middle stump.'

The Duchess did not say, '*He* nearly got her'; one must not fuss about one's chicken's skin. Instead she said, 'Poor Giles!'

'Yes; you must believe that I didn't think Sandford would call for his story in that formal fashion. At least it must have amused Clay. But to get back. We must acquit Clay of attempting – at that early stage – to get another man hanged. He was simply out to establish an atmosphere of crazy, passionate crime, and to indicate one or two suspects to keep us busy. And all this, remember, was provisional; just in case it should prove that there was a big stake to play for.

'Well, there was. We don't know how or when he got to know – though if we get at the network of spying of which he was a part we may learn yet. I suspect that before the play began he knew not only that Auldearn had this document but also something of its tenor and physical appearance. In fact, I think the original plan was a plan of *substitution*. But it was to be thoroughly violent; it was to involve murder – that was part of the fun. And by this time, I suspect, the Merkalova had become a mere lieutenant. She would do what she was told, however desperate the orders were. And this, then, was the plan –'

'One sees,' the Duchess interrupted, 'how right Giles was to see the whole thing as somehow implicated with the theme of the play.'

Appleby smiled. The Duchess was evidently resolved to see justice done to the unfortunate Gott. 'Quite so. Only the relevant aspect of the play was not the theme of private revenge but the theme of statecraft. There really was a fight to the death between Hamlet and, well, the rulers of Elsinore – or Scamnum.

'But this, I say, was the plan. The document was on Auldearn's person. Very good. When Auldearn was alone on the rear stage the Merkalova was simply to shoot him from the shelter of the curtains; shoot him and make off instantly. Clay, lingering on the front stage just long enough to demonstrate that he could not himself by any trick be responsible, was to slip through to the rear stage and get the document. He reckoned to have only Bose there before him; and Bose he could send running for help. The advantage of the arrangement is obvious. It tended at once to cut out any notion of theft. For if one thought of theft one would instantly remark that Auldearn had been shot in such circumstances that the assailant could not have reckoned on time to steal anything before the entry of Clay or Bose.

'Having once got the document his plans depended entirely on what was or what was not suspected. If they didn't search Auldearn's body he could reckon that no theft was suspected; that the murder was passing at its face-value as a crazy crime by the author of the messages. In that case he would bank on getting out of the hall without a general search, or at least on getting the document to a confederate in the audience who would get out unsearched. But if they searched Auldearn's body and so gave signs of suspicion he meant, I think, to fall back on a bogus document he had prepared. He would hide that in the scroll – which he would have kicked away so that it had not been searched – and then see that the scroll was discovered. If the bogus document was accepted for the moment and anxiety thereby dispelled then again there would be a substantial chance of getting away without a general search. And, finally, he had the resource of the Merkalova's little camera. If the worst came to the worst he hoped to be able to withdraw to a dressing-room and photograph the document – not, technically, an easy task – and later get the tiny camera successfully away. He may have had some plan that gave him a substantial chance of that: I can't hit on one but I'm sure Giles could.

'Well, that – with a slight failure of plan to which I shall come – was how things stood when, just after the shooting, Clay hit on a more attractive technique. And if you think he acted fantastically you must remember that about the document per se he didn't care twopence. All he wanted was to be supremely clever in the eyes of Melville Clay.

'The first thing he did when this new technique came to him was to scrap provision for the old. He packed off the Merkalova's superfluous camera – packed it off through the instrumentality of Mr Crispin. That was a superb move.' Appleby paused, rather – the Duchess thought

– as Lionel Dillon might have paused at the mention of 'The Burial of Orgaz'; paused in a sort of professional homage. 'It was the move of a man with the brain – well, with the sort of brain I should like to have. For it prepared the way for the *tour de force* by which he sent the Merkalova sweeping in on us in Mr Crispin's room to exclaim, "Gervase, have they found out?" and throw the camera on the bed. That scene, of course, linked Mr Crispin and the Merkalova well-nigh indissolubly together in my mind, and when I learnt that Mr Crispin could not be suspect as a spy I automatically acquitted her in that direction.' Appleby looked ruthfully at the Duchess. He liked her. 'In fact,' he said, 'I think there's some possibility of this case becoming known at the Yard as Appleby's Waterloo.'

The Duchess laughed. 'I hope so; my sympathies won't stretch further than Giles and Nave this morning. But I don't believe it. You're word-perfect already and obviously going to write an astoundingly wise report. And now, as you kept saying to everybody yesterday, please go on.'

'Clay got rid of the camera, then, and no doubt burnt the bogus document, just as Miss – but that is irrelevant. Then he waited to put across the great performance of his career. There, sitting by herself in the front row and isolated from the audience, was the Dowager Duchess, a very old lady constantly nodding off to sleep. And beside her was Bunney's machine, purring away – so to speak – and ready to record anything murmured into it. And several people had gone to speak to the old lady; it didn't seem to count at all as communicating with the audience. So Clay waited till she had nodded asleep again after Biddle's draught, walked over the front stage, sat down solicitously beside her, made scraps of soothing conversation that the nearer people could hear – and meanwhile, bit by bit, read the whole document to Bunney's contraption. He would hold the paper, I suppose, concealed in a programme – and the whole effect to the people behind would be that of two or three minutes' courteous attention to an old lady. Presently he went away and came back with old Mr Cope – a beautiful completing of the effect. Then he simply put the document in the scroll where it would presently be found. If Bose had not found it Clay, no doubt, would have done something about it himself.

'But he had by no means got clear yet. For the Duke, despite the belated discovery of the document, still took precautions. He sent the audience away, without allowing any communication between them and the players. And then he kept the players in the hall until I arrived from London. By that time Clay had slipped the cylinder out of the machine – to do that unnoticed would not, with his peculiar abilities, be difficult – and was walking about with it. And by this time he guessed there would be a search. It is dreadfully humiliating to have to record that he thereupon got the thing away effortlessly under my nose. He simply dropped it in an empty coffee-urn which Bagot, quite automatically, would take away when bringing a full one – and which the constable at the door would, equally automatically, let through. It was all rather fantastic – too fantastic for me, certainly, as I stood there on the stage solemnly watching Bagot's exit. But remember, again, that Clay was not a common spy prosaically anxious to filch securely and make his money; he was a reckless and inspired creature playing the game of his life.

'And so the first act ended. There had been, from Clay's point of view, two unforeseen turns to it: the Merkalova had shot Lord Auldearn not from the shelter of the curtains but from right out on the rear stage itself; and the substance of the document was now, of all places, on a wax cylinder in a coffee-urn somewhere in the Scamnum offices. And the first of these unforeseen turns gave Miss Sandys her chance and the second gave Lady Elizabeth hers.

'The Merkalova was not quite first-class; she was not quite worthy of Clay. She was liable to muff things slightly. For instance, when she made that descent on us in Mr Crispin's room she went wrong twice. She was a little too pat, so that I had an obscure feeling that it was a put-up job. Not that that did any harm; it merely kept my thoughts centring for a little longer on the fictitious Crispin–Merkalova conspiracy. A more serious slip was a story she let fly about Miss Sandys; it was a serious slip because it tended to keep the spy idea alive. She was liable, then, to muff things slightly and one is not surprised that Clay charged her with letting Lady Elizabeth through their trap last night when actually Lady Elizabeth was not very far away.'

'I'm pleased with Elizabeth,' said the Duchess. 'It was intelligent.'

'It was genius. But the point is that the Merkalova was afraid of *missing*. And that's what Miss Sandys got to. While Giles and I were finding fine theories to account for the murderer stepping right out of cover and under the possible observation of Bose – the iron-cross, gloating-avenger, Fate-in-*Les-Présages* theory, and all the rest of it –

while our minds worked like that Miss Sandys's worked like this: *Why break cover to get closer? Because you're afraid of missing.* And then she asked: *Why are you afraid of missing at that comparatively close range?* And she answered – with incomparable brilliance and disinterestedness if you consider her feminist attitude: *Because you're a woman.* And then she went further in what has been the purest detective process in the case. The revolver had been found. There would be no finger-prints on it. How does one avoid leaving finger-prints? Either by wiping the object afterwards or by wearing a glove. A glove is best, because one mightn't succeed in rubbing prints off adequately if pressed for time. The men had no gloves but the women had: they came straight to the hall to change from what had been rather a grand dinner. After the search they left mainly in their player things. Gloves would still be in the hall. So she broke into the hall with Mr Gylby, found the Merkalova's gloves, and convinced herself and myself – if nobody else – that the right-hand glove smelt ever so faintly of gunpowder – as in the circumstances it might just conceivably do. Miss Sandys had us beaten badly there and the wise report you speak of will have to say so.

'Now the other point – the cylinder in the coffee-urn. Clay knew the ways of big houses and knew that no footman up at two a.m. was going to clean out such a thing; it would be put by for the appropriate maid or boy in the morning. And he knew, roughly, where he could find it in the small hours. What he didn't know was the severe nature of Mr Rauth, who likes to lock things up. As a consequence of that he had to break into the pantry where it was and so leave traces of himself. And to avert suspicion from what he had really been after he broke open a tin of biscuits, filled his pockets with them, and later transferred them to the box in his bedroom. And that was his undoing. For Lady Elizabeth, who was familiar with the precise dispositions in these matters imposed, again, by the excellent Rauth, knew at once that he must have been the raider of the pantry. And Clay made the slip of denying it.

'Now review the position of yesterday morning. Clay had the cylinder: later in the day he managed to hide it in the cow-house. The danger arising from Bose's having seen the Merkalova shoot was over, for the simple reason that he had killed Bose. What, then, had he now to do? Nothing but sustain if possible the impression that the whole affair was one of private vengeance? Did the police, indeed, any longer suspect anything else? He got his answer to that when he looked out in the morning and saw that the house was closely guarded. He knew then that we had some substantial suspicion. He may have guessed that we had intercepted a message we had in fact intercepted: the message promising delivery of the goods. If, then, we knew that there were spies his best course was to persuade us that they had been unsuccessful. And to that end he contrived another intercepted message. I had ensured that no long message could be flashed out from Scamnum in the night. But for this purpose only three or four words were necessary. And they went – a few flicks of a shaving mirror – from Piper's bedroom window to Horton Hill. And so the second message was got deliberately into police hands: the spies had been unsuccessful; the murders were quite another affair; all chance was gone. He had to send the message from Piper's room; it was the only one available to him that commanded the hill. But it was a big risk, the sort of risk he loved. For Piper, if a shade slow, has a brooding and analytical eye. And – in fact – hours afterwards Piper *saw*.

'To substantiate the particular picture of the crimes he was trying to build up he had risked dragging Bose's body about the house. And now he had only one substantial anxiety. When he had delivered one of the messages through Bunney's box he had not foreseen what part the box was later to play. And at any time now there might occur to someone the possibility of investigating the voice which Bunney held recorded. I doubt if he cared twopence for that in itself. But it involved another danger. For as soon as Bunney was given his box in order to put this idea into practice he would discover that the final cylinder recording the interrupted play was missing. At all costs that must be avoided until the cylinder with the document was got safely away. Hence the attack on Bunney. Clay boldly broached the matter at breakfast and then made sure that for twenty-four hours at least Bunney would be silent. Of course he stole the "curious message" cylinder. Doing so killed two birds with one stone; it removed any possible danger of the identification of his voice; and it gave a motive for the attack on Bunney that offered no suggestion of a connection with the spy-theme. And there, incidentally, was the one thing I positively stuck at in Giles's theory: that Bunney had been mistaken for me. And I was just trying to work out the implications of that – that it must be a conspiratorial crime, that it might be a spy crime after all – when, well, when the final whirlwind overtook me.

'Clay made one other move to keep up the Revenge theory. He had the habit of strolling into people's rooms and yesterday evening he strolled into Nave's. Nave was in his bath. And on the table was a Shakespeare open at the play-scene. Nave, you see, had tumbled to the anagram-business before anyone else; trust a psychologist for that. He knew somebody was out to incriminate him and he wondered what more might come. And he found himself going over his Shakespeare in a fascinated sort of way, noting "ravens", "revenges", and so forth. He had just looked at this most apposite of all lines – almost fatally, he had just laid his finger on it – when Clay came in and saw it. The temptation was overwhelming; he sent the sixth message over the telephone from the Raven's own room.' Appleby paused. 'And that was a definite move to get Nave hanged. In other words, Clay was a cowardly scoundrel as well as a very, very able man.

'And now I must go and say good-bye to Giles. *Death at Scamnum Court* has not made good hunting for either of us. It has been Ladies' Day. Miss Sandys got the Merkalova. Lady Elizabeth got Clay.' Appleby rose. 'And the Duchess of Horton, in the middle of a very terrible night, remembered how to tell a story as the Duchess of Horton can.'

Jean was packing suitcases into the back of Elizabeth's car: Elizabeth was packing dogs into the front. And the talented author of *Death at the Zoo* and *Poison Paddock* came rather dubiously down the steps.

'Straight away, Elizabeth?'

'Straight away. They'll run for Kincrae early, I think, and I'm going ahead. By paternal decree. The affair must be blown away from the maidenly mind.'

'I wish it could be blown away. I've made a most frightful –'

'Giles, is Nave annoyed?'

'No. The unkindest cut of all is there. It's all a matter of scientific interest to him. I don't believe, ideologue though he be, that he's capable of one flicker of enmity towards any living creature. And we're going for a walk together after tea to talk it all over. Think of that.' Gott's fingers strayed nervously through his hair; he looked shyly at Elizabeth. As Nave had said: painful lack of knowledge how to proceed. 'It's nice to see you with a whole skin, Elizabeth – praise heaven and Piper.'

'Oh yes,' said Elizabeth, 'Piper was all right. And I owe him an idea too.'

'An idea?'

'Yes; if he hadn't tried to make fun of you at breakfast yesterday – about Pygmalion and his statue, you remember? – I should never have thought of the Pandemian Venus.'

Elizabeth climbed into the car. Then she sighed – her mother's sigh. 'Giles, it's such a pity. That it wasn't true, I mean. It was such a good story.'

'I say, don't pile it on.'

'But it was. It *ought* to have been true. And you can tell Nave I think so when you take your walk.' Elizabeth turned to see Jean safely stowed; pressed the self-starter.

'Good-bye, Elizabeth. And I hope you'll truly blow it out of mind – our play and all that followed.'

'Perhaps we'll have the play again, Giles.' Elizabeth slipped into gear.

'You'd be Ophelia again – even if I produced it?'

'Even if you played Hamlet, Giles – mad, mad Hamlet.'

Elizabeth let in the clutch; the car glided forward. And Gott stepped back.

'Nymph, in thy orisons,' he said, 'be all my sins remembered.'

The Daffodil Affair

Describe the horoscope, haruspicate or scry,
Observe disease in signatures, evoke
Biography from the wrinkles of the palm
And tragedy from fingers ... especially
When there is distress of nations and perplexity
Whether on the shores of Asia or in the
Edgware Rd.

The Dry Salvages

Note

Part 1
Primrose Way

I

The room was void and unquickened; it was like a room in a shop-window but larger and emptier; and the man who sat at the desk had never thought to impress himself upon what he entered every day. Comfort there was none, nor discomfort either; only, did the occupant deign to qualify the pure neutrality of his surroundings, it would surely be austerity that would emerge. The spring sunshine turned bleak and functional as it passed the plate-glass of the tall, uncurtained windows.

The windows were large; the big desk lay islanded in a creeping parallelogram of light; across this and before the eyes of the man sitting motionless passed slantwise and slowly a massive shaft of shadow. Perhaps twenty times it passed to and fro, as if outside some great joy-wheel were oscillating idly in a derelict amusement park. And then the man rose, clasped hands behind him and walked to a window – high up in New Scotland Yard. He looked out and war-time London lay beneath.

With science the crane or scoop or derrick had been perched amid the skeletal remains of a large building; from this point of vantage it struck and shovelled ingeniously at a neighbouring structure whose ruin had stopped half-way down. It was possible to be sad, to be indignant; and many who walked those streets were making the biologically more useful discovery of anger. But a practical-minded man could confine himself to approving or critical appraisal of the speed with which the tidy-up was accomplished – and the man at the window looked superficially as if he might be like that. His movements were economical, impersonal, abstract. His glance, if considering, was unclouded by speculative care. But on his brow was a fixed contraction; this he had carried from desk to window, and now there was neither hardening nor relaxation as he looked out.

Hudspith looked out and took it all in. He looked out and as a practical man placed it: there was this and that contingency to fear, to hope for, next time. And as a moralist Hudspith placed it: his lips framed a word. Wicked. Undoubtedly it was that. But was it evil? He thought not; he grudged to the mere fury and blindness of it that absolute word. During fifteen years Hudspith had controlled the file of police papers which dealt with the abduction and subsequent history of feeble-minded girls. Here lay his anger, and as he looked out over London he saw, in effect, only the shadow of this. Year by year the anger had burst deeper until it was now the innermost principle of the man. He confronted sin that was double and gratuitous. For, given social conditions which were common enough, it was tolerably easy to seduce, strand, swop, sell, hire out girls whose wits were reasonably about them. And so the meanness of going for the feeble ones was – well, exasperating. Evil was exasperating. Or rather, perhaps, it was exasperating that so few people were aware of it.

Their minds stop short of wickedness – thought Hudspith, looking out over London. More of them are aware of God, of Immortality, of the Ideas of Reason, than are really aware of evil. And yet these things, as someone has said, are mere superstructure and superficies compared with the fact of evil ... Hudspith did not go to church, but this knowledge of evil made him, in fact, a violently religious man. He pursued his particular police job, sordid and depressing as it was, with very much that dangerous metaphysical intensity which Captain Ahab put into the pursuit of the White Whale. Other things passed him by, not impinging – like his room.

And now there was this girl – the girl with the outlandish name: Lucy Rideout. Once too often she had ridden out ... Hudspith smiled bleakly – unseeing and unaware – into the bleak sunshine.

A half-witted girl.

'A horse!'

John Appleby, two storeys below, looked incredulously at the old gentleman who had recently been reinstalled as Assistant-Commissioner. 'A horse?' repeated Appleby. Never before had he been asked to go out and look for a horse.

The old gentleman nodded, indecisively; he looked Appleby cautiously in the eye. Things had changed. There were quite a lot more sahibs in lower places, and a few more rankers in higher places, than in the old days. He attached little importance to such things. But every now and then it could become awkward – if one wasn't minding one's p's and q's. 'Yes,' he said; 'a horse.' His tone was doubtful, as if some qualification must follow. He paused, as if in search of something that could be enunciated with confidence. 'Sit down,' he said.

Appleby sat down. 'There's Ambler,' he suggested hopefully. 'I believe Ambler has had a lot of experience with horses. When Crusader disappeared just before the Derby in thirty –'

The Assistant-Commissioner shook his head. 'No, no; it's not that sort of horse. Not a valuable sort of horse – not at all valuable. And, in a way, it's not really an official affair.' He began to scratch his chin doubtfully; checked himself. 'As a matter of fact, it's my sister,' he said ambiguously.

'Ah.' Appleby felt a growing dislike of this shadowy equine problem.

'My sister lives in Harrogate. Tiresome sort of place.' The Assistant-Commissioner was obscurely apologetic. 'Know it, I suppose.'

'I have an aunt living there, as a matter of fact.'

'Indeed.' The Assistant-Commissioner took a calculating glance at his own toes. 'I wonder,' he ventured, 'if she knows –'

'I believe she knows Lady Caroline quite well.'

'What a coincidence!' As he made this imbecile remark the Assistant-Commissioner scrutinized his toes more severely than before. He was not at all sure that this made the matter easier. He decided on a shift to humour. 'You don't happen to know,' he asked, 'if your aunt has a favourite cab?'

'I don't. But I think it very likely.'

'Well, Caroline has – or had. She was attached to a particularly sober driver with a particularly quiet horse. At one time when Miss Maidment rang up the stables – I should explain that Maidment is her companion – I mean I should explain that *Miss* Maidment is her companion –' The Assistant-Commissioner paused, perplexed, 'What was I saying?'

'You had got to the point, sir, at which Miss Maidment would ring up the stables.'

'To be sure. Well, at one time she used to ask for an open landau, a respectable man and a quiet horse. But latterly she has simply asked for Bodfish and Daffodil.' The Assistant-Commissioner paused. 'Bodfish and Daffodil,' he repeated. 'The former was the driver and the latter the horse. That goes without saying, I suppose. One can imagine a Mr Daffodil, but nobody ever gave the name of Bodfish to a cab-horse.'

'No, sir.'

The Assistant-Commissioner appeared dashed. 'Look here,' he said, 'I know it sounds tiresome. But just you listen. There's a quirk in it later on.'

Appleby, who quite liked this old gentleman, endeavoured to smile with cheerful interest. 'I suppose, sir, it is Daffodil who has disappeared?'

'Quite right. At first my sister was told the animal was dead. She was distressed, because the creature was a favourite, and not at all an old horse.' The Assistant-Commissioner hesitated. 'In fact, she felt rather like the poet.'

Appleby smiled – genuinely this time. 'Quite so, sir. Fair Daffodil, we weep to see you haste away so soon.'

The Assistant-Commissioner nodded his head emphatically, much pleased with the success of his cultural reconnaissance. 'Exactly. Exactly – my dear man. At first, then, they said the horse was dead – apparently feeling that the mention of anything shady would be bad for trade. Now, my sister is inquisitive – or what a politer age used to call a person of much observation. She sent for Bodfish, intending to learn the manner of the brute's death. Bodfish came to see her – and I am sorry to say he was drunk. It had taken him that way. Caroline at once made Maidment – Miss Maidment, I should say – ring up the stables for a closed cab, a respectable driver and a quiet horse. She then drove Bodfish home, gave Mrs Bodfish a receipt for brewing cocoa in a particularly wholesome and attractive manner, and went on to make searching inquiries of Daffodil's owner. When she learnt that the animal had been stolen she – well, she sent me a somewhat urgent telegram. Scotland Yard, apparently, came at once to her mind. Natural, having a brother there – I suppose.'

'Very natural, sir.'

'Of course I replied that the local police were the people. So, if you please, she went to see the Chief Constable, taking her solicitor along with her. Seemingly nothing much had been done in the matter of Daffodil. And the Chief Constable, who had hard-worked officers to protect, was pretty stiff with Caroline. Not at first: I gather he tried heading her off by explaining some of the jobs he had on hand, and letting her in on a harmless war-time secret or two. But Caroline, who is even more specifically pertinacious than generally curious, held to her theme. It was *aut asphodelos aut nullus* with her. I believe her motive was quite selfish and practical: Daffodil was the only horse in Harrogate in which she really had confidence, and she was consequently determined that Daffodil should be traced. Too determined, I gather, for in the end the Chief Constable had pretty well to turn her out. So she went home, thought it over, dictated a stately letter of apology through Miss Maidment – and was thus in a position to present herself without absolute indecency on the poor chap's doorstep once more on the following afternoon. He was a bit baffled.'

'As one would imagine, sir.'

'Quite so. And I think he tried a spot of irony – suggested Scotland Yard. Caroline explained that she was already in communication with me. I fear he rather crumpled up, and really did – er – pass the buck. In short – well, it is difficult, you know.'

'Yes, sir.'

'My sister lives in the most modest way. As peers go we're nobody in particular, as you know.' The old gentleman smiled charmingly. 'But then she is the widow –'

'Quite so, sir.'

'Which means that among her brothers-in-law –'

'Clearly, sir. You would like me to go down?'

The Assistant-Commissioner sighed unhappily. 'It *is* difficult, isn't it? And, you know, you look a bit tired.' This was outrageous, but true. 'And you can't always be after those whopping big affairs. A man who manages in a twelve-month to fight a battle on a Scottish moor, and get wrecked on a desert island, and –'

'Of course I'll go if you wish it, sir.'

'Just for a week-end it's a nice quiet place enough.' The Assistant-Commissioner, here touching perhaps maximum discomfort, thrust his toes despairingly out of sight beneath his desk and looked at Appleby in frank dismay. 'You might even *find* the horse, I suppose.' He shook his head perplexedly. 'Caroline would be pleased – but then would it be tactful to the local men?' He smiled wanly. 'I leave the finding of Daffodil entirely to your discretion. The creature is said to be worth fifteen pounds. And that reminds me.'

'Of the quirk, sir?'

'Just that.' The Assistant-Commissioner brightened. 'It really is a bit remarkable. Like those tiny but disconcerting puzzles they used to take to Sherlock Holmes. In fact there's really a mystery in the Daffodil affair – and mysteries don't turn up here every day, do they? Oceans of crime in islets of anything like genuine mystification.' He paused, obscurely troubled by something in this image. 'The place is what is called a livery stables. Means just a business you hire from. But there's the older meaning of a place you put your own horses to board. And somebody was doing that. Captain Somebody who has to do with tanks down there but likes to get on a horse from time to time. In a loose-box next to Daffodil he had an animal that was worth hundreds of pounds. And this brute was stolen *first*.'

Appleby looked up sharply. 'You don't mean that –?'

'Yes. This whopping valuable brute was stolen in the night. In the morning there was a great rumpus, and nobody much bothered about Daffodil or the stable any more. Anything of the sort would have been like locking –'

'Quite so, sir.'

'And then in the course of the day up drove one of those motor-things for horses, returned Captain Somebody's brute, and carried off Daffodil instead – this without anybody being more than vaguely aware of what was happening. Apparently a mistake had been made the first time. Daffodil was the wanted horse.'

'And Daffodil is really worth almost nothing?'

'Apparently not – except to my sister's sense of security round and about the streets of Harrogate. Not very old, apparently – but broken-kneed or winded or something.'

Appleby shook his head. 'I doubt whether Lady Caroline ought to have confidence in a horse that has been down.'

'My dear man, she no doubt likes its face. Anyway, Daffodil was not a valuable horse.'

'There could be no question of pedigree, stud purposes – that sort of thing?'

'Good Heavens, man! Bodfish – I mean Daffodil – wasn't – um – that sort of horse.'

'I suppose not.' Appleby got up. 'It does seem a little queer. I'll catch the first train on Friday.' He paused by the Assistant-Commissioner's door. 'There's nothing else you can tell me about Daffodil?'

'As a matter of fact there is. It's an odd thing to say about a horse. But it appears – this despite Caroline's good opinion of the creature – well, that it was rather a half-witted sort of horse. What would you say was implied by that? Don't know much about the animals myself.'

Daffodil, the half-witted horse. Appleby wandered down the corridors of the Yard and seemed to see – for indeed he was tired – a host of these dubious creatures in his inward eye, tossing their heads in sprightly dance, curvetting and bowing to an equal number of Captain Somebody's whopping valuable brutes. A policeman could not but be gay in such a jocund company ...

A half-witted horse.

2

In vain the soft warm air washed over Superintendent Hudspith; he marched unmollified from one investigation to the next. It was June, and for another man Piccadilly Circus might have been filled with the ghosts of flowers: violets in little bunches wafting on bus-tops to distant suburbs; roses to be carried off by sheaves in limousines; carnations that slip singly down St James's, glow duskily from tail-coats in the bow-window of White's, adorn tweeds in the rustic Boodle's, vie with the more appropriate orchid in the Travellers' – haunt of those hardy souls who have journeyed out of the British Islands to a distance of at least 500 m. from London in a direct line. But these wraiths were nothing to Hudspith's purpose. Fleetingly he allowed himself a glance of suspicion down Jermyn Street, as fleetingly a nod of sanction at the Athenaeum – and stumped down the steps and across to the park. The park was like green stuff spilt on a counter, shot with the sheen of a long fragment of blue-grey silk. The water-fowl were there as usual; statesmen paused in perambulations to observe their habits with attention; shadowing detectives, distantly known to Hudspith, exercised their corresponding vigilance behind. Hudspith marched on. His visual field was all inward and shadowy – no more than a floating wreath of cheated girls. Sometimes they had been drugged, hypnotized; and sometimes they had been robbed of nearly all their clothes ... Hudspith marched – as if behind Queen Anne's Mansions, beyond the Underground's clock, somewhere near Victoria station maybe, blew and wallowed that elusive Whale.

Rideout: it was not, Hudspith thought, what you would call a tony name. On the other hand the address – a block of service flats here on the fringes of Westminster – suggested substance; and if the Rideouts were substantial the more substantial would be Hudspith's severity. He had received no particulars; it was his habit to disregard the first, and often confused, report that came in; he had learnt, however, that there was a mother, a Mrs Rideout – and by this he was obscurely pleased. Mothers, when there were mothers, were commonly greatly to blame. Although Mrs Rideout could scarcely be herself the Whale, she might yet be abundantly deserving of one or two preliminary harpoons. Hudspith was accustomed to limber up in this way. He quickened his pace, turned a corner, and his objective was before him.

The Rideouts were in the humblest station: there lay something of disappointment in this. Mrs Rideout was employed as a cleaner and her daughter as a waitress, and normally they lived 'out'. But recently their home had disappeared in the night; this had moved Mrs Rideout to announce her intention of withdrawing to her sister's in the country; whereupon the management of the flats where she was employed, being much in need of such services as Rideouts supply, had provided restricted but sufficient living quarters on the premises. Through the basement, past the ironing-room and the two small storerooms, the temporary abode of the Rideouts would be found.

Hudspith, having learnt so much from a melancholy porter whose own living quarters appeared to be in a lift, descended menacingly into the cold, the half-light and the gloom. It was familiar territory. Like the poet, but perhaps from a more pressing professional necessity, he was much aware of the damp souls of housemaids; he knew how easily perdition attended their despondent sprouting at area gates. And he knew – he told himself – all about Lucy Rideout, the half-witted waitress. Unsettlement, cramped quarters with an uncongenial parent, inadequate privacy, the constant sight of expensive or at least prosperous living upstairs, the drift of male guests – themselves often unsettled, uprooted; in all this – and in the pictures, the glamorized advertisements, the pulsing sexy music – the story lay. Had he not probed it a hundred times? And Hudspith marched on, confident in his abundant experience, his often-tested technique. Hudspith marched against the demons – all unaware of the curiously literal way in which, far in the distance, demons awaited him.

Mrs Rideout had friends. Almost might she be said, in upstairs language, to be receiving – for two ladies were coming away as Hudspith reached the door; a third, approaching from some other angle through this subterraneous world, was making a ceremonious claim for admittance; and from inside there came a murmur of voices and a chink of cups. Here however was nothing to confound the experienced investigator; it would be untoward were Mrs Rideout found enjoying her sensational sorrow in solitude.

'Good afternoon,' said Hudspith to his fellow visitor. 'A sad occasion this, marm; very sad indeed.'

'What I asks,' said the visitor, 'is – where was the police?'

'Ah,' said Hudspith. 'Where, indeed? But they're here now, missis.' With subdued drama he tapped himself on the chest. 'Come along.'

The woman, who had been about to open the door, paused round-eyed. 'Toomer's my name,' she said. Her voice sank to a whisper. 'Would it be worse than death?'

Hudspith frowned austerely. 'That remains to be seen.' And he opened the door and ushered Mrs Toomer – she was a dim-featured, almost obliterated woman – into the Rideout home.

It was possible – or it ought to have been possible – to see at a single glance all that was to be seen, for clearly in this one room consisted all the territory that the Rideouts, mother and daughter, enjoyed. It was long, narrow and of considerable size, lit by a filter of light from windows which hovered uncertainly near the ceiling; there was a bed at each extreme end, and a table and arrangements for cooking near the middle. There was little that was remarkable in this. But Hudspith, if unaware of his own habitual surroundings, had a trained eye for domestic interiors, and that eye became positively hawk-like when scrutinizing the late environment of levanting or abducted girls. Here there looked to be plenty of evidence. The influence of Lucy Rideout was dominant in the room. Her handwriting, as it were, was not only decisive at her own end; it declared itself unmistakably far beyond any fair line of demarcation, so that one immediately discerned Mrs Rideout's kingdom as a sort of beleaguered fortress within ever-contracting lines. Only here and there was evidence of a species of cautious sortie undertaken, no doubt, since the daughter's departure; a pair of elastic-sided boots had found their way to the foot of Lucy's bed; a small empty bottle of the kind in which ladies are accustomed to keep gin stood on what had served her as a dressing-table; hard by this lay a journal devoted to the celebration of the Christian Hearth and Home. All this was immediately decipherable. But there remained an element of puzzle which Hudspith at a rapid inspection was unable to resolve. And now Mrs Toomer, exalted by the fact of arriving virtually on the arm of Scotland Yard, was contriving introductions to the assembled company. 'Mrs Rideout,' she said, 'this is the police.'

Mrs Rideout was not much over forty and belonged to the inefficient type that contrives to get through life by the aid of a sort of massive unfocussed vehemence. She set down a teacup and looked from Mrs Toomer to Hudspith. 'That's right,' she said, largely and vaguely. 'Yes, that's right.' She exuded that repetitive and dazed acquiescence that makes so considerable a part of the social communion of the folk. 'And I'm sure they ought to do something.'

'That's right,' said Mrs Toomer – and two stout women who flanked Mrs Rideout nodded heads and bosoms in agreement. Human speech is at bottom no more than the individual's demand for reassurance in a lonely world; the sophisticated contrive to extract comforting intimations of solidarity from disagreement, controversy and repartee; the uninstructed prefer much simpler forms of mutual support. When the ritual is in course of celebration – at such a party as was now gathered at Mrs Rideout's – it is a solecism to break the grand affirmative flow of things. And indeed we none of us particularly care for the man who qualifies our suggestion that it is a fine day, or that it looks like rain, or that it is nice to see a little bit of sunshine.

All this the much-practised Hudspith knew. He nodded his head ponderously. 'Yes,' he said; 'something ought to be done. And I'm here to do it.'

'That's right,' said one of the stout women. 'That's what I say.'

'That's right,' said the other stout woman.

Mrs Rideout turned in triumph to Mrs Toomer. 'That's what Mrs Thorr and Mrs Fiddock say,' she said.

Mrs Toomer, who had turned her head in quest of the teapot, nodded skilfully backwards. 'That's right,' she agreed.

'That's right,' said Mrs Fiddock and Mrs Thorr.

Hudspith cleared his throat, preparing cautiously to intrude upon the spell. 'Acting,' he said, 'on instructions received –' The ladies all laid down their teacups, instantly impressed by this wisp of official eloquence. Hudspith slowly produced a notebook. The investigation was launched.

Mrs Rideout called God to witness that she had been a good mother. Mrs Thorr, Mrs Toomer and Mrs Fiddock responded in a sort of trinitarian chorus. Hudspith said grimly that he was glad to hear it, as in most such cases it was not so; he appeared to make a jotting on Mrs Rideout's maternal goodness as if for subsequent scrutiny. Mrs Rideout affirmed that Lucy had always been a good daughter. But everybody knew what girls were nowadays; there was no controlling them; out they would go when they pleased. Hudspith could have written down all this out of his head; he was able to spare considerable attention for a further study of the lost girl's possessions.

He saw the cheap dance slippers; he saw on a nail the pathetic wisp of white rabbit that was some sort of cape. He saw the array of photographs pinned to the wall by the bed: the usual pictures, he wearily thought, cut from the usual cinema magazines. The heroes often wore bathing-trunks now; lying under beach-umbrellas, they leered up at girls who sat with parted lips, entranced. Or in resplendent tails and hair-grease they led their ladies through exotic restaurants while little tables crowded with ambassadors and duchesses made a modest background to the scene. Or momentarily disguised as common mortals they perched, millionaire play-boys though they were, on little stools in small-town drug-stores and scooped at sundaes nose to nose with the beloved. Hudspith ground his teeth as he looked at them. Not the celebrated William Prynne, who wrote some eight hundred thousand words on the theme that stage-plays are the very pomps of the devil, could have felt more ill disposed to this fantasy-world than did Superintendent Hudspith.

It was a gentleman who had lived in the house, Mrs Rideout thought. A foreigner, she thought. And for some time she had known Lucy was carrying on. Lucy had taken to coming home later than she should. Whereupon she – Mrs Rideout – had said – and Mrs Toomer would witness that she had said ...

Hudspith's pencil still traversed the paper. But his glance strayed now to the other walls. Over the fireplace hung Bubbles; that would be Mrs Rideout's fancy. Midway between this and Lucy's end of the room was one of those colour prints in which faintly draped figures are disposed pensively on marble terraces in a blaze of noon-tide light; behind them is a very blue lake, behind that very white mountains, with behind these again a sunset or sunrise thrown in for extra effect. Hudspith had failed to cultivate the plastic arts; nevertheless he recognized that this abomination and the magazine photographs belonged to one world. His glance ran on – and before another and smaller reproduction paused, perplexed. Momentarily disregarding Mrs Rideout's monologue, he walked over to it. A line of print on the mount told him that this aloof and lovely person had been painted by a certain Piero della Francesca. He shook his head, obscurely disturbed.

But Lucy had just gone on going out. In all that black-out too. And then the night before last she had gone out and not come back again. But she had left a note in the cocoa-jug saying . . .

Saying, thought Hudspith, that she was going to be happy and not to worry. He walked over to Lucy's bed, where stood a little book-case. Three rows of books, all nearly new. He bent down. *Sesame and Lilies, The Decline and Fall of the Roman Empire, After London, Cowper's Letters, The Advancement of Learning, Madam Bovary* . . . Hudspith frowned and looked at the next shelf. *Swiss Family Robinson, Little Women, Mopsie in the Fifth, Mopsie Captain of the School, Doctor Dolittle's Voyages* . . . The books were equally new; Mopsie's final adventures had been published in the present year. Hudspith turned round, aware that Mrs Rideout had said something out of the ordinary. 'Cocoa-jug?' he said. 'Are you sure it wasn't the teapot?'

Mrs Rideout was emphatic; so was Mrs Toomer, who had been present at the discovery.

'It's nearly always the teapot,' Hudspith paused, suspicious and alert. 'When do you drink cocoa, marm?'

In the Rideout *ménage* cocoa was drunk only at night. So that was it: not the breakfast teapot but the evening cocoa-jug – in other words a good twenty-four hours' start. The little piece of elementary con-trivance – surprising though this may seem – placed Lucy Rideout at once among the intellectual *élite* of Hudspith's young women. And yet he had been given to understand –

The third shelf was almost on the ground; Hudspith stooped to ex-amine it and his brow darkened. He knew *those* books, and it had not been his fault if the Home Secretary did not know them too. His eye went doubtfully back to the picture by the man Piero della Francesca, and it was a moment before he was aware that Mrs Rideout had stopped talking and that now the person called Mrs Fiddock held the stage.

With an evident sense of drama Mrs Fiddock had set down her cup. 'I seen them and I 'eard them!' she said.

It was a sensation. Mrs Fiddock looked slowly round, enjoying her triumph. Then slowly she wagged a finger at the amorphously vehement Mrs Rideout.

'I seen and I 'eard what it's my duty to diwulge in the presence of this 'igh officer of the police.'

'That's right,' said Mrs Toomer and Mrs Thorr.

And Mrs Rideout nodded her own vaster acquiescence. 'That's right,' she said.

3

Hudspith licked his pencil and congratulated himself on the irregularity of his own methods. It was contrary to correct procedure to slip in on Mrs Rideout's tea-party in this way, but what signifies a little latitude when it is Leviathan himself that one pursues? Hudspith took a final look at the very bad books on Lucy Rideout's lowest shelf and turned expectantly to Mrs Fiddock. 'Quite right, marm,' he said. 'You must out with anything you know about this poor girl.'

Mrs Rideout began to sob – energetically and very rapidly, as if bent on repairing an oversight which had only just occurred to her. Mrs Toomer, having looked round vainly for a handkerchief, handed a tea-towel. Mrs Thorr said 'There, there!' and 'There then!' and 'There now!' to everybody in turn. The tempo of Mrs Rideout's grief changed; she was really weeping; presently the discovery of this so surprised her that she fell abruptly silent. The room waited expectantly.

'This,' announced Mrs Fiddock, 'is a very painful occasion for me.'

'There now!' said Mrs Thorr.

'And I hope that none here will say I did anything I didn't ought. For I only done my duty.' Mrs Fiddock paused. 'As a citizen.' She paused again to admire this linguistic triumph. 'It was in the lounge of the Crown.'

'The lounge!' said Mrs Thorr and Mrs Toomer and Mrs Rideout.

'It was more than a week back,' pursued Mrs Fiddock with dignity, 'that I had occasion to enter the bottle and jug. Now as everyone knows – or everyone except this gentleman here – there's an 'atch in the bottle and jug that gives on the private. And the private has a door into the lounge. And sometimes you sees right through.'

There was an interruption while the ladies went into committee to verify these topographical statements. Depraved old wretches, thought Hudspith. Liquor, he thought. Come out on a case like this and always there's liquor round the corner. But he nodded with a large and false approval at Mrs Fiddock. 'Very observant, missus,' he said; 'very observant indeed.'

Mrs Fiddock gave a gratified bow. 'And there, Mrs Rideout, was your Lucy with that flashy furrein-looking man that was in number nine. Bold as brass, he was, and I didn't think there was any good in it.' She hesitated, momentarily confused. 'It seemed to me I had a duty to do.'

'I don't remember,' said Mrs Rideout suspiciously, 'as how you ever said anything about it afterwards.'

'I had my duty to do,' reiterated Mrs Fiddock more firmly. 'I walked round to the lounge, dispoged myself behind the haspidistra and ordered a glass of port.'

'There then!' said Mrs Thorr. Her admiration might have been directed either to the shameless curiosity of Mrs Fiddock or to the financial solidity and social confidence which this proceeding revealed.

'And I 'eard what I 'eard. "Did you ever 'ear," 'e says, "of the isle of Capri? I got an island just like that." That's what I 'eard 'im say.'

Mrs Toomer raised her hands, instantly credulous. 'Lord!' she said; 'fancy having an island all your own.'

'"Where is it?" says your Lucy – which was the first words I 'eard 'er say. "Where is it?" "It's difficult to describe," 'e says. "But you go to South America first."'

Hudspith's pencil snapped at the point. Rage filled him – against these awful women, against the imbecile Lucy, against the unspeakably threadbare simplicity of this professional seducer's patter. 'Mrs Fiddock,' he said benevolently, 'this is very valuable information.'

'And then neither of them said anythink, and I thought I'd best take a peep round the haspidistra. 'E was smiling at her confident like. And your Lucy she didn't say nothink. She just 'itched her skirt another hinch above the knee.'

Hudspith compressed his lips. Mrs Toomer made a shocked noise on the front of her palate. Mrs Rideout again sobbed.

'It was just then that the young fellow brought the port. "Well, ma," 'e says, "picked a winner? And shall I bring the cigars?" "Young man," I says, "I know my place, and 'opes that others does the same." So 'e went away and I listens again.' Mrs Fiddock paused. 'But what I 'eard this time,' she said dramatically, 'I can scarcely bring myself to let pass these 'ere lips.'

Mrs Thorr leant forward on her chair; the half-obliterated features of Mrs Toomer sharpened themselves in expectation; the tea-towel in Mrs Rideout's grasp suspended itself in air.

' 'E leaned back and lit a cigarette. And then 'e said what made my very blood run cold. "I could do with two or three of you," 'e said, – "and that's what I'm going to get!" And then 'e gave an 'orrid laugh, like 'e might give to a bit of fun that was all his own.'

A moment's profound silence greeted this appalling revelation. 'A slaver – that's what he is,' said Mrs Toomer.

'Or a regular Bluebeard,' said Mrs Thorr.

Mrs Fiddock, her imagination fired by the literary success she had achieved, leant forward. 'Do you think,' she asked hoarsely, 'he drowns them in a barf?'

Maternal solicitude is an awful power. Mrs Rideout, who had risen to her feet in agitation, took two sideways and three backward steps – and was thus able to fall upon her bed in a fit. Mrs Rideout roared; Mrs Thorr and Mrs Fiddock snivelled; Mrs Toomer gently beat her breast and uttered wheezy sighs. It is a dreadful thing to die – or even to conduct police investigations – 'mid women howling. The hardy Hudspith looked about him with some idea of throwing water or opening a window. What his eye immediately fell on was the dispassionate gaze of the Piero della Francesca – whence it travelled involuntarily to *Sesame and Lilies* and the historical labours of Edward Gibbon. Momentarily he felt like a man who sinks through deep waters. Then he stood up. 'Be quiet!' he shouted.

Mrs Rideout stopped roaring and snivelled. Whereupon Mrs Fiddock and Mrs Thorr, as if indignant at his trespass, took breath and yelled. Mrs Toomer continued her asthmatic exhibition undeterred. Hudspith banged the table with an open palm. 'Silence!' he bellowed. 'Silence in the name of the law!'

There was instant quiet, as if the women were dispossessed of devils by the incantation. And Hudspith, learned in demonology, went sternly on: 'Anything that any of you says may be taken down and used as evidence in such proceedings as the magistrate may direct. We will now proceed to inquiries on the character and habits of the missing girl.'

The crisis was over. Even Mrs Toomer ceased knocking her breast. Instead, she took the lid from the teapot and peered hopefully inside.

Lucy Rideout was nineteen; so much could be gathered from her mother – who appeared to feel, however, that this represented her fair share of such information as the assembled party might provide. On her daughter's interests and accomplishments she was vague; of her friends she knew little; among a number of photographs in a drawer she found one which, after some consultation with her friends, she was persuaded to assert was Lucy. Often, thought Hudspith, our claim upon the awareness of even close relations is surprisingly marginal and precarious. Nevertheless there was something almost pathological in this woman's attitude to her daughter; it was almost as if the child had been an intellectual problem which Mrs Rideout had long since found it simplest to give up. He scrutinized the photograph with a professional eye. Lucy Rideout was not pretty. Nor, as far as he could discern, did she possess any of the specific types of plainness which have here and there a peculiar appeal. Why, then, Lucy? Presumably because she was half-witted and so particularly easy to spirit away. Only Hudspith thought that if this indifferent photograph revealed anything at all it was the appearance of considerable intelligence. And this by no means accorded with his brief. He turned to Mrs Rideout. "I understand,' he said cautiously, 'that your daughter was never very bright at her books?'

'That's right,' said Mrs Rideout readily.

'In fact, the truth is that she isn't quite –'

'Her books?' interrupted Mrs Toomer. 'Why, she was always at her books, poor dear.'

'That's right,' said Mrs Rideout. 'So she was.'

Mrs Toomer nodded towards the bookshelf. 'See for yourself, mister. She must have bought all them since the Rideouts was blitzed. Always reading, is Lucy. But bad at her books, as you sez.'

Hudspith frowned. 'But if she was always reading –'

'That's why she was bad at her books,' Mrs Toomer looked curiously at Hudspith, as if doubting the perspicacity of one to whom this elementary point could be obscure. 'Always reading, she was. It fairly drove her teachers wild.'

'That was it,' said Mrs Rideout. She nodded, vague but decided. Suddenly she became more emphatic. 'That and her forgetfulness. No one but me can ever know how forgetful that girl is.'

'*Was*, more likely,' said Mrs Fiddock gloomily.

'That's right,' said Mrs Rideout. 'Sometimes she wouldn't as much as know if she'd put her dinner inside her. Something chronic, Lucy's memory.'

'It comes of reading,' suggested Mrs Thorr. 'Just common reading, let alone the sort of reading your Lucy did.' She turned to Hudspith. 'Lord Bacon and Gibbon,' she enumerated, awed. 'And Shakespeare and the German Gouty.'

'That's right,' chimed in Mrs Toomer. 'And fairy-stories, too, and animals what talk. Half a week's wages, Lucy would give, if she saw a nice big book with coloured pictures in a window.'

And the odd thing, thought Hudspith, is that the bookshelves bear out this fantastic confusion of testimonies. He addressed himself resolutely to Lucy's mother, 'My information is that your daughter is weak in the head. Not what they call mentally deficient, exactly – but getting on that way. Is that right?'

'Quite right,' said Mrs Toomer before Mrs Rideout could reply. 'Not mental –'

'Mentals,' interrupted Mrs Thorr, 'goes to school in a car. Lucy never did that, though her father tried for it when he was alive, poor man.'

'That's right,' said Mrs Rideout.

'Not mental,' resumed Mrs Toomer. 'Just a bit cracked like. What you might call terrible serious-minded.'

'That's right,' said Mrs Rideout and Mrs Fiddock and Mrs Thorr. It was their first piece of chorus work for some time.

'Fair childish,' said Mrs Fiddock, speaking as if offering the next logical step in a well-ordered theme. 'Creepy, it was at times. Shy and innocent and ignorant like.'

Hudspith tried something else. 'Your daughter went out to dances – that sort of thing?'

'That she did,' said Mrs Rideout. 'And that flighty she'd get that there was no holding her.'

The lips of Mrs Toomer, Mrs Thorr and Mrs Fiddock parted in affirmative incantation. Hudspith plunged again. 'What other interests had she?'

'Plays,' said Mrs Rideout.

'Ah – she went to the theatre?'

Mrs Rideout shook her head violently, apparently intimating that there were degrees of eccentricity of which even her Lucy must be acquitted. 'She made 'em.'

'Made them?'

'In bed at night. Since we came here it's fair driven me crazy. Whisper, whisper, whisper.'

'What sort of plays?'

Mrs Rideout considered. 'Diatribes,' she said. 'Diatribes and sometimes another as well.'

'You mean plays sometimes with two people and sometimes with three? What sort of people.'

'They got very queer names.' Mrs Rideout shifted uneasily on her chair, as if obliged to contemplate something she had long felt it more comfortable to ignore. 'Poppet is one.'

'Yes?'

'And Real Lucy and Sick Lucy is the others. Sick Lucy doesn't seem to know much. They're always telling her what happened before.'

Superintendent Hudspith was not a learned man. But he had read the appropriate textbooks in a number of odd fields. And now – almost as if dazzled by the great lights that had come upon him – he gazed at Mrs Rideout and her friends with an unseeing eye. 'Well,' he said, 'I'll be damned!'

'That's right,' said Mrs Toomer.

Hudspith's inquiries were prolonged and it was dusk as he turned east along Victoria Street. Anyone glancing at him as he passed the Army and Navy Stores would have suspected first drink and then somnambulism – for he walked as in a trance. This beat the band; it was the very mark and acme of the evil with which he had to cope. He believed himself well-read in all the quaintness and curiosity of vice; his files were a veritable museum of *recherché* sins; he was the familiar of devils more grotesquely caparisoned than any that ever appeared to St Anthony. But the ingenuity of this – of this vest-pocket promiscuity or compendious polygamy – he had not met the like of before . . . So he walked down Victoria Street growling, ready positively to bark – and conceivably up the wrong tree.

Sesame and Lilies and the *Swiss Family Robinson* and the books on the bottom shelf. *After London* (what would that be? – wondered Hudspith, staring fixedly and vacantly at Westminster Abbey) and *Cowper's Letters* and *Mopsie in the Fifth* ... And suddenly the sheer technical difficulty of what the adversary had achieved revealed itself and forced from him a sort of reluctant admiration. Did you ever hear of the isle of Capri? It was clear now that this could not have been the whole story by a long way. But then perhaps it had been a matter of simple force in the end; despite the note in the cocoa-jug, perhaps the girl had been kidnapped after all.

Hudspith looked up at Big Ben and took no comfort from still being able to read the time on it. London slid past him: high up, the last glitter of day; round him, news-boys and sand-bags, cavities and crowds; far below, the purposive hurrying of the underground and the odd pleasing smell that hangs round the stations as you pass. People glanced up at the sky; Hudspith stared through it, scanning some ultimate battleground of good and evil to which the heaven of heavens is but a veil.

Fetichists. Men who insist on knock-kneed women, on bow-legged women, on one-eyed women ... and now this. Hudspith climbed flight upon flight of stairs rapidly, in a sudden cold sweat. He marched along a corridor – was hailed through an open door. 'Hurrying?' said a harassed voice. 'After another of the vanishing ladies?'

Hudspith snapped an affirmative reply and strode on. But the harassed voice stopped him. 'Well that's nothing. They've put me on a vanishing house.'

'A vanishing house?' Hudspith turned reluctantly round. 'What the deuce do you mean?'

'I mean that somebody's pinched a house – a whole blasted house!' The harassed voice rose to a note of extreme exasperation. 'And a thoroughly crazy house at that.'

4

The best connection was by Leeds. But Appleby, because the thing had been put to him as a holiday, went by York. The wait there was over an hour, and that would be time for a stroll up to the Minster. Also, he remembered a tea-shop with remarkable muffins; and although muffins are largely a matter of butter, he hoped for the best. With this judicious balance of spiritual and material satisfactions in mind he left the station.

The city walls were still there. Naturally so – but nowadays one went about in that frame of mind. The city walls were there, and in places as fresh as if they still expected culverins and demi-cannon to be brought against them hourly. Cromwell, thought Appleby vaguely as he crossed the Ouse. Extraordinarily difficult really to imagine the siege of an English town. But then how oddly things lie in the womb of time: any amount of small change from Roman legionaries' pockets was dug up when they started making the railway station. A great massacre of Jews, thought Appleby as he passed the reticent façade of the Yorkshire Club. They had just time to kill their own wives and children and then the mob were on top of them. In England that was eight hundred years ago. He glanced down Coney Street. There was little traffic at this hour; shop-keepers, who had never read manuals on scientific salesmanship, stood at their doors, unashamedly at leisure; it was all very tranquil, very secure. Laurence Sterne, Appleby thought. And there is something in walking at random about a city, he thought, that makes one's mind turn thus idly over and over, like Leopold Bloom's.

On the left, a huddle of half-heartedly ecclesiastical buildings. On the right, the unbeautiful but beneficent York City Dispensary. And in front, the Minster. The poet Shelley had called it a monstrous and taste-less relic of barbarism. But then Shelley's was an appallingly rational and scientific mind. And perhaps they had been telling him about the Jews . . . Appleby climbed the steps.

When he came out he stood for a moment blinking in the sunshine. A baker's cart rattled past; it might have reminded him of the muffins; instead, it merely recalled Daffodil and the dubious investigation in pros-pect. Why, he asked himself, should you prefer a quiet cab-horse to Captain Somebody's whopping expensive brute? Well, you hired a cab and you went to a party and you told the man to wait. Then you stole your hostess's diamonds, deftly wrapped them in a wisp of hay and pitched them through the drawing-room window at the creature's head. The creature at once devoured the unexpected luncheon, thus un-wittingly becoming your accomplice in crime. It only remained –

Appleby shook his head at this unpolicemanlike fantasy, and found that he had wandered into that narrow and winding street which has the most interesting shops. This bookshop, for instance: *A Good Warm Watch*

Coat – that was Laurence Sterne again; Francis Drake's *Eboracum* of 1736 – one would have to be fairly prosperous to buy that. And that antique shop – he crossed the road. Such places were not quite what they were in the great days of those wandering scholars, the fabulous horn-rimmed Americans of the twenties. Perhaps they will be back again in the fifties, Appleby thought; and paused to glance in. Warming-pans, coffin stools. The pomps of death: dissolution had once been a comfortably solid affair. Now it was papier-mâché coffins and zip-fastening shrouds. He knew a psychiatrist who, in the early months of war, had been required to treat nervous children in a hall stacked with these conveniences ... Another shop – and this time Appleby stared. The same sort of wares were exposed for sale. But suspended in the centre of them was something different. It was an ancient broom – the kind that is no more than a bundle of twigs or faggots bound to a handle.

Undoubtedly it was a witch's broom. And this sudden coming upon such an object in a shop window was like the beginning of a deftly told tale of the supernatural. Appleby, whose mind was perhaps no less rational than Shelley's, frowned disapprovingly. And as he frowned he became aware of somebody looking at him.

It was a shrunken and dusty man; he stood at the shop door so vacantly and patiently that he might have been something put out to purify in the sun. But he was looking at Appleby with a slowly gathering alertness, rather suggestive of a rusty machine beginning to turn. 'Good afternoon,' he said – and added mildly: 'Are you a tourist?'

The word has taken to itself a sinister quality: if you are a tourist you may well be suspected of carrying a fountain-pen filled with tear gas or a short-wave receiver concealed in your hat. And the vast annoyance of Daffodil and Bodfish and Lady Caroline lay heavily on Appleby's mind. 'No,' he said severely; 'I'm a policeman.' He looked gloomily at the broomstick. 'How,' he asked, 'did you come by that?'

The idle question had quite unexpected results. 'Oh dear, oh dear!' cried the dusty man in despair. 'I knew there must be something wrong!' He took a shuffling step backwards. 'I suppose you had better come in and see the cauldron too.'

Appleby opened his mouth to say that neither broom nor cauldron was any interest of his. But even as he did so professional instinct asserted itself. Never let any little odd thing go by. 'Certainly I must see the cauldron,' he said sternly. 'And anything else concerned.'

The dusty man ran an agitated hand through his hair, removed what appeared to be a cobweb from his right ear, and uttered a gulping sound suggestive of mingled submission and distraction. 'You see,' he said, 'one has to be on the look-out for anything that will attract the eye – of a genuine sort, of course. And there was no doubt of the provenance of the articles in this case.'

'No doubt of the what?'

'The genuineness of their history, sir, as proved by the different hands they had been through. I know the family well enough. But I should have been more careful, all the same. The whole thing was queer, I freely acknowledge. Why, even the horse was queer.'

'The *what*?'

'The horse, sir. Very queer indeed was the way that horse behaved.'

Appleby took a deep breath. 'It is about that,' he said, 'that we are going to talk.'

The first few yards of assembled antiques were reasonably well groomed; behind that everything was most woefully weighted with gathered dust. The stock-in-trade was miscellaneous, congested and arranged with a fantasy which must have been of the genuine unconscious kind. An Indian idol sat up in a four-poster bed, stretching out a multiplicity of hands as if demanding early morning tea; a row of stags' heads had Georgian coffee-pots and spoon-warmers depending from the antlers; through the half-open door of a grandfather clock peered the articulated skeleton of an ape or baboon. Your first surrealists, thought Appleby, are necessarily those who purvey curios in a restricted space. And you can achieve similar effects by dropping a bomb on a well-ordered museum. Perhaps some psychic and infantile bomb is responsible for the pictures of Miro and Dali. Perhaps – He remembered that he had come in here to listen to a confession. 'Things look rather quiet,' he said in an accusing voice.

'They *are* quiet,' said the dusty man. 'Really very quiet indeed,' he added with anxious candour.

'Still, you have sold a couple of china dogs.' On a very dusty table Appleby had noticed two oval islands such as the posteriors of these creatures would cover.

'We've been watched!' The dusty man's voice had risen to absolute despair. 'Shadowed!' He slumped down on a stool beside the grandfather clock; the door slid to; inside the bones rattled dryly, as if the whole were a nightmarish memorial of mortality and time. 'After thirty years of respectable trading, much of it with the nobility and gentry of the county – to say nothing of the Dean and Chapter. It's hard, sir; really hard.'

'No doubt.'

'And the Metcalfes are well known to be most respectable folk.'

'Ah.'

The dusty man rose heavily, and from inside the clock the bones rattled again like a sepulchral aeolian harp. 'Of course there is the old story about them. I'm a Haworth man myself and I've known it since a boy. I'm far from denying the queer sort of celebrity they've enjoyed.'

'Wouldn't you say,' asked Appleby gravely, 'that as Haworth celebrities the Metcalfes have been rather outshone by the Brontës?'

'The Brontës! Let me tell you, sir, that the Metcalfes were celebrated through the whole Riding when the Brontës were still hoeing potatoes in Ireland. Why, it was in 1772 that Hannah Metcalfe barely escaped being boiled in her own cauldron. And that was just fifty years after the last recorded execution for witchcraft in these islands. As for the cauldron, it's just behind you. And now I ask you: do you blame me for giving five pounds for the lot? As a Haworth man, mark you, and not caring to see the antiquities of the district disappearing in a caravan.'

Appleby turned round and examined the cauldron. It was a massive iron affair and would doubtless have accommodated Hannah Metcalfe comfortably; certainly Turks' noses, lizards' legs and similar prescriptive ingredients would have made but an inconsiderable bubble and boil in the depths of it. Appleby peered at it more closely. 'It looks to me,' he said unkindly, 'as if it had been cast in Birmingham about fifty years ago.'

'Oh dear, oh dear!' The dusty man was even more distressed than before. 'No doubt there has been a certain element of showmanship involved. It's common enough in such places, after all. The bed in which the great man was born: that sort of thing. And if you have a celebrated witch in the family, and people regularly paying sixpence to see her kitchen, you naturally do a little fitting up from time to time. Not but what I freely admit I ought to have had nothing to do with it. Hannah Metcalfe – *this* Hannah Metcalfe – is a bit strange by all accounts. She looked strange in the caravan. What with her and the horse –'

'We must come to that. Now, I wonder' – and Appleby laid a soothing hand on the dusty man's arm – 'if you would tell me the whole story? I'm not at all inclined to think you acted improperly in any way. But the whole story would be a great help – in something, you know, quite unconnected with the broom and cauldron.'

The dusty man looked both relieved and perplexed. 'Well, it must have been a week ago last Thursday, and I was just taking down the shutters when I saw this caravan coming down the street. And that, you know, was rather surprising in itself. For we're a bit out of the way, and anything that turns down here is usually looking for something in particular. But from what followed in this case it didn't seem to be like that.'

'I see. But if the caravan was trying to slip through York in an unobtrusive way – might that account for it?'

'I dare say it might, sir. Anyway, the thing was going past at a quiet walk and there were two men in front and suddenly one of them calls out. "I've got an idea," he said. "Look at that shop." "Which shop?" says the other, and the first man replies, "There: number thirty-nine" – which of course is myself. And it was then that the horse – a quiet-looking horse enough – began to behave queer. It stopped – and the fellow hadn't pulled it up that I could see – and took to nodding its head like an idol. It went on nodding and the two men seemed to be having an argument. Then one of them shouted at me. "Hi," he said, "you there; here's something ought to interest you." It wasn't very polite, but then in these days' – the dusty man shook his head mournfully – 'it's something to be taken any notice of at all. So I crossed the street. "Look here," says the fellow, "you'll have heard of Hannah Metcalfe's cottage? Well, most of it's here, and for sale." And at that he reached behind him and outed with the broom. "We've got Hannah herself, for that matter," he said, "only she's already booked." "She died a hundred and fifty years ago," I said – for I thought it was some silly sort of joke. And at that there was a wildish kind of laugh from inside, and the young woman stuck her head out. It gave me quite a turn. And of course it was Hannah Metcalfe all right – the young one. "Good morning," she said. And if I remember aright, sir, it was just then that the horse stopped nodding – sudden-like. I don't mind saying that I was beginning to find it a bit strange.'

'No doubt,' Appleby was finding it a little odd himself. 'About this witch's cottage business – what are the facts on that? I gather the old Hannah Metcalfe was a celebrated witch?'

'Just so, sir. And her descendants have always lived there and made a bit out of the old story – though respectable folk enough, as I said. Of course there's the story that the witchcraft or whatever it is has been more or less hereditary, cropping up from time to time. It's wonderful what people will believe.' And the dusty man looked round rather nervously at the cauldron.

Appleby eyed him curiously. 'Yes,' he agreed; 'it is wonderful. And this younger Hannah had that sort of reputation too?'

'Yes, sir – among the uneducated, of course. And I'm told she believed it herself. You see, she's the last of the Metcalfes, and has been living alone in the cottage for years, showing the cauldron and all the rest of it. Such surroundings, you'll agree, might well put uncanny ideas in a girl's head. Anyway, here she was in this caravan, sticking her head out and laughing, while these two fellows argued about I couldn't quite gather what.'

'Ah – that's a pity.'

'Well, sir, roughly it seemed like this. They'd had orders to collect the young woman and seemingly they'd collected a good many of her effects, so to speak, as well. But now they'd somehow found out that these weren't wanted, and when one of them saw an antique shop it had occurred to him to turn a penny by doing a deal. The other seemed to be suggesting that this would lead to trouble – but now young Hannah put in a word. "That's all right," she said. "You turn all that stuff into beer for all I care. I'm off to something different." "There you are," says the fellow who was trying to do the deal. "All fair and square, as you see. And you can have the lot for five pounds." "All right," says the other fellow, nodding approval. And, do you know, sir, the horse seemed to approve too, for it began stamping on the gound with one of its forefeet – just as if it were giving a round of applause.'

'It sounds,' said Appleby seriously, 'as if the horse was bewitched.'

'Very good, sir – very good indeed.' The dusty man laughed with considerable uneasiness. 'And that's the whole story. This Miss Metcalfe might be behaving a bit strange, but she seemed nowise out of her wits and I knew her to be the owner of the goods. So it ended with my giving five pounds for the broom and the cauldron and two or three other things you can inspect. If the Metcalfe cottage was being broken up there seemed no harm in being in on the dispersal.'

'None at all.' Appleby was staring thoughtfully at a table weighed down with elephants' tusks, snuff-boxes and Dresden shepherdesses. 'But tell me: did you have any further talk with Miss Metcalfe herself?'

'No – or nothing with any sense to it. After the things had been brought out I did try to pass a conversational remark. "So you're off to see the world?" I said – something like that. And she looked at me mockingly, as you might say. "That's just it," she said. "Did you ever hear of the isle of Capri?" And with that she disappeared inside the caravan and I saw no more of her.'

Appleby frowned. 'The isle of Capri? It seems a far cry from Haworth. And not too easy to get to in these days.'

'I think, sir, she might be speaking in what you would call a meta-phorical way.'

'Very probably.' Appleby glanced at his watch and saw that he would have to hurry for his train. He did not want to miss it; Bodfish, Daffodil, and even the Assistant-Commissioner's sister had taken on a much more beguiling colour in the past half-hour. 'It is possible that you will hear more of this.' He looked at the dusty man and remembered how out-rageously he had intruded upon his little mystery. 'And meanwhile I wonder if you could sell me a – a teapot?'

But his choice was abstracted. The odd matter of Miss Hannah Metcalfe had pretty substantial possession of his mind.

5

The telephone wires rose and fell, and beyond them the dales swept past, fluid and subtly circling. It was on the white ribbons of road and lane that Appleby kept his eye – expecting always to see, symbolically receding, a caravan and a temperamental horse. There was little reason in the expectation. But then neither had there been reason in what hap-pened in York. Policemen rarely make long and expensive journeys in search of unimportant quadrupeds. They do not commonly come upon traces of their quarry in wholly unexpected places and in a wholly fortuitous way. And Sir Robert Peel himself still slumbered in the womb of time long after witchcraft had ceased to be matter of their serious concern.

The witches have departed, leaving no addresses; the last of them is now somewhere diminishing into distance, headed for the fields of amaranth and asphodel – and with Bodfish's Daffodil as an appropriate guide. Hannah Metcalfe has gone; down these receding vistas she has grown smaller and smaller, as did the Good Folk before her.

And so much for the fantasy of the thing. What of its sober reason? One departs from one place because one designs – or because somebody else designs – that one should arrive in another. The witches, then, are arriving – at addresses which are yet to seek. And equally Daffodil is arriving, and the problem is to find out where. For behind the abductions, thought Appleby, there was enterprise, enterprise as well as – perhaps rather than – mere caprice. And efficiency. If the removal of Captain Somebody's brute had been a piece of bungling, at least the error had been repaired with confidence and speed. And if you want to smuggle an undistinguished horse across country it is not a bad idea to clap it within the shafts of a caravan. Incidentally, you will need all the ideas you can think up. For England today is a country in which even slightly mysterious manoeuvres are singularly difficult to perform. At the top of that little church tower on the hill is the squire or the pub-keeper or the blacksmith, his imagination keyed up to suspect the ingenuities of enemy action in anything a bit out of the way. As far as interfering with Lady Caroline's carriage-exercise is concerned, or in point of persuading Yorkshire maidens that they are bound for the isle of Capri, the times could scarcely be more thoroughly out of joint. And so if the witches and the half-witted horses are arriving *now* there is likely to be some particular premium about their doing so ... Appleby was groping round this obscure conception when the train ran into Harrogate.

There is a pleasing element of the unknown in the approach to big hotels. They may contain an exiled court, the ghostly counterpart of a government department, a great London school, or even a thousand or so people busy making things. But Appleby found only what such an establishment normally holds out, and presently he was wandering across the Stray, somewhat at a loss. He must present himself to the local police and tactfully explain that he was the consequence of humouring earls' daughters who inappropriately demanded the services of Scotland Yard. After that he was committed to visiting this exigent lady herself, and after that again would come the tiresome business of duplicating inquiries which had doubtless already been made in a thoroughly efficient way. Finally, he could not leave Harrogate without paying a duty-visit to his aunt, a person of pronounced character and intimidating early associations.

But this was his mission only in its original or diplomatic aspect. Unless – as was, after all, likely enough – the horse of Miss Metcalfe's caravan was distinct from the horse of Bodfish's open landau – unless this was so the case had taken to itself a certain body, a marked beguilement, in a wholly unexpected direction. Meditating this, Appleby decided to postpone the business of introductions until he had sought enlightenment on this prior point. So he consulted a note-book and made his way to the livery stables from which Daffodil had been stolen.

The stables belonged – with the sort of muted absurdity which went with this whole business, Appleby felt – to a Mr Gee; and Mr Gee, an elderly man of cheerful appearance, was discovered in the middle of a yard, contemplating a sleepy dog with an air of the greatest benevolence.

'A nice dog,' Appleby said.

Still benevolent, Mr Gee swung round. 'Dish-faced,' he said in a voice of unfathomable gloom.

'Ah,' said Appleby, rather at a loss.

'And undershot.' Mr Gee preserved his highly deceptive appearance. 'Pig-jawed, in fact.'

'Well, yes – I suppose he is, a little.'

'She.'

'Ah.'

'Cow-hocked. No feather. Apple-headed. Pily.'

'Pily? I suppose she is. But still –'

'Pily is the only good thing about her. Apple-headed. No feather. Cow-headed. Pig-jawed. What do you think of the stifles?'

'I'm afraid,' Appleby said modestly, 'I don't know anything about dogs.'

'I'm afraid you don't,' said Mr Gee gloomily. He continued to radiate the appearance of good cheer.

'At the moment, as a matter of fact, I'm more interested in horses.'

'You don't look as if you knew much about them either. Taxis I should say was more your line.' Mr Gee, maintaining his air of mild euphoria, began to move away.

'And one horse in particular. I've come about Daffodil.'

'Gawd!' said Mr Gee, and quickened his step.

'Did they try to buy Daffodil first?'

Mr Gee stopped. 'You mayn't know a poodle from a chow,' he said. 'But you're a sensible man. It took the others half an hour to think of that one. And of course they did. What would be the sense of all that stour to steal a horse you knew wouldn't fetch above a ten-pound note? They offered me thirty.'

'And you refused?'

'Of course I refused. Do you think I want to be taken up? It's contrary to the provisions of the Act.'

Appleby, if he knew little about horses, had necessarily to know much about the law. And this particular piece of legislative wisdom was new to him. 'You supposed it was illegal? I hardly think –'

'It was contrary to the provisions of the Act.' Mr Gee was obstinate. 'Twenty pounds for nout is certain sure to be contrary to the provisions of the Act.' He spoke as if from some depth of mournful experience. 'I'd have been taken up. What else is the likes of you paid to go about after? Taking people up over the Act.' Mr Gee's beaming eye looked very shrewdly at Appleby. 'Police everywhere,' he said. 'Gawd!'

Appleby, feeling the shoe-leather thicken under his feet and a shadowy metropolitan helmet hover on his brow, concluded that Mr Gee was a man to reckon with; he contrived to combine a mild mania with an accurate appraisal of men. 'Well, Mr Gee, we'll say you felt the thing to be irregular and would have nothing to do with it. And the result was that the horse disappeared. I don't want to know how or when, for I've no doubt at all that has been gone over already. But I want you to tell me something about the horse itself.'

'About Daffodil?' Mr Gee's cheerful face clouded, so that it was logical to suppose he was about to attempt a stroke of humour. 'Well, I always suspected rareying with Daffodil – though, mind you, it may have been galvayning all the same.' And Mr Gee stooped down and fondled the ear of the dish-faced dog.

Appleby sat down placidly on a bench. 'My dear sir, I quite realize that an erudite hippologist like yourself –'

''Ere,' said Mr Gee, 'civil is civil, I'll have you know. And none of that language in my yard.'

'Very well, I'll say nothing at all.' Appleby took out a pipe. 'But I'm staying here until you give me a reasonable account of that horse.'

Mr Gee looked deliberately about him, plainly searching for a par- ticularly ponderous shaft of wit. 'The trouble about Daffodil,' he said at length, 'was always in the carburettor. And for that matter I never cared for his overhead valves.' And at this Mr Gee laughed so suddenly and loudly that the pily dog rose and took to its heels.

'Come off it.' Appleby filled his pipe. 'A joke's a joke, Mr Gee. But business is business, after all. And I may tell you I hate the stink of petrol. I mayn't know about galvayning – but I'd take a cab every time, just the same.'

The effect of this mendacious statement was immediate. Mr Gee sat down on the bench in a most companionable way. 'I'll tell you what,' he said – and lowered his voice. 'I never half liked that horse. There were old parties that liked him and would order him regular. They thought him almost 'uman. But if there's one thing I like less than an almost 'uman dog it's an almost 'uman horse.'

'I see. By the way, how did Daffodil come to you in the first place?'

'I had him of a man.' Mr Gee spoke at once darkly and vaguely. 'It would have been at Boroughbridge fair, I reckon.'

'But you don't know anything about his previous owner?'

'I reckon I was told.' Mr Gee was gloomily silent. 'I suppose you come from London?'

'Yes.'

'And I suppose you've heard of the Cities of the Plain? Well, add all the lies was ever told in London, mister, to all the hanky-panky Sodom and Gomorrah ever knew – and that's a horse fair. So you may take it that anything I was told about Daffodil down Boroughbridge way isn't what you'd call evidence. I've bought horses, man and boy, for forty years. And I shuts my ears and opens my eyes.'

It was clear that on what the dusty man would call the provenance of Daffodil there was little to be discovered. Appleby tried another tack. 'How was he almost human? Was he particularly intelligent?'

Mr Gee shook his head emphatically. 'Nowise. I don't think I ever knew a horse more lacking in – well, in horse sense, if you follow me. And that's what I said to the police when they first came after him. "The horse was half-witted," I said, "and if he's gone I'll cut my losses." And now I say it again. For who wants a half-witted, almost human horse?'

Appleby looked in some perplexity at Daffodil's late owner. Mr Gee seemed to be suggesting the same relation between human and equine intelligence as Swift had expressed in his celebrated fable of the Yahoos. And yet Mr Gee was far from being a person of literary mind – nor did the quality of his humorous sallies suggest a taste for the finer ironies. So Appleby tried again. 'I find it difficult to picture this animal at all. Just *how* was he almost human?'

Mr Gee looked cautiously round the yard – very much, Appleby recalled, as the dusty man had looked round at the cauldron. 'He knew his numbers,' said Mr Gee briefly.

'How very strange.' Appleby found it difficult to hide his satisfaction. 'You mean that if, for instance, you happened to mention a number in Daffodil's presence he would stop and nod or paw out the sum of the digits involved?'

Mr Gee nodded. 'You've got it. "How much to Starbeck?" a fare would ask Bodfish. "Five bob," Bodfish would say. And, sure enough, Daffodil would nod five times. Unnatural, I call it.'

'It sounds,' suggested Appleby cheerfully, 'as if Daffodil had once been a horse in a show.'

'But that's not all.' Mr Gee laid a hand on Appleby's arm. 'Now, listen,' he said. 'Nobody believes in the uncanny nowadays, do they?'

'Certainly not.' The proposition was extremely doubtful, Appleby thought; but nevertheless it was judicious to agree.

'Well, then, can you explain this? Daffodil knew the numbers you was *thinking* of – just as well as the others. Indeed, more accurate he was on them, Bodfish says. It would be like this. Bodfish would be driving someone to John's Well, say. And "I'll stick her for three bob," he'd think to himself. And then Daffodil would pull up and do his three times nod or stamp. When he was driving Daffodil, Bodfish had to keep figures out of his head, he says. Now, what do you think of that?'

Appleby thought it rather less remarkable than the first instance of Daffodil's powers. But as explaining this would require something like a psychological and physiological treatise, he thought it better to refrain. 'Mr Gee,' he parried, 'did it never occur to you that these peculiar powers made Daffodil an unusually valuable horse? Imagine the thing in a circus. Members of the audience are invited to come up, hold Daffodil by the bridle and think of a number. And then Daffodil taps it out. The trick would make any showman's fortune.'

'It so happens,' said Mr Gee with dignity, 'that I'm not a showman.

But if Daffodil is valuable the way you suggest, then you know something about them in whose hands he was before. They weren't show people, or they wouldn't have let him go.'

Appleby got up. 'Mr Gee, you ought to have taken to my profession.'

'There's compliments you can return,' said Mr Gee, 'and there's compliments you can't.'

6

What they call a Parthian shot, Appleby said to himself as he made his way back to his hotel. And, as far as this evening was concerned, a *coup de grâce*: beguiling as the affair of Daffodil and the witches appeared, he had seen enough of it for that day.

It was the violet hour, and across the Stray the last bath-chairs were striving homewards. Conch-like and creeping, they choicely illustrated in their controlled diversity the beautiful social complexity of England. The coolie element was provided in the main by seedy old persons drawn from various strata of the deserving and undeserving poor; there was an admixture, however, of well-found private menials. These latter, Appleby noticed, tended to push, whereas the seedy old persons pulled. Pulling is more efficient, but its associations are quadrupedal and lowering; in pushing alone can a certain dignity and aloofness be preserved. With traction and propulsion the seedy persons and the servants laboured towards their goals: hydropathics and hotels, guest homes, boarding-houses, apartments, lodgings, furnished rooms. And the bath-chairs too had their hierarchies and orders; a system less of caste than of class – in which there is always the inspiring possibility of rapid rise and always the less cheerful probability of gradual decline. Here and there an enterprising person had contrived to smarten up his stock in trade; but more commonly these vehicles had come down in the world – the varnish cracked, the wicker-work prickly, the hood peeling, the horsehair and kapoc coming out in wisps. And through this scene of struggle moved the haughty aristocracy of the kind; bath-chairs, with doors and with elaborate windscreens of wood and glass, so that the occupants, dimly discerned, showed like dingy mezzotints in drear mahogany frames. The bath-chairs, spoking outwards like a mechanized column deploying, bore away from the focal baths and pump-rooms old women who clutched library novels, ivory sticks, triumphantly tracked packages of chocolate peppermint creams. And on the pavements, politely yielding place, were old men of respectable dress and tenuously maintained bank balances; these exercised dogs; prowled in quest of evening papers, of tobacco; cast ancient professional eyes at the multiform signs that even Harrogate stood to arms. England was carrying on.

And Appleby was hurrying to dine. He would have an early meal and go to a cinema and see something really silly – something silly enough to make Daffodil and Hannah Metcalfe look comparatively sensible when he returned to them in the morning. Certainly no more of them tonight.

'John;' called a commanding voice from behind him, 'come here.'

He turned to face the roadway, and his heart sank at what he saw. It was – it could not be other than – an open landau Two elderly ladies sat expansively and side by side on the principal seat. Opposite to them, and – although she had a whole side to herself – in a more contracted position, was a female figure in a mouse-coloured hat. And on the box, tightly wrapped in rugs like the young of some savage tribe, perched a fat man with a liquid, a frankly tap-room eye.

'How are you, aunt!' said Appleby. 'I was just on my way to call.'

'No doubt.' The disbelief of Appleby's aunt was unoffended and matter of fact. 'Lady Caroline, let me introduce my nephew, John.'

Lady Caroline bowed. She was in the dilemma of those who must combine dignity with a bad cold; her nose and eyes were uncomfortably reddened and she had apparently chosen clothes to match: this gave her an alarmingly combustible look. 'Maidment will make room,' said Lady Caroline commandingly.

'Miss Maidment,' said Appleby's aunt politely, 'will you make room?'

The mouse-hatted lady contracted herself yet further into a corner and Appleby realized with dismay that he was expected to embark. The landau smelt of horse and dust and eucalyptus; it moved off with a creak.

'Miss Appleby,' said Lady Caroline, 'do not you think that Bodfish had better avoid James Street with that horse?'

'Miss Maidment,' said Appleby's aunt, 'Lady Caroline thinks that Bodfish had better avoid James Street. The horse.'

Miss Maidment twisted round on her seat. 'Bodfish,' she said severely, 'you had better avoid James Street with that horse.'

Bodfish, without uttering or turning round, put up a hand and raised his hat some inches above his head. Lady Caroline turned an appraising eye on Appleby. 'We are without confidence in the horse,' she explained. 'Particularly Miss Maidment. She had an experience with a horse. When young. Maidment – my bag.'

There was a search for Lady Caroline's bag. Miss Appleby took no part. But presently she spoke. 'My dear,' she said, 'remember how often you find it –' She broke off and looked meaningfully at Lady Caroline.

'Bodfish,' called Miss Maidment sternly, 'stop.'

The landau was brought to a halt and Lady Caroline prized some inches from her seat. The bag had undoubtedly been beneath her. She got out a handkerchief and blew. The equipage drove on. 'Mr Appleby,' said Lady Caroline sternly, 'you are from London?'

'Yes. I came down today.'

Lady Caroline blew again. 'The tubes are congested,' she said.

'Yes. But not so badly as they were.'

Lady Caroline frowned. 'Young man, do I understand that you are a physician?'

'Lady Caroline,' explained Appleby's aunt, 'refers to her chest.'

'I beg your pardon.' Appleby was quite unnerved by this mis-understanding. 'I'm a policeman. I've come about Daffodil.'

'You are the person' – Lady Caroline looked at Miss Appleby and coughed – 'you are the officer whom my brother was to send?'

'Yes, Lady Caroline.'

'Dear me. My dear' – she turned to Miss Appleby – 'I think Bodfish had better attend.'

'Miss Maidment, Lady Caroline thinks –'

'Bodfish,' said Miss Maidment threateningly, 'pray pay attention.'

Bodfish raised his hat. The quieter streets of Harrogate ambled past with the jerkiness only experienced in cabs and ill-projected films. Appleby, jolting hip to hip with the Assistant-Commissioner's sister's companion, reflected that carriage exercise was not altogether a con-tradiction in terms. And Lady Caroline, having again blown, leant for-ward and tapped Appleby on the knee with a decorously gloved hand, 'I must tell you that I have had more satisfaction from the Cruelty to Animals than from the police.'

'To the Cruelty to Animals,' said Miss Appleby, 'one subscribes.'

'No doubt. But one pays taxes for the police.' And Lady Caroline fixed her glance severely on Appleby's tie, an expensive one from the Burlington Arcade. 'We support the police.'

'In a sense,' said Appleby mildly, 'the police support your brother. So it evens out.'

Miss Maidment contrived a nervous sound in her throat. And Lady Caroline sat back abruptly. 'My dear,' she said, 'I believe your nephew has something of your own wit. But that he has your sufficient sense of decorum I will not at present venture to add. And now, what I was about to observe. The Cruelty to Animals have been most active. And they have arrived, so far, at the remarkable sum of one hundred and eighty-one pounds.'

Appleby looked perlexed. 'I'm afraid I don't understand you.'

'They have traced Daffodil through what may be described as a little Odyssey.' Lady Caroline paused, as if reconsidering the propriety of this word. 'What may be described,' she amended, 'as a veritable Chevy Chase. It appears that in the present posture of our affairs – Bodfish, are you attending?'

Bodfish raised his hat.

'It appears that in the present posture of our affairs –'

'In war-time,' said Miss Appleby inoffensively.

'Thank you, my dear. It appears that, at present, moving a horse clandestinely about the country is a matter of substantial difficulty. This has made it possible to trace Daffodil at least some little way. And much expense seems to have been involved. Conveyances were bought and abandoned as part of a carefully contrived scheme. That sort of thing. I am informed that at least a hundred and eighty-one pounds was spent in this way before Daffodil reached Bradford.' Lady Caroline looked suspiciously at Appleby. 'But this is information which the police already possess.'

'I haven't seen the local men yet; I determined to see *you* first, Lady Caroline.' Appleby, thinking this rather a happy stroke, allowed himself the ghost of a wink at his aunt. 'But I am surprised the animal was taken to Bradford. I knew for certain that he turned up later at York – which is pretty well in the opposite direction.'

'Daffodil was traced to Bradford, and from there some way on the road to Keighley.'

'Keighley?' said Miss Appleby suddenly. 'There is something rather interesting in that. John, you are no doubt aware of it.'

Appleby looked at his aunt with suspicion; there was that in her tone which recalled to him searching investigations into his historical and geographical knowledge long ago. 'I'm afraid,' he said, 'I can't think of anything particularly significant about Keighley.'

'No more there is. What is significant is that Daffodil should last be heard of going from Bradford *towards* Keighley. Because that, you know, would take him uncommonly near Haworth.'

'Haworth!' Appleby sat back so abruptly that his elbow almost dug Miss Maidment in the ribs.

'Exactly so. I am glad you see my point.' And Appleby's aunt turned to Lady Caroline. 'John is, of course, accustomed to putting two and two together. It is his profession. And when he brings his mind to bear upon our unfortunate loss – Bodfish's unfortunate loss –'

Bodfish raised his hat.

'– he at once asks himself what is *peculiar* about Daffodil. And the answer is this: that Daffodil is a *peculiar* horse. A *gifted* horse. In fact, a *queer* horse.'

'I cannot agree, dear Miss Appleby,' said Lady Caroline with dignity, 'that Daffodil is a *queer* horse. But *gifted*, certainly.'

'We will say, then, that Daffodil has unusual powers. And Daffodil disappears. Observe what John does. He will put two and two together if he can. He turns to his files – Scotland Yard, as your dear brother will have told you, is full of files – and seeks for any *context* in which this disappearance of Daffodil may be placed. In other words: have there been any similar disappearances of queer or gifted horses recently? And if not of horses, then of queer and gifted creatures of any other kind? He makes one significant discovery. Recently, and in this district, a young girl has suddenly and unaccountably disappeared from her home – we all read of it, you know, in the local papers. A gifted and decidedly queer girl. In fact, a witch.'

Lady Caroline blew. Miss Maidment made a noise as of muted alarm. Appleby merely gaped.

'And this young female of unusual powers lived near Haworth. How impressed, then, was John when he heard that Daffodil had last been seen moving that way!'

Lady Caroline frowned. 'This is most peculiar. And certainly above Bodfish's head.'

Miss Maidment turned round. 'Bodfish,' she said judicially, 'we do not require your attention longer.'

Bodfish raised his hat.

'But this,' continued Miss Appleby placidly, 'is only the first stage of John's inquiries. He has consulted his colleagues; assistants have been turning over press cuttings' — suddenly Miss Appleby opened her bag — 'as I may say I have been doing myself.' She paused, and Appleby was momentarily aware of an infinitely ironical glance. 'John has been particularly struck by the case of Lucy Rideout, a young girl who recently disappeared — having been, as it would seem, procured for immoral purposes.'

'Maidment,' said Lady Caroline, 'such things ought not to afford embarrassment at your mature years.'

'Now, about this girl is something very odd indeed.' Miss Appleby consulted the first of her cuttings. 'It appears, as the result of elaborate investigations carried out with great scientific skill by a Superintendent Hudspith, that Lucy Rideout represents a remarkable case of dissociation. She is not so much one person as two — or perhaps three — persons; and she must have been — um — correspondingly difficult to seduce. But seduced she was, having been led to believe, as it appears, that she was to be taken to Capri — a disagreeable resort, but one with romantic associations in the minds of the lower classes.'

Appleby was looking round-eyed at his aunt — much as Sherlock Holmes must have looked at his brother, the remote and quintessential detective. 'Capri,' he said, '— to be sure. And did you say dissociation?'

'Yes. What is sometimes called multiple personality.'

'Dr Jekyll and Mr Hyde,' said Lady Caroline. 'Or consider Miss Maidment. Maidment, suppose yourself passionately to desire some unlawful delight.'

Miss Maidment wriggled on her seat — but not at all as if she were contriving to obey this injunction.

'And consider yourself as having, at the same time, a conscience which forbids such indulgence. You are torn between conflicting forces. You are like the souls of the dead in the old stained-glass windows; the angels are tugging at your hair and the devils at your toes. You follow me, Maidment?'

Miss Maidment made an indecisive noise; it acknowledged the theological trend of her employer's remarks by being faintly devotional in tone.

'The strain is great, and you let go. You let yourself go in the middle; and where there was one Maidment there are now two.' Lady Caroline frowned, apparently finding this a displeasing thought. 'But of course you still have only one *body*. The two personalities share it, each taking sole possession for a time. In this way the licentious and the puritanical Maidment each gets her turn, and a certain degree of nervous conflict is thus eliminated. You see, Maidment?'

Miss Maidment again made a noise; then – unexpectedly – she contrived speech. 'I don't understand it at all. It sounds to me much more like being possessed by evil spirits.'

'Lady Caroline's description of the condition is excellent,' said Miss Appleby. 'But Miss Maidment too has made a significant observation. I have no doubt, John, that you will take account of it. Plainly, it has its place – as has another item on which you are certainly informed. I mean the Bloomsbury affair.'

'Ah,' said Appleby.

'What the newspapers' – Appleby's aunt again consulted her cuttings – 'have been calling the Mystery of the Absconding House.'

'Miss Appleby,' said Lady Caroline severely, 'houses do not abscond. Dishonest servants abscond. You are confused.'

'I do not think I am, dear Lady Caroline. This house has undoubtedly *made off* – and very possibly to Capri. Moreover, it is a haunted house. A most substantial eighteenth-century house in a Bloomsbury square. Dr Johnson once investigated a ghost there. And now it has been stolen.'

'Houses may not be stolen, dear Miss Appleby. The proposition is absurd.'

'In normal times it would no doubt be so. But at present it is quite feasible to steal a house. This house was stolen in stages. One night it was intact; the next morning the roof had disappeared. In London at present such things are not, it seems, at all out of the way. The next morning much of the upper storey had disappeared. And so on. People remarked upon it as an uncommonly unlucky house – it was so regularly hit. But by the time the ground floor was vanishing the thing had begun to excite speculation. There was so remarkably little rubble. Then one night the basement went, and there was nothing but a hole.

Inquiries were made and there emerged the indisputable fact that the house had been stolen. It appears that during air-raids there is a good deal of noise and confusion. Buildings are falling and lorries are hurrying about and what are called demolition squads are at work. The opportunities for stealing a house are quite unusual. But it must be expensive. The theft of Daffodil becomes a small thing in comparison.'

'Daffodil,' said Lady Caroline, 'is a *horse*.'

'No doubt. But a queer horse. And Lucy Rideout is a queer girl. And this house of which I have been telling you is a queer house. And all of them have been stolen within a few days of each other.' Miss Appleby put the cuttings away and shut her bag. 'I am glad to think, John, that you have the matter in hand.'

'Yes, aunt,' said Appleby.

Part 2
Whale Roads

I

The ocean was empty and unruffled; it was like the sky but emptier – for sometimes across the sky would pass a small high cloud. The ocean was always empty. Every twenty-four hours, and with startling abruptness, the ship emerged from the long black tunnel of the night into this other and cerulean void; every twenty-four hours, without a glimmer of protesting light, she disappeared again. Just such a monotonous voyaging Appleby remembered in a scenic waterway of his youth; so long in a winding papier-mâché tunnel, so long floating beneath some dome-like structure garishly lit from below.

With closed decks and sealed portholes the ship would nose through the night, a throb in the centre of her and a thud and a swish, a thud and a swish everlastingly at her side. And everlastingly by day the prow rose and fell, rose and fell across the horizon towards which she drove with an energy growing daily more mysterious in its evident transcendence of any merely human scale of effort. The prow rose and fell. And always there were two men watching, their immobile bodies thrown against a background now of sky and now of sea. They were looking for submarines. And now for long stretches of the day Hudspith was there beside them – Hudspith too watching, but with an eye that swept neither to port nor starboard, Hudspith looking straight ahead at the Lord knew what. Buenos Aires, Appleby thought, Rio de Janeiro, phony social experiments vaguely reported from far up the Parana. Hudspith was one of those people upon whose nervous system the sea had a marked effect. Appleby would be glad to see him on dry land again. One does not want a loopy colleague when embarked upon so distinctly rummy an investigation as the present.

We have followed a Harrogate cab-horse across the equator, Appleby said to himself, and have no idea where it is leading us. *Wohin der Weg? Kein Weg! Ins Unbetretene.* That was Mephistopheles, and ought to appeal to Hudspith – before whom it was clear that the Devil might appear in visible shape ... Appleby moved to the rail and looked down at the sea. The Whale Road, the Angles had called it. But the road was invisible; there was no road; the ship drove mysteriously towards a goal beyond the present reach of sense. And rather like that was the hue and cry after Daffodil.

Appleby thought of it chiefly as the Daffodil affair – no doubt because Hudspith so singly saw it as the affair of Hannah Metcalfe and Lucy Rideout. But actually, thought Appleby, it was the Affair of the Haunted House. In that lay the promise of future contact with a somewhat complex mind. For it was not as if the absconding house were a mere decorative flourish or grace note. Its theft must have cost incomparably more than the abductions of Hannah, Lucy and Daffodil put together. Not that it had been particularly difficult. Just expensive.

It sounded, said Appleby to himself as he paced the deck, like one of the impossible tasks imposed upon the heroes of fairy stories. Steal a large Bloomsbury house and walk out of England with it – this in time of war. But it had been war that made the stealing easy; when whole streets are vanishing, a single house is scarcely missed. And the walking out of the country with it depended on war too. What happens when an English port is blitzed? The rubble is promptly shipped to America as ballast and used there as the foundations of new docks and quays – a sober fact so fantastic that one would hesitate to put it in a magazine story. Your churches are bombed; whereupon they become the causeways across which A A guns are rolled aboard your waiting freighters. It is very odd; and makes it just possible for an ingenious person – or organization, surely – to make off with an edifice once critically inspected by Dr Johnson. But why steal a reputedly haunted house? Appleby could see only one reason. And it cohered with his present view of the matter – or ought he to say his aunt's view? – no better than with Hudspith's.

From somewhere aft a bugle sounded. Hudspith turned and strode across the fo'c'sle head. At least he still ate. Appleby stared again at the vacant horizon. One could easily lose one's bearings. All at sea, as they say. Obscurely he wished for a familiar landfall – as if that would help. Table Mountain, hanging in the sky like Swift's floating island. The litter of gigantic lettering on the quays of Manhattan; Brooklyn Bridge, Liverpool and its monster hotels. The low, dun, saurian ripple of land which Australia rolls into the Indian Ocean. If the ship could raise one of these, he felt absurdly, then the unaccountable fragments of this business might come together in his mind. But what lay before the ship's prow was South America, and of South America he knew nothing. Nor was he sure that it was in South America that this chase would end.

The saloon was empty; he sat down and let the weeks of tedious investigation trickle through his mind. The haunted house had gone to Boston and thence to Port of Spain; after that it had disappeared. Hannah Metcalfe and Daffodil had last been heard of in Montevideo. But Lucy Rideout had been reported – though uncertainly – in Valparaiso, and perhaps there was significance in that. He looked up as Hudspith slumped darkly down beside him. 'What would you say,' he asked, 'to Robinson Crusoe's island?'

'Roast Hazel Hen,' said Hudspith sombrely. But this was to the steward.

'Juan Fernandez,' continued Appleby. 'Are they particularly immoral there? Because it looks as if our rendezvous may be somewhere in that direction.'

Hudspith shook his head and said nothing. Bodfish himself, it occurred to Appleby, would be as entertaining a companion. The truth was that Hudspith, learned in the depravities and perversities, had invented a new one – and was foundering beneath the additional burden. The seduction of feeble-minded girls he had supported for years, but the seduction of a plural-minded one was too much for him. Lucy Rideout, he believed, had been carried off for some person so vicious as to relish a mistress who was now one woman and now another. One could probably search all the volumes that booksellers discreetly call 'Curious' without coming upon anything quite so odd – and here was Hudspith obsessed by the thing as if it were an ultimate manifestation of evil. Appleby waited until Hudspith's plate was before him and then tried a little reason. For it is desirable that policemen should be reasonable – and particularly those sent expensively across the world on detective missions.

'Look here, I grant that your hypothesis would be sound and sufficient if Lucy's affair stood in isolation. But it doesn't. It's linked to Hannah Metcalfe – to begin with, by the single word "Capri". And Hannah Metcalfe is linked to the horse; she travelled with it. Just admit that and then ask yourself: how does the horse fit in with your notion of the vice racket?'

Hudspith, who was eating with great intentness, paused briefly. 'I could tell you things about horses,' he said darkly. His eye was far away; it might have been conversing with the shades of Caligula and Heliogabalus.

Appleby sighed. 'Lucy and Capri. Capri and Hannah. Hannah and the horse. Hannah has witchcraft in the family. Lucy evidences a morbid psychology of a kind which former ages accounted for in terms of demoniac possession. The horse has some power of hyperaesthesia which can be seen as an uncanny ability to read thoughts. And all these and a haunted house are picked up in England and spirited off in the direction of South America. These are the facts, and I ask you to explain them – particularly the house.'

Hudspith was studying the menu with a faintly pathological concentration. 'Of course they hang together,' he said. 'Nobody denies it. And I suppose if a man has a taste for demented concubines he may have a taste for a crazy house to keep them in. You don't know the lengths to which these wealthy degenerates will go. You ought to see the private movies they have made. You ought to see –' Hudspith broke off and sat glowering at some inward vision. Then he fell to eating with a slow, disconcerting avidity. Loopy, Appleby thought. St Simeon on his pillar, with the phantasmagoria of all the sins of the flesh circling round him. A great mistake to keep Hudspith on that stuff all these years – particularly when he had such a taste for it. Turn him on to forgery. Turn him on to embezzlement. Too late.

'Hudspith –' he began, and stopped. The other passengers had come in; with bowings and mutterings they were sitting down at the narrow table. The ship belonged to the class of fast cargo vessels that provide for six or eight passengers of retiring disposition – persons disliking floating hotels and averse from dances and sports tournaments. And at present there were Miss Mood, Mrs Nurse, Mr Wine, and Mr Wine's secretary, Mr Beaglehole.

'Warm,' said Mr Beaglehole; 'decidedly warm. Not a day for woollens, Mr Appleby.'

All the passengers laughed discreetly. In time of war travellers about the world commonly cease to be travellers and become missions. And of these there are two kinds. The first, the confidential mission, everybody knows about – and everybody knew that Appleby and Hudspith were a confidential mission engaged in marketing Australian wool. The second sort of mission is the hush-hush mission. And this is the real thing. The persons here have a *mana* from which issue absolute and extensive *tabus*: their whence, their whither and their why may be neither questioned nor mentioned; they must be considered as utterly without a future or a past, as ephemerides of the sheerest sort. This makes conversation difficult and repartee more difficult still. Appleby agreed that it was a warm day.

Mrs Nurse said that the warm days were nicer than the very hot days. Mr Wine, who seldom said anything, said nothing.

Miss Mood said nothing. She crushed her clasped hands between her knees and looked at Appleby with a penetrating glance. Really with that, Appleby thought. It was as if matter of scientific interest was being detected near the back of one's skull.

'The very hot days are rather tiring,' said Mrs Nurse.

About Mrs Nurse, it occurred to Appleby, there was something slightly peculiar. He frowned, conscious that in this lay the beginning of some obscure train of thought. Only a microscopic proportion of the human race ever crosses the South Atlantic Ocean; to do so is – however faintly – a distinction in itself; commonly this distinction is linked to the possession – however infinitesimally faint – of some specific trait or bent or characteristic in the voyager. But in Mrs Nurse nothing of the sort was detectable. It was impossible to conceive of any reason why she should now be thus floating on the waters. On the other hand it was equally hard to endow her in imagination with any more appropriate habitat. She called for nothing in particular. To posit a middling sort of suburb in a middling sort of English provincial town would be to risk far too positive an assertion about Mrs Nurse. Not that she was in the least enigmatic – that was Miss Mood's line – or in any way elusive. The apotheosis of the commonplace was a vile phrase. But it was the best that Appleby could find when considering Mrs Nurse.

'It is calm,' Mrs Nurse said.

It would be difficult to think of a more neutral remark than that, or of a more colourless way of making it. And she was physically colourless too – the colours one might see in a pool in an uninteresting place on a dull day. She was –

'Calm,' said Miss Mood tensely, 'is an illusion – a mere mathematical abstraction. It is simply an axis upon which spins the mortal storm, the great electrical flux which those who live call life.' She set down a glass of tomato juice and looked at Hudspith. 'You, I am sure, understand and agree with me.' Miss Mood's voice as it delivered itself of this gibberish was husky and glamorous, like something recorded on celluloid. Hudspith humped his shoulders, jabbed with fork and sawed with knife; he hated this awful woman as much as if she had been a celebrated bawd. But Miss Mood had clearly got him wrong; her turning to him had all the lush confidence of a tropical creeper's spiralling at the sun. 'Mind-stuff is alone pervasive,' she said. 'There is nothing else in the etheric world.'

Appleby felt a faint jar throughout his system – rather as if he had been pulled up in full career by the sudden recognition of an unexpected short cut. For between two bites of hazel hen he had apprehended the truth about Miss Mood. The woman was going where Hannah and Lucy had gone.

That was it. She and Hudspith and he were, so to speak, all in the same boat. And this was a thing likely enough – boats not being too plentiful these days. If the traffic to the pseudo-Capri was at all heavy – and already it had the appearance of being so – then parts of it were almost certain to converge quite far out on the Whale Roads. And a woman with that sort of eye and vocabulary – for there had been this sort of etheric-world stuff several times before – was just right for Daffodil's stable.

Appleby, chewing on this abrupt intuition, let his glance circle his other companions. If it were logical to suppose this of Miss Mood, then might it not –

The man called Beaglehole was looking at Miss Mood with dis-approval. There was far from being anything out of the way in that. And yet about the manner of Beaglehole's disapproval it was possible to feel something puzzling. Appleby's eye travelled forward to Mrs Nurse, the commonplace and pervasively negative Mrs Nurse ... and suddenly he perceived the truth about her too. He looked at Mr Wine – there was only Mr Wine left – and as he looked at Mr Wine, Mr Wine looked at him. There are indefinable moments in which one feels that one has dropped the shutters just in time. Appleby felt this. For a second he continued to look at Wine blankly, and then he looked at Hudspith. Hudspith's eye was more discernibly than ever upon his private whale – the creature blew and spouted in the gravy. And so much for individual inspection. It remained to consider all five of his companions simul-taneously and by a *coup d'oeil*. Tolerably achieving this, Appleby felt that it would be well to go up and get some air.

2

Sea and sky were as usual; the prow and its watchers went up and down as before. But Appleby paced a deck mysteriously transformed; he was like an actor who steps from the diffuse and rugged structure of actuality into the economy of a well-made play. For here, all unexpectedly, was the problem – or part of it – neatly under his nose again. Beaglehole had looked at Miss Mood with disapproval, the sort of disapproval with which a shop-walker might regard a counter ineptly piled with *demodé* goods. That was it. Miss Mood with her particular patter of the etherial world was booked for the bargain basement. Lucy Rideout and Daffodil would be much more catch.

Beaglehole, in fact, was what in commercial language is called a buyer, and Miss Mood and Mrs Nurse were his latest haul. The case of Mrs Nurse – said Appleby to himself in the sudden illumination that had befallen him – the case of Mrs Nurse was clear. She was a high-class medium – which meant an honest and peculiarly simple woman who was yet capable, in certain abnormal or trance states, of ingenious and sustained deceptions. That was it – or that was it in uncompromisingly rational terms. Mrs Nurse was just the type: a shallow pool under the waters parted and sundry problematical depths were revealed. Mrs Nurse would sit in a darkened room with bereaved mothers and sensation-seekers and inquiring Fellows of the Royal Society. Strange voices would come from her; voices voluble, hesitant, coherent, fragmentary, pathetic, pompous, fishing, shuffling. And people would listen as they had listened ever since the days of the Witch of Endor. One hears his wife speaking. One makes a verbatim report. One weeps. One smuggles a microphone. One offers banknotes. One plans tests with a manometer, a sphygmograph, a thermoscope . . . In other words, Mrs Nurse was a steady selling line.

And somewhere over the faintly serrated blue of the horizon the spirit of enterprise was assembling a large-scale psychic circus. No other explanation would quite fit the facts – as Appleby's aunt, placidly shuffling her press cuttings, had known. The scale was large. There was no sign that Mrs Nurse and Miss Mood were aware of any special relationship with Beaglehole; if Beaglehole was buyer, there were agents in between. Among these passengers, indeed, there was only one overt relationship:

Beaglehole was secretary to the gentleman down in the sailing list as Mr Emery Wine. Almost certainly this brought Wine in. In fact the hush-hush mission of these two was odder by a long way than the workaday imagination would readily arrive at ... Appleby, rounding a corner of the pilot-house, found Mr Wine regarding him with mild attention from a deck-chair. And momentarily his confidence flickered. The man looked so uncommonly like a hush-hush mission of the most respectable sort.

Hitherto Mr Wine had not been cordial; his attitude was one of polite preoccupation and reserve. He was a slight man, well groomed without preciseness, and his manner at times suggested a tempered gaiety which was no doubt on appropriate occasions his most charming social card. And he smiled charmingly now. 'I am a good deal interested in your friend,' he said unexpectedly.

'In Ron Hudspith? Well, that's quite right.' Appleby's slow and easy colonial manner dated from a careful study of Rhodes scholars long ago. 'Too right, Mr Wine. You couldn't have a better off-sider than Ron.'

'You are close friends?'

'Cobbers,' said Appleby solemnly. 'And our dads before us. Ron's dad was a well-known identity Cobdogla-way. You know Cobdogla, Mr Wine?'

'I'm afraid not.'

'Ah.' Appleby contrived the kindly, if quizzical and slightly contemptuous, stare merited by one to whom Cobdogla is but a name.

'What interests me is that your friend appears to be of an unusually intense and brooding nature. To a stranger it would seem to suggest – well, almost a mild mania. I hope I don't offend you.'

'Yes?' Hearing his own richly ironical voice Appleby recalled that a pose too was necessary; he strolled forward and contrived to offer an iron pillar support. 'Ron saw a good deal of the back-blocks as a lad. He was a jackeroo on his uncle's station for years.'

'Indeed.' Mr Wine's was a civil convention of understanding.

'Boundary-riding most of the time. It marks them, you know. Don't see a soul for weeks on end.'

'Ah, I see.' Mr Wine was enlightened. 'The Bush.'

'The Malee,' said Appleby severely. 'And sometimes the Spinifex.' As he offered this refinement of fancy his glance went rather anxiously towards the companion-way from the saloon. The appearance of his cobber

Ron at this moment might be unfortunate. 'You ought to meet some of the old-timers there, Mr Wine. They're so used to solitude and silence that two of them will meet and pass a night together in a humpy without exchanging a word.'

'Dear me!' said Mr Wine, and added, '– in a what?'

'A humpy,' Appleby repeated firmly. 'Sometimes they go a bit strange. Visions – that sort of thing.'

'Indeed! And is your friend at all affected in that way?'

'You're telling me.'

'I beg your pardon?'

'Too right, he is. You've seen him up there by the bows, Mr Wine? That's where he goes when it takes him.'

'I'm very sorry to hear it.' Mr Wine was now leaning forward attentively. 'And his visions are about – ?'

'Ah,' said Appleby, suddenly ironical and reticent.

Mr Wine relaxed and offered some observation on the course of the steamer. Appleby, still supporting that steamer's superstructure with his shoulders, had leisure to reflect on his own rashness of the past few minutes. He had hurled the unwitting Hudspith into a fantastic role – and this was far from being the less reckless because Hudspith at present really had a loopy side to him. He had taken upon himself the burden of an impersonation far trickier than was required to support a vague association with Australian wool. And he had done all this partly out of boredom and the residual sense of the Daffodil affair's being something of a holiday; and partly as the consequence of a sudden and extravagant plan. If Beaglehole was a buyer, then Wine was a talent scout – perhaps his own talent scout. And to have a friend who would score high marks in the psychic circus might be the quickest way of getting there. Hudspith, if his mind was set on tracing Hannah and Lucy, must be prepared to put an antic disposition on. And Cobdogla would be his kindly nurse.

At this moment Hudspith appeared and strode past them with all the glowering concentration that Appleby could desire. And Mr Wine watched him with what was surely the covert interest of the impresario. 'I believe,' he said, 'that a sea voyage often exacerbates such conditions.'

'It makes me feel a hundred per cent myself.' Appleby endeavoured to exude the curious animal luxury that Cobdogla breeds. 'But I've no doubt you're right. Nothing to the outback, though. I've known plenty men turn queer there. And beasts too, for the matter of that.'

'Beasts. You surprise me.' Mr Wine's eye was still on Hudspith as he skirted No 1 hatch.

'Horses.'

Mr Wine's gaze swung slowly round. 'Horses? You have found horses go peculiar in the – the out-back?'

'A horse doesn't like solitude any more than a human, Mr Wine. He gets bored just like you or me – and then he'll do queer things. Why, I've known a horse teach himself his numbers just through being bored. Like counting the tiles on the lavatory floor.'

'You saw the horse gradually learn to count?'

'I wouldn't say that. It was quite a mathematician when I saw it.'

'Dear me.' Mr Wine was looking absently at the sea. 'It did simple multiplications – that sort of thing?'

'Just that.'

'Then it was one of the Elberfeld horses.'

'Elberfeld horses? It was one of the Dismal Swamp horses, Mr Wine.'

'My dear sir, it was one of the Elberfeld horses.' Mr Wine spoke with what was at once polite decision and the liveliest interest. 'They were dispersed, and I suppose one may have strayed even to your Dismal Swamp. Perhaps you never heard of Clever Hans, Mr Appleby? He was the first of a remarkable line of so-called thinking horses in Germany at the beginning of the present century. They caused quite a sensation in their day.' Mr Wine smiled faintly to an irresponsive ocean. 'Krall wrote a book about them, *Denkende Tiere*, and there was even a learned journal, *Tierseele*, taking somewhat wider ground. And now tell me: what did they think of the creature at Dismal Swamp? Were there any reactions of what might be called a superstitious sort? Old women thinking the brute inspired – that sort of thing.'

Appleby eased himself on his pillar and looked at Mr Wine with as much appearance of inattention as he could muster. An hour ago he had believed himself a week's steaming from any hope of contact with his quarry; and now here was detection at positively breakneck pace. 'Superstition?' he said. 'You're telling me. There were old women who thought the devil was in the horse.'

Wine nodded. 'The Elberfeld horses have impressed more than old women, Mr Appleby. There was Professor Claparède. And what's more there was Maeterlinck, one of the first intellects in Europe. He was con-vinced that the phenomena were supernormal.'

'You mean what they call psychic? I thought all that stuff had gone bunk years ago, same as table-turning and ouija-boards.'

'My dear Mr Appleby, there are appetites which are perennial.' Wine shook a wise and indulgent head. 'Table-turning yesterday, astrology today – and tomorrow who knows what? Possibly *Denkende Tiere* again.'

'But surely you don't think there's anything supernatural about a counting horse?'

'Certainly not.' Wine's reply was dry and sharp. 'The thing is merely paranormal.'

'Yes?' Appleby contrived a promptly ironical reception for a strange word.

'These horses have one or another sense extraordinarily developed. Sometimes it is a visual hyperaesthesia; more commonly a tactual. They can be trained to act upon minute sensory impressions – imperceptible signs which a showman will give. But that is not all. They can act upon such impressions involuntarily and unconsciously given. Put your hand on such a horse's neck, or hold it on a taut rein. Then *think* of a number – say five. The horse will promptly signal five, perhaps by neighing or pawing. And the explanation is very simple. You are unable to *think* five without at the same time *acting* five. Ever so faintly, your whole organism is a pulse counting five. And the horse gets the message. Various effects of calculation can, of course, be built up on that basis.'

'Yes?' Appleby, who was far from questioning this simple physio-logical truth, got all the arrogant agnosticism of Cobdogla into the word.

'Yes, indeed.' Wine was almost nettled. 'And exactly similar mechan-isms lie behind much so-called thought-reading. Look at any memoir of a Cambridge man in the eighties and you will find the phenomenon ranking somewhere between a solemn scientific experiment and a parlour game. Professors played it in each other's drawing-rooms. You leave the room and the company hides something. You return, lay a hand on the cheek or temple of someone in the know, and occasionally you are mysteriously guided or steered towards the hidden object.'

'Isn't that what they call telepathy?'

'Telepathy implies a certain distance – often a distance over which it is difficult to conceive any physical agency acting. This is merely a matter of subconsciously interpreting minute muscular actions.'

'Well, that's really interesting.' Appleby straightened up and stretched himself lazily. 'And you seem to know a great deal about it, Mr Wine.'

Wine smiled – so quickly that Appleby suspected something like the expunging of an involuntary frown. 'One remembers odd scraps of information and desultory reading when one is on a voyage. Don't you find it so? The empty ocean induces an empty mind, and much inconsequent stuff floats up. There is another flying fish landed on deck. It is astounding that they can leap so high.'

Appleby agreed – and was inwardly convinced that more than a flying fish had been landed since luncheon. In fact he himself had landed a very queer fish indeed. A fish with most problematical innards. And he had a strong impulse to out with a knife and venture some radical incision; to go flatly on, say, from oddly endowed horses to witches. But that would be wanton. He had already gone too far with the holiday spirit – the figure of Hudspith, once more brooding in the bows, was there to attest it. So Appleby spoke of flying fish and porpoises, and when these tenuous subjects were exhausted he took his leave of Wine and strolled down the deck. Hudspith must be spoken to presently – and the interview might not be altogether easy. Undoubtedly he would particularly object to becoming Ron. Still, it might have been Stan or Les. And policemen must put up with such things.

Twice Appleby circled the deck, and twice he passed an Emery Wine who had retreated into his habitual abstraction and reserve. But at the third time round this problematical person looked up. 'Mr Appleby, you don't happen to have seen Beaglehole.'

'No – not since lunch-time.'

'I must go and find him; we have papers to look at. An excellent fellow is Beaglehole, but we have not much except our business in common. And on a long voyage it is perhaps more pleasant to have a personal friend as a companion.' Wine rose from his deck-chair. 'I think you said that Mr Hudspith and yourself were close personal friends?'

'Yes.'

'Intimate friends?'

'Yes.'

'Very pleasant,' said Wine vaguely. 'Very pleasant, I am sure.' He looked away to the horizon – with calculation, like one weather-wise and planning to exploit a distant gale. And then he smiled his new and charming smile and walked away.

Appleby stood for a moment by the rail and looked down at the sea. Mrs Nurse's remark lay beyond dispute: it was calm. It was as placid, as unruffled as the small talk of Mr Emery Wine. And yet there was not an inch of its surface that was not in motion; the surface undulated and hung and slipped, gained momentum and lost it, flattened and tilted with a subtlety of movement defying analysis. And over the horizon was a great deal more of the same thing. A large complex affair ...

A large solid house, pleasantly proportioned no doubt, proclaiming still the rational good-taste of the eighteenth century. Nothing in all this obscure adventure was nearly so puzzling as the theft of 37 Hawke Square. It was here that the crux would lie. And fortunately more was known about the vanished mansion than about Hannah Metcalfe or Lucy Rideout.

Appleby went below to his cabin, took from a drawer a heavy book of severely scientific appearance and began to read.

3

... At its maximum in the summer of 1866, after which time the appearances became fewer, and finally ceased in 1871. Towards the end of this period the figure, which had at first looked lifelike and substantial, became shadowy and semi-transparent. There was also a gradual cessation of the phenomena that had occurred during these years, namely sounds of the dragging about of heavy weights, and unaccountable lights.

Here it is difficult to deny considerable weight to the evidence, for the persons concerned were well-educated for the most part and – it appears – well-balanced without exception. Indeed one of them, Sir Edward Pilbeam, was a person of scientific eminence; and it may be remarked that he came to an investigation of the phenomena not through any previous interest in psychic matters such as might be held to indicate an innately suggestible mind but simply through the accident of his extended visit to Lady Morrison. It must be observed, however, that in one particular the Morrison case cannot be classified as a true 'haunting'. Certainly the phantom appeared at different times to different persons in a particular locality. But Lady Morrison's first experience had become matter of common talk some time before her butler related his adventure in the wine-cellar; and none of those who subsequently claimed to have seen the 'ghost' did so in circumstances which positively exclude the hypothesis of suggestion or expectation.

Much more remarkable – and that on several counts – is the series of supernormal events associated with the famous No 37 Hawke Square, Bloomsbury. Here we have, what is rare in the evidential sphere, a close analogue of the traditional 'ghost-story', like that of Pliny (*see Appendix H: Phantasms of the Dead in the Classical Period,* §5, *Athenodorus*), which connects some tragedy in a particular house or place, with the vague and often confused accounts of sights or sounds which perplex or terrify the observer. We have too, as in the Morrison case, that gradual 'fading out' of an apparition which some investigators – rashly, as it would appear to the present writer – take as evidence of what may be termed the 'delayed mortality' of the spirit; its power to survive, but only for a time, the earthly tenement from which it has passed. But what more particularly distinguishes the Hawke Square case is this: that there is well-attested record of two similar, but distinct and unconnected, hauntings of the premises, *and that the second took place at a time when all record of the first had passed from any living memory*. It was not until 1911, when Dr Hayball published his well-known *Grub Street Gleanings,* that the story of Colonel Morell was recovered from a hitherto inaccessible manuscript source. Up to that date no scholar had as much as heard of it; and we must note with amusement that Johnson (who had already suffered his unfortunate experience in Cock Lane) hid the incident from Boswell as successfully as did Mrs Morell from the rest of the world. Knowledge of the Morell haunting, we repeat, was recovered in 1911. The Spettigue haunting covered the years 1888 to 1892. The evidence will thus lead many (with what degree of discretion we shall not at present attempt to estimate) to this conclusion; that certain buildings are endowed, as it were, with some special psychic sensitiveness; with an atmosphere peculiarly conducive to super-normal appearances. This has, of course, long been held of medieval castles, church precincts and the like. But the case of the Hawke Square house is somewhat different. Neither in 1772 nor in 1888 did the house possess any of the conventional associations of a 'haunted' place. Yet in both those years phenomena occurred. And what Dr Spettigue recorded towards the end of the nineteenth century is oddly like what Mrs Morell recorded of quite distinct protagonists in the eighteenth. *But of Mrs Morell Dr Spettigue could have known nothing*. It is this that makes 37 Hawke Square something of a *locus classicus* in researches of the present sort.

Light striking upwards through the porthole passed in endless faintly moving washes over the low cabin ceiling; the electric fan turned monotonously from side to side, as if watching invisible tennis; somewhere a bell rang remotely; near at hand a partition intermittently creaked. But Appleby, pausing at the foot of a page, heard and saw none of these things. Instead he heard banging as of innumerable doors down giant corridors; that throb, upon which the ear imposes its own patterns, of aircraft flying very high; voices in shelters saying 'It was a bomb all right, that one.' And he saw the streets of Bloomsbury in silhouette against the burning City; saw Bloomsbury under fire: here a church going, here a college library, and here – just here in this corner of a minor square – the flash and smoke and din-obscured labouring at what was surely the most bizarre activity ever undertaken by rational men.

But was it indeed rational, this genie-like purloining of 37 Hawke Square? Or was it as crazy as the world to which one might so easily be conducted by an over-attentive study of Dr Spettigue and Mrs Morell? Appleby read on.

Our only record of the first haunting is contained in a single letter made available by Dr Hayball. This, although somewhat allusive in nature, is fortunately the product of a logical mind:

To Mrs Morell

Dear Madam, – I write to inform you that I have this day, together with Mr Francis Barber, terminated my three nights' sojourn at No 37 Hawke Square. The intelligence now to be conveyed – namely, that during this period no untoward appearance was observed – I know not well whether you will receive with disappointment or relief. Had the apparition of Colonel Morell in fact manifested itself we should have had some additional assurance that the matter lay beyond the grossness of imposture or the prevalence of *infectious* imagination. As it is, we are very little furthered in our inquiry and it has now to be decided what, if any, action it is proper that you should take. But first, and that you may be assured of my writing from a sufficient apprehension of the facts, I will briefly consider the course of what has taken place.

The death of Colonel Morell, although sudden, aroused in the first instance no suspicion, nor had it occurred to you in any way to connect with it his occasionally expressed anxieties about the Italian man-servant who, with his wife, has since quitted your service. And it was only after your chance communication of that anxiety to the late Colonel Morell's fellow-officer Captain Bertram that this gentleman was first visited by the apparition. Let me remind you, dear Madam, with such gentleness as this painful subject requires, that the ideas of *sudden death* and *poison* lie sufficiently near together in the *arcana* of the mind to be readily brought together when there is offered so striking a link as *absconding Italian*. Were Captain Bertram a man of fanciful mind – and of this his return to India prevents my forming an opinion of my own – the raw materials of romantic fiction lay ready to his hand.

But we are told that the apparition of your dead husband appeared not only to his old friend Captain Bertram but also to a number of other persons of respectable character who have testified to the fact; but with this difference – that whereas to the Captain the vision unfailingly called out for vengeance against his poisoner, in the presence of others it was mute or heard only to groan. The Captain saw and heard things, to him, equally familiar. Is it perhaps easier to conjure up an unfamiliar voice?

A total disbelief of apparitions is adverse to the opinion of the existence of the soul between death and the last day; the question simply is, whether departed spirits ever have the power of making themselves perceptible to us, and whether we are here confronted with an instance in which this has occurred. It is wonderful that five thousand years have now elapsed since the creation of the world, and still it is undecided whether or not there has ever been an instance of the spirit of any person appearing after death. All argument is against it; in its favour we must set many voluntary solemn asseverations. And even so it is in the present case.

I advise you to persevere in your resolution of selling the house; and to take no further action than this. You speak of a duty of *laying* the ghost, or doing that which will afford it relief from having to walk the earth. But this is the shadow of superstition and such as is encouraged by writings carelessly profane: as the happiness or misery of unembodied spirits does not depend upon place, but is intellectual, we cannot say that they are less happy or less miserable by appearing upon earth. Nor can I approve the argument that the apparition, being supernatural, is tantamount to a divine injunction to pursue the supposed murderer of Colonel Morell. For the spirit, if spirit there be, is at best a *questionable shape*, bringing we know not whether *airs from heaven or blasts from hell*, and with *intents wicked or charitable* to an unknown degree. If you will but consider the painful issues which a doubtful criminal prosecution would bring you may well feel Hamlet's doubt: *Be thou a spirit of health or goblin damn'd?* I suppose, in short, that in the pursuit of merely human justice we should regard evidence only mundane and rational. But here I touch on matters so awful that I would not venture to give an opinion did I not find myself supported by my friend Dr Douglas, who, in addition to his own distinguished abilities, enjoys the superior qualification of being Bishop of Carlisle. I am, Madam, your most humble servant,

SAM JOHNSON

JOHNSON'S COURT, FLEET STREET,
March 20, 1772.

So much for the Morell haunting. It is not remarkable in itself, or is remarkable only for the wise advice which it produced. We must credit Dr Johnson with suspecting that if Colonel Morell was indeed poisoned by his Italian servant, the wife of the Italian servant was not without her place in the affair, and from the canvassing of such a 'painful issue' he sagaciously dissuades the widow. Had he given more information on the 'persons of respectable character' we should have been grateful, but this was not to be expected in a letter of the kind he had set himself to write. For the rest we must please ourselves with the picture of the Sage and his faithful negro servant keeping their three nights' vigil in the empty house.

And now we come to the Spettigue affair ...

Again Appleby paused in his reading. The engines had taken on the deeper throb which seems to come in the late afternoon; it was as if they were preparing for their long, tireless haul through the night. Again a bell rang and overhead there was the pad of a quartermaster's feet going forward; from the little saloon below came a chink of cutlery and rattle of plates. Dinner would be at seven-thirty; there would be the usual jokes about the metamorphoses of Roast Hazel Hen. Appleby frowned. There was over a week's steaming before them, and three times a day he and Hudspith would gather round the board with Wine and Beaglehole and Mrs Nurse and Miss Mood – with these and with the wraiths of Hannah Metcalfe and Lucy Rideout. And Daffodil. Roast Hazel Horse ... Appleby pulled himself awake and returned to 37 Hawke Square.

And now we come to the Spettigue affair, which is more striking in itself and gives retroactive significance to the sketchy case of Colonel Morell. At this time, more than a hundred and twenty years after the events we have been considering, the Hawke Square house was in the occupancy of Mr Smart, a merchant, who had married the sister of his close friend Dr Spettigue. There were several young children – a circumstance from which arose one of the most curious aspects of the affair. For the house, like others of its kind, had a central staircase winding round a narrow well. And Mrs Smart, like other careful parents similarly situated, had provided against accident by causing a net or lattice to be placed across the well at the level of the first and again at the third (or nursery) landing. During the summer of 1888 the whole family had repaired for a holiday visit to a hotel in Yarmouth, the servants (other than a nurse) being placed on board-wages the while. During this period nothing remarkable seems to have occurred, and Mr Smart was said to be in particularly good spirits, even playing cricket with his children on the beach. When the holiday was over – and following the usual custom of the Smarts on such occasions – Mr Smart returned to town a day earlier than his family for the purpose of 'opening up' the house – an operation of some intricacy, it will be remembered, during Victorian times. He was to await the arrival of the servants in the afternoon, sleep at his club, and his family was to return home on the morrow. This, we repeat, was the established procedure. But when the servants arrived on this occasion they found their master dead on the marble floor of the hall. The nets or lattices spoken of had been removed and there were indications that Mr Smart had fallen from the top storey.

Suicide and murder seemed equally possible as agencies in this sad affair, and at the inquest an open verdict was returned. Those taking the view that Mr Smart had been done to death saw significance in the time of the fatality: on this day of the year – and perhaps on this day only – was Mr Smart likely to be found alone in his own house. But on the other side it was maintained that this was far from weakening the case for suicide. For by taking his own life under those precise circumstances Mr Smart would so far have contrived to mitigate the shock to his family as to ensure that the discovery was made by servants and not by any of those more intimately concerned. Moreover the removal of the lattices and subsequent luring of the victim to the top of the house appeared an un-necessarily intricate method of committing murder, while the removal of the lattices by Mr Smart himself was consistent with a rational plan for taking his own life with a greater measure of decent privacy than would be compatible with, say, casting himself out of a window.

It were idle at this distance of time to speculate on the facts of Mr Smart's death as given above. Suicide appears to have been the solution at first accepted by his friends, and this chiefly on two counts: Mr Smart seemed to be without personal enemies or any irregularity of private life; and his private affairs did upon examination prove to be embarrassed. It seemed likely that, had he sur-vived, a considerable change in his style of living would have been necessary; and this, it was felt, might have weighed unduly on his mind. As it was, this financial stringency was to have remarkable consequences after his decease.

We have mentioned Mr Smart's friend and brother-in-law, a Dr Spettigue. This gentleman was in medical practice in the vicinity and he possessed at the time a growing family which made increasing demands upon the available space at his residence in an adjoining square. It was therefore arranged that he should rent consulting-rooms from his widowed sister in the Hawke Square house at a figure which should materially assist her annual budget. This estimable family arrangement was completed some three months after the death of Mr Smart, and the two houses were connected by a private telephone line, then something of a novelty in London. It was hard upon Dr Spettigue's entering in occupation of his new professional quarters that the phenomena began.

The apparition which was to appear so purposely to this competent and level-headed medical practitioner must be reckoned one of the most remarkable of which we have record – and this chiefly because of its combining the character-istics of the literary and the veridical ghost. Like most phantasms of the more respectably authenticated sort it was shy, fluid and indefinite in appearance, being commonly no more than a gliding luminous column viewed from the corner of the eye. Often, indeed, the phenomena were not visual but auditory merely, and consisted in those raps and suggestions of the movement of heavy bodies with which the reader is now so well acquainted in the better class of phantoms. On the other hand his ghost spoke, and spoke to a purpose – in this imitating those of its fellows incubated solely in the imaginations of novelists and literary men. To be brief, it was the sustained endeavour of Mr Smart's ghost to secure vengeance upon his murderer.

For some time the manifestations were perceptible to Dr Spettigue alone. Occasionally the apparition would present itself plainly in the form of Mr Smart, and then it appeared unable to speak. But at other times and more commonly – and as if conserving its psychic force for aural impression – it was a vague appearance only, an appearance from which proceeded the very voice of Dr Spettigue's dead friend – only having (Dr Spettigue thinks) 'a somewhat more settled gravity' than during life. The words were always the same. 'I was murdered, Archibald, murdered,' the voice would say. There would then be a pause and it would add: 'I was murdered by –' But at this point the voice would invariably falter and break off – in such a way that it was difficult to determine whether it was through compunction or some failure of memory that the vital information was withheld.

It will not escape the recollection of some readers that the late Mr Andrew Lang, an acute if light-hearted commentator on supernormal phenomena, at one time published a facetious essay in which it was suggested that the futile and unaccountable conduct of many supposed ghosts might be attributable to a species of *aphasia*, or inability to express certain thoughts in words by reason of some specific mental disease. Significance therefore may be attached to these facts taken in conjunction: (1) Lang's essay may have been in the conscious or unconscious recollection of Dr Spettigue; (2) Dr Spettigue was a physician, familiar with the conception of *aphasia*, a fact which might help to fix Lang's whimsical notion somewhere in his mind; (3) although numerous other observers *saw* the supposed ghost of Mr Smart, only Dr Spettigue *heard it talk*.

The subsequent history of the second Hawke Square haunting may be recounted in few words. The manifestations extended over a number of years but with diminishing definition and intensity, finally dying away into merely wraithlike appearances and feeble rappings and scratchings. But this was not before the phenomena had come within the perception of a surprisingly large number of persons, including at least two casual patients of Dr Spettigue's in whom any state of specific expectation is most unlikely. One of these, indeed, who was brought into the Doctor's surgery after having been knocked down by a hansomcab, had that morning stepped off a boat which had brought him home from a ten years' sojourn in China. This is extremely interesting, but so too is the circumstance that neither Mrs Smart nor any of her children was ever perceptive of any supernormal phenomena whatever. The fact of the haunting, as was inevitable, became widely known, and was naturally associated with Mr Smart's mysterious death. But the words heard by Dr Spettigue were wisely suppressed during the lifetime of those concerned, the interests of scientific inquiry being at the same time safeguarded by a confidential deposition made to the Logical Society's committee for psychical investigation. The *Proceedings* of this body contain a very full report.

4

A museum, Appleby said to himself as he closed the book. A sort of ghost museum neatly housed in a rebuilt 37 Hawke Square. Lucy Rideout in the basement illustrating possession by demons; Mrs Nurse holding a seance in the drawing-room; Miss Mood crystal-gazing in the pantry; Hannah Metcalfe floating from room to room on a broomstick; Daffodil tap-tapping in the back yard; the spectres of Colonel Morell and Mr Smart toasting Yarmouth bloaters before the kitchen fire. And no doubt there would be more exotic exhibits as well: Maori *Tohungas* and Eskimo *Angakuts*, Peay-men from British Guiana, Dènè Hareskins from North America and *Birraarks* from Australia. All with their attendant spirits: *kenaimas* and *mrarts, jossakeeds* and –

And Uncle Tom Cobley and all, thought Appleby, abruptly standing up. The thing was fantastic; it was as fantastic if one believed in ghosts as if one did not. And no one would believe such a story for a moment ... He put the book back in its drawer. Writing with a nice, dry, scientific tone. Interesting, without a doubt. And perhaps rather alarming as well.

The cabin door opened and Hudspith came in – Hudspith fresh from the rising and falling prow. And Appleby spoke at once. 'It's Wine,' he said. 'It's Wine who has made off with those women. He's forming a monstrous museum of ghosts and marvels the Devil knows where. Mediums and Medicine Lodges, bugs and bogles.'

Hudspith sat down; his eye, returning from remote distances, focused slowly on Appleby; and almost as slowly his mind focused on the significant word. 'A museum? I shouldn't be surprised. You'd hardly believe what some of them collect. There was an old man in Brussels –' He checked himself. 'Did you say Wine?'

'Emery Wine.'

Hudspith shook his head; his eye could be seen setting out again on its long journey. 'Impossible. He's not the type – or rather not one of them. There are three types of man that traffic in women –'

'But I tell you this affair has nothing to do with trafficking in women. It has to do with trafficking in marvels. This museum –'

Hudspith nodded – very absently. 'I could tell you things about museums. There was an old man in Brussels –'

'My dear Hudspith, keep him for a limerick. We're confronted with something quite different. Wine, or somebody for whom Wine is acting, is assembling a museum of the uncanny in general. Anything within that category is welcome and no expense is being spared. And now I'll ask you two questions. Do you know why Wine has a secretary called Beaglehole?'

'Of course I don't. The question's idiotic.'

'It's an etymological matter. Beaglehole is a corrupt form of Bogle Hole, which is good Scots for the lair of the demon. Wine is very choice in everything he gathers round him, and always on the look-out for a good specimen. And that brings me to the second question. Do you know why he's particularly interested in you?'

'In me? He's nothing of the sort. I've scarcely exchanged a word with him.'

'But I have. We've become quite friendly and I've told him about your visions.'

'Visions!' Hudspith sprang to his feet. 'Is this a joke?' He sat down again abruptly. 'I don't have visions. I may look as if I do, but I don't.'

'So much the better. This is a matter in which the appearance is all. And I have assured Wine that you have visions as a regular thing – largely because of the lonely life you led among the sheep up Cobdogla way.'

'Wherever is that? And why ever –' Hudspith was staring at Appleby with the expression conventionally called open-mouthed.

'Australia, I should think. Or perhaps Tasmania or New Zealand. We must look it up at once. Anyway, that's your background.'

'I think you've taken leave of your senses. And I don't know anything about colonials.'

'Well, to begin with, they don't call themselves that. And for the rest you have just to remember that they are people of open hearts and closed minds. Stick to that and the impersonation ought to hold. And if you can really make an impression in the visionary way, I think there's a good chance of your getting an invitation.'

'Do you mean that I'm to endeavour to step into a show-case in this museum you're imagining?'

'I do.' Appleby was matter of fact. 'Simply because it's your shortest route to Hannah and Lucy – to say nothing of Daffodil. You see?'

Hudspith was far from seeing, and it took Appleby a further half-hour to expound his case. Even then Hudspith was dubious. 'It's all very well,' he said, 'but you must remember I don't know anything about visions. And if this fellow is what you take him to be he's likely to have the whole subject at his finger-tips.'

Appleby nodded, and once more felt that he had, perhaps, been decidedly rash. 'Of course any analogous phenomenon would do. I suppose you couldn't levitate? Float out of one window, you know, and in at another.' He tapped the drawer before him. 'That's what the celebrated Home did in the presence of the Master of Lindsay and Lord Adare.'

'Ships,' said Hudspith tartly, 'don't have windows.'

'Or there was Lord Orrery's butler. He showed a marked predisposition to turn himself into a balloon. They locked him into a room and could hear him bumping about the ceiling. They went in and found that several people clutching his shoulders were insufficient to hold him down.'

'Look here,' said Hudspith, 'do you believe all that?'

'I do not. But does Wine? And then there was St Joseph of Cupertino. Any chance pious remark would set him off. He would give a loud yell, bound into the air and float about indefinitely. At first his superiors took a dark view of it. But later it was officially decided to be extremely edifying.'

'It had better be visions,' said Hudspith resignedly. 'Though I don't see why we shouldn't simply follow Wine up in a more regular way.'

Appleby shook his head. 'The truth is that we have only the most tenuous line on anything criminal so far. Hannah Metcalfe is of age, and at a pinch they could probably square Mrs Rideout. That means that if the girls were free agents and there was no intent to exploit them sexually there just isn't a case at all. Of course people aren't allowed to steal houses. But it would be hard to persuade a commonsense jury that a house which may plausibly be held simply to have disintegrated through enemy action has really been found at the other end of the globe. And as for Daffodil – well, everybody knows that a horse is almost as chancy a proposition in a law-court as on a racecourse.'

'In other words,' said Hudspith, 'this museum may be crazy but can't be established as criminal. So why fudge up visions? Much better go home and report no go.'

'Not at all. You may find something decidedly criminal if you get yourself favourably established there. And besides' – Appleby looked shrewdly at his colleague – 'we don't in any case know that these girls aren't getting a raw deal. Even if they were picked up primarily as museum pieces –'

Literally and figuratively, Hudspith rose. 'Very well. And as you seem to have brought a good many books on all that –'

Appleby rummaged in his suitcase. 'I think I can recommend Gurney and Myers. They describe about seven hundred decidedly queer coves, so you ought to find something to suit your type. I'm inclined to recommend bright lights and voices. They seem to crop up at any time, whereas actual phantasms are inclined to save up for special occasions – like announcing some death at a distance.'

'I see.' Hudspith, Appleby was pleased to notice, had abandoned his brooding expression for one of much cunning. 'Well, as it happens, this *is* a special occasion. It's your birthday.'

'It is nothing of the sort.'

'Look here, if you say I have visions, can't I say you have a birthday?'

Appleby grinned. 'I suppose that's fair.'

'Good. It's your birthday. And Cobdogla never knew such a party as there's going to be tonight.'

'Well, well,' said Appleby – and went on deck wondering if he had been inclined to under-estimate his colleague. Hudspith in his younger days had doubtless been constrained to drink much beer in the interests of criminal investigation, but that he should plump for conviviality as a means of forwarding the present inquiry was a surprise. Perhaps a party would be a good idea in any case, for there was now something decidedly oppressive in the air.

More than ever the South Atlantic was calm, a sort of channel-passenger's dream. The sun swam copper-coloured in a western sky which had gone strangely olive; it was like a farmer peering through a hedge, only there were no crops visible, nothing but the unharvested sea which lay flaccid and inert about the ship. The ocean, said Appleby to himself, walking aft, is our master symbol of energy. Watching it, we draw into ourselves a pleasing sense of power, as we may do from some vital companion. *There is society where none intrudes By the deep seas, and music in its roar*. And when it fails to roar there may result comfort for our stomach and semi-circular canals, but the society lapses and our spirits feel indefinably let down.

The conclusion of this marine meditation found Appleby at the after end of the short promenade deck. Here there was a sort of open-air extension of the smoke-room, glassed in on either side, with a hatch for obtaining drinks behind, and having, as if by way of diversion, a frontwise and elevated view of the little sun-deck provided for third-class passengers. Here one could sit before dinner, sip sherry or cocktails and scrutinize the unimportant proceedings of these obscure persons below. The dispositions of the human species are frequently extremely odd, and the curiosity of this instance was perhaps enhanced by the fact that the third-class passengers, like their elevated fellow voyagers, could number no more than some half-dozen. One got to know them quite well; it was like owning an aquarium or a small zoological park. For instance, thought Appleby, settling down without a drink – for the coming party was something to approach with caution – for instance there below him at the moment was the Italian girl. One could see that she was handsome; that she was dirty it was at this distance necessary only to suspect. And in a peasant girl who has beauty a little dirt is of small moment to a well-balanced mind.

Appleby watched the girl. Without positively removing his mind from conscientious reflection on the mysterious proceedings of Mr Emery Wine he watched the girl below him, and rather regretted that daylight was beginning to fail. Eusapia – he knew that her name was Eusapia Something – was alone on the little deck, and she paced it with a lithe restlessness which, in this relaxed steamship environment, was extremely fetching. A gluteal type, such as would offend one's taste in a ball-dress. But that was the tyranny of the fashion-plate; Eusapia as she was, and with all Calabria behind her, was very well. Would the wife of the Italian servant of Colonel Morell – speculated Appleby, dutifully veering towards business – have been as attractive? And what would the colonel have thought in 1772? And what was Colonel Morell to Mr Wine

– or he to the wraith of Mr Smart, who had so amiably sported with his children on the sands at Yarmouth? These were questions more than speculative – they were questions demonstrably meaningless – but meanwhile Eusapia there was a palpable physical fact.

She paced the deck in a white tunic cut low and tight across the breasts and a black skirt that swung to her ankles; she paced the deck with a strange restlessness and a glance that went impatiently now out to sea and now among the shadows that were losing definition and merging at her feet. It was chilly; somewhere on the starboard quarter the great bronze sun had dropped below the horizon, reddening the while; its last segment, as if suddenly molten and flowing, had spread out in a momentary line of fire that heralded the dark. This Appleby knew without turning. He was watching Eusapia still. She had moved to the side, and sat on a bollard with her back to the rail. She sat in the swiftly gathering dusk, still and isolated. Behind her was the bare rail and a sheer drop to the sea; the empty deck was all about her; and above stretched infinite space. She sat very still, and it grew darker, and she was a silhouette against the yet faintly luminous sea. Her hands lay side by side on the darkness of her lap. And Appleby saw that there was something hovering above her head.

It was white and faint, like a puff of vapour; it took more substance and might have been a dove; it circled above Eusapia's head and poised itself as no bird could do. The thing trembled, vibrated, rose and fell like a ball held in the jet of an invisible fountain. It spiralled upwards and outwards, dropped like a stone and disappeared, showed itself again motionless in air some three feet before Eusapia's knees; it rose in an arc and hung at the same distance above her head. Again it circled. Eusapia's hands, pale as acacia flowers, lay motionless on the black stuff of her dress.

Appleby sat as still as the girl below him. His pulse was not quite normal; there was an unusual sensation in the scalp; almost certainly a chemist would find in his bloodstream elements not present a few moments before. Which was interesting – for he had fallen to watching the girl with nothing more perhaps than a fleeting sexual interest; certainly with no expectation of the uncanny. And yet the performance – this performance in a strangely empty theatre – had instantaneously worked. It is strangely easy to penetrate to magical levels of the mind.

The cities of Rome, thought Appleby – keeping his eye steadily on this now so-interesting young woman the while – the cities of Rome – all the cities that ever stood where modern Rome now stands – existing still in perfect preservation, each simply superimposed upon the one preceding it: Freud had said that the human mind was like that. Well, it was possible at times to shoot right down through them like a miner plunging to his seam ... Now he could only just see Eusapia by straining his eyes. The thing was circling and hovering still.

It circled and hovered perhaps three feet above her head, and her hands were on her lap. Suddenly, and for a second only, one hand disappeared; and simultaneously the thing rose some three or four feet higher – it would now be touching, perhaps tapping at, the ceiling of a moderately lofty room. Appleby waited for no more; he rose and made his way cautiously forward between the deck-chairs and the davits. Perhaps the weather had helped to give Eusapia's flummery effectiveness. The atmosphere was at once chill, dry and heavy; something was in the air.

From the smoke-room came voices. People were assembling for dinner. But Appleby wanted a few minutes more of solitude, and he slipped into the deck pantry, where he could light a cigarette. It was a cubby-hole of a place, and he paced it restlessly – up and down and a step sideways to avoid the weighing-machine ... He stopped. About the weighing-machine there was something suggestive. The man Home again – that was it. When Home had made tables rise in the air without apparently touching them it had been shown that his own weight nevertheless went up by the weight of the table. In fact for all that side of the business there was always a simple physical explanation. Of course the machinery of Eusapia's little show was of the slenderest importance: still, it would be nice to know.

The bugle sounded and he went below – but still so preoccupied that Beaglehole had to speak to him twice on the stairway. And this pleased Beaglehole, for it opened the way to a joke. 'Wool-gathering, Mr Appleby? You know, I've seldom met a man more devoted to his profession.'

'Yes?' said Appleby, remembering Cobdogla.

There can be great power in this word, rightly inflected – and Beaglehole laughed rather uncertainly. 'But, seriously, it has been a sleepy sort of afternoon, don't you think? I haven't felt so lazy for a long time.'

'I beg your pardon?'

'I said I haven't felt so lazy –'

Appleby slapped an open palm with a clenched fist. 'There!' he said. 'I've got it.'

'Got it?'

'Only the particular wisp of wool I've been groping for.' Appleby smiled cheerfully. 'Did Hudspith tell you it was my birthday?'

5

It is very easy to pretend to be more drunk than one is; at one time or another most undergraduates have managed it. There is no great difficulty in simulating extreme drunkenness when one is entirely sober. But to pretend to all the successive stages to tipsiness and intoxication on no basis of fact is a task requiring considerable virtuosity. And it was this task that Hudspith, for reasons best known to himself, had undertaken. As dinner progressed he appeared to be getting drunker and drunker on the ship's much-tossed and shaken wines.

Appleby, in whose honour this exhibition was taking place, watched it with admiration and some trepidation. The performance was, in its way, as finished as Eusapia's, and it was clear that Hudspith had been at it before. In fact he was reviving some star turn of his earlier career and packing a great deal of science into the show. The drink was disappearing undeniably fast, and almost certainly into Hudspith's stomach. Perhaps as the level rose so too did that of some half a pint of salad oil that he had swallowed off-stage. Or perhaps he carried round some dis-intoxicant drug for use on just such occasions. You didn't know where you had Hudspith – or not once you succeeded in pushing back the cheated girls to the frontiers of his mind. For then his youth returned to him and he became a police officer with a positively alarming imaginative technique. Appleby had conjured up Cobdogla, which was probably really on the map; Hudspith was now having a great deal to say about a township called Misery, which almost certainly was not. Misery was an altogether more go-ahead place than the neighbouring Eden. Hudspith doubted if there was a rival to it short of Pimpingie or Dirty Flat. And these were a hundred miles away and over the range.

'The range?' said Beaglehole, mildly curious. 'What range is that, Mr Hudspith?'

Hudspith put down his glass. 'My range,' he said carefully. 'Mine and Uncle Len's.'

'Oh – I see.'

'But it's all mine now,' Hudspith made a wavering gesture which embraced vast distances and at the same time contrived almost to brush the nose of the intense Miss Mood. 'And I can put a sheep on every tenth acre.'

'Isn't it difficult,' Mrs Nurse asked comfortably, 'to pick them up again? Such long runs for the dogs.'

Hudspith merely breathed heavily.

'Your Uncle – ah – Len died?' asked Beaglehole.

'He didn't die,' said Hudspith. 'He perished.'

'He did a perish,' said Appleby corroboratively and idiomatically. It was he, after all, who had started this desperate masquerade, and he must in fairness back Hudspith up. 'Ron found his bones.'

'Some of them,' said Ron with heavy drunken accuracy.

Miss Mood made a sound as agonized as if her own bones were being picked in whispers. '*Which?*' she asked huskily.

'The troopers,' said Hudspith, ignoring this, 'wanted to have it that Uncle Len had been murdered. But it was just a perish, all right. You see, the blacks won't go into the range. It's haunted.'

'What by?' Wine spoke, sharply and for the first time.

There was a moment's silence, Hudspith at this juncture finding it necessary to drink deeply. 'The Bunyip,' said Appleby. 'Haunted by the Bunyip.'

'That's right, the Bunyip,' said Hudspith.

'And what is the Bunyip, Mr Hudspith?' Wine's question was directed uncompromisingly at the late Len's nephew.

Hudspith set his glass down slowly. 'The Bunyip is something not many white people can see,' he said. His tone held a momentary sobriety which was effective in the extreme.

Miss Mood, at least, rose to it. 'And *you*, Mr Hudspith?' she breathed.

The answer was a loud bang and rattle. Everybody – except perhaps the monumentally placid Mrs Nurse – jumped. Hudspith had outrageously thumped the table and was roaring at the steward for a fresh bottle of wine. It was fortunate, Appleby reflected, that the captain appeared to prefer the company of his officers and was not dining in the saloon that night. Hudspith banged again, and there was nobody to stop him; he banged a third time and shouted, so that even Mrs Nurse looked about for her bag. But before the company could break up he had suddenly turned quiet and maudlin. 'Shame to spoil John's birthday. Man only has one birthday in the year.'

'Too right,' said Appleby, who felt that he ought not now to be quite sober himself.

'Never mind about seeing things,' Hudspith flapped a hand at Miss Mood rather as if she were a fly. 'Much better have a song. All join in song. All join in –'

'All join in "Waltzing Matilda",' said Appleby, fairly confident that this particular piece of antipodean local colour was correct. And he struck up by himself:

'Once a jolly swagman camped beside a billabong,
Under the shade of a coolibah tree;
And he sang as he sat and waited while his billy boiled,
"Who'll come a-waltzin' Matilda with me?"

'Up came a jumbuck to drink at the billabong;
Up jumped the swagman and grabbed it with glee;
And he sang as he shoved that jumbuck in his tucker-bag,
"You'll come a-waltzin' Matilda with me."

'Up came the Squatter, mounted on his thoroughbred;
Up came the troopers – one, two, three!
"Where'd you get that jumbuck you've got in your tucker-bag?
You'll come a-waltzin' Matilda with me."'

'Rather a sinister song,' said Wine. 'Or at least with a suggestion of developing that way.'

'Is the billabong the same as the Bunyip?' asked Miss Mood.

Appleby, who was not prepared to venture an answer to this, embarked on another verse. Hudspith joined in – not very articulately, but that was explicable.

'Up jumped the swagman and dived into the billabong.
"You'll never take me alive!" cried he.
And his ghost may be heard if you camp beside the billabong,
Singing, "Who'll come a-waltzin' Matilda with me?"

'"Waltzin' Matilda, waltzin' Matilda,
Who'll come a-waltzin' Matilda with me?"
And his voice may be heard if you camp beside the billabong,
Singing – "Who'll come a-waltzin' Matilda with me?"'

Hudspith applauded vigorously – so vigorously that the general attention became focused on him once more. 'Bravo!' he bawled. 'Bra –' The word died oddly on his lips. His hands, which had been gesticulating, dropped limply to his sides. It seemed uncomfortably probable that he was going to be suddenly sick. Presently, however, it was clear that he was in the grip of some other sensation. His features worked, but it was in perplexity rather than physical distress. Expectant, troubled and oddly absent, he was staring at the stairs of the saloon.

Appleby again thought the performance tip-top. But one had to remember that the audience consisted of something like a panel of experts. Perhaps it would be best to take the part of Lady Macbeth recalling her hallucinated thane to the proprieties of the banquet. 'Ron,' he said loudly, 'how does Matilda go on?'

With a perceptible but unexaggerated jerk Hudspith returned from whatever experience had befallen him. 'Matilda?' he asked blankly. And then he smiled expansively at the company. 'Once knew a smart girl called Matilda.' He leered drunkenly. 'Once took a little girl called Matilda across to –'

This time Mrs Nurse gathered up her bag and rose. 'It has been a very nice party,' she said. 'And now Miss Mood and I are going into the little drawing-room to have our coffee. Good night.' Mrs Nurse put much placid decision into these last words, and Miss Mood followed her – perhaps not without a shade of reluctance – from the saloon.

Hudspith filled his glass, unbuttoned his waistcoat, lowered his voice. 'Once knew a little girl called Gladys . . .'

It was past ten o'clock. Appleby drained his coffee, put out his cigarette and left the smoke-room for a breath of air. Matilda and Gladys, girls not without interesting idiosyncrasy, were now points remote on Hudspith's amatory pilgrimage, and he was regaling Wine and Beaglehole with the fruits of more recent researches. In these matters Hudspith had, after all, a great deal of vicarious experience: more than enough to stock all the smoke-rooms of all the liners afloat. And Wine and Beaglehole were passive listeners – Beaglehole because he liked it, and Wine – conceivably – because he had designs of his own. Wine was a person who had as yet not at all emerged; he was an unpredictable quantity; and that he was really in process of being outflanked by the present fantastic procedures it would be hazardous to assert.

'Well, what do you think?' Hudspith too had come out to breathe, and his voice, disconcertingly sober, came cautiously from the darkness.

'Absolutely awful. Dirty Flat and those rangers aren't owned by people at all like you and your Uncle Len. They're owned by people rather like the lesser country gentry of Shropshire – only there are about six Shropshires to a gent. Still, I must say you do the getting tight rather well.'

'Wait till you see the getting un-tight. That's much more tricky.'

'No doubt. And will you tell me what Matilda and Gladys and the rest are all about? And do you realize that tomorrow, when we're all sober, I shall have to try to hold up my head as the intimate friend of a self-confessed lecher?'

Hudspith chuckled cheerfully. It was evident that his bogus confessions were having the most beneficial effect on his nervous constitution; he had, in fact, discovered what was virtually a new variety of psycho-therapeutic method. He chuckled again, cheerfully but cautiously still. 'Wait and see. There'll be an important moment in about twenty minutes. But the big show is timed for midnight.'

Appleby sighed, for he would have liked to go to bed. 'Very well. It's your do.'

Hudspith's shadow melted into darkness. His voice came floating back from near the smoke-room door. 'Chin chin,' it said.

The night was dark, and Appleby blinked into it. Hudspith bubbling with the raffish idiom of the nineteen hundreds was a mildly surprising phenomenon. But then so, and in an equally dated away, were a calculating horse and an Italian medium specializing in materializations. A witch and a girl possessed by demons were exhibits more 'period' still. In fact – said Appleby to himself as he paced the blacked-out deck once more – this ship has the nineteen-forties dead astern and is heading for the past at its full economic speed of eighteen knots. The Time Ship: master, Emery Wine. It sounded like H. G. Wells ... He took several turns about the deck and returned to the smoke-room. Hudspith's voice greeted him as he entered. 'I like them young,' it said.

'I must say I like them young,' he repeated – and Appleby saw that the process of getting un-tight had begun. For a trace of uneasiness, perhaps of shame, had come into the deplorable saga. Hudspith, though still talking defiantly, was looking at the silent Wine and Beaglehole with an occasional furtive sideways glance – as a man may do who is presently going to realize that he has been making a fool of himself. 'There was a girl in London,' said Hudspith, raising his voice with a sort of desperate and fading arrogance. 'Just a few months ago. Lucy, her name was . . .'

Rather abruptly Appleby plumped down on a settee. Perhaps he had been dull. Certainly he had not realized it was all heading for this.

'Lucy?' said Wine, profoundly uninterested. 'Do you know, I believe this is the first Lucy you've mentioned? Whereas there have been four Marys and three Janes. Beaglehole will correct me if I am wrong.'

'And you wouldn't believe' – Hudspith's voice went higher as he ignored the sarcasm – 'you wouldn't believe how young she was – sometimes.'

Wine laid down his cigar. 'Sometimes?' he echoed.

This time Hudspith lowered his voice. 'Lucy was a damned queer kid. That was what was cute about her. You never knew where you were with her. Sometimes as grave as a judge. And sometimes – well, she might have been twelve. Poor little Lucy Rideout!'

Hudspith was staring mournfully at the ceiling – which meant that he could trust his colleague to make such observations as might appear. And there could be no doubt about the palpable hit: Appleby was instantaneously convinced of that. Between Wine and his assistant there had passed a glance of the most startled intelligence. The nightmarish birthday party had justified itself at last. And the Daffodil affair, lately as ragged and flowing as cirrus clouds, stood now solid before Appleby as he sat – solid too with something of the symmetry of a carefully precipitated crystal.

And now Hudspith was shifting restlessly on his seat. Again he had the look of an uneasy man, but this time his air was not quite that of one dawningly aware that he has carried his liquor singularly ill. He had something of his old brooding appearance, and his eye seemed as if looking half fearfully into distance. 'And there's a funny thing about that girl,' he said. 'Several times today –' He broke off, rose and walked fairly steadily round the smoke-room – a rapidly sobering man. 'I suppose that's why I've been talking,' he resumed inconsequently.

There was a moment's silence. Wine was carefully relighting his cigar. 'You were saying,' he prompted, 'that several times today –'

But Hudspith had strode to the farther end of the room, poured himself a cup of black coffee and drained it. And now when he turned back he was visibly still further chastened. 'You mustn't mind my yarns,' he said. 'Will get yarning after a party. You know how it is. Too much girl and then this damn long voyage.' He stood before them, ignoble but rational. 'Tell you snake stories now, if you like.' Again he shifted uneasily, was momentarily absent. 'Or game of cards. Fixes the mind. After a long party nothing like a hand or two before shut-eye. Come 'long, John.'

Appleby came along, noting that it was just three-quarters of an hour short of twelve. Beaglehole suggested poker; Hudspith demanded bridge and carried his point, so that presently he was demonstrating very convincingly those peculiarly rapid powers of sobering-up which some men possess. It was a dull game, for small stakes, with Beaglehole making occasional bets in the prudent manner of a commercial man, and with Wine displaying an orthodoxy so consistent as to suggest some hidden absence of mind. Hudspith himself was now as sober and normal a businessman as ever came out of Auckland or Sydney. And over the deserted bar the clock ticked steadily towards midnight.

Deep below them the engines throbbed and the slap and hiss of water came faintly up; occasionally they could hear the high note that a ship's rigging seems to take on only south of the line. Perhaps bridge does fix the mind, but bridge at midnight and in mid-ocean can strangely emphasize the isolation of a voyage. Close round about, sleeping or at watch, is the tiny company to which one is attached. Beyond, and stretching past the bounds of any concrete awareness, is the utterly alien deep. We are accustomed to think of the distances of inter-stellar space as alone baffling to the human imagination. But after a fortnight at sea we know that we have traversed distances equally transcending any realizing power of the mind. Through the night the engines drove with their mysteriously unfailing power. And the four men flipped their pasteboards on the square of green baize.

Hudspith was partnering Appleby. He was laying down his hand for dummy. And as he finished doing so he looked past Appleby's shoulder and smiled – smiled with evident pleasure and perhaps a trace of surprise. 'Lucy!' he said. 'I didn't know –' He broke off, frowned, spoke again with sudden anxiety. 'What are you doing? What are you doing with that –'

Appleby, although he ought to have been looking at Wine, swung round despite himself. The door was behind him and it was closed. Behind the door, he knew, was a curtain, and behind that an outer door, also closed. But Hudspith, it was almost possible to swear, had been looking at the deck directly beyond. And now he had sprung to his feet and was passing a hand across his eyes. 'She had a gun,' he said hoarsely. 'There were trees ... palms ...' Dead sober, he looked at his companions. 'I'm drunk,' he said. 'Damn drunk – sorry.' He turned round, pushed his chair back clumsily and stumbled from the room.

As a piece of acting it was absolutely first class. Appleby, although he felt an inclination to cheer, contrived to whistle. 'Poor old Ron!' he said. 'I never knew him get it as badly as that '

Beaglehole rose. He looked both scared and angry – which is no doubt how the sceptical do look on such occasions. And when he spoke it was more aggressively than usual. 'He'll be seeing pink and green rats next. It's a mistake to drink anything but whisky on a ship.'

'Not at all.' Wine, who was stacking cards while staring thoughtfully before him, shook his head. 'This has the appearance – at least the superficial appearance – of something rather more interesting than that. What is called, I believe, casual veridical hallucination of the sane.'

'You mean second sight?' asked Appleby.

Wine shrugged his shoulders. 'My dear man, that is a term from superstition and folk-lore. If we positively believe in such things we shall no doubt use these old words. I prefer the description science gives to something it still regards as extremely debatable.' He turned round. 'Midnight, you will notice. I wonder if your friend's Lucy is still alive? Or has conceivably just died? People who investigate these affairs would no doubt like to know.' He yawned. 'And now what about bed?'

'Sure,' said Appleby and turned towards the door. Suddenly he stopped and laid a hand with innocent familiarity on the other's shoulder. 'But say, Mr Wine, you knew all that jargon about those horses – and now you have the jargon about this. Perhaps you're a bit of a hand at investigating these things yourself?' Appleby let his hand drop, but not before he had felt Wine's muscles grow momentarily rigid. Whatever reply came would be the product of rapid circulation.

'Investigate spooks, Mr Appleby? Dear me, no.'

'Spooks and thinking animals and various sorts of mediums – that sort of thing.'

Wine's eyelids flickered. Then he smiled. It would have been a snubbing smile had it been a shade less merely amused. 'Dear me, no. Beaglehole, shall we be talking too freely if we say that we have more important work than that?' And Wine laughed pleasantly. 'Good night, my dear sir. Good night.'

6

Appleby swung himself out of his bunk and sat on the edge. His hands lay on his knees and the morning sun shone on them. 'You see?' he said. His right thumb almost imperceptibly moved. 'You see?'

'Yes, I see.' Hudspith had just returned from an early prowl on deck. 'But I *don't* see what sort of contrivance –'

'A lazy-tongs. Something that Beaglehole said put it in my head. It used to be quite a popular toy, and nowadays they make elevator doors and things on the same principle. Something rather like a pair of scissors with a piece of lattice-work pivoted to the blades. You close the scissors – a movement of the thumb will do it – and the whole affair shoots out and extends itself a surprising distance. Open the scissors and it retracts itself and folds up. Eusapia was practising with a contrivance like that.'

Hudspith shook his head. 'But surely such a thing would quickly be found out? No conjurer could get away with it.'

'A physical medium isn't a conjurer. Or rather he is a conjurer who imposes conditions which no theatre audience would put up with. He sits in next to complete darkness. His limbs may be held, but he can claim a supernatural origin for all sorts of calculated physical convulsions. And if he is too strictly controlled – for instance if he has had to agree to a careful search before a seance – he can simply announce that the spirits are on holiday for that day. Eusapia is this special sort of conjurer and Wine knows it and is carrying her off to join his circus.'

'Which places Wine. He collects frauds.'

'No.' Appleby shook his head decidedly. 'The thing is not quite so simple as that. Perhaps no known physical medium has ever been exhaustively investigated by scientists without the exposure of fraud. But there are highly intelligent investigators who maintain that with these people fraud is a sort of emergency line of defence. Mediums – roughly speaking – are paid by results. It is conceivable that they are genuinely the channels of supernormal agencies to which the methods and attitudes of scientific investigators are antipathetic. When the mediums are hard pressed by the scientists the supernormal agencies desert them. And then, to sustain their reputation, the mediums resort to trickery. There is thus a case of sorts for continuing to investigate the phenomena even of persons who have been frequently exposed as fraudulent. Wine may know that Eusapia is a little twister and yet his intentions may be those of a serious investigator.'

'Or they may be those of a showman.'

'Exactly. We may be on the track of the Strangest Show on Earth. Something of that sort. But the question is – is Wine on the track of two inquisitive policemen who have begun their dealings with him in a deplorably holiday mood?' Appleby rose and stretched himself. 'I'm going to have a bath. If I meet him I'll ask him.'

'Don't do that.' Hudspith spoke with serious concern. 'Don't, I mean, do any more forcing of the issue at present. You've claimed to know a relative of Daffodil's and I've claimed to know Lucy Rideout –'

Appleby laughed. 'My claim is quite harmless. But the laws of slander are absolutely savage against yours. And from a man whose mission in life is the defence of British maidenhood –'

Hudspith held up his hand. 'Bawdry,' he said with dignity, 'will get us nowhere. I am simply insisting that we've strained coincidence to breaking-point and must go easy if he's not to spot us. I don't think I ought to have had that vision of Lucy last night. I'm afraid I was a bit carried away.'

'Not exactly that. You did contrive to get out of the room on your own legs. And so, for that matter, did Wine. I mean that he wasn't at all bowled over. Beaglehole was much nearer letting some cat out of the bag. Wine is a deep one. And just what he's thinking – or planning – at this moment I can't at all guess.'

'That's because you don't get up early enough. He's been trying to send a wireless message.'

Appleby was picking up a large sponge; he held it suspended in air. 'A wireless message? He must know he has no more chance of that than of taking over command of the ship.'

'You forget that he's ostensibly on some sort of hush–hush job. And to get a message away he's been straining any authority he possesses.'

'It looks as if we've upset him all right. Did they send him away with a flea in his ear?'

Hudspith frowned at this vulgarism – and then fleetingly smiled. 'What you might call half a flea. They told him it was absolutely impossible to send out wireless messages anyway. The atmosphere is electrical.'

Appleby stared. 'Isn't that what they say in a diplomatic crisis?'

'This time it's meant literally. I had all this from the first officer. There's some sort of electrical disturbance in the offing quite outside his experience. That's why the air felt so queer last night.'

'It's nice to know it wasn't just the drink. But isn't it pretty queer still?'

'Decidedly. I think you're quite likely to be electrocuted in that bath.'

Appleby chanced it. And as he lay in the warm salt water and watched its obstinate refusal to dip and tilt with the ship he realized how significant that attempted wireless message was. It went some way towards explaining the theft of 37 Hawke Square.

Mrs Nurse picked up the milk-jug. 'I suppose they make it out of powder,' she said. 'I'm afraid I don't think it at all nice. Particularly in tea. I don't think tea is at all nice on steamers.' She put the jug down again. 'Has anybody noticed the funny sky?'

'I never saw a sky that colour before,' said Wine.

'It's not so much the colour,' said Miss Mood, 'as the way it seems to go all wavy when you look at it.'

Beaglehole nodded. 'You need go no farther than the wireless aerial to see something damned queer. Lights like little blue devils running and jumping on the wires. Mr Hudspith mayn't believe it, but they're really there.' Beaglehole as he said this looked swiftly at Wine, as if to make sure that this was the right line to take. Then he laughed uneasily and thrust away a plate. 'Uncommonly oppressive, isn't it? Makes you feel queer. No appetite.'

'Feel queer?' said Mrs Nurse – and appeared to consider. 'No, I don't think it does that.'

Miss Mood's nervous hands played with a large amber necklace. 'The astral influences,' she said sombrely. 'It may be some great disaster. But I think one ought to eat.' And she tore the paper cover off a roll.

'These disturbances do happen in the tropics,' said Wine. 'I believe they are not yet very well understood. But I don't think Miss Mood need apprehend disaster.'

Miss Mood was clearly not reassured; instead of eating her roll she was tearing the little paper bag into fragments.

'Feel queer?' said Mrs Nurse again.

Appleby, who had been eating bacon and eggs stolidly, turned to Wine. 'A funny old day, all right,' he said. 'A real cow.'

'I beg your pardon?'

'And gets at the nerves. I've known the same sort of thing during a dust storm.'

'That's right.' Hudspith nodded heavily. 'And I've known Uncle Len say –'

'The fans!' Beaglehole was pointing excitedly. 'Did you ever see –'

It was warm and the fans were going – but now suddenly they could be seen only through a spiralling fuzz and crackle of electrical discharge.

'Did you ever see –' Beaglehole, still dramatically gesturing, was interrupted in turn by Miss Mood. Miss Mood screamed. She screamed because, from the table before her, a little snowstorm of paper fragments had risen and was circling round her head. For a moment her startled face was like a pinnacle seen through an eddy of gulls. And then, like gulls coming to rest, the little scraps of paper had clustered on her amber necklace.

It was distinctly odd. But the behaviour of the placid Mrs Nurse was odder. 'Queer?' she said faintly, and fell back in her chair with closed eyes. A moment later they had opened again, but the pupils were upturned and only the whites were showing. 'Queer?' she said very faintly, and her body jerked itself upright. 'Near,' she said in a new voice. 'It is very near.' Her voice deepened again and took on a foreign intonation. 'The Emperor says it is near. He says Beware. No, he says Prepare. The Emperor wants you all to know that it is clear. He understands it all. The Emperor understands everything. We understand everything here. The Emperor advises prayer. It is very near now.' There was a long sigh. 'I feel all hollow,' Mrs Nurse said in her ordinary voice. 'I feel all hollow,' she said piteously.

Appleby, who had started on his last rasher, turned again to Wine. 'I expect you know the jargon of this too, Mr Wine?'

'No doubt she will come to herself presently.' Wine uttered the words non-committally and then took refuge behind a coffee-cup.

'Would you call it a trance?' asked Hudspith. 'Uncle Len once knew a woman –'

Like an erupting geyser Miss Mood went off into high-pitched laughter. Peal after peal of it rang horridly through the saloon. And then it ceased as abruptly as it had begun. Breathing rapidly, Miss Mood sat rigid and with a dilated eye.

'Now there's another strange thing,' Appleby was almost owlishly placid. 'Talking of your Uncle Len, Ron, my Uncle Sid had a cowgirl just like that.' And Appleby nodded towards Miss Mood.

'A cowgirl?' said Wine. He spoke, Appleby thought, a trifle wildly, as if the situation were becoming too much for him. There would come a point at which you could bowl over Wine.

'A cowgirl. And when she went like *that*' – and again Appleby nodded at Miss Mood – 'you could do *this*.' And Appleby's hand went to the lapel of his coat and produced a pin. 'This,' he repeated – and leaning across the table he pushed the pin firmly into Miss Mood's arm. 'Ron, have you got another?' He felt in his pocket. 'Or if one has a pen-knife –'

'Really,' said Wine, 'I don't know that you ought. Clearly Miss Mood is in a condition of hysterical anaesthesia. But you must consider –'

'There!' interrupted Appleby admiringly. 'There's the right jargon again. But does it occur to you, Mr Wine, that for a small boat like this –'

'Just look at her hand, now,' said Hudspith, pointing at Miss Mood. 'What would she be doing that for?' Miss Mood's right hand was moving oddly on the tablecloth.

'I think if I had a pencil' – Appleby felt in his pockets – 'and a piece of paper she would produce automatic writing – something like that. Mr Wine, you agree?'

'No doubt,' said Wine.

'Well, as I was saying, isn't it odd that on a small boat like this there should be –'

'Where is the girl with the golden hair?' said Mrs Nurse, beginning again. 'Where is the girl with the golden hair? Where is the girl with the golden hair?'

Miss Mood, still rigid and still making scribbling movements, began to sob. There was a crackle of electricity from the fans and the atmosphere was permeated with a faint singeing smell.

'Here is Mentor to speak to the girl with the golden hair. Hurry. Mentor says hurry. There are thwarting influences. Where is the girl –'

There was a tumble of steps on the staircase and Beaglehole, who must have slipped out some minutes before, blundered in. 'That Italian!' He addressed Wine in a despairing flurry. 'She's behaving just like this in the third-class saloon. Something to do with tambourines. And a table. Turning a table . . .'

A long reverberating crash drowned his words — a crash as if some Titan had banged a tambourine, as if the very table of the gods had been upset. Again and again the thunder rolled, and daylight flickered feebly between great flashes of lightning. Then there was a hiss of falling water. The curious atmospheric conditions that had led to so much eccentric behaviour on the part of the protégées of Mr Emery Wine were resolving themselves in a straightforward tropical storm.

'I was saying,' said Appleby, 'that in a small ship like this one would hardly expect —'

'Quite so,' said Wine.

'One would hardly expect to find so many birds of a feather. Unless, of course, they were travelling together to a conference or a clinic or something of that sort. But we don't know that Mrs Nurse and Miss Mood —'

'Exactly,' said Wine. 'It is curious, no doubt.'

'We don't know that Mrs Nurse and Miss Mood believe they have anything to do with each other. And now it seems there's a similar sort of woman in the third class. It makes one think —'

Wine took him by the arm. 'My dear Mr Appleby,' he said, 'you and I must go on deck and get a breath of air.'

7

Rain gurgled in the scuppers and drummed on the sun-deck overhead; beyond, it fell in torrents from a sky watery and still lit by a faint lightning; the South Atlantic Ocean looked terribly wet.

'It must frankly appear,' said Mr Wine, 'that we are not what we seem.'

'You mean Beaglehole and yourself?'

'I mean Beaglehole and myself on the one part and Hudspith and yourself on the other part. The phrase is a trifle legal, but expresses the state of affairs very nicely. By the way, I must introduce you to Eusapia. She is quite charming. Dishonest, of course. But in pretty girls moral qualities are not so awfully relevant, are they?' Wine smiled urbanely at Appleby.

'But perhaps it is your friend whom I should introduce to Eusapia. I believe she would obliterate even Gladys from his mind.'

Appleby looked at Wine squarely. 'I don't know that our conversation can usefully take on this tone.'

Framed against a sheet of rain-streaked plate-glass, Wine gave a faint and mocking bow. 'I stand corrected. But scarcely in an idiom familiar to Uncle Sid and Uncle Len.'

'Uncle Sid and Uncle Len are all nonsense.' Appleby, thrown initially on the defensive, determined to make robust work of it.

'I wouldn't say that,' Wine was courteous. 'They seemed to me very credible – and creditable – approximations. Perhaps Uncle Len's bones were a bit steep – but then odd things no doubt do happen in those parts. May I offer you a cigarette?'

Appleby took a cigarette. 'Has it occurred to you, Mr Wine, that it is a serious matter to hold yourself out as being upon a government mission in time of war when in fact your business is quite different?'

'But we can't all of us *really* go on war missions. And unless doing so ostensibly, you know, it's now extraordinarily difficult to get about at all.' Wine struck a match. ' "Some to the wars, to try their fortune there, Some to discover islands far away." The words are Shakespeare's. Perhaps they will elevate what you call the tone of our discussion. And incidentally – isn't it a discussion between the pot and the kettle? Do you and Hudspith really know much about wool?'

'Possibly not. But at least we are travelling on fairly significant business. Otherwise, and at the present time, I would rather be at home.'

Wine shook his head. 'Home-keeping youths have ever homely wits. I am inclined to recommend the islands far away. Indeed, I hope to persuade you to accompany me there. Why not? It may be we shall find the Happy Isles.'

'And meet the great Achilles whom we knew?' The words were idle, but Appleby's brain was working quickly. Some unknown factor, some odd misunderstanding, must surely lurk in Wine's proposal.

'Conceivably even that. Achilles and Hector too.'

'And other shades – like Mrs Nurse's Mentor and the Emperor?'

'Ah.' Wine frowned considerably, so that Appleby wondered if he was thinking up a little more Shakespeare. 'Now we come to business, don't we? That the storm should affect all these queerly organized people was not, I suppose, so very odd. I confess to having felt unsettled myself.

But both Mrs Nurse and Miss Mood in trances simultaneously, and then word of Eusapia misbehaving too, really was a bit overpowering. As I say, it may be admitted that we are not altogether what we seem.'

'Nor are our relations what they appear to be. Neither Mrs Nurse nor Miss Mood shows any consciousness of standing in a special relationship either to each other or to yourself. And yet there can now be no doubt that, together with the Italian girl, they form a sort of convoy under the escort of you and your secretary. Perhaps they don't know about you.'

Wine nodded. 'Well, as a matter of fact they don't.'

'Such concealment is rather strange, to say the least. You have employed agents or decoys to send them travelling where you want them.'

'Just that, Mr Appleby. And of course there was Lucy Rideout too. I must admit that I was very disturbed by your friend's ostensible experience last night – very perturbed indeed. In fact it is only in the last few minutes that I have seen the thing as being an ingenious hoax. And I am disposed to think that you know about the calculating horse from Harrogate. Of what else, I wonder? Have you heard of Hannah Metcalfe? She's a witch. Indeed she is.' And Wine smiled his unruffled smile.

The thing had the speed of mechanized encounter. And the man was not confessing at random; he had an object in view; perhaps it was that of rushing one off one's feet. And – telling all this – what did he know or think he knew? Appleby put out a feeler. 'You think Hudspith never really met that Lucy Rideout?'

'I don't say that at all. I do say that last night he was very skilfully fooling us.'

Appleby threw away his cigarette and took a quick glance at his companion. There was something in the man's tone as he made this last statement – some quality of combined hesitation and emphasis – which was obscurely significant. 'In fact, Mr Wine, you think my friend Hudspith one big hoax? He isn't subject to abnormal experiences at all?'

'I think nothing of the sort. Otherwise –' Wine broke off and hauled a couple of wicker chairs across the little shelter deck. 'Shall we sit down? And perhaps go back to your own part in the affair? After all, turn about is only reasonable. And I think it is admitted that your concerns are not really with sheep – except perhaps in a metaphorical sense.' Wine smiled again at Appleby – and for the first time Appleby thought it an ugly smile. It was ugly and also puzzling – puzzling because based on some misapprehension as yet unrevealed. Or was there misapprehension? Was Wine rather *feigning* a misapprehension? To arrive at a right answer to this might be vital. And perhaps the best thing would be to take a bold step.

'Perhaps, Mr Wine, you take Hudspith and myself for plain-clothes policemen?'

'Ah,' said Wine.

'In which case you wouldn't be far wrong.'

'Ah,' said Wine again. And then suddenly he sat back in his chair and laughed. His laugh was genuine and of the kind that attends the discovery of intellectual absurdity. 'My dear fellow, may we not be a little more frank with each other than that?' Suddenly he sat forward again and touched Appleby lightly on the arm.

'Listen,' he said.

Part 3
Happy Islands

I

PLOP ... PLOP ... The waters bubbled evilly and the heavy sound was indefinably sinister – but each time it was followed by a delighted clapping of hands. 'Another one!' the girl cried out. 'And another one! Oh, look at its nose – and its eyes! Mr Wine says they have little birds that pick their teeth for them. Oh, look at its great tail!'

The waters were dark and oily round the steamer, and unmoving except where the great creatures dropped and splashed. 'Another one!' cried the girl. And the man at the wheel – who stood all day at the wheel, aloof and dreaming – the man at the wheel laughed at her suddenly and richly. *'Lagarto,'* he said; *'lagarto, señorita.'* He swung the wheel, and the whole crazy little vessel creaked; swung it again so that one of the paddles insanely clattered; gave a final tug and they were round another bend with the interminable river stretching before them. For some reason they hugged the south bank, low, steamy and densely wooded. On the north the horizon was nearly always water. They were now two thousand miles up-stream, but the mind revolted at the knowledge. *PLOP ...* 'And *another* one!' cried Lucy in ecstasy. Her clapping raised a flock of pink and yellow parrots from the tree-ferns.

Reclined under an awning in the stern, Mr Emery Wine benevolently smiled. Then a thought seemed to strike him. 'Lucy,' he called out, 'have you written to your mama?'

'Oh, yes, Mr Wine.'

'That's right, my dear.' Wine's glance turned meditatively on Hudspith, who was gloomily scratching his jaw. 'She writes to her mother every week – *one of her* writes to her mother – and I try to see that the letter catches the Clipper. Mrs Rideout is a very good sort of woman. Perhaps you know her?'

Hudspith frowned. One who had romanced so freely about the virginal young person in the prow might well find this question embarrassing. It was true that since coming on board Mr Wine's steamer sundry mendacious explanations had been given. Nevertheless Lucy remained somebody whom Hudspith could not quite look in the eye.

'Of course,' said Wine, 'I had to act a little high-handedly in getting her away. After all *your* lot might very well have got in first if I had at all stood upon forms. Competition does make one a little unscrupulous at times. But now I believe that Mrs Rideout and I understand each other very well. It was one of the things which amused me when Appleby made his little joke about being a plain-clothes policeman. I reflected that there was really very little the police could get me on.'

'There's the horse,' said Appleby.

Wine laughed gaily. 'I stole the horse. But whoever heard of a man being convicted of absconding to South America with a broken-down cab-horse? The thing would fall to pieces as an evident absurdity. No; if you were a policeman – and if Hudspith here were another – I think you would find it difficult to nail me.' He pulled at a soft drink. 'Do you know, Hudspith, I sometimes think that you're rather *like* a policeman? But then at one time I thought you looked quite the Cobdogla type. It's never wise to let appearances count. Take Radbone, now. What would you make of him? I mean judging by the outward man?'

'We've never met him,' Appleby said.

Wine sighed. 'Really, my dear fellows, how absurd you sometimes are. Radbone employs you to keep an eye on me – and I must say I think it's carrying a healthy scientific rivalry rather far – and then when you're detected you turn uncommonly coy . . . Lucy, would you care for a glass of lemonade?'

'Oh, yes, please, Mr Wine.'

'But my point is that Radbone is a dull-looking man who is really uncommonly able. I don't mind confessing that at one time I feared he would get hold of the majority of the material. It's scarce, you know.' Wine lowered his voice. 'Take Lucy there. I doubt if there are a couple of others like that living. Or take Mrs Nurse. One can find any number of Eusapias. But a first-class non-physical medium crops up only once in a generation.' Wine rubbed his hands together softly. 'First-class laboratory and clinical material, gentlemen – first-class material. And I think I have your lot beaten now. I don't think Radbone can reply. Which is why I'm asking you to come and have a look. You can go back and tell him about it.' Wine laughed with high good humour. 'I'm really most obliged to you for coming. It's a devilish long way there – and back.'

'We think it will be very interesting,' Appleby said.

'I really think you will find it so. Jorge' – and Wine turned to a servant – 'you had better fetch Miss Rideout a rug; the air is becoming a little chill … I think you will find it interesting. The *Encyclopaedia Britannica* will tell you that nowhere in the world does there exist a properly equipped laboratory solely for the purposes of psychical research. You will soon know better.'

'And Lucy,' Appleby said.

Wine frowned. 'I beg your pardon?'

'She will soon know too. But why? I mean that it's difficult to see just how Lucy is orthodox psychical-research material. She represents a rare but fairly well-understood morbid condition – that of one individual split up into several personalities. Once upon a time it was thought of as possession by demons, no doubt. But I should have imagined it to be pretty well off the slate of serious psychical inquiry. Lucy is psychopathology, not psychics.'

'Ah,' said Wine – and his glance travelled over the side of the steamer, rather as if he were seeking inspiration among the alligators. 'But there is the historical point of view, you know. One must consider that.' He nodded largely and vaguely in support of this obscure statement. 'And then there are affiliations.' His voice gained confidence. 'When these strange voices speak through Mrs Nurse are we really in contact with an unseen world – or is Mrs Nurse momentarily in Lucy's case? You see?'

Appleby saw. And he saw that the man knew his stuff. Whatever was Wine's game – and it was surely not quite what he claimed – the fellow had the science of the thing adequately enough. Was he what he held himself out to be – and something more? Or was he not what he held himself out to be at all? It was conceivable that a man might devote himself to the organization of large-scale psychical research: many first-rate intelligences had become absorbed in it. It was conceivable that such a man might have a rival called Radbone, and might go to strange and even bizarre lengths to secure a sort of corner in the necessary human material. But was it conceivable that such a man should concentrate his activities thousands of miles up an appalling South American river? Was it conceivable that he should carry off to such a fastness a Harrogate cab-horse and a Bloomsbury mansion – to say nothing of two men whom he declared were spies of his rival, but as to whom there was a recurrent little joke about plain-clothes police? It was a long way up the river – and a long way back. Wine had taken them straight from the liner to his own craft. And now here they were ... Appleby, who did not greatly mind tough spots if only they were odd enough, sat back and sipped comfortably at his Maté tea. To all these questions – and others – answers would appear.

Lucy was having a rug wrapped round her toes; Wine nodded approvingly, set down his glass, and sighed with content. 'Poor old Radbone!' he said. 'Do you know, I think I'll send him Eusapia as a Christmas present? I could wish him a nice little crumb of comfort like that.'

Hudspith eyed his host with unforced gloom. 'You seem to feel that you've got Radbone thoroughly down.'

'I wouldn't say that. He's a smart man – though a smart man with a weakness. A weakness fatal in this particular field. The fact is, he's credulous. He doesn't know it, but he's credulous. Deep down, Radbone is hungry for wonders. And in a scientist, you'll agree, that is sheer contradiction and nonsense.'

'But isn't it a hunger for wonders which actuates you too?' Appleby had looked up sharply. 'If you don't hanker after ghosts and marvels why take all this trouble? You can hardly take much pleasure in carrying off Mrs Nurse if you regard yourself as a confirmed sceptic.'

Wine shook his head impatiently. 'My dear Appleby, you must give the matter a little more thought. My attitude is objective. And I am a scientist. That means that I am not interested in anything outside nature. If there are, in fact, ghosts, then ghosts are in nature and to be brought within the rule of natural law. But Radbone has a sneaking nostalgia for something outside nature – thrills, creeps, mystery for the sake of mystery. He wants his ghosts to be uncanny to the end; to produce the same emotional effects in the laboratory as in the peasant's cottage.' Wine had risen and was speaking almost with violence. 'So his attitude and mine are poles apart. It is contended that there are certain classes of phenomena which are unaccountable. These classes of phenomena may or may not exist. But if they do exist they are certainly *not* unaccountable. The laws governing them can be discovered – and that is my job. Radbone, despite his ability and his eminence, is fundamentally no more than a silly woman at a seance. He seeks not the truth, but the thrill. You follow me?'

Appleby modestly intimated that he followed.

'You must forgive me being a little carried away.' Wine let his scientific fervour soften into a whimsical smile. 'And now I think I shall go down and change.'

Hudspith watched his immaculate panama disappear down the companion-way. Then he turned to Appleby. 'I say,' he murmured cautiously, 'do you believe in this Radbone?'

'It would be nice to. If Radbone is an invention we can hardly be his agents, can we? Which would mean that we had walked nicely into a trap. With our eyes open, of course.'

'No doubt there's comfort in that.' Hudspith was keeping a wary eye on Lucy Rideout.

'I think myself that Radbone has a sort of existence.' Appleby's eye too was on Lucy as he spoke. 'If so, it greatly complicates the whole affair.'

'Heaven forbid that it should be more complicated than at present appears. And for my own part I don't believe in Radbone and his rival push a bit.'

'No more do I. The existence I attribute to Radbone is – of another kind.'

Hudspith stared. 'Well, if he doesn't exist, then we've admitted to being the agents of a ruddy fiction.' Hudspith frowned at himself as he fell into this improper language. 'I've even had to vamp up some story of having angled after Lucy there as Radbone's agent before Wine got in on her. And your birthday party is supposed to have been a trap all on that same fiction's behalf.' He paused. 'Do you know, I'm beginning to take quite a morbid interest in those alligators.'

Appleby laughed. 'Whereas Lucy's interest is far from morbid. It's as spontaneous as that of a child at the zoo. But you don't think that Wine will make away with us simply because we are policemen disposed to tax him with somewhat irregular methods of assembling what he calls laboratory material?'

'I do,' said Hudspith. 'And – what's more – you do too.'

Appleby laughed again. 'As Uncle Len was so fond of remarking: you're telling me. Or, as Uncle Sid would put it: too right.'

'There are bright spots, I suppose. I'm glad that that awful woman Mood is coming up on another boat. To have her counting up the bones after the alligators had been at work –'

'There wouldn't be any bones. The digestive system of the crocodile family is the most powerful known to zoology. The bones are dissolved within a few seconds of going down.'

'It's wonderful how you can always produce the relevant information.' Hudspith stared sombrely at the clotted vegetation trailing past the port rail. 'Can we really be bound for an island?'

'We can – though it must be admitted that Juan Fernandez was a bad guess. The river runs to whole groups of islands; full-grown archipelagos right in the middle of the continent. And of one such it appears that Wine has possessed himself.'

Hudspith heaved himself to his feet. 'Has it occurred to you what it must all cost? The thing is far more like big business than scientific research.'

'Quite so. And that brings in the alligators again. The ruthlessness of science tends to expend itself on white mice and guinea-pigs. It's in big business that you find a really concentrated effort to throw one's rivals to the crocodiles.'

Hudspith rubbed his jaw and was silent; then he turned and made his way below. But Appleby sat on under the awning and watched the mists rising along the river-bank. The day was over, and its heat and its clarity ended in noisome vapours. Steamy and miasmal, the stuff came first in scattered wisps or in the finest and least perceptible of veils. And then almost immediately it was everywhere. The landscape, familiar and unchanging through the long day, was obliterated as if some great hand had let a curtain fall. A kind of treacherously luminous darkness fell.

And that was it. Appleby sat very still, looking out over the waters. That was it. The man had chosen with a certain symbolical fitness when he pitched his lair here.

PLOP.

'Another one!'

Appleby was lost in thought; his lips were compressed and he gazed sternly before him. But now his expression softened. 'Lucy,' he called gently, 'won't you come and talk to me?'

2

'Lucy –' Appleby said, and paused. 'Young Lucy –' he said, and paused again. 'It is young Lucy, isn't it?'

Lucy Rideout nodded.

'Are you glad you came, Lucy?'

'I'm glad; I think it's fun. Do you know St Ursula's?' And Lucy looked up at Appleby, friendly and unembarrassed.

'No; I don't know about St Ursula's.'

'It's a girls' school, and it goes round and round the world in a great steamer. They have a lovely time. Of course it isn't really true. It's in a book.'

'I see.'

'But this is really true. And I do think it's fun. There's lemonade whenever you like.'

'That is very nice. But what about – about the others? Do they like it too?'

'Sick Lucy hates it. She kept on trying to run away at first. But now, of course, she has her studies. She's doing Latin with Mr Wine.' Young Lucy spoke with a sort of reluctant respect. 'That keeps her quiet.'

'And –'

'Real Lucy? Real Lucy is terribly thrilled. But she's scared too, I think. Only since you came –' Young Lucy hesitated. 'She would be dreadfully angry if she knew I told you this.'

'Then perhaps you had better not tell me.' Appleby looked at the child-like young woman beside him with considerable perplexity. Conversation with Lucy Rideout – conversation with the Lucy Rideouts – was really a job for a specially trained man. The amateur, even when he understood the situation, was constantly liable to trip. The cardinal thing to remember was that there was only one Lucy in existence at a time – a Lucy who regarded the two Lucys commonly in an objective and friendly, but occasionally in an exasperated manner ... 'If it would annoy her,' Appleby said, 'you had better hold your tongue.'

'She's in love with you.'

'Oh.' Appleby was considerably at a loss.

Young Lucy's eyes danced mischievously. 'I think if you wanted –'

'Be quiet.'

Young Lucy looked hurt. 'I'm sorry. I don't know much about that sort of thing – not yet. And it's a terribly long yet. I'm twelve, you know. And I seem to have been twelve for years. Sometimes I think that the others are getting all the fun. And sometimes I'm glad and think it would be horrid to be like the others and old.' She paused and frowned, profoundly perplexed. 'But mostly I just wish it was all different and that there weren't any others. And I think the others feel that too. Since we got to know each other, that is.'

'I see. And when did you get to know each other?'

'At first there was just real Lucy, and for quite a long time after I came she knew nothing about me, though I knew about her. It was better after we did both know each other. Then after a long time sick Lucy came. We neither of us knew anything about her and she didn't know about us. Not even that we – we *were*, I mean. That was the worst of all. Then we got to know her and hated her. And then she got to know me, but not real Lucy. That was funny.'

'It was rather strange, my dear.'

'And there was something else that was funny. It was rather a good thing, I think. Sick Lucy was awfully clever. But she didn't remember anything. She didn't know anything about anything before she came. We had to teach her by leaving messages. We wrote things down about ourselves, I mean, and she read them, and so she got to know things. Nowadays sometimes two of us can sort of talk to each other. But it's dreadfully muddling.' Young Lucy looked at Appleby, cheerful and very pathetic. '*I* like you, too,' she said. 'May I ask you something?'

'Of course, Lucy.'

'How many are there of you?' Lucy's glance was now timid, hopeful.

Appleby looked at the deck, suddenly held by a great and growing anger. Here and there in the great cities of the world were specialists who could deal with all this; who could see their way through it as one sees one's way through a mathematical problem. The girl could be healed; made whole; made one. But she was being carried off to an archipelago in the middle of South America ... 'There's only one of me, Lucy,' he said.

The corners of her mouth dropped. 'There seems to be *nobody* else –' Her glance wandered; she clapped her hands. 'Flamingos!' she cried. 'Oh, aren't they beautiful!' She gave a little gasp and shudder. 'Mr

Appleby,' she said, 'can you tell me about the death of Socrates?'

The alligators plopped unregarded; the flight of the flamingos was now a whirr of wings. The servant called Jorge – a villainous-looking fellow – had drawn mosquito-curtains round the little deck and lit a lamp. There was a powerful smell of cooking forward, so that one could almost believe that the paddles were monotonously slapping at a great river of gravy. But Lucy Rideout appeared to have no thought of dinner; her gaze was fixed intently on Appleby.

'And he said that whether death was a dreamless sleep, or a new life in Hades among the spirits of the great men of antiquity, he counted it equally a gain to die.'

'And that is all?' Sick Lucy's face, strained and anxious, was pale in the light of the lamp.

'It is all I can remember, Miss Rideout.'

'Thank you; you are very good. I know so little. My people were poor and without education. And I myself am subject to – interruptions when I try to learn.'

'Indeed? But that is true in some degree of all of us.' Appleby knew that this Lucy was extremely reticent.

'Mr Wine says that he has a great library on his island. He says that he has hundreds of books' – her voice was awed – 'but still I wish that I had not come. The Latin is very hard. Do you know *amo* and *moneo*?'

'I knew them once.'

'It is for always that one must know them. I think that I know *amo* now.'

'You know what it means?'

Sick Lucy drew the rug about her. 'I love,' she said in a mechanical voice, 'thou lovest, he loves.' She was silent for a moment. 'There is so much that I want to learn.' Her voice had a painful precision of one who has doggedly studied books of grammar. 'But I am hindered – the others hinder me.'

'Very much?'

'I do not wish to speak of it.'

'Then let us speak of something else.'

'The others hinder me. Young Lucy is greedy. She is greedy for time. She would push me back – back into –'

'Yes?'

'Nothing,' said sick Lucy in a low voice. 'Back into nothing. Into not being there. I have to fight. And it is difficult. With me it is *amo* and *moneo*. But with her it is flamingos, an alligator – things felt, seen. She is young and does not know things. But she has life. I am afraid sometimes that she will win. You understand?'

'I think I understand a little.' Appleby's voice was almost as low as Lucy's. 'And –' He hesitated, for it seemed inhumane to speak of another of the Lucys as real. 'And besides young Lucy . . .?'

'There is real Lucy. I do not wish to speak of her. She is bad.'

'Bad?' said Appleby gravely.

'With her it is men.'

'I see.' Appleby found that his eye was avoiding the physical presence before him. For one who was not a professional psychiatrist the thing had its occasional extreme discomforts. 'But I don't think –'

'I mean that she might go bad. It is a great anxiety. Will you – will you be careful?'

There was no more than a monosyllable in which to reply to this. But there was a great deal to find out. Mrs Nurse and Miss Mood and the beguiling Eusapia had been spirited away, and it was problematical when they would be encountered again. At the moment only the Lucys were available for interrogation. And which was the one on which to concentrate – which was the most likely to have gained any inkling of the real purposes of Wine? Not that Appleby had the technique to conjure up one particular Lucy; he must take them as they offered. And so he tried now. 'Miss Rideout, what do you recall of how this journey began? Who first suggested it? And – and to whom?'

'I do not wish to speak of it.' Sick Lucy drew the rug about her closer still. 'Mr Appleby, will you please tell me about the Golden Sayings of Marcus Aurelius?'

'. . . and that the fountain of good is inside us, and that with a little digging –'

Lucy Rideout stirred sharply. 'Hoy!' she said, 'you're not talking to *her*, you know.'

'My dear, I thought I was.' Appleby spoke gently but warily. 'It's rather an easy mistake to make. She *was* there, I promise you, only a few seconds ago.'

'Bother her.' Real Lucy's accents were unrefined but not displeasing. 'And bother the little nipper. Not that she's a bad 'un; we used to have high old times together until that prig came along. But listen. Have they been saying things about me and you?'

'Well – yes, they have.'

'You needn't kid yourself, Jacko.' Real Lucy was robustly cheerful. 'Even in the present restricted society.'

'You may call me John if you will. But if you call me Jacko I will not speak to you again.'

'John, John, whose side are you on? Shades of the prig! That's poetry.'

'I'm not on any side. I think you should all get together.'

'And the more we are together the happier we shall be? No, thanks. Do you know why I came away?'

Appleby shook his head. 'No – but I want to. Why?'

Real Lucy thought this a favourable moment for a move; she came over and sat on the arm of Appleby's chair. 'Probably you think it was for a bit of fun?'

'That has occurred to me.'

'Well, it wasn't. I know a thing or two about girls who have gone off like that. And at first it seemed that it *was* just that – as long as it was the foreign-looking young man, you know. But then Mr Wine turned up, John, he's a wrong 'un.'

'I know he is. But why –'

'But not that sort of wrong 'un. You see, a girl that likes a bit of life and fun has to look out for herself. And know about people. And here was Mr Wine wanting to carry me away to the isle of Capri, and yet he wasn't after – well, you know what I mean. He was after something deep of his own.'

'You were quite right, Lucy. He's after something very deep – and rather horrible. But it has nothing to do with trafficking in girls.' Real Lucy, Appleby saw, was more intelligent by a long way than her sisters; in fact she was a possible ally. 'So you saw it was something pretty deep and the mystery interested and excited you. Life was rather dull, and then here suddenly was an adventure. Was that it?'

Real Lucy laughed softly and began to stroke Appleby's hair. 'I wish we could dance,' she said.

'Stick to the point, my dear.'

'I am.' Suddenly she bent down and kissed him on top of the head.

'I was just thinking that you are clever and rather nice, and that you would never think of me as a girl-friend because of the young 'un perhaps turning up.'

'You're quite right again. But go on.'

'Then listen. I came away because I thought I might leave those two behind. I'm tired of them, I can tell you – that silly kid and the prig. Perhaps they're good sorts in their way, but one does like a little place to oneself. I thought that if I came somewhere and did things they'd both hate that, then they might get sort of discouraged and go away. But it hasn't worked yet, has it? Young Lucy just thinks it no of end fun, and the prig is having a high old time with Kennedy's Shorter Latin Grammar.' Into this last statement real Lucy put a sort of whimsical venom which was not unattractive. 'No cinema, no radio, no boys – I mean, hardly any boys.'

'No need to apologize.'

'In fact this boat is a prig's paradise, and for a kid it's better than a free pass to the Zoo. So not much seems to have come so far of the plan for a change of – of –'

'Environment. I think it was a clever plan, Lucy. But rather a leap in the dark. The new environment might be all in favour of one of the others. And then where would you be?'

'Nowhere, I'd be nowhere, as likely as not. But you have to take a chance. And I'm the real one, after all. I think I've got most chance in the end. If I didn't feel that I'd drown myself – and them.'

'You mustn't do that. Nor that either; Mr Hudspith wouldn't like it' – and Appleby removed her hand from under his chin. ''Tell me, Lucy – why did you never go to a doctor?'

'A doctor?' She stared at him. 'I'm never ill.'

'I see.' Real Lucy was so intelligent and so competently spoken that one could forget the absolute and crippling ignorance general in the Rideout world. 'It will be dinner-time in five minutes.' He had looked at his watch by the gently swaying lamp. 'Lucy, what do you think is Wine's game? Has anything ever happened that has given you any idea of what he's really about?'

She looked serious – so serious that Appleby thought for a moment that sick Lucy had returned. 'He gets together other people who – who are different.'

'I know that.'

'And also –' She broke off. 'Jacko – John, I mean – did you meet a man called Beaglehole? Yes? Well, he's one sort of man I understand – though it's not the sort that my sort of girl sees much of. Beaglehole is money. He does everything for money – just for the sake of the idea of having it. Wine is different. I expect he wants money too. But he wants something else much more. He's the kind that takes hold of you hard and pushes you about until you're just how he wants you. But also he's not.'

'Not?'

'Not that. I've said he's not that. He's that and different.' Real Lucy was struggling with some difficult abstract conception. 'It's as if' – she paused over this unusual piece of syntax – 'it's as if he felt like that not about a girl, or about girls, but – well about everything.'

'You mean that he has a terrific desire for power.'

'Oh, John, I knew you were clever.' She touched him on the ear. 'If only –'

Above the plash of the paddles there sounded the chime of a little silver bell. And Lucy Rideout sprang to her feet. 'Oh, Mr Appleby, isn't it fun having dinner so late! When it's dark! And will there be melon?' She clapped her hands. 'The little, round, baby melons?'

And Appleby followed young Lucy below.

3

Like a paradox tiresomely sustained, the river widened day after day as the little steamer puffed and paddled towards its source. The river widened, but was filled with treacherous shoals; they kept now to midchannel, and sometimes there was a water horizon on either bow. Once they passed a canoe with fishermen – men brown and naked and lean – and once so many canoes that Mr Wine had a case of rifles brought on deck. But it was an uneventful voyage.

The days were hot, and by night there was a soft warmth under brilliant stars. Mosquitoes did not come out so far; the decks were clear of curtains and the awnings disappeared at dinner-time; later the crew assembled on the fo'c'sle deck and chanted to the sound of a sinister little drum. Hudspith more than once remarked that the alligators were becoming sparser – but without appearing to derive much comfort from the fact. Perhaps his melancholy was coming upon him again. As he had spent much time on the liner staring out over the prow, so now he would gaze fixedly over the stern and down the double wake of the steamer. Appleby supposed that the old Sirens were operating. In Buenos Aires Hudspith had once been on terms of most profitable co-operation with the chief of police; in Rio there had occurred a notable sequel to his most famous clean-up in Cardiff. And he was growing thinner, Appleby thought; so that the alligators stood to lose by further delay.

And other things might be suspected to be growing thinner: notably the story about Radbone, the rival scientist. Not through want of the sort of sustenance which one might conceive to be afforded by the steady accumulation of circumstantial detail. Wine had quite fallen into the habit of embroidering on Radbone. There was a regular saga about the man, and one with sufficient interior consistency to speak much for the intellectual powers of the story-teller who lazily and extemporaneously produced it. Unfortunately Appleby and Hudspith were scarcely in a position to give it the dispassionate appraisal of literary critics; the saga had a sort of aura of alligator which made it uncomfortable hearing. Nevertheless something useful emerged. Emery Wine was a conceited man.

He had trapped them. He knew that they were policemen concerned with Lucy Rideout and Hannah Metcalfe and perhaps other aspects of his affairs; he believed that he had dissimulated this knowledge and convinced them of his conviction that they were emissaries of a rival scientist – a rival scientist whom he had invented for the purpose of his trap. He was unaware that his explanations were a little too bland and his stories a little too tall. In fact he had under-estimated the perspicacity of his opponents. But then he could afford to neglect the possibility that this was so. Duped or aware, they were caught. His own problematical stronghold was in front, and behind were hundreds and hundreds of miles of the alligator-infested river.

But Wine was conceited; and the fact was interesting even if not helpful. If he was a wrong 'un he was a wrong 'un on a large scale – on the largest scale that wrong 'uns can achieve, it might be. But he was not, as the largest wrong 'uns commonly are, of the double-guarded, cautious and invulnerable sort. He gave rein to an imagination in the matter of Radbone. And imagination might destroy him yet.

There would be something of imagination in a plan for building up here, in some fastness remote from global warfare, a great organization for the study of the teasing borders of natural knowledge. The voices speaking through Mrs Nurse, the roguery and hypothetical something else in Eusapia, the ancient business of Mr Smart and the yet more ancient business of Colonel Morell: these were all but scattered examples of that class of phenomena commonly called supernatural – phenomena never perhaps convincingly and massively demonstrated but yet clinging obstinately to the fringes of human belief in almost every country and age. A spiritualist 'seance' behind the closed curtains of a modern drawing-room has very little to commend itself to an educated mind: the spirits communicate only a nauseous twaddle, and the physical manifestations have constantly the air of – and frequently a proved source in – a trivial if ingenious conjuring. It is only when the student or investigator takes wider ground, when he finds amid remote times and cultures startlingly analogous performances with the identical residuum of stubbornly unaccountable fact, that he may come to be impressed. A group of scientists, puzzled by some 'paranormal' manifestation in twentieth-century London, finds that in seventeenth-century Africa this identical quirk or quiddity in nature has puzzled Jesuit missionaries as intelligent, as acute and as sceptical as themselves. The rub is there. The rub is there, thought Appleby – and from this pervasiveness of the thing rather than from any impressiveness in individual instances does it maintain its status as a legitimate field for scientific inquiry. And there would be something of imagination in a plan for large-scale assault upon this shadowy corner of the universe.

It had never been done. Rather oddly if one considered the momentous issues which could conceivably be held involved, it had never been done. Here and there had come an endowment for such hitherto irregular investigations – but always, it would appear, there had been mismanagement or ineptitude, and the effort had faded out. Telepathy, for instance, had been studied experimentally and at considerable expense. But the investigators – Radbones of a sort, as it would seem – had inadequately meditated the terms of their problem, so that the result presented merely a new field for dispute. And yet in this strange and baffling branch of knowledge the time was probably ripe for some major clarification, and there would be imagination in a really big drive on it.

Yet all this was nothing – or was little – to Emery Wine.

Big industrialists, Appleby said to himself as he looked out across the unending river, are accustomed to keep a few 'pure' scientists in a back room. In their private and cultivated capacities they may even patronize them a little from time to time. Nevertheless the status of these workers is low; they are kept for the purpose of rounding an occasional awkward technical corner, and if they make a 'discovery' they are likely to see it promptly locked up in their cultivated patron's safe – 'discoveries' being as likely as not to jar the wheels of industry. And so perhaps it might be with Wine and any genuine science which his industry might support. For Wine had – or was going to have – an industry. That was the point. And the men in the back room were not going to be very important. Unless, perhaps, some unforeseen crisis came. There was that to be said for a world in the melting-pot. It sometimes turned the back room into the first-floor front.

There were men who would take the sword and with it conquer the world for their countrymen or themselves. Such men were a nuisance always, and in a world of high-explosive they were a calamity. But always History – a sentimental jade – would give them a little glory: that amid an ocean of tears and blood. Emery Wine was planning a conquest conceivably just as extensive. But decidedly there would be no glory. To few men – thought Appleby, looking sombrely out over the river – had there ever come a plan more absolutely bad.

There were men who had attempted to make what is called a corner in some necessity of life – say in wheat. But to this man had come the conception of making a corner in poison. The thing had a gambling element, as such cornerings commonly have: Wine had to bank on calamity and a gathering darkness. But the plan was clear. It was as if in the fourth century of our era, watching the decline and fall of world order in the empire of Rome, some cunning man had concentrated in his own hands all the promising superstitions, the long-submerged and half-forgotten magical instruments of the twilight ages of the mind.

And yet it was not quite that; the conditions were different. Today order and science and the light of knowledge might go, but in the chaos there would remain a network of swift communications, a wilderness of still turning and pounding and shaping machines. The great presses would still revolve and the radios blare or whisper. Whole systems of mumbo-jumbo would spread with terrifying rapidity: already were not weird systems of prediction, grubbed up from the rubble of the dark ages, printed by the million every day? Grant but the initial collapse on which this bad man was counting, and the spread of sub-rational beliefs would be very swift. Power would go to him who had the most and likeliest instruments of superstition to hand. And here – were one's organization sufficiently vast and sufficiently efficient – even a comical cab-horse, even an inwardly riven and tormented cockney girl, might have a useful niche in the new and murky temple. A corner in ghosts, a corner in witches, a corner in *denkende Tiere*. Somewhere in front of this hot and stinking little river-steamer lay the first concrete fashioning of this vast and corrosive fantasy. Round any bend now they might come upon the unholy base or depot, the laboriously accumulated reservoirs of the Lucys and Hannahs and Daffodils – unaccomplished works of Nature's hand, abortive, monstrous, or unkindly mixed. The project, if he had read it aright, was extravagant beyond the compass of a story-teller's art. And yet it was not ungrounded in the present state of the world. As a commercial venture it was dangerous; perhaps what the City used to call double dangerous. But one could write a tolerably persuasive prospectus for it should such a bizarre job come one's way.

Take the Bereavement Sentiment – take that, said Appleby to himself as he watched young Lucy fishing from the side. There are graphs of it, for insurance companies as well as sociologists find such things useful. The peak year in western Europe was 1920. And it was at that time that the papers were full of strange elysiums, cigar-and-whisky empyreans, *revenants* who reported lawn-tennis tournaments on the pavements of paradise. And it was at about that time that such bodies as did exist for the objective study of psychical evidences were inundated with members themselves far from objectively disposed. There are times when every man prays, whatever his settled belief or disbelief may be. And there are circumstances in which many men, and many women – And here Appleby stopped. The best thing, perhaps, would be to go below, and knock on the door of Wine's cabin, and enter, and shoot him dead, and possibly achieve the additional satisfaction of pitching his carcass to the alligators before his retainers interfered.

That – thought Appleby with his eye still on Lucy Rideout – would be very nice. Only the train of speculation leading up to it might be all wrong after all. In a way it ought to be all wrong. The comedy of Lady Caroline and Bodfish, the episode of the York antique shop, the extravagant disappearance of 37 Hawke Square, the deplorable adventure of the birthday party, the untoward consequences of the electrical storm: none of these things alone had the quality – had anything of the key or tone – of this to which they were leading up. Nevertheless Appleby felt that the truth was assuredly here. An examination of the facts led to it as certainly as the long reaches of this river led to Wine's Happy Islands. And the mere scale of the thing made it susceptible of no other explanation.

But the man had miscalculated, Appleby thought. He was banking on what intellectuals of a high-flown kind liked to call the End of our Time. The probability was that this itself was a miscalculation. It is true that times do come to an end, but the thing happens far less frequently than people expect. History is full of periods which appeared to contemporaries agonal and conclusive, but which the text-books were eventually to describe as no more than uncomfortably transitional. Now things were uncomfortable enough, and for the first time since the creation every continent and every sea was under fire. But in the end of his time or his country, his language or his civilization or his race, Appleby was not very disposed to believe. If Wine was counting on that sort of absolute subversion he had probably made a mistake.

Conceivably, however, all this was to attribute too great an imaginative element to his schemes. Under whatever circumstances the guns ceased fire, and whatever of his foundations Western man preserved, in the remaining superstructure there would for long be confusion and darkness, wildered wits and shaken judgements enough. Once more, it simply came to this: had a bold man but his organization ready he could reap an immense harvest of wealth and power.

Think of Sludge. Appleby rose from his chair and paced the little deck. Think of the original of Browning's charlatan. In the midst of the immense solidity of the Victorian age he had been able to work up an extremely profitable hysteria in places astoundingly close to the very centres of English culture. Noblemen had solemnly sworn before committees that they had seen him float in and out of windows or carry live coals in his hand about the drawing-rooms of Mayfair. And the tone of all that — England's first spiritualist epidemic — was most oddly like the tone of more recent movements. In the period between the wars, a period in which much of stability had already gone, it had proved possible to build up — and in the same dominant social class — hysterias of essentially the same kind. This time it had not been spooks; rather it had been a species of cocktail and country-house revivalism even more antipathetic to the rational mind. But the tone was the same; one had only to read the documents to realize that. And it showed what could be done. The ranks of these unstable and disorientated revivalists were full of persons of earnest purpose and sincere conviction. But doubtless the gentlemen who had sworn to the levitating Sludge had been like that. The thing was not thereby the less aberrant, the less dangerous to all that Western man had achieved. And now, should Wine get going —

'So here we are.'

Appleby turned and found his host beside him, pointing over the prow.

'Welcome, my dear Appleby. Welcome to the Happy Islands.'

4

'My own headquarters,' said Wine, 'are on America Island.'

'America Island?' Appleby was gazing far up the river. There appeared to be a land horizon straight ahead.

'Yes. It is the largest of the islands. And then comes Europe Island. Perhaps you will be most interested in that. Particularly in English House. You see, we have found it best to organize our research on a continental, and then on a national or state basis. On America Island, for instance, different groups concentrate on the problems and — ah — possibilities of different parts of the continent. Would Radbone have carried the thing thus far? I think not.'

'Almost certainly not, I should say.'

Wine nodded, seemingly much pleased. 'Take the Deep South, my dear Appleby. The problems are naturally quite different from, say, those of New England. And so we have a Deep South House and a New England House, with a competent man in charge of each. You must prepare yourself for something on quite a considerable scale. We have been at work for a long time.'

'I see. Would it be right to say that the collecting of material, as you call it, has gone a good way ahead of the actual investigation?'

'Well, as a matter of fact, it has.' Wine had glanced swiftly at Appleby. 'When I speak of having competent men in charge of each section I am thinking in terms of field workers rather than of first-rate laboratory men. The material *is* getting somewhat out of hand. Particularly in German House.'

'Indeed?'

'It ought really to be called German Mews.' Wine gave a gay little chuckle. 'Most of the thinking Animals are there – our friend Daffodil among them. Germany was always the great place for that sort of thing. You must have a calculating horse or prescient pig if you want really to impress a Prussian academy of science. And at present we have, I must confess, nobody who really understands the creatures, or can make any headway with their investigation. And that is just an example.' Wine, now gloomy, shook his head. 'Scientists are frankly short with us. And Radbone has some of the best men.' He paused. 'Which is why, you know, I asked you and Hudspith to come and see.'

'But we are not scientists.'

'No doubt. But you have Radbone's confidence. And – well. I must tell you frankly that I have the possibility of some sort of merger in mind. I hope that when you have seen how far we have got that you will go – or that one of you will go – and see if it can be arranged. Go back to Radbone, I mean, with my proposals and your own account of the place.'

'I see.' As Radbone almost certainly had no concrete existence, this was scarcely true. Appleby was far from seeing. But it was to be hoped that he was merely anticipating a truth. If Wine was to be worsted in his own stronghold it was urgently necessary to solve the riddle of such an unexpected proposal as this. But perhaps it had little or no meaning; perhaps it was merely more patter until the two men who had come so inconveniently on his tracks could be most simply eliminated. 'I see,' said Appleby again, and in as considering tones as he could assume.

'I may have spoken lightly of Radbone. But that is only an indiscretion of professional rivalry, after all. I do think that he possesses some final and serious intellectual weakness. But he is at least a magnificent deviser of experiments.' Wine looked Appleby directly but unconsciously in the eye. 'And, after all, a good experiment is everything.'

'No doubt.' Obscurely, Appleby felt disconcerted. And for a moment he had an impulse to be very frank. He would state baldly that he and Hudspith were police officers and that Wine's game was up. Even in the throes of war the British Government would not let two men disappear into the blue. They would be traced; they would be traced thousands of miles up this river. And the Happy Islands, however remote and undisturbed, were certainly sovereign territory of some friendly state. So that, in fact, the game was already up and Wine had better come quietly ... Appleby meditated this and decided: Not yet. For it was a last and desperate card, and could be played at any time.

'It will be nearly an hour before we can tie up' – Wine was looking through binoculars as he spoke. 'So do you go and find Hudspith, there's a good fellow – and we will celebrate the end of this tedious journey in a glass of champagne. With Lucy to help us. Only there had better be ginger pop, too, in case it is the young 'un who is about. Lucy is rather charming, is she not? To tell you the truth, I was rather glad to be able to send those other ladies by the first boat. Eusapia, I fear, was better out of your friend's way.' And Wine, thus gay and mischievous and considerate at once, gave orders for a little feast. The champagne was excellent, and there were tiny biscuits and a pot of caviare into which one dug with a knife. Most of the time Wine talked of Radbone still. But not quite as he had recently fallen into talking. It was as if he were now aware that there was some danger of this mysterious rival's being taken for a shade. And so he was building him up again as solid flesh and blood – establishing him as a real man to whom a real embassy might sensibly be sent. And there were no more jokes about plain-clothes policemen.

America Island was about two miles long by half a mile wide. From each of its shores it was possible to see the corresponding bank of the river, as well as something of the smaller islands farther up. Some of these lay two or three abreast, so that from the air the whole group must have presented the appearance of a single large fish leading a family of varying size downstream. There were several groups of buildings, and the island had been substantially cleared – as had also, it would seem, the river-banks beyond. Something of cultivation had been attempted, but this effort belonged to the past. From the little jetty where the steamer had drawn up there was a short, straight road to the first building. And here, sitting in the shade of the veranda, were Beaglehole and Mrs Nurse, drinking tea. For a few minutes there was an amiable and efficient bustle of welcome. The servants were greenish brown and must have been of some native tribe untouched by Spanish blood; the air was heavy with exotic scent; from the back of the house there came a species of throbbing howl conceivably intended as musical entertainment. Nevertheless, Appleby thought, it was all curiously like arriving on friends in Hampshire for the week-end.

'We chose this house,' said Beaglehole, 'because it is in the Californian style. There's something more commodious upstream, but it looks as if it were meant for Cape Cod. And one has to consider the climate. I hope you won't feel cramped here for a few days. It's been necessary to arrange it like that.'

Wine was taking round a plate of sandwiches. 'Beaglehole,' he explained, 'does all the running of things in a domestic way. We regard him as a steward or major-domo in that regard. Mrs Nurse, I believe these are gherkin. But here are tomato should you prefer.'

'*Chose* this house?' said Hudspith, who had formed the habit of regarding his hosts through a suspiciously narrowed eye. 'Didn't you build the place?'

'Dear me, no.' Beaglehole shook his head, amused. 'That would have been very poor business indeed – and not at all the sort of thing scientists can afford. We bought up the whole place for a song. It belonged to a Teuton called Schlumpf. He was going to start one of those Utopias people think up from time to time, and he got a concession on the islands and did the building. He was practically king of the place. You see, we're a long way from law and order here.'

Wine frowned. 'The Republic certainly doesn't make itself felt in these parts. So we insist that the King's law runs instead. And we have no trouble – no trouble at all, I assure you. There are some rather unruly remnants of tribal folk about, but they leave us alone. We are a very tranquil – ah – research station.'

'Ah,' said Hudspith – and added suddenly: 'What if one of your guests – Daffodil, say – announced that he wanted to go home?'

Beaglehole abruptly lowered a sandwich and raised his voice. 'Schlumpf,' he repeated. 'His idea was that there should be an island to each country concerned and that people should follow their own mode of life there, living in their own sort of houses and so on. But on the river-banks they should work co-operatively and get to know each other in that way. Of course it didn't work. And we took over.' Beaglehole grinned. 'We *do* work.'

'Schlumpf slumped.' Wine smiled engagingly as he offered this witticism. 'And we saw how usefully we could take over the structure of the place. But of course we had to give up the clearing and colonizing part of the scheme. It was quite impracticable, anyhow. For – to be quite candid – Schlumpf was a scoundrel.'

'A scoundrel?' said Hudspith. 'Dear, dear.'

'A scoundrel, I am sorry to say. The Utopia was chimerical; what his Utopians paid to be allowed in was real and substantial. So we drove a hard bargain with him without any compunction at all.'

'It must be nice,' said Appleby, 'to feel that you have turned his shady schemes to good.'

'Very nice,' said Mrs Nurse, brightening at the sound of her favourite word.

'Very nice indeed,' said Wine evenly. 'And now we must think about finding you quarters, though I have no doubt Beaglehole has it all arranged. Mrs Nurse, I expect you know your way about sufficiently well now to take charge of Miss Rideout?' Wine paused as if to emphasize the propriety of his dispositions. 'And where is Miss Mood? I am sure we are all looking forward to seeing her again.' He beamed at Hudspith and then glanced at his watch. 'But Beaglehole, my dear man, perhaps we can steal half an hour to see to a little unloading first. If you are all quite comfortable, that is.' And Wine put on his panama and led his assistant away.

Hudspith, who was holding a sandwich suspiciously between finger and thumb, looked after him frowning. 'Well, I'm damned!' he said.

'Mr Hudspith!' Mrs Nurse's glance went warningly to Lucy, and her tone was severe. Then she was placid again. 'What a nice man Mr Wine is! It was such a pleasant surprise meeting him again.'

Appleby was strolling round the veranda – apparently idly enough, but actually to discover if the party could possibly be overheard. Now he halted. 'Mrs Nurse, you had no idea that it was by Wine that you were being –' He paused, searching for the right word.

'Retained? I had no notion of it. But people do often arrange these things in strange ways. Particularly the sceptical – I suppose because they are a little ashamed of their inquiries. But I think this is going to be quite nice. Not that I like working for the researchers. Few mediums do.' Mrs Nurse was perfectly matter of fact. 'They make real communication so difficult with their conditions and their disbeliefs. You understand? Thwarting influences and all sorts of stupid little spirits break in. And that makes it so tiring.' Her voice was dispirited for a moment. 'Often I am so tired. The feeling just before and afterwards can be very dreadful, Mr Appleby. But still' – she smiled cheerfully – 'I think this is going to be very nice.' She turned to Lucy. 'And I think you will like it too, dear. Come along.' And Appleby and Hudspith found themselves alone.

'Well,' said Hudspith, 'I *am* damned. And do you believe all that about Schlumpf?'

'I rather think I do. Wine and Beaglehole are like ourselves now, and being as economical in their fibs as may be. For instance, I don't imagine they stole this house from California and another from Cape Cod. They've stolen only one house – and stealing one house is a large order enough. But Schlumpf's fantastic notion dovetails in with 37 Hawke Square neatly enough. Do you notice that Wine has never mentioned Hawke Square? He thinks we know nothing about it; perhaps that no one knows anything about it; that it just hasn't been missed.'

'But it was in the papers.'

'For once his intelligence service must have tripped. He thinks we know nothing about it. And that is immensely important to him.'

'I really don't see –'

'But I do. I think I do.' Appleby was on his feet again and pacing restlessly about. 'And it's not at all comfortable. Still, it's a line. And a line is what we want.'

'Would you mind explaining what's in your head?'

'Not a bit; it's just what I propose . . .' Appleby paused, walked to the edge of the veranda and stared up the river. 'Europe Island. Jungle and tree-fern and pampa and alligators and cobras. And a very substantial London mansion rearing itself in the midst of them. It's grotesque. But not quite as grotesque as if Schlumpf hadn't thought to dot the vicinity with Cape Cod bungalows and Highland crofts and Swiss chalets.' He turned back. 'Do you know what makes a first-class experimental scientist?'

'I don't know that I do.'

'The ability to exploit existing conditions. And Wine intends to do that. Thanks to Schlumpf a Bloomsbury house perching itself here is not outstanding and inexplicable in itself. It takes a sort of protective colouring from the chalets and crofts. We shall be taken there and think it nothing out of the way.'

'But –'

'Listen to me.'

And Hudspith listened. At the end he was staring at Appleby almost open-mouthed. 'I can hardly believe it,' he said. 'It's like a dream.'

Appleby smiled. 'I should put it stronger than that myself. Say a dream of dreams.' His voice sank grimly. 'And it just depends on the masons whether there will be a long, long time of waiting till my dreams all come true.

5

Hudspith took a turn about the veranda. 'But if what you say is true –'

'Let me go over a bit of it again.' Appleby held up an index-finger. 'He knows we are police.' He held up a second finger. 'But he doesn't know we know he knows.' He held up a third finger. 'He thinks he has hood-winked us into believing that he believes that we act for Radbone; he thinks we believe that Radbone exists; he thinks we believe in the fundamentally scientific character of the whole affair. That is how the position stands now.'

'I suppose you wouldn't be disposed to call it at all complicated?'

'Only when reduced to these compressed verbal terms. The actual situation is fairly simple.'

'And we must be fairly simple ourselves – or he must think we are – if we are really to believe that the whole thing is some vast scientific investigation. Scientists just don't behave in such ways, except in strip fiction.'

'Quite so.' Appleby took a final dab at the caviare. 'And I doubt if the disinterested-investigator stuff will hold for another twenty-four hours.

These islands are a sort of vast, veiled concentration camp into which Wine is packing every atom of mumbo-jumbo he can collect. Later he will purvey mumbo-jumbo – the locally appropriate mumbo-jumbo – wherever it is called for. Thames and Congo will be all one to the vast organization he is building up. But such a plan cannot really be disguised for long as a sort of grandiose laboratory experiment. He has brought us here, and if we live we are bound to find out. Think of all the contradictory baits which must have been laid; think of all the different terms on which his mediums and conjurors and prodigies must be retained here: terms ranging from full complicity through deception to duress. Apparently we are to be shown over the works – and somebody is bound to give the show away. But it won't matter to Wine.'

'Unless –'

'Unless we announce that we are police and so make it impossible for him to simulate ignorance. Then he would, in a way, be baffled. I mean in the particular little scheme on which he is at present engaged. But if we continue to appear to believe that he believes that we believe in Radbone –'

'I think it would be better without what you call the compressed verbal terms.'

'Very well. His plan – this particular little plan – requires simply this: that one of us should leave the islands while genuinely believing that there is a Radbone. We may know that the scientific business is bunkum; but we must believe in Radbone, even if in Radbone as another rascal merely.'

'Put it like this.' Hudspith frowned in ferocious concentration. 'We have to appear to be saying to ourselves: *What smart policemen we are: we have tricked him into thinking we are the agents of some other scoundrel called Radbone – and on the strength of this one of us is going to get away and bring both Wine and Radbone to book.*'

'Exactly. That will give him the conditions required for his experiment.'

'For his scientific experiment.'

Appleby laughed warily. 'Yes. The paradox is there all right. And in it lies our chance.'

'Ah. I don't know that I'd call it a chance. But perhaps that's another compressed verbal term. We'd have just as good a chance trying to chum up with the alligators.' Hudspith walked away and stared down the road to the jetty. 'No sign of them yet. What about chumming up with some of the material, or exhibits, or whatever he calls them?'

'What indeed. We might manage to start a revolt. And perhaps you'll begin with Miss Mood.'

Hudspith scowled. 'I think Mrs Nurse would be better. She strikes me as an honest woman.'

'In her everyday character I expect she is. But she is also extremely simple and somewhat lethargic. I should prefer to seek an ally in Lucy Rideout.'

'Which?' Hudspith's question was perfectly matter of fact. For long ago the minor oddities of the world of Mr Wine had ceased to surprise.

'Real Lucy. I fear her moral character will not long be of the best –'

'Ah,' said Hudspith – the old Hudspith.

'But she is lively and intelligent and would be a good pal.'

'Um,' said Hudspith suspiciously.

'And if we could get rid of sick Lucy and the young 'un – perhaps without Wine knowing it – we might find ourselves with quite a strong card.'

'My dear chap' – Hudspith stared in astonishment – 'don't you know that the curing of such a case may occupy a skilled alienist for years?'

'No doubt. But there is one fairly simple technique which might work. Lucy – real Lucy – has an inkling of it herself. You decide which personality you want to preserve and then you discourage the others whenever they appear.'

'Capital.' Hudspith was sarcastic. 'Why not kill them out-right?'

'Even that mightn't be impossible. Sometimes hypnotism is used to put the undesirable personalities to sleep. But the thing might be done by making sure they always encountered an uncongenial environment. I gather that real Lucy set off on her travels with just some such plot in mind. Now, if we could cure Lucy and make her reliable – so that she would always be real Lucy, I mean – and at the same time conceal this from Wine –'

'I don't think I ever heard a more impracticable and irrelevant scheme in my life. You might just as well set about curing that Italian girl of playing tricks with a lazy tongs.'

Appleby sighed. 'Perhaps you're right. But it would be nice to cure Lucy, and I think I'd like to try. Of course it would take time – and materials!'

'Materials?'

'Yes. A Latin grammar for young Lucy. We know that's available. And to sick Lucy I would insist on reading about Mopsie in the fifth. Sooner or later each would be disgusted and retire from the scene.'

'And real Lucy, on the other hand, would have to be pampered – quite given her head?'

Appleby nodded solemnly. 'I consider that a certain amount of giving real Lucy her head would be the right therapeutic method. Do I hear our friends returning?'

'Damn our friends.' Hudspith had strode over to his colleague and stood looking down at him suspiciously. 'And I don't like your scheme at all. Real Lucy is an extremely flighty girl. Over-sexed. You can't say that I don't know them.'

'Certainly not.'

'The sort that men give dirty books to on the chance –'

'In fact, you think she should have nothing but Mopsie too?'

Hudspith relaxed. 'It's sometimes difficult to remember that you must have your little joke. I suppose it takes the mind off the alligators.'

'Ah – the alligators.' Wine's voice came cheerfully from the bright sunshine beyond the veranda, and a moment later he had sat down beside them. 'There is rather bad news about that. We have lost some valuable material to them while I have been away. The Bonteen sisters. Thought-readers with a really remarkable technique. But it appears they would most indiscreetly bathe in the river. One would have thought that a very little professional skill would have told them just what was in the creatures' minds. And now' – Wine shook his head and his smile was at once rueful and charmingly gay – 'we know just what is in the creatures' tummies.'

'You mean that the – the Bonteen sisters have been eaten?'

Wine nodded. 'And Beaglehole is particularly upset. He hates waste. Replacements are becoming so hard to get.'

'Like French wines, and the toothbrush handles that used to come from Japan.' Hudspith spoke with heavy irony.

'Exactly so; it is most vexatious. And not so long ago we lost two of our best clairvoyants. I don't think Miss Mood will be half so good. I suppose you've heard of Mrs Gladigan and Miss Molsher?'

'I can't say I have.'

'Well, they have been far our most serious wastage so far. Not that a certain amount of interesting scientific matter didn't emerge. It was like this.' Wine stretched himself comfortably in his chair. 'Mrs Gladigan and Miss Molsher were in a very remarkable physical *rapport*. It would work up to about a radius of thirty miles – a most interesting thing. Miss Molsher would go into a trance and one would stick a pin, say, into one of her limbs – much as Appleby here did to poor Miss Mood. And Miss Molsher, like Miss Mood, would be quite insensible to the pain. But Mrs Gladigan – sitting, as I say, perhaps thirty miles away – would immediately feel the appropriate sensation in the corresponding limb.'

'Very remarkable,' said Hudspith gloomily; 'very remarkable indeed.'

'Not at all, my dear fellow. Phenomena of that sort are not at all out of the way. Radbone will assure you of that. But what was exceptional was this: as soon as Mrs Gladigan felt the painful sensation to which Miss Molsher had been subjected she was able to make her way to her.'

Appleby frowned. 'You really mean that? –'

'Yes. It was simply like a bloodhound following a trail. With no previous knowledge of Miss Molsher's whereabouts Mrs Gladigan would nevertheless be guided directly to her – buying railway and tram tickets and so on as occasion required. Her explanations of how it came about were, as you may guess, vague. She seemed to imply a species of magnetic attraction between the limb of Miss Molsher actually injured and the corresponding and sympathetic part of her own anatomy. And such was the main accomplishment of the ladies when they consented to join us here – for the purpose of ruthlessly objective scientific investigation, it is needless to say.' Wine smiled. 'Well, the investigation turned out to be ruthless enough. But I don't know if you could call it scientific. Some would say that it was a little too unpremeditated for that. I think I have mentioned that we have some troublesome native tribes?'

'I think you have.' Hudspith was rubbing his jaw.

'I am sorry to say that some of them are very unpleasant – very unpleasant indeed. And before we could begin our experiments designed to test the supposed powers of the ladies, Miss Molsher disappeared. She had borrowed a canoe and very rashly gone off on a morning's expedition in it up one of the tributaries. As soon as she was missed of course we organized a search. But all in vain. We could find no trace of her. And it was about a week afterwards that Mrs Gladigan began to experience pains – somewhat sharper than usual – now in one limb and now in another.' Wine paused and glanced at his watch. 'Dear me!' he said; 'how pleasant. It will soon be quite a feasible hour for a glass of sherry.' He paused again. 'What was I saying? Ah, yes, about poor Miss Molsher. Well, we got out the launch, and a gun or two, and Mrs Gladigan steered. But it was soon apparent that something had gone wrong. She was quite at sea. Or perhaps a hunting man would say that she was at fault – badly at fault. We cast – that would be the word – now up the river and now down. And when at length we landed Mrs Gladigan was in yet more evident distress. She appeared attracted now to one and now to another point of the compass. Hudspith, my dear fellow, you look pale. I fear you have had a tiring day. This wretched heat! – it is the one great drawback to the place.'

'That and the savages,' said Appleby.

'The savages? Oh, yes, of course. That evening we heard that they had dispersed. Some had gone in this direction and some in that. Cannibals? Yes, I rather think they are. And Mrs Gladigan too did not survive. Brain fever carried her off a few days later. Of course without Miss Molsher she was a person of very limited utility. Still, it was sad. And the experiment itself – if we may be allowed to call it so – was tantalizingly inconclusive. One could hardly venture to send it to a learned journal, do you think? As I remarked to Beaglehole at the time: if only she had been able to lead us to an abandoned limb! But here are Mrs Nurse and dear little Lucy come out to join us again.' He rose and clapped his hands, and instantly a servant appeared with a decanter and glasses. 'We dine late. It is the Spanish habit. And to give one an appetite there is nothing, I always feel, like lingering talk over a glass of sherry.'

6

The following morning was given to a tour of America Island. Besides the buildings put up by the unscrupulous Schlumpf there were several, more strictly utilitarian in appearance, which were the work of Wine. And of these the most impressive was his private research block. It comprised a library, a museum, rest-rooms and living quarters for the subjects under observation, a room for the projection of films, and a laboratory. It was of this last that Wine was particularly proud.

'My dear Appleby,' he said, 'pray notice the floor.'

Appleby looked at the floor. It appeared to consist of polished slabs of wood some eighteen inches square.

'Now walk across it.'

Appleby walked – somewhat gingerly, but without noticing anything untoward.

Wine moved to the wall and touched a button. 'Now try again.'

Appleby tried again, not without memories of boys' stories in which, upon such an occasion as this, yawning pits would incontinently open beneath the hero's feet. And decidedly there was now something odd about the floor. Nevertheless he got safely across.

'Later I will take you into the basement and show you the mechanisms. But at the moment I need only explain that each of these slabs is actually a tolerably accurate balance. Should we place a table here and sit round it in the dark, and should you then be prompted, say, to tie a thread to your handkerchief and pitch it to the other end of the room, the fact would be recorded down below – and so would the trailing return of the handkerchief as you hauled it back across the floor. And here is the cabinet' – Wine had moved to where a heavy black curtain cut off one corner of the room – 'and behind it the rest of the paraphernalia that physical mediums are so tiresomely insistent on. As you may guess, our best cameras are here. You notice that everywhere the roof is high. That gives scope for the wide-angle lenses. I wonder if Radbone has learnt much from the technique of aerial and infra-red photography?' Wine smiled charmingly. 'I have.'

'Very interesting,' said Appleby. 'But do the mediums like it?'

'Commonly they know nothing whatever about it. And now notice this.' Wine opened a cupboard in the wall and revealed some intricate electrical apparatus. 'I have no doubt you know that one of the grand difficulties in a long seance is distinguishing between one hand and two. Hudspith, when you rub your jaw in that way I know you are a little at sea. So let me explain what happens during a typical experiment. The laboratory is almost dark, and the medium sits at a table just before the cabinet. I am on one side, and one of my assistants is on the other. My right foot is on the medium's left foot, and my assistant's left foot is on her right foot. And each of us holds one of her hands. The medium writhes about; she is allegedly in the grip of some supernatural force. And I assure you that presently, although my assistant and I are convinced that we are in contact with a separate hand, it may very well be that we each have got hold of the same one.' Wine shook his head. 'There is really nothing like a little psychical research for convincing one of the fallibility of the human senses and of the difficulty of really unintermittent concentration. But, fortunately machines are inexorable. I dare say you've seen in the shop windows radio sets that can be set going by a passer-by simply waving his hand in front of a particular spot on the glass? This machine refines a little upon that not very difficult principle. Let the medium get one hand below the level of the table – which unfortunately is what she probably wants to do – and at once this machine –'

'Poor little Eusapia,' Appleby interrupted. 'I'm afraid she hasn't a chance. And that she should be brought all that way for this.'

'Eusapia is said to be full of the most elementary wiles. But it's just possible there may be something else as well.'

And it's just possible, thought Appleby, that there may be at least a little green cheese in the moon. But who would build a costly observatory on what he held to be the off chance of making such an observation? Or who, wishing to convince others of the fact, would build in the middle of nowhere? Yet this laboratory, in which Eusapia's lazy tongs would presently be exposed with the aid of balances and infra-red light, was no mere flimsy screen. It really was an elaborate unit for the research Wine professed. And in this lay the truth about Wine.

If there were three Lucy Rideouts, there were – in a sense – three Emery Wines also. And the name of one of these Wines was – again in a sense – Radbone. When Wine spoke of the insufficiencies of this fictitious scientist he was simply drawing a picture of one of the Wines. Perhaps consciously, or perhaps unconsciously. But there it was.

There was a Wine who was a scientist, a Wine who really wanted to know. And there was a Wine who was a gangster, a Wine who wanted to exploit and grab. But to these two Wines, the scientific and the predatory, there must be added a third: an imaginative and credulous Wine.

Out of spiritualism and allied interests of the mind he was going to form a vast racket. The thing was feasible: nevertheless it was bizarre and extremely out of the way. What had led him to so remote a project? The same bent that really led the scientist into such territory: an obscure impulse to believe – an impulse which would dispense with intellectually respectable evidence if it dared. When Hudspith had simulated seeing an apparition of the sort traditionally associated with the death of the person seen, Wine had been so far carried away as to attempt to verify the thing by radio. The attempt had been entirely futile, for a cast-iron regulation had been against him; it therefore demonstrated something other than a coolly critical mind in face of a possible supernormal occurrence. In fact on that morning Wine had given much away. Again, he had revealed this streak in his make-up through the picture he had drawn of Radbone. And he had revealed it once more in his fondness for putting across tall stories – of which surely the tallest and most irresponsible was that recent one of Mrs Gladigan and Miss Molsher.

And yet, later that morning – and as he and Hudspith were being conducted somewhat hastily over other parts of America Island – Appleby thought a good deal on the history of those unfortunate ladies. The mortal remains of Miss Molsher departing to stew-pots at various points of the compass and the resulting bafflement of Mrs Gladigan's psychic perceptions: the notion was rather more absurd than horrible. Wine had spoken of it in terms of an abortive experiment, and though it was doubtless a fantasy, yet the conducting of experiments by Wine was a fact – a fact to which the elaborate laboratory testified. There was something in Mrs Gladigan and Miss Molsher: they were a sort of allegory, Appleby told himself, of that aspect of Wine's activities with which he himself was scheduled to be most intimately concerned.

'We have half a dozen rather interesting people over there' – Wine was pointing to a long, low building near the water's edge – 'but I think we had better not visit them just now. The fact is that they are really rather tiresome.' He sighed. 'A few will prove to be interesting, but all are rather tiresome. It is one of the depressing conditions of our work.'

'You mean,' asked Hudspith, 'that they're discontented? They'd like to get away?'

'To get away?' Wine looked politely puzzled. 'Of course they would leave if they wanted to. Actually I believe that most of them feel they have fallen on their feet. All have some rather special nervous organization in one way or another, and the result commonly is that they are misfits in the workaday world. Here we provide a special and carefully-contrived environment which I doubt if they would wish to change. They are tiresome simply because they are an edgy and temperamental lot. And I'm not sure that working with them one doesn't take on something of the same trying nervous organization.' Wine turned to Appleby and smiled blithely. 'If you find me – or Beaglehole – a bit queer, you know, you must put it down to that. Perhaps we shall come back here another day. I should at least like you to meet Danilov. He promises some most interesting results. On the other hand, he is perhaps the most temperamental of all.'

'A medium?' Appleby asked.

'It is really difficult to say. He has the gift of tongues – an endowment common in legend and folk-lore, but which I have never met elsewhere. A language will come to Danilov perhaps for an hour, perhaps for a day or even a week. Then it will vanish and another will take its place. Curious, is it not? There is never more than one language at a time – or rather never more than one in addition to his basic Russian. The speaker of whatever is the strange language of the moment understands himself but has no Russian. The Danilov who speaks Russian understands none of the other languages spoken.'

'Very odd,' said Appleby.

'Suppose Danilov to be visited for the moment by French. You can converse with him in either French or Russian, but you can't converse in French about what has just been said in Russian, nor in Russian about what has just been said in French. You see? Either the man is indeed visited by tongues in some supernormal manner, or the different languages contrive to exist in separate compartments of his mind.'

'Do you know anything of his history?'

'Yes, indeed. He was born in Denmark, his mother being English and his father a Spanish engineer. When he was four the family moved to Greece, where he had a German nurse who went mad and ran away with him to Egypt. Later he was adopted by a wealthy Russian who had married a Dutch lady long resident in France.'

'I see.'

'But later on his life became somewhat unsettled and he roamed about the world a good deal. He was back in Russia at the time of the Revolution and was wounded in the fighting. In fact a bullet passed through his brain, and for some time he couldn't talk at all. It was when he recovered from this that he began to exercise his peculiar gifts. But he himself is firmly convinced that it is spirits.'

They were walking uphill; perhaps it was because of this that Hudspith could be heard breathing heavily.

'And of course spirits it may be. One ought never to jump to conclusions on the strength of fragmentary evidence.' Wine chuckled. 'I am taking you this way so that we can get a bird's-eye view of the islands. This hill in front of us rises to about four hundred feet.'

'I'm inclined to think,' said Appleby, 'that you expect Hudspith and me to rise to more than that.'

'Ah.' Wine walked some paces in silence. Then he chuckled again. 'I think we are getting to know each other very nicely.' Again he walked in silence. 'Just think, my dear Appleby, what one could do with Danilov as a sort of evangelist. He roves about the world – perhaps with a little choir or orchestra – and languages come and go as he moves. It's tremendous.'

The breathing of Hudspith became heavier still. Appleby, glancing sideways as they walked, noticed with some alarm a fixed contraction on his brow. It seemed only too likely that the cheated girls had been usurped. Hudspith had found a new Whale.

7

They climbed higher. America Island took form beneath them: an irregular oval of blotched green and brown framed in the yellow of the incredible river. On the summit was a little clearing of which the borders were low palmetto scrub and Papaw trees and feathery palm. Parrots flew chattering over them; unknown butterflies hovered; and everywhere was the sweet scent of the Espinillo de Olor. That the island had been cultivated could be seen – but the orange groves, laid out in quincunx form, were now eroded and forlorn, yielding to a stealthy pincers movement of which the spear-heads were a tangled *monté* of low trees wreathed in creepers; this with a marching army of criss-crossed bamboo behind. Unguarded, nothing human would last here long; nature would sweep in with something of the pounce of Eusapia's lazy tongs, and the Happy Islands would be as they had been before ever Domingo de Irala and the Conquistadores had come this way.

Upstream, the other islands stretched westward; the nearer appearing securely anchored in the flood; those farther away floating uncertainly between air and water. Each was blotched and brown and green, featureless and scrubby except for here and there an aracá or a commanding palm, but with many of the strangely assorted buildings of Schlumpf's fantasy showing clear in the shadowless light of noon. That queer project had been ragged and untidy and evanescent; superimposed upon it could be seen evidences of the yet queerer but efficient and considered project of Emery Wine. Plain frame buildings had been added here and there; each island had a small uniform jetty; a purposive network of wires ran between the houses and spanned the channels on high-masted buoys; here and there a launch darted on the obscure business of the community. For it was a community of sorts; man dominated this corner of the wilderness and nature took second place.

But the majestic river floated on, and a few miles downstream the world was a solitary haunt of tapir and capibara, of vizcachas sitting at their holes and of flamingos contemplative on stilt-like legs. The river was an unending world of yellow water and Pampas-grass and willow, of strange birds – macaws and Magellanic swans – and stranger fish – bagre and dorado, pacu and surubi. The river and its multitudinous life was a world unending. But the river also was no more than a dully-variegated thread winding through the immeasurable monotony of what from this eminence could be clearly seen: the great green ocean of high and waving grass which made the larger world of this part of the South American continent. It was a far cry from Lady Caroline and the dusty little antique-dealer of York.

Wine seated himself in the shade of a solitary Ñandubay. 'You are looking down,' he said, 'on all the kingdoms of the world.' The words were spoken without magniloquence and without either the irony or the gaiety that the man was wont to affect. Appleby, withdrawing his gaze from the farthest verge of the rippling pampa, looked at him curiously – as one may look at somebody interesting and new. 'And the glory of them,' said Wine. His finger made a circle in air – a small circle which seemed to define no more than the group of islands below. 'So why should you and I pretend to each other any longer?'

'It does seem unnecessary,' said Appleby. And Hudspith nodded – not at all like a man who believes that only such successful pretence stands between him and the incomparable digestive system of the crocodile.

'Radbone and I are after the same thing; so let us admit it. And let him admit that here' – and again Wine's finger circled – 'I have got ahead of him. Let him admit that and come in. He sent you to spy out the land. And now' – and a third time Wine's finger circled – 'it is before you. All the kingdoms of the world, graphed and taped.'

Appleby looked down on the islands and electric wires and launches, on these as a stray and tiny atom of human activity in the great void of green. And he saw the atom as a rebel cell in the vast organism of human civility, a minute cell or nexus of cells, definable still by a circling finger, but having the potentiality for unlimited and disastrous proliferation. Here the thing was growing in treacherous concealment, and presently it would send off down the great river, as if through a bloodstream, armies that should attack every weakened centre of a riven and exhausted planet. It was a large picture, and not a pretty one. 'Certainly there seems no necessity to pretend,' Appleby repeated.

'Did I once remind you that home-keeping youth have ever homely wits? When I was a young man I visited Egypt and I visited Rome. And I saw how the resolute man invents gods to put his fellows in awe. I saw what of splendour and power could be built out of the infantile recesses of the mind. I looked at what Milton accurately calls the brutish gods of Nile – and then I looked at the pyramids. By observing how children irrationally fear a dog or a beetle, by probing a little the vast unreason of the unconscious mind, able men had gained all that overlordship and command. I saw it as men must often have seen it before me. I saw it as Faustus saw it.'

'Ah,' said Appleby. 'Faust. But there are those who believe rather in Prometheus.'

'And I went to Rome.' Under the shadow of the Ñandubay, Wine sat staring unseeingly before him, far too absorbed to heed an obscure interruption. 'My plan came to me there. It was as I sat musing in the ruins of the Capitol, while the bare-footed friars sang vespers in the temple of Jupiter –'

The man was the soul of charlatanism, Appleby thought. Spouting Gibbon. Always making a tall story of it. And yet practical and efficient and ruthless. In fact – But better hear him out.

'– that I saw it could all be done again. I saw how such a dominion could be built up more rapidly and surely, because more scientifically, than ever before. Two things were necessary. First, a command of – or better a corner in – all those oddities and abnormalities which must be the instruments for building up a popular magical system. Mrs Nurse and her voices, Eusapia and her conjuring, Danilov and his gift of tongues; all that material one must hold ready and organized. And, second, there must be a softening process. All successful attack, unless it is to rely on sudden and devastating surprise, must be preceded by that. And alone one could not manage it. There must be the hour as well as the man.'

But the point, thought Appleby, is this: is the man, without knowing it, himself the product of the hour? And is the softening process not the source of the plot as well as its instrument? Was not Wine in some measure involved in his own twilight – and was he not vulnerable in terms of this? The point lay there.

'But the solvents had been at work long before my mind contacted the situation. For decades the great institutional systems of belief had been crumbling. You remember Christianity?'

Hudspith, to whom this flamboyant question appeared to be addressed, glowered darkly. But Wine was not in an observant mood.

'How exquisitely the rational and the irrational were held together there! What an instrument it was!' Something of Wine's gaiety had displeasingly returned, and he spoke as a connoisseur might speak of some rare vintage which had passed its allotted span. 'But things fall apart. The centre cannot hold. Mere anarchy is loosed upon the world.' He paused, apparently because this was a quotation and to be savoured. 'And so we can begin again.'

There were times at which the man had a certain impressiveness of perverted imagination. But at other times he was merely odious. And this, no doubt, was only another facet of the fact that there were several Wines. 'And so,' said Appleby, 'you begin again.'

'I begin wherever the softening process yields an opening. And there are openings in almost every country. There are openings in all classes – or sections, as I believe your Uncle Len would rather say. The different fields have, of course, been carefully studied; just as carefully as if we were proposing to market a new face-cream or soap. In the main it will be spiritualism for the upper class and astrology for the lower. Spiritualism is comparatively expensive – and can be extremely so – whereas astrology is quite cheap. The middle classes will have the benefit of a little of both. For rural populations we shall rely chiefly on witchcraft. What is sometimes called the intelligentsia has exercised my mind a good deal. Yoga might do, and reincarnation and the Great Mind and perhaps a little Irish mythology. But the problem is not important, as there are likely to be singularly few of them left. What we shall have to consider – and that, gentlemen, from China to Peru by way of Paris, London and Berlin – is simply Barbarians, Philistines and Populace. The classification is not one of the most up to date, but I fancy it is sufficient. I may say that the United States, in which even Barbarians are lacking, is going to be the simplest proposition of all.'

'Do I understand,' asked Appleby, 'that you are going to start your own Church?'

'Hardly that. But I may say that it will be more like a Church in some countries than others. For instance, in America, we shall gradually take over the churches – the buildings, I mean – themselves. But in England I believe that they would be useless to us, even those that still have roofs to them. In England we shall take over the Music-Halls. Have you ever sat among an English audience during a good variety show? A favourite comedienne singing a sentimental song, with a ventriloquist and a bit of conjuring to follow, can get pretty near the sort of atmosphere we want to achieve. The audience fuses into one cheerful and gullible monster. It is true that the Music-Hall has fallen into a decline, but into nothing like so steep a decline as the Church. We shall make it one of our major centres. And the other will be the Pub. Do you remember Wells's story of the man who tried to perform a miracle in a pub – and it worked? I think he ordered a lamp to turn upside-down. We shall see to it that all our pubs have lamps like that.'

Hudspith stirred uneasily, as if particularly outraged at the thought of hanky-panky in pubs. For some moments nobody spoke; in the heat of noon the viuditas and cardinales had ceased to sing; there was silence except where, directly beneath their feet, a tuco-tuco pursued its subterranean monologue like a gnome.

'The inverted lamp.' Wine had taken off his panama – and with it had shed his facetiousness, so that he was staring across the river, absent and absorbed once more. 'It might be our emblem. One by one what men have taken to be the true lamps are going out, and only the topsy-turvy ones will give any light at all. But are they topsy-turvy, after all? Or have we followed false lights for a thousand years or more?'

The fellow had taken the trouble, thought Appleby, to provide his rascality with a sort of philosophy. And they were going to be treated to it now; if only Hudspith had his professional notebook and pencil a valuable treatise might be preserved. He settled his back against the great tree. Suddenly overhead a teru-tero was calling – the plover of the pampa – and obscurely the tuco-tuco answered from below. Between them the well-modulated voice of Wine held the middle air.

'Take a piece of paper and make a pin-hole and look through the hole at a lighted lamp. Move the pin, head upwards, between the lamp and the paper until it is within your field of vision as you peer. What happens?'

Hudspith, whose eye appeared to have been probing after the tuco-tuco, looked up frowning. 'You see the pin-head upside down.'

'Exactly. Actually it is the image of the lamp which is inverted upon the retina. But our intellect rejects this and insists on seeing the pin head-downwards. It thinks a pin upside down less unlikely than a lamp upside down. And what the intellect rejects shall be our emblem: the inverted lamp.' Wine's voice dropped – dropped as if dipping towards the burrowing creature below. 'Light after light goes out, fire after fire is extinguished. And this gathering darkness has been the work of Science. That is the paradox. The Christians had a very clear picture of things. The simplest peasant could take it in and the subtlest schoolman could spend a lifetime interpreting it. It was simple and permanent. But then Science came along and substituted something difficult and provisional. Decade by decade the picture became more complicated and shorter lived – until now neither the learned nor the simple at all know where they stand. And it is thus that Science puts out the lamps of reason; it is thus that Science is a vast softening process, a vast clearing the way for world-wide superstition. Science offers no fixed points of belief. And Science, in the popular mind, is the sphere of the unaccountable and the marvellous. Have you studied the strip serials? Nothing could be more significant. The Scientist is always there, and he is nothing more or less than the old Magician. He belongs to our camp. And we shall use him. Under our control he will become part of what the world most needs.'

Appleby got to his feet. 'And that is?'

'A handful of simple and thorough-going superstitions, backed by conjurers, freaks and prodigies.' Wine too rose. 'What a pleasant gossip we have had! But now I must go down to the boat. I think you will find luncheon waiting for you. And will you make my apologies to the ladies?'

They watched him go briskly down the hill. And Hudspith snorted

'– so vigorously that the tuco-tuco beneath his feet fell silent. 'Softening process!' he said. 'I'll soften him.'

'On the contrary, it is only too likely that he will soften us. Light after light goes out, including two luminaries from Scotland Yard.' Appleby stretched himself in the sunshine. 'Or, if you prefer it, light after light has gone out already, including several in our friend. As the old books used to say, his mind is darkened.'

'You think he's mad?'

'What is the test? If his fantasies are unworkable – as I rather think they are – then he is mad. But if he could bring his scheme off, or even bring a sizeable fragment of it off, we should have to allow him a sort of perverted sanity of his own. I thought he might have made a little more of that stuff about science and superstition – because of course there's something in it. And if he isn't quite so impressive as he ought to be it's because he fails as the thoroughly objective exploiter of the situation as he sees it. He reckons the uncanny can move the world. Why? Primarily because it can move him. The truth is, he's the kind that would blench before a ghost.'

'And I would beam before roast mutton and a pint of bitter in the Strand. But I'm as unlikely to have occasion for the beaming as he for the blenching.' Hudspith stopped as if to scrutinize the syntax of this. 'We can't whistle up a squad of ghosts to corner him.'

'I suppose not.' Appleby took a last look at the islands and started off down the hill. 'But as far as the roast mutton goes there is likely to be some quite reasonable substitute cooking now. One can't complain of short rations.'

'Talking of short rations' – Hudspith had fallen into step beside him – 'has it occurred to you that in all this business nothing much has happened so far?'

'Nothing happened?'

'No one pulled out a gun or smashed a window or pushed someone else over a cliff.'

'Over a cliff? I don't think I've seen any. But perhaps we *have* been rather quiet.' Appleby paused to watch a charm of humming-birds mysteriously suspended at the lips of flowers. 'Would it be a good thing, I wonder, to take the initiative in brightening things up?'

8

Half-way down the hill Hudspith halted. His indignation had got the better of his appetite. 'The cheek of the man!' he said. 'Telling all that to people he knows are police officers.'

'He doesn't know that we know that he knows.' Appleby tramped on and made this familiar refrain a marching song. 'He thinks we think we have tricked him. We are Radbone's men. *We* have persuaded him we are agents of a man of whose existence *he* has persuaded us. And that gives the basis of his plan – or that little bit of his plan which concerns you and me. If we believe in Radbone, and believe Wine believes we're his men –'

'The experiment will work.'

'Just that. It will be colourable that he should send one of us off to do a deal, while the other remains as a sort of hostage. But any suspicion on our part would be a spanner in the works.'

'A spoke in the spook.'

'Just that.' Appleby nodded placidly at this cryptic remark. 'But, talking of expectation, I really must insist on luncheon. So come along.'

Luncheon was excellent; nevertheless it was consumed in an atmosphere of gloom. Something had bitten Beaglehole, who glowered at his companions with frank dislike. Mrs Nurse was tired and without spirits even to pronounce things nice. Opposite to her sat Lucy in an abstraction, her mind turned perhaps on *moneo* and *audio*, perhaps upon Socrates or Marcus Aurelius.

'This Schlumpf,' said Appleby, cheerful amid the glumness, '– did he build European-looking houses on what you call Europe Land? Did I once hear Wine say something about English House?'

Beaglehole looked up warily. 'English House? Yes – and damned odd it looks. It's the larger part of the sort of house you might find in a Bloomsbury square.'

'What an odd idea! Surely something rural would have been more in the picture?'

'The man was loopy.' Beaglehole spoke ungraciously but carefully, with evident knowledge that for his employer here was delicate and important ground. 'And there it is. One of those big houses built about a gloomy sort of well with a staircase going round and round.'

Mr Smart's staircase, Appleby thought – and Colonel Morell's before him. 'It sounds,' he said aloud, 'a very costly affair to erect.'

'Enormously so, no doubt. But the whole house isn't there.' Beaglehole caught himself up. 'I mean, they build just a sizeable part of such a house. And with old materials, I fancy. In places it looks quite genuinely old.'

'Dear me.'

'Dear you, indeed.' Beaglehole, still unaccountably disturbed, was openly rude. But he continued to give his explanations with care. 'As a matter of fact, the constructing or reconstructing or whatever it was seems to have been uncommonly badly done. We had a storm some months ago, and a good part of it came down. Awkward, because we have a lot of material for English House. Men are just finishing working on the repairs now.'

Appleby felt an impulse to smile confidentially at the savoury mess of fish before him. As an explanation of awkward fact that 37 Hawke Square was still going up this was no doubt as good as could be contrived. 'It sounds pretty queer,' he said. 'I'm rather looking forward to seeing it.'

Beaglehole put down his knife and fork. 'You'll see it, all right. And damned nonsense it is. Bah!'

'Bah, indeed,' said Appleby cheerfully. It was plain that there were matters upon which Beaglehole and his employer failed to see eye to eye. And it was not difficult to guess what these were. With the proposition that a good experiment is everything Beaglehole had no patience at all. 'And you have a certain amount of what Wine calls material waiting to move back into English House? The exhibits weren't blown away in the storm?'

Beaglehole pushed back his chair; he was even more irritated than before. 'One's gone,' he said. 'A confounded –'

'Gone? More wastage?' Wine had returned and was standing in the doorway looking at his assistant with a sort of easy dismay. 'Don't tell me that the alligators have got old Mrs Owler – or the Cockshell boy – or little Miss Spurdle?'

'The alligators have got nobody. But that Yorkshire vixen has decamped. I told you there would be trouble with her. They lost her after a couple of days. She's been gone for weeks.'

Wine frowned, now genuinely displeased, and turned to Appleby.

'The girl called Hannah Metcalfe. I sent her on a couple of sailings ahead of us. A mistake. An intractable person I ought to have kept an eye on.' He smiled wryly. 'You can tell Radbone we're at least not a hundred per cent efficient.'

'And it's not her alone.' Beaglehole was calmer now. 'She took a horse with her.'

Wine sat down, his brow darkening. 'Not Daffodil?'

'Yes. That's how she managed it. She sneaked over to German House in the night, nobbled the brute and a saddle, and swam the river with him. After that she had the pampa before her. But she wouldn't go far with an old cab-horse, you may be pretty sure. The Indians will have got her by this time. There's some consolation in that.'

Mrs Nurse, vaguely apprehending, looked distressed. Hudspith was concealing signs of massive disapprobation. And Appleby looked dubiously at his fish. *Did you ever hear of the isle of Capri?* She had said that. *The Happy Islands.* Well, at least the girl had made a break for it. Perhaps it would be well to follow suit.

'I find no consolation in the poor girl's death.' Wine was looking sternly at his assistant, and it occurred to Appleby that he was speaking the simple truth. 'Such talk is vindictive nonsense. Her death is useless to us.'

'At least it means that nothing will be given away.'

'Rubbish. If she got through to the coast she would be judged merely demented. And alive she was valuable – very valuable indeed. She might have been brought round. And she had guts. There was the makings of a Joan of Arc in her – our own sort of Joan of Arc.'

'Tell me,' said sick Lucy plaintively, 'about the voices of Joan of Arc.'

No one replied, and in the brief silence Appleby felt an uncomfortable pricking of the spine. 'After all,' he said at random, 'she mayn't be dead.'

'I hope not,' Wine reached for a decanter. 'Death is sheer waste – *useless* death.' For the fraction of a second he looked Appleby straight in the eye. 'Do you know, I think we'll all move to Europe Island in the morning?'

There was murder in the air. And that afternoon Appleby committed two murders. It was time to take the offensive, after all.

Near the upper end of the island the departed Schlumpf had caused a bathing-pool to be constructed – an elaborate little place, presumably in the Californian style. To this Lucy Rideout – young Lucy Rideout – had betaken herself shortly after luncheon, and here Appleby later found her practising diving with only a modicum of skill. For a time he watched her – watched that which was common to the Lucy Rideouts – flopping into the water and scrambling out. Sometimes she chattered to him, and her chattering was a twelve-year-old child's. But the body which curved and slid and panted before him was a grown-up woman's – the body of a grown-up woman and of a woman spontaneously physical. In fact, real Lucy's body. In that tenement of clay the other Lucys were misfits ...

Lucy Rideout flopped and scrambled and panted; tired and gasping, she lay on warm concrete and closed her eyes against the sun. She opened them, and suddenly they were sick Lucy's eyes – strained eyes which looked disconsolately down at a bright red bather, at a full and abounding body. She reached for a towel and wrapped it round her shoulders. 'About Socrates,' she said, 'and what he said about being dead –' She looked up – pathetic, unhealthy, tiresome. And Appleby found that he had murder in his heart.

There had been such a lot of sick Lucy lately; it was as if real Lucy had miscalculated in her notion of what a change of environment might do. Sick Lucy was winning. And although an interest in Socrates and the Sages is generally accounted highly estimable, Appleby was tired of it. He was tired of it as would be – he believed – a physician by this time. And he would take the responsibility of killing it if he could. This Lucy's head he would hold under that glittering pool until it breathed no more. Or he would do some equivalent thing. 'About being dead?' he repeated. 'Socrates was interested in what happens after death; in whether anything happens. But he wasn't like Wine. He wasn't prepared to kill people in order to find out.'

'What do you mean?' Sick Lucy had sat up and was looking at him with dilated eyes, suddenly trembling and deadly pale.

'Wine wonders if there are really ghosts. He has stolen a house where twice in the past the ghosts of murdered men are said to have appeared to friends. He himself is going to have a man killed there in order to find out. I am going to be killed without Hudspith knowing or suspecting – and will Hudspith see my ghost? Or the other way about. It is what Wine calls an experiment.'

'I don't believe it. I don't understand it. I don't wish to hear it or speak of it.' Sick Lucy was cowering horribly in upon herself. 'I wish to continue my Latin, to be told about –'

'You didn't know Wine was like that? You didn't know the world was like that?' Appleby had leant forward and was almost whispering into Lucy Rideout's ear. 'It is only one of Wine's experiments. Others will be on you. He teaches you Latin just to keep you about – to keep you alive until he is ready. You understand? He has to keep on encouraging you, or the others would drive you away – drive you into nothing. They are stronger than you. For a long time now you've only been kept alive by believing in Wine and the things he teaches you. Well, they are all false. That stuff isn't even Latin at all. You could never learn Latin – only gibberish. Your mind is too feeble. Your whole life has only been a sick flicker. But it has interested Wine because it is a freak life. What would happen if you died? Would there be three ghosts? He is interested in that sort of thing. You see? And there are other things about the world that I will tell you too. Listen . . .'

She had given a last little cry . . . infinitely horrible. And he looked down on her sprawled body and felt himself faint with compunction and fear. But, ever so faintly, the body was breathing. Perhaps – The breathing was less perceptible, less perceptible still, had surely ceased. Seconds stretched themselves out interminably. He turned away his head in despair.

'Jacko.'

He looked at her, and she was still pale as a corpse. But her eyes were open; were awed; were full of intelligence and life.

'Jacko – John' – the voice was faint, excited, alive – 'something's happened; something's happened to the prig.' Her voice rose in sudden triumph, complete conviction. 'She's dead.' Real Lucy sat up and laughed – happily and exultantly laughed. And then she was weeping uncontrollably – bewildered and bereaved.

But Appleby sat still and waited, like a fantastic sniper beneath the Tree of Life. Presently young Lucy would appear. She was tougher than sick Lucy had been; it would be less easy to hold her head beneath the glittering pool. He sat still and waited, thinking with what words a child could best be killed.

'Dead?' said Hudspith and paused, startled, in climbing once more the little hill.

'Dead.' Appleby looked westwards to where the farther islands were swimming into evening. 'You remember how I suggested that two of the personalities might be systematically discouraged? That's slow murder, though it's an orthodox clinical method. In this case quick murder proved possible. Single lethal doses of discouragement sufficed. And two things are left: an extremely curious moral problem and a valuable ally. Ought I to be hanged? The question will have significance only if the alligators are cheated of their due. As for the ally, there is no doubt of her. Real Lucy – sole Lucy, as one will think of her for a bit – may be a little lacking in modesty. But she has plenty of intelligence and resolution. Wine's plan pleases her very much.'

Hudspith puffed as the ascent grew steeper. 'Then I don't think much of her taste.'

'I mean that her mind can cope with it. It gives her intellectual satis-faction, just as it does you or me.'

'It's not likely to give you any other.'

'Be thankful for small mercies.' To the west the sky was molten, so that the great river seemed to pour from a cauldron of gold. 'I still keep on remembering things that fit in. I remember how Wine once told me Beaglehole and he were only acquaintances – something of the sort. He wanted to make sure – Cobdogla or not – that you and I were fast pals. Friendship was a prominent element in both the Hawke Square haunt-ings; it was to a more or less intimate friend that the full manifestations were accorded. The ghost of Colonel Morell spoke only to his friend Captain Bertram, and the ghost of Mr Smart only to his brother-in-law and friend Dr Spettigue. So when Wine saw that we were troublesome policemen and at the same time friends, he took the opportunity of killing two birds with one stone.'

'Or of throwing two birds to one alligator.' And Hudspith laughed – morosely but at greater length than the witticism justified. 'Not that one brace of friends would yield sufficient material for the great Hawke Square experiment. I don't doubt that a whole series of incidents is planned. Come to think of it, what about Mrs Gladigan and Miss Molsher? Perhaps they were really used that way. Perhaps Miss Molsher's ghost and mine will play hide and seek up and down that staircase.'

Hudspith, it struck Appleby, was developing quite a vein of fantasy. Doubtless it was the exotic environment at work. They were at the top of the hill now, and the river, still golden to the west, flowed dark and unreal beneath them. Mamey and Papaw, castor-oil plants and feathery palm were casting long shadows; the chatter of the chaja and the bien-te-veo was dying; soon it would be night and a universe of fireflies and stars – fireflies multitudinous and fleeting; stars remote and enduring, like the abstract ideas of these, laid up in a heaven of dark deep nocturnal blue. 'Miss Molsher?' said Appleby prosaically. 'But Hawke Square has only just gone up. You and I are guinea-pigs one and two.'

'Unless –'

'Unless he can be headed off the whole thing. After all, this genuine experimental side to the man makes only part of the picture. His racket, his Spook Church, his preparing his grotesque instruments of power: the greater part of the man is in that. And all of Beaglehole; he cares wholly for the practical and nothing for the speculative side. He regards it as the boss's weakness, and so perhaps it is – though it is his fascination too. Now, suppose the major project in some sort of danger –'

Hudspith shook his head. 'At the moment it appears to me invulnerable.'

'Don't be so sure of that. If the major project were imperilled, then Hawke Square, costly though it must have been, would no doubt go by the board for a time.'

Hudspith sat down and leant his back against the now almost invisible Ñandubay. 'Would you say,' he asked dryly, 'that you and I are making plans?'

'Certainly. And we have a good deal of freedom of action – and shall have as long as we succeed in giving the impression we believe in Radbone. We are unlikely to do anything desperate so long as we think one of us is to be let leave this place to negotiate with him. For instance, here are you and I conspiring together in solitude and nobody trailing us. I have a revolver in my suitcase and nobody has rifled it. We could kill Wine. We could kill both Wine and Beaglehole. Might not that break the back of the whole thing?'

'Not necessarily.' Faintly Appleby could see his companion shaking his head. 'We don't know what able lieutenants, what carefully nominated successors, what absentee directors there may be. But it would certainly be the end of us. There must be a pretty big gang of scoundrels scattered over these islands to control what Wine is pleased to call his material. We'd never shoot our way out.'

'I agree.'

'Of course we might contrive a revolution and organize the material behind barricades. But for the most part it's unknown, loopy and unreliable. Except for Lucy – and she's material no longer, according to you.'

Appleby said nothing. It was very quiet on the island and the river made no sound. Within scores of miles there might have been stirring nothing but the indefatigable mole. And yet the island was full of noises – the obscure noises of the South American night, seeming to come always from unknown distances, like murmurings indistinguishable whether of hope or fear.

'The sober truth,' said Hudspith, 'is that we must hope for something from without. A *deus ex machina* to wind the thing up happily after all.'

Again Appleby said nothing. It was dark and, far below, the mole was groping like a spirit perturbed.

PLOP.

Perhaps Hudspith shivered. 'Alligator,' he said.

But Appleby put a hand on his arm. 'Listen.'

And there was a new sound – a near-by sound from the river below. Silence succeeded and then it came again. There could be no mistaking it.

'Yes,' said Hudspith soberly. 'A horse.'

Part 4
Everlasting Bonfire

I

The horse whinnied in the dark. At the sound, a third time repeated, the tuco-tuco beneath their feet ceased like a demon charmed. Stillness was round them like an unruffled pool – a pool beyond whose margins hovered uncertain presences, the enigmatic murmurings of vagrant winds through distant colonnades of grass. The horse coughed.

'It's swimming,' said Hudspith.

Below – far below, it seemed – lights shone in the late Schlumpf's residence in the Californian style. One light might be Wine's and Beaglehole's; they would be sitting with papers before them, augmenting their strange plot. One might be Mrs Nurse's – Mrs Nurse feeling nice, feeling all hollow, feeling tired. And one, Appleby knew, was Lucy's – illiterate real Lucy with a big book before her, spelling out with concentrated intelligence the significant history of 37 Hawke Square. Lights shone on farther islands. Far away a beam of light briefly circled as a launch moved about the upper fringes of the colony – Australia Island, Asia Island, the Lord knew what. Something splashed. Something slithered and heavily respired. A single clipped word was spoken by a human voice. Silence fell again and was prolonged.

'A horse and rider.' Hudspith spoke low. 'But who would put a horse in that infested river?'

Against darkness the fireflies flickered, tiny inconsequently-roving points of light like a random molecular peppering revealed by some laboratory device.

'Who indeed?' said Appleby. 'Or who but a crazed Yorkshire girl!'

They waited, straining their ears. Somewhere on the island a radio had started disgorging the hollow and bodiless bellowings of an announcer tuned too loud – news from the China Sea, from Samara, from San Francisco ceaselessly circling the world, flooding it at the flick of a switch. The faint and hollow bellowing came up to them like the sound of water aimlessly bumping and bouncing in distant caves, but they listened only for a footfall or the quick clop of hoofs. They heard still the bodiless booming and the distant pampas sounds, and once the tuco-tuco stirred briefly below, and then, startlingly near, they heard in the darkness an intermittent short crisp tearing crunch – a noise baffling for seconds, and then suddenly not misinterpretable; the noise of a graminivorous creature cropping as it moved. And then they smelt horse.

The creature stood beside them: a presence, a faint whitish cloud – a warm horse-smelling cloud. If it was saddled and bitted it had been wandering with the reins on its neck; if it had a rider the rider was invisible, dark against the night. Appleby's eye followed the uncertain upper outline of the cloud and rested where the background lacked its powdering of stars. There was indeed a rider, a rider who sat immobile, gazing down on the scattering of lights which marked the headquarters of Emery Wine.

'Good evening,' Appleby said.

A faint jingle, as if a hand had tightened on a rein, was the only reply.

'Good evening,' Appleby repeated. 'Do you remember the shop in York, where they sold the things from old Hannah Metcalfe's cottage? It must be nearly four months ago now.'

Again there was no reply, but the whitish cloud moved. The whitish cloud which was horse elongated itself at the tip and four times dipped in air. The Daffodil of Bodfish and Lady Caroline had not lost his skill.

'And now,' said Appleby, 'here we are on the isle of Capri.'

'Mock.' The voice was husky and deep and not unmusical. 'Go on mocking. But come no nearer. I am not alone.'

Hudspith was scrambling to his feet. But Appleby put a restraining hand on his arm. 'Not alone?' he said. 'Well, there's Daffodil, of course.'

'There are the demons of earth and water and air.' The girl's voice was deep, assured, level. 'You think that in your little room with the cameras and the trembling floor you command the demons. But you are wrong. They are commanded by me.'

'We are not the friends of Wine. And we have no interest in demons. We don't believe in them. We are going to get you safely away – back to the Haworth you were foolish enough to leave.'

The answer was a low laugh, and when the voice spoke again the laughter was in it still – malicious, triumphant. 'You are the friends of Wine. All here are the friends of Wine – or all except the demons in whom you don't believe.'

Obscurely the invisible girl was having it her own way. A spell was forming. Appleby tried to break it. 'My dear Miss Metcalfe –'

Her laugh came again. His words broke against it. 'Listen,' she said. 'Listen to the demons of earth.' Slightly the patch of starless sky shifted, as if the girl were leaning over the neck of her horse. And Daffodil whinnied. And instantly from far below, from beyond the banks of the yellow invisible river, from round the farther islands came a deep faint throb – a throb so deep as to be less a sound than a mere muscular sensation in the ear. 'The demons of earth,' Hannah Metcalfe said. And the throbbing – like the distant beat of many drums – died away.

It was odd; it was so very odd that Appleby found himself cautiously testing the control of his vocal organs before he spoke again. 'And the demons of water?' he asked.

Once more Daffodil whinnied – and whinnied again. And instantly upon the deepest darkness where the great slow river flowed there floated a hundred streaks of pale fire. The streaks curved to arcs, to circles, to rolling and intersecting wheels of phosphorescent fire. 'The demons of water,' said Hannah Metcalfe, 'and the demons of air.' As she spoke the dark sky beyond the river became alive as if with meteors, became alive with red and angry smears and shafts of fire. They rose, curved and fell, and the stars were uncertain and pale behind them. For seconds only the thing lasted, and then Night resumed her natural sway. Out of it came Hannah Metcalfe's voice, graver now. 'Is one of you Beaglehole?' it asked.

'Neither of us is Beaglehole.' Appleby's voice was steady. 'We are the enemies of Beaglehole and Wine.'

'I do not believe you. Here all except the victims are the friends of Beaglehole and Wine. Are you victims?'

'We are police officers.'

'That is nonsense. You are the friends of Beaglehole and Wine. Tell them. But tell Beaglehole above all. Tell him I do not forget. About the ship.'

'We know nothing of the ship.'

'The little ship which sailed from Ireland. I would not go. I did not like the men. Beaglehole made them bind me. And he had a whip. Tell him I do not forget. Tell him that only the victims shall escape and be given their rightful place. All the rest of you the demons are going to take.'

'Miss Metcalfe –'

She laughed. The cloud – the cloud which faintly smelt of Bodfish's open landau – stirred, faded, dissolved. There was a long silence and then the voice, grave and malicious at once, came faintly up to them. 'The demons,' it said. 'The demons of earth and water and air.'

They groped their way downhill, sober and silent. It was only when the lighted windows took definition before them that Hudspith spoke. 'I don't suppose –'

'Of course not.'

'In that case –'

'Quite so.'

Perhaps Hudspith was rubbing his jaw. 'We don't know quite when she escaped. But she's a quick worker.'

'And with decided powers of organization.'

'Joan of Arc.'

'Ah.'

'The horse would help.'

'The horse?'

'Tricks. A magic horse. When the Spaniards first came quite ordinary horses created no end of a sensation.'

'Um.'

The veranda was in darkness but from a corner came the glow of a cigarette – a cigarette rapidly and nervously puffed. Appleby addressed it. 'Hullo,' he said cheerfully.

The cigarette dipped and took flight into the night. Beaglehole spoke. 'Is that you two? You're prowling late. Where have you been? I thought I heard something damned queer. And did you see something in the sky?'

'We walk by night,' said Appleby. 'What could be more appropriate in a haunt of ghosts and spirits? Of course it's dangerous. The right-valiant Banquo walked too late.'

Beaglehole swore. 'Did you hear anything, I say? Did you see anything?'

'We heard the owl scream and the crickets cry. Is Wine about? He would enjoy a little culture. But perhaps it's time to go to bed – to sleep, perchance to dream.'

'Damn you,' said Beaglehole. 'What the devil are you talking about?'

'Something queer. They say five moons were seen tonight.'

'Five moons!'

'Four fixed, and the fifth did whirl the other four in wondrous motion.'

'Bah! You must be tight.' And in the darkness Beaglehole turned away.

'Take care,' said Appleby softly. 'Take care, sirrah – the whip.'

There was silence. They were alone again. 'Well, well,' said Hudspith. 'I never knew excitement took you that way. Quite like Prince Hamlet putting his antic disposition on.'

'If a man were porter of hell-gate . . .'

'What?'

'I suppose he would be rather like Beaglehole. Don't you dislike Beaglehole much more than Wine? It's because he's without a meta-physical – or superstitious – side to him. A porter of hell-gate with no belief in the everlasting bonfire.'

'No doubt,' said Hudspith vaguely, and yawned. 'But I think we'll call it a day.'

2

The launch pushed off; the engine spluttered and roared; above the Ceibas with their bunches of great purple flowers rose macaws, blue, red, and yellow, to hover against a morning sky of amethyst and gold. Nature was in one of her painfully frequent gaudy and tasteless moods. But Lucy Rideout clapped her hands and shouted. 'Oh, look at their wings!' she cried. 'Oh, look at their lovely beaks!'

Out of the corner of his eye Appleby saw Hudspith shiver. The real and only Lucy Rideout had still a substantial memory of her deceased sisters; she acted them, as one might say, to the life. Wine, debonair and amiable in the stern, could have no inkling of the latest wastage in his material. But to one in the know Lucy's impersonations were a little eerie. And were they not perhaps hazardous as well? Thus encouraged, might not Lucy's ghosts walk; sick Lucy and young Lucy indeed revisit the glimpses of the moon – even achieve some shadowy resurrection in that now glad and eager body in the bows? But by such thoughts Lucy herself was clearly untroubled. She was single and whole; she was in on such counter-plot as could be contrived; she was having a marvellous time. And now she turned to Hudspith with suddenly serious eyes.

'Mr Hudspith,' she said plaintively, 'tell me about the Discourses of Epictetus.' She wriggled a little nearer Appleby. It was all outrageous fun.

And Hudspith rubbed his jaw and frowned – but before he could offer any suitable reply Wine leant forward. 'You can see it now,' he said. 'English House. Or perhaps it should be called Schlumpf's Folly.'

Fantastic against the morning, rectangular amid the curved and coiled luxuriance of the place, soot-begrimed in the clear air, 37 Hawke Square reared itself somewhat shakily before them. A large house hastily demolished and in its old age transported across the Line can never look quite the same again – particularly when originally designed as a unit in the middle of a row. But there it stood, discernibly something out of Bloomsbury, and presumably carrying with it sufficient of the spirit of place to justify the psychic experiments of Mr Emery Wine. It might have been simpler to endeavour to take over the house where it originally stood and try out a murder or two on the spot. Perhaps Wine had mistrusted the metropolitan police. Or perhaps he had simply obeyed a collector's instinct to have everything cosily around him. Anyway, there was the house – and so pitched that the yellow and unending river almost laved the vestigial remains of its basement storey. Here had died Colonel Morell and that unfortunate Victorian merchant, Mr Smart. The place looked, too, as if its conscience might be heavy with the doing to death of sundry general servants; their ghosts, brandishing brooms or ceaselessly hauling scuttles of coal from floor to floor, might well haunt the premises with obstinate venom.

'I am particularly fond,' said Wine, 'of the simple and severe lines of the front door.'

Appleby looked at the front door – the door through which, nearly two hundred years before, Dr Samuel Johnson and his negro servant Mr Francis Barber had departed from their fruitless vigils. And of course the bodies must have been brought out that way. But where hearse and mourners had stood there were now only reeds and water and alligators. In fact the front door – it had been given a new coat of green paint, and in the centre, very shiny, was the brass head of a lion champing a ring – the front door had more of Venice than of London: one would have found the appearance of a gondola more appropriate than that of a Sedan-chair. Still, it was all very colourable, and there was even smoke coming from the chimneys. And Appleby looked at it steadily. Then he turned to Wine. 'The man who did that was quite, quite mad.' He paused. 'Don't you agree?'

Wine looked thoughtfully at his finger-nails. 'Well – of course I should not care to defend the sanity of old Schlumpf. I scarcely knew him. And the thing looks pretty mad. But one can never be quite sure. There may be something more to the maddest-looking project than immediately meets the eye. Don't you think so? Hudspith, my dear fellow, don't you agree with me?' Wine smiled whimsically at the inarticulate reply given to this last appeal. 'But at least one would not have it otherwise; the thing is so pleasingly odd. Of course there is a good deal that is odd about our own project – Lucy, my dear, I think you should put on your hat – and Schlumpf's anterior oddities make perhaps too much of a good thing. That is why Beaglehole there is such a comfort. There is nothing odd about him. A solid businessman who keeps our feet on earth – or on deck as we puff up and down our interminable river.' Wine was talking gently and apparently at random. 'Which reminds me: the steamer is going down with Beaglehole tomorrow. So I fear you will not have much time to explore more of our oddities or of Schlumpf's. One of you, that is to say.'

'One of us?' said Appleby. The launch was curving inshore; presently 37 Hawke Square would tower above them like a menacing cliff.

'Either Hudspith or yourself. I want one of you to go and contact Radbone just as quickly as you can. Have you listened to the news lately? There really isn't much time to lose; our merger, if we can agree upon it, had better be soon.'

'Perhaps we ought both to go?'

Wine cocked his head, as if this were a sound suggestion which had not occurred to him. 'Perhaps so. And yet I don't know. There is so much that I could discuss with one of you. I think we could draught a complete plan. No' – his voice was politely final – 'I really think not. We must save all the time we can. But which of you had better go?'

'I don't think it makes much difference,' said Hudspith.

'No,' said Wine amiably. 'I don't think it does.'

Deserted and echoing, and with its ill-assembled doors and floors and wainscoting rattling and creaking in the dry wind of the Pampas – it was thus that Appleby had instinctively thought of the new 37 Hawke Square. But it proved to be more than fully occupied. Miss Mood seemed, since her last appearance, to have multiplied herself by some process of fissure natural to the lower forms of life; she was to be found on every landing. And – although Mrs Nurses are rare – there were several Mrs Nurses. It had to be remembered that 37 Hawke Square was also English House, and that in material for operating in England Mr Wine was peculiarly rich. Mediums and thought-readers and prodigies wandered on every landing and popped in and out through numbered doors. Moreover it was probable that for every person thus visible there was another altogether too odd or erratic or unreliable for present view. The place was, in fact, crammed like a cheap lodging-house. And this, thought Appleby as he stood on the first-floor landing after luncheon, made the situation more than curious. Perhaps it offered unexpected scope for manoeuvre. Certainly it straitened the enemy's plans.

'Jacko!'

He looked up and saw Lucy beckoning from the next landing. She was conspiratorial and happy. He went up and joined her. 'Have they given you a decent room?'

'Not bad. In the attics. It's funny about this house. Come up to the top.'

They climbed.

'It's funny about habit.'

'About habit?' Real Lucy's English prose, Appleby reflected, had a touch of young Lucy still. It was at once infantile and cogent, like the more lucid performances of Miss Gertrude Stein.

'It's funny about a step you think is there in the dark when it isn't – isn't it?'

'When you try to take a step down that isn't there? It can give you quite a jar.'

'Yes. Well, I get a jar when I keep on trying to go below-stairs and there isn't a below-stairs. You see, the house we all lived in before the blitz –'

'All lived in!'

'Mum and me and the others.'

'Of course.'

'It was just like this, and of course below-stairs and the attics were our parts. And now there is no below-stairs; just three or four steps and then it ends off. I suppose it was all they managed to steal of the basement. Still, there's all the attics. Let's go right up.'

They climbed higher. The English material of Emery Wine flitted past, banged doors, talked, sang, somewhere played a piano. It's funny about this house, Appleby thought. It's funny –

'Jack – about Mr Smart.' They had reached the top, and Lucy leant over the balustrade. 'This is where he fell from. It's not really a well, is it? Not much more than a slit.'

They stood approximately on the spot from which, in the London of 1888, an unfortunate merchant had fallen to his death. A cross, thought Appleby, looking down, marks the spot. It was funny about Mr Smart. And it was, indeed, hardly a well. What one saw far below was a narrow rectangle of tiled floor.

'Of course,' said Lucy, 'you'd go right to the bottom. But not quite – quite clean. There'd be bumps.'

The observation was correct; probably there would be bumps; probably the body would go bumping down like a ball on a pin-table. And this, somehow, was nastier than a single plunge; and smash.

'Of course,' said Lucy, 'he may try poison, like the other man – the colonel. But I don't think so.' She was frowning down at the tiny pattern of tiles below. He looked at her curiously. 'But I don't think so,' she repeated.

'Why not?'

'Because the – the case of Colonel Morell is less certain. I think he'll try to – to reproduce the more striking one.'

Striking, thought Appleby, was the word. He glanced round the landing. There appeared to be nobody about. 'You're probably right.'

'Though of course he might just do something quite different. The – the –' She paused, at a loss for the right abstract words.

'The conditions of the problem would still hold.'

'Yes. But somehow I think it will be the staircase. So think what he has to do. And suppose it's Hudspith.'

'Suppose it's Hudspith,' said Appleby gravely.

'Well, Hudspith has to go off with Beaglehole on the steamer as if for a long journey. That means no more Beaglehole for weeks. And that's important – if we can work it.'

Appleby was looking at her with narrowed eyes. He had colleagues as competent and economically-minded as this. But not many of them.

'And then Hudspith has to be brought back – or persuaded to come back. And nobody here must know. And he must be pitched down here and killed, and still none of all these queer people must know, and then there must be a lot of waiting while you think he is just sailing down the river. It was ages before Dr Spettigue –'

'But that was because Dr Spettigue didn't move into his new consulting-rooms for quite a time.'

She shook her head. 'That's not quite right, Jacko. I mean, we don't know the ghost would have appeared any quicker even if Dr Spettigue had moved in at once. Perhaps ghosts take some time to pull themselves together. Particularly after –' And her glance went down the long drop to the hall below.

'You're quite right. Wine must be prepared to wait weeks or even months for results from this particular experiment. And, mind you, it's no more than a side-line with him; a little weak hankering after pure science in a predominantly practical man. Interesting chap, Wine.'

Lucy shook her head impatiently. 'Don't be cool and detached, Jacko. It's just showing off. And – and beside the point.'

Appleby looked at his late patient and victim with respect. 'Go on,' he said.

'The point is this. Hudspith is pitched down there and killed and nobody must know. That means getting rid of the body quick. What will they do? Feed it to the alligators, if you ask me. And what about Beaglehole? He must make himself scarce and keep himself scarce. If you saw him or heard he was about it would be all up with the experiment. The whole thing turns on your not suspecting anything. If you suspected that Hudspith was dead, then you might begin to *expect* a ghost. And the experiment has to be so that there isn't what that big book calls specific expectation.'

'You've got it all up, Lucy. Have you anything to suggest?'

'Well it's pretty clear what *might* be done, isn't it? The question is, can it be worked? We'll try.' She sighed and grinned at him, pale and excited. 'You know, it's a good thing the young 'un and the prig are out of this. They'd be scared stiff.'

'And you, Lucy?'

She stretched herself luxuriously and perilously against the balustrade. 'Me, Jacko? Well, I don't think I'll ever bother to go to the pictures again.'

3

It was dusk among the chimney-pots. Half-close the eyes and it was possible to imagine a whole forest of them; possible to conjure up a whole London below. And perhaps one day London – perhaps one day all the great cities would be like this: some single surviving battered building perched above swamps and grasses which stretched everywhere to the horizon. *After London* ... it had been one of the books of one of the Lucys – the story of a sparse feudal culture scattered over home counties from which the industrial heart had vanished in some unnamed catastrophe ... Appleby peered out over the darkening Pampa. There too, on those last and inaccessible reaches of the monstrous river, were spears and bows and arrows; were the remnants of some primitive and tribal organization. Perhaps the savages would have the laugh on the more complicated and showy structures in the end. Perhaps –

A smut falling on Appleby's nose interrupted this reverie. Down in the bowels of 37 Hawke Square they were burning real coal. Soot and coal-dust were no doubt the appropriate incense of the place and peculiarly necessary while the right psychical atmosphere was being worked up. There was something very close to ritual sacrifice in the fantastic experiment being prepared by Wine. Indeed, a psychologist would say that his conduct was purely atavistic – a mere throw-back to primitive magic – and that the ingenious notion of an unusually drastic experiment in psychical research was the merest rationalization. But whatever it was – thought Appleby, sitting on the laboriously transplanted leads of 37 Hawke Square – whatever it was, it *was* – and in a very pretty state of forwardness. And there was only one thing to do.

They must go to Wine and tell him that his experiment was pointless – pointless because they knew all about it. They must tell him that they knew Radbone to be nonsense; that they were known to be policemen; that they were policemen with a powerful backing behind them; that they had accompanied him up the river knowing all about his game; that their superiors knew all about his game; that diplomatic means were being taken to smash it now; that his best chance was to fade out quietly without committing a capital crime. Government would step in and liquidate his enterprise, but with luck he himself would not be successfully pursued.

Appleby reeled it off in his own mind – and disliked it. The perfection of Wine's experiment, it was true, they had power to smash. To no unsuspecting friend in that house would the ghost of a murdered man ever appear, or fail to appear. At their first word spoken all that laborious project of Wine's would be in atoms. But beyond that the position was bleak. Wine was very little likely to be intimidated. He would know, almost as well as they knew themselves, how long and tenuous was the track from the Happy Islands to Scotland Yard. In a world at peace the pursuit of two missing officers would be inexorable indeed, but would be slow. Under present conditions Wine – whose whole vast project was a gamble – might well reckon that his own powers would be deployed and triumphant long before they were run to earth here in their vulnerable cradle.

The river flowed past the front door of 37 Hawke Square. The alligators plopped within earshot of its dining-rooms. Such incongruities, deliberately contrived by a logical if perverted mind, had an insidious power to paralyse the will, to baffle the intellect. But not Lucy Rideout's. Lucy enjoyed a saving ignorance. She knew far too little of the world to be in danger of sitting back flabbergasted. And she knew enough of melodrama and had enough of native wit to contrive sufficiently surprising answering stratagems of her own. One might do worse than give Lucy her head.

A shadow moved among the chimney-pots. Wine had emerged on the roof – an incongruous figure in his quietly immaculate tropical clothes. 'Appleby, is it you? I am glad you have found this amusing vantage point.' Wine sat down easily on the leads. 'Who would ever think to survey the heart of South America from the roof of a London tenement? And yet here we are, and there South America is.' He waved his hand whimsically before him. 'Utterly irrational, but a fact. And all the most potent facts are utterly irrational. That is our theme. Men made steam engines by observing and exploiting the way things actually work. We are going to make far more potent engines by observing and exploiting the way things are spontaneously imagined to work. Consider the stars, my dear man.'

Appleby looked up at the darkening sky. In a few minutes now the stars would be hanging there, would be hanging there whether one was considering them or not . . . 'The stars?' he said vaguely.

'Consider the stars. What is it natural to believe of them? What notions about them come spontaneously into men's minds? Clearly the notions of judicial astrology. Compared with them the notions of Copernicus and Newton, of Kepler and Einstein, are temporary, local and eccentric in the highest degree.'

'But the notions of Copernicus and his followers work. Their predictions come true. Whereas with the astrologers –'

Wine interrupted with a wave of an amiably dismissive hand. 'The human race, my dear Appleby, is much too shock-headed, and has much too short a memory, to take much notice of whether predictions are fulfilled or not. All it wants is a certain quality in the predictions themselves. They must have a magical and irrational element of sufficient substance to satisfy the magical and irrational appetencies which make up nine-tenths of the content of the human mind. That is what we are going to provide – Radbone and you and I.'

'And Hudspith.'

'And Hudspith, of course.' Wine was silent for a moment, as if his mind had gone off on some other train of thought. 'Has one of you by any chance got a revolver?' he asked suddenly.

'I have. But I don't think Hudspith has. Would you care to borrow it?' Appleby spoke easily, but with a mild unconcealed surprise. If Lucy's hair-raising plan was to be adopted it was necessary to appear utterly unsuspecting of danger.

'Dear me, no. It has simply struck me that some rough census of weapons is desirable. The truth is, there are rumours about the surrounding natives which I don't quite like.'

'I hope they haven't caused any more wastage?'

'No: the trouble is rather that they appear to be lying very low. It makes me think they may be meditating some attack. And though they are not visible by day, there are stories going round of rather queer things being seen and heard at night.'

'Queer things? That sounds right up your pitch. Perhaps they just want to pull their weight in your brave and irrational new world.'

Wine laughed – perhaps a shade uncertainly. 'After so much of Beaglehole it is really delightful to talk to somebody who can make a joke. But, seriously, I am a little perturbed. They undoubtedly ate those two women who were so interestingly *en rapport*.'

'Miss Molsher and Mrs Gladigan?'

'Yes. And now they have most certainly eaten the Yorkshire girl who escaped with the horse. That is most upsetting in itself, for really she was a most promising witch. But what I am afraid of is that the thing may give them an ungovernable taste for white man in the stew-pot. I believe it does sometimes happen that way.'

'No doubt. In fact, an abstention from cannibalism, if one takes a broad enough view, is probably temporary, local and eccentric in the highest degree. And if the savages turn really spontaneous we are all likely to be turned into cutlets.'

Wine's laugh was perceptibly harsh this time. 'Quite so. We don't want magical practices *too* near home. Perhaps Hudspith may congratu-late himself that he is going downstream in the morning. He, at least, won't be eaten by cannibals.' Wine paused. From the river below came the faint *plop* of an alligator.

'But for us who remain you think there is real danger?'

'Only of inconvenience and a tiresome scrap. The savages are believed to exist in quite considerable numbers, and in these upper reaches have never been brought under control. But fortunately they are quite without any sort of directing intelligence.'

'Ah.' Appleby knocked out his pipe and looked up at the heavens. Yes, the stars were there – armies of unalterable law. And, perched obscurely on his grain of dust in space, he winked at them. 'Fancy,' he said. 'Fancy a Yorkshire witch ending her days in an American savage's cauldron. Irrational, isn't it?'

Hudspith snapped down the locks of his suitcase. 'I wonder why it should be me?' he asked composedly. 'Of course Wine came to realize that my having a vision of Lucy that night was a hoax. But I feel he went on believing those stories of yours about my being that sort of man.'

'In a way you are that sort of man.' Appleby, sitting on his bed in the small hours, spoke softly across the room. 'You're a moody devil with an abstracted eye and a bee in your bonnet about abducted girls. It gives you quite a distinguished air. And I don't doubt Wine regards you as psychically sensitive. Nevertheless you are going to supply the ghost and I am going to be the percipient: there's no doubt of that. Probably the theory is that only psychically peculiar people have the makings of good ghosts. Come to think of it, ghosts are seen by all and sundry in the most unselective way. If they're seen at all, that is.' Appleby paused in order to give some attention to loading his revolver. 'Whereas as often as not a ghost has been a person of some mark. I think you must take it as rather a compliment that you have been cast for that particular role.'

'Cast is the word,' said Hudspith. 'But not so much a role as a bump.' He laughed loudly at this complex of puns, and then checked himself as the sound echoed startlingly in the night. 'You know I can't help feeling an element of waste in the thing.'

Appleby laid the revolver on his bed. 'Very natural, I'm sure. All condemned men must regard the projected execution as a quite unjustifiably lavish expenditure of life. They must feel that a decent regard for economy positively requires that the thing be commuted to a kindly rebuke.'

'I don't mean quite like that. Do you ever read detective stories?'

'Lord, lord! What sort of talk is this? No, I haven't read a detective story for years.'

'I read quite a lot. Recreative, I find them.' Hudspith had switched off the light and was speaking out of the darkness. 'They quite take one out of oneself, if one's in my line.'

'I see. No ruined girls.'

'Not many ruined girls. They don't sell. How many people would you say have written detective stories?'

Appleby yawned. 'Hundreds, I should imagine.'

'Quite so – and some of them have written scores of books. Folk with intelligences ranging from moderate through good to excellent. A couple of women are quite excellent; there's no other word for them.'

'Is that so? I say, Hudspith, it must be deuced late.'

'And what would you say those hundreds of folk are constantly after?'

'Money.' Appleby's voice, if sleepy, was decided.

'They're constantly after a really original motive for murder. And here one is. I'm being murdered to further the purposes of psychical research; murdered in order to manufacture a ghost. It's a genuinely new motive, and none of them has ever thought of it.'

'Probably someone has. You just haven't read that particular yarn. Good night.'

'But I haven't explained what I mean. About waste, that is.' Hudspith's voice continued to come laboriously out of the night. 'Here is a perfect detective-story motive, and yet we're not in a detective story at all.'

'My dear man, you're talking like something in Pirandello. Go to sleep.'

'We're in a sort of hodge-podge of fantasy and harum-scarum adventure that isn't a proper detective story at all. We might be by Michael Innes.'

'Innes? I've never heard of him.' Appleby spoke with decided exasperation. 'You might employ your last hours more profitably than in chatter about the underworld of letters. Go to sleep. Go to sleep and dream of the nice boiled egg they send to the condemned cell on the fatal morning.'

Hudspith sighed and for a time was silent. 'It's all very well rotting,' he said at length. 'But about this idea of Lucy's – do you think it will work?'

Silence answered him.

'Do you think it will? After all, it's a matter of some importance from my point of view.'

But again there was silence. Appleby was asleep.

4

Boiled eggs had been prominent on the breakfast-table, and while discussing them Wine had gone over in considerable detail the terms which Hudspith was to propose to his employer Radbone. Hudspith had made jottings in a notebook, scraped out his second egg and gone stolidly on board the little steamer. And no one could have guessed he guessed he was flirting with death. He stood beside Beaglehole in the stern, and sometimes he waved and sometimes Beaglehole waved, and quite soon they were indistinguishable dots far down the river. Wine, whose farewells had been openly affectionate, retired to administrative duties for the day. And once more Appleby climbed the little hill and sat himself down beneath the Ñandubay.

Hudspith was gone. A policeman who believed himself not to be known as such, he was gone as the result of what he believed to be a successful ruse – was gone, as he believed, to bring back troops and police and the rule of law to the Happy Islands. But in all this he was deluding himself. Radbone was a fiction successfully imposed upon him. And he was going to his death – a curious death, useful to science.

Such was the picture of the affair as it presented itself to Wine now. And how did Wine see Appleby? As another policeman who believed himself not to be known as such, a policeman who had only to go on pretending to believe in Radbone, a policeman who had only to sit tight in unsuspicious-seeming ease until his colleague returned with abundant help. But in all this but another deluded policeman. For to Appleby no Hudspith would ever return in the flesh. Only to an Appleby wholly unapprehensive, whole unsuspicious of his friend's death, there might one day appear Hudspith's ghost – a ghost calling for revenge. To others as well the ghost might manifest itself, but it would be to Appleby, as to Captain Bertram and Dr Spettigue, that some definite revelation would be attempted. Hudspith was to die, and thereafter the unsuspecting Appleby would be under scientific observation. Has he seen anything? Has the spirit of his murdered friend managed to communicate with him? These would be the questions asked. And all this as a sort of side-line to Wine's vast organization. The man sat down there, marshalling and docketing his growing army of clairvoyants and astrologers and miracle-workers to strictly practical ends. But he had this little weakness for real science. And hence the strange transplanting of 37 Hawke Square and Hudspith's present voyage ... Appleby gazed down the river. The little steamer had rounded a bend. There was only water, yellow and empty, to be seen.

Appleby filled his pipe. He lit it and puffed and thought about Hudspith's death. It was important to get this melancholy event quite clear.

Hudspith must die here. It would be no good cutting his throat fifty miles down the river – else might his ghost vainly haunt a solitude broken only by the flamingos and the scissors-birds. And not only must he die here – here in 37 Hawke Square – but here too must violence first be offered him. Wine's scientific thoroughness would insist on that. The murder must, so to speak, begin and end here.

Hudspith, then, must be brought back all unsuspecting. And quietly; nobody must know. Not one of the teeming occupants of the house must know. Even thoroughly reliable accomplices must be at a minimum – for the more of these there were the more possible would it be that the experiment might be vitiated by the operation of telepathy. Minds knowing of the murder might communicate to Appleby an obscure alarm.

Hudspith must be murdered here. *And he must know it.* Appleby frowned as he hit upon this point. If you do not know that you are being murdered it is conceivable that your ghost will never know that you were murdered. Hudspith must be brought back all unsuspecting; he must be made aware that his murder is imminent; he must be murdered with the knowledge of as few persons as possible; his body must be disposed of safely and instantly; all must be as if he were still smoothly dropping down the river in the company of Beaglehole.

These were the conditions of the experiment. Most of them Lucy had worked out already; and Lucy had seen how drastically they limited the enemy's power of manoeuvre. How could the thing be done?

Appleby looked up into the empty South American sky. It needed an aeroplane, he thought.

The steamer could not come back. But Hudspith must come back. Suppose, then, that Beaglehole affected to remember some vital point in the proposed deal with Radbone which Wine had not cleared up. Suppose that, some way down the river, a plane of Wine's opportunely turned up. Suppose Beaglehole proposed a quick hop back in this to the Happy Islands and then a return hop before the steamer had gone much farther on its way. This would serve to bring an unsuspecting Hudspith back and – what was equally important – it would serve to get Beaglehole quickly away again after the murder. For nobody must know of Beaglehole as mysteriously returned and hanging about. The moment Hudspith was murdered it would be desirable that Beaglehole should make himself scarce. And for this a plane would be the thing. An amphibian plane could come and go in darkness. And Wine was almost certain to possess one. It all combined to bring Lucy's plan within the fringes of the feasible ... Appleby knocked out his pipe and started down the hill. Lucy Rideout was all right. One knew where one was with her – now. But what of Hannah Metcalfe – and Daffodil? He looked out over the dark luxuriant fringe of the river to the infinite spaces beyond. An army could manoeuvre there.

Black coffee is the best vehicle for administering a surreptitious sleeping draught, and at half past eight that night Appleby gave the appearance of drinking a good deal of black coffee. An hour later he told Wine and Mrs Nurse that he was feeling sleepy. And half an hour after that again he was in bed. He was in bed and in darkness – for the night was very dark. He lay in bed thinking of the curious turn which it was proposed that things should take. Finish was required; there must be a constant care for convincing detail. And Appleby put out his arm and turned on a little lamp by his bedside. He tossed an open book, spine upwards, on the floor. It would be thus with a man whom an opiate had surprised.

Everything was very quiet by eleven o'clock; so quiet in this over-populated house that it was tempting to believe there must have been laudanum all round. The sluggish river slapped half-heartedly at the stone steps before the front door of 37 Hawke Square; a light wind intermittently clattered in some metropolitan chimney-top contrivance overhead; far away the creatures of the South American night called to each other sparely and without conviction – the call of wild things perpetually half awake on the off-chance of alarm or catastrophe. For Appleby it was an off-chance too; it would mean a hitch if he were called out into the violent stream of things that night. But he was very wakeful.

Wine came at twenty past eleven. He tapped at the door – lightly; slipped into the room – softly; spoke – very quietly indeed. 'Appleby, my dear fellow, I hope you don't mind –' He was across the room and by the bed; and now he said nothing more. Appleby, breathing heavily, sensed him as sitting down. And then he felt a touch, light but purposive, on his wrist. Wine was feeling his pulse.

Constantly one had to remember that it would all be very scientific. The way to avoid surprises was to remember this. Doubtless this pulse-business would be repeated at frequent intervals during the next hour or so. For, hard by the sleeping man, stirring events were presently to accomplish themselves. How interesting – how scientifically interesting – if that pulse quickened to some obscure intimation of drama from the waking world!

Wine must be watching him intently. And as Appleby visualized that intent glance he felt his own eyelids flicker as those of a man heavily asleep ought not to do; he contrived to stir uneasily, groan, and bury his head in the pillow. And what, in fact, would his pulse tell? Wine was a hard man to cozen.

The light from the bedside lamp still seeped faintly through to Appleby's retina; outside the room, on the second-floor landing, another faint light would be burning. But everywhere else there would be a velvet blackness now; only from high overhead the river would show, perhaps, as a streak of dullest silver. No doubt a skilful pilot – Appleby listened. From far down the river came a murmur of sound that grew momentarily in volume and then faded away. There was silence and then far off a bird cried. A bird cried and another answered; many birds were calling, and the blended sound made the same murmur but louder, so that it drowned the sullen slap-slap of the river and the creak of the London chimney-pot overhead. But again there was silence, and then again the murmur grew, louder still. Colony by colony up the long reaches of the river the birds were coming awake and crying and then once more sinking to rest. High above them something was passing – and now a new vibration could be felt, a new sound heard. The faint quick throb of the engine grew. And again Appleby felt the touch on his wrist.

The engine cut out. Seconds passed. Now the plane must be on the water. But nothing more was heard, and the lengthened minutes crawled interminably by.

'Appleby!' It was Wine's voice, sudden and commanding hard by Appleby's ear. But this was something abundantly to be expected, and the sluggish movement of the head which alone resulted must have been convincing enough. For now Wine took Appleby's right arm and cautiously pushed up the sleeve above the elbow. Something cool, firm, binding was applied and faintly the arm began to throb. More science. A mere finger on the pulse was not enough; here was one of those gadgets which gives much more accurate information on how the human engine behaves ... Minutes passed again, and then a sharp jarring sound came up and in through the open window. That was a boat, thought Appleby; Hudspith and Beaglehole had arrived. And *that* – there was a click and a distant bang – was the front door opening and closing. And in a moment there would be footsteps on the stairs.

Mr Smart's stairs – the stairs up which that respectable merchant had mounted on returning from his good-humoured holiday at Yarmouth. And now Hudspith was coming up, with Beaglehole, maybe, a couple of treads behind him ... The throb in Appleby's arm changed its tempo; nothing could be done about that; Wine must make what he might of it. And now they were outside on the landing and there seemed to be a pause. Here they would have to halt if the proposal was to knock up Wine in his bedroom. Would they go higher? Beaglehole had a room on the next floor – the floor where Mr Smart's nurseries had lain. Could a pretext be manufactured out of that? Appleby strained his ears. Yes, they were going up. Wine sat very still.

A murmur of voices floated briefly down. Voices in talk – and then a voice in surprise, in anger, in alarm. There was a split second's silence, and then a queer crack or smack followed by a thud. Silence flooded the house, was broken by a deep gasp as of a man raising a burden. Then a brief slither, a bump, a slither again and again a bump. And finally, from below, one single and very horrible sound.

Appleby rolled over, groaned and again lay still; the performance gave some little ease to his nerves. Probably there were beads of sweat on his face; of that too Wine must make what he would. Steps were descending. They went past the landing and down again without hurry but without pause. And then the front door must have been opened once more. For from outside came up a heavy splash. The incomparable digestive system of the crocodile genus was being invoked – and perhaps the affair held no worse moment than that ... A very long pause followed. On those smooth marble slabs, transported so far for this far-fetched destiny, a good deal of mopping up would have to be done. But presently that too was over, and up from the river came the low plash of oars cautiously plied. The sound died away, and as it did so the pressure on Appleby's arm relaxed. Wine was packing up his instrument. Now, with the quiet satisfaction of an investigator who has successfully laid the foundations for an important experiment, he would take himself off to bed.

Breakfast was even better than usual. There was melon in monster slices which the servants had cut so as to give an appearance of quaintly serrated teeth, and Wine, though a modest host, had to confess himself quite proud of the grilled trout. Mrs Nurse placidly poured coffee at the head of the table. Behind her, through the incongruous urban window, the morning showed fresh and lovely, an almost English affair of cool breezes and fleecy clouds. On one of the nearer islands, nestled in greenery, there could just be distinguished a *Schloss* and a *chalet* pleasantly recalling the curious fantasy of the late Schlumpf. Everything was smiling and cheerful. Only Lucy Rideout looked a little worn and pale. Sick Lucy had looked rather like that.

'How charming it will be,' said Wine, 'sailing down the river this morning. I declare I quite envy our friends. Mrs Nurse, another trout? They are toothsome but small. Or will you take a boiled egg?' He looked round the table in momentary perplexity. 'I am sure I saw boiled eggs. But here is what looks like quite a capital ham. Lucy, my dèar, a slice of ham will certainly help you on with your Latin later in the morning. We seem quite to have dropped our Latin lately. And quite soon we must begin German. A language full of interesting shades. What do you think, now, is the difference between *essen* and *fressen*?' Wine looked gaily round the table. 'It's *essen* when we eat the trout and it's *fressen* when the alligators eat us. I wonder if they thought to put some of these delicious little fish on board the steamer? Hudspith, I am sure, would be not unpartial to them.'

The man had a macabre imagination which seemed at the moment too much even for Lucy's robustly melodramatic taste. She pushed away her melon – it had rather an alligator-like look – and slipped from the room. Wine watched her go without curiosity; already it was on Appleby that most of his interest was concentrated. How long did a ghost take to get going? Perhaps there would be a preliminary period of obscure intimations. Or perhaps it would walk in as promptly as the shade of Banquo. Appleby, like Wine looking round vaguely for the boiled eggs, frowned sombrely. *Fail not our feast* ... What if the dead man should really walk? And he in turn pushed his plate away – a gesture more expressive than elegant – and left the table. The dead man ... Appleby disliked the idea of homicide.

Lucy was on the veranda, and he went up to her with a question in his eye. She nodded – cautious, careful and excited. 'Dead,' she said.

'Instantaneously?'

'Quite.' Her glance became troubled. 'Jacko, about those eggs –'

'Eggs?'

'Was it too risky to pocket them? After all, he must –'

Appleby smiled faintly. 'One must take risks.' He paused. 'Do you know, Lucy, I'm rather troubled about – well, about the ruthlessness of the whole affair.'

She looked at him, wondering. 'But it was one or other of them. Or probably it was him or all of us. And I'm certainly not going to be done for if I can help it. After all, you must remember I'm only just beginning as – as a person.'

'That's true, Lucy. And good luck to you.'

'And now we've gained a lot of time, and perhaps we'll be able to wind the whole thing up. All we have to do is to keep on stealing eggs and things without being noticed.'

Appleby laughed. 'This ghost must eat. By the way, where is he?'

'I've got him hidden in my room. And we've got the plane hidden too.'

'There was a pilot?'

'No. Beaglehole piloted it himself. So afterwards we just taxied up the river and into a creek.'

'But, good Lord, he's never –'

'He seemed quite good at it. But he's worried about being concealed in my room. He doesn't think it quite – quite proper.'

'No more it is. But, bless him, I don't suppose anyone since Casanova has had more frequent occasion to hide himself in girls' rooms than Hudspith.'

'Who was Casanova, Jacko?'

'Never mind.'

5

Undoubtedly time had been gained. The liquidation of Beaglehole at the moment when Hudspith was to be liquidated had been a master stroke in its way. Hudspith, preserved, could live on filched boiled eggs indefinitely. And Wine, by the very conditions of his experiment, was obliged to wait patiently upon events. No doubt there would be a limit to the scope of the deception achieved. The Beaglehole who was to have flown down the river again had presumably tasks to perform and reports to make; when these were unachieved Wine's suspicions would be aroused; and although various explanations of Beaglehole's disappearance could be imagined, something like the true explanation would certainly present itself to his late employer as one of the substantial possibilities.

Time had been gained, thought Appleby – and once more he frowned over the way the thing had been done. Beaglehole – disagreeable wretch that he was – had been murdered by an aggressively moral policeman and a green and engaging girl. It was true that he had been murdered in the act of committing murder; true that the killing of him had been in a certain sense an act of self-defence. Any other way of attempting to deal with the situation would probably have been fatal to the ultimate interests of law and order. Still, Beaglehole had been deliberately killed as the result of a course of action carefully and ingeniously thought out beforehand. Legally that was homicide in some degree. Morally it was murder. Or so Appleby thought it wise to think. A policeman, if forced to essays in manslaughter and assassination, ought to view them somewhat on the sombre side ... And Appleby looked out over the green and yellow of the incredible river. Anyway Beaglehole's death, whether criminal or not, had been all one to the alligators.

Time had been gained – but was it certain that the commodity was a useful one? Time to reconnoitre the full strength of Wine's organization but did they not already know that it was too strong to fight through? They had played for time while knowing that time was not a particularly attractive proposition; had played for it because there seemed nothing else to play for. They had won it, and it remained a dubious gain. But in the same match they had won something else. They had won not an indeterminate extension of the affair, but an instrument for abruptly writing *Finis* to it. An instrument, thought Appleby, out of the very last chapter of a schoolboys' story. In fact, an aeroplane ... And Appleby, strolling across Europe Island, glanced over his shoulder. Not far behind him Wine was taking an after-breakfast walk in the same direction.

And likely enough Wine or another would always be there now. In this fantastic community Appleby had become an object of major scientific interest, something far more beguiling to the psychic investigator than Miss Molsher or Mrs Gladigan had ever been. A man who at any turn may encounter a veridical ghost is abundantly worth keeping an eye on. And this is likely to be annoying to one whose thoughts turn much upon a conveniently hidden aeroplane.

Appleby paused and waited for Wine to overtake him. Had it fuel and oil? Of course Hudspith should slip away with it in the night; that would be the ideal thing. Only Hudspith, by whatever inspiration he had contrived to taxi the craft into hiding, was certainly incapable of controlling it while air-borne; that, tiresomely enough, was an accomplishment which only Appleby himself possessed. And his skill was their best chance. Once get the thing into the air and it should be possible, however unfamiliar a crate it was, to get some sort of flying start down the river. It would be a matter of dodging surveillance – surveillance which would be particularly carefully maintained at night. For it is then that ghosts and spirits walk. Perhaps, thought Appleby, as he prepared to receive one of Wine's most cordial smiles, perhaps the dodging could be done. But somehow his faith in the aeroplane was small. He had tried to terminate adventures in the simple fashion of juvenile fiction before. And always something had gone wrong. It was as if the adult universe wasn't constructed that way. Of course there was one other method of concluding this deplorable adventure of the Happy Islands – a method much too odd to commend itself to the realism of youthful minds. But a method he had better get going on now. 'A pleasant day,' he said; 'but with a hint of something rather oppressive, don't you think?'

'Perhaps so.' Wine looked absently at the day. 'I hope you slept well?'

'Thank you – yes. Rather heavily, in fact. I suppose it is the Pampas air.'

'No doubt.' Wine shot out a hand which neatly caught a mosquito on the wing. 'I do not always sleep well myself on the Islands. I find them a great place for dreams. And dreams – after one has thoroughly studied them, I mean – are tiresome when they come in legions. Do you dream?' The question dropped out casually. 'Or dream here more than usual?'

Appleby appeared to consider. 'No, I don't think I do.'

'Last night, for instance, when you say you slept particularly heavily: did you dream at all then?'

'I'm sure I didn't. Or I think I'm sure. But I suppose one has many dreams one doesn't remember. I believe people have been studied and examined while asleep in an effort to discover whether they really dream all the time or not.'

'Indeed?' Wine was more vague than a man of science ought to have been. He pointed up the river. 'I take particular delight in those Magellanic swans.'

They walked together for a time in silence. Time. They had gained time. But obscurely Appleby was sure that he didn't want it – or not much of it. Why not push straight ahead? They were passing through a little grove. Not a bad spot, a grove. For some seconds he walked in an abstraction. Then suddenly he stopped, swung round, stared behind him. It was the evolution of a moment, and he was pacing forward with Wine once more. 'Those mists,' he said casually; 'they seem to hang about quite late among the trees.'

'Mists?' Wine's eyes faintly widened. 'Ah – to be sure.'

Not that one must go too fast. There was the prime difficulty that something like this trick had been played on Wine before. He had been credulous over Hudspith's supposed vision on the night of the birthday-party; surely he would be on his guard a second time. Still, the point was that the credulous side to him was there. And it might be played upon to the point of complete nervous upset. The experiment – perhaps it ought to be called the counter-experiment – was not easy. But it was beguiling. And a fairly direct road to it might be best. Appleby lit his pipe. 'What would you do,' he asked, 'if you saw a ghost?'

Wine's eye followed a humming-bird. 'A ghost?' he said. 'What a curious question!'

'I don't know what put it in my head.' Appleby frowned. 'I suppose this. Here you are proposing to trade in superstition – to batten on it in a very large way. In fact you are going to cash in on the un-canny on a hitherto unthought-of scale.'

'Well, I suppose it will be some time before I rival our theological friends in their heyday. But on a fair scale, certainly. Incidentally, I don't think you put it very prettily. Batten is a horrid word.' Wine smiled cheerfully. 'But I think you were saying –'

'That you are proposing to exploit the supernatural for profit.'

'Just like Radbone and yourselves.'

'Quite so. Has it occurred to you that it is all rather disrespectful?'

Wine came to a halt. 'I'm afraid I don't follow you, my dear fellow.'

'You claim to have an open mind on the whole thing. You conduct experiments in a thoroughly scientific manner. You wouldn't do that unless you supposed it possible that the whole supernatural structure of traditional superstition and belief may, in fact, exist. Suppose it does. Suppose your experiments yield unmistakably positive results. Suppose, as I say, you see a ghost. Where does that take you?'

'Some way farther along the path of science, I suppose. I have added to human knowledge.'

'You have indeed. You have demonstrated to yourself that you live, after all, in a magical universe. Not a materialist and rational universe, in which we clearly do the best for ourselves by grabbing what we can of the here and now. On the contrary, you live in an unaccountable universe, one much more like that of what you call our theological friends. Really believe that you see a ghost, and you are bound, on reflection, to see that you see a great deal behind it: malignant spirits, jealous powers. Suppose Hamlet really saw his father's ghost: where did that ghost come from?'

'From sulphorous and tormenting flames – if we are to believe Shakespeare, that is.'

'But if a real ghost were to appear in your laboratory, could you say it didn't come from the same place?'

'I don't know that I could.'

'In fact you would find yourself in a new universe, and one in which the practical side of your enterprise would look much less smart than it does at present. For if the universe is, after all, a spiritual or spiritualist universe, then exploiting spirits and spiritualism for material ends is –'

'Disrespectful was, I think, your word.'

'Just that.' Wine, Appleby reflected, was not to be easily bowled over by a nerve-war. Still, some undermining might be going on. 'Think of Faust. He peered too far into the way things work.'

'And was carried off by demons.' Wine chuckled and resumed his walk. 'As a matter of fact,' he said presently, 'I do at times think of Faust. Your train of thought is not unfamiliar to me. But you put it rather well.' He walked for some time in silence. 'And after all, my dear Appleby, you are in the same boat. I wonder what *you* would do if it was *you* who ...'

He paused, and Appleby looked at him innocently. 'If it was I who –?'

'Nothing, my dear fellow; nothing at all.' They had turned back and were now in the little grove in which their conversation had begun. 'Mist?' he said. 'Do you know I didn't notice it?'

'Mist,' said Appleby. 'I saw a wisp of mist where there wasn't any.

And I felt the morning obscurely oppressive when it was quite lovely. I don't know that you could have done better yourself.'

'Ah,' said Hudspith.

'I'm sure he couldn't,' said Lucy. 'Not that I don't think Mr Hudspith very clever.'

'But it was a mistake.' Appleby shook his head sombrely. 'One wants to go after an element of the unexpected. The ghost of Hudspith appears to his friend Appleby. It repeats the pattern of the other Hawke Square affairs. The experiment yields a result which has been envisaged. And though it may not be comfortable for Wine to have to decide that the universe does, after all, contain unaccountable powers, still, the disconcerting result has been foreseen by him, and there will be a certain reassurance in that. His equilibrium is much more likely to be upset by something which is both supernatural and *unexpected*. *He* sees the ghost of his victim; *I* fail to see the ghost of my friend. Something like that.'

'Ah,' said Hudspith again. Somewhat gloomily, he was peeling the shell off a boiled egg.

Lucy crossed the room from the door where she had been listening. 'It's a pity about the sheets,' she said.

'The sheets?'

She pointed to the bed. 'Nice pastel shades. But one wants a good old-fashioned white sheet for a ghost.'

Appleby sighed. 'Somehow I don't think we'll ever catch Wine in a sheet, however snowy. What's our plan? Nothing less than to make him repent. It's almost absurd.'

'Faust was scared into deciding to burn his books.'

'My dear Lucy, wherever did you learn that?'

Lucy frowned. 'I don't know. But I could tell you quite a lot of funny things like that. Things about Socrates and Marcus Aurelius and –'

'I see.' Her former sisters were rapidly growing dim to Lucy Rideout; already they had merely the quality of intermittently remembered dreams. In another twenty-four hours it looked as if they would have joined Miss Molsher and Mrs Gladigan on Wine's somewhat rapidly growing list of wastages. Which was satisfactory, but not immediately to the point. Appleby rose. 'I must be off. There's a fellow watching for me at the end of the corridor, and he might get curious if my visit to Lucy lasted too long. Wine won't repent. Ghosts won't make him believe that trading in ghosts is disrespectful and dangerous. He won't shake hands with us and retire into private life. But even one ghost – and that merely in pastel shades – might cause him a bit of a flutter for a time. Remember the birthday-party and how het-up he must have got for a bit.' Appleby turned to Hudspith. 'This plane – will it have gas?'

'Presumably so. Beaglehole was certainly going to fly straight back in it. That, of course, is what Wine thinks has actually happened. Beaglehole was going to fly straight back without anybody except Wine knowing that he and I had as much as been here. It would be the obvious thing to have enough fuel to begin with to make the double trip.'

'It depends on the capacity of the tank. But we'll hope for the best. The plane is our real hope, such as it is. While everything runs smoothly here it's no go; I'm watched much too carefully to get away. But tonight we'll spring our ghost and hope for fifteen minutes' chaos. Then we make a break for it.'

Hudspith nodded. 'But must it really be a sheet? I doubt if that's at all the current fashion with ghosts.'

'Nor has been for centuries. No, this ghost shall have risen dripping and bloody from the river.'

'It doesn't sound at all comfortable.'

'There will be a reek as of the inside of a charnel-house – no, of an alligator. And a rush of chill air.'

'I don't see –'

'To say nothing of a phosphorescent glow. I think Lucy and I can work it all out this afternoon.' Appleby moved to the door. 'And now eat your last egg – my dear fellow, as Wine would say.'

6

Positive seduction would be immoral. And under the present conditions of constant surveillance it would be moreover, if not impracticable, at least of a daunting impudicity. So what had it better be? A cash proposition was a possibility. Or one could try threats. Or contrive some sort of appeal to professional vanity ... Appleby, strolling over Europe Island, shook his head. If he knew anything of the type, sex it would have to be. The promising beginnings of a vulgar intrigue. Hudspith could offer much technical advice. But then Hudspith would disapprove. For that matter Appleby disapproved himself. He was prepared to admire, but reluctant to pursue – in this being like the majority of prudent men past the first flush of youth's irresponsibilities. Still, the girl must be nobbled. Appleby strolled on.

She lived in a sort of convent. This was an initial difficulty, though likely to be an eventual advantage – for decidedly she must be feeling rather bored. And probably annoyed: the food would be wrong and, likely enough, they made her take baths. This last would be all to the good. But meantime there was a high, white wall. Appleby climbed it and sat on top. He waved cheerfully. And the dark-skinned person who unobtrusively followed him everywhere this afternoon, and who had quickened his pace as he began to climb, grinned sardonically and sat down on a tump of panicle grass. Appleby waved again; or perhaps it might be better said that he made a gesture of a frank and Latin sort. For there she was. He jumped down on the other side and advanced upon her. Whereupon the dark-skinned man got up, scaled the wall in his turn and settled down to a grandstand view from the top. Well, let him. '*Buenos tardes,*' he said.

It was long after dinner. A little fire – a real coal fire – had been lit in the small ground-floor room used by Wine as an office and study. And he and Appleby were alone, sipping whiskies and sodas in the soft light of a standard lamp. Wine was growing increasingly affable. 'I hear,' he said, 'that you have been visiting our Southern European friends.' And he chuckled good-humouredly.

'I really don't know how you can have come to hear that.' Appleby did his best to reply with a sort of shame-faced caution.

'My dear chap, I must really apologize. With so many queer fish about the place – scores and scores of them, I am happy to say – we have necessarily become something of a police-state. The staff are all spies by instinct, and they keep a smart eye on new-comers in particular. I fear one of them has been zealously trailing your good self. It is very absurd, of course – but that's how my little piece of information comes to me.' He chuckled again. 'I hope you found it interesting?

And not too tiring?' Wine threw another piece of coal on the fire. He was being very man-of-the-world.

'It struck me as rather conventual.'

'Exactly. It is what I aim at over there. With half a dozen or so girls brought up in Mediterranean conditions it seems the best way to cope with what might be a difficult situation. Not that I at all object to their having a visitor from time to time, my dear chap. There is some very promising material over there – I mean from our professional point of view. Some very promising mediums of the lower class. And well-behaved on the whole. Just sometimes I have to threaten to bring over one of the Fathers to give them a talking to.'

'One of the Fathers?'

'Our nearest neighbours.' Wine had hesitated for a moment before he replied. 'There is a Jesuit mission station about eighty miles due north, over difficult country. Actually we never communicate. But the girls know they are there, and go in considerable awe of them.'

Appleby stared thoughtfully into the little fire. This was news. And clearly it was authentic – something, perhaps, which Wine thought it no longer necessary to conceal. But it would be better not to show too much curiosity. 'There was the girl called Eusapia –' he said tentatively.

'Aha!' Wine pointed his glass at Appleby with a gay and whimsical gesture. 'To be sure. Well, well, well.'

'But I rather wish I hadn't gone. Coming back I had a queer sort of feeling of something wrong. Not anything to do with those girls. Rather with this house.'

Wine's eyes narrowed suddenly. 'Wrong here?'

'Yes. As if something had happened . . . I really can't explain.' Appleby paused, let his eyes travel uneasily round the little shadowy room. 'Funny thing, sex. Makes you feel guilty. Only the sense of guilt takes on all sorts of queer forms. Doesn't it?'

'I suppose it does.' It was a cautious rather than the man-of-the-world Wine now.

'Sometimes you just feel that everything has gone sinister.' Appleby frowned, nervous and puzzled. Would Hudspith, he was wondering, put up a better show than this? He doubted it. 'But, come to think of it, I had very much the same feeling earlier in the day. It was when we were walking through that little grove this morning.'

Wine was sitting very still in his chair. But his voice was casual still. 'My dear chap, it's probably nothing but liver. I wouldn't indulge these Freudian notions, if I were you. Guilty and creepy feelings because you've been kissing a girl behind a hedge is all nonsense. Have another drink.' He got up and reached for the decanter. 'And shall we turn out this lamp? I think few things are more soothing to the nerves than simple fire-light. We hardly need warmth tonight, but the glow and flicker are pleasing to exiles like ourselves.'

Exiles. The undiscovered country from whose bourn no traveller returns . . . From the tessellated hall of 37 Hawke Square, gloomy beneath the frowning landings that led up to the nurseries of Mr Smart, came a faint and rapid whir – the sound of a grandfather clock preparing to strike. And then came the chime. It was midnight.

'Midnight!' said Wine. He set down his glass. 'Perhaps we ought to turn in. Hasn't the door blown open?' He twisted round in his chair. The door had certainly opened: it showed as a rectangle of darkness in the dimly fire-lit wall. And a breeze cool and faintly damp, as if it carried a fine spray; a breeze suddenly strangely chill . . .

'Odd,' said Appleby. 'The temperature does seem to drop at night. But such a really cold wind –'

He stopped. For the breeze was no longer chill merely; it was an arctic air, a wind chill as on a Russian steppe . . . And abruptly Wine was on his feet. 'The smell,' he said hoarsely; 'my God, the smell!'

'Smell?' said Appleby. There was indeed a smell, a sudden indescribable reek as of the grave, a thick and seeping vapour as of vermiculation and decay. 'Smell? I don't notice anything. But it is uncommonly cold. And I do feel damned queer.'

Wine sat down again. 'You notice the cold, but not the smell?' he asked. In the flicker of the flame Appleby could see him frowning in some final effort of the dispassionate intelligence. Was the cold veridical – an objective fact? And was the smell a subjective concomitant? The fragmentary scientist that was in Wine could be seen on his features, doing battle with dismay. Everything was very quiet. From somewhere beyond the blackness of the open door came a long, deep sigh.

He was on his feet again and had swung round. 'Did you hear that?'

'I can't hear anything.'

'Look!'

There was a glimmer of greenish light in the doorway; it concentrated itself, took form and was a man. Or it was the phantasm of a man, immobile and framed in darkness. It was, thought Appleby, very like a good conjuring trick — dangerously so if the spectator's mind was cool. 'Wine!' he cried. 'What the hell are you staring at? Wine!'

The room reeked still. The phantasmal Hudspith advanced. Water dripped from his muddied and blooded tropical suit; one side of his face was a ghastly mush of orange and blue. Slowly, he was raising an arm.

'Can't you see?' Wine was clinging to the back of his chair.

'See?' Appleby stared blankly at the door. 'You're mad. I see nothing. There's nothing to see. Your blasted laboratory and your experiments have driven you out of your mind. Why couldn't you keep to the racket, you poor mut, and leave tinkering alone? Radbone credulous. Bah!'

The phantasm was pointing. And it spoke. 'I was murdered,' it said in a deep voice. 'I was murdered, Appleby, murdered —'

Wine screamed — screamed with his eyes strangely fixed on the phantasm's head. Part of the head was missing, as if it had been smashed or blasted or gnashed away. And yet not missing . . . for a great fragment of skull, as if reluctant to accept dismemberment, floated in air above the wound, 'I was murdered,' said the phantasm; 'murdered by —'

Wine screamed again; he turned and stumbled towards a desk. He grabbed; he held a revolver in his hand and was firing; he was pulling the trigger wildly while the shaking and reeking barrel pointed aimlessly at the floor. There was a crash from behind Appleby and another door burst open. Two men were in the room; one of them the dark-visaged man who had trailed him all day. Heedless of him, they ran towards Wine; Wine was now lying on the floor; outside the nightmarish and flickering room the whole crazy house sounded of tumult and confusion. After all, thought Appleby, its whole constitution was such that it would go quickly on the jump . . . He turned and slipped quickly into the darkness of the hall.

'It's only a rowing-boat,' said Hudspith. 'We might have managed to get one of the launches. But we'll be quieter in this.'

'I don't know that quiet is much needed.' Appleby mopped his forehead in the darkness as they pushed off. 'There's the deuce of a row.'

It was true. As if panic had propagated itself by mysterious means, the whole group of Happy Islands was in tumult. The clamour struck up to the stars and everywhere were strangely moving and darting lights. They pulled powerfully at the oars.

'Jacko' – Lucy's voice came from the darkness of the stern – 'your Italian friend did you proud.'

Appleby laughed softly. 'She certainly did. And on credit too.'

'What do you mean, on credit?'

'Never mind. How did she manage that cold wind?'

'Mr Hudspith understands it.'

'Ether.' Hudspith was peering anxiously up the river. 'Ether stolen from the medical stores and stood before a big electric fan. The alligator-stink disguised the smell.'

'And the alligator-stink?'

'Lucy will answer that one.'

'Never mind,' said Lucy.

They rowed on. Wine's collapse had caused a confusion almost un-accountably abundant; all the darkness was filled with tumult and cries and splashing. Appleby frowned into the night, opened his mouth to speak, changed his mind and was silent.

'I think it's the next creek,' Hudspith said.

'Good heavens! Wasn't it risky leaving it as close as that?'

Hudspith laughed shortly as he tugged at his oar. 'Not half so risky as trying to pilot the thing any farther.'

'Taxiing a hydroplane isn't all that difficult.'

'Lucy will tell you what it felt like.'

'It felt like death,' said Lucy briefly.

'Or like driving a racing car fitted with skates through a maze in the dark.' Hudspith turned round and peered ahead once more. 'Easy, all.'

They had taken two turns up a broad backwater, and the nearest island was now some distance behind them. But still the night was mysteriously alive and moving; the sky flickered oddly; there was a great deal of shouting from directions hard to place.

'If we can get it air-borne,' said Appleby, 'we shall do something.' His voice was anxious; the plane was their one hope; and still he was

obscurely unable to feel faith in it … The little boat drifted round
a final gentle bend and he rubbed his eyes. For there the plane was
– authentic, real and waiting. Only there was something odd about
it. The night was starry as always, but here in the backwater it was
very dark. What was odd about the plane was that it was *visible*.

It was silhouetted against a dull red glow. And in the sky were points
and trails of light, shooting arcs of reddish fire. A cluster of these rose,
fell. A tongue of flame shot from the tail of the plane; another rose
beside it; there was a third in the cockpit. The plane was blazing.

And behind them as they rested on their oars there was a splashing
in the river; Appleby turned to see a half-circle of dark bobbing heads.
That, of course, was it. The general tumult was explained – as was
the destruction of their only likely link with the outer world. But it
was not a moment for reflection. He tapped Hudspith on the shoulder.
'Into the bank!' he cried. 'And out and up.'

The little boat grounded in mud; in a few seconds they were scrambling
in a *monté* of tree-fern and bamboo, and it was very dark. But back
a little from the water the terrain would be clearer, and it was
necessary to see even at the risk of being seen. They were not being
pursued, unless it was stealthily – and in that night's operations the
period of stealth seemed to be over. From the Islands the clamour was
now indescribable, and from somewhere farther along the bank came
a savage and exultant singing. They stumbled on and were climbing;
they were on the brow of a little hill, bare save for one vast tree,
spreading and shadowy. They staggered under it and, momentarily
safe from espial, looked back. Hudspith grunted. Lucy gasped and laid
a hand on Appleby's arm. It was an extraordinary sight.

Very clearly the assault, so strangely timed to coincide with the shock
of domestic confusion on Europe Island, had been completely successful.
The heritage of Schlumpf, the dominion of Emery Wine, was everywhere going up in flame; the sky already glowed as from one vast
bonfire; a pall of smoke was gathering over the river. The windows
of 37 Hawke Square glowed luridly – glowed as with an indignant
glare at this second night of outrage within a mere fragment of time.
The peace of the Augustans had seen its birth; it had known the long,
strenuous tranquillity of Victorian days; now flame and destruction had
pursued it from continent to continent.

The savages were intent to destroy. But they were not, it seemed, intent to kill. Clearly on the nearest Island – and distinguishably on Islands farther away – they could be seen bearing off, violently but with a sort of strange and ritualistic respect, the abundant and various stock-in-trade of Wine's now fallen and ruined enterprise. Naked and in groups, dark-skinned and powerful, they bore away billowy women and frightened girls and bewildered men. Mediums and palmists, thought-readers and scryers and astrologers; they were being borne away as by devils in an old window; were vanishing in a confusion of contorted limb and frantic gesture, like Sabine Women in a tapestry unrestrainedly Baroque. The clamour of the strange pervasive rape echoed over the river and the pampa; the flames waxed and mounted; the stars were dimmed.

'Look!'

Lucy was pointing. Just below them, and nearer the river, was another low hill. And in a sudden flare of light – it was probably the flame reaching the petrol in the plane – they saw a single figure standing immobile, surveying the scene.

'The witch,' Lucy said.

And it was Hannah Metcalfe. She stood very still and watched the bonfire with slightly parted lips. On Beaglehole and his whip, on Wine and the isle of Capri, she had achieved her revenge.

Hudspith stirred sharply. 'My God!' he said. 'She's demented. Only a devil would plot such a thing.'

Appleby nodded. 'Perhaps so. And only a very powerful and talented person could carry it out. I believe –' He stopped and laid a warning hand on each of his companions. 'Listen,' he whispered.

The sound was very close. It came from the other side of the great tree. And it was the neigh of a horse.

In the flicker from the distant fires the creature showed cloudlike and uncertain. There was a flare of light, and they saw it clearly; it was erect, prancing and magnificent. Suddenly Lucy called out; of the three of them her senses appeared to be the keenest. 'Jacko, look!'

Appleby turned. The backwater was still behind them. And now, in front and steadily advancing, was a great sickle of dancing flames. Its significance was clear: a long line of savages was converging upon them with lighted torches, and there was no line of retreat. They must have been detected by those bobbing heads in the water; now they were to be rounded up. Appleby eyed the distance. 'Five minutes,' he said; 'we haven't got more than that.' There was a jerk at his shoulder; he turned and eyed the great horse; the animal was tossing its head strangely in air. 'One, two,' said Appleby; 'three, four, five – by the lord Harry, it's Daffodil!'

'Daffodil?' said Hudspith. 'Nonsense! Daffodil is a broken-down cab-horse. This is as fine a creature –'

'It's the pampa. It was the same with the Spaniards when they first came. They landed a lot of sorry jades –'

'They're nearer,' Lucy said warningly.

'– but after a month or so of the pampa air –' Appleby broke off; he was working at the horse's tether. 'Hudspith, I've rather lost my bearings. Which bank are we on?'

'North.'

'Then perhaps we can do it. Do you ride?'

'No.'

'But you can hang on to a stirrup-leather. Imagine you're an infantry-man charging with the Scots Greys.' Appleby was in the saddle. 'Steady, Daffodil, steady! Lucy, up you come. And yell, all of you; yell like mad.' With difficulty he turned the horse's head towards the advancing line of fire. The creature reared, came down, curvetted like a colt. And Appleby gave it the rein. 'A Daffodil,' he shouted, 'a Daffodil!' They charged nightmarishly down the hill. Savages danced and yelled in front. The hooves of Daffodil thundered below and Hudspith held on as to a hurricane. Behind them the glare from the burning Happy Islands obscured Orion and climbed to touch the Southern Cross.

7

'Surprise me?' The Jesuit Father looked innocently at Appleby. 'No, I cannot say you do that. Except perhaps in the matter of the horse. It was an uncommon feat of endurance. One feels that he deserves a flagon of wine, like the animal in Browning's poem. You admire Browning? I think of him as an Elizabethan born out of time. He has that theatrical vision of Italy and the Papacy which is so essentially of the Elizabethan age.'

'I hate to think of all those poor creatures carried off by the savages.'

'It is curious that he could do so little in the dramatic form.' The priest shook his head, cultivated and austere and comfortable. No doubt, thought Appleby, he could discourse thus adequately on the poets of half a dozen semi-barbarous nations – and was glad to do so when the rare occasion should occur. 'But I beg your pardon. You were saying –? Ah, yes; about the poor people who have been carried off. There is little chance of rescuing them, I sadly fear. In any temporal sense, that is to say. You see, those tribes come from pretty far to the south-west. We never contact them. But I assure you that their prizes will be given a very comfortable time. They will be treated as gods.'

Hudspith took his eyes from the little sun-lit cloister-garth. 'Is that comfortable?'

'Humanly, it may not be so bad. We must pray for them, of course.' The priest was silent for a minute. 'You see, all the natives hereabouts have the most enormous appetite for marvels. It amounts to an em-barrassment at times, I do assure you.' He smiled gravely, a man who would not readily be put to a stand. 'And they are very numerous. They will absorb hundreds of holy men and miracle-workers without the least trace of spiritual or intellectual indigestion.'

'That,' said Appleby, 'is just what Wine believed the world at large was ripe to do.'

'I think we can look after the world at large.' The priest smiled again. 'You and I,' he said politely.

'It's an odd end to the thing. For a moment I was inclined to call it poetic justice. But it's not quite that.'

'It has a certain artistic fitness, Mr Appleby. To say more than that would be – injudicious.'

Lucy Rideout, rather alarmed in strange surroundings, looked timidly up. 'I'm dreadfully sorry for Mrs Nurse.'

'She shall be particularly remembered.'

Lucy blinked, very much at sea. 'And you think that Mr Wine –?'

'It is likely that he will have been killed. We heard little of him, but undoubtedly he bore a bad name. And hereabouts, believe me, that is a fatal thing to do. I am wondering about the girl who was believed to be a witch. She must have obtained great power. Her, I believe we can rescue. In such matters, when they are important, we are not without means.'

'You think Hannah Metcalfe important?' asked Appleby.

'She has much talent, and among those people might be an instrument of much good. She shall be found. And instructed.' He smiled again and rose. 'And now you are tired, I am sure.'

Time had passed, and even Harrogate was not quite the same. Here and there a bit was missing. The enemy, uncertain of his reception in more martial quarters, was occasionally contriving to chasten the spas of England – chosen haunts of a war-mongering plutocracy. And even Lady Caroline had changed with the times, wearing a steel helmet as she took her daily carriage-exercise in the open landau.

'Dear Miss Appleby,' said Lady Caroline as she stood on the steps of her modest but distinguished hotel, 'have you seen my muff? Maidment used to look after it for me.'

'No, my dear. I fear you have to look after it yourself nowadays. And you must not regret Miss Maidment too much. The auxiliary services do such wonderful work.'

'No doubt. But I fear that Maidment has been much actuated by a desire for the society of men.'

'Dear me!'

'I had frequently remarked it. Where is Bodfish?'

'Nowadays, Lady Caroline, he appears to like to walk Daffodil up and down before taking us up. Sometimes to *trot* him up and down. But here they are. Have you noticed that the carriage never seems to keep quite still?'

'Bodfish,' said Lady Caroline sternly, 'have a care.'

'How eager Daffodil is to be off!' said Miss Appleby. 'The carriage quite hits one in the back.'

'I am afraid,' said Lady Caroline, 'that this paltry bombing is having an undue effect upon the nerves of the populace. Have you noticed now nervous people appear to be in the streets? Our own modest progress might be a charge of cavalry. Did you notice that policeman at the corner? He positively leapt for the pavement as we passed.' Lady Caroline settled herself with some difficulty in her corner. 'I am not sure that the springs of this landau are quite as they were.'

'I agree with you.' Miss Appleby swayed in her seat. 'But it is a great comfort once more to be assured of a quiet horse.'

'Quite so,' said Lady Caroline. 'I declare there is quite a wind blowing;

I had not remarked it before we started. And in what poor condition the street must be.'

'How fast we are going! Here is the Stray already.'

'To be sure it is. And the traffic is considerable. Have you noticed how red Bodfish seems to go sometimes round the neck? Can it be that he has returned to beer?'

'There *is* rather a lot of traffic. And do you notice how much of it appears to *swerve* at us? One could almost be alarmed.'

'My dear' – Lady Caroline swayed and bucketed and gasped – 'my dear, there is much comfort nowadays in a quiet horse.'

More about Penguins and Pelicans

For further information about books available from Penguins please write to Dept EP, Penguin Books Ltd, Harmondsworth, Middlesex UB7 0DA.

In the U.S.A.: For a complete list of books available from Penguins in the United States write to Dept CS, Penguin Books, 625 Madison Avenue, New York, New York 10022.

In Canada: For a complete list of books available from Penguins in Canada write to Penguin Books Canada Ltd, 2801 John Street, Markham, Ontario L3R 1B4.

In Australia: For a complete list of books available from Penguins in Australia write to the Marketing Department, Penguin Books Australia Ltd, P.O. Box 257, Ringwood, Victoria 3134.

In New Zealand: For a complete list of books available from Penguins in New Zealand write to the Marketing Department, Penguin Books (N.Z.) Ltd, P.O. Box 4019, Auckland 10.

THE MARGERY ALLINGHAM OMNIBUS

Whether he's faced with a deadly game of hide-and-seek in a remote Suffolk house, protecting a retired judge from assassination or an international ring of rather special art collectors, Albert Campion holds his own. His deceptively innocent appearance and mild manners mislead not a few in the three novels contained here: *The Crime at Black Dudley*, *Mystery Mile* and *Look to the Lady*.

'Always of the elect, Margery Allingham now towers above them' – *Observer*

THE NICOLAS FREELING OMNIBUS

Because of the Cats, *Gun Before Butter* and *Double-Barrel* – three gripping high-tension thrillers are included here, and they all feature that most unorthodox detective, Van der Valk. Whether he is asked to investigate an unpleasant case of teenage violence, sent to solve a commonplace murder, or assigned to a dreary town to uncover the author of poison-pen letters, he always gets the cases no one else wants. Cool, amiable and incurably curious, he probes the routine surfaces ... and finds himself in dangerous places.

'Van der Valk remains the most subtle, complex and interesting of fictional police detectives' – Edmund Crispin in the *Sunday Times*

THE PENGUIN COMPLETE
FATHER BROWN
G. K. Chesterton

Here are all forty-nine quietly sensational cases investigated by the high-priest of detective fiction, Father Brown. Immortalized in these famous stories, G. K. Chesterton's little Norfolk priest has entertained and endeared himself to countless generations of readers. For, as his admirers know, Father Brown's cherubic face and unworldly simplicity, his glasses and his huge umbrella, disguise a quite uncanny understanding of the criminal mind at work.

John Mortimer in Penguins

RUMPOLE OF THE BAILEY

Horace Rumpole ... sixty-eight next birthday, with an unsurpassed knowledge of Blood and Typewriters, a penchant for quoting from the *Oxford Book of English Verse*, and a habit of referring to his judge as 'the old darling' ... Rumpole now takes up his pen in pious hope of making a bob or two that the egregious taxman, or She Who Must Be Obeyed (Mrs Rumpole), or his clerk, Henry, won't benefit from. In doing so he opens up some less-well-charted corners of British justice.

'Rumpole has been an inspired stroke of good fortune for us all. – Lynda Lee Potter in the *Daily Mail*

THE TRIALS OF RUMPOLE

Rumpole is back, as irreverent, as iconoclastic, as claret-swilling, judge-debunking, impudent, witty and cynical as ever.

'Rumpole is worthy to join the great gallery of English oddballs ranging from Pickwick to Sherlock Holmes, Jeeves and Bertie Wooster' – *Sunday Times*

RUMPOLE'S RETURN

Has Rumpole really hung up his wig? He is supposed by all and sundry to be enjoying his well-earned retirement in the Florida sun, beside his cherished helpmeet and replete with airmail copies of *The Times*. But the merest whiff of a meaty Blood case and of his sworn enemy, Judge Bullingham, sends the venerable warhorse a-twitching ... and back to the dear old Chambers to take command.

'I thank Heaven for small mercies. The first of these is Rumpole' – Clive James in the *Observer*

Julian Symons in Penguins

THE BLACKHEATH POISONINGS

'A superb detective novel of an original kind, which, while offering the reader as much information as anyone, ends with a surprising and totally unexpected conclusion. At the same time his evocation of this late Victorian epoch – a kind of black *Diary of a Nobody* – seems to ring true in every respect' – *The Times Literary Supplement*

THE TELL-TALE HEART

THE LIFE AND WORKS OF EDGAR ALLAN POE

'Mr Symon's analysis of Poe's divided self is uncondescending, and does not simplify his subject. On the contrary, he rescues Poe from Freudians, symbolists, moralists and other simplifiers. By indicating the ramifications of the two selves, he restores to Poe his depth and mystery. He manages to be both incisive and finely circumspect ... And he even makes you like Poe most of the time' – John Carey in the *Sunday Times*

BLOODY MURDER

'An urbane and scholarly account of the crime novel ... from its beginnings with Poe and Vidocq down to the immediate present' – Michael Gilbert in the *Sunday Telegraph*

'Can be heartily recommended to anyone who has ever enjoyed a detective story or a crime novel' – Kingsley Amis in the *Spectator*